I0608971

The Family at Serpiente

Raymond Tolman

The Family at Serpiente

First in The Serpent Trilogy

SUNSTONE
PRESS

SANTA FE

© 2017 by Raymond Tolman
All Rights Reserved.

No part of this book may be reproduced in any form or by any electronic or mechanical means including
information storage and retrieval systems without permission in writing from the publisher,
except by a reviewer who may quote brief passages in a review.

Sunstone books may be purchased for educational, business, or sales promotional use.
For information please write: Special Markets Department, Sunstone Press,
P.O. Box 2321, Santa Fe, New Mexico 87504-2321.
Body typeface › Granjon LT Std
Printed on acid-free paper
∞
eBook 978-1-61139-504-4

Library of Congress Cataloging-in-Publication Data

Names: Tolman, Raymond, 1948- author.
Title: The family at Serpiente / by Raymond Tolman.
Description: Santa Fe : Sunstone Press, [2017] | Series: The Serpent trilogy
; volume one | Description based on print version record and CIP data
provided by publisher; resource not viewed.
Identifiers: LCCN 2016057498 (print) | LCCN 2017011906 (ebook) | ISBN
9781611395044 | ISBN 9781632931726 (softcover : alk. paper)
Subjects: LCSH: Indian mythology--Fiction. | Domestic fiction.
Classification: LCC PS3620.O3285 (ebook) | LCC PS3620.O3285 F36 2017 (print)
| DDC 813/.6--dc23
LC record available at https://lccn.loc.gov/2016057498

SUNSTONE PRESS IS COMMITTED TO MINIMIZING OUR ENVIRONMENTAL IMPACT ON THE PLANET. THE PAPER USED IN THIS BOOK IS
FROM RESPONSIBLY MANAGED FORESTS. OUR PRINTER HAS RECEIVED CHAIN OF CUSTODY (COC) CERTIFICATION FROM: THE FOREST
STEWARDSHIP COUNCIL™ (FSC®), PROGRAMME FOR THE ENDORSEMENT OF FOREST CERTIFICATION™ (PEFC™), AND THE SUSTAINABLE
FORESTRY INITIATIVE® (SFI®). THE FSC® COUNCIL IS A NON-PROFIT ORGANIZATION, PROMOTING THE ENVIRONMENTALLY
APPROPRIATE, SOCIALLY BENEFICIAL AND ECONOMICALLY VIABLE MANAGEMENT OF THE WORLD'S FORESTS. FSC® CERTIFICATION IS
RECOGNIZED INTERNATIONALLY AS A RIGOROUS ENVIRONMENTAL AND SOCIAL STANDARD FOR RESPONSIBLE FOREST MANAGEMENT.

WWW.SUNSTONEPRESS.COM
SUNSTONE PRESS / POST OFFICE BOX 2321 / SANTA FE, NM 87504-2321 /USA
(505) 988-4418 / ORDERS ONLY (800) 243-5644 / FAX (505) 988-1025

Raymond Tolman

The Family at Serpiente

First in The Serpent Trilogy

SUNSTONE PRESS

SANTA FE

© 2017 by Raymond Tolman
All Rights Reserved.
No part of this book may be reproduced in any form or by any electronic or mechanical means including
information storage and retrieval systems without permission in writing from the publisher,
except by a reviewer who may quote brief passages in a review.

Sunstone books may be purchased for educational, business, or sales promotional use.
For information please write: Special Markets Department, Sunstone Press,
P.O. Box 2321, Santa Fe, New Mexico 87504-2321.
Body typeface › Granjon LT Std
Printed on acid-free paper
∞
eBook 978-1-61139-504-4

Library of Congress Cataloging-in-Publication Data

Names: Tolman, Raymond, 1948- author.
Title: The family at Serpiente / by Raymond Tolman.
Description: Santa Fe : Sunstone Press, [2017] | Series: The Serpent trilogy
 ; volume one | Description based on print version record and CIP data
 provided by publisher; resource not viewed.
Identifiers: LCCN 2016057498 (print) | LCCN 2017011906 (ebook) | ISBN
 9781611395044 | ISBN 9781632931726 (softcover : alk. paper)
Subjects: LCSH: Indian mythology--Fiction. | Domestic fiction.
Classification: LCC PS3620.O3285 (ebook) | LCC PS3620.O3285 F36 2017 (print)
 | DDC 813/.6--dc23
LC record available at https://lccn.loc.gov/2016057498

SUNSTONE PRESS IS COMMITTED TO MINIMIZING OUR ENVIRONMENTAL IMPACT ON THE PLANET. THE PAPER USED IN THIS BOOK IS
FROM RESPONSIBLY MANAGED FORESTS. OUR PRINTER HAS RECEIVED CHAIN OF CUSTODY (COC) CERTIFICATION FROM: THE FOREST
STEWARDSHIP COUNCIL™ (FSC®), PROGRAMME FOR THE ENDORSEMENT OF FOREST CERTIFICATION™ (PEFC™), AND THE SUSTAINABLE
FORESTRY INITIATIVE® (SFI®). THE FSC® COUNCIL IS A NON-PROFIT ORGANIZATION, PROMOTING THE ENVIRONMENTALLY
APPROPRIATE, SOCIALLY BENEFICIAL AND ECONOMICALLY VIABLE MANAGEMENT OF THE WORLD'S FORESTS. FSC® CERTIFICATION IS
RECOGNIZED INTERNATIONALLY AS A RIGOROUS ENVIRONMENTAL AND SOCIAL STANDARD FOR RESPONSIBLE FOREST MANAGEMENT.

WWW.SUNSTONEPRESS.COM
SUNSTONE PRESS / POST OFFICE BOX 2321 / SANTA FE, NM 87504-2321 /USA
(505) 988-4418 / ORDERS ONLY (800) 243-5644 / FAX (505) 988-1025

For Judy Tolman,
My soulmate.

Preface

*T*he setting for The Serpent Trilogy is Aztlan, the home of the Ancestral Puebloans that encompasses four modern states with Chaco Canyon in New Mexico being the center of this ancient world. It was the home of a people commonly referred to as the Anasazi. Named by the Navajos, that means ancient enemies. The history of this ancient world has been lost in the sands of time, however new discoveries are continually being made by archeologists and scientists which enlightens our understanding of those ancient people and, in so doing, rewrites the history of this dynamic era.

Few other regions in this world can boast about such archeological treasures, beautiful scenery, dynamic geology and diverse people as modern New Mexico. Many languages can often be heard wherever people gather in this multicultural landscape. Long ago, forward-thinking and influential individuals recognized the extraordinary cultural heritage of this region. One thing above all that is unique to this region, that cannot be displayed in a museum, purchased or owned, is the profound mysteries that exist throughout this land. One of those mysteries that this novel is based upon is the Native American's metaphysical belief that serpents are shape-shifters, known as Skin Walkers in their natural form. Archeologists have discovered that serpents have been associated with human civilization, on every continent from the earliest of times. From dragons in China to Quetzalcoatl and Kukulcan in South America, they are an enigma to both the archeologists and historians who document such matters. In the American southwest, serpents known locally as Skin Walkers have always been part of the cultures of the Native Americans and currently feared among those communities.

However, this novel explores the dynamic interactions between people far more than serpents. The Serpent Trilogy explores the history of the Americas through the eyes of Penny Anderson, a high school junior, who escapes an untenable home situation and flees across the country to join her Uncle and Aunt in Serpiente, New Mexico. The Navajo Hidalgo, a history detective, who works with the family, tries to warn Penny of the dangers of Serpiente. She persists and, in the end, wins the confidence and hearts of this unique family. As a team they uncover the mysterious creatures that have, throughout history, enjoyed vexing and manipulating humans to evolve into warring creatures for their own evil reasons. In time, using the tools of Science and Native American folklore, the detectives discover the secret to making peace with the serpents. Unfortunately, antiquity thieves discover and attack the serpents, resulting in a new war between the human clan and the serpent clan. The family conducts academic field research that reveals the ultimate truth about the serpents, leading to a plethora of other mysteries. This is part of a cautionary tale of both serpents and humans exploring the premise that good and evil are subjective concepts as well as the possibility that, through cooperation, mutually beneficial solutions are the result.

Long before I decided to become an author, I experienced mysteries while growing up in New Mexico that questioned my outlook on reality and sparked my curiosity in science. As a child I was in awe when I first viewed the beautiful Spiral Staircase of the Loreto Chapel of Santa Fe, which defied construction practices of that time. While deer hunting above Cuba, New Mexico, I found my first dinosaur track, a twelve inch footprint that looked like a huge bird track made in a different age. While visiting the Slick Skillet Turquoise Mine in Manassas, Colorado, I was intrigued as I learned about how deposits of turquoise and other minerals were hidden away during the pueblo revolt. As a student of geology, I wondered what worlds were forever hidden

Part 1

The Legend of
El Montano del Serpiente de Cascabels

*It is not in the stars to hold our destiny
but in ourselves.*

—William Shakespeare

Be wise as serpents harmless as doves.

—Matthew 10:36

Penny's Dream

As I slept I became aware, to my amazement that for some reason flashes of intricately woven patterns of red light appeared in my mind, moving and forming the most detailed tendrils of patterns I could imagine. Normally I would have panicked, experiencing something like this, but I became curiously interested in the light show having never experienced a dream so vivid and inviting. Seeing such transformations was hypnotizing. Then my head bounced just enough to wake me as the Greyhound bus hit a chug hole in the old pavement. Glancing out of the window I could see that the bus was coming into another tiny town, but I could only see the words *San Jon* on a road sign. In the deadly monotony of the trip I had given up trying to keep up with my location. I only wanted to go back to an undisturbed sleep without having to deal with unwanted attention from unruly male passengers. The bus finally came to a complete stop to exchange a passenger; I had never been so bored in my entire life. For just a moment, I was awake, and then as the bus came to a full stop, I fell back into a deep sleep.

Then the filaments of color returned and with the same brain chemistry as someone who realizes the epiphany of a great truth, I discovered I was somewhere else, watching a world coalesce around me. There were two other people who seemed eerily familiar to me. Then, in a burst of colors I suddenly became a character in the dream.

I became mesmerized by the yellow flames of a campfire dancing in the brown eyes of a Navajo man. Except for his eyes he was invisible sitting in the shadows with no real form yet I knew, for some reason that he was Navajo. He looked up at me for just a second, staring into my soul. I ducked his gaze by looking around and pulling my sweater a little tighter over my arms; it was getting cold now that the sun had gone down despite the fire. For some reason I thought to myself that nights in the New Mexico desert should not be so chilly. I glanced uneasily at a young man who appeared to be nervously feeding the crackling campfire, while watching the sparks fly. The sparks flickered upward into the sky producing the most fantastic and intricate swirls of fire I had ever seen, then vanishing into a growing silence. It came to me that only the Navajo seemed at ease in the flickering shadows whereas everyone else felt fear and dread. For a moment I could see many things moving in the otherworldly silhouettes of darkness. Out of the shadows a snake appeared and raised its head as if to strike; it struck but it was too far away to actually strike me. It immediately recoiled and then disappeared back into the darkness.

The panic attack the snake produced lasted only a second but it was incredibly real. Turning and carefully watching where I was stepping, I returned to the confines of the fire circle, casually poking a stick into it creating new spark patterns. I cleared my throat and listened to myself say aloud, "Tell us the story of the serpents, and tell us the legend." Then I said it again but more softly, "About the *serpientes*, please tell us about the rattlesnakes."

The weathered Navajo sighed and began his tale "It is a story of ages past, and a caution. The *serpientes* and the people of this country are old, older than you know. Human clans count their lives in generations, rarely being able to trace their lineage back more than a few hundred years. Human historians can trace their history back only a few thousand years, and scientists can trace human ancestry only a few hundred thousand years. Rattlesnake clans, on the other hand, go back much further.

"Humans have had an intriguing culture, but rattlesnakes have had an enduring culture; their lineage goes back millions of years. To an outsider visiting this lonely planet, the rattlesnake would be considered a far superior creature to the humans. Rattlesnakes have been around a lot longer and are in many ways far more successful than we humans. In fact, I suspect they will still be here long after we are gone! To the human clans with their herpetologists, rattlesnakes can be a mystery and new species are still occasionally being found."

The Navajo took a long drink from his coffee cup before he continued. "Unfortunately for the rattlesnake, we are far too large to swallow. However, for a smart rattlesnake we can easily be absorbed into the local food chains. As predatory creatures, rattlesnakes are deadly and almost invisible, easily blending into the environment until an unwary person walks by. After striking, they steal away and hide, feasting on the life energy that you are losing as you die. They allow their prey, even human prey, to crawl off and die, then, while you are decomposing, your worthless carcass attracts all kinds of smaller creatures who will dine on you. The rattlesnake then dines on them!"

The Navajo seemed amused by his story but the young man and I glanced at each other and shared a feigned grimace of disgust. I found, in that instant that I was absorbed by the mysterious man's eyes. He was young and his eyes were brilliant blue with what looked like cracked glass in the iris.

The Navajo says, "Many of my people, and the people who lived here before my ancestors came, hold a unique perspective, an original view of the world."

The young man tossed another large piece of wood into the fire and everyone watched the patterns that the sparks made, in my altered state of mind the sparks created a maelstrom of delicate red patterns each punctuated with a spark of light. The Navajo continued, "Well before the non-humans, the early, cruel Spanish, and the barbarians from Texas and beyond to the east, it was the old ones who knew the best stories about rattlesnakes. My people are their descendants, and we are now old ourselves. We are isolated in personal as well as cultural patterns. We are living in a universe constructed from lifetimes of experiences, all held between the wrinkled old ears of our elders. They know the best stories about rattlesnakes from living out among them. But what you need to understand is there is far more out there than mere rattlesnakes."

A Visit from a Bruja

I was instantly awake as an elderly lady wearing a veil over her face and dressed in what looked like funerary attire asked me in Spanish if I would move over, letting her sit down beside me. I had no idea what she was saying but her hand motions were crystal clear. I moved out of her part of the seat, as fast as I could. Sitting stiffly, the elderly lady parked her cane between us but didn't release her grip on it. The cane was hand carved with the curve forming the head of a snake. Such an inanimate thing, yet it was on guard, with the triangular head always watching. It seemed to repel any thoughts of touching it or the lady.

Sitting up and looking out of the window I could see nothing; it would be some time before sunrise. Looking at the seat in front of me I wondered if I was still experiencing a dream. I wondered about my sanity. I have never experienced a dream that left me considering my sanity. My mind was in overdrive with nowhere to wander except through my memories. It was as if I had just received an electrical shock.

Looking over, with a flick of her wrist, the elderly lady adjusted the thin black shawl over her face, disappearing into her own world. Within a minute she was snoring softly, her serpentine cane guarding her, still grasped firmly in her white bony hand.

I wanted to remember the vision; it seemed that I was familiar with the men in it particularly with the one who played in the fire, but when he looked at me all I ever saw was his eyes. It seemed that we stood there looking into the fire, listening to the Navajo's words about rattlesnakes. I realized that I could remember everything the Navajo had said even though I did not understand it all. I thought about the word *serpientes*, the Spanish word for serpents and I knew it was also a place where my relatives lived in New Mexico. I could remember what the Navajo said, but I couldn't remember what his face looked like. It was all so new to me. I tried hard to think about the faces of the two men. I knew without a doubt I had never seen anyone like them before.

I was perplexed. Who were these spirits who visited my dream? Oddly, I could remember some details of the dream exactly but other things were very vague. I could remember the eyes of the two men. One naturally looks at the eyes; they are the gateways to the soul, but could not recollect their faces. It seemed that we looked into the fire while the Navajo told his story, and for some reason I was attracted to the one with the cracked blue eyes. Furthermore, I had no idea why I knew that the man was a Navajo. In my experience, growing up in East Tennessee, the only Native American I had ever met was a classmate; popular, smart and athletic. He was well mentioned in the school yearbook. My mother said that his family were Melungions who survived by doing lumber and carpentry work. His mother may well have been Cherokee but she looked to me like everyone else and so did her son. I remember him joking about it when he was filling out the forms every student has to fill out at the beginning of the school year.

The dream had been far too intense; I could remember every detail of the snake, the cold, and the vivid colors; particularly those that came out of the fire but strangely, I could remember nothing about the two men except for their eyes. Sleep was out of the question, I was afraid to sleep. My muscles were tight, like a runner in the starting blocks. I had never experienced a panic attack such as this one before. Slowly I was able to slow my breathing and began to think about the circumstances that led me to a bus stop in San Jon, New Mexico.

Memories are very human. They are a recording of our whole life, the essence of who we are. Most memories are like flowers pressed between the pages of a book. Over time they slowly lose their colors and fragrance until they finally crumble into tiny particles and fall from the pages. Humans sometimes rearrange those memories into meaningful patterns that make sense to us but often have little relationship to what actually happened. We don't remember what really happened, and what we create in our minds becomes what happened. Our memories lie to us. They were not golden times but rather ordinary experiences that are now gold plated. Today's ordinary experiences will someday become tomorrow's gold plated memories.

The things we experience outlast our mortality. Those things are like monuments that people build to honor heroes after they've died. They're like the pyramids that the Egyptians built to honor the pharaohs. Only instead of being made of stone, they're made out of the memories of our essence.

We tend to forget what is uncomfortable and remember those times that were fun. We tend to remember the birth of a child but forget the pain of the labor. Perhaps it is a survival mechanism when we humans totally block out some memories, memories of pain and anguish can disappear quickly but some memories can be indelible. I tend to remember every moment of meaningful experiences, particularly those connected to grand adventures and fortunately, my life was to become a series of grand adventures linked to a family into which I was adopted. Sitting there in the bus as the first tiny hint of daybreak appeared on the horizon outside of the window, I considered my life story, the story of Penny Anderson.

Childhood Reflections

As a child, what few pictures taken of me show a lankly blond girl who would have been labeled as homely. I never thought of myself as particularly good looking. In fact, I thought of myself as being downright ugly and as far as intellect; I was not exactly known as the class valedictorian. I was a misunderstood child who was slowly morphing into a completely different person both physically and mentally.

Teachers at Camp Creek Elementary School complained to my mother that I had too much energy. I would not sit still in school nor did I seem to care. Life offered too many exciting things to explore and I didn't need a teacher to explore everything that life offered. Don't get me wrong, Every once in a while I would take out time to actually look at those spelling words or even watch how the teacher did long division but I sure wasn't about to waste my precious time practicing those skills. I didn't need to. I simply looked at a page in a book and could bring the whole page back in my memory as if by magic.

Much later, I would learn that I had a photographic memory. Unfortunately at the time, a school psychologist labeled me with something called attention deficit disorder; ADHD. The psychologist requested that I be put in special education classes where I could work in a controlled environment. I found myself in classes that were mostly composed of troubled but otherwise ordinary children. I stole the teacher's answer books and memorized them.

Suddenly I was considered smarter than the teacher because I knew the answers to the problems that were in the textbooks that even the teacher couldn't solve; the math teacher needed the teacher's book with the answers to demonstrate how to solve the problems. I felt sorry for her so I returned her books with all the answers in them. The frustrated and embarrassed teacher immediately had me placed back into the regular classroom.

Despite it all, I have fond memories and am proud of my years at Camp Creek and now at the newly constructed East Greene High School. I liked my new school despite the narrow mindedness of the teachers, administrators and the local people who actually ran the school through political pressure.

They disliked change. Before the new school had been built the locals had been embroiled in a major fight between the people who wanted a new high school and those who wanted all the schools to remain elementary school based through high school. A major concern, far more than the quality of education was the future of the football teams.

Winning football teams trumped everything. Many wanted one large county high school which would guarantee a large pool of students to draw from. Instead they wound up with four smaller schools; East, West, North, and South High Schools. They were doomed by the structure of the system to have mediocre football teams. The local town of Greeneville, on the other hand, spent far more money-per student than the county schools. Their football team was in the state playoffs almost every year. Because of this, the citizens of the local town demonstrated a superior attitude toward the county students.

Before the high school was constructed, Camp Creek had many people who still referred to the town as Cold Springs because of a minor civil war battle that had occurred nearby. Located about ten miles out of Greeneville, the county seat of Greene County, Camp Creek consisted of a country grocery store and gas station, several churches, a café, and a school that served grades one through twelve.

Located at the buckle of the Bible belt, and despite the fact that they all prayed to the same God and used the same bible, the citizens of one small community distrusted the citizens of another and felt that trouble would inevitably occur. Maybe, they just wanted to control what was being taught in those schools. They held to beliefs that had been passed down through the generations. Because of that, the schools lagged far behind most urban schools even in East Tennessee.

At least for me, things did change. During my last semester at East Greene, I had made straight A's, one A- in math class and three other A's, in Agriculture class, and the other in physical education, being especially proud of the grade earned in chemistry; an A+. It was a fun class, just a matter of learning the rules of the game and solving many little puzzles. I remember that being only a sophomore and the youngest student in the class I made the highest grade. This made me proud. Most of my classmates would refuse to take the time to learn the rules and chemistry was a class most of the girls avoided, which was one of several mysteries to me. I felt I could do anything the boys in the school did; in fact, I knew I could do a lot better job than most of them. Many of the girls in my school took the attitude that some classes, such as math and science, were meant only for boys, but I knew better.

Memories keep flowing into my head about those days, I had been taught that I could achieve anything I wanted in life by two of the most important people in my life: my father, who kindly took great pains to instill me with lofty goals and ideals while he lived with us, and my physical science teacher, Mr. Dale whom I had encountered the previous semester.

Mr. Dale was different from most of the other teachers at East Greene High School; he wanted his students to learn to think for themselves. As soon as the students walked into the class room, while attendance was being taken, he had his students copy a quotation from a famous person off the chalkboard. His first quotation was, *"I can deal with stupidity, but not with those that are proud of it."* This quotation pretty much described the red neck boys who would stumble into class and drape themselves over their desk, often going to sleep. I often thought that those boys were a waste of time but had to be dealt with. Mr. Dale then wrote five words on the blackboard and asked the students to explain what they meant. *"Then they came for me."* Five simple little words, what could they possibly mean? After we finished copying the quotation, the class discussed what the author was trying to convey. The five words come from an important historical incident during the rise of the Nazis during World War II. Mr. Dale would need to explain and give many examples of what he was talking about. Few of the boys in the room ever realized that he could be talking about them.

We learned from the greatest of philosophers, educators, politicians, and writers in the world. My favorite quotations were from Mark Twain, a classic example of a person who thought for himself. Like Mark Twain, as well as many others, Mr. Dale taught students to make their own choices about life rather than just believe what they were told. Because of this Mr. Dale had made enemies in the community. One deacon of a Baptist church was especially angry with him. What the school officials couldn't understand was that the deacon was also the head of the local KKK. He particularly disliked Mr. Dale because of his liberal thinking. Mr. Dale was continually making a point that we needed to become problem solvers, thinking for ourselves rather than to have someone think for us, but to be tolerant of people who were different from us. He made me believe in myself, even if others didn't believe in me.

Ancient Trails

When I was starting my junior year of high school in the tiny town of Camp Creek in East Tennessee, I had begun to skip my lunches at school, saving the money and secreting it a short distance away in a secure hiding place on a very small trail, behind the farmhouse which led up a sharp rise, rising eventually to a mountain ridge. I don't know why I felt obligated to save that precious money, but something inside of me made me. Perhaps it was a premonition, something that comes into one's consciousness without a reason or rhyme.

Ancient trails crisscrossed the entire mountain like spider webs. Trails that have been used by people as far back as can be remembered. Trails originally used by the American Indians, then early settlers. They were used as hideaways during the civil war and now as hunting trails and places for kids to play. My hiding place, where my purloined lunch money was hidden, was on one of those trails discovered during long walks with my Grandfather. As a little girl, my grandfather and I had explored all of the trails on the ridge and purely by accident we discovered a hollow tree with an opening turned away unseen from the main trail.

As we walked, my grandfather told me stories about the history surrounding our community on the mountain; stories usually about the Civil War. To me, all of those stories were fascinating. The county was named after Nathaniel Greene, a revolutionary war hero. Settlers first came to Greene County as far back as 1772 when early pioneers first arrived on the Nolichucky River and by 1784 the entire area became what is known as the State of Franklin, which later became Tennessee, and is why many streets and buildings have references to the Lost State of Franklin. During the Civil War, Greene County was largely Unionist becoming the winter quarters for General James Longstreet after the Confederate defeat at the Battle of Knoxville in 1863. Not everyone around Greene County was pro Union. Confederate Calvary Commander John Hunt Morgan was killed in 1864 when Union forces surprised him and his officers in Greeneville. Greeneville became the only town in the United States that paid tribute to both the Union and the Confederacy in its courthouse square. Evidence for the war is found all around the county, everything from the Minnie balls, a large caliber shell used by the Union forces that are still occasionally dug out of the ground to the cannon ball that is still clearly visible in the Presbyterian Church wall in downtown Greeneville.

Soldiers from both sides took pot shots at each other along these trails. Grandfather explained that most people think of the battle of Blue Springs near Mosheim as being the great battle that took place in this county; however some of the most vicious fighting occurred on that old ridge overlooking the Campbell farm. It must have been terrifying, discovering that you and your enemy are on the same trail creating an impasse. Fighting in old growth forest is very difficult; solders cannot form a battle line as was the preferred style of fighting during the civil war. Just getting around is usually impossible. The forest is more of a thick jungle here. Neither side could get around the other without a herculean effort. Both sides would eventually need to retreat.

The preferred method of assassination during those days was hiding behind a rock overlooking the ridge, waiting to spot movement on one of the trails. A stealthy army could move to within a few yards of the crest of the ridge without ever being spotted and then a blood bath occurred.

The Cherokee tribes had used those trails and there was evidence that many others had been there well before Columbus. There were people who had lived here eons ago, probably hunting ice age animals, using the ridge as a hunting advantage, and the forest to hide in.

A graceful yet ancient ridge, its flanks and ramparts were covered then, as it is now, in poisonous plants; mostly poison ivy and oak. Ancient travelers would learn to carry ample supplies of jewel weed with them to counter the effects of the ivy. In the past, the entire countryside was forested, not as it is now. In the modern world, the forest appears as islands between farms. The world of the forest creatures is constantly shrinking. A way of life is rapidly disappearing.

As a kid, my friends and I had explored every inch of the ridge. From an early time in my life I could remember taking walks with my grandfather, Papa Nick, following those ancient trails. Starting from the old farmhouse we followed a hardly discernible trail through the woods to a small clearing. From there, we followed the older established trails. Generally, one trail followed the ridge, and another trail followed below, under the rocks that formed the cap rock with smaller trails disappearing down the mountain to other farms and secret places.

One of those secret places was a small cave. Really not a cave at all but an overhang, the cap rock formed a place to get in out of the weather. I remembered playing there many times while Papa Nick would sit, rest, and smoke an old pipe while looking down at our his farm.

Nowadays it was a great place for kids to play, those small assassins. Becoming a teenager, I would enjoy jogging the trails but now as a high school student I rarely ventured into the woods except to hide a bit of money. Soon I discovered that high school required most of my time, but occasionally I still wandered up on the mountain's flanks where I took time to think.

Remembering a particular day, I realized that I couldn't answer to myself why I was saving my lunch money, but for some reason I felt compelled to squirrel it away. The hollow tree made a perfect place to hide a coffee can full of money, but I have often wondered why I felt so compelled to save it. Skipping lunch seemed to be a painful way to save money particularly during afternoon athletic sessions; the only happy person was the wrestling coach who marveled at how I had kept my anorexic body weight down.

High school was my great escape, almost a vacation from the tension of home life. I hardly had to participate or do anything for my A in physical education because of my participation in varsity sports. Although I had played volleyball and softball for years, this year I had also made the girls wrestling team. I was good at it, missing going to state my first year by losing only one match. And the girl who won that match, a senior, went on to take first place in the state meet. The kids suddenly respected me, particularly the boys who would die of embarrassment if a girl beat them at anything nonacademic, making my time at school a joy and I got along with everybody. Everybody, that is, except my mother.

Jealousy

My mother, Mona and I, had lived alone since Mom had split from my father and we had moved back in with my maternal grandparents, Nick and Nora Campbell. Coming back to live with her parents was very difficult for mom.

Mom had left Camp Creek when she was seventeen years old to go to Texas to visit her brother Tom, and she planned on never looking back. She had high hopes and big plans for herself. But reality sometimes interferes with high hopes and big plans; Mom's reality was very different from her hopes and dreams.

She had married my father, Tim Anderson, who worked on an oil rig, after a whirlwind romance. She married him mostly for the security. Getting married and having some guy take care of you was the accepted norm but she was not prepared for the baby or the loneliness that soon followed. My father had to stay at the drilling sites that he worked on for two or three weeks at a time, and sometimes that turned into months at a time. Then he would come home for a few days. The days that he was home were very exciting; he showed mom all of the local sites and kept her entertained. But the other weeks were filled with loneliness. Then, of course, she found out that she was pregnant.

My father was extremely excited about the baby and so was my mom, but she had to go through the long months and the hard times of being pregnant mostly alone. Dad tried to give her all the attention she needed in the few days that he was home each month, but that was impossible. She found herself begging him to stay home every time he left, but she knew that they would be without an income if he stayed. So she learned to keep her mouth shut and began to feel more and more, unhappy as time went by.

She stuck it out for five years. But as I grew older, things between Mom and Dad got worse. Finally, Mom gave up on the marriage to my father and asked her mother if she could come back to live at the farm. Her parents said yes, but Mona felt as if she were a failure, dragging herself and her little girl, me, back home with her tail between her legs.

Dad was not at all happy about Mom's leaving the small house he had bought for her. He seemed to love me very much, even though he had grown tired of Moms constant complaints about his being gone so much. "If you want to run back home to your parents, you need to find a way to get there on your own, because I am not going to give you the money to get there!" I remember him shouting angrily, along with a lot of insults about her not being able to stand on her own. Mom knew of course that her parents would bring their old pickup truck over and haul her things back to the farmhouse. Feeling intense shame, Mom called her parents.

"Are you sure that this is the right thing to do?" said Nora, my grandmother, "No one in our family has ever been divorced before." Mom knew that her mother was thinking about the reaction of the ladies in the First Baptist Church when she came home with no husband and with a little girl to take care of.

"Yes, Mother, this is the only thing that I can do," said Mona, Our grandparents finally agreed, but the whole conversation had made Mom feel like the biggest disappointment to them that she could possibly be. Dejected and disheartened, we returned to the Campbell farm.

When I reached seventeen years of age, with all the hopes and dreams that Mom had when she was that age; my feelings about the whole mess started to change. I remember having a skewed idea of my father, Tim. For all these years, he had been able to swoop in to Camp Creek for a week, spoiling me rotten, and then he disappeared leaving Mom to deal with the repercussions of the spoiling. He bought me toys when I was too little to understand that Mom could not afford them; as I got older he bought me clothes that made the other farm girls in Camp Creek jealous.

When he left, I expected Mom to buy me things just like Dad had. Unfortunately, Mom only had the money that she could earn at the local cafe, one dollar and twenty five cents per hour and tips, and that was not much. Supporting herself and me was a constant worry. We always had plenty of food because of the farm, but extra money for fancy toys and clothes was very scarce.

Mom meant well for me, but was way too busy with her own affairs to take care of a young daughter, or even to show an interest in my accomplishments. By the time she got home from a long day at the cafe she was dead on her feet, and that is when the arguments usually occurred. I wanted to talk about school, boys, and everything a girl could imagine, but Mom just wanted to go to sleep. Even when mother had free time from work there were always complications.

Mom was a very attractive lady, always the center of attention at the cafe. Men frequently asked her out, and I couldn't help but resent it. With grim determination I vowed that there was more to life than marrying some guy who would take care of me for the rest of my life. I watched my classmates and quickly figured out that the boys at school my friends married were far more interested in having someone to take care of them than they were of taking care of their girlfriends. In fact, some of my friends quickly discovered to their sorrow that many teenage boys were only after sex.

Afterwards the boys had no use for the girls; as word got around, which it always did, the only boys that came around were those who wanted to have sex. The responsible boys seldom came around. In this small community once a girl lost her reputation it was impossible for her to get it back.

I was determined not to fall in love and repeat the same old pattern I saw over and over. Early on, I decided that when or if I got married it was going to be a mutually independent, but supportive and nurturing, relationship. We would share responsibilities, both financial and emotional. Life, as well as many people, had taught me to think for myself.

Feeling torn between my father and mother, and the jealousy between the two made everything difficult, leaving me ever so desperately wanting to move to West Texas to live with my father. I idolized my father, but thinking back, I had actually spent very little time with him. Back in Texas, my father was an oil roughneck, so we knew that it would be impossible for me to live with him. I would be alone much of the time because of his work, and Mom justifiably felt that I was too young to be left alone in a strange town full of roughnecks.

However, there was one other possibility that could be pursued. My father Tim had a brother who lived in *Serpiente,* New Mexico, and he and his wife June had invited me to come out to visit many times. Of course I never could actually afford such a trip, but the thought intrigued me. When I approached my mother with the possibility of going to West Texas to visit my dad, the conversation always ended up in a screaming argument, but visiting Ken and June in *Serpiente*, New Mexico was another question altogether; mom simply got quiet and said, "We'll see."

My father thought the move was a great idea and even thought of sending me some money for the bus trip, but my mother seemed to always nix the idea. She actually loved me very much, but the idea of not having a teenage girl to support and discipline was enticing to her. She was still a relatively young woman, and she had frequently gone on dates with some of the men who came into the café. But as I grew older the responsibility of taking care of me had become a heavy burden to her. As I grew older my mother did not like the way some of her dates looked at me. She never went out with those men again, keeping me safe became more and more difficult.

Turner

I always felt very uncomfortable when mother started dating a new man. Most of them were nice, but I felt like a third wheel when they were around and I resented the time mother spent with strangers rather than going to the sports and honors events at school. In my heart I knew it was time to leave, even if it meant giving up my senior year with friends and moving to a place that could have just as well been on the other side of the planet.

The final straw that broke the impasse was when my grandparents, Nick and Nora hired a hand to help around the farm. Turner was a local boy who was eight years younger than Mom. Typical in many ways, he was proud of himself. A good worker, he knew how to operate a small farm and made life much easier for Nick and Nora, however he had one characteristic that made him stand out; he thought he was God's answer to women. He fancied himself irresistible to women. In only a short time he began spending time with mother, literally hanging around the house when he should have been out in the fields. Mom basically ignored his advances, knowing that all he wanted was a one night stand, then he would lose all interest in her and probably move on to another job leaving the grandparents to find another worker.

The problem that Mom could never grasp is that Turner was far more interested in pursuing me than her. It had all started out so innocently. Most southern boys use flirting as a polite way of getting through life. It would not seem uncommon for a boy to flirt with a girl, it happened all the time. Flirting was a way of life with many of the prominent boys in the high school. But after a while, I noticed that Turner wanted to single me out. I always felt like I was being herded to a deserted place where he could be in charge. Invariably anytime he could find himself alone with me he would start some serious flirting.

I made it perfectly clear that I didn't like him at all, but that never seemed to slow him down. Every time mom left to go to work Turner would show up. Many other girls would have given in to him, and had, but I refused to play his game. I belittled him which only made him angry. He became determined to conquer me even if he had to force himself upon me.

Then it all began in earnest, I began to fear for my safety one evening when everyone was gone. He literally chased me around the house tackling me and holding me down while attempting to French kiss me which I thought was disgusting. I rolled him off after a while and then ducked into the bedroom and soundly smacked him in the shins with a softball bat as he charged in. Turner rolled over grabbing his shins and letting out a profanity. Running past him while he was in agony, I darted out the front door and then immediately changed direction heading to the trail so I could lose him in the woods.

Turner appeared at the back door of the house and slowly started up the trail but it was obvious he was still smarting from the baseball bat to his shins. He slowly followed me up about fifty feet then put his hands on his hips, turned and returned to the house.

I hid deep under a cedar tree with my thoughts focused upon an escape to *Serpiente*. I had never lived on a western ranch before, but I certainly knew how to take care of farm animals. The rural community of Camp Creek had allowed me an ample education in dealing with livestock and most of my friends were county students living on small farms. I could ride horses, milk cows, and buck bales of hay with the best of the boys.

Two hours later I watched as Mom returned from the café. Thinking that Turner had left the house I returned but as I entered the front door I was shocked to find Turner sitting on the couch with a smug look on his face and his arm wrapped over Mom's shoulder. Immediately, I knew it was time to go. I returned to my room, braced a chair under the door and made plans.

The Greyhound Bus

*O*n a sunny June day in 1966, I snuck out of the house and caught a ride to Knoxville with a friend. In Knoxville I boarded a Greyhound bus which slowly poked its way to New Mexico. I couldn't afford the direct bus so every little town required a stop with an exchange of passengers. It had taken me over a week before the bus finally pulled into the Tucumcari bus depot.

Looking over I was surprised to find the mysterious lady who had been sitting beside me had now vanished. I could not remember her getting up to leave. The only boarding passenger was an Indian, who for some reason insisted upon sitting directly beside me, again trapping me away from the aisle in a single seat. All I could do was sit there and wonder about his intentions. Suddenly I felt like I had escaped one bad situation only to find myself in another.

"Excuse me!" I said, as the large Indian slid into the seat next to me. "I've come nearly the whole way from Tennessee with this seat to myself."

Usually strangers simply got up and moved to another seat when I asked them, but as the bus filled up with passengers the Indian just stared ahead without saying anything. But he also propped his feet up in front of him, making it impossible for me to get out without crawling over him.

I was perplexed; not wanting to look arrogant and say something really rude, but I sure didn't like being boxed in. I stood up and looked down the rows of seats but couldn't see an empty seat. I decided to pretend to be indifferent to the Indian by looking out the window but soon I couldn't help but glance at him every few minutes. He was dressed roughly, in old jeans with cowboy boots that looked completely worn out. But from his waist up he appeared to have on a new plaid shirt. He was wearing no Indian jewelry, rare I was to later learn. Many southwestern Indians carried much of their wealth in the form of turquoise and silver jewelry. His hair was cut short like a business man allowing me to think to myself that maybe he wasn't entirely wild. Never the less, I was a little nervous, having never been around a real Indian before, not even the local Cherokee Indians that were indigenous to East Tennessee. This fellow was distinctly Native American. I was trapped and I knew it, so I did the next logical thing and slid over to the window and fell into a nervous sleep as the bus pulled out for Santa Rosa.

After a quick stop in *Cuervo*, New Mexico, I awoke as the bus pulled into *Santa Rosa*. It was lunch and bathroom time, and a chance to change seats. But just as I stood to get out, the Indian glanced over to me and said, "Penny Anderson?"

In amazement I replied, "Yes?"

"When you come back I have to talk to you about your uncle," he said. Blankly I stared back at him wondering what to say. How did he know my name? How did he know my uncle? He finally stood up allowing me to gently ease past him.

Away to the restrooms I ran, looking for the elderly lady with the serpentine cane but she had indeed vanished. I decided it was time to eat. Unfortunately, by the time I had arrived in Santa Rosa, I was for all practical purposes dead broke, having used up all but two quarters from my stash of lunch money, saving those to make phone calls.

Inside the bright bus counter the smell of hamburgers being grilled made my stomach growl, having not eaten for two days. I noticed the mysterious Indian sitting at the counter, eating a hamburger while watching the tourists pick at the trinkets in the curio shop adjoining the lunch counter. To the Navajo Indian it was a curious sight, watching people from faraway places like Chicago or New York poke through aisles of Indian trinkets that most likely were made in China or Mexico, certainly not made by Navajo artisans. It must have struck him as curious how people were fascinated by Indian trinkets but were afraid to speak to a real live Indian. Real Indians, he knew, would never use any of the toys that the tourists cherished. Most Navajo Indians couldn't afford such toys and certainly had better things to spend their money on, like food, gas and electricity, when it was available.

I stood behind him trying to figure the man out. Then he turned, without looking back at me and quietly signaled with two upturned fingers for me to come and join him. He then pointed to the empty chair next to him, just as if he knew that I had been watching him. Well, somehow he knew my name and the fact that my uncle lived in *Serpiente*, but he seemed so imposing and mysterious. Now that I really had a good look at him, I realized that he wasn't as old as my first impression had given me, perhaps five years older than me. He was just weathered, as if he had spent a lot of time outdoors.

Deciding to confront him I walked up to him in front of the many people eating in the café and blurted out, "How did you know my name, and what do you know about my uncle?"

He casually glanced up and stuffed another French fry into his mouth while ignoring me. Looking straight ahead I could see his eyes in the reflection from the counter mirror. I recognized those eyes and suddenly felt at ease. I sat down next to him looking into his reflection. He looked straight ahead and said nothing at first. He seemed completely uninterested.

After another slow chew followed by a slow swallow, followed by an even longer sip of his cola, he finally said, "June received a phone call from your mother. Evidently, after searching everywhere the police finally ran into your friend from the high school who gave you the ride to Knoxville. She was brought in as an accessory to a crime. Everyone thought maybe you had been kidnapped. Your friend explained to your mother what had actually happened which caused a confrontation with your friend Turner. Your mother found out what was really going on and called the police and had him arrested. Since then, we have been watching for you to show up. By the way, my truck is in Albuquerque at the bus stop. I'm supposed to, maybe," he said hesitantly with a frown on his face, help you return home."

I stared at him, not saying anything. "OK," the Native American continued, "your uncle, Ken Anderson sent me, but you have to understand that we have a problem out at the ranch."

A problem, out at the ranch, I had never imagined that possibility.

"There are some things...funny things happening out at the ranch, and so he sent me here to talk you out of coming out to *Serpiente*. By the way, my name is *Naalyehe Ya Sidahi*." He looked over at me. I'm sure I had a frown on my face and he followed his name with; "That is my birth name, which most people have no idea how to pronounce or what it means. By the way, it means one who is a trader but all my friends just call me Hidalgo, like the horse or the county in southern New Mexico. I've been called Hidalgo ever since I was a little kid growing up on the reservation, the name just stuck to me." Looking at his reflection in the lunch counter he said slowly, "I don't know how I got that name; it's the name I've been called all my life." And with a flip of his wrist he ordered the waitress over.

Hidalgo

*D*uring my last two years I would eat very little at school. Lunch was often the main meal and sometimes the only meal of the day for many of the local students. My conditioning didn't matter, I was starving. I had run out of money somewhere in Oklahoma and I was already worried about what was going to happen if I didn't make connections with Uncle Ken. But Hidalgo had already ordered a plate of cheeseburgers with fries and large cheery malt. In just a moment the food would be delivered. It was just what I wanted, and immediately I was grateful for the generosity of the mysterious Indian called Hidalgo.

"Let me explain how this works," Hidalgo said, "I had business in Tucumcari so I left my truck in Albuquerque and took the bus to Tucumcari so I could ride back with you and explain the situation to you."

"What situation?" I asked. At this the Navajo wrinkled his forehead and looked off past the tourists.

"This may not be the best time for you come out to the ranch; we are having serious problems with the livestock. I'm afraid that we may have to send you back to Tennessee," Hidalgo said bluntly.

Hearing that, my eyes started to tear up, flowing down my cheeks; nobody seemed to want me around.

Hidalgo continued with his story, "Several summers ago we noticed around the ranch house that all the small animals were disappearing, you know, like rabbits and chickens. We didn't think much about it because it only happened in the summertime, but after a while we started noticing larger animals disappearing. Even John Luna, our neighbor, reported to us that some of his cattle were disappearing."

He stopped talking when the waitress set down a plate with a large cheeseburger and a pile of French fries in front of me. My mouth began to water at the smell of the food, but I knew that I did not have any money to pay for the food.

"I did not order this," I said quickly.

Hidalgo chuckled softly and replied," I thought you might be a little hungry since your mother told June that the only way you could have gotten the money to make this trip was by saving up your lunch money. I didn't figure that amount of money would go very far on a long trip like you have been on."

Softly I whispered, "Thanks," and dug into the pile of food.

While I was eating, Hidalgo continued with his story. "The chickens disappeared from the henhouse, and Uncle Ken and Aunt June had to drive all the way into *Los Lunas* and buy new baby chicks." Hidalgo held up his hand with two fingers sticking out, "Twice they bought new chicks before we started locking them up at night to keep them from disappearing."

"Your uncle has decided that he needs to send you back to Tennessee for your own safety. He doesn't want to be responsible for you. What if you disappeared, too?"

The Ride to Albuquerque

I was flustered, but had learned in high school to stand on my own. "Face your fears and they will go away," my wrestling coach would say. I was determined to see my uncle; besides, he was my ticket to freedom, including the freedom to eventually get to live with my father. Hidalgo was stoic at first, he wanted to avoid a scene and he was already receiving curious looks from some of the older ladies, but as soon as tears started pouring down my face, he softened. Within minutes we were climbing back into the bus. Hidalgo had no choice but to be kind, it could be dangerous to a young Indian or anyone else accused of trying to hurt a defenseless young girl.

Returning to the Greyhound bus, I stared out of the window at the strange scenery around me. In the distance were huge mountains, but unlike in Tennessee, where they would be covered with trees, there was only a sprinkling of small cedars and juniper. Brilliant blood red bluffs capped the flat mountains looking like they had been stained with the blood of ages. They were timeless and mysterious, not inviting as the hills of East Tennessee had been. The few small creeks we drove past, arroyos as they were called in the West; were bone dry.

The ride to Albuquerque was filled with descriptions of what the local ranchers were dealing with. At all the ranches the pattern was basically the same; first the chickens disappeared and so the ranch hands found themselves taking turns, staying up all night watching for coyotes. But not a single coyote was ever seen. Then small calves were found scattered around the range, dead, with bloated bodies. The ranch hands found themselves on night patrols after that, looking for evidence of poachers; not a single thief was ever found, and not a single shot from a rifle was ever fired.

"Tempers were on edge, neighboring ranchers were under suspicion, even though they were losing livestock too. Then winter came and it all mysteriously stopped. But as the heat of summer returned, so did the disappearances. Needless to say, we all have our hands full," said Hidalgo.

"We would prefer not to deal with another responsibility. Your uncle is going broke despite years of hard work to build up one of the best ranches in New Mexico. He would never forgive himself if anything happened to you."

I listened patiently, but my decision was firm. I had to be patient, I didn't have any choice. To return to Tennessee would be a disaster. Now I was seriously worried about my future.

A billboard sign appeared alongside the road; "Mountains ahead, better gas up!" But that last part of the trip through Tijeras canyon where the northern, upper end of the mountains called the *Sandias* and the lower, southern part called the *Manzanos* were dissected, seemed to take only a short while. My mind was in overdrive as we arrived at the terminal in Albuquerque and as Hidalgo had said, there was his old Ford truck parked in a nearby parking lot. Hidalgo continued pleading with me, even pulling out a large roll of money and forcing it into my hand. Handing it back forcefully into Hidalgo's hand, I was defiant; I wasn't going to back down without a fight. We both looked down to the ground for an instant and quickly I opened the door to the pickup truck and climbed in.

Hidalgo stood with his hands on his hips and just watched for a spell, He was amazed at my stubbornness, but also my strength of will. Hidalgo looked at me sitting in the cab of his truck with my arms folded in defiance, a complete turnaround from a few hours before.

Hidalgo playfully walked around to the window on my side of the truck and said, "How do you know that I have not been lying to you? Maybe I'm not really a hired hand out to rescue a young lady, maybe I'm the boogieman out to get you?"

"No, you are not the boogieman," my eyes rolled as I said the words. "You are Hidalgo who works for Ken Anderson, my father's brother. You know way too much, you have described Ken and June exactly. You also described the ranch at *Serpiente*. Your description is exactly like the description I read in a letter from June, and she described the ranch in detail. She mentioned you."

With this realization, Hidalgo threw up his arms and walked around the truck to the driver's side. Hidalgo shook his head and said to me, "You are just like your father. I worked with him in Colorado. He was the one who got me this job with your uncle that has allowed me to send money to my family." He glanced over at me and continued, "We don't want to be mean about all this, but we have a problem out at the ranch and..."

I finished his sentence with, "and you don't want me to get hurt."

I just stared ahead and said, "Fine. If you don't take me to the ranch I'll get there by myself, even if I have to walk."

I knew I had him; playing poker was not new to me, besides I had learned a few things from my mother such as how to handle men, and instinctually I was still learning.

Hidalgo leaned over to me and said, I was not lying about the problem at the ranch house, but so far, no humans have died, as far as I know."

I looked at him but in his soft brown eyes all I could see was concern. He didn't blink. Answering him with a firm and short staccato voice I said; "First of all, a real boogie man would not have been so corny when trying to approach a girl." then I smiled at him.

Hidalgo went limp in the seat, then slowly rising he pushed the key into the ignition, turned the key, and stepped on the starter. The old motor roared to life and we pulled out of the parking lot.

Corey

*P*ulling onto the Old Isleta highway and heading south, entering the Rio Grande Valley, I began to realize that we were in a different world. Except for the long meandering valley that the Rio Grande River flowed through, there was little green anywhere until my eyes traveled all the way to the distant eastern mountains, the *Manzanos*, or Apple Mountains as Hidalgo called them. He explained that over two hundred years ago someone had actually planted an apple orchard on the back side which is how the Mountain got its name. No more rolling green hills with tiny farms like the ones back in East Tennessee! To the west was mile after mile of flat land, dotted with volcanic cones and flat topped black hills where lava spread out like pancake batter.

We turned off in *Los Lunas* and filled the old truck and some Jerry cans in the back of the truck up with gas, Then we ventured off to the west, over the *Rio Puerco* River, and finally turned south again on a dirt road past several black volcanic hills. We traveled between 10 and 35 miles per hour on this corrugated and winding road. In the distance Hidalgo pointed out *Ladrone* Peak, Hidalgo pointed further to the south where the ranch was located, still an hour away on this rutted and sandy road.

By the time we arrived at the ranch house, Hidalgo and I were fast friends. We had no choice, it was a long drive. *Ladrone* Peak was now to the north and the sun was just setting. It was a typical New Mexican ranch, with a very large main house, barn, and several outbuildings. Everything was run down, but that was normal in an area where everything had a function and pretty didn't really count for much. Even in Tennessee the local farms had been small cities to themselves. However, this particular ranch house looked different. Everything was boarded up, with no windows uncovered.

Uncle Ken and Aunt June were there, under the porch along with two small children that belonged to the house keeper, a small boy about ten years old, called Jacob and an eight year old girl with hair so black that it seemed to shine. She was introduced as Rebecca. They were just leaving as Hidalgo and I drove up. Apparently they were being escorted out to their old truck. They loaded into their old truck and waved as we got out of Hidalgo's truck.

Uncle Ken and Aunt June walked out to hug and greet us, but I could feel them pulling my arms and directing me inside the house. As I got to the steps of the porch a man appeared in the doorway. Standing on the porch was a young man who was about the same age as me and really good looking, I thought to myself. He was dressed just like Hidalgo, except that all his clothes were obviously work clothes draped over a muscular body. I was shocked to see those same brilliant blue eyes that looked like cut glass actually looking at me. He had a face with a smile that instantly mesmerized me. I instantly seemed to know him and thought to myself that I finally got to see the face that belonged to those eyes in my dream. Ken and June introduced the young man as Corey.

Uncle Ken later explained to me that Corey's father had been his best friend. Unfortunately, when Corey's parents were killed in a traffic accident a few years ago, he had to decide where he was going to live. Normally he would have simply stayed with his relatives in Albuquerque. He knew he was welcome there. But just on a whelm, Ken and June invited him to stay out at the ranch for a couple of weeks, a vacation, a place where he could be alone to decide what he wanted to do. He never left the ranch, becoming an integral member of the family that ran the ranch.

Aunt June later told me that Corey had turned out to be a great help to them. He was willing to do anything that needed to be done around the ranch, both inside the house and around the rest of the ranch. He was like a son to Uncle Ken and Aunt June, and an older brother to the many small children that seemed to appear around the house during the day. Before the disappearances that occurred, ranch hands would stay over at the ranch doing odd jobs and seasonal work and most of them had children. But now, few were around.

It was getting late when we arrived, but it was obvious that something was wrong. They quickly herded me past Corey and into the ranch house and the door was locked behind us. Inside, sitting at the kitchen table, was my father, with a big grin on his face.

After hugs, everyone sat down at the dinner table, a huge table piled high with an astounding variety of food. There was a sampling of all the Mexican food popular in that part of the country and as soon as all the plates were full I began carefully tasting the strange smelling but delicious food, and a multitude of conversations began.

Finally the talk got around to me. "Penny, you will just have to forgive us," said Uncle Ken. "Something strange is going on around here, and we don't understand what it is."

My uncle explained that all the local ranches were dealing with the same problem, and nobody understood what was causing it. "Our livestock is being killed; small animals are disappearing, and, as of last week, we learned some men have disappeared as well. We can find no trace of what is killing them, but it seems to always happen at night. During the day, nothing happens." This sounded a little frightening to me, but I was too excited about seeing my father for the first time in more than two years to think too much about it.

Later, when everyone else was fast asleep, my father and I talked about what was going on and about what I was going to do. I learned that my mother had called my father in Texas. She related how everyone was in a panic when I left until they finally discovered your friend that had driven you to Knoxville.

Evidently Turner had showed up at the house the next day, which may have eliminated him as a kidnapper. However he got into a huge argument with Mona, punching her several times and demanding to know what Mona had done to his girlfriend, me! Fortunately for us but very unfortunately for Turner my grandparents had driven up, recognized what Turner was up to and called the police. They arrived a few minutes later and slapped handcuffs on him then hauled him off. He is currently charged with assault and battery, home invasion, and after the police discovered a stolen gun in his truck he was confined to a jail where he will be for at least a couple of years.

"Now that Turner is out of the picture, do you want to go back to Tennessee?" my father asked.

I emphatically answered, "No." I was angry at what had happened, sorry for my mother, and wrestling with a dozen other emotions that were all taking a toll. I finally slumped down in the couch and at some point I dozed off, probably due to complete exhaustion.

Miss Snoops

I awoke with a start, wondering what time it was. The last thing I remembered was talking to my father while sitting in a couch next to a huge kitchen table. Now I found myself in a real bed. It was the first time I had slept on a real bed in several days and because of the late hour I had stayed up talking to my father I had slept hard. After catching my breath, I discovered that I was still in my clothes; someone had carried me to bed. It took me a while to sort out everything in my mind. I knew

I had been dreaming but couldn't remember the dream. The dream didn't matter, it was just another dream. Besides, I was waking up in a whole new world.

The room was completely dark except for a pale sliver of light under the door. Fumbling out of the bed I discovered a round cylindrical object on the end table next to the bed. It was a flashlight. Slowly making my way over to the door I looked outside. The first thing I focused on was a skull staring back at me on a shelf. I was in a long hallway with the walls covered with bookshelves. Stepping out of the door and turning, I followed the light but stopped to look around. Books overflowed from many of the bookshelves that seemed to cover every possible space on the walls. Where there were no books or papers on the shelves there was copious amounts of Indian pottery and artifacts, all, I would discover belonging to June.

Looking up and down the hallway I discovered June walking toward me. "What's with the skull," I asked?

"Oh that's Elmer" June answered. Walking over to the skull and plucking it off the shelf, she said, "Look at the teeth, Elmer once belonged to an *Anasazi* Indian. An old Indian, he lived until he was well into his forties. Look you can tell by the way the parts of the cranium have grown together. It is easy to tell how old a person was when they died if you know what to look for. He was very old for an *Anasazi*."

"What killed him," I asked?

"Well I don't know what actually killed him but his people rarely lived more than thirty years. When their teeth wore out they usually died unless they had some-one who would chew their food for them."

I grimaced at the thought of eating food that someone else had chewed. Placing the toothless skull back on the shelf, June said, "Let me show you around. I'm sure you would like to take a shower."

I hadn't had a shower in over a week and felt downright slovenly. June opened a door next to the room I had been sleeping in and exposed a well-kept bathroom with a shower over a tub. "What time is it, I asked?"

"Almost noon, you must have been bone tired last night when you arrived."

I immediately went back into the bedroom and picked up my small backpack, my only luggage, and pulled out my only change of clothes which had been washed out in a bathroom sink.

"Call me when you're ready to come out," June instructed me, "I'll show you around. By the way, your father had to go back to work this morning. He had to sneak off the job to see you. Everyone has been very worried about you, especially your father."

My father was gone, driving the long trek back to Texas to the job that demanded so much of his attention. I felt alone now, in a dangerous place, with no way to get out. What was I to do?

That morning over a plate of *huevos rancheros*, eggs with a spicy red chili sauce, my uncle and aunt explained to me that my father was going to be back as soon as he could. Until then, I was welcome to stay with them. "Please," Aunt June warned me, "Don't go out after dark without someone with you. Until we can figure what is going on here, it is not safe for you to be out by yourself. We are telling you this for your own good. We don't want anything to happen to you while you are here!"

I just listened, but was thinking that when adults didn't want you involved in something, they always said that it was for your own good. Usually they were not telling you the whole story. At that moment I vowed to get to the bottom of what was going on here, whether I had anyone's permission or not. I had just turned seventeen years old, and had been pretty much on my own for several years now.

It wasn't that my mother had been neglectful; she just had other things on her mind. I gradually took over a lot of the cooking for both of us, and if any cleaning got done around the house, I had to do most of it. My mother had a night job and her own life. Mona was a petite woman, with soft curls around her face, blue eyes that always had a twinkle in them, and a figure that most women her age would die for.

On the other hand, I had inherited my disposition from my father, but then, I had inherited my looks from my mother. As I had grown older I discovered that I wasn't ugly. In fact, I had a nice figure as a result of all the exercise from wrestling, softball, and volleyball. I had a very pretty face, not beautiful like my mother, but pretty just the same, and the older I got, the more like mother I looked. In time, it was obvious that I could become a gorgeous woman like her. But I knew a secret, beauty like that is not always a blessing; I knew it could also be a curse.

I was simply independent, having neither the time nor the inclination to deal with boys, boys that were looking for someone to take care of them. I had not had a lot of dates in high school because of my attitude. Most of the boys saw me as a great friend, but knew better than to try to look at me as a dating prospect. Some had tried to get personal with me, but they all soon learned that I definitely had a mind of my own.

My most prominent trait, however, was not looks, but curiosity. Some of the kids at school had teasingly called me Miss Snoops because I couldn't stand being in the dark about anything. I had not had a surprise party in my whole life, because I always figured out what was going on before the party took place. My mother had tried many times to find a good hiding place for the few toys at Christmas when I was just a little girl, but I always found them early and then figured out what they were even before I could read the words on the outside of the box.

But now I was in a new situation. Yet this seemed to me to be the perfect time to put my sleuthing skills to work on an important and very real problem. If I could find out what was going on here at the ranch, I would not only help my uncle and aunt, but maybe my father would see that I was responsible enough to take care of myself and let me stay for a while. I was so excited at the possibility that chills ran up and down my spine. I was determined to show them and decided to start asking questions.

The Ranch House

After washing up, I sat at the kitchen table with Ken and Corey who were just finishing up a light lunch. The table was huge, with twelve chairs around it. It was an amazing ranch house. It was large and modern yet very utilitarian. The kitchen adjoined the living area and again there were bookshelves everywhere with strange looking objects on them. Items such as white Indian pottery with black zigzag lines next to a tri cone drill bit used in oil drilling. The large living area had several large tables arranged for work but all of them covered with maps, papers and books. Built in woodstoves heated the structure and even in the kitchen there was an old timey cooking stove next to a new gas range. I was mystified at the large rounded structure that was in the yard just out the kitchen door. I had never seen a thing like it before. It was about six feet tall with an arched opening that was very smoke stained. June explained that it was a common *horno* or oven used for baking bread in both the Spanish and Pueblo settlements in the Southwest. They particularly used it during the summer months so the house would not get hot. Unfortunately, since the problems had occurred at the ranch it had not been used.

I also learned that what electricity they had in the house came from a car motor in one of the outbuildings that generated all their electricity. During the colder months they rarely used it preferring kerosene lamps and woodstoves.

Despite the hundreds of books and artifacts that covered just about everything, the house was kept perfectly clean. There were work areas and areas to recline. June explained as she pointed to the kitchen, "Just about everything in this house has a purpose. Take those sinks over there." They were huge, used for far more than washing dishes; it was where they worked up meat for the winter months. In fact, she explained, all the meat that is eaten in this house is butchered here and worked up in those sinks. "Everyone here cleans up after themselves." Feeling a blush come to my cheeks I excused myself, went back to the room where I had slept and made up the bed.

Returning to the kitchen I asked about some of the artifacts scattered among the books on the shelf.

"Most of those were given to me years ago. Some of them like Elmer are on loan to me," said June. "In fact, I do not approve of removing artifacts from burial sites. Elmer is used when I give lectures at the universities around here. I sometimes work as a guest speaker in anthropology and archeology classes."

My thoughts returned to the problem at hand. I understood that I knew very little about what was actually plaguing the ranches in the area known as *Serpiente* and wanted more facts to work with. My first thought was to ask everybody as many questions as I could think of. Looking at Corey I implored him, "You know, the more information a person has, the easier it is to solve a problem." Corey just shrugged his shoulders as if he didn't know anything but his eyes gave him away; he looked at Ken almost asking permission to answer my questions.

My eyes also locked on Uncle Ken until finally he responded.

Ken spoke slowly, carefully choosing his words. "I do have a theory but it is a bizarre theory to say the least."

"Good" I said while folding my hands under my chin and batting my eyebrows, "I love a good spooky story."

Uncle Ken started to explain, "We think," then after another long pause he said slowly, "I think it may have something to do with *El Montana del Serpientes de Cascabels*, the mountain of rattlesnakes.

With eyes narrowing and a frown appearing I asked "What is a mountain of rattlesnakes?"

"Well," he slowly cradled his head on his knuckles. "I have only seen that mountain once. It was in late fall, and it was on a miserably cold day." He stopped and appeared to be in deep thought. "There is something to that mountain. It isn't natural."

"What do you mean it isn't natural?" I fished.

Ken locked eyes with me.

"I had a terrible feeling the entire time I was there. I felt like there were thousands of eyes upon me, yet I never saw a thing. It was really just a feeling I can't explain."

After a full minute of silence, I responded with a long, "Yes?"

"The mountain appeared to be a small volcanic cone with a very thin exterior of black volcanic rock. It is eroded in one place exposing an underneath of soft white rock formed with huge gas bubbles. Under a few inches of hard exterior rock, the interior of the mountain is a world of tiny caves. It just stands there, a very small volcanic cone in the middle of sandstone canyon lands. This country is full of small volcanic features. I'm sure you noticed many of them on the way in. Most of them are steep hills with black volcanic rock forming huge mesas. They are perfectly flat on top because the molten lava spreads out like pancake batter when it is extruded from the volcano. But we don't have any cone volcanoes in this area and yet this mountain is a small and perfect cone. It seemed unnatural to me. I was glad to get away from it."

"It has quite a history," June added, sitting down at the table with them. Aunt June, the avid archeologist along with many other skills then added, "The old ones, the *veijos*, those first Spanish conquistadores, knew where the mountain was but kept its location a secret. They had little interest in exploring this area. There was nothing but ruins here even back then. They preferred to conquer living Indian tribes that could work for them, or lead them to El Dorado. They were looking for cities of gold, but all they found were small cities made of mud or adobe. Few traces of gold were ever found in those settlements. The Native Indians in New Mexico knew where gold was but placed little value on it other than to make small trinkets. They apparently traded it off to people who lived in central or South America, where gold became a very important part of their culture."

The Mystery of Chaco Canyon

*U*ncle Ken then added, "Another theory is that they traded their gold to more southern tribes for macaw feathers or sea shells that could be used for decorations or ceremonies. There have been many early explorers that have crossed into the labyrinth of rugged canyon lands, but they all crossed into this area with a certain amount of trepidation. Ancient ruins are everywhere. They are unique to this area because they are like the ruins in Chaco Canyon which is located way to the north of here."

I stopped his explanation by raising my hand, "What is Chaco Canyon?

Ken resumed his explanation, "Chaco is unique, located some fifty miles south of Farmington, New Mexico. Farmington is located on the San Juan River, like its namesake, agriculture occurs there but Chaco Canyon is something entirely different. It is an enigma in just about every way possible. Much of northwest New Mexico is a barren landscape. Arroyos there see no running water except for a day or two a year after heavy cloudburst. The badlands is completely devoid of vegetation except for sagebrush and tumbleweeds. Chaco Canyon lies there, in a basin a hundred miles long."

Ken stared off to another world for a few moments and then continued, "Of all the places in New Mexico that I have been, this barren quarter of the Colorado Plateau is undoubtedly the most unfortunate place I have ever visited. In winter the snow blusters about like fine dust, and the temperatures can drop to twenty below. In summer the rocks get so hot you can't touch them."

Ken looked into my eyes yet he still seemed to be far away. "Looking for remains of ancient cultures one might expect to find nothing there. At most, one might expect to find where the ancient *Anasazi* camped on their way somewhere else but Chaco seems to be the center of the *Anasazi* world. The culture reached a peak in the eleventh century A.D. after they built a vast city there. The people who once lived there built walls with slabs of rocks, fitting them together with a unique style of masonry. They made an art form of it. The stonework alone required thousands of man-hours of work. Masons broke rocks into thin, workable slabs, some of them smaller than your little finger. Laborers hauled baskets of wet mortar and woodworkers stripped timbers and rounded the ends with stone axes before setting them into place. Within an area of ten miles they built thousands of structures including great *kivas* which they used for their ceremonies."

After a moment to swallow some coffee Ken continued. "The roofs to those chambers were constructed with timbers. Those roofs weigh up to ninety tons each. To support the roofs over two hundred and fifty thousand trees were felled in mountains fifty miles away and hauled on the backs of men across the desert."

Ken stopped for another swallow of coffee then refocused on me, "Imagine, hoisting and carrying massive logs in procession to Chaco. It is one of the little things that bother archeologist like June."

June joined the conversation, "When early people excavated the ruins they found enough artifacts to load a train. The people there were importing and exporting goods as far away as South America. All of that construction, yet they have found only a few skeletons there and most of them appear to have come from somewhere else."

June answered with another question, "What did they eat and drink? There is no permanent water there now and it takes massive amounts of water to raise corn or any food crop. They would have had to bring nearly all their food in from somewhere else. Something strange happened there, there are too many unanswered questions."

She stopped talking for a moment. Then she said, "Something terrible happened. It appears that they deserted the place and went north up into southern Colorado for a short while, however something very different and strange was happening there. These were people who lived in constant fear, a terror of something or someone. They moved into cliff houses. Most people believe that they were killed by some terrible disease or some ancient warlike people killed them. Perhaps clan warred against clan until no one was left to tell the story but something very strange happened that is yet to be explained. The entire population appears to have shrunk.

"In time most of them left the entire region, going south into what is now central New Mexico and Mexico, becoming the Salado culture. The Salado culture is the culture to whom the Spanish, brought smallpox and other diseases. Virtually all of them died out. Here in New Mexico there are only fragments of them remaining; mostly the Zuni, Hopi, and various other groups like the pueblo at Isleta that you drove past on the way here. But for a while, they nearly all died off, and their descendants don't really seem to know or won't admit to what happened. To this day it is still a mystery as to what really happened and the same thing appears to have happened to the natives who built the ruins around here."

I mulled this over for a minute then asked, "Could you show me the ruins around here?"

Ken answered her with a stern, "No" He then softened his tone and added, "Well maybe after the summer is over and things settle down around here. Right now I don't want you outside of this house unless one of us is with you. Perhaps this winter we can take you into one of the back canyons and show you some ruins but I don't want you or anyone else in this house to go near that mountain. All I know is that a large population used to live in the canyons to the south of us. All that is left of them is the bones and ruins. Particularly around that one volcanic hill, bones are everywhere, and some of them are human bones."

I knew it was time to turn on the charm, the same charm I had used on Hidalgo. "Just supposing one of you fellows decided to go there, what would it take, I asked while fluttering my eyes?

After rolling his eyes and sitting up straight, Uncle Ken continued, "Exploring

El Montana del Serpientes de Cascabels can only be accomplished by climbing up and down steep canyon walls, but once there, the traveler may find the volcanic cone. The route is dissected by side canyons, quickly losing and confusing any traveler. I have heard stories of a few brave souls who survived a visit to the mountain and told stories of lost friends and missing relatives. They found skeletons along the trails and, as an understanding of what was happening occurred, sheer terror would set in."

"During the eighteen hundreds, the first white Americans ventured into this area. But they quickly stopped coming. Every time a prospector would find a small deposit of gold or silver in the area they would shortly thereafter be found quivering with arrows. The local Apache and Navajo Indians who were wandering near *Serpiente* simply wouldn't allow themselves to be conquered by the Spanish or Mexicans, and certainly not by the newcomers from the east."

Hidalgo, who had been listening from the living room, entered the conversation, "The Apaches would pass by *Serpiente* when running from the authorities, but they never ventured into the surrounding valley. And they certainly would never actually climb upon the flanks of the volcanic hill. It has a mystical or religious significance to them. They feared it. The Navajos and the Apaches could steal anything; sometimes knowing where and how to hide the loot and then disappearing was their greatest skill. They knew that few would venture into the canyon lands of *Serpiente* so they felt relatively safe there but my understanding is they all avoided that particular mountain."

"You're a Navajo Indian aren't you?" I asked. At the moment, I was thinking of the dream that I experienced in far-away San Jon, New Mexico.

Hidalgo pulled up a chair and joined them at the kitchen table answering with a very slow, "Well, yes."

I stared into his eyes trying to imagine what they would look like, twinkling in a campfire light.

Aunt June then leaned over and jumped into the conversation again with, "In time, Penny, you will learn that Hidalgo is no ordinary Navajo Indian. In fact, he is no ordinary person. He is one of the most intelligent and learned persons that I know. We all have deep respect for his opinions."

I looked at Hidalgo as he blushed. He was a little embarrassed.

"Please tell me what you know about the people who lived around this mountain you're all talking about," I asked Hidalgo.

Hidalgo took a sip of steaming coffee, looked off into the distance and started his explanation. "Nothing is left now but ancestral memories and oral traditions, which are slowly disappearing. Although there are many modern Pueblo languages with dialects spoken throughout the southwest, little is known of the *Anasazi* who lived here long ago."

"The *Anasazi* are believed to be one the oldest cultures of this area. We do not even know what their word for rattlesnake was and we have no idea what it sounded like. There are several different languages spoken here in the Southwest now, several official native languages in New Mexico alone. All languages change with time, but the Hopi and Zuni pueblos probably share the closest linguistic links to the ancient ones. The Zuni language, interestingly, has intriguing similarities to ancient North African cultures, which existed over two thousand years ago. Yet some language experts say that it is related to a Japanese culture; but that's another mystery that folks like your Aunt June are trying to solve."

I kept my innermost thoughts to myself. I recognized the inflections, and academic nature of Hidalgo's voice. He talked just like the Navajo in the dream. Did he know that he had visited me in my dream?

Anasazi Life

*U*ncle Ken said with a serious tone in his voice, "Before you think about going into the back country of *Serpiente* you had better educate yourself to the people who lived there. Let's see what you can learn in the next few weeks and then we might talk about letting you go there, but not without Corey and Hidalgo and not until cold weather sets in."

I was starting to get angry but decided not to show my anger but rather to take this as a challenge. I thought I would bait my uncle Ken with a couple of questions. "First of all, what is so complicated about being an Indian? And secondly, what makes these Indians any different from Indians elsewhere? We have Cherokee Indians who live in Tennessee and they live just like the rest of us."

"That's true, answered Ken, however the world you grew up in is very different from this world and if you go back a millennium the world you grew up in would be entirely different. First of all, the world that you grew up in is green and lush with plenty of natural game and food that can be found in nature. Go out to the back pasture where the canyon opens up and live by yourself without camping gear, food and only the creek for water and you wouldn't last a week. Most young people wouldn't last a day."

June who by this time was feeling a little sorry for me entered the conversation with, "To us, being an *Anasazi* would not have been much fun. We tend to forget how easy it is for most people to acquire water and food. Many ruins have been found near large rivers such as the Rio Grande or the San Juan, however many large settlements have been found where there is hardly any water at all. Chaco, for example, is one of those places. Small tanks or *tinatas* of water can sometimes be found in surrounding hills but often their water came from seeps. They had to strain their water out of the sand letting the sand settle in a large container and then skimming the useful water off the top. Sometimes there would only be a drip spring to support thirty or forty people. Some ruins have been discovered where it is a complete mystery as to where they got their water. They were obviously experts at using their water carefully; mostly for cooking and drinking, seldom would there be enough for bathing."

"As for food, any modern grocery store has foods that an *Anasazi* would never have dreamed of. Potatoes originally from Peru, bananas from South Brazil, milk and dairy products, the ancient *Anasazi* would never have encountered these wonderful foods. We live in one of the most isolated areas of New Mexico yet we can easily drive into Belen or Los Lunas and go to a supermarket where we can buy whole bags of food if we choose too. Around here we raise all our own meat and depend upon our garden for fresh vegetables. But then, we have irrigation wells here. We buy in bulk and carry it back in the bed of our trucks. How did they transport their food?"

"They had to walk everywhere. Remember that the Spanish brought over horses from Europe and they were not used until a thousand years later. There was no such thing as a fat Indian. They lived on the edge of starvation all the time, but particularly in the wintertime and particularly here in the Southwest. Even when food was found it was usually a slim variety of food, for example only wild onions in the early springtime."

I thought about this for a minute then asked, "Well, just what did they eat?"

"Theirs was an extremely bland diet, except for the three sisters as they are called. Corn, squash and beans were the only vegetables which they grew, where they could grow food, but mostly they lived entirely off the land. Even pinto beans which provided protein were not introduced until much later. However, your Uncle Ken's challenge to you is not a hard as you imagine. If you were a determined person you could easily live off the food that is in the south pasture."

I had only a blank look to offer at these revelations. I've always thought that

Native Americans had plenty to eat; after all, it was the Indians that saved the early English creating a holiday everyone knows of as Thanksgiving.

June explained, "As you walk around the edge of the pasture you run into a thorny brush that produces small beans. The natives relished those beans which were usually eaten raw. In the forested areas there are acorn nuts and piñon nuts from the pine trees that grow there. They collected the nuts and made delicious flour out of them that was added to stews and made into tortillas. As you drove into Los Lunas you and Hidalgo drove through a swamp covered in cattails. When pulled out of the mud the roots are edible. Then there is tuna."

This brought my head up with a look of confusion. "What a minute, I know that there are no oceans around here."

"That's true," said June but there is prickly pear cactus growing all over the place and the little red fruit they produce is packed with nutrients. The name for these berries is tuna."

Ken added, "Those tuna also contain seeds. To me, they taste like tomato sauce."

June continued, "The prickly pear pads themselves are quite edible and eaten in Mexico all the time. They are quite good when flowered and fried. They actually raised cactus in order to eat the flowers and the little red buds that appear on them.

Ken added, "Everything has thorns on it but on bad years we burn the thorns off and feed them to our cattle. Even *cholla* cactus is edible, prepared in a number of ways, but you have to get rid of those thorns. For hundreds of years the only food the *Anasazi* raised was corn and squash. But again, you need to understand that their corn was different from ours. Blue corn was often raised because it could be planted almost a foot deep in the soil where it was moist. Regular corn was planted in shallow holes, with several seeds in each hole which produced cobs about the size of your little finger."

"Like you see in Chinese food," I interjected.

"Yes, but their corn was the forefather of modern corn," added June." They planted corn in bundles so the outer stalks would protect the inner stalks."

Ken added. "They also had peppers, did you know that there is more vitamin C in peppers than in just about any food, including any modern food. The problem was obtaining a steady supply of food. The entire mass of the *Anasazi* was in constant migration which is one of the reasons there are Indian ruins all over the Southwest. They had to travel to gather food. Localities around a permanent settlement would quickly run out of small game such as rabbits and deer. However a young brave could easily feed himself if he was constantly wandering. They probably ate mesquite beans or anything green they could find to counter the effects of a constant meat protein diet. Wintertime would have been a serious problem for there is very little vegetation. Constipation followed by headaches would have been the result."

"When native people were first put on the reservations often they were given large doses of Epsom salts. The magnesium sulfate would clean them out but they still lived primarily on small game. Deadfalls were commonly used to trap that small game. Rabbits, ground squirrels and mice were commonly consumed."

"What about bows and arrows," I asked. June answered me with; "Bows and arrows were introduced during the Basket maker III period, which occurred about 450 A.D. I don't know about you, but how many bow shots would it take to finally hit an animal on the run? Think about it, they would spend most of their time acquiring something to eat. Even if they were able to kill a larger animal, how would they preserve the meat? Sure, they made a lot of deer jerky but have you ever tried to cook with jerky? Again, the *Anasazi* were very small, thin people who lived on the edge of existence."

I stood up and walked over to the living room where Hidalgo happened to be sitting, listening to our conversation. Reaching down and stabbing Hidalgo in the ribs above his small pot belly I laughed and said, "Not all Indians are skinny."

Hidalgo grabbed my arm and pulled me down on top of him; tickling me like a rough housing kid. After the tease settled down, Hidalgo replied with a hint of laughter in his voice, "After the white man introduced all manner of food around here our people grew as tall and fat as you white people. There is a problem here that you need to understand. If your people had survived since eternity by barely living off the land and suddenly you had plenty to eat, your body couldn't deal with the sudden prosperity. Have you ever eaten Indian fry bread? All it is, is dough fried in grease. Like doughnuts, it is extremely fattening. Navaho's have barrel chest by nature, but now we are also fat because of the massive amounts of rich food we eat. Our bodies are not used to eating white man's food. Just like you all, we relish what we can't have."

I answered with a snort, "So it is our fault, huh!"

Hidalgo answered me with, "It's not my fault that there are so many good cooks around here."

Frowning, Ken continued his explanation. "Even in places where food could be easily grown and local game was available, they were extremely limited in the food they had available to eat. Squash, mesquite beans, and the food plant that they domesticated; corn. The entire *Anasazi* people were being bothered by much more than dealing with the vagaries of environmental issues such as lack of rain or too much rain. Cold winters and searing summer days certainly bothered them; not to mention the problems of war with other peoples."

June interjected, "But something was really bothering the *Anasazi*." She emphasized the word really. "One theory I encountered recently involved corn. Corn or maize for most American Indians is considered sacred. In fact, many of their pictographic murals and petroglyphs include images of corn. Modern day Indians have corn ceremonies and corn dances. Currently, they think that corn originated in Eastern North America but it was really domesticated in Mexico. It returned six hundred years later fully domesticated and became the basis of survival for the *Anasazi* as well as all cultures in North America. There is a theory that many of the inhabitants of Chaco and other communities were suffering from a brain condition from eating only corn."

"Chaco Canyon is located in a desert and because they were not living in an agricultural area virtually all of their food had to be imported. The easiest and probably the only food that could be carried long distances would have been corn. Outlying settlements probably traded corn for something in Chaco. The problem is corn lacks the key amino acids, lysine and tryptophan. When eaten exclusively, levels of serotonin in the brain begin to drop leaving the person in a state somewhat like sleep deprivation. Imagine what it must have been like; all the elders who were the tribal leaders lived almost exclusively on corn. Imagine your leaders having nothing to eat, every day, except corn."

I thought about all of this for a minute then piped up, "So, if I can survive in the back pasture for a week eating only the local food you would have confidence in me?"

"Well it would help," answered Ken.

"Fine," I said, "Let me round up some cooking pots I can use over a fire and turn me loose."

Ken followed my proposal with, "I suppose you'll need a sleeping bag, tent and matches?"

"Well sure," I responded.

June looked at me and said, "I hate to burst your bubble, but the ancient *Anasazi* didn't have tents, sleeping bags and matches. Even if you could start a fire without matches what are you going to cook your food in? Pottery wasn't invented around here until the Pueblo period about 750 A.D. All we could allow you to take with you is the clothes on your back. We couldn't even let you wear shoes."

"No shoes!" I exclaimed.

"No, you have to make your own by weaving plant fibers," said Ken with a smirk on his face.

"I responded hopelessly, "Maybe I'll take you up on your challenge this fall."

Turning to Hidalgo, I wondered how many times I would think about my dream when asking him a question and said to him; "In the meantime, tell me more about this place called *Serpientes* that this ranch is named after."

Rattlesnake Clan

"*The legend of *Serpiente* began as a racial memory among those most ancient of American Indian cultures. Oral traditions were recorded in those tribes, far removed in time and distance from those curious people who stumble into *Serpiente* now. Unlike the rest of nature, humans and coyotes are attracted to interesting places. Driven to satisfy their innate curiosity, they explore every feature of the natural landscape. This explains why they are always in trouble."

"Of course, coyotes are much better at problem solving and escape than any human! They are, and have always been considered the tricksters among the many clans of creatures who co-habit the world. In the ancient, as well as in the modern world, coyotes compete with humans."

Uncle Ken then added to the story while Hidalgo gulped a rapidly cooling cup of coffee, "Perhaps the mountains themselves provide a warning for those who learn to read them. *Serpiente* is a strange and mysterious place, accessible only by ancient and secret trails. Seen from the air, the only way to see the lay of the land, travelers observe monotonous miles of rugged sandstone canyons. The most forlorn and inaccessible part of the region is *El Montano del Serpientes de Cascabels*, a stark volcanic cone in contrast to the surrounding sandstone canyon lands."

"The earliest of people, those ancestors who lived in this maze of canyons, built cities there, cities now in ruins now buried under sand. They walked secret trails carved through the sandstone canyons leading to waterholes, streams, and lush green valley's where they grew their food. The climate was generally much wetter thousands of years ago and back then growing food like corn and squash was much easier. They lived there for thousands of years, prospered, and evidently lived in harmony with everyone."

We were all silent as we pictured ancient cities in the windswept canyons. Hidalgo broke into Penny's vision of the ancient cities by saying to Aunt June, "If I can have just one more cup of that wonderful coffee, I'll tell you the rest of the story."

Aunt June got up, walked over to the stove, and poured Hidalgo another cup of coffee, adding the sugar and cream just like he liked it. After a sip of hot coffee Hidalgo continued, "The legend goes that the Rattlesnake clans had always lived in the canyon, but in time the rattlesnakes that lived on the black mountain changed, growing larger and smarter. They warred with the other rattlesnake clans, eventually eliminating all other rattlesnakes near *El Montano del Serpientes*."

"For many years the human clans who lived in the canyon lands had benefited from their relationship with the rattlesnake clan of *Serpiente,* but when the world changed and the seasons began to be colder and much dryer, trouble occurred. The human clan began to discover that their children were disappearing. The Rattlesnake clan was thought to be stealing and eating the smaller children. Indeed, perhaps in desperation, some members of the Rattlesnake clan were stealing the babies, but no rattlesnake trails were ever discovered at the scene of the crime, only paw prints left by the coyotes. Yet, the rattlesnake clan was blamed, and soon there was war. In time, only the oldest and wisest humans were still alive."

Pausing to sip the coffee, Hidalgo continued, "It is said that the human clan eventually conquered the rattlesnakes by killing all but the baby rattlesnakes, which they carefully raised as their own children. In time the rattlesnakes became dependent upon the humans, who provided all the food for them. Thereafter, for a thousand years, the human clans and the rattlesnake clans lived together in peace, and in time they prospered. The human clan even grew wealthy. The rattlesnakes, being creatures who naturally lived in deep and secretive places, knew where all manner of minerals and gemstones where hidden, and they obediently shared these with the grateful humans, even guarding the treasures for the humans within *Serpiente*. In this way, the ancient human clan lived peacefully with the Rattlesnake clan for many lifetimes, slowly accumulating treasure."

Another sip of coffee preceded the final part of the story. "After a while," Hidalgo continued, "the coyote clan grew envious. They were the ones who had actually been stealing and eating the children, and now they were outnumbered by both the human and rattlesnake clans. They began stealing children again. Unfortunately, even more warlike human clans, my ancestors, migrated into and discovered the clans of *Serpiente* and all-out war occurred. The human clans moved from the valley floors into cliffs and the most secret of places, but to no avail. All the peoples of those most ancient human clans were killed."

I was by now completely perplexed. I had never heard stories like these before, even though in school I had learned about many eastern tribes, such as the Cherokees, who once roamed throughout Tennessee; they did not have similar stories as far as I knew.

Uncle Ken said, "When the first Anglos came into this area, stories circulated that there were many secrets in the *Serpientes*. People suspected that there were great treasures to be discovered there. Maybe the rattlesnakes now guard the treasure, hidden deep within the maze of caves under *Serpiente*."

Finishing his coffee, Hidalgo continued, "After a while the children of this last human clan began to disappear. Upon realizing that the rattlesnake clan was secretly warring with them, they left the area, leaving petroglyphs to warn others who might stumble into the vicinity. In time, all knowledge of *Serpiente* died. The legend ended, the people vanished, and nothing of the story was left except ruins and petroglyphs. For the last two thousand years, all knowledge of *Serpiente* was lost to the world. It was not revived until the Spaniards arrived much later."

I could only think to myself that the stories were indeed the most confusing and perplexing stories I had ever heard except for my dream that occurred on that dreadful bus trip. For some reason all of these stories seemed very important. Whatever was causing the animals to die seemed very real. By now, I had examined several dead animals for myself. They all looked the same. Not a trace of what was killing them could be found. I needed more information.

The Artifact

I settled into the routine of life in *Serpiente*, quickly making friends and making myself useful. During the day the ranch was run just like any ranch. Newly bought chickens were let out of the henhouse and allowed to run loose in the yard, just like chickens always do. But, each night they were rounded up and enclosed in the henhouse, which was boarded up so nothing could get in or out. Small calves were enclosed in the barn, which was sealed. Horses and larger cows were left to fend for themselves.

As the hot days of summer became more intense, we found more and more dead animals in the fields and the disappearances of small animals peaked. Then as fall approached, it all slowly subsided. But the ranch families around *Serpiente* were still wary; something was out there and few of them would entertain any ideas of mysterious rattlesnakes or coyote clans. Stories like those were just fantasy to the local ranchers.

I couldn't stand the tension created by this fearful mystery. I had to solve the problem. First of all, I couldn't stand to be cooped up in a ranch house every night during the hottest part of the summer, living in fear. Second, it just wasn't in my personality to ignore a challenge. I love the outdoors just like my father does, and so I began to spend some time every day exploring the countryside. It was interesting and very different to me.

My favorite place to explore was the back pasture of the ranch where a canyon with a tiny stream of water flowed out of it making a serpentine turn and then miles below the ranch disappeared into the sand. In the distance the land became a labyrinth of deep canyons, each with secrets to hide. There, I found my first petroglyph, stick figures of humans and snake-like forms. From Hidalgo I learned more about Indian lore; from Corey I learned the skills that a real cowgirl needs to explore the country. But I was always under strict orders to return to the ranch house each night, where the whole family locked themselves in.

One afternoon while looking for petroglyphs, I discovered a tiny arch in the rock below my feet. Getting down on my knees I dug the soft sand away and discovered pot shards. Within a moment or two I discovered that they all fit together to form a ceramic vessel. I examined them, turning them over and over in my hand; black geometric designs drawn on a white pot. I kept putting them together until I realized what I was looking at. Each of the geometric designs was actually a snake. The heads of the snake converged at the lip of the vessel. It startled me when I figured it out. Gathering it all up I put the pieces into a large pocket in my backpack.

From Aunt June I had learned more and more about the *Anasazi* pottery. Used for over 700 years white ware pottery is the oldest pottery made by the *Anasazi*. It is made from gray Cretaceous clay with a slip of white kaolin clay.

The pottery in the ranch house always fascinated me. I always felt artistic myself and was intrigued by the designs on the pots. In the ranch house I discovered several piles of shards, in box tops, as if waiting to be reconstructed, glued together to show the work.

I offered to reconstruct the vessels but June suggested that I had more important things to do. I learned that colorful decorative vessels are not just pretty pots; they are pieces of social architecture. In their designs and styles you know who the maker and owners were or who they were trading with. Potshards are like calling cards, a person versed in pottery can tell you exactly what ruin or at least what region a shard came from.

Generally, in the north, bold black on white ceramics in the tightly painted geometry was made. South of Chaco, and many generations later, reds and buffs would be produced with highly stylized figures of humans and animals, polychromatic pottery appeared in the Southwest in the form of black and white designs painted on red or orange backgrounds.

I returned to the ranch house that night, putting my things away and then joining June in the kitchen to prepare dinner. Later, during dinner, I decided to show off my find. Taking the pieces out and reconstructing the pot enough to show the design painted on it. It all created quite a sensation, but after all the talk was over, June casually reached over and placed her hand on top of mine.

"I can tell you exactly where you found it," June says. "I found the shards there years ago. I examined the pieces and then returned them exactly to where I found them. I would appreciate it if you would return them."

Puzzled, I asked "Sure, but why do you want me to return them? Besides, there are boxes of pot shards all over the house. What is the difference?"

"Well," June explained, "All of these collections were made years before the Antiquities Act was enacted." Looking around the living room, June attempted to explain the significance of the pots and piles of pot shards scattered around the house. "Many of them were already here when your Uncle Ken bought this ranch from Mr. Miller, a fellow who looked somewhat like Gaby Hayes; a face full of whiskers and a rowdy disposition. He built the building that is now used as the chicken pen and lived in it for many years. Like everyone else in this area he naturally collected artifacts. After all, once someone discards something it is up for grabs by others. When he became ill and had to move into town, we acquired the property at an auction in Belen."

"To tell you the truth, I had never seen the place, I was a little intimidated but once I saw the site I fell in love with this place. As with all ranches in New Mexico water must be in abundance in order to support agriculture and cattle. That small creek that you like to hike to sinks into the sand around here where it is easily pumped out of the ground. Most people new to this area think it is pretty desolate but actually there is an ocean of water under out feet. Ninety-nine percent of the water that flows down that canyon actually flows underground.

I said "Well that explains some of the artifacts around here but this place is full of them."

June looked at me and lowering her eyes and admitted that she had indeed been a collector years ago, but as she learned more about archeology, first as a student and later as a professional, her entire attitude had changed.

"One of the things that changed my perspective about collecting artifacts came about from a conversation with a gentleman over in Zuni," said June. He said, "How would you feel if I dug up your grandmother, mounted her bones on a piece of ply board and put her up for display."

"I really have mixed feelings about it all," admitted June. Most of the antiquities that end up in museums such as the Smithsonian Institute are never viewed by the public. Many of the artifacts here are on loan to me from universities, I use them for lectures, and after all I am an archeologist. It is legal for me to possess them but the difference is I have never sold a single thing. You have to understand that there is a tremendous market out there for artifacts." She reached over and picked up a single black on white pot and asked me if I had any idea how much it was worth.

I examined the artifact for a moment then threw out the number of fifteen dollars.

"Actually," grinned June, "it is worth over ten thousand dollars."

June explained further. "Legally, people are not allowed to collect artifacts. When they do they are invariably lost, destroyed, or become scientifically useless. In the United States, it has been illegal to remove artifacts without permission from public land since 1906. That 1906 law reads that, 'To remove, excavate, injure, or destroy historic or prehistoric ruins or monuments is against the law. Any collector who finds an object on lands owned or controlled by the Government of the United States must have government permission to remove it.' As a professional archeologist, I have that permission but that doesn't mean I would remove artifacts. We own that land that you found the shards on but I still follow ethical practices."

As usual, I was amazed at the logic that June used. The next day, after the sun came up, I collected the pot shards I had found and returned them to their sandy grave.

Falling in Love

I became more and more intrigued with Corey. He was a soft spoken young man with brilliant blue eyes and strawberry blond hair with streaks of lighter blond in it from being out in the hot sun of the Southwest. Corey accompanied me on my many explorations around the ranch and the areas around the ranch that were within walking distance, but we were always careful to be home by nightfall so we didn't worry Uncle Ken and Aunt June.

One thing about living on a ranch is that everyone works hard and even more importantly, everyone eats well. I was now rapidly approaching my eighteenth birthday and getting prettier by the day. As Hidalgo one day said, "I had the rugged good looks of an all American outdoor girl but there was much more to consider." I don't think he was talking about my intellect.

When I was in high school back in Tennessee I had always been surrounded by boys, but they were just friends. Now there was something different about the way I felt about Corey. I was very careful to keep my feelings well hidden from Corey and the rest of the family, but as the summer wore on and we spent more and more time together, hiding my feelings grew harder and harder.

Corey was special in many ways, gentle yet strong, quiet yet outgoing and very smart. Not the kind of smart that is seen as arrogance, but rather the inner smart of someone who never had to brag about himself. Nobody ever had to tell him what to do; he always seemed to intuitively know what to do and did it. It was almost uncanny. Corey would always hand you the tool you needed before you asked for it. Often he would do whole jobs, such as putting new leathers on the windmill, without ever being asked. He was very young in years, but very mature in his work ethics. Every evening Corey and I both worked on our home schooling, spending many hours sharing information. I had begun to admire Corey more and more until one day I realized that certain urges were occurring.

Exploring the ranch and finding out about this area of New Mexico with him had been the most fun I had ever had. I loved just sitting and talking to him about anything. We could talk for hours about the smallest things, but right now we were both focused on the problem at hand. Real families do not lock themselves in their homes at night in fear of what is happening outside, particularly on a ranch a hundred miles away from a city.

It was only a matter of time until Corey and I started to make plans to sneak out at night, not to do what kids at our age normally do, but to discover what was killing the livestock and making the ranchers live in fear. Who was to stop us? Corey and I were, for all practical purposes, adults, who could do what we wanted to do. And so, in small steps, we began to explore the vast wastelands of the canyons that make up *Serpiente*.

Rattlesnake Research

Fall was coming, and with the chill in the air the problems of disappearing animals and dead livestock seemed to vanish. Each day more and more frost appeared on the brown grass that the cattle were eating and eventually small animals could be seen around the ranch.

Deciding to do some research, Corey and I took one of the ranch pickups and made the long drive into Albuquerque where we could quietly sit in the public library and take notes. From my reading I discovered a world of information about rattlesnakes.

In the American southwest there are many examples of animals and plants that display brilliant colors, warning possible predators to keep away. They are all, as a collective lot, poisonous, and they advertise their deadly business to avoid being eaten. Then again, there are a few who, despite their deadly abilities, choose to vanish from sight and disappear from scrutiny, to be invisible to all until that deadly moment when they choose to come out of hiding and strike their prey.

Rattlesnakes are the prime example of these, striking and injecting their prey with a hemotoxin that leads to a rapid cellular breakdown resulting in internal hemorrhaging. Some specialize in nerve poisons or neurotoxins that inter the body's neural network and turn off vital organs. I was surprised to learn that most rattlesnakes contain a cocktail of toxins that do both. There are even rattlesnakes that deliver venom that causes nightmarish hallucinations with mystical and terrifying visions. Most victims of this rattlesnake's bite report flashbacks years after the initial bite.

Rattlesnakes are unique among New World pit vipers, having a series of horny interlocking joints at the end of the tail which make a sharp rattling sound when shaken. After each shedding of skin a new rattle is created. Surprisingly, the rattlesnake is deaf; it cannot hear its own warning sounds.

There are many varieties of rattlesnake. The most common is the prairie rattlesnake, comparatively small in size with the top of his head covered with plates. The banded rattlesnake is the common species found in the eastern United States, and is possibly the inspiration for monolithic structures built in rattlesnake motifs by the ancient Mound-builder culture. I began to think more about that last fact. As I read, the more I realized just how important snakes; particularly rattlesnakes were to ancient cultures, even to the tribes that occupied my home state of Tennessee. Snakes were on the minds of virtually all ancient cultures throughout both North and South America.

Rattlesnakes of one species or another can be found anywhere between southern Canada and Argentina. One species, known to science as Crotalus, is quite another creature altogether, with the top of its head covered with scales. The diamond back rattlesnake sometimes reaches six feet in length and is named for the diamond-shaped marks on its back. It inhabits many southern states, particularly in the American southwest, where it receives respect from all creatures. A mere 100 milligram injection of its venom will kill an adult human. A far less conspicuous rattlesnake, the Mojave rattler can kill an adult human with as little as 10 milligrams of venom.

Again, thinking back to Tennessee I thought of the only two snakes I had personally encountered; a slow moving non-poisonous snake encountered when around creeks that indeed looked very dangerous and black snakes. Black snakes were very aggressive and fast. I thought of a friend, Tater as everyone called him, who was picking up a bale of hay and just as he brought it up to chest level in order to load it into a truck he found himself face to face with an enraged snake. Several bites later he found himself sick but not deathly sick. He would never load hay again.

Rattlesnakes are all rather thick-bodied, large, triangular headed snakes of sluggish disposition; they are not inclined to bite unless disturbed or in pursuit of prey. They are cold-blooded and really would prefer to be secreted away, digesting a fat rat.

Rattlesnakes normally live around herding animals. It is thought by some biologists that the rattles evolved in order to keep the snake from being stepped on. They are one of the God's most noble creatures, certainly more noble than many human beings.

Some humans will hurt you in a number of ways, without the slightest provocation or conscience, yet of all the animals in the world, only the rattlesnake will warn you before striking. Like the Texas flag with the motto, 'Don't Tread on Me,' rattlesnakes are perfectly up-front with their intentions, a position many admire and which few humans adhere to.

From my short experiences with snakes I knew that visitors or newcomers to the southwest will usually either kill any snake they encounter or run from it. Many of the locals kept cats around the house to keep snakes away; unfortunately for those who live in isolated country, the cats attract coyotes, which in turn attract coyote hunters with their traps, chemicals, and bounties. Coyote hunters attract the attention of environmentalists, who attract the attention of the news media, who attract the attention of lawyers and their accountants, and the debate rages.

Old timers, those wise folks with family roots firmly embedded in the desert country, have been taught from an early age to respect any snake. I learned that in the southwest, everything works in distinct cycles producing patterns in nature that tell the climatic history of the region. The story can be read in a piece of wood through the science of tree ring dating called dendrochronology. The history of climate can also be read in lake-bed sediment or in individual human remains where stories can be told by studying craniums or by the wear on the layers of teeth.

The librarian realized that Corey and I were doing some serious research and brought us a small stack of stories about rattlesnake encounters within New Mexico. One newspaper article addressed a law suit that was currently taking place in Albuquerque. Apparently, on the first day of the New Mexico State Fair, a small girl, who had been the first person to ride a bumper car at the carnival, got into the car expecting to have the time of her life. Instead it cost her life. Getting into the toy car was certainly not a problem for the child but as soon as another car smacked into it a rattlesnake that had been hiding in the nose of the car struck her several times. The child of course died well before she could be taken to the hospital. All of this was causing new regulations to be proposed. Inspections would be required of everything before the opening day of the fair.

From the Truth or Consequences Newspaper, a town named after a television show, I read one particularly sad story about an eight year old boy who was fishing out at Elephant Butte Reservoir. The family of the eight year old had set up a car camp along the shore and had returned to the camp after catching several small fish to prepare for dinner. The small boy had remained at the shore with fishing pole and a can of worms.

Unfortunately he ran out of fishing worms so he walked up and down the shore until he came to a pile of drift logs. Turning them over he found, what he thought was, more fishing worms. Pocketing a handful of them he returned to where he had been fishing. Unfortunately, the worms turned out to be baby rattlesnakes. The child collapsed after being struck many times on his hands and leg, dying before his parent could figure out what had happened.

In a scientific journal I was handed was an article that talked about the possibility that soon DNA and chemical studies would be able to pinpoint where any human remains came from because of the chemicals dissolved in groundwater which would act like fingerprints, identifying where the person's drinking water came from. These chemicals are incorporated into the very bones of an individual. The patterns are always there and could be read like a book to anyone with the wisdom, equipment and education to interpret them.

The sediment from lake beds tells the story of dry years and wet years, of droughts and floods, of what the environment was like long ago. Wet years produce lots of grass, providing food for the rabbits and rodents, which in turn provide food for a large carnivore population such as rattlesnakes, coyotes, and hawks. Then there is a long drought with intense competition and die off until the next wet cycle begins.

Rattlesnakes, being cold-blooded, fare well in drought conditions, obtaining fluids from their prey. The most important service they render is in consuming rodents that carry the fleas that are the host which carries the plague. The reproductive voraciousness of rodents is amazing; without the help of snakes in preventing the spread of this disease, drastic action would be required. Drastic actions usually result in a negative ecological impact. God's noble creature actually has, in the long run, saved infinitely more humans lives than he has ever taken.

Rattlesnakes have been here for a long time. The remains of a petrified rattlesnake from the Blackwater Draw Museum of Eastern New Mexico are on display, in mute testimony to its presence during Ice Age New Mexico. Of course, rattlesnakes were here long before the last Ice Age. Dinosaurs watched where they were stepping.

There are, as one might well imagine, some major disagreements in the field by biologists concerning rattlesnakes; take for example, color. The rattlesnakes along the red wall formation of the Grand Canyon are hematite red in color, allowing them to blend in with the natural background. In a different location, with rocks from another age such as the yellow Jurassic, Morrison formation, the same rattlesnakes have taken on the background color of yellow, making them difficult to see. The shadowy Bosque, the cottonwood forest along rivers, can produce yet another variation when the snake is somehow able to conceal itself on a shadowy, littered and brushy trail.

In terms of disposition, there are again wide degrees of disagreement on what a rattlesnake will or will not do. 'If you put a rope around your camp at night, a rattlesnake won't cross it,' an old cowboy once patiently explained. Why wouldn't it? Human smells have never seemed to bother them before. Why would a rope help? Of course, when camping out a cautious person might be inclined to put down a rope, just to be safe. But then, maybe it's the smell of horses or cows on the rope that the snake avoids.

Snakes want to avoid animals that may accidentally step on them. They are attracted to warm-blooded prey, usually small critters such as field mice, rats and an occasional lizard. When hunting, they are very opportunistic and infinitely patient. In the southwest and in particular, Texas, New Mexico, and Arizona, the best known species of rattlesnake is *Crotatus atrox*. Many times in the distant past, volcanic eruptions produced a hematite-red ash, staining every grain of exposed sand. The ash from those early volcanoes produced a red layer of soil that can be traced all the way to the east coast of the United States. The red rattlesnake lives in those blood-red, hematite stained rocks that are exposed throughout the southwest. This creature retains a profound, universal impact on the American Indian's metaphysical world. Investigations into aboriginal culture in the Southwest have discovered traces of the rattlesnake motif in decorative work from the earliest times.

Until recent times, the Hopi Indians of Arizona practiced snake dances that enthralled tourists in the Grand Canyon area. They still practice those dances, but now they are secreted away from the curious stares of the enthralled and photo-happy tourists. I couldn't help but wonder what the fascination with rattlesnakes really was. Was there more to it than modern archeologist realize?

Ancient Dragons

June offered Penny an interesting insight into rattlesnakes. She related this story, "I was working at a site up by Aztec and noted to another worker there that there were many gopher snakes around. Then after a few days they suddenly all disappeared. Shortly thereafter, rattlesnakes started to be found; everywhere. While excavating the bottom of a *Kiva* I found several snake skeletons stretched out without heads. Normally when a snake skeleton is found, it is curled up. When we informed the local Indian helpers they wouldn't come and look. The natives refused to enter and wouldn't explain why; they simply got their stuff together and left the site. They never offered an explanation; making me think that there was much more to it than they were willing to say.

Around the year 1100 A.D. there seemed to be something very strange happening around the entire world that had to do with serpents. In the southwest, snake pictographs and petroglyphs appeared on rock surfaces all over the region. In Cahokia near what is now St. Louis the mound builders constructed huge monuments with a meandering snake eating an egg as the focal point. The problem is, the huge mound could only be seen from above, making it impossible for people to see it. Yet the megalithic mound was constructed with one thing in mind; the snake. The mystery is why was the snake effigy so important to those people?

In South America entire cultures were evolving with flying snakes at the center of their culture. Even their pyramids had built in snakes that appeared along the stairways that appeared to move as the sun sets or rises, setting them in motion as the rock shadows appeared to move. In Meso-America the symbols were found everywhere. Even in China, a blossom of dragons appeared with wings that made them terrifying.

John Luna

I had chosen to go on long fall hikes around the ranch house venturing further and further up the sandstone canyon at the back of the pasture. This day I was watching the tiny creek that flowed out of the mysterious bowels of the sandstone canyon. The creek was swollen, flowing with tiny ripples in places. Usually disappearing into the sand, I knew it would flow far into the distance, perhaps flowing into the Rio Puerco and then later into the Rio Grande. The turbid water I was watching would, sooner or later, meander all the way down to the Gulf of Mexico, evaporate and eventually return in the form of new clouds to start the process all over again.

Suddenly I was confronted by a large Hispanic fellow atop a black horse. It was impossible not to stare at him. He seemed like someone out of a western movie with a rifle in a scabbard and a revolver in a holster hung low around his hips. Stopping his horse in front of me, he took his sombrero off bringing it across his chest until it settled low in his extended arm.

"*Como estas*," he said with a grin that suddenly appeared under a large bushy mustache.

I had no idea what he was saying. I had not taken Spanish classes in high school before I left Tennessee and was now wishing I had. But the rider took sympathy with me and asked in perfect English, "How are you?"

I answered with a timid, "Just fine and you?" Meanwhile I was looking for an escape route but realized that I didn't have a chance of outrunning a man on a horse.

"*Me nombre,* eh...my name is John Luna. I live over there." He pointed to the distant rolling hills crisscrossed by many small arroyos. Then he asked, "How are June and Ken doing?"

Instantly I felt safer. "They are doing fine. Do you know them?"

"Oh sure, they are old friends." He paused for a moment and stared at me making me feel a little uncomfortable. "What is a good looking girl like you doing wondering around in this God forsaken place?"

I walked over to him and explained that I was staying with the Andersons until I could live with my father, Tim.

"Oh I know your father; he is a very good man. A hardworking man, I really like him. He has always said kind things about me."

This gave me a little more confidence and so I walked even closer to him. He looked down at me and with a grin on his face and says, "You are not afraid of me?"

"Not really I said; if you make a move for your gun I will be all over you. You will be blind for the rest of your life and feel like a castrated cow." This threat elicited a rumble of laughter from deep inside of him. He dismounted and we sat together on a large fallen limb from a cottonwood tree.

"It is true that I love beautiful women, and you are certainly beautiful, but..." He patted his chest, pausing to form the correct words. "I am really just a big teddy bear who loves to talk to all women, especially those who are not afraid to talk back to me."

By this time I was feeling pretty good. I had never been complemented on my looks by anyone outside of the immediate family and of course Turner who was nothing but a vague memory. I asked John Luna again, "Just who are you?"

"Well, he answered, I am a *borrachon veijo*." As he said it he stood up reaching for his saddle bag where he produced a pint bottle of whisky. He took a long pull from it then offered it to me. I shook my head no and starting to get up. "Stay around for a while and talk. I am harmless. Trust me I wouldn't hurt a friend of Ken Anderson. He would shoot me, *muy pronto*," he said with emphasis. "Besides I have no one to talk to out here except this stupid horse. He has a brain about the size of a walnut and is very short on words but big on sneaking back to the horse stall for his oats."

"What are you doing out here?"

I began to explain what the situation was at the ranch house choosing my words carefully not to tell him everything but rather trying to turn the conversation into questions about the disappearances.

Luna gave me his point of view on it all, "Oh, I don't believe that all this has anything at all to do with rattlesnakes. First of all there are no snakes out at this time of year and to tell you the truth I haven't seen a rattlesnake out here for at least two years. In years past, they were all over the place. One small hill next to my creek used to have a den of snakes that lived in it. When one of my cows stumbled over it she fell though. When her head came back up she looked like she had whiskers which turned out to be rattlesnakes. The cow lived but lost a lot of weight and walked around with a huge swollen head for a month or so."

"The thing is," he paused for a short moment to allow the thought to sink in, "all the snakes have disappeared around here. Something else is killing animals including many of mine." He thought about it for a minute, took another pull off the pint bottle of whiskey adding, "They sure look like rattlesnakes got to them though. I have even found the two puncture marks on them; they swell up and then die. If it is rattlesnakes killing them they must be very venomous because normally a larger animal doesn't die from a rattlesnake bite, but these animals surely died. The problem is I can't find any traces of rattlesnakes around here. It is a mystery to me. Where did the rattlesnakes go, and if the snakes are gone what is killing the animals around here now?"

I asked him, "How do you protect yourself at night?"

"From what," Luna answered with a laugh.

John Luna got back on his horse asking me if I would like a ride over to the ranch house. I answered him "Maybe next time, right now I just want to finish my walk."

John Luna repeated his motions with his sombrero and yelled "*Vayo con Dios* as he galloped off toward the Anderson ranch house. I knew what that Spanish saying meant and truly appreciated it.

The Cliff Dwelling

*A*rmed with the knowledge Corey and I ferreted out of the library, we began to explore further and further into the *Serpientes*, until finally we began spending the nights camped out in the canyon lands. Each canyon was different, despite the monotonous yellow and red sandstones that made up the walls of the canyons. It was a wet winter; snow that had accumulated from many small snowstorms was slowly melting in deep canyons. All of the canyons had tiny streams in their valleys that fed large pools as the water collected behind rock falls. After heavy rains those tiny streams could become raging rivers which is how most of the canyon carving occurred. Usually, during the late summertime the canyons would be bone dry, except for the largest of seeps or pools. We were able to see all manner of wildlife around these pools.

Everything seemed normal out in the countryside away from the ranches, but everywhere humans lived something strange was happening. Around ranch or farm houses, virtually all the farm animals and wildlife had vanished. It was as if the ranch houses where the humans lived were being purposely selected.

While we explored the canyons, it became clear to Corey and me that there had been many people here before us. Granaries and small Indian ruins were everywhere. Also, the floor of the canyons had obviously been shaped to a degree by ancient humans who grew corn and squash and all manner of food there. We made a game of studying the rock carvings, or pictographs, which covered the rocks near these ancient ruins.

In an earlier conversation, Hidalgo had explained that contrary to common belief most of these symbols were not simply doodling, writing, nor were they necessarily spiritual in nature. Some symbols were simply directional signs, placed to mark a trail, identify territory, or perhaps to show the way to water, important places, or some other natural or cultural feature. Other symbols identified tribes or clans; some symbols were used to record important events in the life of the clan, such as a memorable hunt or an extraordinary deed, the way we might write a newspaper article or send a greeting card. Furthermore, unlike most pictographs that are merely scratched on the rock, these pictographs were not merely scratched but rather were chiseled into the rocks forming petroglyphs. Someone had spent considerable time carving these figures. They were meant to last for all time.

Two symbols were common in the pictographs: one was a glyph that looked like clasped hands; easily seen by putting one hand inside the hand of a partner and looking down at the design it makes, a universal symbol for friendship used by all cultures throughout history.

The other was rattlesnakes. In one bizarre case, Corey discovered the clasped hand symbol with one hand being a rattlesnake. This seemed creepy to me, I could not imagine a situation where humans and rattlesnakes would be friendly to each other.

The more we explored the windswept canyons, the more of these rattlesnake motifs we discovered. "We must be entering the clan of the rattlesnake people," I joked, not realizing just how true my statement was.

Besides the many small *Anasazi* ruins we found a multitude of granaries where the ancients stored their food, usually well up on the canyon walls, in inaccessible places where animals couldn't get to them. It was on one of those trips that we discovered, by a serendipitous event, a collection of Indian ruins, high up in the cliffs in a natural cave enclosure. Finding the ruins was a story in itself.

Trying to find a bit of privacy to answer a call of nature was my least favorite part of camping trips, so I had climbed up the side of the canyon into what appeared to be a jumble of rocks while Corey waited patiently below. Instead of the semi-private natural ladies' room I expected, I found a tiny slit opening going back into the sidewall of the canyon. My curiosity got the best of me and so I decided to see if I could climb through the slit and see what was on the other side.

The slit in the rock was so narrow I had to walk sideways past the sheer rock walls that towered above me on both sides. Only a few feet further in, the canyon opened up. Then around a curve in the rock cliffs, high up on a sheer cliff, was a vast cave-like structure with Indian ruins.

It was a huge flat shelf about twenty feet deep in the middle, tapering out on the ends until there was not enough room for a foothold. Covering the entire maze of ruins was an overhanging rock roof. The entire cave was south-facing, allowing the sun to warm everything on frosty but clear winter days, while in the summertime the cave would be shielded from the sun, which was higher in the sky at that time of year. This ingenious solar heating would make the cave a great place to live, I thought if you didn't mind having to climb a sheer cliff just to get into your house!

I could not wait to go to tell Corey what I had found. Making my way carefully back though the slit in the rock walls I shouted, "Corey! Quick, come up here!"

Corey burst into the opening wild-eyed and panting, clutching the .22 rifle he had brought to shoot small game for our suppers. "Penny! What's wrong?!" he gasped.

"No, silly," I giggled, "Nothing's wrong! Look!" I pointed up at the slit in the rock.

"Dang, gal, you nearly scared me to death!" Corey began grumbling, but then he looked, really looked, through the slit in the rock.

"Who...how?" he began, and then just stopped and stared at the slit in the rock that I was pointing at. Coming into the canyon at such an extreme angle it would have been invisible from the canyon floor

After Corey went back to tie off the horses that he had been holding, he retraced my original path and climbed until he was at the base of the sheer cliff, where I was waiting for him.

We searched the cliff bottom until we found what we knew must be there; footholds that were carved into the face of the cliff; the only way up. The problem was that the footholds didn't start at ground level. A solitary person would have to pull himself up with his arms to gain that first foothold, which was about six feet up. Obviously, one of two things had happened at some time in the past: either the floor of the canyon had eroded and dropped down, or the people were afraid of something or someone climbing up to their homes. They had made it as difficult as possible for anyone, or anything, to access their homes. Luckily for us we could help each other to climb up.

Corey carefully lifted me up to the first of the footholds, where I worked my way up to the floor of the ruins. Then I lowered a rope down to Corey, who just as carefully worked his way up the face of the cliff. We were amazed at what we discovered there; unexplored ruins. Not a footprint could be found, only a fine dust that covered everything. These ruins were very different from other ruins we had explored, where everything of use or value had been stripped from the ruins by those thieves of time, pottery hunters.

I had learned many accounts of these antiquity thieves, or pottery hunters, in our studies at the library and from Aunt June. They are unscrupulous people who locate sites where ancient peoples lived and strip them of any artifacts that appear to be of any value. They then sell the artifacts to collectors. By taking this evidence of past civilizations away from where it was originally found, these thieves of time interfere with legitimate exploration that would extend our understanding of these ancient people. Antiquity thieves have always been despised by real archeologist.

There appeared to be many rooms, tiny by modern standards but cozy as well as functional. I walked up to one of the T shaped doorways, so low I had to bend at the waist to enter. I remembered what June had shared with me about *Anasazi* ruins. The first T shapes were at Pueblo Bonito, and later they spread to the remainder of the Colorado Plateau. The T door appeared later in Mayan sites such as Palenque in southern Mexico. A number of sites with the strange doors have been discovered in Peru. They appear to designate privileged space, perhaps something ceremonial.

"These people certainly did live in fear," I said. "I realize that *Anasazi* people were much shorter than we are but the only way to enter these rooms is by getting on my knees. If someone was inside and they wanted to, well, an intruder would be a sitting duck for a tomahawk to the head. You can't go in without exposing the back of your head."

Corey answered with, "Yeah, that's obvious. I wonder why, or what, or even who they were so scared of?"

"And what's the deal with the T-shapes?" Corey never answered the question. He didn't know the answer. No one does.

Inside, the rooms looked as if the people had just walked away and left them without looking back. Make shift tables still had beautiful pottery with petrified food in them. Tiny cores from ears of corn were strewn everywhere. Along the walls was bedding that had turned into a mat of rags and dust. Bits of clothing made from plant fibers were still hanging from pegs in the walls, with piles of tattered lumps of woven cloth on the floor under them. In one room I discovered a pile of black obsidian rock that would have been shaped into arrowheads or stone implements with edges sharper than surgical steel. Corey, being a student of geology like his late father, identified it as obsidian from Jemez Volcano. Jemez produces perfect black glassy rock that was perfect for making arrowheads. The nagging thought that came to Corey was why they would bring obsidian all the way from Jemez Volcano which is located well above present day Albuquerque. "That was a long way to walk just to get chunks of rock," he thought. Surely there was perfectly good obsidian somewhere in the volcanic hills surrounding *Serpientes* that could be found.

On reflecting, Corey remembered June telling him of a mystery she had encountered. They had found proof that the people from Midwestern settlements had traveled by canoe over two hundred miles into Yellowstone to collect peculiar pure black obsidian. He also thought of something Aunt June had said to him about Jemez obsidian rock; it has been found in the form of arrowheads as far away as the east coast. In Corey's mind he felt that there must be something else to it, there are too many other materials which can be made into arrowheads.

Then, in a small natural alcove just above the floor, in the wall, Corey found a tiny shrine with pieces of raw turquoise. Picking up the turquoise he thought he recognized it as some he had seen before from Arizona. Turquoise can be easily identified by the matrix, that is, the patterns formed by other minerals. Each turquoise mine produces its own particular patterns and colors.

There were also several small green crystals he wasn't sure about. They looked like emeralds but Corey had never heard of emeralds being found in this part of New Mexico. From his knowledge of the history of New Mexico he had learned that Cabeza de Vaca had written that while in southern New Mexico his party was presented with five emeralds, shaped like arrow heads. The Indians had said that they were from high mountains toward the north, where they traded for them with feather brushes and parrot plumes and they said that there were villages with many people living there. But the only place he could think of where emeralds were actually found was North Carolina where spectacular deposits had recently been found. There were also some small figurines, about an inch and a half wide that had been sand cast from gold. All but one looked like animals in nature and of course the most common was of snakes. The odd one had the cast of a head with tinier heads hanging like ear rings from the ears.

Since it was late, we made camp in the ruins for the night. Early the next day, we climbed above one of the ruins and examined some pictographs along the back wall. The rock carvings showed fifteen strange human like creatures of all sizes, with broad shoulders tapering down to tiny feet. To me, they looked bizarre with zig zag lines and spirals superimposed on the bodies. Completely surrounding them in an arc over them was the serpentine figure of a rattlesnake.

The image struck both of us as strange. What could it possibly mean and why was the rattlesnake carving so boldly and prominently displayed? We looked at each other. Did this carving mean something? Was there a connection to the current problems at the ranch house?

During the journey into the canyon, we had found small rattlesnake pictographs everywhere, but this pictograph was huge! Clearly these people were obsessed with rattlesnakes, but why? Finally Corey nervously turned to me and said, "Uh, Penny, have you noticed anything particular about the rattlesnakes on this trip?"

I thought a minute, and then a feeling of puzzlement came over me, "We've been exploring these canyons for some time now and we've seen hundreds of rock rattlesnake pictographs, but we've yet to see a single skin shed from a rattlesnake much less a live rattlesnake!"

Corey agreed with my point with, "At this time of year they are all hibernating. I wouldn't expect to see snakes out here but I sure would expect to find traces of them, mostly where they would shed their skin, adding another button to their rattlers. I haven't seen a trace of a real snake out here."

An Attack by the Antiquity Thieves

During the afternoon the winter air turned chillier and the first small flakes of snow began to fall. Corey and I explored a bit further, but we knew we would soon have to return to the ranch house. Just a short distance down the main canyon we were following, we came across another set of ruins. These were easily spotted, with granaries clearly visible on the canyon ledges above. Stopping and tying off the pack animals, we explored these ruins room by room. But these ruins had been picked clean, with nothing but shards of pottery lying around.

We were just turning to leave when the rocks above Corey's head seemed to explode. A sharp crack shattered the silence as the sound of the bullet caught up to it. Corey pulled me down as we dived behind the walls, fervently wishing he hadn't left his rifle with the horses. Corey's face was bleeding from a tiny crystal of rock that was ejected from the impact of the bullet. Who could possibly be shooting at us and why?

We lay against the cold sandstone rock for several minutes, scared and confused, expecting someone to show up at any moment, but no one shot at us again. Just after dark we crawled out of the rock ruin and were surprised to find our pack animals still tied off. We looked around for someone, but couldn't see anyone. But we did find something else; a rolled up sheet of paper was tied to the side of the saddle on Corey's horse. I opened it and read the menacing words, "Keep away from our stuff!" It was signed *Tu Ladrone*.

Obviously the shot was a warning from pottery hunters, those thieves, or *ladrones*, as the Mexicans called them. They obviously thought Corey and I were competition, stealing the pots that they wanted to steal.

That evening Corey and I traveled as far as we could, far away from the ruins, before setting up camp. A full moon came out, but we remained hidden, camping next to the canyon walls, leaving us in a moon shadow. Watching the glittering reflections in the shallow and mostly muddy steam at the bottom of the canyon, we lay awake with our minds in overdrive, thinking about the mysterious ruins, the shooter, and of course the rattlesnakes.

By now, both Corey and I had a new theory, a theory that involved serpents with bells on their tails, but the shooter complicated things. It was a mystery as to how the thieves were getting into the ruins. Obviously they were coming in through a different canyon but it was many miles away from any jeep roads that Corey knew of.

Corey and I decided that we needed a new plan of action; one that would somehow protect us from the thieves, yet one that would allow us to solve our mysteries. It would be almost a month before we could return to further investigate our discoveries. But this time we would be prepared.

A Return to the Cliff Dwelling

A month later we returned to the canyon where we had found the ruins. This time when Corey and I went exploring we were prepared with winter gear loaded onto pack horses and with Hidalgo accompanying us. He was more knowledgeable, experienced, and he understood the back country better than most people. He was a skilled outdoorsman, an experienced marksman; furthermore, he held a burning curiosity about the ancient Indian ruins. We took rifles and all manner of camping gear thus taking two days longer than it had taken Corey and me to make it to the ruins. We didn't want to accidently blunder into the thieves. We camped that night at the base of the cliff houses spending several hours re-exploring the ruins. Hidalgo was fascinated by the pictographs.

"They tell you more than meet the eye," said Hidalgo. "My ancestors were the Navajo who made war on the older *Anasazi*. But we respected and learned from them. We learned about their world through their pictographs and dealing with them personally. I suspect that some of them were headhunters and cannibals."

When I asked Hidalgo about pottery hunters, his answer was simple: "How would you feel if your grandparents, along with their burial possessions, were dug up from their graves and put on display?" This question opened the door for a long, involved conversation about science versus private rights. Then there were conversations about the need for better enforcement of The Antiquities Law. New laws were currently in legislation, proposed in order to discourage the pottery hunters.

The miles passed quickly under our horses' hooves, but soon we found ourselves at the site of the unexplored ruins that I had discovered in the side canyon.

Unfortunately, we quickly discovered that changes had occurred during our absence. As soon as we climbed up to the floor of the ruins we spotted a pile of trash; potato peelings, egg shells, and empty cans littered the rock floor. The ruins had been systematically ransacked, with everything of value gone. Even the small piles of unprocessed obsidian rocks were missing.

"What possible use could obsidian have been to them?" Corey blurted out in frustration. But the essence of the ruin was still here, particularly the rock drawings showing the rattlesnake encircling the anthropomorphs, those carvings of people that lived here long ago.

Hidalgo studied the rock panel for several minutes before saying anything. "It looks like the humans who lived here were surrounded by the rattlesnakes. Maybe they lived up here," he said, gesturing to the rooms, "So they would be safe from the snakes. Or maybe the humans had an alliance with the rattlesnakes and the encircling snake is a symbol of their territory. I don't know, but one thing is for sure; they were terrified of something or someone or they wouldn't be living up here."

By our fourth day out, tramping through a thin covering of snow on the ground, we discovered several other ruins that seemed impossible to get into; we didn't explore them because we hadn't brought rock-climbing equipment. As we explored, we saw places where the snow had completely melted away, exposing the trail under our feet. The canyon floor was littered by a layer of small bones.

Quite unexpectedly, we came upon what appeared to be a very small volcanic cone sticking out of the middle of a valley, surrounded by sandstone outcrops. The black volcanic cone was almost perfectly formed, with what appeared from ground level to be a perfect small caldera at the top and glassy smooth sides that didn't look natural at all.

Most volcanic rock is bubbly and angular, but the sides of this cone bore smooth black rock. Very black, the small hill looked almost artificial, looking totally out of place in the yellow and red sandstone country. We walked slowly around the mountain, looking for anything odd and noticing several odd things. The hill really wasn't a cone; it was more like a rounded-four sided pyramid. Another odd thing about it was that only the outermost few inches of rock was black, the eroded side was still where Uncle Ken had said it was, white with thousands of bubbles. We also noticed something that was not there.

Normally volcanic rock is perfect for pictographs, but on this volcanic rock not a sign of human marks could be found. Standing out in stark contrast to the surrounding countryside, the mountain had always had a dubious distinction, more than just the oddity of being the only black volcanic hill for miles around. We walked around the base of the mountain with our boots crunching on small bones which seemed to litter the ground everywhere. Nothing but bones, bones everywhere.

We were getting ready to leave when I noticed something in the corner of my eye. Caught between two dead branches was a snakeskin unlike any I or the rest of us had ever seen before. In shape, looking like any other snakeskin, except that each scale was like a tiny mirror, reflecting everything around it. Penny put it against different colors, and each time the color was reflected in the glittering scales. Lying on the ground, it was almost invisible, reflecting the colors around it.

Unlike other rattlesnakes that slowly adapt to their surrounding color, this snake must have totally blended into the background color. This snakeskin came from a truly stealthy rattlesnake, a snake no one had ever seen before, an unworldly snake.

I pocketed the snakeskin while Corey and Hidalgo made the short climb to the summit of the mountain. What they found was a typical crater, except for one thing: there were thousands of small holes located around the inner rim. Fortunately for them, rattlesnakes hibernate in the winter. Little did they know that just beneath their feet were thousands of sleeping serpents, all members of the rattlesnake clan; the hill wasn't a volcano, it was a nest.

The Death of John Luna

The first warm days of summer were approaching. After finding the strange snakeskin, Corey, Hidalgo and I were convinced that somehow these new rattlesnakes were responsible for the disappearances around the local ranches. However, it is one thing to think something and another to prove it. Besides, no one had actually ever seen a mirrored rattlesnake or anything else killing the livestock. But obviously something was causing the deaths, and the mirrored rattlesnakes were our best working theory.

Corey, Hidalgo, Ken, June, and I sat around the kitchen table many evenings during the remaining days of winter trying to come up with plan to deal with the rattlesnakes that were sure to make their appearance as soon as the weather got hot.

We examined the snakeskin over and over. No one had ever seen a snakeskin with the qualities of the skin they found. The snakeskin was, for all practical purposes, alien.

Back at the volcanic cone, as the weather improved day by day, new alien creatures began to appear. Around the scattered ranch houses in *Serpiente*, the smallest of animals began to disappear. These were followed by larger and larger animals, until it was obvious to everyone that all animals were disappearing again. No rabbits sprang out of the brush as a rider passed. Even the birds disappeared when nests with eggs in them became a thing of the past. Our family had begun to seal themselves at night as a precaution against the mysterious antagonist, but we were feeling more and more certain of what we were dealing with; a new kind of rattlesnake. But the business of running a ranch still had to be taken care of, and since the small community of ranches that were located in a twenty mile radius were all losing cattle and money they had decided to pool their resources, when possible, as insurance against defaulting on their ranches.

When it costs more to operate a ranch than it earns, eventually it is abandoned. Even with pooling their resources, the smallest of the ranches were doomed by the disappearance of their livestock. Not long after that the whole area becomes a ghost town. The west is full of ghost towns. When the minerals or resources being mined runs out or the population over reaches the carrying capacity of the land, the community dies. At this point, *Serpiente*, the ranch, was well on its way to becoming a small ghost town along with all of its neighbors.

After the sun was well up, Uncle Ken called me into the living room to do a chore for him. "We need you and Corey to go over to the Luna Ranch and ask John if he can meet with me and some other landowners."

"Sure," I answered, "As soon as I finish cleaning the kitchen I'll find Corey and head over." I had run into John Luna several times since I had first met him and come to really like him. Despite a very rough exterior, Luna was the biggest teddy bear I had ever run into. I had never been around someone who could tease like Luna yet I felt perfectly safe around him. I had quickly realized that the sexual innuendoes in his teases were a complement, not an advance.

The only truck that still had a good tank of gas in it was Hidalgo's old Ford. He had left the keys in it since no one ever stole anything that far out of town; besides the truck had been given to him by Ken several years before and we were only going a few miles.

After an eight mile drive to the other side of the tiny creek that flowed out of *Serpiente* Canyon we finally arrived at the Luna Ranch, discovering a problem right away. The first cause for apprehension was the front door which was wide open, causing Corey and I to look at each other.

"Maybe he is out in the horse stables," Corey said. So pulling up in the yard we slid out of the truck seats and headed to the stables. What we found there was appalling. Luna only owned one horse, Midnight, which he took care of even if he had to skip meals himself.

We found the horse lying on its side, nearly dead. Something had gotten to it during the night and its face and neck were swollen to nearly twice its normal size. The commotion of Corey and I walking into the horse stall caused the animal to begin jerking its head and legs trying to get up. But within only a few moments it suddenly stopped moving at all. Midnight, John Luna's horse, had died. After a cursory search of the horse barn showed that nothing seemed amiss, we headed back to the house.

John Luna was there. Except for a sheet wrapped around his middle, he lay naked in his bed, dead. It was easy for us to trace what had happened. Something had come through the front door that he had left opened. Luna was bitten many times by something, then left to die.

Luna had fired several shots at something in a panic. He must have been terrified at something as he had managed to shoot himself in the foot. There were five bullet holes in the wall where the slugs had blown the plaster away. The sixth slug from Luna's revolver had passed through Luna's foot imbedding itself in the metal bed post. He obviously had shot himself while trying to escape the intruders. The empty revolver was still gripped tightly in his hand.

I was too shaken to examine the body but Corey took his time and gave Luna an examination that would make a medical examiner proud. Luna's head had swollen to twice its normal size and on his face and neck were several puncture wounds; two small holes side by side, just like the fang marks a large rattlesnake would leave. Corey hugged me while I tried to recompose myself, but I was having trouble fighting off the tears that flooded my eyes, "Luna was killed due to over a dozen rattlesnake bites."

"Any other evidence of snakes," asked Penny?

"Well, let's look," answered Corey.

They could find nothing in the house but out in the yard they did find a short trail of impressions in the soft sand exactly like crawling snakes would leave, all headed in the direction of *Serpiente* Canyon. Then the trail just stopped as if the snakes had disappeared.

A drive into Belen in order to notify the police, followed by a funeral would occupy all of us for the next week. When the real medical examiner finally made his way to the ranch house he simply declared the death was due to rattlesnake bites but he was amazed at how the bites were inflicted. Rattlesnakes are solitary creatures who work entirely alone. In his view, Luna had been murdered by someone who had obviously brought the snakes in and dumped them in Luna's bed. But of course, that really didn't make any sense either. In the end the death certificate listed his death as cause unknown.

Dr. Rebecca Hartsell

Early on a summer morning, Ken and June loaded us all up into the family car, the only vehicle they owned that would seat everyone. All the other vehicles were work trucks used to haul everything from hay bales to cattle. We traveled to Los Cruses to visit New Mexico State University by way of the small town of *Magnalena* and then *Socorro*. After dropping Corey and I off at the university, June and Ken spent some time shopping for some clothes that they desperately needed, including some shirts for Hidalgo and some gifts they needed to purchase to pay off gift debts from wonderful friends. We started asking questions as soon as we ran into someone to talk to. In particular we hoped that someone at the University could provide insight about the snake skin, or have an idea of how to get rid of the rattlesnakes, but we also knew that we had to be careful what we said and to whom we talked.

After we arrived we discovered that we should have planned to be more specific about who we were going to talk to We had no idea who could help us. However we were smart enough to go directly to the office of information in the administration building.

After determining that Corey and I were not new students at the university, the flustered receptionist, who was manning the information desk, had no idea where to send us, but a young lady who was seated at a small desk working her way through several piles of mailers offered a suggestion. "Dr. Wyerhouse sometimes talks about snakes in his classroom. I don't know what he actually does with them but he might be able to direct you to someone who can answer your questions. You also need to visit the biology and agricultural schools.

Dr. Wyerhouse, turned out to be an English professor who apparently liked to scare his students by talking about rattlesnakes. After I explained the situation to him, he suggested using a new invention, an atomic bomb. This seemed like a great idea until a student awaiting an appointment to discuss a low grade on a paper overheard the conversation and politely but firmly explained how radioactive isotopes travel through food chains. Besides, since the rattlesnakes lived deep underground, the explosion couldn't possibly hurt all of them. In the end, the rattlesnakes might even be genetically altered and somehow become even worse. Dr. Wyerhouse, who was a little embarrassed, countered the conversation by suggesting using poisons but his suggestion was, again, immediately ruled out by the student, "Poisons invariably enter the food chain and kill many other creatures. Besides, how do you poison a rattlesnake? Rattlesnakes prefer to eat live creatures, and would more than likely ignore a dead carcass stuffed with poison."

Some of the solutions were even more bizarre; Dr. Frankel who overheard and walked in on the conversations offered an opinion. "Drive them out with a high pitched noise," he defiantly announced.

Dr. Wyerhouse lifted his head up from the table and said, "Even I know that rattlesnakes are deaf, besides even if we could drive them out of the caves, what's to keep them from regrouping somewhere else?"

"Oh, I didn't think of that," replied Dr. Frankel. He followed his last questions with, "Well, then, what about an electric fence?" And so the meeting went on, with no consensus as to what to do. The student who had offered his earlier opinions interjected himself into the conversation again with "You need to see Dr. Hartsell in the biology department." Corey and I left the office wondering about the fate of the young student.

Dr. Rebecca Hartsell turned out to be a new research professor. She was on the cutting edge of many university projects and was intrigued by the snake skin. Dr. Hartsell spent some thirty to forty minutes examining it. "I have never seen anything like it," she finally said. "It really looks like some of the stuff they are working on in Albuquerque at Sandia Labs. They are working on stealth technology, trying to make everything from soldiers to airplanes invisible."

She did, however, make one important discovery about the snake skin. Under ultra violet light the skin glows, almost like bioluminescence. "The same thing happens to scorpions. In darkness they are invisible but they glow under a UV light. She also proposed that the reason the snakes only came out at night was because of the protective skin. When light was shined on it during the day, the scales would act like mirrors; in the dark it would be totally invisible. In the end, no real solutions were found but now we had a tool to make the snakes visible. The local ranchers would have to find their own solutions. But more than anyone, solving the problem was left up to the family that I had been adopted into.

As the summer got hotter, the men learned how to spot the rattlesnakes by using flashlights adapted with ultraviolet light filters. They were amazed to discover that on a hot summer night several could be spotted in the yard. By covering their horse's legs with a stiff boot material, they were able to ride around the house and into the pastures after dark. The heavy leather simply made it too hard for any snake to bite into the flesh. With those horses they could explore at night when the snakes were active. They would ride out into the pasture then turn on their flashlights. The flashlight beam would reflect glittering sparkles of light from the skin of the rattlesnakes. Even the moon could occasionally cause a dull sparkle by reflecting off the mirrored scales. This enabled them to literally hunt the rattlesnakes at night with small rifles, staying far enough away not to spook the horses.

Many of the rattlesnakes were killed, but in only a short while the rattlesnakes learned to slither down nearby holes at the approach of any larger animal. They could feel the vibrations of the approaching horses for quite some distance. As the baby rattlesnakes started to grow, the problem only worsened. Several close calls occurred when one of the men would almost step on a rattlesnake or pick one up with a bale of hay in the barn. The snakes were fearless, harder to spot and harder to hit with a bullet than the native rattlesnakes, and the canyon lands crawled with them. Except for an occasional coyote, all the smaller animals again disappeared from around the ranch house.

Finally, my natural curiosity aroused, I asked a simple but obvious question, "Why are they attacking the ranch houses? They don't seem to be bothering animals out in the pastures unless they have human smells associated with them. Why are the rattlesnakes warring with humans?"

The Undulating Serpent

The first apprehension was a result of finding a hose loose. The gas clothes dryer that June used in the wintertime had an exhaust that was held to a floor bracket with a ring clamp. It would take a massive amount of effort to dislodge the clamp without taking a flathead screwdriver and unscrewing the screws. Yet, there it was loose and just lying there on the floor. Any animal that could get under the house could have entered the house without a soul knowing it until it was too late. Uncle Ken was angry. "There is just no way that a snake could get that hose off, I put it on myself and I know I did it right," he exclaimed in frustration.

A snake does not need much room to hide; in fact, they are masters of camouflage and stealth. The humans spent two days searching the house with UV lights but never found anything. Every bed had to be torn apart, every drawer had to be taken out with the contents looked through and every piece of pottery had to be examined for the possible presence of a rattlesnake. They found nothing but the many things that they had put away somewhere and then forgotten where they had put them.

Nothing happened for the next two weeks. Then a most peculiar thing happened. I had gone to bed early that night, lying in bed for almost two hours before actually drifting off to sleep. My mind was in turmoil thinking about all of the events that had occurred. Finally I drifted off into a sound sleep but was awakened when I thought I could hear a mouse in the room. At the moment, it had never occurred to me that a mouse could have gotten into the room, as I continued to wake up and find my senses; I realized that there couldn't have been a mouse in the house. The doors and windows were all screened or boarded over. Reaching over to my end table I picked up the flashlight I always kept there. It still had the UV filter on it. As I turned it on I quickly noticed several rattlesnakes on the floor. In terror, I sat up and quickly noticed that the door to my room had been opened. Just then, one of the snakes head popped up at the foot of my bed. As the other snakes appeared to flee from the UV light, this particular snake literally poured itself on the bed. Much larger and thicker than any rattlesnake I had ever read about, I discovered that I couldn't make my body move; I was frozen with fear.

The snake raised its head, as if ready to strike, but instead, it moved its head slowly back and forth as if trying to hypnotize me. It was a phantasmagoric scene, the snake glowing under the lighting the flashlight provided. The slit eyes showed like glowing red embers never blinking, holding a cold and cruel focus. I remember thinking, Snakes do not undulate before they strike, why was this snake making loops with its head?"

The snake had an effect on me, as if it was trying to communicate something primal. I couldn't understand what the snake wanted but I did have the distinct impression that the snake was intelligent. I finally regained self-awareness and realized I was gripping the covers in my hand. In an instant as the snake dipped its head, I managed to throw the covers over it and ran out the door. Scanning with my flashlight so I could avoid any other snakes, I almost ran head first into Corey who stood there with only his shorts on, staring at the floor. In less than a minute, Ken and June came running out of their bedroom with their heads bent over in search of snakes on the floor. The only person that had not appeared was Hidalgo so everyone went to his room in order to see how he was doing.

We found Hidalgo in bed, wrestling with an imaginary snake just inches from his face, only there wasn't a snake there. He was having a nightmare. After waking up a very sweaty Hidalgo, we all just looked at each other for a moment. How could they have all experienced the same intense dream? The dream was so real, and the details they all shared were astounding. In everyone's dream the snake had risen from the end of the bed and seemed to spill out on top of the bed covers. The only difference had been in Hidalgo's dream. He actually had grabbed the head of the snake and was rolling around with a death grip on it. Then the next thing he remembered was Corey shaking him.

Corey had a look of puzzlement on his face as he whispered quietly, "Now I understand why Luna shot his foot. He thought he was shooting a snake. But, those were real snake bites that he received, I don't understand."

I volunteered a guess, "Maybe his snakes were real and of course, he did have that revolver with him. None of us had a gun with us".

"Well, that is not entirely true." Hidalgo interjected, "I had my police issue with me but I never thought about using it. In my dream the snake was on me too fast."

"One thing I do understand," says Ken. "If those snakes can make all of us have the same dream at the same time, there is much more to this than any of us ever thought. They are controlling our minds."

June nodded her head up and down in agreement. "We really have discovered something strange here. Let's search the house." Not finding anything, not even a loose hose, we finally relaxed and began to ponder the situation. Sleep finally returned just as the sun began to show on the horizon. The actual mystical snakes that had caused the dreams had already begun their long journey back to their nest.

The Confrontation

All summer long the humans and the rattlesnakes warred with each other. Finally, the first cold days of fall returned, and the snakes began to disappear again. Corey, Hidalgo and I decided they had to return to *Serpiente* to see if there was a way to get rid of the rattlesnakes for good. On a frosty November morning, we loaded our pack animals and headed back toward the volcanic cone.

It was a trip that seemed much shorter now that we knew the way. Since it was winter we had no fear of being attacked by the rattlesnakes.

Returning to the ruins that I had discovered, we retraced our steps to the bottom of the cliff. There we tied a rope to our packs after securing the animals and climbed to the ruin shelf to find a cozy room out of the wind to sleep.

Pulling up our packs, we soon found ourselves huddled around a small fire while coffee boiled, steaks with potatoes fried, and anticipation peaked. What would tomorrow bring? Could we find a way to either get rid of or make peace with the snakes? That evening there was another light snow and we slept deeply. We knew that nothing could reach us where we slept, which is why the ruins were there in the first place. Even a rattlesnake cannot climb a sheer wall.

The next morning we lowered our packs and sleeping gear to the frosty ground at the bottom of the bluff, gathered it all up, and headed out to the main canyon to feed and load the horses. When we got to the place the horses had been tied, however, nothing remained except tracks!

"Two men," Hidalgo said, "And they led the horses away with them." Without hesitation they stashed their heaviest gear and started after the men and horses.

Hidalgo still had his trusty 30-06 with him, and Corey had a 357 magnum pistol that he had carried ever since that first shot landed above his head when he and I first encountered the pottery hunters. He also had used it on night patrols looking for rattlesnakes. Still, without the pack animals and horses, it would be a long walk back to the ranch. We desperately had to find where our animals were being taken.

We were angry. Hidalgo and Corey were not about to allow someone to take advantage of us like that. They suspected that the culprits were the same people that took the pot-shot at Corey and me on our previous trip. Even I was furious. We were bound and determined to have a confrontation with the pottery hunters, the only other people we had ever run into in *Serpientes* except for the thousands of ghosts.

Fernandez and Garcia

We took off on a long hike following the tracks left behind in the thin layer of snow through the main canyon in the area. Many hours later, with burning feet and red faces, we caught sight of a small whiff of smoke coming up over the curve of the canyon in front of us. Creeping over rocks and through the small cedars that lined the canyon, we soon discovered horses tied up to some salt cedars. Behind the brush that was lining the tiny seep stream was a cavernous hole in the rock, where two men were busy cooking a meal. I looked over at Hidalgo and whispered, "What are we going to do?"

Hidalgo said, "That's easy," and whispered his quick plan. Corey took off in one direction and Hidalgo the other. I held my ground.

As soon as everyone was in place I called out to the two men. "Hey, you guys, I want my horses back!"

The two men, not expecting two young kids to put up any fight, were taken aback. Profanities in Spanish echoed off the curved rocks of the campsite, along with a fast flurry of activity. With guns in hand they jumped to their feet and defiantly stood their ground. Peering toward the direction my voice had come from, the one I would later discover was known as Jose Garcia yelled out to me, "Come in and get your stuff, we might even party a little bit."

I yelled back, "Sounds like fun, only I would need a real man to party with!" At that, the one named Garcia let a round go with his old 30-06 rifle. "Do you really want to mess with us?"

The noise echoed up and down the canyon walls. The other one, Don Fernandez, stepped toward my voice with a big grin on his face and said, "Cover me and I'll get us something for dessert!" Thinking that the girl was alone or that the boy was with her but unarmed and hiding, Fernandez felt brave and reckless. They had never dreamed that the girl and boy would actually pursue them, much less challenge them; besides they were armed, and they assumed that Corey and I were alone and defenseless.

As soon as Fernandez took a step forward, Corey stepped out of the rocks beside him with his pistol aimed directly at the Mexican's chest. His friend Garcia turned to fire at Corey, but Hidalgo aimed and shot at his knee. The knee appeared to explode, with blood and bone pieces flying everywhere.

The battle was instantly over; with one shot Hidalgo had evened the score and won the upper ground. Immediately the men started pleading for their freedom. Garcia was carried to a horse and unceremoniously slid into the saddle, while the other one turned to get the bundles of loot they had stored there. "Leave it," Hidalgo yelled in a commanding voice. In utter frustration, his companion pleading for help, Fernandez grabbed the horse's reins and headed out of the canyon. They would need to find a doctor immediately, or the situation would get far worse for the one named Garcia. He would spend the next few days in absolute agony as the horse carried him back to civilization. He would spend the remainder of his life with a distinct limp.

At the campsite, Corey, Hidalgo and I found crates and sacks full of Indian relics pilfered from the ruins. Several of the sacks contained priceless relics, even jewel-encrusted ornaments. Hidalgo took particular interest in a small sack full of green jewels.

"Do you know what these are?" he asked. Corey examined the jewels and exclaimed, "Emeralds! Where could they have come from?"

Hidalgo was mystified. "I wonder how they found these stones. Most Indians in this area valued turquoise; it has a religious meaning to the people. But I don't understand how they could have acquired these." Pocketing the small bag of emeralds, the three of us pondered what to do with the loot that the pot looters had left there. One bag contained items that they recognized as belongings of a local rancher.

"These are mean people," says Hidalgo, "we will have trouble with them again." We looked through the plunder, took out the most portable articles, and decided to hide all the rest in a small rock cave with a doorway that would have been unnoticed from only a few feet away.

Small Sticks

That night, we camped under the rattlesnake ruin that I had originally discovered. Now we knew what had happened to the local men who had disappeared; they had been murdered. Perhaps they too had wandered into the canyon looking for something and had stumbled into the pottery hunters. How many people had the pot-hunters disposed of? We could only guess as we went down a list of people that we knew had disappeared, and that was the ones that we knew of. How many more were there?

"I should have just killed them both right there," Hidalgo said, looking toward the site of their earlier battle. Thinking that we were indeed very lucky not to have been killed ourselves, we pondered our next move. After eating my portion of stew, I began to re-explore the cliff ruins that we had named rattlesnake ruins. I started walking from room to room, but then I decided to walk out onto the narrow cliff of rock formed near the edge of the ruins. There I pondered a sight that before now we had all ignored.

"Hey, you guys!" I yelled. As Hidalgo and Cory walked over I pointed to the narrow floor and asked a simple question. "What are all these small sticks used for?"

Hidalgo and Corey bent over to examine the sticks, which were all rotted over time with very few clues as to what they were used for. They were as mystified as I was. So I started digging into the fragile remains. "What a minute," I said, "Look at those tiny skeletons." Buried inside of the pile of rubble, we found a number of small skeletons, some of a rat like creature and some of birds.

Hidalgo was mystified. "In all my years, I have never seen anything like that. Why would people living in a cliff house cage small animals that would be useless as food?"

We returned to the tiny fire we had built by bringing up scraps of wood from the canyon floor below us. Sitting around the fire, we looked at each other for any sign of inspiration.

Finally I said, "What if they were not raising the animals for food? What if they were raising the animals for someone, or something else? What animal eats rats?"

All three of us looked at each other in the flickering firelight and said, Rattlesnakes!

Blood Sacrifices

Hidalgo pulled out the bag of emeralds, which would be worth many thousands of dollars, and said, "I don't understand it. Early people respected the rattlesnake, but they left them alone. Even if they were providing them with food, why would the rattlesnakes care? Rattlesnakes are not very smart creatures!"

"That's true;" said Corey, "but these are not typical rattlesnakes. Why would they only attack the human settlements, and not simply eat wild prey like regular rattlesnakes do?"

Hidalgo said, "At least I believe I understand now why the pot hunters didn't have to deal with the rattlesnakes."

Corey and Penny looked at him in confusion. Corey asked, "How did they avoid running into them?"

Hidalgo answered, "They only hunted pots in the wintertime. In the summer there are usually a few people who wander into these canyons chasing cows or sheep or just to explore. The pottery hunters didn't want to get caught. Not only that, most of those fellows have other jobs they do in the summer. My guess is, with the rattlesnakes causing problems, some of the local ranchers wandered off into these canyons looking for answers. Obviously they died for their efforts."

Corey said thoughtfully, "That still doesn't explain why the Indians raised small animals or how they lived in peace with the rattlesnakes."

Hidalgo said, "It also doesn't explain how the ancient ones accumulated so many jewels."

In this moment I had an inspiration and I said, "Sure it does. It's just a hypothesis, but what if the oldest Indians made peace with the rattlesnakes? What if they achieved peace through some kind of trade? The rattlesnakes and the ancient race needed each other; the rattlesnakes provided protection from other human tribes, and of course a snake can go to many places underground. What if, somehow, the rattlesnakes provided the underground wealth and the humans provided small animals for the rattlesnakes to eat? What if, from the rattlesnake's perspective, the humans were making blood sacrifices to them?"

Corey responded with, "I don't know. First of all, why are the rattlesnakes just recently becoming a problem around *Serpiente*?"

Hidalgo smiled and stood up, throwing his hand out in front of him. "I know, don't you two get it?"

Corey and I looked at each other and shrugged our shoulders.

Hidalgo said, "Think about it. What animal in nature eats rattlesnakes?" He answered his own question, "Coyotes! They are the only animals out here that will naturally attack and eat a rattlesnake, but during the last twenty years or so they have been hunted nearly to extinction."

"I get it!" I said, "When the coyote population dropped, the rattlesnake population exploded, and that's why the snakes have recently appeared around here! Before, the coyotes kept their numbers in check. I have wondered why I've only seen a couple of coyotes since I moved out here; they have all been killed off, and the ones that are left are very timid. They run from any human they encounter."

Corey said, "So what do we do, import coyotes? I'm sure the local ranchers will love that. After all, coyotes also eat baby cows and sheep."

They went to sleep that night mulling the problem over in their heads, trying to come to a practical solution. I kept thinking about the idea of blood sacrifices. Every ancient culture that I had read about in my history books had some kind of blood sacrifices. Even in the Bible there were verses that involved blood sacrifices.

The Proposal

Early the next morning, I started the conversation by proposing a solution. "I think the local Indians actually used the rattlesnakes to help them. It may have taken them a long time, but they figured out how to live in peace with the rattlesnakes. I believe those little wooden cages are the solution to our problem. A real scientist would conduct an experiment in order to get demonstrable, measurable, and repeatable results. I propose an experiment in which we actually leave food for the rattlesnakes and see what happens!"

"Sounds awfully dangerous to me," Hidalgo thoughtfully countered. "We would have to come out here during the summertime and leave the food where the snakes can get to it and see what happens. How are we going to keep the rattlesnakes from getting to us?"

"Well," I said, "The Indians lived up here in this cliff for a good reason; it's the night time when these snakes come out."

Hidalgo turned and answered, "Yeah, but it takes two nights of camping to get to this ruin. Just getting here is going to be a problem. And have you thought of what your uncle and aunt are going to say when we tell them about this hair brained plan?"

Corey said, "We have another problem. How do you build a cage that doesn't let the rats or mice escape, and still lets the rattlesnake in?"

Hidalgo answered his question with, "If you turn loose a dozen or so baby chicks, where are they going to go? We only need cages to transport them here."

I promptly answered the questions with, "I'll bet we would be safe as long as we travel during the day and at night zip ourselves into tents. As long as we don't go out in the dark or leave a zipper undone, we should be fine until we reach the cliff ruins."

Hidalgo added, "We have all the way until spring to figure everything out. Right now we have far more pressing things to worry about. What if Fernandez and Garcia decide to come back for revenge? The one good thing we have to show your folks is this," he said, holding up the bag of emeralds. "There is a small fortune in this one bag, and we didn't even look through all the other bags. Your uncle will be able to get his ranch back in order with the money these jewels are worth."

Corey looked up at them and quietly said, "You both know that the real problem is going to be to convince all the local ranchers around here not to shoot every coyote they see. I've certainly shot my fair share of them."

"Hidalgo casually whispered, "I have never killed a coyote. Many Navajos have beliefs about coyotes."

I said, "My bet is that once the coyotes start preying on the rattlesnakes again, sooner or later, a balance will occur, just like there used to be."

"It may take a few years to get a, what did you say, a 'demonstrable, measurable, and repeatable' result to that question?" said Hidalgo.

We then started the long ride back to the ranch house, where we gathered all the local ranchers up and discussed the situation with them. Ranchers came from many miles away, most of them unaware of the problem the ranchers in *Serpiente* were dealing with. Most everyone disagreed about the coyotes. Old habits and ways are hard to change. Not only did most of the ranchers think it was a good idea to kill the coyotes but they wanted everything dead, except for their farm animals. As usual, money was the common denominator. They would kill anything that threatened their livelihood. The meeting was full of debate and bitter arguments. One fellow left the meeting shaking his head, saying that he had never heard of such a "dammed fool" plan. He didn't believe that there was such a thing as rattlesnakes that could be invisible, and he dismissed everyone as having a case of mass hysteria.

The one thing we didn't mention or talk about was the treasure we had discovered. The last thing we wanted was an invasion in the back country of even more pot hunters. Everyone knew it was illegal to steal things from Indian ruins, but, like a lock that only keeps an honest man honest, the law would only work for a few. It was hard times, and a few would not be able to resist the temptation.

The Experiment

That spring everything picked up at the ranch at *Serpiente*; for the first time in several years Ken and June had plenty of money to keep the ranch going and Hidalgo had a new house built for his mother and father, who lived on the Navajo reservation. Suddenly they were the envy of the neighborhood, even if their nearest neighbor was now fourteen miles away.

Corey and I put the money we made from the sale of the emeralds into a bank account in Los Lunas, where we could use it in the future to pay for our college education or to start a business. At this point in our lives neither one of us was sure of our future, but there was something else happening. Corey and I were spending more and more time alone together. Rumors started to fly as the little ones around the house occasionally caught the two of us doing more than just holding hands. Love was in the air, but we both knew we had major problems to solve before that love was going to go anywhere. Besides just because I was in love with some character in a dream, doesn't mean it was going to happen in real life.

Hidalgo, Corey, and I made plans for our return to the canyon that summer, collecting special cages that would allow something like the head of a rattlesnake to enter but the spring loaded door would not allow a mouse to escape. We found ourselves in the business of actually buying and raising mice and baby chicks. The occasional neighbor who dropped by thought we were a little crazy, but that didn't matter, our plan was in play. Then the day came when we were ready to put our plan to the test.

Loading up our horses with their odd looking leather boots on and bringing several mules loaded with cages full of mice and camping gear along with us, we plunged into the canyons of *Serpiente* once more. Camping at our usual spots, we noticed that no one had been in the canyon before us; not a track of a human could be found. What we did find was a few coyote tracks, and at one point Hidalgo saw just a glimpse of one before it disappeared into the labyrinth of brush and rocks.

We traveled during the day, setting up camp early in the afternoon. Carefully each night we zipped up our tents so that not even the tiniest creature could get into them, and we stayed there until well after sunrise the next day. By late in the third day, we reached the Indian ruins where we hoisted everything up to the rock shelf.

Hidalgo observed, "Well, at least we don't have to find a tree to hang the cages from. You would think this canyon was full of bears rather than rattlesnakes." Everyone finally had a blissful sleep out in the breeze using our sleeping bags and pads to lie on.

The next morning the experiment was on. We hiked to the base of the black hill where we set out several cages with terrified mice and baby chickens in them. We also turned a multitude of baby chicks loose for bait then we returned to the ruin.

It was a long night filled with anticipation as well as some dread. We had no idea what we would find the next day. Everyone did, however agree that we would probably discover all the bait gone and that would be that.

The Results

Early the next day, we hiked back to the volcanic hill just as the last of the rattlesnakes slithered into the cone. We immediately went over to the cages. The mice and baby chicks were all gone, but to our amazement there was something inside of each cage. In several of the cages were small quartz crystals about the size of a small finger nail. In two of the cages we found hematite or fool's gold crystals, but in the last two there was something special. In one was a small gold nugget, and in the other was a large green emerald about the size of a thumbnail.

So this is what the rattlesnakes wanted, a sacrifice of food for what was, to them, trinkets. They wanted food that was easy to get to, without cowboys or coyotes to threaten them. The snakes would not have to travel long distances to make war on the humans or risk war with the coyotes. That first night they seemed famished, consuming all the bait that was left out for them.

The next night we put out the rest of the cages and collected a few more trinkets, including another, slightly smaller, green emerald in exchange; but not all the terrified mice had been eaten. We soon discovered that in time, we would need to bring fewer and fewer mice and baby chicks as the summer progressed. Like all snakes, these snakes digested their food very slowly.

One evening Hidalgo, Cory and I went back to the rattlesnake pictograph.

"Now I understand it," said Hidalgo, "The people who lived here had a working relationship with the rattlesnakes. "The snakes actually offered them protection from more warlike human clans and provided jewels and some gold that they used to fashion ornaments and religious objects. The circle of the snake also represents the balance between the two clans."

"And the coyote clan was the thing that kept them all in check," said Corey, "sort of a balance of nature."

I said, "Sure, just like in nature, too few rattlesnakes and the mouse population explodes exponentially. Mice carry fleas and then when they invade the human population and problems begin, such as the black plague that decimated much of Europe during the dark ages. Serpents would eat enough of the mice to restore the balance of nature.

Too few coyotes and the rattlesnake and mouse populations explode, yet too many coyotes and some of the coyotes will starve. Until, of course, people come along and killed most of the coyotes, which caused a population explosion of the rattlesnakes."

During the next summer, every other weekend we brought a caravan of mouse cages to the volcanic mountain known by the old ones as *"El Montano del Serpientes de Cascabels,"* the mountain of the rattlesnakes.

We collected and inspected the cages that had been left there before to see what the rattlesnakes had left for us. On occasion we found something of great value, a nugget of gold or a gemstone of some value.

The ranches around *Serpiente* became safe again. People were no longer afraid of the night and could allow the smaller farm animals to graze around the community of buildings that make up the ranches without fear of them disappearing.

Yet a common fear among the ranchers kept them out of the canyons, and shortly coyotes began to reappear in the canyon lands that made up *Serpiente*. They seemed to relish the freedom of the canyons without fear of being shot at. The rattlesnakes stayed in a smaller and smaller area until they finally never left sight of their nest.

Don Fernando and Jose Garcia were not seen there again, at least for that year. They managed to hide away in a small adobe and rock house that was invisible to all except those that knew its exact location. But the damage that they had caused to the archeological history of the area was immeasurable and was evident everywhere that ruins could easily be found and access was easy. Great debates would occur as to what they had done with the loot they had plundered. Where and to whom were they selling the plunder?

During explorations of the canyons Corey and I, using climbing gear, found two other small ruins that had not been ransacked. Even they had some small piles of crystals hidden in tiny nooks in the walls of the small rooms. But the vast majority of the ruins had been destroyed. With the money the thieves had already made from stealing the artifacts, and the nature of human greed and vindictiveness, we knew deep in our hearts that someday there would be another confrontation. We knew that, in time, we would have to deal with Don Fernando and Jose Garcia again, but we could at least hope that the thieves had learned their lesson. Meanwhile, I found myself a full-fledged member of a new family.

Part 2

Discovering America

Look like the innocent flower. But be the serpent under it.
—William Shakespeare

In reality, all fights come down to two basic issues that have little to do with the content of the arguments: One person feels that he or she is being unfairly controlled or feels neglected.
—Advice from Penny's Grandmother, Nora Campbell

A Balance of Nature

During the weeks and months following the conquest of the rattlesnake clan, the coyote clan also prospered. Coyotes naturally took advantage of not being killed on sight. The area ranchers stopped shooting coyotes on sight, unless, of course they were up to mischief. Without human intervention a balance of nature returned to the area known as *Serpiente*. Regular rattlesnakes soon returned to the canyons living off the small rodents, lizards and other small animals that all rattlesnakes relish. They also made the humans much more careful when they were outdoors. Humans all had to learn to look before they sat on old logs or entered a dark shed, but regular rattlesnakes never appeared close to the mountain. It was not known whether they instinctually stayed away from *El Montano del Serpientes de Cascabels*. Had serpents who lived there manipulated their minds, or maybe nature was just taking its course.

Larger snakes do eat smaller snakes, even of their own species. Death to them occurred as they discovered themselves being suddenly swallowed and then slowly being digested. The mysterious mystic serpents stayed within the bounds of their personal territory. Perhaps they considered the mice and baby chicks brought to them as some kind of ritualized sacrifice. They quickly learned to never leave the mountain because it welcomed an attack by the coyote clan. Nor did they feel a need to war upon the human clan. Within the time of a summer, they had learned to stay within the confines of the mountain.

No one had any more dreams with glowing snakes in them. They were much more than just a new species of rattlesnake. These were not normal snakes; the speculation was that they were not from this world, that they were alien. In fact after experiencing the simultaneous dreams where the serpents entered their dreams at night, everyone was in awe and intimidated by their power.

We referred to them as serpents because they were not regular snakes. The human clan obligingly brought them food twice a month, which the snakes seemed to relish. They digested their food very slowly; soon it only took two mules with loaded cages full of mice and baby chicks per visit to feed them.

They rewarded the humans with symbolic objects from the mountain. Finding something left by the snakes was always a delight for the humans who lived at the ranch house known as *Serpiente*. It was a symbiotic relationship. The vast majority of crystals and minerals they received from the serpent clan were pretty, but useless, usually white quartz crystals and iron pyrite crystals known as fool's gold which made up the majority of the volume of their accumulating treasure, but sometimes the snakes delivered pretty green crystals known as emeralds as well as the occasional gold nugget. As long as this relationship could be maintained, the Anderson family, a family made of members closer to each other than most blood families, grew wealthy both monetarily and emotionally.

The Secret

We all took great satisfaction in solving the mystery and it was immediately agreed upon to keep our discoveries a secret. Only our immediate family would know about the secrets of the mountain and the serpents. The emeralds and gold were cashed in Albuquerque where June and Ken had a banker friend who agreed not to ask questions about where the gemstones and nuggets came from. To allow others to know would invite disaster as greedy humans always seem to find a way to destroy another's livelihood. My Uncle Ken, along with Aunt June, was now able to think about reconstructing the ranch. It had become truly neglected and tumbled down and several structures desperately needed repairs. New calves were now appearing and eventually they would actually show a profit on the cattle they were raising. Eventually they wouldn't even need the treasure that was being accumulated from trips into the backcountry. Even without the money that the cattle produced, they were making a good living wage on just the interest the precious stones had created.

After many long and hard days, spent clearing a road up the main canyon,

Hidalgo and Corey were able to drive a wagon load of small animals to within a half mile of the nest. That last half mile actually consisted of climbing up one very steep canyon wall and then descending down another. A trail had to be constructed that allowed everything to be hauled on the backs of mules. Building even a decent mule trail took many days of hard work. Being that close to the nest, camping out at night was seldom done, they were still spooked. As soon as the sun set, they got into sealed tents not coming out until well after sunrise.

Hidalgo and Corey took over the job of driving the team of horses that carried the cages of rodents that provided sustenance for the strange mystical serpents. Eventually, Ken and June developed the confidence to travel to the mountain. Upon arrival, at base camp they would load everything onto mules but one of the boys had to lead the mules up the precarious walls of the canyon. It was dangerous work. Often they decided to simply load the cages on mules to begin with, saving them from having to repack the mules.

It was hard work leading the mules over the mountain. Once at the base of the mountain they would exchange the cages left from the week before and see if there were crystals present and pocket them. Leaving many cages with a small rodent in each one, they then dragged the mules back to the ranch house. Sometimes several weeks could pass without finding anything of real value but sometimes they left the mountain several thousand dollars wealthier.

Dragons

*C*orey and I continued our research, but nowhere else in the world did anyone know of serpents such as those in *Serpiente* but we discovered that we were living in a world where its' ancient inhabitants made snakes a central part of their cosmology and we were starting to come up with new theories as we learned even more. Throughout history there were many civilizations that had some form of serpent in their cosmology. In religion, mythology, and literature, serpents and snakes represented fertility. As snakes were observed shedding their skin they became symbols of rebirth, transformation, immortality, and healing.

Serpents were guardians of temples and sacred places, probably because when threatened, snakes such as rattlesnakes and cobras hold and defend their ground making them natural guardians of treasures. Asclepius, the god of medicine and healing, carried a staff with one serpent wrapped around it, which has become the symbol of modern medicine.

The venom of the serpent is thought to have a fiery quality similar to a fire spitting dragon.

The word dragon derives from an ancient Greek word meaning 'to see' meaning the glowing eyes can see beyond the obvious. The Aztec and Toltec serpent god *Quetzalcoatl* had dragon-like wings, much like its equivalent in K'iche' Maya mythology; they were feathered serpents. Even sea serpents were considered. Cryptozoological creatures were once thought to inhabit the oceans of the world. Even in smaller bodies of water they were thought to still live, such as the Loch Ness Monster.

The vision serpent was a symbol of rebirth in Mayan mythology. Through its associated rituals they felt they could create a doorway to the spiritual world and assume its power. In Ancient Egypt, where some of the earliest written records exist, the serpent appears from the beginning to the end of their mythology. Their primal snake goddess *Wadjet*, the Egyptian cobra, was depicted on the crown of Egypt. The Rainbow Serpent is a major mythological being for Aboriginal people across Australia. It ruled the underworld and did things like make fruit trees bloom. The Minoans Snake Goddess brandished a serpent in either hand. Serpents figured prominently in ancient Greek myths. Medusa was a vicious female monster with sharp fangs and hair of living, venomous snakes. According to Nordic mythology, the serpent *Jormungandr* was thrown into the oceans where he grew so big that he was able to surround the earth and grasp his own tail. *Jormungandr's* arch enemy was the god Thor. Even in Africa, the chief center of serpent worship was a serpent creature known as *Dahomey.*

In what would become America, the Native American tribes gave reverence to the rattlesnake as grandfather and king of snakes who is able to give fair winds or cause tempests. Among the Hopi of Arizona the serpent figures largely in one of their dances. The rattlesnake was worshipped in the Natchez temple of the sun and the Aztec deity *Quetzalcoatl* was a feathered serpent god. In Meso-American cultures, the serpent was regarded as a portal between two worlds.

Due to my growing up in East Tennessee and going to Sunday school with my friends, I was aware of many references to serpents in the Christian Bible, such as in the Garden of Eden, but we were beginning to think that there was much more to all this than just myths. We couldn't help but wonder why people like the Mound Builders would have built such a huge monument to serpents if all they were thinking about was a myth. Located near what is now the city of St. Louis, next to the Mississippi River, is the ancient settlement known as Cahokia which emerged about the same time as the Chaco Canyon phenomenon occurred in New Mexico. Serpent Mound was constructed there, an enigma to archeologists. We couldn't help but to wonder about the intersection of time considering the vast distances between them. In time we learned of many cultures that were fascinated by serpents.

The Canyon Pool

It was early spring and Corey and I had decided to take a few days off and do some backcountry camping in the canyons behind *Serpiente*. This time however, it would be just for fun. Packing our horses for a short trip was, as always, a lot of work but we enjoyed the freedom of exploring the backcountry. What we really enjoyed on those trips was exploring the canyons for Indian ruins. Even after numerous expeditions exploring the many canyons surrounding the ranch house we still found unexpected treasures there, even occasionally finding an unexplored ruin.

With the problems associated with artifact thieves behind us we did our explorations at a leisurely rate, savoring our freedom to explore. Camping had become a ritual for us. Becoming creatures of habit and using the same skills that we would later use while exploring rivers, we had become professionals. Nothing was ever lost, or forgotten, or left at the ranch where it did no one any good.

After spending a week or so in the backcountry we would return to the ranch house and rediscover the joys of civilization. Little things, like home cooked meals, or air conditioners, real beds, or even the company of others had become a treat all over again. We learned one of the most valuable lessons that outdoor people learn; that most people do not appreciate the modern conveniences in life until they have to do without them. But as would happen on many backcountry trips that we enjoyed, destiny would take a hand in what we were doing and change our lives all over again. This was one of those trips.

The deep canyons that cut into the countryside behind the ranch house formed serpentine, undulating patterns which is why the area was called *Serpiente*. It became our playground. On the last trip into the back country we had discovered a large pool of water in the bottom of one of the side canyons. But it was not just a typical pool of water often found in backcountry canyon country. This particular one was huge, with a tiny waterfall of crystal clear water cascading into it. It was somewhat of a geological mystery and beautiful.

Pools like that are usually only found on large desert rivers such as one we enjoyed in northern New Mexico on the Canadian River. There, Mr. Wooten, a friend of Uncle Ken, had invited all of us to his ranch for a couple of days last summer. That first day there we had spent an enjoyable day buying and selling livestock, then after dinner Mr. Wooten drove us from the Wooten ranch house over to the Canadian Canyon where, after a short climb down the escarpment of sandstone bluffs we dropped down into the floor of the canyon.

As we were following the meandering channel that had cut into the solid sandstone, it suddenly dropped off the edge and plunged into a large pool dozens of feet deep providing a perfect diving platform for the young at heart that would enjoy the pool. It was a popular place for everyone in the area to enjoy; even Boy Scout groups would camp there and enjoy the pool as all young people love to go to the swimming hole.

This pool at *Serpiente* was similar but the waterfall was tiny in comparison. However after heavy rains it would become an impressive waterfall gouging out an impressive bowl in the rocks below, larger than an Olympic swimming pool. The water then over flowed past a hundred yard sandy beach that was in the shade of the overhead rocks during the afternoon. It was a perfect place for a large group of people to meet and it was obvious that we were not the first to discover the pool. Many Native Indians from different times had enjoyed the pool, probably for the same reasons as Corey and I.

A perfect place to play, the pool had everything a young couple who were in love could want as long as you were willing to spend a couple of days hiking and backpacking to get there as well as dealing with the sand that seemed to get into everything. Little did we know what great discoveries were to be found. It had become my personal discovery that the world is a mysterious and interesting place. One never knows when they might discover a mystery and have a new game to play.

We set up camp and enjoyed the day just loafing around. We would swim for a few minutes, and then get out of the cool water. Warming in the sun for a moment we would then escape the blazing sun by retreating into the shade of a rock shelter and read for a while.

Corey got impatient, which was a trait he often demonstrated, and decided we should explore the bluffs and small smattering of Indian ruins that were around us. We put on our hiking shoes, packed small possible packs, packs that contained everything that we might need in case of an emergency, and took off exploring the canyon around us.

We noticed that the walls of the ruins were in the classic Chacoan masonry with T shaped doors. Evidently this pool was a very important meeting place to the native Anasazis who lived here. The ruins were much better constructed than a typical ruin but were completely empty. We were not sure whether pottery hunters had beat us there or the Anasazi only used the place as a meeting place, leaving nothing behind. We were casually walking upstream and climbing over the rocks and boulders following trails laid down by the ancients when we found ourselves standing in the shade under a sheer rock bluff. Located above the pool and waterfall we discovered a huge flat area. The flat rock floor there, about the size of a basketball court, appeared to have been scoured smooth, probably by flooding water. Off to one side was a huge rock overhang forming a perfect amphitheater.

A meeting place, I thought. That is when, after taking a long drink from our canteen, I looked up and saw pictographs covering the rocks far above us, hundreds of them. The problem was, the glyphs were up high, imposing the obvious question, how in the world did they get up there to carve the rock? We knew that in other places, we had seen similar inaccessible rock carvings. The ancients probably made ladders by carving notches into logs and then leaned them on to the bluff to gain access.

As we wandered up the canyon floor we discovered rock drawings covering the sheer bluff for about a quarter of a mile up the canyon. Occasionally the carvings were so ancient that the floor of the canyon had actually eroded away leaving the pictures high on the rocks. In other places the canyon had filled in to cover older drawings so that only the tops of them were visible to the observer. It all seemed natural enough; a lot of water had come through this canyon at one time or another.

Most of the drawings were chiseled deep into the sandstone rock forming petroglyphs. Many had paint covering them made from pigments found in nature. Unlike modern paints, these colors seemed not to fade in the sunlight. Most of the rock art was typical of this area, I immediately found several that I could easily identify such as the classic clasped hands demonstrating friendship, swastikas which had no relation to the ones made infamous by the Germans in World War II but rather the much older migration symbols. The glyphs were classic Anasazi symbols however many of them were odd, as if done by artists from many different areas. We easily recognized the double crosses that signified dragonflies, frogs, bighorn sheep, geometric designs and an amazing array of anthropomorphs; designs of people who appeared to represent many different tribes.

One entire section of the bluff contained connecting spiral circles not unlike the ones I had seen in a picture of ancient Celtic ruins found in Great Briton. The ruin called New Grange, was constructed over 5,000 years ago and is older than Stonehenge and a thousand years older than the Pyramid of Giza located in ancient Egypt. As usual, I wondered if there could have been a connection but realistically I knew that there was a three thousand year difference between these ruins and the ones in Great Briton.

The most famous glyph in the Southwest, known as *Kokopelli* was present in many places. Sometimes bent over, with a hump on his back and sometimes with a phallus as large as the flute he was playing. There, of course were rattlesnake symbols along with ghostly people who were usually triangular in shape, big at the top and tapering to tiny feet. Some of the anthropomorphs or human like characters had peculiar antenna like structures that have always mystified the observer as to what they are or mean. Some were more intricate than any Corey or I had ever seen whether in real life or in books. But in the dead center of them was one set of carvings that were different. There were letters from an ancient alphabet. There was an M with an elongated last mark, a four, a T, a nine, an L, a backward K, and another M with the peculiar elongated last mark and a backward E. This assortment of letters was Greek looking, similar to some English letters, but made absolutely no sense at all. It appeared like writing they had seen in textbooks at the University. Was it Greek, Hebrew, or some other language? We could only guess, but one thing was for sure, it didn't belong there. Deeply stained with desert varnish it was obvious that they were ancient carvings. It was something that should have been found on another continent and in another time. We had another mystery to solve.

Discovering America

Dinner was ready, fried chicken, mashed potatoes, sausage gravy, green beans, and dinner rolls; all my East Tennessee favorites. The familiar food made me a little homesick. I was beginning to miss the time I had spent in East Tennessee with my mother and grandparents. Time seemed to have healed my experience with Turner; I felt that in a fair fight I could easily beat him particularly since I had been practicing martial arts with both Corey and Hidalgo and could almost hold my own against them, besides Turner was still in jail.

Everyone was anticipating our story of the adventure and what secrets we had discovered. The ranch house was buzzing with excitement as the children that belonged to the ranch workers ran everywhere instead of walking. Hidalgo as usual was stirring his classic cup of coffee that he drank with every meal and stoically watched the whole circus. Meanwhile Aunt June and I hurried ourselves to set the table. Shortly, we all finished off the last bite of chicken to be brought out.

"Must be something pretty interesting that you found, you've been walking around with grins on your faces all afternoon." said Ken.

Kidding him, Aunt June said, "Maybe they found true love out there, or maybe they have an announcement to make. Who knows, maybe Penny is expecting a child or something."

Ken laughed out loud at the thought and said, "I don't think so, I think they want to finish their college before they get married and tied down with children, besides Corey has his own ideas about marriage and I haven't any reason to think he is in any hurry to get tied down."

"Like you," countered June who had a chuckle in her voice.

So with great anticipation we sat around the table slurping down delicious fried chicken with an occasional tease. Everyone laughed after every bit of ribbing except for Hidalgo who simply sat with a grin on his face. Somehow he knew another adventure was on the horizon. Everyone ate until we couldn't eat anymore and finally the time came.

"We found some interesting pictographs," I announced. June smiled and said "You've got to be kidding; this entire state is covered with Indian graffiti. Those Indians were just like kids, they had to leave their marks on every flat rock that they could find."

"Yes, I said, but these are different."

"How so," said Hidalgo who hadn't said a word up until now and was the only one who was really taking them seriously.

"Well," said Corey," First of all let me tell you about our secret place." With that he went into great detail about the large pool that was formed in the bottom of the canyon, about the ruins and finally, about the Indian pictographs that were there. He particularly made a point to describe the large flat area above the waterfall and the Chacoan styled ruins.

"Well it's true that style of building is entirely out of place there. That is a mystery in itself." Ken finally stopped him in mid-sentence with, "Look, you led us to believe that there was something really amazing up there. Cut to the chase."

After a long pause I explained. "Some of the markings are not Indian. They look like Greek letters. It looks like someone wrote a message there at the same time the pictographs were made but it is completely different than Indian markings."

Corey went on to describe some of the letters. "There were backward letter E's and a leaning number four and funny constructed M's. I have never seen anything like it.

"Well I have." said Uncle Ken. "A few years ago I was hanging out with a fellow by the name of Bill Holliday. Looking at Corey he said, "He is a distant relative of yours, a cousin or something like that to your late father. He took us out to a black volcanic mesa just west of Los Lunas, part of the Huning property. There is a large rock there that is covered in funny writing.

Hidalgo said, "You mean *Cerro Los Moqujino*, or in English the hill of the strange writings?"

Ken replied, "Oh, you have seen it too? Hidalgo nodded, "yes" and Ken continued. "Many people around here have seen it." Looking at Corey and me, he explained. It was located on a volcanic mesa along the very road that you have turned on to get to Serpiente many times.

Corey said, "I never heard of it and you mean we have been driving past it all this time and I didn't even know it?

Uncle Ken says, "That's true."

Hidalgo then followed with, "You realize, I hope, that people have paid very little attention to that rock because it has been thought to be a fake. Very few people, especially anthropologist or archeologist believe that Europeans came to America until Columbus stumbled onto our shores. But many Indian tribes have oral traditions of Europeans coming to America well before Columbus. Penny, you should know this, the Cherokee Indians have always had a tradition that white people preceded them in the occupation of East Tennessee."

I didn't know that fact but decided not to advertise my ignorance. "Well I was aware that settlements in the extreme northeast of America are proving to be Vikings. They appear to have been built hundreds of years before Columbus stumbled into the new world."

"That's very true," countered June, "Even Columbus is said to have been inspired by stories he heard about earlier explorations by Vikings and even by the Irish. According to Eastern Tribes, whites lived along the Little Tennessee River and they had fortifications down the Tennessee to the mouth of Chicamauga Creek. Oconostota, the great Cherokee chief states that his grandparents and father said that the whites were called Welsh; that they had crossed the great water and landed first at the mouth of the Alabama River and made their way to the mountain country.

Some tribes of the Cherokee Indians down in Georgia even believe that they are descended from ancient Hebrew peoples who came to Americas thousands of years ago. It would change all of history and then school teachers would need to have new history books printed. Think about it, who really discovered America? Everybody lays claim to that honor. Hidalgo added with a smile, "Actually my ancestors only discovered America after migrating down from Canada a few hundred years before Columbus."

I was fascinated by this description of my old homeland. Immediately I was intrigued and wanted to know more. I asked him what else they knew about the ancient history of the country I was born in.

Hidalgo shrugged his shoulders and added, "Well I don't know much more, but I do know that supposedly a Prince Madoc who was chronicled by Welsh bards as early as the late fifteen hundreds, was supposed to have come to America. In fact, part of Britain's claim to America came about as the discovery and settlement of the Welsh under Madoc shortly after the eleven hundreds. I even read, while in the library in Durango once, that in 1818 a Roman coin was found on the site of the present town of Fayetteville, Tennessee, on the Elk River and not far from the site of an ancient fort."

Ken looked out of the front window of the ranch house and followed Hidalgos points with, "You realize that by finding another set of markings, and if those markings can be authenticated, it would give more credence to the mystery stone in Los Lunas.

"Well, the markings we found had the same amount of patina as the rest of the rock carvings. Right now, I want to learn more about that Los Lunas stone," I said with undisguised excitement, while Corey's head went up and down in an affirmative motion.

Uncle Ken looked at us and answered thoughtfully, "It would be a lot easier for us to drive out to the mystery stone than it would be to pack into that back country. Let's all drive out there some time and take a look at the mystery stone. I need to go into town tomorrow anyway and I'll see if I can set up a meeting at the Los Lunas Mystery Stone with Bill Holliday. He knows as much about the place as anybody I know.

Bill Holliday

Three days later, after a lunch was prepared and packed, we all piled into the Jeep Cherokee and headed north to Los Lunas. After almost reaching the blacktop road into town we turned off and took the road that normally goes out to the Huning Ranch and the Indian Site known as pottery mounds. Despite antiquity laws, for many years the curious, school kids, family and Scout Troops had been going out there to collect pottery shards. Pot shards were everywhere, literally buckets of them.

Driving off that dirt road we took a smaller rutted road over to the base of a large volcanic mesa, typical for this area except that this one overlooked what at one time was a vast Indian village where thousands of people lived alongside the Rio Puerco River. Nowadays it was just pastureland and desert. We soon spotted Bill Holliday sitting on the tail gate of his pickup truck, taking a sip from a thermos bottle.

Corey was excited to meet a relative he had never met before. After a warm embrace and some frantic shaking of hands along with introductions, they opened the small pedestrian gate that Huning had erected in his fence to keep his cattle from getting out and we all started walking up a well-worn rocky trail. Corey and I, just like all kids, ran ahead prompting warnings from Aunt June to look out for rattlesnakes.

Bill Holliday knew the area well, and he should have. He had served as the sheriff of Valencia County and knew every nook and cranny. Friendly and jovial, he was like many of the locals, strong and firm yet the biggest tease one could imagine, he reminded me of an Anglo version of John Luna. Constantly looking for an excuse to tease one of the kids, he also wasted no time in getting around to Corey and me. He knew when young people were in love and he relished teasing us. I had learned long ago to ignore this kind of teasing. Like my friend John Luna, I took it all as a compliment and dished it right back.

Taking only a few minutes we found ourselves in front of a large slab of volcanic rock with ancient script written on it. "What does it say, I asked?

"Well, replied Holliday, "according to those who study this stuff, they say it is the Ten Commandments and the smaller inscription (he pointed) says Yehweh is our Mighty One." He turned and looked at me and said, "You realize that if this was actually written by an ancient scribe it would give direct proof that a connection existed between the Americas, through explorations of mariners, with the Middle East. It would indicate that after sailing across the Atlantic Ocean, explorers as early as 3500 years ago came to this area."

I asked, "Exactly who wrote it?"

Holliday answered with, "Well, nobody really knows, all we know is that it is an ancient Hebrew writing. By the way, you read it from right to left." We studied the rock for some time noticing that the exact same letters were present in the petroglyph Corey and I had discovered.

"Is it real, I mean did ancient people come all the way here from the Middle East, thousands of years ago?"

Holliday mulled it over for a minute then answered, "Well, according to some scientist who have studied it, its' real. Even the local Indians have a tradition about it." While looking at Hidalgo for approval he continued, "According to Native Indians down in Isleta, the rock was a mystery even to them long before modern Anglos came into this area. But then, there is also a rumor that around 1920 or so a group of students from the University came out here and carved it as a practical joke.

The problem is the local Indians; they have a tradition and knowledge of this place that goes back much farther than that date. They claim it was covered by lichens and was ancient when they first discovered it and it is obvious that there were many people here in antiquity, there are markings all over the place."

Seeing that he had an entranced audience Bill Holliday continued, "According to local history, the inscriptions were first seen by European settlers as far back as 1800. Florencio Chavez, a former resident of Los Lunas claimed that he had been shown the rock by his maternal grandfather, Simon Serna, whose father had seen it as early as 1800. Serna himself was pretty old at the time he saw it."

After a pause to take another sip out of his thermos bottle Holliday continued, "Frank Hibben of the University of New Mexico examined the rock back in 1936 and at that time the rock was half covered in sand and covered with lichens. Unfortunately many people have been here since that time. Someone took a steel chisel and cleaned out the grooves removing the patina making it impossible to scientifically date the inscription."

"There is also the thing about the eclipse," Holliday says. "In the year 2017, the citizens of New Mexico are going to be entertained by one of the most dramatic events which nature has to offer. In that year, according to Astrophysicists who know about such things, we will experience a total eclipse here in the Los Lunas area. During this kind of experience, the stars come out and are clearly visible in the middle of the day. An eclipse has occurred here before. Two thousand years ago it happened here. Surely the Anasazi saw it. From rock art found around the state, such as in Chaco Canyon, there is evidence that early people witnessed the event and in their own way recorded it for the rest of eternity."

"The thing is, if you take the Mystery Stone seriously there is evidence that non-Indian people also witnessed the event. Recently the remains of the red ocher people were discovered on the east coast in an area where no previous discovery of them had been known. In Brownsville, Texas there are rock carvings overlooking the Rio Grande where it deposits its water into the Gulf of Mexico. Those rock carvings or petroglyphs have a distinctly European influence. However they are disappearing quickly due to erosion and vandalism. It seems that for some myopic reason every generation of us humans think that we have all the right answers and those other poor unfortunate ones that have come before us didn't know anything. Many feel superior only when making others appear; smaller."

Bill Holliday pointed at the trail that continued up the steep hill and said, "There is more to look at on top of the hill."

I was intrigued at what the top of the hill looked like. I knew that at one time it was the top of a seething volcanic flow but what I found there was interesting.

Bill Holliday explained as he pointed, "The top of the mesa is a fort. If you look closely you can see where a defensive fort has at one time been built. Of course there is little left now but you can certainly see the outlines of buildings that stood here a long time ago.

June ventured a theory, "They look like European defensive works, like Masada.

I asked, "What is a Masada?

"Well, answered June, the ancients Israelites constructed a massive fort on top of a sandstone mountain similar to this one. They fought off the Romans for several months until the Romans built a giant ramp so they could bring siege machines to the top of the mountain. When they finally got there they discovered that all the Israelites had committed suicide rather than being captured by the Romans. To this day, Israel's version of the CIA is called Masada in honor of their ancestors.

Intrigued by what they learned everyone took a few days off and backpacked into the canyon where the pool was located. June was particularly intrigued by the pictographs. Over the years she had come to the conclusion that it wasn't a question of who had discovered America first, but who hadn't discovered America, well before Columbus.

A Real Family

Both Corey and I had to make decisions about our future. I was just in the prime of my young life and it was obvious that I was having an effect upon the young men I encountered. Hidalgo, on one occasion even said that I was a strikingly beautiful woman and he was actually serious when he said it. I rarely went into town but when I did I noticed that every boy I met did a double take. I was beginning to acquire that beauty that makes it difficult for a boy my age to sit and talk to me without being tongue tied. I was healthy and growing financially strong, and Corey had become my best friend. But the relationship was starting to change. We were beginning to look at each other differently. Not just a childhood infatuation but rather a mutual admiration. There was much more to it than just the physical attraction. We had become partners in life, depending upon each other for all kinds of things. We were becoming soul mates.

Both Corey and I had finished our high school education but it was by taking tests sent by mail. We were home schooled, a necessity in this very isolated ranch country. This all seemed rather matter of fact for Corey but for me I missed sharing my senior year with old friends, and the sports I was always involved with would have been the crowning accomplishment of my senior year. With my grades I could have won scholarships. My entire life could have been different. I missed a multitude of friends, school dances and homecoming, a formal graduation rather than just simply receiving the diploma that arrived in the mail several weeks after I had completed my studies. I thought about the Robert Frost poem "The trail not taken," and wondered about the trail I had not taken. Later, I was to learn that I had already learned from Aunt June and Uncle Ken more than most college graduates.

Deep in my heart I even missed seeing my mother. Remembering the days leading up to my trip to Serpiente, the arguments, the yelling at each other and the hurt feelings bothered me but I was older and more mature now. We could put our differences aside.

Both Corey and I wanted to go to college, but the responsibilities of living in Serpiente had, until now, taken up all our time. Now, we had time and more importantly money. Now we had the freedom to consider our futures but most importantly in our hearts we were conscious of our real treasure; biologically unrelated souls that had become a real family and lived in a place called Serpiente.

Hidalgo's Dilemma

*N*ow that he was financially secure and with his help his mother and father were now more secure, everyone seemed happy but Hidalgo, who wanted much more out of life. Unlike many other Navajos, Hidalgo had a 'you only live once' attitude. He decided to return to his personal studies.

Being a Navajo, he had a very Indian view of the world. He lived in a metaphysical world very different from most other people, whether Indian or white. He still made a point to return to the reservation occasionally to take part in ceremonies such as the Blessing Way. Having a fancy car or house, meant nothing to him. He read constantly, a trait he had picked up from Ken and June who kept a personal library in their house. While other people spent their time staring at a plastic box with moving pictures of other people's lives in it, he preferred to ride the countryside taking care of the ranch and thinking his own thoughts. He was accomplished in his own personal studies, he always took a book with him on those rides and when the sun climbed into the sky making it too uncomfortable to work he would hide away under the shade of a tree or cliff and read. Hidalgo was truly a self-educated man.

Before coming to work for Ken and June on their ranch, a job that my father had arranged, Hidalgo had worked in Durango, Colorado as a deputy sheriff, a job he had enjoyed at first but soon found boring, dealing with the same drunks and petty thieves over and over, The tourists were fascinating to work with, at first, but soon that too became predictable. The tourist also made the same stupid mistakes, over and over and that was frustrating, but his biggest complaint about the job was the mischief that the kids on vacation got themselves into.

Young kids, usually teenage boys, were being turned loose in a tourist town, usually without their parents having the foggiest ideas what they are doing. They were always getting into trouble in very predictable ways and when he tried to help them his personal belief system and his job came into conflict.

It was always the same. The boys would get caught shoplifting, drinking beer or smoking marijuana, or even just fighting among themselves. They were then arrested. If their parents were fairly wealthy they could buy their way out of trouble with the help of one of the local lawyers who specialized in such work. But for most, and the more serious offenders, they were always put into a juvenile facility that was operated by a private company.

Sometimes a person who was committed to spend a month there would find themselves serving almost a year before they were released. The guards were the ones who decided if an inmate was rehabilitated or cured. Meals cost the correctional facility about ten cents apiece yet it cost the parents one hundred and fifty dollars a day for their children to be there, all court mandated. The more inmates who occupied the facility and the longer they stayed in jail, the more money the facility made.

The facility was always filled with teenagers. A portion of that extra money that the facility made was then kicked back to the judge who sentenced them there and the judge was becoming wealthy because of the kickbacks. Everyone seemed happy about this relationship between the county and the facility, but it didn't set right with Hidalgo.

Hidalgo had heard of a system that the Native Indians used in Alaska. There, minor offences were treated just like anywhere else, the youngster or his parents paid the fine. Some even spent time in a correctional institute just like in the lower forty eight. But hard core offenders were treated very differently. They were handcuffed, put aboard a small boat and then driven through icy cold water many miles away to a deserted island. There, they were left a small supply of food in a small cabin with a wood burning stove, a table, and a bunk.

Being totally alone with no one else to blame for their problems, the offender was put into a survival situation. They were left there for months on end requiring them to take personal responsibility for themselves. The consequences of their actions were severe. If they loafed, they went without food. One young man in a fit of anger burned down the cabin just to be stubborn. When the first snow started to fall he found himself building another cabin with the very limited resources that were at hand. He was responsible for his own actions good or bad. The program worked, when they were allowed to return they were very changed individuals who had lost the hate and greed that sent them there.

Hidalgo's last year on the force had left him in a quandary whether to stay on the job or move on. When the corrupt judge was finally discovered through a tax audit it was discovered that he had been putting his money into an island estate in the Cayman Islands. By putting his money there he had avoided paying taxes and when discovered he quickly left the country. It was the final straw for Hidalgo.

During the time Hidalgo was working in Durango, he spent his free time taking classes at Fort Lewis, the local college. There he studied law and criminology as well as his personal favorite subject, Native American history. At one time, Hidalgo even considered becoming a lawyer and then returning to the Navajo reservation and representing other Navajos who were constantly getting into trouble. That was the way it was, the same Navajos getting into trouble over and over. But more than anything else he wanted to become a detective. Maybe even a private detective.

Hidalgo could not reconcile his feelings about justice and the way the county operated, so when the opportunity occurred he left the job. Hidalgo moved to Serpiente, after meeting Penny's father who was in Durango taking a couple of days off from his job at the drill hole. Penny's father had managed to get himself into a jackpot when a young lady and he collided on a busy sidewalk. In the excitement Penny's Father hadn't noticed that the girl had slipped her hand into his pocket and relieved him of his wallet that was passed off to her boyfriend. That wallet contained some fourteen hundred dollars. He reported the pickpocket to the police and Hidalgo was assigned to investigate the incident.

Several hours later Hidalgo found the pickpocket and returned his money to Penny's father. Since it was the end of Hidalgo's shift, Penny's father invited Hidalgo into one of the local restaurants where they had dinner. They started talking and spent several hours over dinner talking about a wide variety of subjects. When my father mentioned the possibility of a job in Serpiente, Hidalgo jumped at it.

Living on the ranch with Ken and June was heaven for Hidalgo. He made far less money, but he liked ranch work. He could pursue his own interest including going into Socorro or Albuquerque whenever he wanted to and most importantly he was still in a position to help his parents.

The Wedding Announcement

We had worked all summer long taking care of the mundane jobs of running a ranch and the weekend trips to Serpiente Mountain when finally, cooler weather was setting in. Corey and I had time on our hands so we packed all our personal belongings into a truck and headed to New Mexico State to attend college.

Enrolling for classes was a special treat, a personal accomplishment. I had no idea what I was going to major in, all I knew was that although I was good at just about everything I set my mind to several areas of study held an interest for me. I was leaning toward biological science or even an English degree, but was also considering archeology because of my tutorage from Aunt June. For a while I even considered studying art. During my classes, I discovered I also liked to write and would forever-more keep a personal dairy of all my activities as well as hundreds of small drawings.

While there and in a way not to offend Corey, I even went out on a few dates with some of my classmates, but they didn't impress me. They all seemed like kids who were really at school as an escape from Mom and Dad and the possibility of a job.

There were those professors that impressed me. Some of them reminding me of some of my favorite high school teachers whom I had met when I lived in Camp Creek in East Tennessee.

I tried out for the college Volleyball team. Being a college sport it was much harder than any sport I had played in high school but, when the cuts were made, to my amazement I had made the junior varsity. I was offered a small scholarship, but I turned it down fearing that it would commit me to staying with the team for four years. Besides I could afford the tuition and I felt that the scholarship should be used for someone who needed it more than I did.

No matter how hard the job or how boring or even dangerous the assignment was I could always count on Corey. Corey was there for every volleyball game and soon most of the other boys just gave up trying to pursue me. It was obvious to all concerned that Corey and I were destined to be a couple.

We studied, we played, and sometimes we even fought with each other. Especially when I noticed that several of the girls on the volleyball team were flirting with Corey. This made me fell neglected and jealous and Corey didn't even seem to mind. In fact, after a while he seemed to encourage it and that is what made me mad. But we always made up afterwards. Especially since Corey never actually went out with any of them unless they were in a group and I went along. I secretly decided that I was not going to take a chance and lose Corey to another college girl. I suspect that secretly, Corey was thinking the same thing about me.

During winter recess instead of hanging around town we packed up the car with gifts for the workers' kids and books for Hidalgo and returned to Serpiente. We had an announcement; we had decided to get married.

Preparing for a Trip

"When are you getting married," asked Hidalgo?

Waiting for Hidalgo's grin to slowly subside, Corey answered with, "Well we haven't quite decided yet."

"OK' says Uncle Ken, "Where and when are you going to get married?

"We haven't really made any plans yet, "I answered for him. All I know is I brought up the subject with Corey, and he said he had no idea; that we needed to finish college, that he really wasn't ready yet, that I wasn't ready yet, that we were too busy, and finally that he just didn't want to talk about it. He got really quiet and moody so I waited a few seconds then simply said to him that if he wasn't interested in marrying me I was going to find someone else who would marry me. He then proposed to me within sixty seconds."

Uncle Ken looked at Corey and said to him, "And you are really in agreement with that story?"

"Yep," says Corey.

"You realize that you were trapped like a rat," says Ken.

Corey answered with, "Maybe, but I have to tell you, I cannot stand the thought of Penny getting married to some other guy, and I do not want to live without her. I love her. I have always wanted to marry her and that's that!"

June finally got into the conversation with, "Have you kids made any plans at all?"

I answered with, "Well I'll tell you the truth. I...I stopped in mid-sentence and began my sentence all over again, "We have been thinking about making a trip back to East Tennessee. Corey has never been back East and I miss my friends. Besides I would like to see my mother. I might enjoy showing Corey some of the sights around my home. Then after we get married we'll return to school, and maybe get an apartment in married housing and continue our education at the University."

So instead of returning to spring session of college we spent the next month working around the ranch in Serpiente, making plans, and packing for the trip to Tennessee. We bought a new pickup truck for the trip figuring that it would be more practical and could be to good use after the trip. After all, we still worked at the ranch in our off time.

Early that spring Corey and I packed up our truck and headed across the country to Camp Creek, Tennessee. It was a much more pleasant trip than I had made last time. That long trip on the bus now seemed to have happened a lifetime ago to an entirely different person. Corey and Hidalgo agreed that Corey and I would visit with my family for a little while, plan the wedding in East Tennessee, and then Hidalgo, who was to be our best man would use a new pick-up that he had bought to drive to Tennessee for the wedding.

Corey and I enjoyed the drive to Tennessee, taking many side trips, so that we could take in all the sights that a seventeen hundred mile trip could afford. But I had mixed feelings about confronting my mother. We had not communicated with each other since I left, other than the postcard I had sent to her after I had arrived in Serpiente. Other than that postcard there had not been a word between us. I had a gut feeling that it could be an ugly scene when I arrived.

Mona

When we finally arrived in Tennessee, Corey was amazed. Having lived in New Mexico all of his life, the greenness of Tennessee was a revelation to him. The tall trees, the wide, green fields, and the rolling hills and tall mountains were a source of amazement. He had never in his life seen anything like it. It took his breath away. From the time we entered Tennessee, I began to get more and more nervous. I had mixed feelings about this trip. Seeing my friends would be great fun, and I could not wait to introduce Corey to all of them, but the meeting with my mother was going to be awkward.

Despite my nervousness, when we entered Nashville, we both wanted to stop for the day to see some of the sights. We had read about the Parthenon, but neither had ever seen it. The Parthenon is a replica of the original Greek building newly erected in Nashville. We also wanted to see Opryland. We both were music fans and I was looking forward to shopping at the Mall. We spent a day in Nashville and then headed east toward Camp Creek and my mother.

Entering Greeneville, I was amazed at how much the town had changed in just three years. Houses now occupied places that had been open fields when I left. There were new gas stations and businesses that had not been there when I lived there before.

Driving through town it was only a short time until we arrived in Camp Creek which looked just like it did when I left it. When I got to grandfather and grandmother's farm, I was surprised to find that my mother no longer lived there. My grandparents seemed to have aged more that I had expected. Farm work had taken its toll on both of them. I introduced Corey to them and my grandmother fixed glasses of tea for us all. She also brought out a freshly baked coconut pound cake to share with us that made me think that I had forgotten how good Grandmother's cooking really was, and just how much I had missed southern cooking.

Grandmother told me that Mona had finally found the man she had always looked for. His name was Jed and he and Mona lived in Greeneville, the county seat. My grandparents seemed to like Jed a lot and seemed happy that Mona had finally grown up. Grandmother called Mona and told her that I had come back to Camp Creek for a visit, and Nora insisted that Corey and I go to see her, so in about an hour, with directions to Mona and Jed's house, we got back into the truck and headed back to Greeneville.

When we got to Mona's house, Mona and her new husband, Jed were waiting on the porch. I introduced my mother to Corey and Mona introduced both of us to Jed. Jed was a big man, who towered over Mona's height. I would have called him plain with wiry grey hair and big ears, but after I got to know Jed, I understood why Nora had been drawn to him. He was a gentle giant who worshiped the ground that Mona walked on. He did anything that Mona asked without any complaint and was extremely protective. He had acquired the café where Mona had been working when I left Camp Creek. He was someone who treated her like a queen and had plenty of money to spend on her, he let her be the boss. I was sure this was the man of mother's dreams.

The visit was uncomfortable at first, but as the afternoon wore on we became easier with each other. I told Mona and Jed about my trip to New Mexico and our

Native American friend, Hidalgo. I mentioned to my mother that I had become very interested in the Native American cultures out west and that Corey and I had learned much about the subject from Hidalgo, but I carefully did not mention anything about the serpents. I did not believe that was a subject that would make her comfortable about her daughter returning to the west.

Mona and Jed asked us to stay with them for dinner and we agreed. After another scrumptious southern fried chicken dinner, my mother and I told the men to take their dessert into the living room while we washed the dishes. This gave mother and daughter a little time to talk.

"Mother," said I hesitantly," I realize now that a lot of the arguments between us were my fault. I believed that I was all grown up and I didn't believe that I still had a lot to learn about the world."

"I understood at the time and I understand a lot better now," answered Mona. "I still had a lot to learn myself and I don't feel that I am through with the learning process yet." Don't get me wrong," Mona was very hesitant about her next remarks, but I felt that it was important for her to express her opinion. "Why are you in such a hurry to get married? I got married to your father when I was young like you are, and look what a mistake I made."

I felt a rise of anger as I answered, "What's the matter Mama? You were much younger than I am now when you first got married. Don't you like Corey? I love Corey and he understands me better than anyone I have ever met. He is gentle and kind and the best friend anyone could ever have. We have been friends since I first arrived in New Mexico. Besides, look around you. Most of the girls I went to school with here are all married."

Mona interrupted, "Everything that you say about Corey may be true, I don't doubt it, but how many other boys have you dated seriously? He seems like a nice boy, but you are both very young. Don't make the same mistake that I made, by marrying the first boy that you have ever dated and as for the other girls around here, they always get married because they are expected to get married even if they can't afford too. It is the grandparents who wind up raising those children that are produced. Even if he is 'the one,' you may regret your hurry in the future, and if you don't, he might. There is an old saying, 'You have to kiss a lot of frogs before you meet your prince,' I am living proof of that saying. Learn from my mistake. Go back to school. If he loves you, he will still be in your life. If not, you are better off without him. Fear is a very poor reason to get married."

"Mother, I can't understand you," I yelled, "you used to want to have nothing to do with my life and now you want to ruin my life. Corey and I know who we want to be married to right now and we are not going to change our minds. Leave us alone, and stop meddling." With that I ran into the living room and said to Corey, "We are done here. Let's go back to Grandmother's house."

Corey and Jed had been having a similar conversation in the living room, but Jed was a little more careful about his opinions, because he knew that he was still an outsider in the family. As soon as I came into the living room, obviously very upset, Corey jumped up and put his arms around me. He too had had enough of this conversation and was more than ready to leave.

After we got into the truck and pulled out of the driveway, Mona began to cry. "I really just want what is best for my daughter, but she will not listen to anything I have to say," she sobbed.

"Honey, Jed quietly comforted her, "Very often kids her age have trouble believing anything their parents tell them and you are in a difficult position because she has been away for almost three years. She may have heard more than you think, and she may remember some of it later, when she is not so upset."

I was very quiet on the way to my grandmother's house hardly saying a word to Corey. I was deep in thought and so was Corey. More of my mother's talk had gotten into my brain than either of us had believed. Was this the right time for Corey and me to get married? Did I trap him, when I told him that if he didn't marry me, I would find someone else? Did Corey really want to get married, or for that matter did I? Corey and I had had a wonderful adventure the last three years. We learned a whole lot about ourselves, each other, and the world around us, but did that make us ready to be a married couple?"

Corey was having some of the same thoughts. He knew that he loved me very much. He felt comfortable with me, more than with any other human being, but he had felt so alone when his parents were suddenly killed and I had felt the same way because I was also away from my immediate family. Being away from my parents had made Corey feel lonely too. Being isolated on the farm with only Hidalgo to hang out with had started to get old. Had either one of us experienced enough in other relationships to measure our relationship? I thought back to my dreams I had on the way out to New Mexico. It seemed that Corey was in that dream but I could never be for sure. It seemed that something was plotting against our marriage. What kind of an evil entity could that be?

Lost in our own thoughts, we arrived at Nora and Nick's farm. Nora saw as soon as we came into the kitchen door that something was wrong. "I bet Mona said something that made Penny mad," thought Nora. "That daughter of mine never knows when to keep her mouth shut." She decided to bide her time and talk to me when she could get me alone. In the meantime, Nora decided to bring up a thought she had while we were gone thinking that maybe it would take our minds off of dealing with Mona and Jed.

To Marry or Not to Marry

"I had an idea while you were gone," Nora said brightly, "that might interest you both. You told me that you had become very interested in the culture of the Indians out west. Why don't you explore the culture of the Cherokee Indians in North Carolina? It's only about three hours away, and you might find it as interesting as the Native American culture out west. Nick and I would enjoy taking you to visit Cherokee, North Carolina for a couple of days."

I glanced at Corey and said, "I think Corey and I had better talk this over before we give you an answer. How about we go for a walk and discuss your idea? Visiting Mona and Jed today turned out to be a very stressful occasion, as I expected it to be and I could use a walk to help me relax. By the way Corey, what in the world was Jed talking to you about?"

"Well actually he seemed to have some pretty good advice. He said to live in the moment, that I should not attach myself to physical things, that I should treat others the way I would like to be treated, find happiness in the service of others, make the most out of today, follow my dreams, and don't take myself too seriously and that I should be aware that there are hypocrites and manipulators in the world." Corey grinned shyly and said, "It all sounded like some great ideas to me. But I was not expecting to be put on the spot by Jed. The conversation hit some sore spots and I will need some time to figure them out. A walk might clear my head a little bit too."

Still being young lovers we went out the kitchen door and slowly started down toward the dirt road that ran through the farm land. "What else did Jed say to you?" I asked, and I knew that Corey heard the concern in my voice.

"He asked me if I really wanted to get married this young, he replied hesitantly. He just got me to thinking about it. "Neither of us has graduated from college yet, and while that is not unusual, I know that both of my folks wanted me to graduate from college and you will be the first one in your family to graduate from college. Don't you think that all your family would be proud of you if you finished? Wouldn't it be fun for you to do the things that you didn't get to do in high school only on a much grander scale?"

I interrupted him with tears in my voice, "You sound as if you have changed your mind about wanting to marry me. Is that what you are trying to say? Is the wedding off?"

"No," said Corey impatiently, "That is not what I am trying to say. What I am trying to say is; why are we in such a blazing hurry to get married? We are only twenty. We have the rest of our lives to be married."

"But if you really loved me, you would want to be married as soon as possible so that we can spend the rest of our lives together," I cried. You are just looking for a way to get out of this marriage. I do not want to talk to you anymore tonight and maybe not ever again!"

With that I turned and ran sobbing loudly to the farmhouse. Nora and Nick heard the kitchen door slam as I ran up the stairs to my bedroom. "Maybe I had better go up and see what is wrong with her," Nora whispered.

Nora tapped quietly at the bedroom door, afraid that Corey might be there with me trying to console me. Nora could hear the sobs in my voice as I whispered, "Come in."

Nora came over to the bed where I lay alone crying softly and put her arm around me. "What's the matter honey? Did you and Corey have a fight?" Nora whispered softly.

"He doesn't want to marry me anymore Grandmother," I wept, " Jed had a talk with him this afternoon while we were at mother's house and now he is talking about going back to college instead of getting married. I hate Jed and Mom. They were both dead set on keeping us from getting married and now, they have convinced Corey that it is a bad idea. Mom has always thought that she has a right to run my life, and she doesn't." I hiccupped between sobs. "Grandmother, Corey is the only one in the world who has ever understood me and now I am going to lose him because of Mom," I continued, "Mona took me away from my father when I was little and now she wants to separate me from Corey, too. Why doesn't she want me to be happy?"

"Don't be so hard on your mother," Grandma said hesitantly. "We all look at life through our own experiences. Your mother loves you, but she does not want you to make the same mistakes that she did. She got married at about your age and it was not the right thing for her. Now, she is scared that you will wake up in a few years and realize that you have made the biggest mistake of your life. We all try to learn from our mistakes, and often we try to force our children to learn from those mistakes to. Sometimes timing is everything but unfortunately you don't know it until it's too late. Besides, this whole situation just doesn't sound like you. You were the one who always kept a clear head about boys."

"Let's talk about you and Corey now," Grandma went on. "What did he say to you tonight? Did he say that he did not want to marry you; or that he didn't love you?"

"No," I flatly pleaded, "but he might as well have said those things. He said that he thought we should finish college before we get married. If he really loved me, he would want to marry me right now. What if he finds another girl that he loves more than me while we are in college and doesn't marry me at all?"

Grandma had tears in her eyes, too when she responded, "Where did this scared little girl come from? And who is she? The Penny who left for New Mexico knew just what she wanted out of life and what the man that she would marry would be like. She could do anything that she put her mind to and was not going to depend on any man to take care of her. I know that you love Corey and I believe that he loves you. If that is true, waiting awhile to get married will just make your love stronger, and if it is not true, wouldn't it to be better to find out now than after you are married and maybe have children to think about?"

"You have given me a lot to think about, Grandma," I sniffed.

"I'm sure that the Penny I know and love very much is in there somewhere," chuckled Grandma. "Give it some time and let's go check out Cherokee, North Carolina. I think you and Corey will both enjoy the trip and maybe you will reach some conclusions along the way. Your whole life does not need to be planned in the next ten minutes."

When Corey came back about an hour later, I heard the kitchen door open and shut softly. Running down the stairs, I hugged him tightly. "I am sorry that I ran away when we were discussing things. That is not the way to get things settled. I am also sorry for trying to trap you into marriage. I love you very much and I still believe that we can go to college and also get married, but if you want to wait, then we should wait,"

We talked softly so we wouldn't wake the grandparents. "I am not saying that we should not get married," whispered Corey, "just that we need to think about not getting married right away. You don't need to worry. I love you more than I can ever imagine loving anyone. I'm not trying to break up with you. I am trying to do what is best for both of us, and if you really believe that it is absolutely necessary that we get married while we are here in Tennessee, then I will marry you. I don't ever want to lose you, but I don't believe thinking about it for a few days will hurt anything."

"I think you are right," I agreed and going to Cherokee and looking around would be a good way to spend a few days. Grandma suggested that we leave tomorrow afternoon and spend a couple of days exploring and I think it is a wonderful idea."

Corey agreed and we both went to our bedrooms to try to get a little sleep. This day felt like it had been forty eight hours long instead of twenty four, and the trip to Cherokee tomorrow would be a long one too. I didn't think that I could sleep but exhaustion took over and I was fast asleep as soon as my head hit the pillow. Corey on the other hand felt a deep relief that this crisis had blown over at least a little, he was feeling very alone. He knew that the discussion would have to continue later, but he was looking forward to exploring the history of some of the Indians of the East.

Nick and Nora got up at five the next morning. While Nick took care of the farm animals, Nora packed a wonderful lunch of country ham biscuits, fresh tomatoes, potato salad that she had made the day before, and baked beans that were made from scratch, the country way.

After finishing with the milking and feeding of the animals, Nick came into the kitchen door and asked Nora, "Have you called Mona and Ken to make sure that they will take care of the animals?"

"I am waiting until they have a chance to wake up," replied Nora. "You know that since they became 'city folks', they don't get up this early in the morning, especially on a weekend. I'll call them around eight. Corey and Penny will probably not be up before then and it will take them a little while to get ready."

When eight rolled around and all the chores were finished, Nora called Mona. Do you and Jed mind feeding the animals for a couple of days while we run over to Cherokee, North Carolina and take Corey and Penny with us?"

"Why are you going over there?" questioned Mona.

Advice

"Penny has developed an interest in Native American people, since she has been out West; it has something to do with their work as historical detectives. We just thought she and Corey might enjoy learning about the Native Americans who lived around here."

"Has Penny given up this crazy idea of getting married?" asked Mona with a sigh in her voice. "I tried to talk to her about it when she and Corey were here, but as usual she did not listen to a thing I said. I just don't know how to get through to that girl."

"Yes," chuckled Nora, "She's just as stubborn as the seventeen year old girl that I once knew. Whatever you and Jed said to those two kids has really got both of them as prickly as a porcupine. I think Penny heard a lot more of what you said than you thought, but now is not the time to put more pressure on either of them. Let them have a little fun in Cherokee and think about whether or not they want to get married on their own."

"O.K. replied Mona. "Maybe you are right, but the whole idea of her making the same mistake I did and getting married for all the wrong reasons scares me to death."

"I understand, but if you will remember your father and I tried to tell you some of the same things that you are trying to tell Penny and you wouldn't listen either," continued Nora. "You are going to have to trust that she has a good head on her shoulders, and that whatever they decide Penny and Corey will do what is best for them. You can't make another person's decisions for them even if they happen to be your daughter. Now, what about feeding the livestock?"

"No problem, Mom, maybe the couple of days away from Camp Creek will be fun for you and dad too. It has been a while since you have taken some time out from that farm and just had fun. Don't worry about anything. Jed and I will take care of things," promised Mona.

As soon as she got off the phone, Nora called up the stairs. "Penny, Corey, time to get up and get ready. We will be leaving for Cherokee in about an hour so that we can get there before it gets dark."

With everything finally packed in the car, Corey, Nick, and Nora and I were on the road to Cherokee. On the curvy mountain roads, Nick figured it would be about three hours before they reached their destination. The old Dodge that belonged to

Nick and Nora had about 75,000 miles showing on the odometer and had been taken care of by Nick himself, but it was a farm vehicle, and had been used pretty hard. Nick did not push it too hard over the mountain roads.

At first the atmosphere in the car was unusually quiet. The easy banter between Corey and I was absent this morning. We talked hesitantly about the weather and what we would do when we got to Cherokee until abruptly I questioned, "Grandma, how did you and Grandpa know that it was the right time to get married?"

Nora paused for a minute and then answered, "Circumstances had a lot to do with when we got married." She remembered with a faraway look in her eyes. "Your grandpa and I grew up in Camp Creek on adjoining farms. We went to elementary school together and sometimes as we got older our fathers would help each other out. During busy times like haying and such everyone who was old enough to work on both farms would go to one farm and help with the harvesting there, then they would all go to the neighboring farm and finish there."

"Even when your grandpa and I were too young to lift the bales of hay and put them on the wagon, we would walk along behind the wagons and pick up loose hay and put it in a sack for immediate feeding to the farm animals. Nothing was wasted on either farm."

"So you see," continued Nora, "Your grandpa and I spent a lot of time together even when we were very young. As we got older it seemed natural to kind of 'hang out together' as you kids call it now. By the time we finished school, most people just assumed that we were a couple and we did too. I'm not saying that neither of us ever went out on a date with anyone else; we both saw other people from time to time, but no one knew us better than we did each other. We had been best friends almost from the time that we were born, so we knew each other pretty well."

"That's how Corey and I feel about each other," interrupted Penny. "We feel like you and grandpa; we belong together."

"Wait just a minute," replied Grandma. There is more to this story. Do you remember that I told you that there were circumstances that intervened in this story? Well, the biggest of those circumstances was World War II. Being of healthy mind and body and nineteen years old, your grandpa enlisted in the army. I wanted him to marry me before he left, but your grandpa refused. He said that too many things could happen while he was gone and that it would be better to wait until he got back to the states."

"And you know that I was right" interjected Grandpa with self-satisfaction in his voice. "Look at how many young girls was left as widows with small babies after that war and how many of them cheated on their husbands out of loneliness while they were gone, not to mention how many got divorced because of girls the husbands got involved with while they were gone. I admit that I saw some of those girls while I was overseas. Loneliness was a constant companion along with fear. And anyone who tells you that he was not afraid is a liar. Spending some time with a pretty girl does not mean that I didn't still love your grandmother, but sometimes female company was a way of making me feel better and I grew up a lot during that war. I think I have been a better husband because of the time spent away from your grandma. As I grew up, I realized that she was the only woman that I wanted in my life, but when I made that choice, I had the experience and knowledge to make that decision."

As they continued their journey, Grandma continued the story, "During Grandpa's time away, I got to know more people my age. "All the young people who were left in Greene County worked to support the men who had gone to war. We wrote lots and lots of letters, both to our friends who had gone to war and to young men whom we did not know. We made care packages of things like soap, shaving cream, wash clothes, chewing gum, hard candy and other things that we thought the soldiers might like to have. We also baked goodies like homemade candy and cookies to send. In doing so, I got to know a lot of people that I had not met before, both men and women. Mostly we all went out to grab a coke at Cole's Drug Store or the Big Top, but I also went out with a few of the guys that could not go to war because they were Four F. Those dates helped me to decide that your Grandpa was the man for me, but I am glad I got to go out with a few other guys so that I could be sure that what we thought we had together; was truly real."

At this point Grandpa interrupted the story with the words, "I went out with some other girls while I was overseas. It was a lonely time and when I finally got a three day pass in France, it was fun to just talk to a pretty girl. It didn't mean that I loved your Grandmother any less, but it did pass the time and taught me a little something about what other girls are like."

Grandma then took up the story again. "Some time apart to grow sometimes makes a real love a whole lot stronger and if it falls apart during that time, then it wasn't real at all."

Corey and I were deep in thought the rest of the way to Cherokee. Grandma and Grandpa rented two rooms in a small motel, one for Grandma and me and one for Corey and Grandpa. Grandpa and Corey carried the bags to the two rooms and Grandma and I unpacked. Then we all went out to the little café located right beside the motel to get sandwiches for supper. After supper we decided to turn in for the night.

Grandma was almost asleep when I softly said, "Thank you for the story today.

It was not exactly what I expected to hear, but it certainly gave both Corey and I something to think about."

"Penny," answered Grandma, "No one but you and Corey can decide what is best for the two of you. Life is a grand adventure and every one of us has to make our own decisions and then live with the consequences. We all make some good decisions and some that we later regret. The best thing that you can do is be honest with Corey about how you feel and hope that he will be honest with you. Now, get some sleep and you will feel better in the morning."

Cherokee History

*T*he next morning, we all discussed what we wanted to do on our first day in Cherokee. "I want to visit some of the shops that I saw coming in to town," said Grandma. "They had some handmade pottery that I would like to see."

"I have heard that there are some gem mines and that tourists can pay a fee to look for gems and then keep whatever gems that they find when they leave, said Nick. "I would like to check that out."

The geologist inside of Corey was intrigued and he definitely wanted to learn more about emeralds that were mined nearby but he figured he had plenty of time. "I do not know much about the Cherokees," replied Corey. "I read something about a Cherokee Indian Museum on a brochure in our hotel room. I would like to check that out."

"I'll go shopping with grandma, I laughed. I can probably find something to take back for Hidalgo, Uncle Ken, Aunt June, and maybe even some gifts for the kids that always accumulate around the ranch house. Then tonight I want to play Indian Bingo. It costs a little money, but I think it would be fun." At this remark Corey frowned.

"That is a stupid waste of money," he retorted with anger in his voice. "Why do you want to just throw your money away?"

At the anger in his voice I flushed with my own anger. "I will not spend a lot of money playing bingo, but I want to see what it is like. It sounds like fun to me, besides it is my money anyway."

"I know it is your money, argued Corey, but if we get married, I do not want my wife wasting money on foolish things like Bingo."

"Well, maybe we are not getting married if you feel that way." I shouted and stormed out of the café.

Corey looked at Nick and Nora and apologized. "I don't know how Penny can be so unreasonable, but I think that I will go to the museum and let her cool off for a little while."

After Corey left the café, Nora shook her head. "If he tells Penny that she is being unreasonable, there may not be a wedding."

Nick and Nora decided that they would go back to the motel room and look for me. When they got there I was in the room that I was sharing with Nora.

"Do you still want to go shopping?" I asked Grandma.

"Only if you feel like it," she replied hesitantly.

"I am not going to let Corey spoil my day" I said with a sigh. "Let's go shopping."

As the two women left the room, Nora caught Nick's eye and rolled her own eyes. "While we women go shopping, why don't you check out the gems and meet us back here about lunch time?" Grandma said with a parting wave.

In the meantime Corey was fuming, he was mad at himself thinking that he was acting strange, not like himself at all. Why should he care if Penny spent some money? He wondered why he had allowed himself to get angry about it but then maybe it was a matter of principle. He walked around town for a while and then stopped into the Cherokee Indian Museum. He read about the "Trail of Tears," a time in history when Andrew Jackson ordered the Cherokee people moved to a reservation in Oklahoma. Corey was fascinated by the story. It saddened him to read of the many people who died on the trip and the unhappiness of those who survived. Considering the fact that the Cherokee Indians were highly civilized, in fact far more civilized than many of the invaders from Europe who stole their land from them; there is no wonder there is still resentment to this day. They had been treated as badly as the people were exploited in Germany during the last war. When gold was discovered in Georgia, it sealed the deal for the Cherokees. Their civilization was over. Corey thought back to early Southwestern history and the Pueblo Revolt. History seems to always be repeating. People enter another land and look down on and mistreat the people already living there. People were always greedy, wanting what the other person has.

Corey's Fall

$\mathcal{W}$hen Corey looked at his watch, he was surprised to learn that he had spent three hours in the museum. He hurried back to the hotel hoping that Penny had cooled down and given up the idea of going to play Bingo. After all, he reasoned, she would come to her senses. He was sure of it.

When he got to the motel, no one was there. There was a note on the dresser of his room. It said, "Grandma and I have gone shopping and Nick has gone to look for places where he could explore information about gems. We are planning to meet for dinner in the restaurant adjoining the hotel and then I am going to treat my grandparents to a visit to the Bingo Parlor. We would like for you to join us, but if you do not choose to go, we will see you at the motel after we finish playing bingo. I am not sure when that will be."

Immediately Corey was angry again, mostly because of his own foolishness. He knew that if he went to join us, we would have another fight and he did not want that to happen. "I need some time to think," he thought to himself.

In exploring Cherokee, a very small town nestled in the Smokey Mountains, Corey had noticed several hiking trails that led out of town and into the local mountains. He decided to take a small hiking pack which was in the trunk of the car. Being summer time, with no rain expected, he figured on a leisurely walk through the woods might help him think more clearly and he thought that it might even do me and him a lot of good. He even thought about spending the night in the woods somewhere. He carefully wrote a note to Penny explaining what he was going to do and locked the door.

He decided to walk a trail that followed a small creek. As he walked along the trail he was deep in thought trying to ease his conscience about me and the fight that we had. "I don't believe that I was unfair," he thought to himself. "We all agreed to be frugal with the money that we got from our adventures besides I don't believe that Penny's grandparents were comfortable with going to the bingo parlor." He of course was lying to himself. He knew he was being a fool about it all, but Penny was acting so utterly strange to him he couldn't help himself.

Little did he know that I was feeling the same strange feelings. Corey continued the argument with himself. "Penny's grandparents went to the bingo games just because Penny wanted them to go. They are just going to waste money. But then, I too have wasted a little money; after all, I wanted to come out here to take a vacation too. Vacations cost money. We both understood that before we left New Mexico. Why should I have the only say as to what we do with our money? It is her money too. I have never tried to tell Penny what to do before. She is a very independent woman, and for me to try to control her would be a big mistake. If we are going to get married, we need to work this out. We need to give and take."

As Corey was deep in thought he was not watching the trail. This is a big mistake but in the mountains of Western North Carolina at dusk it can be a fatal one. Unlike the forests that he was used to in the dry southwest, here the forest floor is covered with moist, decaying leaves covering up decaying vegetation and small vines. This makes the forest floor slippery in places. Added to the upgrade caused by the rise of the mountains, a hiker must pay attention to where he is walking, especially one who is not a native of the area.

All of a sudden, Corey stepped into a small hole and caught his toe under a vine. He lurched forward expecting his foot to come loose but it didn't. Instead he stepped sidewise in order to avoid falling down. Unfortunately that step was off the trail.

For a second, he thought he could rescue himself but the rock he grabbed to stop his fall rolled off the edge of the trail and before he knew what was happening, he was falling headfirst down the side of the mountain.

It was a sheer drop down into a dense tangle of brush and small trees. Unfortunately, on the way down he managed to almost impale himself, on a small stump. He immediately felt a sharp pain in his side but his inertia carried him though the tree branches. When he hit a large enough tree to break his fall, he was hurting in a number of places. He couldn't untangle himself; it seemed as if he was caught in a spider web of enormous proportions made out of branches covered with ivy vines. Extrication from the branches proved to be impossible for the moment.

He instantly realized that his chest was really hurt. "Probably a broken rib," he thought to himself. "Not too bad, but it is going to make it a pain to get back up to the trail without help." He then worked at righting himself but when he put weight on his foot that he had stepped into the hole with, he felt a searing pain going up and down his side. He thought he had broken his ankle. He was in serious trouble and he knew it.

He laid there for some time assessing his injuries. He heard what he thought was someone or something walking on the trail. The first thought that came to him was about a warning he had received from Penny's grandfather about bears. Fear gripped him. "Hello," he yelled, "Is anyone up there?"

After a long pause a small voice trailed down to him.

"Are you talking to me?"

"Yes," Corey answered!

"What are you doing down there, are you hurt?"

Corey was so relieved to hear someone else he almost fainted. "I tripped and fell off the trail. Can you help me? I don't think I can get back up to the trail by myself."

Corey finally saw a silhouette of a small man looking down at him. The man sat down on the edge of the trail sliding over the edge producing a small shower of gravel as he pushed off and slid on his butt. As Corey finally was able to see the man he noticed that he was a Native American, probably a Cherokee many years older than himself.

"What brought you to this situation?" asked the Cherokee.

"I was just hiking to clear my head," replied Corey. "When I have some difficult thinking to do, I often get a clearer picture of the problem when I am out in nature. And," he paused, "and I have some tall thinking to do, possibly the most important thinking of my life."

The Cherokee smiled a wry smile. "Sometimes, the ripple of a mountain stream, the sound of the wind in the trees, or the smells of the woodland can help a person figure out the difference between what is right and what is wrong. The closeness of nature is very important to my people. Nature has guided us through life and helped us to get through some very difficult times."

As the Cherokee man carefully felt Corey's ankles, ribs and legs, Corey introduced himself. "I am visiting from New Mexico and am staying with my future in laws in Camp Creek, Tennessee. My girlfriend's family thought it would be a good idea to come over here to learn about the people who live here."

"Yes, they are lazy, crazy people, uncivilized and sometimes dangerous. They are always trying to steal anything they can."

What the Cherokee said bothered Corey, but he didn't feel like arguing with him. It hurt too much. He could hardly hold himself up without hugging at the tree branches that were covered with vines. Slowly, a hop at a time with the Cherokee helping, he managed to reach the floor of the canyon. On the way down he learned a few things, mostly about pain. It turned out that he was only about twenty feet from the floor of the canyon but it was almost straight down. Even with the Cherokee helping him it was almost impossible to get through the thicket of small trees and brush and it was getting dark before they reached the bottom.

Once settled on a rock, Corey caught his breath enough to finish his conversation. "You know, at Serpiente in New Mexico my best friend is a Navajo who has taught me a lot about his people. I certainly don't consider his people as lazy, crazy, uncivilized and sometimes dangerous, always trying to steal something."

"I was speaking of white people" replied the Indian with a grin on his face. "Spend some time walking in my moccasins and you will understand. When the white man discovered this country Indians were running it, no taxes, no debt, women did all the work, and white man thought he could improve on a system like this?"

Corey quickly decided it was time to change direction with the conversation. "My name is Cory Anderson. My girlfriend and I are visiting her relatives before we get married and we thought it would be a good time to find out about the Native Americans in this part of the country."

"That is the first I have ever had someone talk to me about marriage and Indians in the same breath," the Indian said with a grin. "My name is William Owl and I am a woodcarver. I was looking for cedar stumps when I heard you calling. I have lived around here all my life and I sell my carvings at the Artist's Colony in Gatlinburg, Tennessee. The animals hide in the wood and it is my job to get them out."

Owl had finished his examination of Corey's injuries and he said in a worried voice, "I don't think any of your injuries are serious, but the sprained ankle and the broken rib will make it extremely difficult for you to get back up to the trail even with my help. It's getting late and as you can see, the sun has gone down. I think that it is going to be dangerous trying to get back tonight. I believe that we should build a small fire and stay here until daylight; then I will go to Cherokee and get some help."

Corey reluctantly agreed, "I also have a tarp and some provisions in my pack. I was wearing it loose when I fell and now it is somewhere down here." They looked around and spotted the backpack lying in the cold waters of the creek. He was lucky the water hadn't carried it off. "I left a note for Penny that I might spend the night in the forest to think, so she will not be worried. In fact, no one will look for me until late in the day tomorrow."

William Owl rescued Corey's pack then cleared off a small space so Corey could lie down. Above Corey he rigged the tarp, even though there was no rain called for, it would suffice to keep the dew off of him. He would be much warmer now even without a fire.

Corey always carried a small first aid kit in his pack. He took out a small cloth and some alcohol swabs. He tried to wipe all the dirt and leaves out of his open scratches and wounds. Every movement caused his rib to send a twinge through his whole body.

"You need something else; I'll be right back," says Owl. He returned after about fifteen minutes with handfuls of jewelweed. Corey was already starting to itch. He had never encountered poison ivy before, but the Indian showed him how to rub the sap all over. Despite the jewelweed, which should be applied immediately after exposure, Cory would be in for a new experience for the next few days.

The trail is closer to the creek about a hundred yards down the trail. Do you think, with my help, that tomorrow you could make it that far?" queried Owl.

"It is not going to be easy, but with the trees and you to hold on to, I'm sure I can make it," said Corey uncertainly. "First thing tomorrow morning, help me stand up and we will see how it goes from there."

William Owl

The following day William Owl awoke just as the sun was coming up. Corey had spent the night in restless fits of scratching the ugly red rash that was taking over his body. Owl put his hands under Corey's arms and gently lifted. When Corey tried to put some weight on his ankle he got lightheaded and nauseous for a moment and slumped to the ground.

"I think I had better put a splint on that ankle before you try to put any weight on it. I don't think it is broken, but a splint will prevent more injury," said Owl with wrinkles of worry on his forehead. He went to search for some relatively straight sticks to use for splints. Corey meanwhile untied a short section of rope off of the tarp. In a few minutes Owl was back with several sticks that would work for a splint. He tied them tightly around Corey's ankle and lifted him by the shoulders again. This time the pain was manageable. By holding on to the trees as they climbed down the creek bank the two men managed to get to the place by the creek where they could climb back to the trail. It would be a long day, hopping all the way down the trail that Corey had so easily walked up the day before. He was very grateful that the Cherokee who had found him was an experienced hiker like himself, although Corey's mistake was a very rookie one.

Suddenly the busy town of Cherokee was in front of them and another couple volunteered to get under Corey's arms for a last effort to get to the parking lot where the hike began. Corey was relieved to be able to get the weight off of his ankle. But the more he relaxed, the more he realized that he hurt all over. "Thanks," he said to Owl "I don't believe I would have made it even to the creek without your help and spending the night dangling on the side of the mountain is not my idea of a good time."

Owl says, "No problem," he turned around and walked away. Corey thought he would never see him again.

Corey managed, with the help of a passing policeman who found him sitting on the curb of the parking lot, to take him to the local emergency room. There the doctors dressed his broken rib and wrapped his foot. They also gave him some ointment to relieve the intense itching that had consumed him.

The Motel Room

The next few days Corey spent lying on his back on a bed in a motel room nursing both his ankle and ribs but also his ego. He expected sympathy from me but it didn't happen. I acted like I was a little embarrassed by him. Now his feelings were seriously bruised. When I returned from the Indian bingo games I found the note Corey had left and was consumed with anger. I convinced myself that he was returning to Serpiente without me. We had packed up to return to Camp Creek when I noticed the door to Corey's room was just slightly open. Thinking the cleaning ladies were working in there I opened it just enough to take one last look in there and to my astonishment I discovered Corey lying in bed.

"I thought you had left to go home," I blurted out.

"No, answered Corey, I left to climb up in the hills so I could get myself into a jackpot!"

We all stayed another day, just to make sure that Corey would be taken care of, but we had to return to Camp Creek in order to take care of the farm animals that by this time would be sorely neglected. Corey couldn't move while the rib fracture healed but fortunately Nora, my grandmother took pity on him and made arrangements to have food delivered to him. Corey discussed with them what the Cherokee who had rescued had said to him. Nick and Nora could not offer a clue as to why the Cherokee had such pent up animosity for the white people who lived in his community. I went home with Nora and Nick in order to help on the farm, agreeing to return in a day or two to rescue Corey and with that Corey found himself entirely alone in a motel room.

After only a day he was tired of the room service food but every time he got out of bed he found himself fighting the pain from his ribs. Although there was a television in the room it hurt too much to mess with it. In only a day he found himself bored with it, preferring to stare out of the window looking at tourist as they passed on the sidewalk in front of the motel. The only people he spoke to was a young Cherokee girl who delivered food and cleaned up the room. He had never been so alone in his life.

The Trail of Tears

The following night Corey was having secret thoughts about whether or not I would return at all. That evening he rolled out of bed and dropped down on his knees, which was the only way he could get up, and went to the bathroom. Returning to the bed, doing everything in reverse he looked from the bed and discovered William Owl sitting in the chair next to it.

For a moment he simply stared at Owl, he looked older and feebler than he had remembered. Finally, working up his courage he asked, "How did you get in here?"

William Owl grinned and answered his question. "My granddaughter is the one who has been bringing your food to you and cleaning your room. She told me about you and I wanted to talk to you."

"Great," responded Corey who was grateful for any company. "What do you want to talk about?"

"Oh, there are a couple of things I wanted to share with you," answered Owl. "First of all I wanted to explain to you why I made the comment about the people who live around here. I fear that I gave you the impression that I disliked all white people; that is not true."

"You mean the comment that white people are lazy, crazy, uncivilized and sometimes dangerous, always trying to steal something," responded Corey.

"Yes," replied Owl. "That is of course what your people have said about the Cherokee as well as all people who are different than you."

"Well, responded Corey, I'm sure that is true. I am not a historian, my expertise is in geology. My father was a geologist in the petroleum industry back in Texas and New Mexico."

William Owl looked at him and said, "There is something special about both you and the young lady you were with, and I'll try to explain that later, you need to understand that by the time the English actually arrived here," he pointed with both hands down meaning where they were at the moment, "almost all of our people had died or were dying."

"What do you mean," asked Corey.

William Owl began an explanation; "Small pox, measles, influenza, bubonic plague, trachoma, diphtheria, malaria, amoebic dysentery, typhoid fever, cholera, chicken pox, yellow fever, scarlet fever, and whooping cough. American Indians were dying from what were childhood ailments in other parts of the world. Only a tiny fraction lived through the epidemics. For example, when Thomas Jefferson made a tally of Virginia's forty tribes from 1607 after Captain John Smith made contact, to a count made in 1669 by the Virginia assembly, the tribes had been reduced to one-third their former numbers. "My people began to wonder about their own Gods, they seemed to be no match against the white man's Gods. My people did not understand how diseases were passed from one person to another. We believed one cannot give a disease to another any more than a wounded man can give his wounds to another."

"Lewis and Clark, who were sent out to explore new territory discovered that smallpox had arrived there long before they did. Even as far away as the Columbia River in the far Pacific Northwest in April 1806, Clark came upon a large, ruined village and the few, pox scarred survivors of a terrible epidemic that had roared through three decades earlier. Disease had reached that remote corner of North America long before the Europeans, liquor, war, or land grabs. You see, nearly three centuries earlier, people like Hernando De Soto had brought disease with them.

It all may have started in Mexico City, and by the time it exhausted itself of victims seven years later, it had killed American Indians trading at remote Hudson's Bay Company outpost in far northern Canada by way of long established trade networks.

Before the introduction of the white man into the southeast the Cherokees were the absolute rulers of this part of what was to become the United States. The Cherokee conquered all previous tribes of people who had lived here eons ago and either drove them out or subjugated them. The Cherokees in 1828 were not savages. In fact, we assimilated many European-style customs, including the wearing of gowns by Cherokee women. We built roads, schools and churches, had a system of representational government, and were farmers and cattle ranchers. We were in many ways, more civilized than the foreign invaders. We even had a Cherokee alphabet, the 'Talking Leaves' that was perfected by Sequoyah."

It should not have surprised Corey about the command Owl had of the English language as well as his vast knowledge of history that Corey was unaware of. After all, William Owl had spoken English all his life and he had been steeped in the history; it was the history of his own people. He continued, "After gold was discovered in Georgia, in 1830 the congress of the United States passed the Indian Removal Act. Although many Americans were against the act, most notably Tennessee Congressman Davy Crocket, it passed anyway. It was President Jackson who signed the bill into law.

We Cherokees attempted to fight removal legally by challenging the removal laws in the Supreme Court and by establishing an independent Cherokee Nation. At first, the court seemed to rule against us, as if we were not a nation, which we obviously were. In Cherokee V. Georgia, the Court refused to hear a case extending Georgia's laws on the Cherokee because they did not represent a sovereign nation. Then in 1832, the U.S. Supreme Court ruled in favor of the Cherokee Nation. In this case, Chief Justice John Marshall ruled that the Cherokee Nation was sovereign, making the removal laws invalid. We rejoiced but then learned that we would have to agree to removal in a treaty."

"By 1835 we Cherokees were divided and very sad. At that time, most of our people supported Chief John Ross, who fought the encroachment of whites starting with the 1832 land lottery. However, a few of my people actually wanted to move to another place. They actually thought there would be places they could go where they would not have to deal with the white people."

"A treaty was signed by members of a Treaty Party in 1835, giving Jackson the legal document he needed to remove us all. The treaty was ratified by the United States Senate and that sealed our fate. Among the few of your people who spoke out against the ratification was Daniel Webster and Henry Clay, but it still passed by a single vote. In 1838 the United States began our removal to Oklahoma, doing what they had intended to do all the time. General Winfield Scott arrived here in 1838 with 7000 soldiers and the invasion began.

Men, women, and children were taken from their land, herded into temporary stockades without food or even places to relieve themselves. Then my ancestors were forced to march a thousand miles. We would have all died but our chief made an urgent appeal to Scott, requesting that the general let our people get into smaller groups. By moving in smaller groups they could forage for food. They arrived in Oklahoma during the brutal winter of 1838. About four thousand of my people died as a result of the removal. The route they traversed and the journey itself, of course, became known as 'The Trail of Tears'."

"We killed many of our own chiefs who had worked with the whites after we realized what had happened. Perhaps that helps to explain why many of us American Indians have such a low opinion of the whites. We are now locked out of most of our homeland as well as our culture."

Corey ended the conversation by adding; "And so a county formed fifty years earlier on the premise...that all men are created equal, and that they are endowed by their Creator with certain unalienable rights, among these the right to life, liberty and the pursuit of happiness, brutally closed the curtain on a culture that had done no wrong."

William Owl sat and starred at Corey for a moment then changing the subject of the conversation, he added, "Don't give up on your girl. She is under the influence of a serpent, a demon but she doesn't know it. Here," he handed Corey a small amulet that appeared to be a tiny carved owl with a leather string tied in a loop around it. "She should wear this around her neck, she needs protection. Give it to her to wear when you see her." With that said, and without an explanation, William Owl walked out of the motel room, closing the door behind him.

Hidalgo's Arrival in East Tennessee

A day later, Corey was feeling much better, particularly after grandmother and I retrieved him from North Carolina. Borrowing Grandpa Nick's cane, he decided to get out of the house and exercise his sprained ankle. That evening Corey and I slowly walked up the trail behind the farm house where we could be assured some privacy. There, I stood and studied the stars on the edge of the Milky Way Galaxy, contemplating my position in the universe. Was it wise, like thousands of girls before me, to blindly take a plunge into married life as I was about to do? Or, like a select few, perhaps I should test myself by traveling to the edge of many new worlds and there possibly find my real love, my purpose in life, and perhaps even God. I was entertaining quite a personal dilemma.

My recent preoccupation with getting married was a complete paradox within myself. It elicited feelings of doubt, panic, and worry, and yet I sometimes drifted into a feeling of elation when I thought about a release from those fears. Like my wrestling coach had said, "Face your fears and they will go away." This is just another fear for me to face. In the quest for a solution to my problem, I thought to myself that perhaps tonight I would discover my place at the edge of the universe. Here among the stars, I was dealing with that ultimate challenge, to pick the right path, but for now I was content to look down to the man in my dreams, the greatest love in my life, Corey.

Corey appeared to have gone to sleep. Oh well, I laughed at myself. I had been warned that men treat their women that way. I walked over to him and kicked his shoe.

"Are we going to get married? I demanded as a tease.

No, he answered. Then he started to add something to his answer but I was already storming down the trail. After a few steps I stopped, turned around and spoke. What I heard coming out of my mouth sounded strange even to me. "Come on, time for us to get back down to the farmhouse. This problem isn't going to solve itself, nor is it going to be solved tonight or ever. I am not going to fight this anymore."

Without saying a word, Corey rose to his feet, catching up and attempting to slip his arm around my waist. I pushed it away and continued down the trail muttering; "Well, if you don't want me, I can find someone else who does!"

Corey, who was still limping badly, forced himself to catch up with me and said. "I have something I would like you to wear."

Turning around I grabbed the tiny owl amulet and thrust it into my pocket, then I turned and stomped down the last of the trail leaving Corey far behind me. When I got back to the farmhouse I climbed a set of stairs and then entered through a side door directly into my room.

Meanwhile Corey was hurt, confused and scared. Perhaps, he thought, it was time to get back to Serpiente. Entering the old farm house kitchen through the back door he was amazed at what he found inside. There sat Hidalgo eating a homemade pretzel with coffee, as if nothing was out of the ordinary.

As Corey reached over to shake hands with Hidalgo, he yelled for me to bring in a fresh cup of coffee.

I was angry at this point, how dare Corey so nonchalantly to ask me to bring him a cup of coffee. I was completely unaware that Hidalgo had arrived from New Mexico. As I crept down the stairs I heard him repeat the request; "Penny, how about getting me some more of that coffee?" Thinking it was just Corey, and still more than a little angry, I got the coffee out of the kitchen, and went into the parlor and threw it on Corey. It missed Corey but the hot coffee landed all over Hidalgo.

Hidalgo who had a worried look on his face began wiping himself off and then laughed, "That sure is a bad waste of good coffee."

"Hidalgo," I exclaimed, "What in the world are you doing here; we thought you understood that you were not supposed to come out here unless we decided to go ahead, and get married."

Hidalgo contemplated the situation for a moment then asked the obvious question. "Well, are you going to get married?"

"Yes, interjected Corey in a firm voice, but not now," he emphasized. "We have way too many things to do first."

Without thinking I reached into my pocket and pulled out the amulet Corey had given me. It was a small carving of what appeared to be a very hard bone, looking somewhat but not exactly like a tiny owl with a leather string strung around it. I had forgotten about it in all the excitement of the moment. Pulling it over my head so it hung under my chin I experienced an epiphany. I looked at Corey and simply said "For some reason, and it is a mystery why, I have been acting like a huge fool. For some reason I got it in my head that I had to get married right now. Looking back for the last few days I must have been a horrible host.

"But as far as what you just said, thank you, I couldn't agree more." Corey and I hugged, which brought a chuckle from Hidalgo.

"Can I see that amulet?" Hidalgo asked.

"It's something Corey gave me," Penny explained and handed it to him.

Looking at Corey, Hidalgo asked him where he had gotten it. The question brought a long explanation from Corey about William Owl and what he had said to him.

Hidalgo examined the small amulet then said, "Owls are usually thought of as symbols of death. There was a long pause in the conversation then he continued, "But owl amulets are sometimes used as a protection from death. If I were you, I would wear it"

Corey explained what William Owl had said about a demon bothering Penny.

"Has he ever met you?" Hidalgo asked me?

"No, all I know is that he is someone that helped Corey after he fell and that he seemed kind of mysterious."

Hidalgo again said, "Wear it and see if things don't change." He seemed to be the mysterious one now.

My grandmother, Nora came into the parlor at just that moment, seeing Hidalgo she was deeply embarrassed by the coffee still dripping off of him. She grabbed a kitchen towel and further embarrassed Hidalgo by wiping up his lap. After taking a moment to fend off my grandmother, he began his explanation as to what he was doing in East Tennessee.

"After you left, Aunt June and Uncle Ken took off a couple of days and visited the canyon with the pool that you and Corey discovered. She found something there."

"What do you mean she found something there?" I asked.

"Well, answered Hidalgo, "You know that she is quite versed in Indian rock carvings."

"Sure," said Corey, "We all know that but what did she discover? We had already told her about the old Greek or Hebrew writings on the panel."

"That's true," answered Hidalgo "But after she was able to really examine the rock carvings she discovered that they were from tribes from all over the Southwest. She even discovered a Toltec symbol there. It looks like something right out of a Mayan panel. Evidentially peoples from all over the place met there."

"True, but that wouldn't have brought you seventeen hundred miles out here," says Corey.

"No, I may suffer from butt fatigue for some time now. But you see, she told a friend of hers, a fellow archeologist from the University of New Mexico, and now everyone wants to know the secrets of the place. She was contacted by some people from a group that call themselves the New Mexico Historical Society; they are offering her a reward of ten thousand dollars. What they want back is publishing rights to her field notes. Just think, a guaranteed, published book with, of course, royalties. The royalties from the book would be worth far more than the cash reward. It could be the chance of her professional lifetime.

"I don't understand," I asked, "Exactly why does all that bring you out here?"

Hidalgo answered, "There is circumstantial but growing body of evidence that there were people here well before Columbus. In fact, as you pointed out once before, they know that the Vikings made journeys to the extreme northern portions of the east coast. Archeologists are currently excavating ruins that these early visitors left there even as we speak."

Hidalgo pulled a piece of paper out of his pocket and began reading out loud, "There are many clues which have been discovered which are accepted in other cultures and strands of science, but not in the pragmatic unyielding, and often biased archeological science of western culture."

"Early explorers, probably of Persian but possibly Egyptian, Middle Eastern, or even of African descent have voyaged into the Gulf of Mexico and then explored northward, following the aboriginal trails or rivers into the interior. Did they leave documents in the form of hieroglyphs carved into rock which prove they were here; if they did, why did they choose the routes that they took and what were they looking for"?

"You mean European contact," interjected Nora.

"It doesn't matter, any contact before Columbus," answered Hidalgo. "The first thing we need to do is to start finding any information we can about discoveries out here and then get the information to June for documentation."

Nora setting down her kitchen towel and with a thoughtful look on her face interjected, "Perhaps I can get you started. I read an article in the Greeneville Sun about a recent find at a place called Bat Creek, Tennessee. According to the article, professors say that carbon dating of wood fragments and other evidence found a century ago in an ancient tomb prove that Hebrews sailed to America centuries before Columbus." Grandma walked over to a small china closet that had a large stack of old newspapers on it. After setting several papers aside she announced, "Here it is," and began reading out loud.

"Cyrus Gorden, a former Dartmouth College professor of Judaic culture, proposed a theory this year after studying inscriptions on a stone." She walked back to her rocker, sat down and continued reading; "The inscription is important because it is the first scientifically authenticated pre-Columbian text in an Old World script or language found in America."

"According to the article, they also found brass bracelets made from a zinc-copper alloy used by the Romans from 45 to 200 A.D. They theorize that the Hebrew sailors were trying to escape Roman repression after a rebellion in 73 A.D. Gordon believes the sailors landed in the southeastern United States, were forced inland because the coast was settled by American Indians and got as far as Louden County, here in Eastern Tennessee."

"The Bat Creek tomb was first unearthed in 1889. It contained nine skeletons, with the heads of all but one pointing north. Under the skull and jawbone of the south pointing skeleton were several objects, including the inscribed stone."

"It says here, Gordon's work has been ignored because it is so controversial.

The prejudice against the idea that someone came before Columbus is so enormous it's practically impossible to overcome."

Hidalgo complemented her by saying, "That is exactly the kind of documentation that we are looking for."

"I'm confused, Grandma asked, "What do they mean the prejudice about the idea that someone came to the United States before Columbus is so controversial?"

Hidalgo set back in his chair and answered her. "Before modern dating methods were invented, no one knew exactly how old a historical site was unless there was some actual historical document of some kind that told them. They are using radioactive isotopes now in order to tell. They have matched up radiometric with tree ring dating and they can now date objects going back many thousands of years very precisely. Yet they don't even know for sure how long the local natives have been here in Tennessee or where they came from. Well, I am from Dine, now located in New Mexico." he continued with a grin. "The problem is most of what we are looking at is rock carvings that cannot be dated by any method. They are easily faked. It has become a tradition among professional archeologist that Columbus was the first to discover America. Archeologists are now at war over the date 1492. Most professional archeologist won't touch stuff like the Bat Creek Mystery Stone because they are quickly labeled as pseudo or fake archeologist. Anymore, it takes people who are not dependent upon the money provided by institutions to make new discoveries. That is why groups like The New Mexico Historical Society offers rewards. They want to stir up interest. Besides, the more discoveries we make; the richer all our histories are."

"I suppose if someone could prove that their ancestors discovered America first, they could possibly lay claim to this entire country," says Grandma.

"Fat chance, those politicians aren't going to let that happen," chimed in my grandfather Nick with his rather matter of fact way of talking. "All of this puts you into a particular position, doesn't it Hidalgo?"

"No," answered Hidalgo, "Native Americans own property because that is the way American operates, but our ancestors had no concept of owning land. If you think about it, the idea of ownership is only a legal term anyway. Like money, you can't take it with you."

"Anyway, historical detectives consider what they do a privilege. They are explorers. It is more than a job, it's an adventure. A historical detective is unlike an archeologist who documents discoveries. We make discoveries."

"And that would be you all," exclaimed Grandma who now looked at everyone in a whole new light. She was suddenly seeing me in a whole new light; her grandbaby was truly a grown woman. Nora was proud. As her mind worked, she was now seeing my whole family in an entirely different way.

"Yes, Hidalgo said, "They sent me out here to conduct research. We are supposed to run down any leads out here while June conducts ground research out west." We are now officially historical detectives."

Penny interjected excitedly. I like the sound of that, you mean we are going to get paid for doing what has, up till now been a hobby?"

"Uh huh," answered Hidalgo, "Unless of course, you intend to immediately get married, move into a trailer house somewhere and start raising a bunch of babies like all these other little girls around here.

Corey countered his tease by saying, "We intend to do just exactly that, but we are waiting on you first, after all, you are older than us."

Hidalgo grins and says, "There is more to life than making babies. There is plenty of time for that but I want to discover America first, make contributions, and then settle down. Besides, I want to be able to provide a good living for my wife and children when I settle down. I want to be able to tell my children stories about what we did and see the pride in their eyes."

In an instant, everything seemed perfectly clear in my mind. Instead of dread, I now had joy in my heart.

Reaching over to Hidalgo, I took the amulet back and placed it around my neck.

"I don't know what it is but for some reason it seems to ease my mind.

Corey says, "Well, it's supposed to drive away a demon that is bothering you."

"All I know is it seems to be working!" I exclaimed and placed it under my blouse next to my heart.

What is in a Name?

I woke up early to noise coming from the kitchen. Throwing a robe over my shoulders, I ventured into the kitchen to see what was going on. There, I found my grandmother, Nora, teaching Hidalgo how to prepare country style biscuits. While they cut the biscuits out of the dough with a small tin can, Nora was explaining how they could be prepared in a Dutch oven. After the biscuits were put into a greased pan she began an explanation on how country sausage was made. As she highlighted particularly gruesome parts of the process she would look to Hidalgo to see if she could get a reaction. This brought a laugh out of me; I had watched Hidalgo do both preparations many times while back at the ranch. I sat down at the kitchen table to enjoy the show. Nora began asking questions about the Navajos.

"Do your people still live in tepees," Nora asked?

"My people never lived in tepees, you must be thinking of plains Indians like the *Lakotas*. They now live in houses that look somewhat like the houses around here," answered Hidalgo.

"Do you still scalp people?"

"Only when they deserve it," answered Hidalgo. Hidalgo answered her questions as best that he could but I noticed a devilish grin on his face. He loved the entertainment and went out of his way to make himself a good guest.

"Actually many of my people live in traditional houses made of timbers called Hogan's and some of them live in mud houses."

"What, mud houses?" Nora was obviously mystified as to what Hidalgo was talking about.

"Sure, they are often made from adobes or mud bricks that are laid just like the bricks around here.

"Don't they melt when it rains," Nora asked. "Aren't they terribly ugly and uncomfortable? How could you possibly live in a mud house? How do you keep clean?"

Hidalgo, who had been grinning suddenly looked serious and says, "Adobes are made from mud and straw in an asphalt emulsion which makes them water proof. Besides, most adobes are plastered over. In Santa Fe and Albuquerque there are mud houses that are priced in the hundreds of thousands of dollars."

Nora had nothing to say after that bit of information but after a few moments she asked Hidalgo an odd question. "How do you feel about Corey getting himself a squaw?"

"A squaw," countered Hidalgo who was feeling terribly playful, surely you don't mean to say that you want your granddaughter to be referred to as a squaw? We all have a much higher regard for her."

Nora blankly looked at Hidalgo and said, "Isn't a squaw the wife or does that word just work for Indians."

Hidalgo decided to play with this for a while. "Well, first of all there is no such thing as Indians here in America unless they came over from the country of India.

Actually the term is a misnomer that goes all the way back to Columbus who was obviously confused as to where he landed."

Nora says, I'm sorry, obviously you would rather be called Navajo."

Actually it must be a very confusing nomenclature to many here in the East. The name Navajo is a Tewa word that was used by the natives who were settled in the Southwest long before the Navajos came into that area. The name Navajo means thieves or takers from the fields. Actually we call ourselves Dene which means we the people. Anglos are often confused by Native American names, take Apache for example. Apache is a Zuni word for enemy. Apaches also call themselves Dene. You will discover that Penny, Cory and I often talk about the Anasazi Indians who lived in the canyon lands to the south of Serpiente. Most modern people now prefer the name Ancestral Puebloans. I realized it is all very confusing, but imagine what it is like for us. Most so called Indian names are actually names that Europeans have given us. For example, the name Delaware; the British named those Indians after Lord De La Ware who was a brave military leader. Indians who live in Canada call themselves Inuits, rather than Eskimos which means those who eat raw flesh. The Sioux call themselves Lakotas, meaning allies or the people, but their ancient enemies, the Ojibwes, called them Nadouwesioux which means little snakes or enemies. The French shortened the name to Sioux. The Ojibwes refer to themselves as Anishinabes or the people of creation. By the way, on the way here we passed a small community called Mohawk which actually means cannibal. The Mohawks actually call themselves Kaniengehagas, the people of the place of flint.

In southern Arizona for example, the Papagos means bean eaters, a name given to them by the Pimas, another Arizona tribe. The Pima by the way, were called Pima which actually means "I don't know' which was apparently their reply when asked their name in Spanish by early explorers. The term you used to describe your grand-daughter, as 'squaw,' actually means a prostitute or something even worse. By the way, the only tribes that I know of that are called by their real names are the Hopi or peaceful ones and Havasupai which means people of the blue green water, referring to their home among the beautiful waterfalls in a side canyon of the Grand Canyon."

"Oh my," Nora says, "I have been using that dreadful term all of my life and didn't know any better. Grandma immediately went back to working on the biscuits but Hidalgo could see she was raising her eyebrows every few minutes and muttering to herself which brought a mischievous smile to his face.

Returning to the bedroom to get dressed, the events of the previous night came back to me. I was a little embarrassed by the emotions I had demonstrated. It came to my conscience that if I had gotten married right away I would be living in Camp

Creek near my family. I would be able to demonstrate to all my old friends that I could be just like them. I could do what was considered normal, living close to my family. Living close to my grandparents had been especially intriguing to me. I thought to myself, why? Why was all of this suddenly so important to me? It was as if someone or something wanted me to drop out of the race, to disappear, to become another girl raising kids in another cheap trailer house.

I then thought of Corey. His whole life was a world apart, living on a ranch in New Mexico. He could never escape his responsibilities; everyone there was dependent upon him. I had ignored my own values that had made me special in the first place. Life was becoming a grand adventure, why should I leave a life of adventure with certain romance in order to relive my mother's life. I would no longer be a member of a team. I didn't like what I saw when I glanced at myself in the vanity mirror.

When I reentered the kitchen Corey was there, looking up at me a little warily he said to me, "How are you this morning?"

"Terrible," I answered. "I have been thinking about what I have been putting you through, I'm sorry."

"No problem," Corey replied.

Hidalgo, who had been preoccupied setting the table and who hadn't said a word asked me then. "Have you ever considered that someone or something didn't want you to return to Serpiente?

I thought about it for a minute then answered, "Well, It seems like the idea of getting married, right now, and staying here in Camp Creek, got stuck in my head. It felt like an obsession. Now that I think about it all, I am mystified. It seems like a silly idea to me now. I truly am embarrassed about it all."

Hidalgo looked at her and said, "Perhaps your actions were being directed without your even knowing it. Has it occurred to you that Corey may be dealing with a demon also? It is not in his nature to be concerned about such trivial things as losing a couple of dollars playing a game like Bingo. That sort of thing is common to many of my people. It is as if an evil spirit places those ideas in your heads. Maybe they are afraid of you and don't want you to return home."

I thought about that for a minute, particularly about the part about returning home. Serpiente had become more of a home to me than any place I had ever lived. I pulled the owl amulet over my neck and handed it to Hidalgo. Hidalgo was fascinated by the object, turning it over and over in his hand and then handing it back to me. "I would appreciate it, if you would keep this with you at all times. There is something special about it, I don't know what but it is special."

"Sure," I responded. Serpiente was my home now. I could always return to

Camp Creek anytime I wanted to. In the light of day it all seemed clear to me. Perhaps something was playing with my mind, I could only wonder, thinking about my dream for a second. I had never told them about the dream I experienced on the way to Serpiente. But, one thing I knew, Hidalgo knew about things like that. He truly was an unusual Native American.

Judaculla Rock

*M*y vacation had turned into a job, but suddenly I was feeling better about myself. Perhaps a demon had been influencing me, playing games with my mind. Now those recent ideas about getting married right away seemed ridiculous. I was also realizing just how close I had come to losing Corey or ruining not only my life, but his as well. I promised myself that I would be a much more responsible person in the future, especially when it concerned other people's lives.

It would take a couple of days to rig Corey's truck out for the task at hand. We found a place in nearby White Pine where a camper shell could be installed on the truck so we didn't have to deal with rain and the expense of motels every night. Yet we were not really back on the job as one would expect. Both Corey and Hidalgo wanted to explore. This part of the country was all new to them. Appalachia was as old and mysterious to them as Chaco Canyon was to an Easterner. So it became a vacation with a purpose.

We preferred camping out whenever possible or practical. We had plenty of money but all of us had grown up being very frugal. Old habits are hard to break, or as Nora said, "Waste not, want not." Besides there would be plenty of time spent in towns where we could enjoy ourselves.

One might expect the situation to be a little odd, especially for Hidalgo, who could have easily found himself, going along on a honeymoon. But because we had worked so intensely together for the last three years it seemed like all we did was change work sites. And despite the fact that I had grown up in East Tennessee I had never actually seen any of the sites we were now planning to explore, in fact, like most of my old friends I had never been more than fifty miles away from home.

We were seeing and learning new things and had many questions to answer; no one knew why the oldest pyramids built in America occurred in northern Louisiana or why Ice Age Clovis style materials were mysteriously being discovered in Virginia. In fact, more Clovis age sites were being discovered along the east coast than out west and the long held idea that those people had come over to America from Asia through Alaska was being questioned more and more. Certainly the vast majority of Native Indians had crossed over the Bering Straits but there were nagging questions about older contacts. We had read that during the last ice age sea levels were several hundred feet lower than they are now but it still would have taken a herculean effort for early people to have crossed the Atlantic Ocean. These were obviously mysteries to be solved.

Our first day trip was over to Caney Fork Road in Jackson County, North Carolina. My grandmother, Nora wanted us to see one of two mysterious sites that she had seen as a little girl.

One site was the Judaculla Rock. There we found a large boulder about 40 feet in circumference that was covered with rock carvings. Since the local Cherokee Indians had no idea what the carvings and diagrams meant, we knew it was of great antiquity. We studied the carvings carefully trying to match them up with the rock carvings that we were familiar with.

Even Hidalgo was stumped; he suggested that maybe the carvings were some sort of treaty between earlier people who lived in North Carolina well before the Cherokees.

I thought that one diagram appeared like a hand pointed to the last pictograph, and was showing the way to a place; it was a map. We drove the long drive back to Camp Creek intrigued but with no real answers. On the way home Grandma looked at Hidalgo and said, "Here I thought you were an Indian and could read Indian writing!" Hidalgo rolled his eyes.

Hidalgo made an attempt to make my grandmother understand about Indian writing. "When Columbus first came to the continent, there were an estimated five hundred languages being spoken. Currently there are about thirty four, seven in New Mexico alone. He asked Grandma if she could speak Spanish.

"Heavens no," Nora responded.

"Well, I can, along with several other languages but I can't put my mind into the mind of a person living thousands of years ago. Besides, the symbols seen on the rock represent something in the mind of the author. Who knows how many thousands of years ago that rock was carved and what was in the mind of the writer?"

Then with a mischievous look on his face Hidalgo asked her, "Have you ever seen English as it was written long ago? Can you read old English from five hundred years ago, or even read Shakespeare in its original print?

Nora could only say that she couldn't read Shakespeare well in any language.

The Old Stone Fort

We found ourselves filling a large cardboard box with piles of photographs and articles containing tidbits of information. In the Southeast there were few American Indian ruins for us to explore. These Native Americans lived in a vast forest, never using stone to build their structures. But I discovered that there exists in East Tennessee, as well as the entire Eastern United States, fortified mound works. The one we were to visit was situated in an excellent strategic position overlooking steep bluffs, located on the plateau between two forks of whitewater streams that combine to form the Duck River.

We explored the "Old Stone Fort" near Manchester, Tennessee, where one of the rare instances of a primitive work built in the remote uplands could be examined. It has no mounds within its large enclosure yet it was evidently designed to withstand a long siege. It is built in the forks of the Duck River, on the brow of a ravine, and it could hardly have been better placed by a military engineer. The name, "Old Stone Fort" is a misnomer, for the walls are made of earth, like all other primitive ramparts; the core of the earth fortification is stony rubble.

It has one entrance, an intricate gateway, cleverly designed to be hard to attack and easy to defend. On our visit we learned that some have been inclined to think that Old Stone Fort was erected by a band of Spaniards who strayed far inland. This is very unlikely. It required a massive amount of work to construct. Yet why it was built remains a mystery. All that anybody can say conclusively was no Indian dwelled there in the times we are aware of, and there are no Indian dwelling sites found anywhere nearby.

Both Hidalgo and I recognized it immediately as an ancient meeting place, much like the canyon pool that Corey and I had discovered in the canyons south of *Serpiente*. It was clear from literature at the 'fort' that many modern people had tried to connect the fort to biblical events or to ancient Hebrews or Phoenicians that had wandered into America.

Hidalgo became angry talking to one fellow who insisted that he was an expert on ancient America. What was so strange to Corey and I was that the fellow was a fellow Native American, a Cherokee Indian. "We Cherokees have always had a tradition that white people preceded us into the occupation in East Tennessee. Whites lived along the Little Tennessee River and they had fortifications down the Tennessee to the mouth of the Chicamauga Creek. Oconostota, the great Cherokee chief believed that his grandparents and father say that whites were called Welsh; that they had crossed the great water and landed first at the mouth of the Alabama River, and made their way to the mountain country."

The old Cherokee further explained that even earlier a Prince Madoc who was chronicled by Welsh bards put his ideas into print as early as 1584. In fact, part of Great Britain's claim to America, rather than some Italian by the name of Columbus was based upon the discovery and settlement of the Welsh under Madac shortly after 1170. According to this person, Prince Madoc taught the natives to build the structures known as Mounds all over the Eastern United States. Hidalgo knew better than this. Native Americans didn't need instruction from others on how to build their megalithic structures. It took very little time before they realized that most mysterious places could be attributed to the Woodland Indian culture. The mystery was why did they build structures such as the old stone fort or in places like Ohio, why were there giant effigies of serpents there?

While there we discovered the possibility of an Irish fellow by the name of Saint Brendon the Navigator who is said to have ventured into the area of the United States about 484 A.D. supposedly he came over in skin boats. Evidence is found all over the eastern states in the form of dug out enclosures and writing found on rocks. An example of the writing is *Caros*, shaped like a large "R" which is a combination of two letters, an "X" and a "P" which are the first letters of Christ written in *Ogham* text that were used in Ireland at the time. But then, writing was being found all over the country. In Oklahoma there were reports of *Ogham* writing that we would eventually examine.

We all had some real questions. Not only were writings discovered at Bat Creek, but in such places as; Morristown, Tennessee. There was a rock inscription there that appeared to be the same as an inscription found on a rock in a mound near Grave Greek, near West Virginia in1838. The writing on both rocks had been interpreted as being from ancient Semitic or Iberian people with the same thing written on both of them; "Mound in honor of Tadah. His wife caused this engraved stone to be inscribed." Could there be two people with the same name? Hidalgo immediately decided one or both of them were fakes. But there were other sites that were even more mysterious.

In 1891 in present day Bradley County, an Isaic Hooston Hooper discovered a wall on his property. The wall was discovered covered with mysterious inscriptions interspaced with pictograms of exotic animals, and sun symbols. The experts determined that the writings were a form of old Hebrew written by scribes from an ancient culture. They theorized that the giant document had been created in a desperate attempt to preserve their cultural knowledge and history for future generations to rediscover. Some experts thought the wall was between four thousand and four thousand and five hundred years old, constructed by one of the lost tribes of Israel. Others thought that the writing was actually tracks left from burrowing worms, making it a natural phenomenon.

The next few days we took in several sites, all either enigmatic rock carvings that were undecipherable or Woodland sites that were part of the Mound Builders. The Mound Builders were a culture of early American Indians that were centered in Cahokia along the Mississippi River. Fragments of their culture are found all over the eastern United States. The mystery is in the date. Throughout the entire world many cultures peaked in the eleventh century at about the same time. It was the same time that the Chaco Canyon phenomenon occurred. Why did they all simultaneously appear after thousands of years of dull Paleolithic culture?

Several theories have been proposed for this, such as the appearance of a supernova on July 5th, 1054. It was so brilliant that it was easily visible in broad daylight and at night was the most brilliant object in the sky. People who expound this theory say that the ancient people seeing such natural phenomena interpreted this as a religious sign and changed their way of doing things. Most archeologists believe a favorable climate was the reason cultures flourished but apparently no one theory can account for what happened throughout the world.

After this trip we returned to Camp Creek, early the next day we packed up a few odds and ends and headed toward Bulls Gap then on to Morristown. In Morristown we turned due north going through the Cumberland Gap, the route that Daniel Boone had pioneered on his way into Kentucky. To us we were all traveling over new roads, pioneering a route to Manchester, Kentucky.

The Red Bird River

The Red Bird River is the main tributary of the south fork of the Kentucky River, running over a bed of rock, gravel, and mud. The river winds through the Daniel Boone National forest draining the eastern half of Clay County, Kentucky.

Canoes often float the river in late fall and spring, the river being best described by river runners as a busy Class I with almost continuous riffles, small waves, and shoals. At higher water, several of the shoals and small rapids may be classified by river runners as borderline Class II. The Red Bird is not known as a whitewater river. Rarely there do you see those intrepid kayakers who love to flirt with death, showing off their skills.

In the Red Bird River you are far more likely to see a solitary fishing rig with crusty old souls with wrinkled faces and fishing poles in hand, wondering why in the world some foreigner like you is floating through their favorite fishing hole. The Red Bird Valley is one of the most beautiful in the Daniel Boone National Forest, with steep hills looming above the river and lush vegetation everywhere.

Setting up a car camp alongside the banks of the river was easy for us. Without mules or horses to deal with and plenty of excellent camping gear along with cold drinks in a cooler, we were in heaven; the kind of heaven that most young people never get the chance to experience. We were discovering America, and we might even get paid for doing it.

There were no stars out that night. When the water temperature is warmer than the air temperature above a river, everything is smothered in a shroud of fog. The mood of the river had changed along with everyone else. Visibility was only a few yards. While the three of us sat on the edge of the river an absolutely silent apparition appeared.

An ancient derelict boat was drifting downriver through the mist, silently slipping along in this eloquently mysterious river. A homemade fishing rig, an anachronism to today's plastic and aluminum boats, floated into view, meandering through the maze of gravel bars. Even after several minutes we still couldn't make out the old man who was commanding the fishing rig. Everyone felt a little nervous; we had heard stories of arguments, shootings and disappearances along rivers. We didn't want to startle the apparition; an altercation was the last thing we wanted to be involved with.

As the old fisherman drifted into within a few feet of us, Hidalgo cleared his throat to allow the man to know that we were there.

"Hello, came a voice from the apparition; then a face appeared with long disheveled grey hair and beard. "I'm just fishing, not bothering anyone."

Hidalgo answered him, "You are not bothering us, come on over and let's chat awhile, besides I'm getting tired of dealing with these two lovebirds, looking at Corey and me. They don't seem to want to talk to me, just hug each other.

The old man was more than willing to talk to Hidalgo. "The fishing should be really good tonight but I haven't caught a thing, I haven't eaten anything since early this morning and it doesn't look like we are going to have anything to eat tomorrow morning, much less tonight. You got any extra grub to eat?"

"Sure," answered Hidalgo. Corey and Hidalgo helped him out of his home made watercraft and Hidalgo signaled for me to bring some food from the trucks. Upon examination of the boat, it was apparent that the old man was sincere. He had no gear other than a homemade fishing pole and some cans which presumably had fish bait in them. A boater in this vast emptiness of humanity, what was he doing there?

Not really knowing what to say, the old man explained that his wife of forty years would each day drop him and his old boat off upriver and he would float downriver to catch their daily supply of food. "Can't afford to go to those stores in town," he volunteered. "Besides they always cause trouble for me and Lily, my wife. We prefer just to live out here during the summer and return to our cabin in Hancock County over in Tennessee when it gets cold. Say, are you an Indian or something? You look different than these hillbillies around here."

Hidalgo didn't quite know how to answer him but he explained that he was a Navajo from New Mexico and then started to explain what they were doing there. "We have come here to examine the mystery rock in Manchester."

"Yeah," he responded. That old rock was part of the cliffs overlooking the river and has been there for many years. Nobody really knows who carved the pictures on it but I suspect that they were early white people who came into this area. What some people believe though, is that ancient Phoenicians made the journey across the Atlantic to the Gulf of Mexico. Desiring to explore the new lands they had discovered they paddled up the Mississippi until they encountered the confluence of the Ohio River, from there they continued until reaching the Kentucky River. Always taking what appeared to them at that time the biggest fork of the river, they continued until they reached this river, the Red Bird River. This land was given the name Kaintuckee by the first pioneers of the 18th century because that was what all the Indians called the territory."

"The Phoenicians discovered wild turkeys here that resembled peacocks that lived in their homeland. Because the birds were similar, they named the place Tukkiy. The word was spelled "Kentuck" by the first historian, John Filson. The Virginia Assembly spelled the name "Kentucky" when it became a county of the state of Virginia."

"Anyway, years ago the whole rock fell down when they were constructing the road through here. They loaded it up on a large truck and hauled it into Manchester so they could draw tourist in."

Listening and enthralled by the conversation, I had already returned with an armload of French bread, cheese, ham, and a large bag of potato chips. As we sat and watched, the old man began wolfing down food, pausing every few seconds to stuff a morsel into the pockets of his tattered jacket. Obviously the man was famished and was trying to hide some of the food for his mate.

I returned to the truck and gathered up another supply of food which I put into a cardboard box that I placed into the floor of the old boat. Noticing what I was doing, he stopped stuffing bits of food into his pockets and appeared to be very grateful.

Hidalgo had noticed that the old man's face was very dark, made even darker because of his white hair. "You are not one of the local hillbillies are you," asked Hidalgo?

"Be careful," many of them would get into a fight with you if you used the word hillbilly even thought they might brag about being a hillbilly themselves. "No, he answered, "I am a Melungeon."

Mystified, Hidalgo asked him "What in the world is a Melungeon?" The old man was hesitant in his answer; he seemed to be afraid to explain himself as if there was something terribly wrong about the fact that he was a Melungeon.

"Ask around, people will tell you about us. I hate to be unsociable but my wife has not eaten as much as I have. Thank you for the food and company." With that he climbed back into the relic of a boat, pushed off and began paddling, rather than just drifting, with the current, disappearing into the fog.

Melungeons

*T*he following day, after breakfast, we returned to Manchester, Kentucky where we pulled up to a very small but public library. Inside we got directions to the Manchester Mystery Rock and collected several small publications that were for sale by local authors. Sitting down at one of the tables the library provided for people to read, we browsed thought the short pamphlets we had acquired and Hidalgo read through one small book about Melungeons he discovered on the shelves.

From the booklet: "Melungeons are a Tennessee mystery people who were living alongside the Cherokee Indians when the first Scotch-Irish peoples moved into this area. Melungeon people themselves, have always preferred to have been associated with descendants of Portuguese pirates or sailors. Early on, they anglicized their Portuguese names to those of settlers in the Marlboro, South Carolina area. Whether they were pirates or merely shipwrecked sailors would have made no difference. Their only safety lay in changing their names. With the passage in 1699 of the stringent anti-piracy laws, rope happy citizens were apt to act first and think afterwards. They appear to have settled near the headwaters of the Pee Dee River some time before the American Revolution and to have drifted north into the mountainous areas of East Tennessee.

It was a rough time for them. Not only were the land transfers still in a state of confusion at the present, so was the confusion over the color line. In 1844, three hundred and ten free persons of color were listed along with whites, slaves, and all others which meant Indians.

They were classified as mulattos because of their dark coloring. As such, they were required to pay taxes, but were not allowed to vote or hold office and of course Negroes were not legally citizens until after the Civil war. During the Civil war the Melungeons were ruthless guerrillas, preying on both sides of the conflict."

One quotation caught Hidalgo's eye; "Early in the last century, when the white folks first came here, the Melungeons was already here, holding all the good land in the creek bottoms. The white folks were covetous of that good land, but didn't want to just take from the Melungeons, brutal like. Well, it wouldn't abeen no trouble if the Melungeons was ordinary heathen Indians. They would a just kicked 'em out. But here they was sorta living like civilized folks, and they was speaking English, and some were believing Christians. But their skins were brown on account o' their Injun blood. So the white folks begin sayin' nobody with nigger blood could vote, hold office, or testify in court. Then they went to court and before long they got hold o' that good bottom land. So, there wasn't nothing' left for the Melungeons to do but move up on the ridges."

In the last few years, due to the modern serological studies, the mysteries of the Melungeons have partially been solved. They are indeed descended from Portuguese.

The Manchester Mystery Stone

After prompting by the locals, we learned a few things about the Manchester Mystery Stone. Indeed it had rolled down to the main rode during construction and was carried to the town. It was even rumored that it was being considered for a documentary for PPS television. This particular slab of lenticular sandstone has many carvings of what is believed to be a Phoenician message written from over two thousand years ago. There apparently is several ancient languages involved, making the writing almost undecipherable.

From the pamphlet I read out loud for everyone's benefit. "The Golden Age of the Phoenicians lasted for only about three hundred years. Born in about 1,150 BCE, from the fusion with *Cherethites* and *Pelethites,* it was nearing its end by about 850 BCE. For three hundred years the cities of Lebanon had been independent and had become rich solely on the basis of a few small ports and a coastline of about two hundred and fifty kilometers, a bare minimum of land and possessions. Seen in this light, 'wonder' is inadequate to describe their achievements."

"The Phoenicians have always seemed rather an uncanny and mysterious people, particularly to the Greeks. The Hellenes could not understand how this tiny race had succeeded in building up an empire which spread over almost the entire area between Gibraltar and the Lebanese coast, and it was all the more difficult to understand because their empire was so elusive."

"The Phoenician empire was not built upon great cities and ports but rather dense networks of trading routes, routes over large bodies of water whose only visible trace was the wake left by a fleet of fragile ships. Where evidence of Phoenician cities has been discovered, they were always sea oriented. The land served these people as a base from which they could launch themselves into their true element, the ocean. The

Phoenicians, or more exactly, the most important of many tribes which later came to make up the Phoenician race, came, as far as we know, from the Sinai, between the Gulf of Suez and the Gulf of Aqaba."

"Deserts seem to make good incubators for the human race. The Bible describes migrations of this Bedouin tribe. The question of how this nomadic people from the desert took to the sea is a mystery. A precondition was wood suitable for building ships, amply provided by the abundant cedars of Lebanon. A simple process therefore; they came, they conquered, and from nomads of the steppes' became 'nomads of the sea.' They gradually developed from the small beginnings of primitive coastal navigation to the navigational techniques which later enabled them to extend their empire from Lebanon to the Mediterranean and even across the Red Sea to the east coast of Africa. All of this occurred between the period of 1200 B.C. and 900 B.C."

Exploring Eastern Pre-History

We learned of many mysterious sites and discussed plans to explore them. We had planned to go north all the way to the Viking sites, documenting them and hopefully getting some research leads. Along the way we planned to visit universities, historical sites, museums and anywhere else where we could ask questions. We had learned long ago that showing up in person often produced interesting meetings with people who would discuss the subject off the record. We were working, yet it seemed like play to me. Everyday seemed to have a new adventure and learning experience.

One place we wanted to visit was in New Hampshire, located on a farm and was being billed as the Stonehenge of America. No one knew who had built it. But some of it seemed no different than many other large structures found throughout America. After some exploration of the site people had found small tunnel like structures that allowed a beam of sunlight to focus on an alter rock at the summer solstice. Was it built that way on purpose or was it just a coincidence?

The site also had a rock structure that for all purposes appeared to be a sacrifice alter. The problem was it could also be a table used by farmers to butcher hogs or other animals. The groove along the edges of the rock would collect the blood from the animal that would be processed into such epicurean delights as blood pudding.

One site, however, definitely did seem to have some merit. Off the coast of Halifax, Canada an ingenious treasure trap was discovered on Oak Island. In 1795 a teenager found what appeared to be an underground shaft which later revealed alternating layers of flagstone and timber. Thinking that possibly pirate treasure was hid in it excavations took place but after a certain depth, the shaft would fill in with water preventing the workers from continuing excavation. It turned out that the core shaft had feeder tunnels stretching to the ocean deliberately flooding the areas once one of the tunnels was hit.

Experiments with red dye traced three connected tunnels and it was soon assumed that more tunnels would be found further down. Despite all that, money poured in from investors such as politicians the like of Franklin D. Roosevelt, movie stars such as John Wayne and other businessmen hoping to be a part of a new discovery and treasure. Being unable to dig deeper to access the treasure the workers used drills and cameras in an attempt to discover what was down there. They reported finding strange markings on stones, fragments of paper with an unknown lettering on it and they supposedly caught a glimpse of what appeared to be tools, some which looked ancient and others with futuristic appearances. It is said that they even managed to bring up a piece of gold chain. They were also able to determine that there were higher than normal concentrations of mercury and radiation. Whatever was buried at the bottom of that hole is truly a mystery and considering the amount of work that must have been involved in building the site, something incredibly valuable was hid there. But then again, it might just be a natural sinkhole with nothing in it: which due to the amount of money used in its exploration is why it now is called the money pit.

The Answer in the Food

After spending the morning in the library we decided to find a good restaurant where we could enjoy a good meal without the chores of cleaning up afterwards. I opened the conversation with a simple question.

"Hidalgo, you don't really believe that outsiders discovered America before Columbus, do you?"

His answer surprised both Corey and me. "First of all, I believe that Native Americans discovered America well before the last ice age. Their achievements stand for themselves. We conquered and adapted to this entire continent eventually dividing ourselves into many tribes, speaking over five hundred languages. At that time the world's oceans were hundreds of feet lower than they are now, the water being locked up in the ice sheets that covered all of Canada and much of what is now America. It is highly unlikely that these early settlers came all at once; in fact there is mounting evidence that some may have arrived here some forty thousand years ago. Certainly they were here some eleven to fifteen thousand years ago. The real question is; how they got here. Some people are now saying that they didn't just walk over, many of them may have followed the coast all the way down to South America in kayaks. Food is much easier to obtain along a coast line than in the interior of the continent."

"I thought they were killing large animals like mammoths and bison which were in abundance," Corey says.

They did, but have you ever looked at migration rock carvings found all over the southwest? They look like swastikas. Unlike my people, the Navajo who migrated south from what is now Canada, the *Anasazi* appear to have entered America from the south, not the north.

"But what about people other than Indians," I asked.

"The coast line of America is littered with thousands of ships which are just now being explored due to the development of modern diving equipment. There is much mystery as to when all those ships got here. Besides there are Native American legends, especially in South America, that speak of other peoples from across the oceans that have visited them. For example, who discovered America? One legend which persists in the legends of nearly all Indian cultures is the stories of Viracocha and Quetzalcoatl. They were bearded white people and flying serpents who supposedly taught the native peoples great things and then returned to where they came from, promising to return some day. But there are other tantalizing mysteries to solve. There is research currently going on about a European people known as the *Solutreans*. The *Solutreans* culture may have come from present day France and Spain from roughly 21,000 to 17,000 years ago. They were known for their distinctive tool making which was characterized by bifacial, pressure-flaked spear heads. There is evidence that they may have influenced the development of the Clovis tool making culture in the Americas.

I thought about this for a while and agreed that the mystery certainly would not be solved that day without evidence other than rock carvings that could be easily faked.

Hidalgo then grinned and reaching over stabbed the sweet potato I was eating with his fork and said. "There is your concrete proof; you are eating it."

Laughing, I stabbed back at my sweet potato and said; I don't know what you're talking about but you can't have my sweet tater."

Hidalgo pulled his fork back and set back into his chair. "Let me explain. Everyone knows that corn or maize was domesticated here, probably somewhere here in the eastern states but what many people don't think about is that sweet potato that you are eating. They have been found all over the Pacific Ocean on islands as diverse as Easter Island and Hawaii. The sweet potato was domesticated along with all potatoes in what is now Peru. How did they wind up all over the Pacific? Obviously ancient Polynesians came to this continent way before Columbus discovered America."

Hidalgo continued. "Actually, almost everything on your plate is a mystery. Do you know where chickens first came from?"

"From here in Kentucky where the first Kentucky Fried Chicken comes from," I answered playfully and with a grin on my face.

"Well, countered Hidalgo, great tasting chicken certainly does but the first chickens were domesticated in Southeast Asia, yet they are finding chicken bones at archeological sites in South America. How did they get here? There are many mysteries such as how copper that came from the Great Lakes region has been discovered on ancient boats in the Mediterranean. Or why *Jomon* pottery that was developed in Japan is found in Ecuador. Not only that, but archeologist have discovered diseases in mummies that they know came from Japan. To this day there are Asian features in the local *Valdura* Indians that live in Ecuador." The real question seems to be not who discovered America before Columbus, but rather who didn't."

"I don't know," countered Corey, "but we promised that before we went to Cahokia we are supposed to check in with the ranch. I'll call my relatives in Albuquerque and see if they have heard anything from June and Ken."

A few minutes later he returned with a worried look on his face.

"What's up, asked Hidalgo.

"We have a problem, answered Corey.

A Return to El Montano del Serpientes de Casabel

Corey and I traveled in our pickup truck while Hidalgo drove his truck all the way back to Serpiente but on the way we made some decisions about what we were going to do with our lives. We had money as a result of the emeralds so we didn't need regular jobs. We wanted to do something special. Hour after hour we talked it over and finally it dawned on us that what we enjoyed more than anything else was solving mysteries; usually within a historical setting, having grand adventures, and detective work. While we were finishing our college we would be historical detectives and of course we had Hidalgo to help us. What could possibly go wrong?

We found out what could possibly go wrong almost as soon as we entered the old ranch house. Both Ken and June were subdued with mixed emotions. On the one hand they were thrilled that we were home. On the other hand, they were obviously worried.

"Our thieves are at it again," announced Ken. Ken explained that the last two times that they had tried to go to *El Montano de Serpientes* they had been shot at and were unable to complete their normal rounds at the mountain. The authorities had been called but as usual, they were too far out in the country for them to really do anything. One policeman simply suggested that they shoot back, something that was very unlike June and Ken. Sure, they had a right to defend themselves but the thought of actually killing someone was something they didn't relish at all, besides they might be the ones who would get shot. In the canyons and mountains of Serpiente if someone got shot the body might not be found for months if at all.

Corey and Hidalgo spent the next few days putting a backcountry trip together, making sure this time that they were well armed with rifles, pistols, and determination. They took their time getting underway, making every attempt at secrecy that they could manage. They wanted to be stealthy.

Camping at a different spot than usual the first night, they took turns watching the ridges until well after dark before they all retired to their sleeping bags.

"What a honeymoon, said Corey sarcastically the next morning."
I answered him with "I know what you mean." I had almost forgotten what it was like sleeping out on the hard ground." It was a sarcastic answer, during the last couple of years I had spent almost as much time sleeping on the ground under the stars as in

a bed. Corey was slow getting into the spirit of things. I teased him by saying, "What's the matter? Have you forgotten how to dig a hip hole so you can sleep comfortably?"

We laughed but we also knew we had some serious strategies to plan. We walked over to where Hidalgo should have been sleeping only to discover that he was gone. We fixed breakfast thinking that he would return in a few minutes but it was a full two hours before he finally showed up.

"I need coffee," announced Hidalgo as he sat down.

"Where have you been," I queried? "We have been worried sick about you."

"Well, said Hidalgo after a long sip of coffee that was well sugared and creamed, "I have been scouting the trail ahead. I can't find a trace of anyone. Let's travel on to the next camp and I'll scout from there. By the way, sorry about slipping out on you two but I wanted to give you some privacy and I really think it would be a good idea to scout ahead before we run into someone."

We all then had breakfast, packed up the horses, and slowly retraced Hidalgo's path always looking for the slightest movement or sign of trouble. By the second night we were feeling more confident but the going was agonizingly slow. It took us four days to reach my rattlesnake ruins that I had accidentally discovered over a year before.

We wondered if there was evidence of further activity by artifact thieves there. It seemed unlikely however the thieves had picked the place clean. It made a great camping spot for them as it did for us. As we did the first time we discovered the ruins, we carefully climbed the sheer cliff, using the small footsteps dug out by the ancient inhabitants. These were the most impenetrable ruins in the area yet the trash from the pottery thieves was still there, littering the floor of the ruins. We camped after carefully hiding the horses in a grove of cedar trees well below the ruins.

The next day we walked to *El Montano del Serpientes de Casabel*, the volcanic cone that had been the home of the mirrored and mysterious rattlesnakes. The first thing we noticed was that a large section had been cut out of the side of the cone with a Bobcat. Bobcats are very small and portable bulldozers that can be dropped into the backcountry by using a helicopter. The cut exposed thousands of small tunnels that were the homes of the rattlesnake clan.

Hidalgo said, "Look at this," picking up one of many canisters that littered the ground.

"What are they" I asked.

"Gas canisters, says Hidalgo. Someone has forced poison gas into the rattlesnake dens, and this stuff" he said, holding one up, "is deadly poison."

"Our pottery thieves must have thought that by killing the rattlesnakes they could find treasure inside of the mountain."

Corey said, "It looks like all they found were tunnels going through the pumice. Either the rattlesnakes hid the treasure far underground and only brought out a small amount at a time or they only brought out what they themselves had found."

Overwhelmed by sadness I said with resignation, "They killed the goose that laid the golden eggs."

"That's probably true," said Hidalgo; "I seriously doubt that any of the rattlesnakes survived the gas."

Returning to the cliff ruins where we had left our camping gear we settled in to camp one last night before we returned to the ranch. That evening we built a nice campfire, since we now had no fear of the thieves. The thieves would have left as soon as they figured out that there was no longer any treasure to be found.

We three friends slept well that night. The next morning we sat around the campfire enjoying coffee and a great meal of bacon, eggs and potatoes. Corey and I were pretty sad but in only a short while we noticed that Hidalgo seemed in good spirits. "I don't understand. I realize that we have accumulated a lot of wealth over the last year, but what about the rattlesnake clan?"

Hidalgo grinned and replied, "Last night was a full moon."

"I still don't understand, I said.

"Well," Hidalgo answered with hope in his voice, "You know how those rattlesnakes are almost impossible to see, but they will sparkle when there is light on them. Last night I saw two rattlesnakes crawling along the base of the cliff. If they are male and female rattlesnakes I suspect that our story is not over."

"Wonderful," I said. "I was hoping that as crafty as the members of the rattlesnake clan have proved themselves to be, that they would not all be in the same place at the same time. Besides, they seem to be far smarter and more mysterious than I could even imagine."

A golden era had vanished between the human clan and the rattlesnake clan. What the future would bring I could only guess but it didn't foretell good things for the human clan. These were not really rattlesnakes that we were dealing with, they were an alien life form. They could be highly revengeful creatures.

My relationship with Corey, as well as Hidalgo also changed dramatically. We were now a team and from now on it would not just be my story but rather our story.

The Mystery of Mr. Owl

June looked down at me as she looked through the stacks of papers on the shelf. She was multitasking as usual looking for documents concerning correlational studies involving dendrochronology, climatology and sedimentational studies of the Chaco Canyon site while answering Penny's questions. She truly wanted to know what the area was like thousands of years ago. Was it a free running stream in the bottom of a canyon that was situated in a vast pine forest? Was the area an inviting place to build the oldest structures there by the Anasazi Indians? She was concerned. According to some reports of those who study field mice nest the area was much like it is today; a vast desert with no water except an occasional rainstorm to provide water for the usually bone dry *arroyo* that makes up Chaco Creek. It has been a desert since the last Ice Age. For a moment she thought of the sign erected by the National Park Service; No Fishing! It is unlikely that there has ever been a fish in that particular creek.

I looked up from my notebook and again asked June for her thoughts on marriage. June focused on my question and answered. "What is marriage? Well, it is different things to different people. Did you look up the word in the dictionary?

"Sure but it was a little disappointing, kind of like talking to a lawyer."

June asked, "What did it say?"

"It is a legally and socially sanctioned union, usually between a man and women that is regulated by laws, rules, customs, beliefs and attitudes that prescribe the rights and duties of the partners and accords status to their offspring."

June thought about the definition for a moment and says, "I always thought of it as a commitment of support to another person both emotionally and financially for the rest of your life."

"That sounds a lot like what we have here in Serpiente, "I replied. "None of us are biologically related yet we all have a commitment of support to each other."

"That's true, answered June the only thing is, Ken and I have not had children of our own. We wanted children in the beginning, it just never happened. But then, we have children here all the time, not to mention you, Corey and Hidalgo. Marriage is far more than just a legal contract between two people in order to determine taxes, property ownership; it definitely has its advantages. But then I suppose from the earliest cave man, men have been promiscuous if given the opportunity. It seems to be human nature for them to want to have sex with as many women as they can. But women want the security that marriage provides; someone to help her take care of the children that usually result. Actually there are many advantages that marriage offers, especially from the women's point of view. Married people live a lot longer than unmarried people. They also have fewer physical and emotional problems. And of course being married is certainly better if one considers taxes. Single people always pay more."

"I guess Hidalgo could be a problem to explain if you counted him."

Laughing, June responds with, "Not really, we have always thought of Hidalgo as family. Let me simplify all this for you, marriage is having a soul mate, someone that you truly can share your life with. If you want to know the truth, it takes time to learn to be married. Having a big wedding ceremony is just something to show off with. I realize that in some families it is very important but that is not what makes up a marriage. A marriage is finding a soul mate; the rest is just legal and religious customs. By the way, it looks like Corey and Hidalgo are returning."

A few minutes later Corey and Hidalgo piled out of a truck looking worried.

"What is the matter?" I asked them as they entered the ranch house.

Corey sat down at the kitchen table, his usual place when serious talking was to take place. "I sent a letter to Cherokee, North Carolina, addressed to Mr. Owl. I wanted to thank him for all the help he had been to me. I don't understand it. According to the postmaster in Cherokee there is no such person living there. I then called the motel where I spent those days after my fall and asked if they could give me an address for his granddaughter who worked there and they assured me that no such person ever worked there. I don't get it. I was under the delusion that he had lived there for years and yet there is not a trace of him there. The postmaster, who should know about such things, says that the closest family with the last name Owl is several miles away in an entirely different town but there are no records that there was ever a Mr. Owl in Cherokee.

"Did you contact the local Indian agency or Cherokee Tribal Council in Cherokee?" asked June.

"Well, they did give me the number of a member of the Tribal Council, a Mr. Amadahy but when I called there he knew of no Mr. Owl, I think he thought I was a prank caller."

"Well, he didn't just drop in from the sky," I said, "There has to be a record of him there somewhere. He told you he was a woodcarver and sold his wares in Gatlinburg. I'll bet that if you contacted the business bureau there, they would be able to help you."

"Well, I thought about that but there is no record of a Mr. Owl or even a woodcarving shop. They certainly sell a lot of carved objects in Gatlinburg but there is nothing in the records about a shop that is specific to woodcarving and of course there is no one that has ever heard of a Mr. Owl. He is not listed in any phone book, nor is he in any of the records of the Cherokee tribal council." Corey responded. "I'll keep trying, but for now, I have no idea how to find him, I'm beginning to wonder if he was all just a dream.

Hidalgo finally entered the conversation with one simple statement, "Maybe he was just a dream. Maybe he is a Shaman. Stranger things have happened."

Hidalgo continued, "Well maybe he is just a figment of everyone's imagination, but Penny certainly still has the owl amulet around her neck. How do we explain that?"

Corey who was obviously mystified simply shrugged his head back and forth. He had no idea what had happened even though he had crystal clear memories and even a couple of small scars from his time in Cherokee, North Carolina.

The Wedding

Many times in my life I have laid awake at night thinking about my wedding. Then as sleep overwhelmed me, I would continue dreaming about the wedding that virtually all young girls think about. Everyone I knew was there including Mom and Jed as well as Uncle Ken and Aunt June. Of particular importance to me were Grandma and Grandpa who seemed so proud of me. Hidalgo was the best man who as usual when involved with formal situations was uncomfortable but stoically doing what was expected of him. Many of the people in the audience stared at Hidalgo, not because of distrust or concern but rather because of simple curiosity. All of my friends from high school were there even though they looked a little older than I remembered them and of course many of them carried tiny babies with them. It seemed like the entire community of Camp Creek and East Greene High School, turned out for my wedding. It was so large we had to have the ceremony in Greeneville. Many people showed up and then left when they realized they could never fit into the church despite the fact that it was much larger than our high school gymnasium.

My dress was floor length white satin covered with lace and tiny white seed pearls that sparkled from the reflection of the candles all around the huge sanctuary of the church. The sanctuary would easily hold two hundred people and was packed.

The train on my dress dragged out behind me for about a foot and the veil was held in place by a silver tiara. It was covered with the tiny seed pearls like my dress. My shoes were also white satin with a one inch heel. I was sure that I would look like the princesses in my story books.

I was carrying a large bouquet with white lilies, roses, and baby's breath tied with a white satin bow that hung almost to my knees.

Patricia and Anna, my cousins, were my bridesmaids and they wore blue dresses with the tiny seed pearls on the bodices. They carried small bouquets of lilies and daises dyed blue, and baby's breath.

I fell into a deeper sleep for a while. In my dream I was telling Grandma all about my dream wedding. We talked about the dresses. Grandma in my dream said, "It will be hard to find dresses that are just like you have pictured, and they probably will have to be ordered. Also, they will be expensive. I think that you need to pay for the dresses and give them to your cousins. You also need to pay for the tickets for your cousins to get here. It is not fair to ask them to spend that kind of money on your wedding."

"Have you thought how much the dresses, the minister, renting the church, paying the minister, and paying for the rehearsal dinner, and the reception after the wedding will cost?" added Grandma. I know that you and Corey have the jewels that the serpents have given to you, but do you really want to spend all that money on a wedding, asked Grandma's voice in my head? "Do you really want to spend what you have saved? Isn't there something else that you may need in the future?" My grandmother was always practical even in my dreams.

The following Monday morning without anyone knowing what we were doing, Corey and I drove to the county office of Valencia County and acquired a marriage license then went to the Valencia County Health Department for blood test. A week later, we showed up at a small chapel in Los Lunas with a mystified Hidalgo who had no idea what was going to happen. In the tiniest of chapels a Navy Chaplin married Corey and I while Hidalgo, dressed in work cloths comprised the entire bridal and groom assembly. He was best man, best lady, court, witness and everything thing else that relates to a fancy ceremony. During the ceremony I had a flash, remembering the overpowering vision dream I had so long ago. I had feel in love with the cracked blue eyes and all that came with them. My dream had come true.

Despite it all, we loved the very informal ceremony. It was more in our nature than a gaudy and costly wedding. We decided that we could raise children at any time. We could certainly afford raising them now, and we still had thousands of dollars stashed away in bank accounts in all our names. But for now, we were drawn to something that seemed more important. We were determined to explore the possibilities of actually being historical detectives even thought I wasn't at all sure how it all worked. One thing I was sure of, I was part of a family.

Part 3

Rinconada de Tiempo

No power and no treasure can outweigh the
extension of our knowledge.

—Democritus

The Geology Lecture

$\mathcal{D}$r. Douglas began to ramble as he came to the end of the geology lecture he was delivering to sophomore and junior students. He knew that with these students he couldn't get too technical with his lectures yet he expected real accomplishments from them when it was time for the final exam. He had exhausted the subject of stratigraphy, the science or study of rock layers. Yet having several more minutes to fill during the afternoon lecture, he allowed himself the luxury of drifting from the subject of today's topic. It was a favorite ploy he used. By combining a personal hobby and the science that he taught he found that he could sometimes engage their interest.

"Whether by hiking, canoeing, horseback riding, or in a multitude of other ways limited only by the imagination of the traveler, realization quickly comes to the knowledgeable and observant traveler that there are mysteries evident everywhere. Incredible ambiguities exist, true puzzles." Dr. Douglas began, and then he stopped for a moment and studied the faces of his students. They appeared to be engrossed in what he was saying yet he didn't want to cross the academic line and wander to far from the subject at hand.

"The Southwestern United States make up a unique area that is rich in geological features and scenery. A close examination reveals hidden worlds out there, with clues in evidence of every conceivable environment, climate, flora and fauna. Just pick up any rock, it will tell you a story, if you know how to read and interpret what that rock is telling you."

An avid field geologist and outdoorsman he couldn't help himself, he had to tell this story as colorfully as he could, and this story had been stuck in his mind for some time.

"In Albuquerque, New Mexico there is a canoe club called The

Adobe Whitewater Club. In their newsletter an article was billed as the first ever decent down the Rio Puerco river. Even by New Mexico standards the Rio Puerco is not much of a river most of the time. It originates as a tiny mountain stream well past the tiny town of Gallina in Rio Arriba County. Below Cuba, New Mexico, without prolonged rain, the Rio Puerco normally disappears into the soft alluvial soil, interspaced with slick deposits of clay in the bed. With rainwater the arroyo could theoretically be run by kayak from Cuba to its confluence with the Rio Grande River near Bernardo. And so to test this possibility, a handful of kayaks were being flushed down this unlikely river that slowly meanders south through sandstone plains that have escaped the lava flows of more recent geologic events. For miles, in many sections of the decent down the river, climbing the banks to escape would be impossible as the river cuts a vertical channel giving the appearance of a deep crack in the earth. The mystery is why would anyone want to run it in the first place?"

A couple of hands went up in the lecture hall from students who were over achievers not realizing that they were not really being asked that question.

Dr. Douglas continued after a short pause to see who was rising their hands, "Plausible answers abound. Perhaps a desperate chance for adventure shrouded by that ideal search for knowledge, research conducted with on the job experience; maybe just plain bravado. One can only guess their motives, but I applaud those river runners, they are a rare group of individuals."

Being a river runner himself, he liked the spin he put into the discussion which helped to generate empathy for the characters in his stories. At this point, he was having fun and apparently the students were too. Being a Colorado school and dealing with young people many of whom had run at least a few of the local rivers around Colorado, they had an idea what it was like. They could relate. Actually, whitewater rafting was one of the fastest growing industries in the state.

"About two-thirds of the way down the river, the people in the article gave up in disgust, probably the result of numerous mandatory portages, too much sun, and let's face it; it wasn't any fun slopping through the liquid mud. But for the knowledgeable, they were floating through a most interesting place. They were floating down a relatively new channel cut through rocks that formed a truly ancient beach. Who knows? Maybe they were at least partially drawn down the river by a fascination of descending through geologic history and arriving at the edge of a vast prehistoric sea."

Looking carefully at several of the students he noticed that they were taking notes again. He thought to himself that they should know better than to take notes when he gets off the subject. There were no test questions on his stories. But their interest made him feel encouraged and self-satisfied.

"It would be at least another seventy million years before humans would ponder the prehistoric scenery." He paused again. "It would be like the pages from your geology book, looking back into particular slivers of geologic time. The clues are also there in the fossil bearing rocks."

"Just south of where we are today, seventy million years ago, there existed two entirely different worlds next to each other divided by a beach. Those worlds were in a perpetual interplay. The beach has changed a lot over the years but at one time it must have been a wonderful place to visit. Cutting the Cretaceous Age New Mexico and Colorado vertically down the middle, the eastern half of the states were covered by a vast Cretaceous seaway; a sea displaying abundant life producing rich fossil beds with much greater fossilization of life than occurs on even modern beaches. To the west of that watery world was a vast Cretaceous desert, with blowing sand stretching as far as the eye could see, reminiscent of the Sahara of today. This surely would have been an interesting if not inviting sight. In the Sahara one can travel for days on a moving ocean of blowing sand. Disorientation, dehydration, and eventually death descend upon the unprepared. In time, the sand cements itself together into sandstone revealing every grain of its formation, ancient wind directions, and climate."

A young lady in the second row started to talk to the person next to her. Dr. Douglas met her eyes and she immediately looked down at her notebook and began writing, several students around her giggled.

"Sand, of all natural forms is most elegant, nature in the nude. A sand dune begins with any obstacle on the surface such as a stone, or bush, or anything heavy enough to resist being moved by the wind. This obstacle forms a wind shadow on its leeward side, resulting in eddies in the current of the air, exactly as a rock in a stream causes an eddy in the water. Within the eddy the wind moves with less force and velocity than the air streams on either side, creating what geologist call the surface of discontinuity. Here the wind tends to drop part of its load of sand. The sand particles, which can be visualized as bouncing, and tumbling along the surface before the wind, rather than flying through the air begin to accumulate and the pile grows higher, becoming itself a barrier to the wind, creating a greater eddy in the air currents and capturing still more sand. The formation of the sand dune is then underway."

"Sand dunes form in amazing patterns, all dependent upon variations in wind direction. Viewed in cross section, sand dunes display a characteristic profile. On the windward side the angle of ascent is low and gradual. On the leeward side the slope is much steeper, usually about thirty-four degrees, the angle of repose of sand and most other loose materials. The steep side of the dune is called the slip face because of the slides that take place as sand is driven up the windward side and deposited on and just over the crest; when the deposit of sand on the crest becomes greater than can be supported by the sand beneath, the sand slumps. As the process is repeated through the years, the whole dune advances with the direction of the prevailing wind, until some obstacle like a mountain intervenes. At this point the dunes, prevented from advancing, pile higher. The great sand dunes at the Sand Dunes National Monument here in Colorado have dunes reaching five hundred feet high. The only higher sand dunes are in Iran, where they attain a world's record of seven hundred feet. However, ancient deposits of sand dunes that have metamorphosed into sandstone are found that are many thousands of feet thick. In New Mexico and here in Colorado much of that sand has been stained blood red due to volcanic ash from ancient volcanic eruptions."

"There is evidence that ancient Nile like rivers did cut through those enormous sand deposits forming unique microhabitats, not unlike the unique desert rivers of today. These ancient river deposits are often mined for the dinosaur fossils they now produce."

"The shoreline of that ancient seaway ebbed and flowed continuously producing fossil beds with alternating layers of fossils from completely different environments. A sandy beach produced gastropod fossils. Later a forest would leave layers of coal, followed by limestone with shark's teeth scattered throughout it. Then this vast area slowly cooked over a long period of time, perhaps with many features similar to the geysers and hot springs of Yellowstone Park of Wyoming, a similarly active zone. Imagine, an immense beach lying on top of a large geothermal area. It must have been a wonderland of underwater hot springs, a haven for biological organisms."

"Underwater geothermal springs on this magnitude would be responsible for producing mineral deposits such as gold and silver on a grand scale. The largest mines in the world today are found in areas having been formed similarly."

"An examination of global maps depicting volcanic sites discloses many hot spots under the earth's crust, found independent of the major rift zones usually associated with subduction volcanoes. Hot spots, forming such places as the Hawaiian Islands and Yellowstone Park have sparked a flood of theories to explain their formation such as impact craters, mantle plumes or sub-crustal rifting. Before those volcanoes appeared what was to become New Mexico simmered for eons producing extremely complex geothermal features that would be buried by seventy million years of sedimentary and later, igneous rocks."

Dr. Douglas glanced at his watch, and discovered that now he only had three minutes left.

"During this time in southern Colorado and New Mexico a giant rift occurred. The crust became thin as this area was pulled apart. In a line going straight down the center of Colorado and New Mexico the area dropped only to be filled in again with sediments from the surrounding mountains along with the lava from thousands of volcanoes. Ten thousand feet high, Sandia Crest which is the eastern edge of that rift zone is just east of Albuquerque and currently it is crowned with Pennsylvanian Age sea fossils. Yet at the base of the mountain is Albuquerque, itself a mile high like it is here in Boulder. Below Albuquerque, some two miles below, are the same deposits of Pennsylvanian Age sea fossils as on top of Sandia Crest. The earth has become displaced that much."

He now began to speed up his presentation.

"The area north of present day Albuquerque is buried by numerous volcanic mountains such as Jemez, Naciento, Mount Taylor and thousands of minor volcanic structures such as dikes and volcanic lava flows. Located on a double geological fault, the last few thousand years has created the Jemez volcano covering much of northern New Mexico and producing the largest continental caldera on the planet, just due north of present day Albuquerque."

"Seas of lava then covered vast areas hiding world after world and, of course, all that lava piled up on top of most of the beach where all those valuable minerals and wonders were hidden. Unfortunately, after volcanoes appeared, the area produced extremely complex geothermal features that would be buried by seventy million years of sedimentary and igneous rock. Only hints of the former world can now be found."

"Today, the Rio Puerco or Pig River cuts down though rock layers of small fragments of that beach. Erosion along the banks, and along numerous side canyons, reveals a confusing stratigraphy of fossil beds. A journey along the Rio Puerco can reveal a wealth of fossils hinting about the life that existed on that ancient seashore."

"There are often strange and secret reasons why a river runner would venture down such a God forsaken river; the channel never taken, except by a curious few. Due to an absolute lack of scenery, whitewater, dangerous indigenous natives, too many mosquitoes or rattlesnakes; the reasons for a runner to attempt a river such as the Rio Puerco may carry a deep philosophical meaning, a scientific inquiry, or imminent stupidity.

The class laughed but nobody got up to leave despite the fact that Dr. Douglas was now past the scheduled end of the class.

"Once upon the water, every person is an island and a world apart, totally responsible for his own life. That is the way it is going to be when you get there. Let's hope that most of you display a physical and mental toughness when we get there. Be prepared to classify and collect a world of invertebrate fossils. This is why we will be going there on your next scheduled field trip. Class dismissed."

One of the ladies who worked in the main office walked over to him as the students picked up books and notebooks and loaded them into small backpacks, "Dr. Douglas, I have some mail that just arrived for you," she said handing him several simple letters. He quickly browsed through them until he came to one that was marked with the return address; Ken Anderson Ranch, Serpiente, New Mexico. That one he immediately opened and read.

Dr. Douglas

"Southwest Airlines Flight 1473 is now arriving at gate 14," announced the overhead intercom as I, along with my new husband Corey, and our friend Hidalgo, waited at the gate. The three of us had become very close friends over the last three years, with Hidalgo being the best man at our wedding. Corey kept glancing at me as they all anxiously watched the entryway from the tarmac for a view of Dr. Wayne Douglas, a geophysicist and amateur archeologist from Denver and a good friend of the Anderson family.

After several people walked through the entryway door, Dr. Douglas made his appearance, a disheveled professor with his carrying bag that undoubtedly contained his most personal possessions, his field notes. He was tall, lanky, and balding, yet with the dark tan he sported, it was obvious he had spent his fair share of time out in the field. He was indeed a field geologist who disliked the time he spent in the classroom teaching students who often had no idea what he was talking about. He would rather be out in the field doing real geology.

I walked up to him and introduced Corey and myself. Hidalgo then reached out and shook his hand Indian style grasping the wrist rather than the hand and slipping his hand down into a regular handshake.

Dr. Douglas seemed in good spirits, he knew he was on the percipience of an adventure, but he was a little amazed at how young Corey and I were, and as far as Hidalgo was concerned he was a little amazed, thinking to himself that this doesn't seem like something a typical Navajo would be involved with. But then, he had spent a lot of time in the field where he had worked with many Native Americans, usually in the oil production business, or dealing with them trying to get access rights to uranium deposits. He even knew a few Navajo words but was far from being able to converse with them in their native tongue.

On the way to the luggage carousal Hidalgo glanced over to Corey and me and said, "You know you can tell a world of things about a person by their hands."

"What do you mean," I replied. "Well, silky smooth hands, mean someone who never does physical labor, which means he would have to be taken care of on a trip like this. You look or feel for the little things like the bump formed where a pencil rides the tip of the index finger or well-manicured finger nails. Dr. Douglas' hands are rough and well calloused, he will be just fine.

They gathered up the professor's luggage from the luggage carousal, and then walked through the corridors lined with milling people to the La Fonda, a restaurant where a young guitarist, Hector Pimental was playing classical and Spanish music on his guitar. They ordered some food from the obliging waitress and settled down to discuss their project.

"I understand that you are the folks that contacted me at the university about a possible new find up on the *Rinconada*. Well, you can make some money from these finds or you can invest a fortune looking for a payday and finally find yourself broke. However what you hinted at in your letter was a connection to the ancient Indians that lived here in New Mexico. Sometimes the real treasure isn't found in gold and jewels but rather in an academic understanding of the ancient people themselves."

Despite the fact that Dr. Douglas was putting the meal on a university money account, they ate rather lightly that evening dining on tacos and diet cokes. Corey and I had accumulated a small fortune while working at our uncle's ranch in Serpiente, however we had been brought up to be very frugal with our money; never spending money on anything they really didn't need. It was a personal choice we had all made. Rather than watching others on a television we had decided, as a way of life, to live our own adventures. We were historical detectives.

Soon we settled down to discuss the situation. "We are dealing with a mine that was hidden by the Anasazi Indians a long time ago. The Anasazi or ancient enemies, as Hidalgo explained, hid gold, silver and turquoise mines in New Mexico hundreds of years ago."

Dr. Douglas finally spoke, "Mr. Hidalgo, I have heard a little bit about the pueblo revolt but I would appreciate it if you could provide insight into it. I would like some background information and your perception on it."

Hidalgo looked a little sheepish but responded with "I'll explain it in detail tomorrow on the way up." With that everyone finished their meal, gathered up the suitcases and duffel bags, which were heavy with gear, and headed to the parking lot, where Hidalgo opened up a brand new four wheel drive Jeep Cherokee truck that had been loaned to them by Uncle Ken. From the parking lot we proceeded to find a good place to spend the night.

The Pueblo Revolt

The following morning after breakfast we historical detectives and Dr. Douglas loaded up the Cherokee Jeep and headed toward Santa Fe, stopping for gas and a few last groceries that Dr. Douglas insisted they get. We were pretty well prepared with the rear of the jeep crammed with all manner of camping gear that spilled over to several bundles of gear tied on top of the jeep. Hidalgo did the driving and with a captive audience and several prompts from Dr. Douglas asking him questions about the pueblo revolt as well as a Navajo view of the origins of Native Indians in North America, Hidalgo finally agreed to share what he knew. As it turned out, Hidalgo had an encyclopedic knowledge of the revolt.

"According to many anthropologists the first people that migrated into New Mexico were of the Sandia culture. It is thought that they came from Siberia across the Bering Straits some thirty five thousand years ago. However, archeologists are now discovering through radiometric dating they may have been here long before that. The remains of cave fires have been carbon dated going back as far as one hundred and twenty five thousand years ago, but anthropologists just don't know for sure. The carbons deposited from those fires are old but they found no artifacts. But then again, how does a fire occur deep in a cave by itself? The earliest Americans apparently followed the coast line all the way down into South America and then migrated back northeast via land routes, probably following rivers into the interior. Many of their artifacts were discovered in a large cave on a ridge behind the crest of Sandia Peak just outside of Albuquerque."

"During the last Ice Age there is ample evidence of these people in the form of spear points actually embedded inside of mastodon bones found near Clovis, New Mexico. Ten thousand years before Christ was born, people were wandering around this area living a hunter-gatherer, life leaving evidence of their presence and even some petroglyphs showing mastodons. New Mexico was very different back then of course. Colder and wetter, it provided all the food they needed. Soon afterwards, many other clans of humans wandered into this area including Folsom Indians that appeared near the end of the last ice age. During this same time the Cochise people migrated into this area. They were apparently the first to settle into communities where they cultivated corn, squash and beans." Dr. Douglas knew all of this but listened attentively anyway.

While dealing with the traffic of Santa Fe, Hidalgo continued his story; "The Mogollon culture followed, which is why their pottery is found all over New Mexico, and at the same time the Anasazi culture took root here. They are the ones we are interested in. Just a few miles to the west of where we are going is where Chaco Canyon, one of the greatest Anasazi cities is located. All Indian tribes warred among themselves as the climate in New Mexico became harsher and dryer. Where you now see desert land the first tribes enjoyed a lush countryside filled with pine trees with game to hunt everywhere. When that lush countryside started to disappear, the people competed for the available resources. This competition for survival led to war among the various tribes."

"Then the Spanish arrived" says Hidalgo, and the tone of his voice changed, his mood became darker. "As far back as 1536 Cabeza de Vaca came into southern New Mexico and that is when the rumors of the Seven Cities of Cibola started."

"In 1540 Francisco Vasquez de Coronado invaded New Mexico looking for gold and the seven cities. In order to get rid of him the local Indians just lied about richer cities elsewhere and he followed that lie all the way into Kansas. Then in 1598 Juan de Onate established the first Spanish capital in the Tewa village of Ohke north of present day Espanola."

"So what was the problem with Spanish," said Dr. Douglas?

"Well, said Hidalgo, at that time in their history most of them were a cruel and greedy people. Most of the young Indian men were put into forced labor raising crops for the invaders. The buildings that the Spaniards lived in were all built by Indian labor at the end of a whip. In fact, many of the women were forced into slavery to take care of the lusty demands of the soldiers. And the priests, Hidalgo hesitated, they had a fanciful idea that all an Indian had to do was to be exposed to the Catholic religion and they would be saved. Saved from what? That book, the bible, supposedly had all the answers but the natives had no written language, had never needed one, and certainly had no idea what a book was, much less how to speak in Spanish! The natives were forbidden to practice their own religion, on pain of death."

We pulled into a gas station just outside of Pojaque for soft drinks and a bathroom break I desperately needed, afterwards Hidalgo continued. "The Pilgrims landed at Plymouth Rock in 1620. Meanwhile here in New Mexico there were over fifty families living in Hacienda styled homes. Most history books that students read don't take that simple fact into account. While the pilgrims were scratching out an existence on small farms on the east coast, Spanish people had been living here in New Mexico, in well-built haciendas, built by the slave labor of the local Indians."

He waited a moment while that simple fact sunk in. "But back to the pueblo revolt, the war began in Acoma when the Indians rebelled from their cruel masters. During that time over five hundred native Indian men were rounded up and the Spanish removed one foot from each of them to induce them into Christianity, then in 1626 the Spanish Inquisition was established in New Mexico. The situation yearly got worse and worse until finally a San Juan Pueblo medicine man found a way to unite the tribes to face their common enemy; the Spanish."

For some time Hidalgo got quiet as he negotiated traffic but soon he returned to his conversation. Everyone listened spellbound to what he was saying while reflecting upon their own experiences.

Hidalgo continued, "The *Encomienda* system in New Mexico allowed the Spanish to seize a portion of every Native's farm crop to support the Spanish missionaries, military and civil institutions. Then there was the *Repartimiento*, which provided for forced Indian labor to work in Spanish fields and weaving sweatshops. Then there was the Inquisition, an all-out holy war on anything that was not Franciscan Christian. This Inquisition spanned the entire 17th century."

"In Zuni," Hidalgo continued, "Over in west central New Mexico, unlike many other pueblos like Isleta, they were one of the last holdouts against the Spanish during the Pueblo revolt of 1680. Geography and isolation is probably why. Throughout the 17th century, Spanish authorities destroyed Pueblo kivas and sacred objects. Religious intolerance, in conjunction with a persistent abuse of pueblo labor prompted several pueblos to revolt. Unfortunately, the Spanish usually crushed them. In 1675, forty seven pueblo caciques, or priest were convicted of practicing sorcery and plotting to rebel against the Spanish. Four of these religious leaders were hanged. The others were whipped, reprimanded and finally released."

"Later real upsets happened when other Indian tribes came to raid. My ancestors, who had migrated from Canada, were now under the Spanish Inquisition and we despised them. It was all out war, everywhere. Not only did we fight the Spanish but my people, the Navajo, fought the Apaches as well as the Pueblo people, everyone was at war. The worst raiders were the Apache and my people, the Navajos."

"My people were hunter-gatherers who came from the north and knew nothing of farming. They did know, however, enough that when they raided a village, they didn't kill everyone. They left enough people alive so that there would be crops to steal again the following year. By 1680 the Pueblo Indians banded together and drove the Spanish out of New Mexico all the way south into Mexico, and that's the way it stayed until Don Diago de Vargas returned to New Mexico."

"When the Indians drove their cruel masters out of New Mexico they systematically hid all the old mines that they had been forced to labor in and only a few have been rediscovered."

Stories of Lost Treasure

Dr. Douglas said, "You have got to be the smartest Navajo I have ever met."

"No," replied Hidalgo," I'm just one of the few Navajos that have ever been put into a position to learn and use what they knew. As Will Rogers once said; all people are geniuses, just in different ways."

Corey said, "I've heard stories about lost mines that the Indians hid. According to what I have read, starting in the middle 1500's Franciscan missionaries came into New Mexico to plant the seeds of religion. During the late 1700's they were still coming in. During this time, young Father La Rue came from his native France to Durango, Mexico. He spent some time administrating and toiling in a small village in Mexico but decided to go north after the crops in his village had begun to fail and the local people began to move out. While in Mexico he befriended an old soldier who had been all over New Mexico and the old soldier told him about a secret he had kept for many years of a rich deposit of gold he had discovered while on a scouting trip for the army. Since the village was failing as a farming enterprise Father La Rue became desperate and decided to venture into New Mexico. In time, he and many of the desperately poor people of the Mexican village made their way north along the

Journada del Muerto and in due time they found the place described by the old soldier and made a camp by a spring.

The men searched the peak and the Basin and finally found the vein of gold. Selecting a spot where observation of them would be difficult, they tunneled into the peak. For several years work went on. The gold was stored, and Father La Rue only spent what was necessary when he went to buy supplies and tools."

"The church, finding him gone from Mexico sent an armed expedition to determine what had happened to Father La Rue and the village. Discovering that he had journeyed north in search of gold they followed him to the general vicinity to where they thought he had gone. One day, one of La Rue's men came into Mesilla for supplies for their village. He soon discovered that a party of soldiers and representatives of the Church were quartered there and that they were in search of Father La Rue and his colony. Returning to La Rue he told what he had learned. La Rue had the mine sealed and the gold hidden so no one could find it."

"It was not long before a Mexican house servant in Mesilla told the soldiers about the colony and the garrison of soldiers who were accompanying the Church representatives headed to the colony. The party arrived and made formal demand of Father La Rue that he deliver to them, in the name of the Church, the mine and all the gold which had been taken from it. The priest refused. He maintained that the gold belonged not to the church or himself, but rather to the people of the village."

"The soldiers at once opened fire. Although Father La Rue's colony was greatly outnumbered, they valiantly fought to defend their rights, refusing to surrender. In the battle he and most of his people were killed. The few who were captured and tortured died in agony rather than reveal the hiding place of the treasure."

"In time, all knowledge of the whereabouts of the mine were lost and forgotten then along came the Apache chief Victorio. Victorio plundered white settlements during the 1870's including isolated mining transports, wagon trains, settlers and even isolated towns. It is thought that he knew of the old mine where the gold bullion was hidden but had little use for it except as a place to hide even more loot. The US Cavalry engaged him in 1880, after which he fled to Mexico where he was killed by Mexican troops, leaving a mystery as to what he done with the loot he captured."

"In 1937, Milton E. Noss, a Hot Springs doctor went deer hunting in the San Andres Mountains and was climbing what was to become known as Victorio Peak when he spotted an opening in the hillside. Supposedly, he climbed down into underground caverns to discover mine workings and gold bars stacked like cordwood, each one weighing from 40 to 60 pounds. There were also Wells Fargo strongboxes containing a multitude of old coins and jewelry."

"He also discovered some twenty-seven skeletons down there, some of them chained to the walls. He managed to get out a number of sacks of the gold bars that were mostly gold and copper. He even turned over much of it to the US Mint in Denver. They confiscated the gold and gave him a receipt for almost a hundred thousand dollars' worth of gold. Ending up with a piece of what to him was worthless paper, he was furious. Fearing that Treasury agents intended to confiscate the other gold bars he had recovered, Noss returned to the cave and hid all the bars he had already recovered somewhere close by. He always claimed that only a small portion of the treasure from the original cave was ever recovered."

"So what finally happened," I asked?

"Well, the usual I suppose," answered Corey. "The U.S. military couldn't get the bars out without tremendous and dangerous effort so they used dynamite in an attempt to open up the mine, but it caved in instead. Noss enlisted another fellow, Charles Ryan to help him. There was gun play after he determined that the other fellow was trying to steal much of the gold for himself. Stories about the place circulated in many of the local newspapers particularly about the gunfight that supposedly took place. But Noss had been killed and only his wife now knew the whereabouts of the mine."

"Then in 1955, concluded Corey, "The area was included in the White Sands missile range and the entire peak and surroundings were fenced off. No one to this day is allowed into the area.

Dr. Douglas said, "So the gold is still there?"

Corey answered, "Not only is it still there, it is now the property of the United States government. You can be arrested for just trespassing on the range. They say it is too dangerous because of unexploded ordinance."

"I suppose," entering in the conversation and not wanting to be left out nor thought of as being timid, I said, "One of the most famous examples of hidden mines is the one that was found is in the Cerillos Hills, east of Albuquerque. There, turquoise has been mined by the Pueblo Indians for the last thousand years." I glanced over to Corey for a look of approval, not getting it I then smiled at Hidalgo who was nodding approvingly.

"That's true, said Hidalgo. "Even the Spanish are rumored to have hidden many things away there. During the pueblo revolt of 1680, the Spaniards from a small mission on the East side of the San Francisco River in the foothills of the Mogollon Mountains secreted a hoard of mission treasure and mined bullion from two area mines. The mines are thought to be located just west of the San Francisco River and

North of the present town of Glenwood. Somewhere in the lower foothills of the Frisco Mountains in the Gila National Forest there is supposed to be a fortune."

I continued my story as the others listened, "Others say that the Spaniards carted the treasure into the foothills of Ladrone Mountain, broke down and buried the entire loot there, wagon and all. Then they traveled using the wagon horses over to the Rio Grande River and headed south to El Paso. But then, some of my sources say they might have been discovered by the local Apache Indians who killed them. Anyway, it's all a mystery and the loot has never been found."

We were slowed down coming into Espanola as a car crash had occurred ahead of us. Attempting to fill in the lull in the conversation Corey spoke up.

"I know another story," said Corey. "Bill King who now lives in Los Lunas tells a story of his father who first opened a mine by Manassa, Colorado known as the Lick Skillet Mine. His father bought the area in order to graze some cattle, but it takes a vast amount of land to raise even one cow there. The soil is extremely thin just like it is where we are going. Under a thin layer of sand and dirt is just plain old lava, thousands of feet deep. One day while traveling across the land he discovered an indention or sink in the land and his curiosity got the best of him so he went over to explore. What he found was a shallow hole that had been covered over by felled cedar trees. Curiously he began digging into them and found a stone ax.

This wetted his curiosity even more so he dug the whole mess out. What he discovered was an ancient turquoise mine that had been hidden by the natives. He reopened the mine as the Lick Skillet Mine because he couldn't make any money until the price of native turquoise went through the roof years later. Now, his grandson is a wealthy man who lives in comfort and Manassas turquoise is highly valued because of the matrix colors in the gem rock."

Hidalgo said, "There were hundreds of mines across the Southwest that were opened by the Indians, mostly turquoise and later gold and silver. The Spanish found many of them but most were kept secret. During the pueblo revolt nearly all of them were destroyed, caved in, or just plain hidden in order to keep the Spanish from discovering them."

"Those early Spanish people were too greedy, and things have changed little. Look what happened to Native peoples all over the United States. They were removed from their lands and deported to reservations, usually the most worthless land that could be found. Then, when gold and silver was found on that land they were relocated to even more worthless land despite treaties or laws that the white man wrote. Now as they find oil or uranium on those most worthless of lands and now that they have become valuable they want us to move again. We are tired of being pushed around, but there is little we can do about it." Empathetically we looked at each other for a moment then Hidalgo suggested we find another café for lunch.

Rinconada

*W*e stopped in Espanola for one last meal that we didn't have to cook for ourselves when Hidalgo said, "I've been talking all morning, its' your turn Dr. Douglas."

Dr. Douglas stopped him mid-sentence with a "Just call me Wayne" followed with "Let me give everyone a little background geology of this area."

"The entire *Rinconada* consists of various types of extrusive igneous rock, mostly sheets of plain old black lava, formed after a series of cataclysmic volcanic eruptions during the late Cenozoic Age. Intermittent earthquake activity further fractured the lava in innumerable places. Those cracks were later intruded with many types of mineralized rock such as quartz or as hot springs which later produced deposits of turquoise and many other precious minerals. This process has continued through recent times, and in places, still continues."

"Jemez, the largest continental caldera type volcano in America is located along the southern edge of the *Rinconada*. It produced layers of volcanic rock in some places thousands of feet thick. The Rio Grande River which courses thought the eastern flank of the volcano has continued in its original course, throughout this part of New Mexico. Down river, and south of the *Rinconada*, the river has changed course many times in the geologic past. At one time it even carried the waters of the Arkansas River which flowed south, down into New Mexico but volcanism in the northern end of the San Luis Valley of Colorado changed its course to what it is today, running into eastern Colorado and finally into Oklahoma. At one time, before the Rio Grande Rift opened up, the Rio Grande River was thought to have run on the back side of the present day Sandia Mountains forming what was to become Lake Estancia. After the last Ice Age the river changed back to the course it now flows. Lake Estancia became salt beds that can still be found southeast of Estancia."

"Under that volcanic rock of the *Rinconada* is sedimentary rock with alternating and interweaving layers of rock from many prehistoric environments. Ancient seas produced limestone sediment imbedded with entombed shells, petrified wood, petrified sand dunes, coal beds, petroleum deposits, and much more."

"Underneath much of central New Mexico, volcanic activity produced a vast geothermal hot spot. This unnatural heat created a geological wonderland of geysers and warm pools for ancient creatures that lived there, such as bathing dinosaurs. An environment somewhat reminiscent of today's Yellowstone region, but much grander, warmer, and geologically as well as biologically active, the heat created vast travertine and mineral deposits throughout this era."

"Even as New Mexico became dryer and hotter at the end of the Cretaceous Era, during the latter part of the age of dinosaurs, this area enjoyed a unique semi-tropical climate with rivers flowing in places now covered with vast flows of lava thousands of feet thick."

"Geologist figure that there is a world of features under all that lava, there are fortunes to be made if only someone could get to them. Until recently, it was assumed that few knew about the mineral bearing rocks that lay beneath the hundreds, and in most places thousands, of feet of once molten rock. But there may be those who apparently know secrets, which is why I am here."

American Indian Roads

While waiting for the waitress to bring out our meals Corey reentered the conversation. "My turn, just because you have a PhD and Hidalgo knows a wealth of New Mexico history doesn't mean Penny and I don't know anything."

Corey said, "There exists now only a thin layer of soil, on top of that volcanic mesa called the Rinconada, that provides a life hold for only the meanest and toughest of creatures both plant and animal. But when people first ventured onto the Rinconada, after the last Ice Age, the climate was much wetter than it is now. It was much easier to live there, with abundant game and a vast forest of cedar and pine trees blanketing the mesa."

"Some of the people found shelter in the cliffs overlooking the Rio Grande River Gorge, looking somewhat as it does today, with cliffs that offer protection from the afternoon sun and prowling enemies. These cliffs overlook deep canyon chasms with many secret places to hide away. The Anasazi built well-worn trails throughout the Rinconada as well as the entire Southwest."

"Recently, high altitude photography has revealed early American Indian roads across the entire southwest and well into Mexico. Many long sections have even been found in places many feet wide; literally roads. But away from the major trade routes, trails are harder to trace, even with aerial photography. Sometimes there is only a trace of a trail, an ancient puzzle that tantalizes and intrigues us to know more about them. Apparently early American Indian trails were everywhere, going to places now secret and unknown. The combined effects of a hotter and dryer climate along with deforestation have all but erased them and many of the trails have disappeared. Even now, few would bother to explore the traces of those early pathways with the frigid winters and searing heat in summer which allows only a subsistence life anytime."

"But the greatest feature of the present day Rinconada is the Rio Grande Box Canyon, a deep chasm created by the tumultuous volcanic tug of war between Jemez volcano and a resilient Rio Grande River. Currently the river is winning. The river begins its decent into the layers of volcanic rock well up into Colorado, leaving deep talus piles of boxcar size chunks of black volcanic rock on the canyon sides. For most river runners the upper box is generally considered un-runable, except by the best of the best, experts in kayaks. They are people who are willing to risk their lives. People who are willing to spend more than one night sleeping on top of an angled volcanic rock because there is no other place to lay down. No beaches, no nothing accept a roaring river with endless class five rapids."

"The lower box is now the premier training ground for the whitewater enthusiast who may someday get to run the upper box. The lower race course section is easily observed from a blacktop road and it has classic river rapids, which at any water level provides thrills for thousands of New Mexico white water boaters."

"Further downriver the river cuts through the southern edge of the Jemez caldera. Along the river anywhere there is a slab of volcanic rock with a smooth surface; one is likely to find designs carved into the rocks. Then there is the Bosque where Espanola is located. Below that, in the canyon, a wealth of petroglyphs or Native American pictures can be seen carved into the rock. They can be seen all the way down White Rock Canyon from the river's edge. Frankly, we may find ourselves searching for one of those ancient trails that can lead us to our destination."

I ate the last of my hamburger, set my drink down, and asked, "What exactly is the story of the Armijo Shack?"

The Story of Armijo

"Well, I learned about this place from my uncle Bo when he was visiting us out at the ranch in Serpiente" continued Corey. "When he was a little boy his folks had attempted to homestead on the Rinconada after moving by covered wagon from Oklahoma. They lived there for about two years and finally gave up, moving on to Albuquerque where it was far easier to find work and make a living."

"A few miles down the road from the homestead was the old Armijo shack, a black tar paper shack with the exterior completely covered with flattened and nailed cans that held the black tarpaper to the re-sawn lumber of which the shack was constructed. The home had a bed, a table, and an old potbellied stove on a dirt floor. Living there was hard."

"Everyone thought Armijo was a little fetched in the head and he was obviously dirt poor. But he was also known as a walker and hiker, a traveler who disappeared for weeks at a time. Maybe he was a poet, but he never worked and was considered by some of the locals as a *borroachon veijo* or old drunk, despite the fact that he was seldom actually seen drinking anything but water. But upon closer inspection, Armijo was nothing like people imagined, certainly not an old drunk."

"One day everything changed for Armijo. While at the trading post in town it was noticed that he was paying for his few groceries and a new skillet with pure gold dust. This is a meticulous procedure, exchanging a weighed amount of the gold for goods and then the difference returned in coins. It was only a matter of time until others began to notice. Yet he would spend only the tiniest amount, from a small bag hung around his neck."

"Like many mysterious people of the southwest, he never spent a grain of dust for more than he needed. He never disclosed or talked about the source of the gold, and no one thought he had more than the dust in that tiny pouch, hardly enough to attack him for. But then, everyone was dirt poor, and desperation causes good people to do deplorable things."

"Late one afternoon, Armijo who had become a friend of the family and frequent visitor, stopped by the homestead for a visit and a meal. There was very little to eat, mainly pinto beans and a few garden vegetables with a rabbit serving as the meat, but Armijo was a particularly modest eater and he always carried a generous supply of his own tortillas. Fortunately for us, he shared them all with the family. They were a treat, fat and brown from the wood stove on which Armijo made them. Armijo never used table utensils, preferring to use a tortilla for everything utilitarian."

"The meal, of course was just a pretense for he and Uncle Bo to sneak out to the woodshed for several rounds of moonshine. In a state of drunken delirium, Uncle Bo and Armijo boasted and laughed at each other's lies, but later Armijo got serious, speaking of different worlds, and places of mystery, and especially one magical place found by pure accident. His story kept the other boys, who were well hidden but within earshot, curious and spellbound. This is that story as heard by Uncle Bo and passed on to me from his memory."

"Like hundreds of others before him, Armijo had prospected the Rinconada for the pink, quartz-bearing rock in which gold was found, and in a few tiny spots, he actually found quartz ore with gold streaks in it, but in most places the gold was too inaccessible or expensive to mine. The easy pickings had already been mined out long ago. Gold of any consequence had never been found along the Rinconada and what was found would require vast amounts of money, water to process, and know-how to get out. Armijo, like everyone, found tiny trace amounts, little or nothing."

"So years ago, he gave up prospecting and settled down to the life of a hobo, that is someone who works part time when the opportunity arises, but usually just lives by camping out and living off the land. In those days this was not so usual. Armijo was a hermit, neither seeking human companionship nor dependency on others and certainly not like so many that had learned to live off the work of others."

"One morning along the banks of the Rio Grande River, after rising from a short meal of catfish, beans, tortillas, and coffee, Armijo carefully cleaned and packed up his personal gear, hid it, and began one of those spring walks he so often took after breakfast, traveling and doing his exploring before it got hot in the day. Not particularly going anywhere or for a purpose. But from this river base camp, the only way out, besides going up or down the river, was to plunge straight up the talus rock piles in hopes of finding trails higher up. So after finding a likely spot Armijo took it upon himself to climb up the canyon wall seeking a cure for his curiosity. It was on one of those short walks that so often turns into an all day affair as he explored on; climbing past house size talus piles that lined the side of the canyon that he discovered something unusual."

"A more uninviting place to explore one could not imagine, but he could see what appeared to be the tops of small pine trees extending beyond the cliff of rocks far above him. The entire mountain had slumped away sometime in the distant past, leaving a small flat area about one third of the way up the canyon. There Armijo could see a tiny island of green in a vast maelstrom of black volcanic rocks. But he was confused about how to reach that area."

"After being pinned to the canyon wall for an hour or so he stumbled onto a sandy path. Not really a path, just a place to put your foot that wasn't up against a rock. A gentler walk at last, but the sand played out, turning into a dead end. He had a bit of an overhang above him. To go further would require some technical climbing of which he was terrified."

The check came, and the pretty waitress filled up everyone's glass with fresh ice and drinks but everyone just sat there spell bound by Corey's story.

"Discouraged and tired, he started back down but then noticed a cut back route. The cut back provided a route unseen by someone climbing up the canyon wall. In only a few minutes, following the new route he found himself on his back, breathing hard, on a flat area of sandy rock. As soon as his breathing finally calmed down he could hear something. Far off in the bottom of the canyon the river made roaring sounds as the water flowed over the rock bed producing tumultuous cataracts. But this sound was a trickle of water, and close."

"As he reached the summit he found a tiny valley of stunted trees and brush, a world the size of someone's small yard, a microclimate with ancient soil. What fascinated Armijo was the trickle of a tiny stream. Completely invisible from the rim of the canyon, this very tiny stream has deeply cut into the soil and through the ions even into the volcanic bedrock. At one time it obviously carried much more water from a mysterious source. The tiny creek was easily stepped over, a deep crack with water flowing down it and disappearing beneath the rocks he had just climbed up."

"Armijo got down on his belly and dropped down as a way to satiate his thirst. He reached down into the shallow water, lifting up handfuls of water. But in the gravel of the stream he noticed a bright metallic rock, gold. Reaching down he pulled out a bean sized gold nugget. His curiosity naturally peaked at the prospect of finding a little gold, reaching down to the stream and running his fingers through the sediment in the gravel he found other tiny traces of color, enough, he thought to himself, that he would return many times. And so he spent the next half an hour or so, mostly on his belly, slowly tracing the tiny stream that meandered up the valley and he delighted in finding the occasional speck of gold. But as he worked his way across the tiny valley, crawling on his belly, it also became evident that the stream was going to disappear under more talus rocks, and he would probably never find where the gold was coming from."

"After the sun went down, allowing the air to cool, he returned to his morning camp where he spent the night, followed by another breakfast of catfish, supplied by his trot line. He gathered up his stuff and slowly hiked back up the talus piles and back into what was now his own private little world where he would spend the next few days. A dreary climb but once on top he was king of his own domain where he could see for vast distances down into the canyon. His gaze was drawn upward over the giant labyrinth of rocks to the top of the next hillside. Cataclysmic events had occurred there long ago; probably an earthquake had collapsed the entire side of the canyon wall, removing and covering the ancient and natural route up and out of the canyon."

"Several days later, he returned to the creek, searching for more traces of gold. Out of curiosity he climbed over every accessible route into the jagged talus pile hoping to find the source of the water. He discovered, in a small slit between two giant slabs of rock, a dark crevasse with cold air flowing out of it into his face."

"Long ago, large timbers had been wedged in this one opening. They were so old that they looked natural, but after closer examination, they appeared worked as if with a human hand, but now they had been there so long that they were easily dug out like so much loose dirt. Digging away what loose rocks and rotten timber he could, and after carefully calculating the chance of encountering a rattlesnake, by poking ahead with a stick. He slid between the slabs of rock, into what appeared to be the floor of a cave."

Armijo's Discovery

*C*orey continued his story, "The cave split here with the tiny stream coming from one direction and a dry floor going into another. The wet cave was too small for him to explore and the other disappeared into inky blackness. He explored it only a short distance when he found himself balancing on the brink of a deep crevasse wondering if he really wanted to go on down. Alone as he was, if he was to become hurt he would undoubtedly die. But after slowly transferring his weight to the rock, Armijo looked into the dark around him. As his eyes became adjusted to the tiny amount of light streaming though the crack in the rock, Armijo was astonished to discover that he was dangling above a deep pit with a large pile of rocks under him that trailed down into a dark and mysterious place."

"Armijo could not go any farther, and began to climb back out. He returned to Espanola where he purchased a few items that he absolutely needed. But his tiny sack he always carried beneath his chin was considerably larger, a fact not unnoticed by some of the locals. But he returned to his old shack and stayed there for several days where he received more company than he had received in years. It would be sometime before he would venture anywhere during the day. Soon, as the summer grew hotter the curiosity of others subsided."

"Returning weeks later armed with kerosene lamps and more matches, Armijo again descended into the cavern. By using a knotted rope he carefully climbed down the pile of rocks and was able to see just far enough ahead to see a dry floor completely covered with rocks, and an inky black cavern disappearing before him into the dust he was creating. He guessed it to be a lava tube; those underground conduits where red-hot molten magma once flowed in a race to obliterate everything it touches, forming lava flows and filling in worlds from other ages. The resulting lava tube could extend into the mountain for miles or end abruptly. He did discover something there that was very interesting, on the wall across the room and just discernible though the dusty air was a petroglyph."

"Armijo explored the large room and discovered many places where cold air came through the cracks between the jumbled rocks but could never find a route further into the cave. Returning to the wet part of the cave, he was delighted to discover several pockets in the floor of the tiny steam filled in with a large quantity of gold nuggets. These he carefully collected until he absolutely couldn't go any farther by squeezing himself past the slabs of rock."

"And that was it," Corey said. "The story ended. But apparently it took very little gold to satisfy him. Or perhaps he feared being killed for his gold. He kept his secret. Uncle Bo was the only person he bragged to and even Uncle Bo didn't believe him. The old man's shack was finally found burned down one frosty January morning, and it was never determined if Armijo was in the shack when it burned but Armijo was never seen again."

"The family notified the next of kin concerning the disappearance. It took months for someone to show up, a brother and a nephew. Where the old shack had burned only a grey pile of ash and trash remained. There, sticking up out of the ash was several pea sized pieces of gold that a recent and rare rain shower had exposed."

"After bringing a bucket and shovel up from the wagon and digging out the dirt, the relatives of the old man were amazed to discover a small fortune in gold dust. After further washing the gold at the homestead, they had several sacks of gold. When Armijo died, he died a rich man. He had collected enough gold to be living a very comfortable life in Albuquerque. Unfortunately when he died the route to the source of the gold was lost with him."

The Cholos

With that said we all stood up and started to leave but we looked over and noticed three young men staring at us with smiles on their faces. One was a burly, unwashed fellow with gold colored ear rings in his ears. One was a very small and literally greasy looking fellow, covered in tattoos, and a third looked clean and business-like. *Cholos*, I guessed almost saying the word out loud. Had they overheard the conversation? As they walked over to the casher the eyes of the three desperados followed them and shortly after they left the café so did the three men, following behind them in a blue pickup several car lengths back.

They followed route 285 at Chimayo north until they came to a rutted road near Ojo Caliente that lead off the main highway, that only a four wheel drive vehicle could navigate. They turned up this side road. The blue truck stopped for a few moments along the edge of the main road then turned back on to the highway continuing north. All four of us let out slow breaths then contemplated the road that was tilted at a breathtaking angle.

Once on top the driving was easy. Before us was a vast panorama of desolation. Nothing but scrub cedars and some local grass with intermittent sand drifts appeared before us for miles. "How could anyone live here?" Dr. Douglas said then answered his own question with, "Well, desperate people will try anything to survive."

"Uncle Bo's family had moved here without a clue as to what it would be like once they got here." said Corey. We traveled for a couple of more miles until we came to some old buildings that had all fallen in on themselves.

"Watch for rattlesnakes" said Hidalgo, and Corey and I immediately exited the one building we had stopped to explore. Corey said, "I've had my fill of rattlesnakes in Serpiente."

We returned to the Jeep and decided it was best to head out to the edge of the mesa overlooking the chasm formed by the Rio Grande River. Following a jeep trail we eventually found a nice camping spot near the rim under a large solitary cedar tree that offered some shade from the mid-day sun and set up camp. That evening, Dr. Douglas took out some topographic maps which here spread out on a portable table.

"The problem is we are looking at a vast canyon with only a couple of trails marked on the topographic map." He pointed to the dashed marks on the maps at the trails now used only by occasional fishermen who would carry a pack containing all their gear along with fishing poles and camp out at the river's edge while escaping the rest of humanity for a couple of days.

It was a lonely place, dropping off precipitately two thousand feet straight down to the river that roared over great rapids. We could hear the tumultuous river all the way to the top. We wondered what it would sound like at the bottom.

Along the river small trees grew everywhere a tiny bit of dirt allowed them to. There were but a few small riparian beaches that afforded space to set up camps for the few fishermen that would make the descent. The climb out would have been a killer, a two to three hour hike going up switchbacks that in many places were extremely dangerous. It was not a climb for the out of shape or faint of heart.

We had dinner that evening of fresh steaks cooked over a small grill we had brought along, then sat down to do some serious planning for the next day's activities. Hidalgo suggested climbing down the trails that the fishermen used to see if they could spot any likely spots where the old mine could have been.

Dr. Douglas answered him with, "The trouble with that is thousands of people have climbed down those trails and they would have certainly spotted the mine by now. We need to try something different. Corey, what did you say about Armijo finding a place that had recently caved off?"

"Yeah," Corey answered, "Uncle Bo said that Armijo said the mine had been covered up by a rockslide with the rocks settling in a very small flat spot, and that it was very difficult to get to."

"Then that's what we are looking for," replied Dr. Douglas, "Tomorrow we hike up and down this edge of the mesa looking for just such a spot."

While they gazed down into the canyon, Corey turned around and started back to the camp, when he noticed, far away in the distance and back toward the old house, a blue pickup truck parked. Turning to the others he said, "We better watch ourselves, I see trouble parked over there and I'll bet they are watching us."

Upon looking at the truck I said, "Yeah, I understand this country is famous for thieves. We better not leave our camp unguarded."

At that, Dr. Douglas walked over to a duffel bag that was propped up against the table and pulled out a .357 magnum that was holstered. Hidalgo walked over to the Jeep and pulled out a small hunting rifle and with that they settled into an uneasy sleep, stirring every time they heard a sound outside.

Deadly Visitors

The following morning the blue truck was gone but the fact that it had been there the previous evening made them all uneasy. We spent the next three days hiking up and down the canyon rim looking for possible sites and access trials to those sites. Each time they took off exploring we left someone in camp to protect our things. Obviously they didn't want to return from one of their treks only to find everything gone and the jeep sitting on cinder blocks with everything of value stripped away.

Being a very isolated place it had happened to others before them. River runners who had enjoyed the tumultuous rapids of the canyon often returned to their camps to discover everything of value gone. On some occasions it was even worse. Single women were sometimes attacked. When the crimes were reported nothing ever happened. The crimes were basically covered up without anyone ever being arrested. In many ways it truly was a modern wild west. There were very good reasons we kept an eye open for visitors.

Hidalgo was the most vigilant as he had personally dealt with the arrogance and greed of unscrupulous characters during his wanderings around New Mexico and particularly during his tenure in Durango with the La Plata County Sheriffs' Department over in southwestern Colorado. He understood that once thievery started in an area it usually occurred like a plague, a pandemic of hurt that was almost impossible to cure.

Each day we packed a lunch and spent the day on long hikes along the rim using the clues Armijo had left us. Looking for evidence of ancient trails, where clumps of scrub trees grew out of the small pockets of soil that occasionally accumulate in depressions. We investigated several possible leads, but each time we found ourselves unable to get to the sites or found nothing after we got there.

We had spotted several pickups and cars on the horizon, most of them simply delivering fishermen to the rim where fishermen then hiked down one of the established trails used to get to the bottom of the Rio Grande Box. Every once in a while one would simply just park and stay near the old settlement where the homesteaders lived. These caused some concern but sooner or later they all left. We were beginning to feel that it was a hopeless search and by the evening of the third day we were sitting around camp, tired and desperate, when well to the west of them, they spotted the unmistakable blue pickup truck we had encountered in Espanola.

"Trouble" announced Hidalgo, and again they all scurried around to get the revolver and rifle kept for protection against two legged snakes.

I asked, "What do you suppose they want? We don't really have anything of real value here!"

Hidalgo answered with, "Sure we do. They know we are carrying money as well as equipment that can be hocked or traded for drugs. Besides, it wouldn't really matter, they probably would steal everything just to cause us trouble, its' all a game to them."

Everyone hid behind something, just in case there was a gunfight, as the old blue pickup slowly crept its' way down the road toward us. Finally it pulled up to maybe fifty or sixty feet from us and then it came to a stop. The door opened and a very elderly Spanish gentleman poked his head out of the door and yelled "You're not going to shoot me are you?"

Juan Mateo Valencia Armijo

Putting a battered old hat on his grey hair and stepping out of the blue pickup he walked over to the camp where everyone had slid out from behind cover. "Let me introduce myself, my name is Juan Mateo Valencia Armijo, and all I want to do is talk to you." Hidalgo signaled him to come into the camp and everyone introduced themselves. "By the look on your faces, I think you thought I was someone else," said Juan Armijo. "Have you had trouble out here?"

"Well yes," said Corey, we were followed by three young and not so friendly looking boys all the way from Espanola, in a truck that is exactly like the one you are driving. We have been worried about them."

"Yes", says Juan Armijo. "One of those boys is my nephew, Enrique. He overheard your conversation about the Armijo mine and naturally it caught his attention when he heard his own name being gossiped about."

I gasped in astonishment, "You mean he thought we were talking about him?"

"Yes," said Juan Armijo, "until you got to the part about the mine, then he was all ears. He tried to catch up to you when you left the restaurant to talk with you but his friends were slowing him down, and there was no way he could follow you in old Lupe here when you turned off 285." He causally glanced over to the old two wheel drive blue truck. "You know there are easier ways to get here. If you come in from the north there is a good dirt road most of the way here. It is used by fishermen, but of course, the way you came is much shorter from Chimayo."

Hidalgo said, "Well, what you want with us?"

Then Corey interrupted the answer with another comment, "According to my Uncle Bo you were supposed to have died in a fire, years ago."

They provided Juan Armijo with a camp chair and a cup of coffee from the stove and he continued his explanation. "You see, the Armijo you are all thinking about was my uncle who did die in that fire. I was just a little boy visiting with my father when we came out and found the old shack and to our amazement some gold in the ashes. There was much gold there, enough to know that my uncle had known where there was more. Unfortunately the secret to the location of the mine has been lost to everyone. Many have tried to find it to no avail. But I have a clue."

I said, "Let me guess, it is located about a third of the way up the canyon walls where there is a tiny steam that is invisible unless you are standing on top of it."

"Oh yes," replied Juan Armijo.

I continued, "And there's the clue about the tiny flat place that grows some small brush."

"Yes," said Juan Armijo, those clues are all true, everyone knows them. *Senoir* Bo remembered well, however I have another clue."

With that information they all just sat and stared at each other. Finally Hidalgo broke the ice by saying, "What do you want from us?"

"Well, it's not like you think," replied Juan Armijo, "actually the story has been in my family for years and I would just like to get to the bottom of it."

I was still a little worried and interjected, "Like Hidalgo said, what do you, want from us?"

Juan Armijo took a long drink from the lukewarm coffee and replied. "You see, the mine has been a mystery in our family for years and with all the people who have attempted to find it everyone has given up, except, I guess, for you all."

Again Hidalgo said with a note of impatience in his voice. "But what do you want from us?"

Juan Armijo again took a long drink from the coffee cup and said, "Satisfaction, that's all. If they found gold those young kids you saw in the cafe would just blow it away, they are all *perazosos*, too lazy to work for anything. But to me, it is important to know about my uncle, my family. Did he really find a gold mine? Yes I think he did but actually I think he really found something far more important."

"Something more important," I asked with a question in my voice?

Juan Armijo shifted his weight in his chair taking a long breath and said, "I'll make you a deal, if you find gold, keep it. But, if we find something more interesting, and I think we will, I want the Armijo name to be attached to it."

Corey and I, Dr. Douglas and Hidalgo all looked at each other in puzzlement. They did not know what to make of the new arrival. Could they trust him? Did he really know anything that would be helpful?

I asked, "Why do you think there is more to this than just a mine shaft with a little bit of quartz rock?"

Juan Armijo answered, "My uncle told us at one time that he had discovered a way to another world, a place where the Indians came from. Many of the Indian tribes around here have a belief that their ancestors came from holes in the earth leading to a middle earth.

Hidalgo agreed, "That's true. The Hopi Indians believed that their ancestors came from a hole in the bottom of the Grand Canyon, but no one has ever found such a place."

Finally Dr. Douglas spoke. "You say you know of another clue to the location of the mine?"

"Yes" replied Juan Armijo, "I have a good clue, you see, my uncle told me stories about Indian trails and ruins he had discovered around here. My clue has to do with that"

We all thought about it for a while commenting on the fact that we were not really looking for gold but rather the adventure in solving a mystery. Money had not been a problem ever since our days at Serpiente. We were all relatively wealthy, but could not resist the chase of another adventure. So we came to an agreement; the gold, if there was any, would be split between them, with most of it going to charity, university studies or in Hidalgos' case to a trust fund for a college scholarships for Navajos and part would be used to help provide for his family on the Navajo reservation.

Juan Armijo finally shared his secret with them. "You have been searching the canyon rim for a trail down into the bottom. What you really need to do is find the trail from Chaco Canyon that ends on the rim. There you will find a petroglyph of a hummingbird carved into the rock under your feet. The trail, what there is of a trail and if there is still a trail, drops down the canyon from the hummingbird."

Corey says "Yeah, that makes sense, but we have walked all up and down this rim and not seen any trace of Indian trails or petroglyphs."

Juan Armijo placed his coffee cup on the table and said, "That's your challenge, to find an Indian trail leading to a petroglyph, and then who knows how hard it will be to find the original trial down into the canyon."

We talked about it all until it was starting to get dark and Juan Armijo excused himself, went over to his blue truck where he had a sleeping bag in the bed, climbed in and went to sleep. If it wasn't for the blue truck sitting there it could have all been a dream. Everyone went to sleep that night thinking about what the new clue meant.

The Anasazi Trail

The next day we drove the Jeep back away from the rim and then started slowly crossing the countryside. There were lots of trails. Cow trails, game trails and even some human trails that took fishermen down into the box canyon, but no Indian trails. It was what everyone expected. Anasazi trails are usually visible only from the air. Like the lines on the plain of Nazca in Peru or the Mojave Maze one could be standing in the middle of one and not realize it. Even though it is flat on top of the Rinconada Mesa it is still a rough and dangerous place to drive across. After a day of this we came back to camp exhausted and low on gas. Thankfully we had an extra Gerry can full of gas waiting for us back in camp.

The next morning while everyone packed up the camp to leave, Corey came up with another plan. Since the trail from Chaco Canyon supposedly ended up at the rim he packed his lunch and hiked along the rim trail again, this time taking a simple broom used to sweep out the floorboards of the jeep with him. He attached a walking stick to it with a piece of wire.

The rim trail was overgrown with brush and local grass but it was also volcanic rock mostly overlain with a thin covering of sand. Since there had been no humming-bird petroglyphs on any of the rocks that sometimes were heaped up along the edge he decided to sweep the loose sand that always accumulated on the rock. Using the other end of the stick he dragged it through the sand leaving a small ditch behind him. It was stop and go, over and over because the hard volcanic rock was crisscrossed by thousands of tiny cracks and each one had to be examined to see if it was natural or man - made. By late afternoon he was exhausted, hot and discouraged but just as he was getting ready to return to camp and declare all was lost he found a crack that was exactly one centimeter wide and one centimeter deep that had a curve in it. In nature all rock cleavages were in straight lines, so he immediately began to sweep it out. Soon everyone noticed his work and joined him in the effort. In a manner of minutes they had uncovered a perfect hummingbird petroglyph. A rock carving that looked machine cut and had been walked over thousands of times by hikers and fishermen all oblivious to the design that someone had carefully cut into the rock under the sand and below their feet.

Within a few feet of the rim, behind some brush that was hiding the entrance; we found the first sign of an ancient trail. Someone had actually carved a six inch wide cut into the side of some hard volcanic rock that would otherwise require some expert climbing to descend. The trouble was, it was late in the day and the trail on their side of the canyon as well as the entire box canyon was deep in shadow from the sinking sun. We covered up the petroglyph with sand to keep others from discovering it and returned to camp. The Armijo mine would have to wait another day but with great enthusiasm and excitement we unpacked the gear and the adventure was on again.

The Passageway

Early the next day the five of us awoke with greater anticipation than we had experienced since the expedition had begun. Eating breakfast in a hurry we gathered up climbing gear and Hidalgo, Corey, Dr. Douglas and I hurried over to the canyon's edge leaving Juan Armijo in the camp on guard since he begged not to have to climb down the canyon. As they left he said "When you get older, climbing hurts more and more but the view is greater than anything a young person sees." They also felt like he would know anyone who drove up to the camp and might actually have a better chance of talking thieves into leaving than we would.

Climbing down a canyon is like climbing a mountain in reverse. When climbing down any steep trail momentum tends to carry you and it is easy to find yourself sliding on some loose gravel and praying you will stop before you plunge off a precipice. The return is safer, but by then, you are already tired, hot, and usually dying of thirst.

The trail ran out about a hundred feet from the rim where a rockslide had occurred, but by then the detectives had already spotted a tiny island of green earth a hundred yards below them. It was not unlike many other small islands easily visible but Dr. Douglas pointed out one simple fact; some of the bushes that grew there required a constant supply of water, a basic prerequisite for the solution to one of the clues.

Returning to the top we decided upon another approach to the island. Old man Armijo had actually discovered the island on a return trip from the canyon so they decided to find the nearest fisherman's trail that would allow descent into the canyon. Three hundred yards north of them they found it. An older trail that was now seldom used because of the loose rocks and gravel next to sheer drop offs that would take your breath away. Easier to ascend than to descend, the trail curved slowly toward the island through a series of sharp switchbacks. The group slowly and carefully followed it down until they were even with the island. There they ran into a problem. The same problem that Armijo had run into, getting over to the island. The side of the canyon composed of angular chunks of black volcanic rock the size of small houses would be impossible to transverse. Searching up and down the main trail we discovered that at some time in the past a switchback had been shortened by about twenty yards or so. Following the older section of the trail it immediately became obvious why, about ten feet of it had caved off leaving nowhere to gain a foothold. Now it was time for the climbing gear.

Corey led the way tethered to Hidalgo. Hidalgo would let the rope out while Corey made a running leap to get to the other side of the trail. He made it, barely. From there they looped the rope around secure rocks on both sides of the drop off so everyone could clip a carabineer onto the rope and slide over to the other side. With Corey pulling a safety rope it was easy to cross but then the trail switched back ending again, below where the upper trail had broken away. Tired but elated we thought we could hear the tiniest trickle of water dropping over rocks, just as Armijo had years ago. We knew we were close but we still had a house size block of lava to get over.

Corey again led the way. Doing a classic chimney technique he worked his way to the top of the rock where he found an old galvanized pipe that had been driven into a crack in the rock. Tying a rope to the pipe offered easy access for the rest of the party. Walking across the block of rock at a forty degree slope into oblivion we made our way across, then we easily dropped down into a small island of land, and there trickling over the solid rock was a tiny stream of water, only inches wide, that flowed under and through a pile of rocks disappearing from view again through the rocks.

We refreshed ourselves with the water then began a serious examination of our surroundings. Looking into the stream we could not find a trace of gold as it had been long ago picked clean by Armijo. We followed it only a short distance where it disappeared into the side of the rocks just like Armijo had said it would.

The work then began. The three men cleared the brush away from the rocks in search of a cave while I explored the rest of the island discovering only a pile of rusted cans that Armijo had left behind on his trips to the cave. Suddenly Corey yelled, "We found it."

The timbers were still there, wedged in a rather small opening. Again, they were so old that they looked unnatural, but after we examined them the wood appeared worked as if with a human hand, but now there were only rotting fragments of wood. Again, the possibility of a rattlesnake came to mind, but they knew that rattlesnakes would only be found at the entrance; once we got into the cave they would cease to be a problem.

We entered the cave after taking out flashlights from of one of the small backpacks we were carrying. Immediately the cave split with the tiny stream coming from one direction and a dry floor going another. We knew the wet cave didn't allow a passage so we began our exploration of the much larger dry cave. Again, we explored only a short distance when we found ourselves balancing on the brink of a deep hole in the floor. With the flashlights we could see that we were standing on a thin edge of rock overlooking a deep pit with a large pile of rocks in the center of a large room under us.

That is when Hidalgo spotted the petroglyph on the wall of the cave far below them. Much like the petroglyph they discovered on the rim, this one was also very different from the thousands of other Indian markings found all over the southwest. It was of a much finer workmanship, more Mayan than Anasazi looking, but definitely American Indian, with a classical descending rattlesnake meandering down in wavy lines past the hummingbird. The rattlesnake stair steps were usually understood to be the route to a river or water, the hummingbird in Mayan mythology was thought to represent warriors. Without sunlight to fade the colors there were still vibrant red colors in the grooves that formed the glyph. Dr. Douglas and Hidalgo studied it in detail trying to decipher its meaning.

Up till now, he had not said much but now Dr. Douglas began taking. "I have seen many examples of lava caves; they are fairly common in volcanic areas such as this. They are formed by liquid magma, cooling on the outside yet still flowing on the inside forming gigantic hollow tubes of rock making a labyrinth of passageways into the once molten and fluid rock. I wonder whether the original cave entrance caved in, blocking the once obvious route. Or perhaps it was caved in and hidden like many ancient mines during the Pueblo revolt. One thing is for sure, there has to be a route to the floor down there."

Corey said, "Well we certainly can just repel down."

Dr. Douglas answered with, "Yeah but is there another way?"

Everyone began searching for a route that had obviously been covered up, probably the last time by Armijo. They began to move many manageable stones. It was a dangerous job, easy to crush one's fingers or drop one on a toe and if one removed the wrong rock the massive stones might come down on you.

But after removing several oddly shield shaped and very thin sections of rock they found what appeared to be a tiny slit in the wall just big enough to allow a small person to pass. After some work we all managed to squeeze through and entered a long narrow passageway shaped like a crescent moon, always curving over to the right at the top, but more importantly, dropping downward. Immediately the walls opened wide enough to allow passage with a cumbersome bent over stoop to match the shape of the passageway. It was an extra shell, a sister lava tube that slowly curved to the right just like the main cave, somewhat like the turn of a giant seashell.

The Volcanic Cavern

*D*r. Douglas stopped in his tracks, "Look at this," he said, and he pointed down to the floor. The floor of the cave had a perfectly level path. Brushing away the sand they discovered the floor had a delicately inlaid rock footpath, not unlike the walls in ruins found throughout the *Anasazi* world, but laid flat. They were mystified, as to where the bright yellow sandstone came from, contrasting so much with the much darker gray and black volcanic rock that was everywhere else. Anasazi and Chacoan in appearance, the trail disappeared under sand and out of the lamps light, but it returned within only a few steps.

In a few minutes we found ourselves slipping past one last tight squeeze and looking back at the light filtering down from the entrance. They were at the bottom of the large room where the petroglyph was on the wall. Again the petroglyph appeared to be machine cut. We walked back and examined it closer while looking for other exits from the room. In the center of the room was a large pile of rocks that had caved off the ceiling and it took only a short time to decide that the only logical way to go was to return the way they had come.

After maybe a quarter of a mile the roof apparently collapsed into the outer cave, but someone had chiseled a passage through the rock. We then came to an entryway of a familiar pattern, the 'T' doorway seen in many southwestern Indian ruins. We had to lean over, exposing the back of the head, like an oriental exposing the back of the neck, to allow passage into the inner caverns. But after just a few yards of uncomfortable walking, the trail stair stepped down to a much larger volcanic cavern.

There, we found ourselves slowly wandering down a long lava tube on an obvious trail. Even the tiniest bits of rock had been removed in the footpath, making it perfectly smooth, but after a while the trail came to an abrupt end, with a shear drop appearing in the floor. The cave had been fractured after its creation. A vertical crack in the floor dropped and descended as far as they could see. Across the void in the floor the floor of the cave continued for a short distance, but was littered with rocks, unused and obviously not traveled. On both sides of the pit were two circular cuts in the rock, where long ago a wooden beam, now gone, supported something. Possibly it had been a large pulley, a block and tackle, or just a place to tie a rope. Someone had gone to a lot of trouble, but the obvious questions kept popping up in everyone's minds. Where would the wood come from, and how did they get it past the narrow parts of the trail? Were there other ways into this place?

We sat perplexed as to what to do. The only way down was into a steep narrow chasm. Hidalgo dropped small pebbles down the precipice, but the sounds were foreign, far off, as if not really striking bottom. We would have to return again to this place; in fact we might have to return many times to safely get to the bottom.

I then said, "Hey you guys look at this." On the wall was the name Armijo, crudely scratched into the rock. This may have been as far as he had got and it was as far as we would get until they came back better prepared. It was time to return to the camp.

The Vertical Drop

It took us two hours to return to the rim where they found Juan Armijo under the cedar tree sound asleep in an aluminum lawn chair he had brought in the back of his old blue truck. Everyone shared the news with him which brought about looks of astonishment followed by contentment. He had wondered all his life about his uncle and just what it was he had discovered and what had eventually happened to him, although the general consensus was that he had died in the fire that consumed his shack. He was particularly interested in the name that Penny had discovered scratched into the volcanic rock.

That evening we traveled back to Chimayo with Juan Armijo with them to find a two inch pipe that they could wedge into the chasm opening so we could repel down the crack. It would be hard work, and then there was the problem of getting back up the deep crack when they were through exploring. We found ourselves having to drive all the way into Santa Fe to find extra rope and while there bought all manner of foodstuffs which we put into coolers to keep cold. We arrived back at the camp after 11:00 pm and immediately went to sleep.

Early the next day after a breakfast that included fresh cantaloupes and milk for our cereal we loaded all our ropes, caving gear, and a lunch into backpacks and started back down the trail. Two hours later we had arrived again at the opening to the cave. The outside temperature was already in the nineties making every motion an effort, but as soon we stepped inside the cave the air was cool, and very tolerable. After retracing our steps through the crescent shaped corridor and finally into the long tunnel we arrived back at the pit. This is the point that most people would turn around. It was not a place for anyone with acrophobia or claustrophobia. The drop appeared to be straight down. Corey and Hidalgo set the pipe into the grooves that someone had provided for them and attached the ropes. After considerable preparation Corey eased himself over the ledge that covered the pit and after dropping down only a couple of feet he immediately discovered perfectly cut, hand and foot holes carved into the hard volcanic rock. They all felt a little foolish for not discovering them before.

Still using the safety ropes, he quickly discovered that as long as you started out, literally on the right foot, there would always be a logical place for your next step. If you started out on the wrong foot you would have to return to the top and start again. It was a vertical wall ladder, one that became increasingly easier to manage as the drop became less steep. Even in the dark, if you searched with your hand or foot, sooner or later you would discover a logical way down the steep rock. As Corey climbed down the wall, carefully playing out his safety ropes, he began to feel much cooler air, and could hear far off echoes. As he neared the bottom of the chasm the decent became easier as the drop turned into a steep slide. Now the cut steps were more like stair steps carved out of the volcanic rock. Finally, reaching a platform he unpacked and lit his battery powered lamp. He realized that he had now dropped into an immense underground cavern. At the bottom of the steep incline he was no longer climbing through volcanic rock but rather the original bedrock of yellow sandstone. This large grotto provided a place to rest and was obviously used as a resting place by others. Leading away from the grotto were trails going off in many directions. He returned to the top where they tied supplies that they would obviously need later and dropped them, tied to a drop rope, a bundle at a time into the pit. Several hours of hard work had already been accomplished and facing a two hour climb to the top we returned again to camp. Tomorrow, we would all brave the pit taking with us one last cache of supplies we might use in the depth of the caverns. That evening I thought about all the circumstances and even the dream that had brought me to this place. It all seemed so much like a dream but then, there was Corey, curled up around me. Not all dreams portend bad omens.

The Cavern

Early the following morning, we repeated the now well-rehearsed procedures, dropping down the trail into the canyon. A couple of hours later we were connecting our carabineers to our safety harness and attaching ourselves to a safety rope. One at a time, we had to slide off the edge of the rock and search with our toes to find a place to put our feet. Dropping down was much easier to do now because of the foot and handholds Corey had discovered but I knew I wouldn't want to try it without the safety rope. It was a terrifying moment. For a second I thought I was back in my dream. After finding the hole in the rock I allowed my weight to rest on it then after another foothold was found, I leaned back and let myself freefall. At the bottom of the drop, I released my safety rope and stepped out of the rope harness slowly dropping down to the stair steps which seemed to be dropping into a large room. Capped by hard volcanic rock, the stairs led down into a grotto. Corey, who dropped down ahead of me, was busy rounding up our packs. The room had one giant stalagmite in the center of it, surrounded by a small pool of water and then surrounded by flat floor. Around the edge of the room, stones had obviously been arranged to form a place for someone to sit or even recline. It was a haven with a ceiling made of black volcanic rock mostly covered with a white crystalline material making it very reflective. The floor and walls were the same yellow sandstone that the upper pathway was made of and there were two obvious exits from the grotto, one appearing to go back up and one appearing to go down. After Dr. Douglas and Hidalgo made the drop, Hidalgo declared that this would be our base camp. No matter where we explored, we would always return to this spot. It was our personal kingdom. Soon we noticed another, smaller petroglyph with exactly the same design as the previous one. But this time there were three rattlesnake motifs carved into the sandstone walls, one a two headed rattlesnake trailing up and the single one pointing down.

Staying together, we explored one of the two major trails leading up from the grotto. After only a small amount of exploration, we discovered that the path meandered uphill and eventually split into two paths. We picked one to explore and explored it until we realized that corridor we were exploring seemed to meander upwards until the volcanic rock reappeared. The cave seemed to be hand constructed in places and certainly went somewhere but where?

Returning to the grotto we explored the main trail that led downhill only far enough to see if it went somewhere. As we dropped down, the yellow rock changed into a creamy limestone rock. Below the volcanic cap, rock had dissolved into immense huge underground chambers. Timidly following the most apparent trail, we descended out of the sandstone into travertine cave rock. We walked along a Swiss cheese world with cave openings going in every direction. Keeping to the ancient trail we began to hear running water. In a short while, we found tiny underground rivulets of water cascading though a world of travertine rocks around them. The deeper we went the more complex the scenery around us became. Reminiscent of Carlsbad Caverns only with actively growing stalactites and stalagmites, it was if they were dropping into worlds created long ago and under many different circumstances. Dr. Douglas was in awe. He was actually seeing a world that before he could only imagine. Based upon what he knew about geology and upon his experiences all over the world they had discovered something extraordinary.

Bordered by delicate formations appearing like millions of tiny Chinese rice gardens, the pathway actually dropped though a labyrinth of travertine formed by mineral laden water. The cascading water caused the delicate and thin walls to vibrate, singing songs to the traveler. The travelers descended a well-worn man made path made of perfectly inlaid yellow sandstone. But after several turns with obvious routes, the trail ended in a broken rock area that required much exploration and wading in icy cold water. After considerable wrong turns, dead ends and some cursing from Dr. Douglas, we were relieved when they found the trail again, but only the last fifty or so yards of it, for it appeared to come to an abrupt end.

We found themselves next to a sandy beach alongside the confluence of two shallow crystal clear underground rivers. But along the edges of the river on this inside curve, were many small houses made of the yellow sandstone rock. Roofless, and with small walls they appeared to be like any small ruins one might find in the southwest. These structures were really just suggestions of homes. Very little privacy is required in a world of perpetual darkness. Inside a cavern, there is no temperature change or weather of any kind, but the air does circulate, sometimes when large storms pass overhead in the other world, there is real wind in some of the tighter places.

As we explored along the cave-like depressions in the rock we discovered many interesting structures. These were not unlike many other ruin structures that we had seen before made out of the local rock, the same rock style that was on the trail, and made of the same intricate inlay pattern like we had seen before in Chaco canyon. Inside the houses, we discovered all manner of wonderful artifacts. All objects such as bowls, articles of clothing and blankets were as they were left. The pottery was highly stylized with a white on black theme decorated with intricate designs looking as if they were made by master craftsmen. Sash belts were lying on the makeshift beds made with much delicate beadwork. Yet these were not homes but rather sleeping quarters for a few families in an eternally dark world. Perhaps they were able to work without the aid of light at all. But what were they working at?

They guessed the water flowed generally south in a great meander with a tremendous amount of side channeling and river braiding. The ceiling was several stories up, or so we guessed and above that it was all capped with volcanic rock. Somewhere, well above that rock, was the modern Rio Grande River, slowly cutting down through the rock, under a bright New Mexican sun. As the river flowed into the inky caverns, we could hear, in hundreds of faraway recesses water cascading over, onto, and into rocks making the familiar sounds of small cataracts and waterfalls. We imagined earlier people exploring these tiny underground rivers.

We crossed over to the sandy beach on the other side and then stepped into the other shallow river coming in from a slightly different direction and discovered an intriguing fact; the water was very warm, almost hot. A delicate steam rose into the air above it. This channel of water was obviously flowing through a volcanically active area north of our location.

I set down in the water to warm myself and exclaimed, "Hot and cold running water. What else could we possibly want?"

"Well, Dr. Douglas exclaimed, just look at the black gravel under you."

Certainly the gravel was black but it also contained tiny sparkling particles of a yellow material; gold.

Dr. Douglas exclaimed in jubilation, "You all realize that there are many personal fortunes of gold in that gravel. If we were able to mine all that gold out of there we would be millionaires many times over."

"How in the world would we be able to get it out of here," asked Corey?

Dr. Douglas mulled the question over for a few moments then answered with, "Well, I don't know. It would be impossible to get machines in here. I suspect that it would have to be removed the old fashioned way, just like the ancients did, one bag at a time by climbing up the chasm and out through the lava tube."

After some rummaging around we found a small creek coming in from a side cavern that flowed next to a huge structure that was carved into the gently sloping but solid rock. A curved cut in the rock at the top slowly meandered back and forth over little pockets in the groves. We were puzzled at first but Dr. Douglas recognized its use after exploring and finding a diversion canal designed to pour water over the petroglyph. Intricately carved and very artistic, the deep groves made a fantastic design and were actually designed to carry water into them. After an examination we discovered inside the groves of the design, in various states of purity, gold. The ancient ones were mining the gold here in the caverns, and washing it here.

Being pressed for time as it was already late evening, we discovered under a make shift bed several leather sacks and to our delight and amazement, they contained pure granular gold. Gold that would be carried by the ancient ones, in leather sacks, to another place where it would be traded for all manner of goods. We wondered who they were trading with, there is little evidence of gold being used by the ancient people who lived here.

We discovered that the ancient trial we had followed eventually continued on the other side of the shallow streams but immediately disappeared into the maze of caverns. These streams might have been flowing during the age of dinosaurs carrying mineral rich deposits along its meandering journey to become part of the water table of the Rio Grande Valley. To the north of them the rivers were obviously cutting through deposits of extremely high grade gold ore, carrying the gold downstream and depositing it in the deepest recesses of the crystal clear streambed.

It was in those pockets of water that we discovered what thousands had been looking for on the Rinconada before; gold. Upon close examination of the stream sediment, we could plainly see what looked like tiny pieces of the finest gold wire. It was everywhere. All we had to do was take the gravel back to the petroglyphic device, turn on the water by moving a single flat stone, and allow it to separate the gold for them, bag it up and then spend it.

We sat down together to mull over their situation. As we did so we turned off all the lights except one to save the batteries for the return trip to the chasm. At that point Corey dropped his flashlight, breaking the bulb and casting them into pitch black, but as their eyes adjusted to the dark they realized something. There was light in the caves, which brought up the next question, where in the world was it coming from? Where they were, on the cold river side, the light was extremely dim, but on the other side, where the hot water channel was coming through, the walls were glowing from thousands of tiny light sources.

"Must be bioluminescence, says Dr. Douglas, bacteria or something. The light must be getting energy from the hot water flowing through here." It was all an awesome sight being able to see the beautiful cave formations without any other source of light. As I neared the source of the light they seemed to get brighter. I then realized that any air movement made them glow brighter.

"Now I know how the ancient ones were able to get around here without torches, says Hidalgo. I was wondering how they were able to stay down here without leaving any soot marks on the ceilings or walls."

We had spent an adventurous day in the caverns and were overwhelmed with what we had found. Then it was time to begin the long uphill climb back to the bottom of the pit, the grotto. Now it would be getting dark outside and we were wishing we had simply brought sleeping bags with us but when we got to the bottom of the pit we suddenly realized that something was terribly wrong. Laying there on the floor was all the rope that should have been tied to the pipe well over two hundred feet above us. Someone had cut the rope. Someone had left us to die.

The Ladrones

*C*orey, as usual, led the way up by carefully climbing up the chasm using the footholds that the ancient ones had carved. Starting at almost a forty five degree incline the chasm quickly shot straight up. Even with the footholds it was a strenuous and dangerous climb. At the top he encountered a problem that he knew he would have to deal with. The rock there formed a slight overhang which is why they hadn't noticed the footholds in the first place as well as the reason the ancient ones had locked a log in place. He would need to somehow toss a rope over the pipe, that, thank heavens was still there. He thought to himself, if whoever had cut the ropes had dropped the pipe there would be no way to get out.

Perhaps they thought it would make too much noise and alert the detectives and their group to their oncoming predicament. He laughed to himself, what difference would it have made? After several attempts he was able to toss the rope over the pipe. Even though it was just a yard or so away he was terrified at the thought of losing his grip and plummeting to the bottom. He fastened the rope he had tied to his belt that got heavier and heavier as he climbed. Secured everything and climbed out. With a safety rope tied securely back in place, I quickly followed, then Dr, Douglas, and finally Hidalgo climbed to the top of the pit. Once there, we began the long climb back to the top of the rim.

Hidalgo muttered, "I'll kill that Mexican when I get there, I never should have trusted him. Why would he want to help us anyway?"

I, on the other hand kept trying to calm them all down. Corey simply led the way looking ahead for any sign of danger and Dr. Douglas who was in the rear was too exhausted to say anything.

Eventually we neared the rim and everyone crept up the trail trying their best not to make any noise. As they looked over the crest they were perplexed. Juan Armijo was leaning against the tree apparently asleep. Walking over to him they quickly realized that there was more to it than that. He was tied to that tree and bleeding from his nose. Startled, Juan Armijo started out by yelling in lightning fast Spanish with a string of what was probably profanities, then when he realized that he was among friends he settled down to explain that he awoke to find two men in camp and one of them was holding a pistol directly at his face.

"They arrived just as you folks dropped over the edge of the canyon and demanded to know where you were off to. So I told them you had gone down to the river to fish. Of course they didn't believe me and punched me several times until I told them you were also prospecting. One of them took off down the trail to find you and the other one ransacked the camp, took everything of value and after the other one who had gone off to find you came back, they took off."

"What did they take off in, ask Hidalgo?

They left in a brown car just like your Jeep Cherokee, maybe a station wagon. I really don't know. I was tied to this darned tree and couldn't really see. I thought they were going to steal my old truck, it was the only one that I had keys to, said Juan Armijo. But, they didn't, they went through everything else. I know they did carry some things and then loaded it into the back of their vehicle."

"They must be mean hombres because they said they had decided to follow you all the way down the trail to see if you had any money on you."

After a short examination of the camp they could find very little of value missing.

"This doesn't make any sense to me" says Hidalgo, if they were thieves they would have grabbed everything and then run. These guys were interested in hurting this expedition. They wanted to hurt us. In effect, they were committing murder. Why would they take a risk like that? Tell me more Armijo, what did they look like?

Armijo frowned then said, "Aw, they were a couple of Mexicans, maybe your age with bad teeth." He was looking at Hidalgo when he said, "One of them had a really bad limp. His left knee if I remember correctly. Anyway, I have never seen them before and trust me I know all the *ladrones*, eh thieves, around here.

We all turned and looked at each other. Finally I asked, "Fernandez and Garcia from Serpiente?"

Hidalgo replied, "Has to be. Who else would have a grudge against us? Who else would have gone to all this trouble?" They decided they were dealing with a real problem then after mulling around camp for a while they made a list of what was stolen and Hidalgo and I headed to Espanola. It was time to talk to the police.

Sergeant Blanco

"What can I help you with?" Said sergeant Blanco who was on desk duty at the Espanola police department and who was giving a curious look at what was apparently an unusual couple; a weathered Navajo Indian and a gorgeous Anglo women with blond hair. He had never seen that combination of people walk in to the building before, and was suspecting that they were angry at each other. He wondered what the Navajo had done.

"We would like to report an attempted murder," says Hidalgo.

"Where did this happen?" asked the Sergeant with the smirk disappearing from his face.

I answered, "We were up on the rim overlooking the Rio Grande Box on the Rinconada."

Sergeant Blanco said with a shrug, "There's not much we can do about things that happen up there, the area is just too big and we have to deal with too many problems here in Espanola. Did you know that last week there was a murder here in Espanola, and we know that there are drugs that just arrived on the streets?"

Hidalgo who had had some experience with police departments looked upwards and said. "The truth is that you aren't going to do anything about what just happened to us, too much trouble for you."

Sergeant Blanco looked a little miffed but answered him with, "The truth of the matter is things happen up there all the time and there is little we can do about it. By the time we get there, there is no evidence. The people who have been victimized have left and the locals won't tell us anything because it is their relatives that are causing the problem in the first place. Stealing from the tourist is a cottage industry there, a way of life for many of them. I can't arrest all of them."

"That's true," said Hidalgo, but you can write up a report on it so that if anything serious happens you will have something to go on."

"Well yes," says sergeant Blanco, "I thought maybe you wanted us to assign an officer to watch your camp for you."

Hidalgo, who was becoming exasperated, retorted. "Did you hear what I told you in the first place? This was an attempted murder, not of just one individual but four of us."

"So you were one of the intended victims?"

"Yes, said Hidalgo with more than a little irritation in his tone, "Look, I worked for the La Plata police department in Durango for a while and I know when we are getting the run around."

A little embarrassed Sergeant Blanco got serious about what he was doing and pulled out an incidence report form and started to fill it out.

Hidalgo and I gave a description of Fernandez and Garcia, along with a cover story of Dr. Douglas, doing some geological work for the university. Afterwards Hidalgo asked, "What do you know of Juan Armijo? He is an older fellow who we ran into up there?"

The sergeant, now being much more cooperative thought for a minute then reported, "Oh yeah, I know of him. He is an eccentric old man who lives in Chimayo. He is quite harmless, although some of his relatives are a little shady."

Hidalgo says, "What about his nephew and his friends?

The sergeant answered the inquiry with, "No, I don't think so, but I could be wrong. I don't know him or his friends. I've never heard any reports on them."

Hidalgo asked, "What do you know about Don Fernandez or Jose Garcia?"

"Who are they and where do they live?" asked the sergeant.

Hidalgo answered the query with, "Somewhere around Serpiente or possibly Magnelena or Socorro, maybe Belen."

Sergeant Blanco excused himself and walked into an adjoining room full of cabinets and said, "Give me a few minutes."

Several minutes later he came back holding several pieces of paper in his hands. "Those guys are bad men and they certainly are in the files, they both have rap sheets several pages long. Garcia and Fernandez have both done time in Santa Fe at the state penitentiary. Actually they are currently wanted for burglary and in Bernalillo County for armed robbery. Where did you run into them?"

Hidalgo and I spent the next few minutes explaining the incident in Serpiente where they were caught ransacking Indian ruins.

"It figures," said sergeant Blanco, "People are trying to find those two characters. It makes sense that they would be laying low yet doing something that makes them lots of money."

The sergeant shared information with us as to where the last known address for the two characters was and then gave us his card. He was now a lot more interested in the situation up on the Rinconada.

Revenge

Returning to camp that evening we drove past every motel they could find along the route back to Rinconada. Our journey was uneventful but every time we saw a brown boxy looking car we became anxious. We pulled into several parking lots in front of motels looking at license plates until we finally came across a likely Cherokee Jeep, but in just a matter of minutes a young couple with small children came out and got into the jeep and drove away.

At one time, a brown Cherokee Jeep drove up behind us. Then it passed us with an elderly lady driving it. It obviously was just another false alarm. We were perplexed at what to do and had to make some real decisions. Returning to camp we unpacked the coolers of iced drinks and food we had purchased, set them under the cedar tree, covered them with wet towels to keep them cool and went to bed. The next morning we again enjoyed fresh food again.

Hidalgo, while stirring his usual cup of well sugared and creamed coffee looked up at everyone and said, "I think we should get what we can out of the mine, while we can before something else happens."

Corey looked up from his ham and eggs and replied, "You realize that if we show up with bags of gold, anywhere, it is going to open up a Pandora's Box of questions from people. Everyone is going to want to know where we found it. This place could wind up looking like a circus."

"Not only that," Dr. Douglas interjected, "What we found is a real treasure even without the gold. Biologist will want to know about the bioluminescence and archeologist will have a field day with the Indian artifacts. In fact, there are very few places like this on the planet, and those petroglyphs tell me that this is not an ordinary Indian camp. Even Chaco Canyon cannot hold a candle to this place. The University professors are going to want to study this. It could make many of them famous."

Hidalgo looked worried as he said, "Our artifact thieves think that we are dead, yet here we are. Sooner or later they will be back and discover our camp is still here with us in it. Then, they will not leave us alone until they know what we have here. The next time they try to kill us they might succeed."

Corey continued, "Next time they may drop the pipe down the hole and it really would be impossible to get out."

I angrily said, "Next time one of us is going to be hiding. If it is me and they show up, I'm going to shoot first and talk later."

Hidalgo says, "That would not be a good idea. First of all, we hid the truth from the police yesterday. Secondly, we can't prove that they tried to murder us. More than likely, knowing the way justice works around here, you would be sent to jail for murder. The way I see it is we need to hide the entrance to the mine and then leave for a while or set a trap for those thieves."

Dr. Douglas worriedly replied, "The trouble with that is, they already know about the entrance to the mine. They just don't know what is down there. Surely by now they have heard the old Armijo mine story from someone around here and have made the connection to the possibility of there actually being gold there. Besides why else would we be here? I don't think we could convince them that we are studying the local geology or just plain fishing at the river. Besides they already looked through our stuff and we didn't bring a single fishing pole. No, they know we are on to something here and they will be back."

I added, "One more thing, they are bound to have made a lot of money selling artifacts they stole out of the Indian ruins down in Serpiente. They have resources and I wouldn't doubt that they would hire some help, especially if they thought they would get even richer. Then there is Garcia, you know he has a score to settle for that bullet Hidalgo put into his knee."

Juan Armijo, who hadn't said a word so far finally looked up and said, "There are options. We can take some dynamite and blow the entrance and come back at a later date or stay and fight them. I don't know about you all but I say let's set a trap for them. Let's give them some of what they have been handing us."

Everyone looked at Juan Armijo and as he looked around the party he could see everyone's heads bobbing up and down in a yes posture. Everyone was angry and wanted a degree of revenge. Juan Armijo then smiled.

The Trap

The next morning while Dr. Douglas, Armijo and I stayed in camp, armed and ready for unwelcome visitors, Hidalgo and Corey took the familiar trail back to the mine. Once there Hidalgo hid himself away in the rocks while Corey made the long climb down into the caverns. Once inside, he collected several leather bags of gold which he packed away into a small backpack he was carrying. He then climbed to the top and pulled the backpack up to the top of the chasm.

He then immediately returned to the entrance, got the all clear signal from Hidalgo and the two of them hid the gold. Then Hidalgo took a turn into the caverns. They did this until they had gathered up all the loose bundles of gold that they could find in the ruins. Carefully hiding all but a small amount they returned to the camp. Once Corey and Hidalgo were back in camp, Dr. Douglas and I loaded into the Cherokee Jeep and headed back to Santa Fe, stopping everywhere we could to make sure that we would be plainly visible to anyone watching. Once in Santa Fe we deposited the gold in an account. While in Santa Fe we purchased two more weapons along with ammunition before returning to the camp.

For the next week we daily took a single small sack of gold into Santa Fe depositing it into a deposit box at the bank then returning, making sure we were seen by anyone who might be watching, but after almost a week of this we began to worry that our bait wasn't being taken. Then on the seventh day, just as it was starting to get dark a brown vehicle appeared on the road back at the old Armijo shack. They built up the fire to make sure that it appeared that everything was normal.

The next morning as usual everyone dropped off the edge of the Rinconada while Juan Armijo causally took a chair and leaned against the cedar tree while pretending to sleep. Sure enough, within a few minutes, Garcia and Fernandez drove up to within about a hundred yards. Fernandez got out of the car and started walking into camp. As soon as he got to the cedar tree he lifted the butt of his gun and hit Juan Armijo in the side of the head with it. The head popped off and rolled over to the camp fire pit.

By this time Garcia had driven into the camp and was getting out of the car. Fernandez, realizing that the head was only a storefront mannequin dressed to look like Armijo, immediately turned to run to the car but the trap was already sprung. Hidalgo and Corey let loose with a volley of shells causing the two *ladrones* to freeze in their tracks.

We were well hidden behind the rim escarpment and offered no target for Garcia and Fernandez. With nowhere to run and little to hide behind they gave up, throwing their hands into the air and dropping down on their knees, just like Hidalgo ordered them to do.

The Kidnapping

We gathered around the thieves with guns at the ready. Corey yelled at them, "Why are you bothering us?"

Garcia spit on the ground, looked up at him and replied rudely, "What do you expect? You messed up the sweetest deal we have had in years down in Serpiente, it was *muchas dulce*. But the real reason, the main reason, is my knee. It hurts me all the time. I will never be able to walk again like a normal person."

Foolishly I walked up to him, got right in his face and said, "What about the people you have killed? They will never walk anywhere again. What about their families who will never get to share their lives with them again?"

Hidalgo started to warn me to get back but I was angry. I let my anger get the best of me. I turned to look back at the others but Garcia made a razor fast move as he pulled a hidden knife out of his belt, thrusting the blade under my neck.

We were suddenly in a standoff.

"Get those keys out of your pockets, demanded Garcia." Flustered but feeling helpless, Dr. Douglas and Armijo pulled the keys to both vehicles out of their jeans and handed them to Fernandez. He immediately gave them a sling over the edge of the cliff. With the sharp blade of the knife still under my chin the two thieves walked over to the car, got in and speed away, with me between them.

The dust rolled up behind the car as the kidnappers speed away, Hidalgo, Cory and Dr. Douglas made a mad scramble toward the edge of the cliff. But just as they got to the edge Armijo finally got their attention.

"Do you really think we need keys to start old Lupe?"

Looking back at him they all turned around with perplexed looks on their faces. Corey asked, "You don't need a key?"

"No," replies Armijo, "Let's go."

With that, they all ran to the old blue truck. With Hidalgo up front with Armijo, Corey jumped into the bed of the truck. Armijo reached under the dash and after a little fumbling with some wires the old truck roared to life and away we went; barely, for the old truck was indeed old and had to be carefully driven over the rutted jeep road to get out to the main road which was itself well rutted and corduroyed. They didn't have a chance; by the time they got back to the blacktop the other car was long gone. Driving until they came to the first backcountry store they stopped, went in, and called the police to make a report. They hoped that Sergeant Blanco would put out an all-points bulletin along with some road blocks, a kidnapping had occurred.

Within twenty minutes a state police car arrived at the store. Shiny and black the car signified to Hidalgo a fighting chance with the *desperados*. They knew they would need help but little did they know where it would come from.

Enrique

Corey was fit to be tied. Two days had passed without a word as to what had happened to me. They did find the keys to their Jeep Cherokee after some grueling searching by using ropes to repel down the slabs of hot volcanic rock. It was then back to work for Corey and Hidalgo, spending everyday driving around looking for a trace of the desperadoes' car and then returning to the edge of Rinconada in order to camp each evening. They were truly feeling the old saying; 'If it wasn't for bad luck, they would have had no luck at all.' Finally everything changed.

Corey spotted it first. On the horizon they could see Armijo's old blue truck slow plodding its way over to the camp. Armijo got out of the truck along with several other younger people, the people that had been in the café, weeks before when they were stopping for lunch. Armijo introduced Enrique his nephew along with his rough looking friends.

Corey asked, "What are they doing here?"

Armijo chuckled and answered, "Have you ever heard the saying that you can't judge a book by its cover?"

"Sure," answered Corey. "Is there something we can do for you?"

"No," replied Enrique, "but we can help you."

Mystified, Hidalgo who by this time was starting to get angry, answered, "How can you help us?"

"Simple," says Enrique, "I know where they are keeping Penny."

With that said they all jumped up jubilantly and the entire tone of the conversation turned to hope.

Enrique continued, "She is being held at a hacienda off the main road. I think it is a relative to one of the men you are looking for which is why you can't find them anywhere. The car is kept inside of an adobe walled in yard. You don't know where to look but you see we have many friends with many ears and eyes. They spotted the car you are looking for and even saw the one who has a bad limp. If you wish we will help you get Penny."

"Let's go," Corey replied excitedly, but Hidalgo caught him by the sleeve of his shirt and pulled him back into his camp chair. "We need a plan before we go barging in, and I really think we need to inform the police. This time I don't want them to get away, and...

Corey interrupted with, "If they have hurt Penny in any way I'm going to..."

"Do nothing," says Hidalgo. "Kidnapping is a federal offence, the FBI will be involved. We need the police to put them away for the next fifty years or so. If they can't, then we will talk of disposing of them, besides if we don't do this legal, we will be the ones in jail instead of them." He winked at Corey and said, "Trust me, I know how this works." With that, they drove into town again to place another phone call to the police.

Ojo Caliente

That evening they met with Sergeant Blanco as well as the State Police and Enrique gave them directions to the hacienda in Ojo Caliente where he had seen Garcia coming and going. Dr. Douglas, Armijo and his nephew then returned to guard the camp. The hacienda was a classic styled home that would be worth half a million dollars in the right location. Here it was isolated and quite some distance off the main road. Run down and slowly falling apart from lack of repairs it was a perfect fixer upper for the industrious soul, but for the lazy people who lived there it had no value other than a hide away from prying eyes.

As soon as they got to the old Spanish styled house the police surrounded the property and several policemen climbed the six foot adobe wall that surrounded the house. A state policeman went up to the door. He no sooner knocked on the door when two young thugs ran out the back door. With nowhere to go they were immediately caught. Everyone then entered the house with guns drawn.

I had been tied to an iron railing which was part of an old bed, unharmed, but extremely dehydrated, angry and in desperate need of a bathroom. Fortunately Corey was there to untie me and after a quick run to a bathroom, we hugged. Hidalgo ran into the kitchen and brought me some water.

"Where are they, ask Hidalgo?"

I answered, "I think they borrowed their cousin's car and were going to go back to our camp. I do know one of them said something about dynamite.

"Dynamite, repeated Hidalgo, what in the world would they to do with that stuff?"

"I don't know, I replied but I don't think they are blowing up tree stumps with it. Who is watching the camp anyway?"

Hidalgo looked worried as he answered, "Dr. Douglas, Armijo and his nephew were going back out there to keep an eye on things. You do realize we have really misjudged those boys. They saved our bacon. Enrique's friend who is Armijo's nephew was the one who spotted Garcia and Fernandez and let us know where you are.

"Sergeant Blanco says, The State Police have two other hombres in custody, let me and my boys go with you." With that said, a caravan of police cars with Corey, Hidalgo and myself following them, headed back to the camp at Rinconada at break neck speed.

The Explosion

The dust could be seen for miles around as the caravan of cars drove across the flat Rinconada but it was a good feeling. We all knew that once someone made their way out to camp there would be no escape, there was only one way in unless they took off down the canyon trails which would lead to the same situation, no way to escape. Upon arrival, the police cars all pulled into a crescent formation facing the camp with the cedar tree in the middle. Sure enough another car was there besides Armijo's old blue truck but no one was in camp. They had all gone down the trail.

Everyone stood around for a few minutes to discuss a strategy as to what to do. Hidalgo said, "You realize, I hope, that if they are inside of the mine there is no way out except climbing up the rock wall. I would be really surprised if Garcia could even make it.

I countered his thought with, "Yes but he is a very determined and vindictive person. I know he wants to know what is down there. They know they can't ever make money from this mine, and what they really want is revenge. They don't want us to prosper from it. They want to hurt us and they don't care who else gets in the way or who gets hurt."

Several policemen along with Sergeant Blanco gathered up some equipment that they carried in the trunks of their cars and they all started single file down the trail with Hidalgo in the lead. Corey and I stayed in camp just glad to be together and alive. I knew that it would have been only a short matter of time until my captives would have tortured me.

After several minutes of anxious hiking they arrived at the small island and there was Dr. Douglas, Enrique and Armijo leaning against a rock wall in the shade.

Hidalgo, who was the first one to get to them asked, "What's the deal? Armijo casually looked up and answered with a single word, "Justice."

"Where are Garcia and Fernandez?" asked Hidalgo. Armijo, instead of saying anything, simply pointed into the mine.

Enrique then joined in the conversation as the last of the policemen dropped down from the rock and crossed over the tiny stream to join them. "We saw them coming so we took off down the trail and hid while they passed us. We then followed them down to the mine. We waited awhile then followed them inside. We waited until curiosity overtook us and we decided Garcia and Fernandez had time to drop down the pit. After they reached the bottom we waited a few more minutes and then cut the rope."

Armijo laughed, and added "Just like they did to you guys, justice. What goes around comes around."

Dr. Douglas moved within an inch of Hidalgos ear and whispered, "You realize I hope that all they are going to find is an archeological site. They will never be able to figure out that the river beds are full of gold gravel.

We also moved the pipe so they couldn't escape," continued Enrique. "They aren't going anywhere."

Sergeant Blanco, who by this time understood the humor of the situation chuckled, "So what we really have now is a rescue mission rather than a hostage situation. Say, that is poetic justice. They walked into the mine until they reached the chasm. Calling down they received no response from Garcia and Fernandez. Sergeant Blanco then snickered, "It's getting late, lets come back tomorrow morning with better equipment and we'll dig some rats out of a hole."

Upon arrival back at the camp everyone decided to leave except for Corey,

Hidalgo, Dr. Douglas and myself. Corey and I were preparing dinner when I thought out loud. "What about the dynamite? We looked in the car the two had left there but couldn't find anything.

At six in the morning the next day the police showed up, this time with a larger caravan than the last time. Yet there was no feeling of panic or even hurry as the men gathered up ropes, and climbing gear that would actually be useless in the cave but like the boy scouts, they felt they needed to be prepared.

Each policeman slung an assault rifle over his shoulder along with a canteen and portable phone in case they got separated. Hidalgo attempted to explain that they wouldn't have any need for all the equipment but they wouldn't heed any of his advice. So over to the edge of the escarpment they walked only stopping at the start of the trail long enough for Hidalgo to point out the route.

They descended over the escarpment with Hidalgo in the lead descending down the now well-worn and memorized trail until they reached the island. Entering the mine again, they again showed Sergeant Blanco the route past the petroglyph and into the long lava tube until they reached the chasm.

Sergeant Blanco was in awe of the cave, but was terrified of the chasm, a vertical crack in the rock going straight down and straight up over their heads for eighty or so feet before it ended. Yelling down into the chasm it was only a short matter of time until Sergeant Blanco heard the voices of Garcia and Fernandez as their voices made their way up to the policemen. Profanities peppered most of what they were saying, mostly in Spanish, but obviously they were two very angry men.

"We are not coming out unless you let us go," yelled Garcia!

Sergeant Blanco causally replied, "We can always leave you there until you starve to death."

Fernandez retorted, "There is light down here, and there is another way out."

Hidalgo countered his argument with, "No, the light is coming from bacteria or something growing on the walls around the warm water river. There is no way out except up this shaft."

Garcia yelled back, "We have dynamite; if you come down here we will blow all of you up."

Sergeant Blanco yelled back, "Well that wouldn't make any sense. You would just manage to blow yourselves up and maybe trap yourselves in there forever. The only way out is for you to let us drop you some safety ropes and then turn yourselves in to us."

Garcia screamed back, "And spend the rest of our lives in jail, no thanks, I would rather die first."

Sergeant Blanco took a long breath of air and replied, "That is just what you will do, die down there." With that a bullet ricocheted up the chasm spending itself harmlessly on the ceiling of the cave far above their heads.

Hidalgo looked at the others in the group and said, "It would be safer just to wait them out. They think there is another way out but that is highly unlikely. We never found another way out and if there was another way out why would the Indians have used this entrance." With that said they carefully placed the pipe back into place and lowered the safety rope. They then went back to the entrance of the mine and positioned themselves for a long wait.

It took three days before a starving Garcia and Fernandez agreed to be helped out of the chasm. It had taken them that long to explore the caverns that were easily accessible and come to the obvious conclusion that the only way out was through the original entrance. They were hungry but could not calm the thoughts of revenge they had.

Sergeant Blanco immediately took them into custody and the entire party started back up the long trail. Everyone was in a hurry to leave but Garcia and Fernandez were in a particular hurry to leave. Everyone simply thought it was just because they hadn't eaten for some time and were desperate for food.

Returning to the main trail and having climbed about a hundred yards up it they felt the explosion before they heard it. Kaboom. Looking back down at the small island they could see rocks flying out and down into the river below. Then, the entire side of the hill began to move in a tumultuous cascade down into the river actually damming it up.

After a few panic filled moments wondering if the trail they were climbing would begin to fall away they stood up and surveyed the situation. As the dust started to settle they could see the river back up and then finally after a few minutes begin to flow over the new rock pile forming a classic rapid that would have to be run by a river runner in order to be downgraded to a class five rapid. The island, along with the tiny creek and most of the trail had vanished along with all hope of ever finding a way back into the lost caverns, gold, archeology sites, and biological creatures from a different world.

Garcia and Fernandez had their final revenge but they would have to enjoy it inside the New Mexico State Penitentiary spending the rest of their natural lives there for kidnapping as well as several other major offences. They would never be heard from again but unfortunately, no one would ever be able to gain entry into the mine again as it was buried under thousands of tons of black volcanic rock.

A Return to Normal

*D*r. Douglas was facing another problem; time. Another round of new classes would be starting back at the university and he would have to return to Boulder. He didn't want to go but he valued his position as professor of geology. They exchanged emergency phone numbers, made some fast plans for future expeditions, mostly in the form of river trips throughout the southwest and he was driven into Santa Fe where he boarded another airplane and returned him to his home. He was more than disappointed, not because of the loss of the gold but rather because of the loss of knowledge that could have been acquired by scientist who would have welcomed the opportunity to explore and learn from such an unusual environment. He knew that another route into the mysteries under the Rinconada would probably never be found. Dr. Douglas didn't want to give up hope anyway. Maybe someday they would find another way into the magnificent caverns. Maybe there would be other Indian roads that would be discovered, leading to even more wonderful places. They all agreed that anything was possible but unlikely.

Hidalgo, Corey and I thanked Armijo and Enrique once more for their help, offering them some of the gold that we had succeeded in retrieving from the mine. Armijo turned it down, but Enrique accepted a moderate amount graciously, saying that he had plans to return to school and making something of himself. Like Penny and Corey, he said, "I have the bug. I want to learn more about my ancestors and the treasures that were lost here in New Mexico."

Hidalgo returned to the Navajo Indian Reservation to spend some time with his mother and father who were now celebrities on the reservation because of Hidalgos adventures. Hidalgo invested much of his newfound riches into a Native American Polytechnic School in Farmington.

Corey and I returned to Serpiente to rest. We wanted to spend some time alone in the backcountry without fear of pottery thieves, rattlesnakes and responsibilities. We knew however, that we had the 'bug,' that virtual infection that enters all who search for unknown treasures, adventures, and mystery. It would only be a matter of time until we would find ourselves out on a lonesome trail following another great adventure and solving another historical mystery.

Part 4

Evil Intent

Nothing is more frightening than a fear you cannot name.

—Cornelia Funke, Inkheart

We always vilify what we don't understand.

—Nenia Campbell, Horrorscape

An Introduction

The entire world watched during August of 1994, as the planet Jupiter was battered by a swarm of comet fragments. Many people were startled by the realization, that the universe can be a very dangerous place. The comet that hit Jupiter with twenty-one fragments delivered to that planet an explosive force equal to about 40 million megatons of TNT. Any one of those fragments would have been enough to destroy the earth, with far more power than the energy of all the nuclear bombs ever built. At this time, scientists have computed probabilities of an asteroid impact on Earth within an average person's lifetime. They concluded the odds to be about one chance in several thousand. It is the size of the asteroid that matters. Too small and an asteroid burns up in the atmosphere or explodes in the air like the one that hit Siberia in 1908. If an asteroid is too large, the earth vaporizes. We humans have always considered the universe to be a very dangerous place, which is one of the reasons why we are what we are.

Unfortunately most modern people have forgotten about the skies. As a species we are oblivious to what goes on up there. Our ancestors who were always out in the open saw much more than we modern people do. In many ancient cultures, such as in Egypt people would keep their animals inside their homes and they would sleep in the cool air on the roofs of their homes, quite literally under the stars. Without air conditioning it was the natural way.

Most high school students in today's world would never be able to spot a planet among the multitudes of stars on a given night. They wouldn't know how nor would they have the patience. Many people have been disassociated with the night time sky as a result of religious beliefs or televisions. There are some, who do not even believe in planets. Planets are of course, the first stars that appear in the night sky and they move from night to night. Considering the scientific advances that have occurred in the last few years it is amazing how pockets of our society have actually chosen to be so dramatically unaware, a preferred ignorance.

Constellations

Corey, Hidalgo and I heard the first sound as a tiny "clink" of rock, although it is highly unlikely that a living creature had moved it. Anyone who spends time at the bottom of a deep canyon hears the miniature rockslides that occur, usually as a result of miniature geological events that occur during wind, ice, water erosion, uneven heating, even plant growth. Then again, a few seconds later, we heard a lesser "clink."

Under the starry sky Corey and I lay together on our tent mats with heads propped up so we would be looking straight up into the clear nighttime sky. Hidalgo was fifteen feet away in the same position, absorbed by the nighttime canvas that nature had painted for us. We were looking at one of the greatest natural spectacles in the world each seeing a different view, even though we were seeing the same thing.

To me, the night time sky was bringing up visions of young lovers, stars embracing stars. Fanciful thoughts toyed with my mind as I gazed into the night sky and I let my imagination run wild. Just married, fanciful thoughts of love were natural for me as it is for all young ladies. The love of my life, my soul mate, was resting beside me.

Corey was connecting dots. The stars made patterns to him like they had done to millions of his forefathers who had undoubtedly done the same thing. Making sense out of random patterns is a human condition we are all hardwired for; Sagittarius, Orion, and Ursa Major which naturally looked like a big dipper to Corey. He couldn't conceive a pattern of a bear in those stars. His mind connected the lower part of the dipper until he spotted the North Star. He knew that as the earth rotated under it all the other stars appeared to travel in concentric rings around this one lonely star, a star that people of the earth had used for navigation for thousands of years.

Hidalgo's mind was taking him back to stories and impressions of events he had experienced as a little boy growing up on the Navajo Indian Reservation. Filled with the memories of ceremonies that only Navajo youths experience, the dots were there but they made entirely different patterns and meant entirely different things to him.

Some of those stars ever so slowly moved, not really stars at all but rather planets that are easily observable as the first dots of light that appear after sunset. Venus, the most easily observed planet, sometimes even changes route, going back to where it came from, a process that scientist call retrograde. This motion mystified all earlier people. Some of the lights in the sky were falling, leaving streaks in the sky as they burned up in the atmosphere. A meteor shower was creating a light show for our evening's entertainment.

Hidalgo's mind wandered to places where early people dwelt. Laying at the bottom of White Rock Canyon, he was surrounded by the magic of Bandelier National Monument. He was thinking of the Anasazi, those ancient people, on whom his people, the Navajo, had made war. He also thought of secrets that he preferred to share with only his closest and personal friends. The ceremonies of his people were in many ways still a mystery to him, particularly those that dwelt in the mist of times forgotten.

He had learned that Anthropologists are confounded as to why the early Anasazi Indians called Chacoans built an utterly fantastic civilization that was abandoned and is now only ruins. What drove them to build these structures in one of the most uninviting and inhospitable places in North America? Why build there?

He thought of the spiral petroglyphs on the Pajata Butte that allowed daggers of light to line up on them. He had read that those early people believed if the daggers did not line up when they were supposed to, then the earth was out of balance and a new time or age would occur. For a second he thought of the Mayan calendar that some interpret as a giant time machine, a time machine that will run out on December 21st of 2012. He chuckled to himself, thinking that they would need to build a new calendar; if their civilization had survived to the present day.

His thoughts drifted to the last time the entire planet underwent dramatic change in the home of the Mayans, the mountains that had once grown lush grass became covered by vast sheets of ice. Later, as the world warmed up, the ice exposed that previous world for all to see. It happened all over the world; Savannas with great lakes and rivers dried up to become the Sahara Desert. Grasslands became bleak deserts; jungles appeared where grass only grew before. Chaco Canyon changed from a vast forested plain with water running down the tiny streambed at the bottom of the canyon, to the bleak desert it is today.

This self-educated Indian was fascinated about those things. He had made it a point since he was young to study the history of the region in which he was living.

Even as a little boy on the reservation, when other children had shown little interest in the stories of the elders and the traditions of his people, Hidalgo hung on every story and ceremony that was told to him. The elders knew that children such as Hidalgo would keep the traditions of the Navajo alive after the elders had passed to the next world.

Hidalgo's mind flashed back to the present, some living creature was creating sounds; a deer, raccoon, bear, cougar, or homicidal manic. Worry momentarily set in, then vanished. A deer, that perfection of stealth, wandered through our camp, apparently unaware of us, as its ever so slight sounds were masked by the churning, bubbling waters of the Rio Grande River. In our enthusiasm to see the meteor showers and evening wildlife, we were emulating the deer herself, so quiet and stealthy.

We all knew of course, it was better to plan canoe trips to coincide with known meteor showers, but if anyone travels into the thin clear air of a desert or mountain top, away from city lights, will be entertained by the numerous meteors that fall through the night sky on any given night.

This was a great night. In the high desert mountain regions of the southwestern United States, beach camps in deep dark canyons with sheer surrounding walls provide shelter for the camper from the glare of light sources from nearby cities. There, in the deepest of shadows, burrowed into a warm sleeping bag looking skyward with clarity of vision we laid there and enjoyed the meteor shower. Without the aid of flashlights, lanterns, televisions, or even a lowly campfire, each of us had time for our own contemplation.

The next morning over the campfire where a breakfast was cooking Corey asked Hidalgo, "What did you think about the meteor showers last night? Penny and I were listening to a radio broadcast from PBS about them on the way down here. It said that meteorites can range in composition from snowballs to vast chunks of metallic rock, reminiscent of the nickel iron core of the Earth. Did you know that some meteors survive the impact with the earth to become meteorites, which are collected usually in places like polar ice fields or deserts? They are studied by scientists. When found, they are worth their weight in gold."

"Curiously, when fragments of meteorites are heated in a test tube, large amounts of gases are liberated, mostly hydrogen and oxygen, which condense to form water, a basic prerequisite for life. There is water, tied up chemically, in the most distant and bleakest of rocks out there. Some of these meteoric fragments have been examined for the presence of fossilferious carbon based organisms, namely meteorites which are thought to have been blasted off the planet Mars by some earlier asteroid impact there. Fossilized microorganisms have been found on those rocks, causing skeptics to demand an earthly origin for these pieces of meteorite."

"That's fascinating," I interjected, "but what do you know about comets? Have you heard that three comets will be visiting the earth before the year 2000?"

"Comets are very different from meteorites" answered Corey. "Comets are astronomical precursors of change, and this seems to be a time for astronomical signs."

Hidalgo started clearing up the breakfast as we talked. "If that is the case perhaps we should all work a little faster on these dishes, otherwise those comets and asteroids may hit before I get these dishes done and we will never get back on the river." Everyone laughed and picked up the pace.

As we all rushed around packing our canoes and getting ready to get back on the river, I thought about how strangely things worked out. Hidalgo, and Corey as well as I were from different worlds. I was a small town, Tennessee girl, Corey was a New Mexico boy, and Hidalgo was raised on a Navajo reservation, yet we discovered that we all had a deep interest in ancient peoples of the world and interest in the heavens and what could be learned from them. All of us had acquired complimentary knowledge in different ways, and each could learn from the other.

Back on the river, Hidalgo took the lead in his canoe because he was more experienced and paddling solo making him more mobile than Corey and me. I sat in the front of the tandem canoe with Corey in the back. This made me the lookout and Corey was the one who actually steered the canoe.

As we neared a bend in the river we heard the tell-tale roar of an upcoming rapid. Hidalgo pulled to the bank of the river to scout the rapid and Corey and I pulled in behind him. We walked around the bend and saw a rapid that extended as far as we could see, with several large rocks scattered throughout. There was one particular large rock right in the center of a wild section of rapid. Because of this rock, I was inclined to walk around the rapid, but when I scouted the way around I found that there was dense brush blocking the way.

We walked back to the bend and discussed the best way to get around the big rock. "I think the right channel is deeper," I conjectured, "It also seems wider than the left passage."

"The left channel is closer to the bank," interjected Corey. "If we tip the canoe, it will be easier to get out of the water from there. What do you think, Hidalgo?"

Hidalgo thought for several minutes, looked at the rock from as many angles as possible, and then hesitantly replied, "It's hard to tell how large the rock is or how much of it is hidden underwater, but I think Corey may be right."

"I bow to your experience," I said to Hidalgo. "I think you are both wrong, but you have been running rivers longer than either one or us." It was a lie and I knew it. We were all learning together.

Having made the decision, Hidalgo pushed his canoe into the water and started toward the rapid with Corey and me following in our tandem canoe. All went well for Hidalgo as he approached the rapid making his way past the rock that formed the rapid, but the back of his canoe scraped the rock on the way. With a chill he realized that the heavier, tandem canoe would not make it over the edge of the rock that he had scraped. He tried to wave to us and let us know that we needed to swing to the right, further away from the rock, but it was too late. Corey could not turn the canoe in time to miss the edge of the submerged rock.

The canoe caught the rock just close enough to the middle to broach. Corey immediately jumped out of the canoe and was trying to push the canoe off the rock, but the fast water swept him off his feet and only by holding on to the side was he able to keep from being swept on down the rapid and away from the canoe. My end of the canoe was raised out of the water. I tried to get out of the canoe but when I tried to put my feet on the rock, the only thing I felt under my feet was water. Frightened, I jumped back in the canoe. By this time Corey had managed to pull himself up to the upriver side of the canoe. He tried again to push it off of the rock, but it would not budge. "Get out of the canoe," he hollered to me, "I can't get the canoe off of the rock with you in it."

I hesitated only a few seconds, then dived into the back of the canoe, which was now in front. As I did, the shift of my weight caused the canoe to lurch off of the rock. At the last second, Corey dived into the canoe and off we went down the river. We were out of control, going down the rapids at a terrifying speed and full of water, but we were off the rock. Corey finally got the spare paddle loose from under the seat of the canoe and steered us to the bank where Hidalgo was waiting with a rescue rope after fishing Corey's lost paddle out of the water and ready to fish one of us out if we fell out of the canoe. I was laughing and crying at the same time as we pulled up to the bank. The adrenaline rush of the adventure made me feel like I was drunk. "Well," I laughed, "I guess that I was right after all." Corey and Hidalgo just sighed, knowing that they would never hear the end of this.

Since everything in our canoe was soaking wet, we decided to camp where we were on the river bank. We hung up the sleeping bags to dry and put out some fishing lines to catch a catfish for dinner. Luckily it was a hot day and the sleeping bags dried out before it was time to get into them.

Hidalgo built a small fire so that I could dry off and we all sat around and continued our morning conversation. Hidalgo said, "Most ancient Americans; the Clovis and Folsum, Anasazi, and later the Pueblo cultures and much later the tribe called the Navajos, witnessed and made attempts to record astronomical signs in the southwest. Those records can be found in the form of petroglyphs throughout the Southwest. A close examination shows that many of the larger ruins were built along astronomical orientations. In South America it is thought that the native cultures based their entire civilizations upon astronomical observations with the locations of ruins being found close to water sources."

"Records were kept throughout the world of such observances. Haley's Comet was visible in the skies over Jerusalem when that city fell to the Romans in 66 B.C. The comet must have sided with the Romans, because they defeated Attila the Hun, in 451 A.D. The comet attended the Norman invasion of England in 1066, early in the present millennium. Mark Twain joked that he came into life on a comet, because he was born in 1835, the year of a visit by Haley's Comet. He left this life on its next pass, seventy five years later, which has prompted some to take his kidding seriously."

"The heavenly bodies in the solar system that fascinate me are asteroids," said Corey. "My teachers at the university said that according to geological and astronomical calculations, an asteroid about 1 mile or 1.6 kilometers across, strikes Earth once every 300,000 years. An asteroid this large would leave a crater over 10 miles across. Nobody really knows what effect it would have on the planet as a whole, but the pall of dust kicked up by the impact might block out the sun long enough to bring on a nuclear winter. Agriculture and commerce would probably cease, and most people in the world would die. I'll bet that the real consequence of such an impact would be far greater than any cinematic re-creation. The consequences of a real impact would be felt for generations, assuming that there was someone left around to experience them."

Conversations About Asteroids

Corey found himself talking while we all unpacked everything making sure water had not gotten into anything. He talked about asteroids based upon what he had learned as a student of geology. "Ever since photographs of the earth and the moon were taken from deep space and made available to the public, much to the credit of the National Aeronautics and Space Administration; many of us have been fascinated by the thin membrane of living matter on our earth known as the biosphere where life recycles itself. From space, with the deep vast emptiness behind it, this biosphere appears to be alive. Indeed, much has been written concerning the Gaia Hypothesis, which hypothecates that the earth is a living organism. In the vastness of space, we ponder whether there are other biospheres out there that would support life. The earth as seen from outer space is strikingly beautiful, constantly changing, however, if I were the operator of that distant camera, I would be looking over my shoulder."

"Consider the following: Our planet resides in an almost invisible swarm of meteoroids and asteroids, with thousands of objects orbiting our sun that periodically cross the Earth's orbit. During a meteor shower, hundreds of small ones can appear and leave their fiery trail in the night sky. The vast majority of them are rice size, and even they leave an impressive trail in the sky. Larger ones do hit the earth, and occasionally hit houses and even people. In some areas of the world, collecting these extraterrestrial objects is the basis for lucrative hobbies. Only rarely does one hit that leaves a crater such as meteor crater in Arizona. According to the paleontological records, very large meteorites impact every few million years, which causes nature to have to start over. An asteroid impact seems highly unlikely since one has not fallen in historic times. However, there is evidence that an impact was observed on the moon and documented by the Chinese, Native Americans, Egyptians and many other sources."

Hidalgo started to enter the conversation but Corey cut him off.

"For weeks after an impact, the moon probably appears as a larger red orb. In the geologic records, massive die-offs have occurred in 26 million-year cycles, corresponding to earth's orbit and probably due to asteroid impacts. This is what apparently happened to the dinosaurs. It will likely happen again. We have some 15 million years or so before the next major predicted die-off episode. In the meantime, a rogue asteroid, one that appears out of nowhere leaving us little time to prepare could most likely hit us. If such an impact occurred, dramatic changes would occur to the biosphere. Life, as we humans know it would certainly have to start over.

I asked him, "What are our chances of being killed by such an asteroid impact?"

Corey answered me, "Some astronomers consider your odds of being hit by an asteroid impact may be as high as one in six thousand, greater than your chance of dying in a plane crash. If of course you do die unexpectedly, it is far more likely to be from very earthbound causes, such as automobile accidents, high blood pressure or gunshots. Does all this worry you?"

Hidalgo and I looked at each other both rolling our eyes and continued setting up tents.

"You probably wouldn't, you are probably not as fatalistic as I am. But let me tell you something, a quick glance at a New Mexico road map will immediately remind you, of the geological features that this state is set in. That large line which goes north and south is the Rio Grande Rift Zone, and right next to it, just above Albuquerque, is Jemez volcano, the largest caldera type volcano in the United States. Obviously it is unique to the state. Was an asteroid the precursor, the cause of the Jemez volcano? What about many of the worlds other volcanic sites? Was Hawaii formed as the result of an asteroid impact, a precursor to its current hot spot activity, which due to plate tectonics, has resulted in a string of volcanic islands, like a string of pearls. The oldest islands have eroded flat while the geologically younger islands have tall peaks. The next Hawaiian Island is currently being built, still thousands of feet below the ocean surface. The same questions are now being asked about Yellowstone super volcano. Did the geological disturbance that created these volcanoes originate deep within the earth or from more lofty places?"

I finally turned to Corey and simply said, I don't know about getting hit by an asteroid tonight but you are going to get hit by me if you don't help us set up camp!"

White Rock Canyon

That next evening we camped along a beach underneath a vertical wall of lava that soared straight up a couple of thousand feet. At the top of the cliffs was an entire town. The town of White Rock is the home of many scientists who work at Los Alamos Laboratories yet they were separated by the vast cliff. We could just as well have been a thousand miles apart. As our camp became enveloped in darkness we again extinguished all sources of light in order to consider the night sky. Discussions again centered upon the metaphysical.

Corey's seemed determined to continue his earlier conversations. "The American Southwest is currently experiencing a rash of reports of strange lights at night, metaphysical locations, cattle mutilations, disappearances, and unidentified flying objects of every shape and description. We even get reports of crashed UFOs with dead occupants that the Air Force immediately whisks away, covers up, and denies; thus creating a media feeding frenzy along with the creation of assorted television shows devoted to the subject. Historically the Southwest has been famous for its unsolved mysteries, long before there were aliens to worry about. It seems to have been a center of unexplained occurrences that baffled the Native Americans, the Spanish, and is certainly perplexing to the peoples who live here now."

Hidalgo grinned as Corey burned his hand on the coffee pot but that didn't keep him from talking. "Phenomena will often occur leaving the observer in a quandary as to what it was, which upon later examination reveals itself. In fact, almost all super-normal phenomena can be explained enlisting the resources of universities, police, and laboratories throughout the world using modern scientific methods readily available to the public. There are, however, a tiny percent of real phenomena that cannot be explained by anyone, therefore the challenge of the mystery persist. Until the end of the millennium and well into the future, there will be an unending parade of disaster films, earthquakes, killer bees, volcanoes, asteroids and comets; and perhaps there are alien spacecraft, riding along on the comets, watching us. Many of these ideas manage to entertain us, but life rarely imitates art. Real environmental change is anything that has an effect upon us, whether positive or negative. When there is apparently nothing we can do about catastrophic change, most of us demonstrate a fatalistic attitude."

I added, "A little like the gallant mouse that was last seen shaking a tiny defiant fist, just before the hawk snatches it up".

Certainly that was the way Corey and I along with Hidalgo approached difficult rapids, especially with fully loaded canoes. It was also the way we approached our lives. We were all new to the science of river running, but we were learning fast. All three of us were experienced with the outdoors with years of experience with pack animals but canoeing was new to us. We knew that we were going for many swims. It was our fate. But running rapids was our choice. We could choose whether or not to put ourselves in this situation, and we must deal with the consequences of our choice. But some things are simply beyond our control, we became fatalistic. It was in our nature as humans.

Corey, who was just about to doze, noticed a moving object just at the horizon. Quietly he whispered to me to watch. "There's another airplane from Denver landing at the Albuquerque airport." But it didn't. Instead it just sat in the sky for several minutes then suddenly darted away.

"What in the world was that, I asked being as puzzled by the light show as Corey." Rising up on his elbows to get a better view, the hair on the back of Corey's neck began to rise as he realized that what he was watching was impossible. Corey whispered, "This all reminds me of the story of the alien spaceship that arrived in Washington and the alien stepped out of it with a book. Everyone was panic stricken by the appearance of the alien until they read the title of the book, 'To Serve Man,' everyone relaxed. They relaxed until they realized that it was a cookbook."

The Gallina Canyon Mystery

A month of ranch work later and after Corey had returned from Los Lunas, New Mexico where he had a mail box at the post office, he walked into the living room of the ranch house and made an announcement. "I may have a new mystery for us to solve."

I was helping Aunt June to prepare dinner and looked up and kidded him. "Let's hope no one is going to get shot at this time."

Hidalgo who had just walked into the kitchen picked up on the conversation, looked at me, and added, "Or kidnapped." Our last encounter with the two characters that were antiquity thieves was still a sensitive memory. The kidnappers were spending time in the New Mexico State Penitentiary and by the time the thieves were released from prison, they would be too old to care.

Everyone was building up the ranch we lived on but we still had plenty of time to explore our new passions; being river runners and historical detectives had been a lucrative hobby but now it was becoming so much more, opening up new and exciting pursuits.

Corey sat down beside me and pretended he was holding me to protect me while Hidalgo grabbed at me, which brought a giggle out of me followed with, "Well, let's hear it." Everyone settled down to hear Corey's story.

Corey pulled out a thick letter he had received and began to explain. "It all has to do with my Aunt Alice and her family that lives in Albuquerque. Oral history is very much alive in the family. Aunt Alice is the repository of all of the oral history. She is the person who in the Holliday family was always the historian as well as the executor of the family wills. As you may guess, the family has been keeping up with our adventures as historical detectives and volunteered a family secret to us. Aunt Alice thought that maybe we could get to the bottom of a mystery that she had encountered."

Hidalgo said, "So this is not really your mystery but one of your relatives?"

"Yes," replied Corey, "However, Aunt Alice would never have written to me about it unless there was something to it. Let me set the stage for you. There are actually two letters here, one from Alice about family stuff and one from her son Richard who wrote down the details of the mystery." With that he began an explanation of the locality of the mystery as he read from segments of the letter.

"The Rio Gallina, located between Cuba and Lindrith, is a tiny desert stream draining a large canyon after summer downpours. Usually there is just enough seep water in it to get your toes muddy or your jeep struck. But in times of flash floods, as with all drainage systems, this tiny stream can become a roaring hematite red torrent of water as it carries everything down its channel to be deposited down river. The Rio Gallina is a tributary of the Rio Chama, a popular whitewater canoe river, with the confluence occurring across the river from Christ in the Desert Monastery." Corey added on his own, "Much of the letter is also about an Indian culture that existed there between the seventh and the tenth centuries A.D. They were a strange people who apparently kept to themselves. According to what Richard was able to discover about them, they did not engage in trade, no Chacoan or any other pottery is found in their villages, and none of their pottery is found anywhere else. Apparently at one time or another, the people who lived there long ago were all massacred, anyway that is what the archeological literature claims."

I jumped into the conversation with, "Does all this mean we are going on another canoe trip, maybe down the Rio Gallina River?"

"Well," said Corey, "the river there is only a few inches deep, however we might run the Chama River."

"Well, we could drag the canoes down the river," Hidalgo sheepishly replied in a tease.

We had taken up river running as a way of exploring the back country. What started as a simple raft trip down the whitewater section of the Rio Grande River, being coached by Dr. Wayne Douglas, who was a passionate river runner and professor at the University of Colorado, had developed into our passion. I loved it. Corey and I had rented a tandem canoe but now we were purchasing our own solo canoes and equipment from a store in Albuquerque. I had insisted upon having my own solo canoe after our adventures in White Rock Canyon.

Referring back to the letter but not reading from it Corey continued, "Aunt Alice and Uncle Boone were deer hunting in Gallina canyon when this mystery occurred. You all know how it is with families like that; deer hunting was a vacation for them. They never went anywhere unless they were fishing, deer hunting, or rabbit hunting. It was what they worked for. Anyway this part of the letter was written by their son, Richard. He is the one who really wants information about what happened to them."

Aunt June and Uncle Ken joined them, all bent on hearing the mystery. The letter read as follows:

"Dear Corey,

I hope things are going well with you and your adopted family. Say hello to everyone for me. Things are fine with us but I can't get this hunting trip we took out of my head and I was hoping you and Penny and that Navajo fellow might shed a little light on this subject for me."

I again started to giggle and poked Hidalgo in the ribs. "I wonder if he means this Navajo fellow or some other Navajo."

"Cut it out." growled Hidalgo who wanted to hear the story."

"If you take the dirt road between Regina and El Vado, New Mexico, you can find, after some exploration, a road over to the Gallinas Canyon. We have deer hunted there a couple of times and every time we go there I have the time of my life exploring the place. This last time we went hunting, I had a schoolmate, Butch Roberts and his parents go hunting deer with us. Where we camped, which is where the jeep road drops down into the bottom of the canyon; there are on top of almost every small hillside, pits dug out of the ground with circular edges lined with stones that suffice for walls. Timbers made from the surrounding ponderosa pines provide rafters. Finally, small branches with mats of grass and dirt make up the roofs. Sometimes rocks cover the entire home so that the unwary person might be totally unaware of the kiva - like home under their feet. Like much of New Mexico, this area has been isolated long enough so that many of the remains of the ancient Indians are still in place, undisturbed after thousands of years."

"My mother, Alice reminisces about her days as a little girl, when the family would go down from Estancia and explore the Gran Quivera Ruins just south of Mountainair. It was a lot of fun for a little girl to run and play on the maze of walls that remained at the site."

"She would get arrested for doing that now." responded Aunt June.

Corey continued reading the letter, "In Gallina Canyon I really wanted to dig into as many ruins as possible. Who knows what marvelous things my friend Butch and I might uncover? Fortunately, as you know, Grand Quivera Ruins and most other ruins are now protected under the Antiquities Act to protect them from little grave robbers such as I was then. Tell your Navajo friend and June that I am sorry for my trespasses but I didn't know any better back then."

Hidalgo said grudgingly, "Well I suppose I can forgive him if he has a good enough story to tell us. Besides he was just like many other kids out there that don't know any better."

Corey continued reading the letter, "This was the place my family decided to go deer hunting again that year. Everyone achieved adulthood or so I thought, through the ritual of deer hunting. At least, that was the way I imagined the world worked, as a boy. Like many other families in the South Valley of Albuquerque, my folks would work all year long in order to take a week off and go deer hunting; our vacation."

"When we arrived the air temperature was moderate, not cold at all. But after setting up camp and spending the morning exploring the local countryside, the temperature immediately dropped. Huge six sided snow crystals persisted in the air throughout the afternoon, covering up any sign of ancient mystery and turning my mind back to what we had come up here for, deer hunting. Slowly, after dark, the sky cleared and the stars came out in the most amazing clarity that memory affords me. It was spectacular! After a heavy snow the night sky is cleansed by each and every snowflake with the tiniest particle of soot or dust in its center. The snow literally cleanses the air."

"And so it was that I found myself camped out with my folks and the parents of my friend Butch, sitting around a campfire one snowy October evening, when the most amazing thing happened. My mother Alice was talking to a captive audience of Butch and me. Lois, Butch's mother, was there as well as my little brother who couldn't remember anything because of his tender age. Dad and everyone else were back in Cuba, New Mexico, trying to get a broken differential repaired on Mr. Roberts' jeep, which was the only way to avoid walking for miles up and down the river when hunting. My mother, Alice was sitting there with the rest of us, looking into the campfire while we were sipping mugs filled with brews of hot cocoa or coffee."

"We had big problems to contend with; first there was the broken jeep, then there was the snow which made travel difficult if not impossible. We weren't really prepared for this drastic weather change, yet we were all having a ball just contending with it. I don't remember exactly what she was talking about, but suddenly, in the middle of a sentence; my mother stopped, looked off to the hillside north of us, and said, what's that?"

"Vision and perception on a crisp, cold, fall evening after a snow can really be acute. This was the kind of atmosphere that astronomers prefer when photographing the stars. You can see for miles with the naked eye, and we all saw the same thing. At first we could see what appeared to be a small orange explosion. A mushroom shaped ball of what appeared to be brilliant fire that got bigger and redder as it rose from the earth. It took a few seconds for us to figure out how far away it was. On the side of the hill this apparition rose through the clear sky."

"Did an airplane crash? My mother slowly asked, as we stared in amazement."

"Probably an atomic bomb, Butch blurted out."

"No, it isn't that far away", I said, thinking out loud, based upon what I knew about bomb testing, which was next to nothing. It was about then that we realized that there was no sound."

"Looks like a jet crash or a gas-well fire," I volunteered. The more we looked, however, the more we became convinced that it was just up the hill from our camp, only a few hundred yards away. It was really close! No sound, no explosion, just a brilliant ball of colors in the general shape of a thunderhead superimposed and reflecting off the snow. The apparition appeared to be boiling with colors emanating from the inside out. I had just walked down that same hill a few hours before while returning from a hike and couldn't remember anything strange about the place."

"The apparition started to change. Deep reds and purples appeared yet not a sound. It didn't expand exactly like a fireball. Reflecting back upon it, I have the impression that it had a high density; it was much heavier than the surrounding air. It was an entity. It was heavy, metallic and sparkly despite its gaseous appearance. Soon, it began billowing out. Within a few minutes it began to flow toward us, with colorful tendrils cascading over rocks and through the trees toward our camp. Phosphorescence, psychedelics, whatever it was, it had lost its brilliant colors after the initial fireball and began to show subtle shades of pinks and lavenders. This shimmering, cascading, no longer metallic fog still seemed unearthly with glowing points of light in it. Perhaps ten minutes passed, which seemed like a lifetime as the mist swirled around us on its way to lower grounds. Little puffs of it jetted up as it passed over the fire. Once at the riverbed it lasted perhaps another twenty minutes or so before disappearing altogether. There just seemed to be a glowing in the moonlight over the riverbed the rest of the evening. No sound or smell, no sensation of heat at all and apparently no after effects except to forever make us skeptical about what we understood as science."

"At least, I am spared the responsibility of defining what it was that I saw. I simply can't." My mother and I discussed the incident many times. I am often reminded of it when seeing high school chemistry experiments, which produce colorful clouds, or even in tiny rainbows of color in the prisms of early dew and water, yet, never with all the same brilliant characteristics of that fateful evening. I never thought that deer hunting could be such a metaphysical experience."

"Last year we returned to the canyon and stopped to talk to a sheepherder who was in front of Unzueta's near the small village of Gallina, who knew what I was talking about. He explained that his grandfather, who also was a sheepherder, experienced the same mystery many times while tending his sheep in Gallinas, but the fellow stopped talking and left as soon as Alice and Boone came out to join us."

"According to a friend of mine, this sort of stuff occurs all over the southwest. He claims to have seen the same sort of stuff while floating down the San Juan River and in a minor way, in Aspen Colorado. Do you have any idea what it was? Hope to hear from you soon, Richard"

"What do you suppose it was," volunteered Uncle Ken?"

I answered, "It sounds like what people see in North Carolina at a place called Linville Falls. There, many people camp out or sit in their cars at an overlook to see lights that appear in the canyon. Scientists speculate that they are plasma balls generated by earthquake activity. In the laboratory, when granite is crushed it can generate tiny balls of colorful plasma. They hypothesize that the entire area is under tectonic stress and the stress creates the ball plasmas. It might be something else though; ball plasma tends to disappear as soon as it comes into contact with anything."

Hidalgo then entered the conversation, "All over the Four Corners region people have experienced strange lights in the sky. My people, the Navajo, have beliefs about them. They call them Skin Walkers, some call them Shape Shifters. They believe that they are witches or *brujas* who can change their form from one creature or another or simply show themselves as balls of light."

Corey asked, "Is that what you believe?"

Hidalgo answered cautiously, "Well I don't really know. Most sane people simply say that beliefs such as those are really superstitions. You realize that I have never actually seen anything like that and I have lived in that area for years. I do know that when I worked for the police department in Durango, occasionally someone would report seeing lights in the sky but they were usually dismissed as nuts. The majority of those reports came from around the San Juan River area which forms the northern boundary of the Navajo Indian Reservation. No one really pays any attention to those reports because most of the people who are floating down that river are partying. One fellow claimed to have seen two moons one evening but then he had drunk several shots of whisky beforehand. Everyone just laughed at him."

I interjected, "Yes but they can't all be crazy or under the influence. Besides, researching the subject would be a great excuse to explore another river." I looked over at Corey who didn't give me any indication at all, which disappointed me, but Hidalgo was curiously excited about the prospect.

Hidalgo said, "I think it would be a great idea if Ken and June would volunteer to provide us with a shuttle and if I could go into Durango for a short while, there is a *bilagaana* I would like to visit." Everyone looked a little puzzled for a moment but he continued his point. "It has been a long time since I have seen this person and I have some unfinished business to take care of."

With that everyone started the practical business of planning a trip to Durango where we would drop off Hidalgo. Then, if all went as expected and we got a required permit from the Bureau of Land Management for the lower San Juan, we would drive down the Animas River toward Farmington where we would find a good put-in, meet Hidalgo, and launch our canoe trip.

The Bilaganna

I did my research. The creation of many classic southwestern desert rivers begins high on the volcanic slopes of the mountains of Colorado where winter snow accumulates following cycles as old as time. Near Wolf Creek Pass, melting snow slowly turns into rivulets. The major contributor to the San Juan River is the Animas, becoming a river from thousands of rivulets near the tourist town of Silverton, Colorado. The river there is not considered navigable because the water actually flows through and under talus rock piles. People have tried it but many of the bodies have yet to be found.

Other tributaries which can produce amazing amounts of sudden runoff below Farmington are the La Plata River, Blanco Canyon, Gallegos Canyon, Chaco Canyon, Montezuma Creek, Recapture Creek, Cottonwood Wash, Comb Wash, Chinle Creek, Grand Gulch, and Oljeto Wash, the watershed is enormous. With such an extremely large drainage area, unpredictable floods can occur at any time. The high water that carries away your icebox on a hot summer day may have come from a thunderstorm hundreds of miles away. A party of canoes only one canyon up stream may not notice the change. Down river, the source of the flood may often be deduced by the color of the river water. The river here is reminiscent of all wise and beautiful women, she returns a gentility and playfulness when approached with preparation, flattery and care; but can be cruel when not properly appreciated.

The river runner must be willing to invest tremendous amounts of time and resources for the opportunity to visit and become intimate with this most unique and grandest of rivers. A visit requires the river runner to come to grips with profound psychological, physical, and logistical challenges. The rapids are relatively easy class I - III at normal water levels. The scenery is spectacular, providing a paradise for the student of geology and there are few places in the United States where the stratum is so vividly exposed. Many great western movies have been filmed there.

This canyon, along with many others in the area, like the Grand Canyon, was formed when the Colorado plateau began to rise some seven to nine million years ago, trapping a much older meandering river. As the land rose, the ancient entrenched river simply kept its original course cutting down through 2000 feet of much older Permian rocks. During its course across the Four Corners area the San Juan traverses a series of geologic formations representing an enormous period of time, from the base of the Cretaceous formations down to exposed rocks from the middle of the Pennsylvanian age. Fossils can be found everywhere often as a beautifully agatized red matrix in gray limestone. Volcanic intrusions further complicate the geology adding to the mystery and beauty of the area such as in the Mule Ear Diatreme area. A volcanic vent pipe, similar to the Kimberlite pipes of South Africa that is mined for the world's best diamonds. It forms a prominent feature of the area as well as a marker into the deep canyons.

In recent years the San Juan area has become an attraction for an increasing number of people of varied interest. The upper part of the run is extremely rich in archaeological sites. Several universities offer authorized field trips into the area for geology and archaeology students, but concern has been expressed recently about our very human habit of loving our archaeological sites to death. The San Juan was the center of much of the Anasazi world as well as the recent Navahos. Modern vandalism has become a problem. Those "Thieves of Time," as Tony Hillerman and others have called then, are still fast at work in this area. Unfortunately there are vast amounts of money available for those who plunder hidden ruins.

A seasonal attraction is sand wave surfing, which at high water makes for a roller coaster ride. In a canoe, the trick is to avoid swamping. You might show up at Sand Island to find a tiny, precious trickle of clear water coming all the way from Navajo dam in New Mexico. Or, you might find a raging brown river of extremely fast water that completely submerges the rapids with sand waves of frightening proportions. Watching large groups is at least as good as going to a circus, sometimes just getting around them while they are in the middle of a summer water fight can be an experience.

The water is usually very warm with summertime water temperatures approaching the temperature of bath water. Eventually the sand gets into everything, even for those who come prepared. Even native people suffered as a brief examination of Anasazi skulls demonstrates overly worn teeth as a result of eating gritty food such as cornmeal which is ground on stones made from the local rock.

According to dendrochronological dating research, the southwest had a much wetter climate in earlier, postglacial years. There is more than speculation that Chaco Canyon and Canyon de Chelly had permanent water flowing through them. One can imagine what it was like. Instead of a desert, the area was a vast forest of ponderosa pine and grass. Rivers which are now nothing but dry arroyos at the bottom of rocky canyons, were spring feed streams with lush vegetation and game abounding. For generations the population grew and the culture flourished. But a climatic change occurred along with deforestation, following a pattern as old as mankind itself. The ancient Anasazi appear to have suffered extensively from over taxing the carrying capacity of their land, particularly after drought.

The river returns a unique and personal impression affecting everyone differently; much has been written and published describing this experience. The mature river runner knows that there are life skills to learn that have little to do with the mechanical aspects of river running, but rather skills dealing with the complex psychological mechanics of interpersonal relationships in a bizarre and alien environment for an extended period of time. But overall, the San Juan is one of the most popular and safe white water runs in the United States and the people who swarm to this river are as varied as the river topography. Occasionally, many languages can be overheard along the river and she assumes an international flavor. Like any river she can be moody, but is treasured by moments provided by elements such as light, color, and atmosphere that come together in just the right chemistry producing dramatic moments and the resulting impressions, reflections and memories.

It was late spring which meant the days were warm but the nights would be cold. The river would be very high and the water very cold. By the time we would finish the expedition some three hundred miles downriver, the days would become long and hot and the river water warm.

After making arrangements to have a hired hand watch things at the ranch, which actually required little effort but rather a responsibility to keep eyes open for the usual problems such as a calf getting tangled up in brush or the daily feeding of livestock, Aunt June and Uncle Ken provided the shuttle.

Ken and June took it all in stride being glad to get away from the ranching business for a few days. They would perform the duties as shuttle bunnies both dropping us off in the river and meeting us later at Clay Hills in southeastern Utah. It was going to be an expedition type river trip, that is, we were not going out to enjoy a couple of days of whitewater, rather this trip would take more than a month or two to complete.

Knowing how Hidalgo enjoyed all the hiking and side trips, they intended to do research along the way getting to know some of the local people who lived along the river along with absorbing the local history and hopefully we would see of some of the phenomenon we had been told about.

We packed dry bags with sleeping gear, dehydrated food and everything we could possibly use on a river trip. Then we loaded the three solo canoes onto a small trailer that we had rigged out just for the purpose and made the connection to the Jeep Cherokee. Early the next day, well before the sun came up, everyone crammed into the Jeep and we all headed to Durango, Colorado with Ken and Hidalgo doing most of the driving.

It indeed was a long trip to Durango getting into a motel late that evening. We normally would have found a camping spot but instead decided to get a room because Aunt June found camping out close to a large town a little uncomfortable, besides Hidalgo wanted to make phone calls to his *biligaana* so he could make connections.

Durango is a tourist town full of restaurants and places for young people to play. Early the next morning we dropped Hidalgo off in front of a house in Durango's suburbs. Without a word of explanation or hardly a good bye he stepped out of the Jeep and with a quick wave he walked up to a door that quickly opened and he disappeared inside.

By this time Corey and I were dealing with another mystery to solve. What in the world was Hidalgo up to? Certainly he had a life of his own but he was also considered family. There were very few secrets between us, but when it came to his *biligaana* he was silent, choosing not to discuss the matter despite several prompts by me. Corey and I felt it was not our place to pry but secretly we were eaten up with curiosity.

The next day, after dropping Hidalgo off, we drove south along the Animas River to scout it. We wanted to see what we were getting into. What we discovered was a river full of diversion weirs that would require many portages. We had been warned about diversion weirs. They were the one deadly aspect of this river. Water that rushed over the top of them would curl back upon itself when it plunged down causing a nasty hydraulic. This caused the unwary river runner to be trapped in a cycle of water that continually pulled them back into the waterfall offering no escape unless one dived deep under the churning water and swam out without a lifejacket.

Rebar and angle iron is also found around diversion weirs making it possible for a canoe or canoeist to become impaled. They heard of one fellow who had been trapped in the reverse current of a weir for several hours until a large limb from a tree branch fell over the edge which he used to push himself away from the waterfall.

We finally found a reasonable 'put in' around the small community of Cedar Hill then returned to Durango where we purchased fresh food and ice for our coolers. We knew the ice wouldn't last but we figured we could buy fresh food and ice along the way. The melted ice would later provide water for us to cook with. There was more to this trip than exploration; it was a personal test, a survival lesson. This trip was something that very few people would do and that is to subject themselves to deprivation and hard times in order to experience personal growth. Naturally, others would think we were crazy.

Early the next morning, we returned to the 'put in' at Cedar Hill where we planned to meet Hidalgo. After arriving we unloaded everything out of the Jeep and began organizing the dry bags. We had learned many river runners' tricks from Dr. Douglas. Each dry bag was lined with a separate heavy plastic bag and was burped with all the air pushed out of them and then we tied them off. Afterwards we sealed the straps on the outside of the dry bags making sure they had a good double seal. A prussic loop with a carabineer holds all the gear together under the lacing ropes. If the canoe is hopelessly trapped the lacing ropes are cut and the gear spills out but is still held together because of the loop. The unfortunate canoeist must then float down the river using the dry bags as floatation; needless to say, winter trips could be problematic.

Finally the whole mess was then laced into the canoes. If they did go for a swim, the canoe could not sink because of all the displaced air inside of the dry bags. This was one of many tricks that had become rituals Dr. Douglas had taught them. This one he himself had learned from a fellow he watched float down the Dolores River on his dry bags after he had inadvertently destroyed his canoe in State Line Rapid.

Corey and I packed our canoes and then Hidalgo's canoe, all the time getting nervous thinking that Hidalgo had misunderstood the meeting place and time, but soon a blue sedan appeared, turning into the small dirt road that offered access to the river. Hidalgo stepped out of the car but a young lady also stepped out. She was a gorgeous lady with blue eyes and long brown hair trailing down the back side of a perfect figure. As they walked over to the canoes Hidalgo introduced her as Jill Thompson.

"Jill works for La Plata police as an undercover agent."

Shaking hands during the introductions I burst out, "I thought you were meeting with a *bilaganna*!"

This, of course brought out a roar of laughter from Hidalgo, "That's right, answered Hidalgo, "a *bilaganna* is a white person."

Confused, I blurted out, "I thought a *bilaganna* was some tribe, or some kind of Indian or maybe a witch doctor."

"Well, she belongs to the tribe that I used to work for, which just happens to be the La Plata County Police Department."

Ken, who was grinning during the whole episode finally said, "Yes but you didn't tell us that it, was a she, and that she was beautiful."

Jill replied, "Well, I have known Hidalgo for some time now and we are really good friends."

"More than just good friends," laughed Hidalgo, which caused a blush to appear on both Jill's and my faces. Everyone started laughing and Aunt June put out her hand saying, "Welcome to our crazy family."

After Jill and Hidalgo embraced each other in a passionate hug and kiss that seemed to last forever he turned to the wide eyed and totally surprised group and said, "Let's get down to business and get these canoes down the river." The three of us put on life jackets, waved, and pushed off into the icy cold water leaving Uncle Ken, Aunt June, and a *bilaganna* named Jill smiling and waving from the bank.

Farmington

We sat on custom saddles made of closed foam that also acts as floatation in our brand new canoes. We also leaned back against our sleeping pads that were sealed inside a dry bag and propped our feet against the coolers. We were very comfortable, only using our paddles to occasionally turn our boats so they didn't float sideways in the current. We were enjoying ourselves with our new found freedom of effortless movement but it didn't last. We soon approached the first of a number of diversion weirs. We would need to find a place to pull off the river, unpack all the dry bags and the coolers and carry them, along with the canoes around the weir. This portage would take several trips while balancing along a four inch wide cement retaining wall while water roared past us over a short waterfall into a hydraulic laced with large slabs of cement with rebar sticking out in odd places.

A channel next to the weir diverted water off to satisfy thousands of acres of farmland. It was a dangerous procedure that would have to be repeated many times but with practice it became a routine. After several similar diversion weirs, we found ourselves coming into Farmington where we finally came to what appeared to be a custom built weir. Custom built for river runners with huge warning signs that warned of the danger of running the weir. A custom built takeout had been provided on the river just for the purpose of portaging boats around. We had already portaged around many weirs that were far more dangerous but here close to town more precaution is taken because of children. Just below the weir was a small campground with picnic tables. Seemingly a perfect place to camp we pulled out and set up our tents to enjoy an uneventful evening under the stars.

We awoke the next morning to a shotgun being fired from the nearest house. Jumping out of our sleeping bags, Corey and Hidalgo grabbed pistols they had brought with them for rattlesnakes, dog packs, and marauding packs of thugs who might, but were unlikely, to bother us. We discovered in the field next to us a man running around firing his shotgun into the air to scare away a pack of ravenous crows that were slowly devouring his cornfield. It was a false alarm. After our hearts stopped racing, we prepared a fine breakfast of steel rolled oatmeal cooked with pecans and fresh rose hips that I had picked along the side of the river. We then packed our boats and headed down the river.

Above Farmington we ran into an unusual scene at another diversion weir. Several young people were swimming in the river along a beach with access to the main road.

Corey said, "Hey they are just enjoying a simple swim."

Hidalgo answered with a wide grin, "Maybe everyone on this river swims that way."

I said with my cheeks burning, "Don't people around here believe in wearing swim suits?"

But after a few curious stares and a wave we were well below the swimmers and coming into Farmington where the river began to braid into many channels. Each channel subdivided through a forest of Russian olive trees until the largest channel we could find was just a few feet wide. We waved at people who spotted us from a parking lot well above the river then continued in search of another campsite.

About two thirds of the way through Farmington we finally came to a lovely site. There, a young man was throwing a stick out into the rapid formed from another weir, and his dog, an Australian sheepdog, would plunge into the river and fish it out. We watched this for about forty or so times and finally the dog who wasn't nearly as tired of the game as the young boy was, disappeared into the brush.

We were now alone despite the fact that we were in the middle of a city. Hidalgo and Corey emptied dry bags that also served as backpacks, and began a hike into town in search of a grocery store to replenish our supplies. When they returned, a small crowd of people had gathered with fishing poles and coolers full of drinks. They hung around, a pleasant group of young families, until late in the evening. There was definitely fish in the river, and as they left to go home they offered me several nice catfish that Corey and Hidalgo cleaned and threw into one of the coolers to keep fresh for tomorrows' breakfast.

The next morning after breakfast and another ritual of watching the young man throwing the stick so his dog could get his daily exercise, we set off again down the river. An enjoyable day ensued. As we floated leisurely we noticed several hideaways that people had built along the edge of the river. Speculation as to what people were doing in those hideaways lead to an almost, but not quite, exploration of one of them. Hidalgo made the point, it is none of our business what people do in those shanties. Below Farmington and the confluence of the San Juan River from Navajo Lake we came upon two concrete embankments on either side of a thin water line that crossed the entire river, the PNM diversion weir. No sign or warning was visible.

"You really don't want to go down there!" Hidalgo casually replied as Corey floated out to the edge of the escarpment. He wasn't trying to demonstrate bravado, rather, he was living proof that fools rush in where angels fear to tread.

"Well, I might try it," Corey replied. Unloading, portaging, and repacking the canoes several times a day was losing its thrill and by this time everyone was really tired of portaging. The advice of Dr. Douglas was always foremost in our minds; "You've got to be safe, any man made dam can be a deathtrap." Hidalgo had of course earlier seen the diversion dam from the road. He had seen the large concrete blocks built into the main channel. He knew they were death traps, particularly to a long canoe.

"It really doesn't look too bad down there from here" Corey yelled at Hidalgo as Hidalgo turned his boat and headed toward the bank while shaking his head all the way. Glumly, Corey back paddled the canoe back from the drop line and followed Hidalgo and me. He was glad he did, the PNM diversion dam suddenly descended down a concrete chute to reappear as a waterfall going over large concrete teeth. Everyone got out of their canoes and walked down a well-worn path until encountering a Navajo family fishing in the white water below the weir. Most Navajo's find it hard to talk to others who do not speak their native language. Although they may appear to be impolite, they usually don't mean to. Actually, the outsider is the one who comes off as impolite. The outsiders appear very aggressive, always in too much of a hurry. Outsiders were always too worried about money. However with Hidalgo with us we made friends very quickly.

One of the older ladies spoke to us in English, "Last summer a raft went off that thing. The ice chest, raft, and all stayed in the white water the whole summer, I don't know what happened to the people."

There must have been some little angel up there that day in the form of Dr. Douglas's advice. His persistence on being the ultimate careful person saved Corey's life.

Below the confluence of the San Juan from Navajo Reservoir and before coming into the town of Shiprock, We encountered the hogback, a large rock formation of yellow sandstone that provides a stark contrast to the usual flatland topography. The Hogback's strike is north - south yet the river had cut perpendicularly, though the formation providing a paradox as to which came first; the mountain or the river?

Leaving the Hogback, everyone was a little dazed, but in good spirits. Spending day after day on a river is a joy but it takes a particular mindset to continue. Thoughts of evenings sitting under an air conditioner while drinking cool drinks seemed to nag at our collective consciences. Hidalgo was becoming more stoic about everything.

The river had so far, provided some strikingly beautiful views of the volcanic spire of Shiprock over the polychromatic mirrored surface of the river. The view was epic! The river at this point flows under some huge gates, which were part of, you guessed it, a diversion weir. Except for the trickle of the overflow stream the entire river was gone. I said to Corey and Hidalgo, "I'm thinking about the movie African Queen, with Bogart dragging the boat down the river with leaches dining on him." The final irony! Why were the river Gods doing this to us, what had we done?

"This trip is over" growled Corey as he threw down his paddle absolutely discouraged. There wasn't enough water to float a toy boat, much less drag a "real" boat like ours which were tiny by almost everyone's standards.

While Corey and Hidalgo unpacked our canoes to move gear out of the danger from the public and their roving pickup trucks, I walked down the streambed. Over the vehicle tracks, the tiny stream flowed around a bend and disappeared. The River Gods, along with the Corps of Engineers, had stolen the river but with a little exploration the obvious was apparent. The main body of the river rejoined the riverbed just far enough down river to allow us the opportunity of doing at least one more long portage. The trip was instantly on again but it was getting late.

The San Juan was transformed into a thick muddy brown beyond Farmington where the La Plata River runs into the San Juan after heavy rains. The river then enters the Navajo Indian Reservation and irrigated farming is replaced by sagebrush followed by overgrazed desert. A couple of camps down the river, we found ourselves confronted by a raging bull that wanted to play with the pretty thing grazing across the river. It's a curious feeling knowing that water only twelve inches deep was separating us from a raging bull that could easily have torn us apart; so much for Bovine love, I couldn't understand why the bull didn't just wade across the river.

The town of Shiprock turned out to be a disappointment from a culinary point of view. We were limited to what we could easily walk to so we settled for greasy fried chicken from a local KFC. In the most extreme southwestern section of Colorado that is imaginable, the river went under the bridge on State Road 160. Stopping to relax under the shade of the bridge, the only shade for miles around, we contemplated the desolation that was before us. Large sandy mesas loomed on the horizons but between them were miles of endless New Mexico scrub land. The river here was lined with Russian olive trees, a useless plant with sharp thorns that would puncture a car tire. Like many imported plants such as kudzu, they all turned out to be more trouble than they are worth.

Russian Olives were part of a useless experiment done many years before when it was thought that they would stabilize the bed of the river. Instead like many plants that are not indigenous to an area they took over. In places one would need to travel for miles down the river before a place could be found to pull over and make a camp. Sand islands often were the only places where the weary river runner could pull over and find a spot to pitch a tent. This was where they would put their survival skills to work living off of the land. We also contemplated another small problem. We were well behind schedule and the permit we had received in order to run the beautiful lower San Juan had a launch date of the 23rd. It was becoming obvious that we would not make that date and had no idea how the rangers would react to a late launch. We resigned ourselves not to worry about it. The worst that would happen is we would have to take off the river and submit a new application for a later launch or simply hang around for a day or two until another party failed to show up and we could take their place.

The Letter

We made camp on a small island well upriver of the small town of Aneth. After a dinner of batter fried rattlesnake and cactus, washed down with one of the few soft drinks we still had in our iceless coolers, I rummaged through my notebook where I kept my personal journal and, among other things, found a description Dr. Douglas had written about his first solo trip down this section of river.

"Dr. Douglas - Shiprock to Sand Island

After arranging shuttles, my brother Bo and his son Neil were kind enough to drop me off under the Shiprock Bridge, even though they had just completed a long grueling week's work. The responsibilities of employment kept Neil from going with me, but rather than waste an opportunity and permit, I was on a solo canoe trip on the San Juan.

Just as it turned dark, and with a little exploration, we found a suitable launch directly under the Shiprock Bridge where we entertained a growing contingent of local Navajos by hastily overloading the canoe. The friendly, but very inebriated Navajos, watched in apparent amazement at the circus provided by me getting ready to launch my canoe.

Finally, just at that point when you really can't see unless you get completely away from light or stare through the beam of the flashlight, I pompously planted myself on the saddle. In an attempt to launch me, Bo tried to push the rear of the canoe with his boot. The canoe, bogged in the mud, didn't move an inch. Bo said with a snicker in his voice, "Well, lard ass, you going to get started or not?"

I love Bo and I've always respected his point of view. I feel safer that way. He is a living character in his own time, respected by his enemies, as well as his friends. Bo Douglas was always the kind of a person who walks off the silver screen, a character in a modern western novel who is the study for the actors who might play such a part. He has always managed to handle himself in a bar fight.

The boat didn't budge and there I sat, wondering if I should step out of the boat getting my feet muddy or just sit there enjoying the comedy of the situation. Meanwhile the Navajos were back into exchanging beers. They would offer us beer out of their brown paper bags and I would offer them a beer out of my icebox. No beers were actually drunk at the time, just passed around in an attempt to cross vast cultural and linguistic chasms. They naturally wanted to float down the river with me, go for a ride; all of us piled up there in a banana styled canoe; standing perhaps. Wondering if this canoe trip was going to get out of town without an incident, I rocked the canoe in the mud for dramatic effect. Immediately, Bo and Neil turned and within a few seconds they would be gone and I would be alone with the inebriated Navajos. Being careful not to step in deep water but rather into the muck, I immediately pushed the canoe into the night.

There were bad eddies under the Shiprock Bridge and being totally self-conscious, I didn't want to make a fool out of myself by swamping the overloaded canoe, but with a few correction strokes the canoe was around the bend of the river. Like Indians on a war party, I could see my Navajo friends scurrying along the river bluffs watching me drift in the fading light.

Darkness was sudden as I searched for a site for a possible campsite. I found it, across the river from a cliff with a road and houses on top. Besides the constant whining of semi truck tires I counted three dogs by the sound of their barks. Cattle sign everywhere, but no dog tracks. I felt safe until about 4:00 AM when I was awakened by a growl about two inches away through the tent fabric. Sitting up to listen, I longed for the comfort of a .357 Magnum, but there was nothing. Since it was getting cold I slipped into a ski bib only to find a tick, which had made the journey with me inside of the bib.

After an uneasy night without a good hip hole and while rolling up the fabric of my tent I discovered a very angry scorpion which I had pitched my tent upon the night before. The fresh coyote tracks in the soft sand behind the tent told the story of a startled coyote.

Sheepherder's weir, the only rapid on this stretch of river was at high water. Constructed by the locals by dropping large rocks into the channel during low water it was like any other natural rapid I had run. After finding a reasonable chute, slipping down and filling the boat with water followed by bailing, I crossed to the river bank down river of the rapid for photographs then resumed my trip down the river to admire the distant cliff dwellings on the river right.

The morning of the third day the sky looked hazy, a sure sign of a weather change, but the wind remained calm all morning. Late in the afternoon a major cold front slammed into the Southwest consisting mostly of cold rain and wind. It is easy to make headway down a floodwater river without wind, but a stiff wind with accompanying sudden gust, makes the Russian Olives lining the banks death traps. All you can do is concentrate on not letting the wind blow you into the spiked sweepers that line both banks. Panic attacks occurred several times as I almost lost the canoe, dipping the gunnels which allowed gulps and rivulets of water in and I didn't dare take the paddle out of the water to bail. I strained to keep the boat lined up in search of a fast retreat off the water, but on this Russian olive lined section of river, retreat wasn't possible.

After several dramatic moments with incredible wind gusts toying with me, I finally saw a strip of road leading to a modern riverside sweat lodge on river right. Could I wait out the storm here? But then, I begin to think. It could be a good place to get shot, or chewed up by a dog. The ranch house was visible just over the hill. It is usually such a simple thing to take off a river but here it was impossible. I continued downriver until it began to make a long turn to the north where I spotted a twelve-foot sand bar. I was desperate. Dog tracks were everywhere, leaving me feeling really spooked but in the dark with just enough room to pitch a tent in the middle of a Russian olive thicket, I was simply too tired to go on.

In a roaring wind I settled in to rest, setting up camp, and even cooking a nice dinner. After dark, the wind pattern changed again, coming in gusts followed by periods of relative quiet. During one of those quiet interludes I nonchalantly cleared my throat; immediately several dogs started barking in unison. Time to move!

I packed fairly carefully and quietly at first, but soon I began to hear voices and the bellowing of an irritated bull. I began packing faster and faster. The bull was being herded into the field where my camp was and arrived with the dogs in a loud thrashing through the salt cedar and Russian olive thickets just as I pulled out in a desperate escape down the river.

Nothing was tied in and the air mattresses were wedged in an inflated heap under my feet. After crossing the river and desperately looking for the next campsite, I finally found a rather large arroyo next to a fence line on river left. Every inch of earth that could be used to pitch a tent became tantamount in importance. There I set up camp the second time that night on the highest bit of dirt I could find and worried all night long about flash floods which, thank God, never came. The following night found me recovering on a nice island at the foot of a large cliff at Montezuma Creek. The danger was over and magic was about to begin.

Dr. Wayne Douglas-University of Colorado"

After I had read the letter out loud to everyone, I looked over at Hidalgo who was grinning. "Do all your Navajo friends do things like that to river runners?"

"No, he answered. Just to the ones who camp on their property without asking for permission. We are very private people, what rights we have, we exercise."

I countered the point with, "Well in that case if we do get into a jackpot, you are the one we send for help."

"Fair enough," replied Hidalgo but what if I am the one who needs a rescue?

Looking at Corey I said, "Then I will get us out. I can usually get men to do anything I want them to do."

Corey says, "There she goes, bragging again."

Laughing, I let my mind wander back to the pages of Louis Lamour's, *The Enchanted Mesa*.

Our daily routine was pretty much the same every day. As soon as the sun came up we all set our sleeping bags out in the sun to dry then prepared a breakfast. As soon as we were done eating, we packed our canoes and dropped back into the coolness of the river. We would float for several hours, stopping occasionally to explore a ruin or interesting place, then about four in the evening we would take off the river at the first shady spot, and I would fix dinner while Hidalgo and Corey would explore the countryside. At one time I noticed Hidalgo picking out pretty red crystals from an anthill. He showed them to Corey then he tossed them back on the hill.

Sand Island

*W*e camped the following evening on an island across from the town of Aneth where I spent the morning continuing my reading of *The Enchanted Mesa*. We packed and left the island much later than planned. During the afternoon we had a layover as we hiked up a side arroyo until we came out at a small settlement consisting of a gas station and general store. Restocking our coolers and dry bags with dehydrated food as well as carrying several water bottles we then made our way back to the canoes and continued down to Sand Island, the usual put in for the fantastic river that was to follow.

At about ten in the evening of the 23rd we arrived at Sand Island, Utah. There were no park rangers in sight. In complete exhaustion we dumped ourselves as well as our stuff on the ground and went to sleep. We hadn't realized that we were in the middle of the launch ramp, the busiest possible place at Sand Island early in the morning, except for the chemical toilets.

She was a cute Ranger, eager, young, and full of ideals, just married, if Hidalgo's guess about the brand new set of diamonds proudly displayed on her hand was any indication. She was full of arrogance often cultivated in those who are in positions of power. We found ourselves replying to her;

"No, we don't have a fire pan. Never use them except when we're out on picnics or canoeing in the winter or changing the oil in our cars;" a major problem was developing.

"The BLM doesn't want fires being built along the river unless fire pans are used to protect the environment. Fire rings are strictly forbidden. Do you realize that once you stain rocks black they stay that way forever?"

It didn't seem to matter that we had no intention of building a fire of any kind. It was summer time and we prepared all our meals on one of the gas fired cooking stoves.

"According to the regulations, I can't allow you to go without regulation fire pans. Are you sure you can even make it down the river?" She never cracked even the slightest smile while looking right past us.

"We put in over there in Durango, Colorado." Hidalgo pointed to the distant east while trying to look as professional and worldly as possible with the last several weeks of dust and perspiration on him.

"This permit says the twenty-third!"

After a long pause the silence was broken by, "We got here late on the 23rd and no Rangers were on duty, therefore we registered our launch and floated to here and camped," said Corey, as we looked up and down the tiny launch ramp which was gathering a crowd of curious onlookers. We hadn't registered our launch but we were hoping she wouldn't discover that critical fact.

I finally said, "Where is a lawyer when you need one?" The crowd was getting out of hand as many of them had also camped near the ramp, hoping for an early launch, but our three canoes were clearly in the way.

The pretty, young ranger consulted with the other Rangers that were on duty then she agreed to an inspection. We brought out all the gear and charm that we could muster and she reluctantly allowed us to go; as soon as we got a fire pan.

I asked the perky ranger how many times she had been down the river. "I don't do river trips," she responded with a distinct sound of distain in her voice. Corey and I packed up the boats and carried them out of the way of the tourist while Hidalgo made the long walk into Bluff, Utah to purchase a fire pan that would never be used.

"Perhaps our ranger will be the last diversion weir we will have to deal with," I said, making sure that the ranger heard it. I have always respected authority but despised those who demonstrated authority with arrogance.

Hidalgo finally showed up several hours later with a brand new oil pan that would double as a fire pan. However he was in no hurry to get on the river as he knew there were some petroglyphs along the sand bluffs not too far from the launching ramp that he wanted to see.

"The native people were not the first to take scalps they learned that from the white foreigners, that invaded this area. The local Indians took heads rather than scalps, a trait that they had in common with the later Aztecs. This place is unique however. The petroglyphs here show head hunters. I suspect that some of the earliest peoples here may have been cannibals who actively hunted outsiders," Hidalgo explained. "Headhunting was an important part of their culture, at least until they became the hunted."

The Circus

Sand Island is not an island, but rather a cottonwood and willow covered sandbar backed with natural bluffs in an ancient meander of the San Juan River. It was used by the Anasazi as a religious and cultural site. During the winter it is deserted but in the summertime, it is a three ring circus. To the casual observer Sand Island can provide entertainment from the continually changing crowd of tourist and river runners. Currently it is becoming expensive to stay at Sand Island. Corey and Hidalgo carried the canoes well down river and set up a camp under a cottonwood well away from the crowds, then they took off hiking down the river in search of petroglyphs returning after only a few of hours of exploration.

During the evening, two young girls started playing Neil Young's, "Old man look at yourself; I'm a lot like you," over and over. Like all men, Corey and Hidalgo enjoy it when a young girl flirts with them but I put a fast stop to the one young girl who was flirting with Corey. Corey smirked and said to the girl, "I can easily hide behind the fact that I am hopelessly in love with Penny, pointing to me and I'm bound to be a disappointment."

The young girl was disappointed. She wanted someone to take her into Bluff where she could find some night life. Obviously, she hadn't spent any time in Bluff, or as most would ask, what night life?

Later, Corey and I watched while the perky ranger showed up to inspect the young ladies' camping gear, the ones who had been playing the Neil Young song. Hiding, we watched as the rangers gave them their inspection. Without realizing that the girls were in kayaks, the problem of fire pans came up again. One of the girls stepped away, disappearing behind tents, and reappeared holding a large metallic object; the proverbial fire pan that just happened to be a lid from a BLM trash can. At this point she was told that kayaks do not require a fire pan if unsupported by a raft.

Turning around and seeing the lid, one of the rangers politely asked, "And how are you going to carry that fire pan?" After a little stumbling at the realization of the obvious lie, the young girl sheepishly returned the lid to the trash can.

Hidalgo soon had a problem on his hands. A sixteen-year-old blond, a 'hottie', who would be more appropriate talking to one of her classmates, asked Hidalgo if he had floated the San Juan before.

"No," he answered her, but before he could step away she asked another question.

"Are you an Indian or something?"

"Yes I am..."

She cut him off with, "Would you help me with my life jacket?" Hidalgo looked helpless at this point. "Would you help me by spreading some sunscreen on my body? Are you going to rescue me if I fall in, are you going to give me mouth to mouth resuscitation?"

Hidalgo just walked away. He said to me, "I needed to be rescued by her mother."

A middle school teacher from California befriended us. He and his 14-year-old adopted Korean son arrived with a canoe duck taped, right side up on top of his car. He seemed eternally grateful for our advice offering us sodas, paperback books and constant entertainment by telling horror stories about teaching. The real questions that was never asked was," What would the paint on the car look like when the duct tape was peeled away or what happens if the canoe fills with rain water?"

One fellow who was obviously experienced about this river came over to the camp and struck up a conversation. He had been down the river many times and offered advice; "Late fall, winter, or early spring canoe trips take you back to what the canyon was like before it was discovered by thousands of new river runners and their families. The contrast of showing up at a completely deserted Sand Island in order to run a river where you know that you will meet no other people can feel terribly spooky and a sad thing to do, but on those trips the runner relishes the companionship of the few fellow humans also in a canyon that looms much larger."

"Winter canoe trips require careful preplanning and teamwork to avoid death from hypothermia. Don't try it unless you are with a very professional team and have time to layover, but the rewards can be momentous. That time of year is a paradise for the photographer intent upon capturing those special moments created though the chemistry of light and weather."

He was an artist with words as well as with oils and brushes. "The contrast of white snow on the many layers of brilliant red rocks or camping near the base of waterfalls that cascade thousands of feet down into the river after late fall rains create magical and very special moments."

We liked him. He was the only person there that didn't need something, want someone, was just plain nosy, or had a bunch of loud children running around playing though other peoples' camps. He continued, "During summertime canoe trips finding a camping spot can be a difficult matter. The side canyons that offer excellent hiking opportunities are the most popular and scenic spots, and the demand for these few spots far exceed the number of actual campsites that exist at any given time. People have gotten into gunfights over the right to camp at prearranged sites. Sometimes it is smarter, if you are not in a big hurry to wait until other campers simply move from a site and then move into it."

"Even at odd months of the year you still see some interesting people. Look hard enough and you can usually see someone making a fool out of him or herself. Take for example what happened one late summer day when I was haunting the campsites at Slickrock.

After setting up tents as far away from the other tents as possible, I went for a walk up the gulch. The sun was out, no wind, everything warming up, and the entire trail was strewn with clear pools with young coeds from the University of Utah. Being Mormon country, I didn't really expect much, but you never know. They were all young college students, mostly girls, acting like they were in a different world. Walking alone, I totally surprised most of them. They turned out to be pleasant but extremely shy. Maybe the sight of an older fellow dressed in survival gear covered in dirt and sweat tended to throw them off; I can't imagine why."

"Several pools, waterfalls, and startled young maidens later, I was amazed to have one of them actually walk up to me and initiate a conversation. She was a tall blond goddess with green eyes and large voluptuous breast just barely being held in place by bandanas."

"Where did you come from" she asked, as I stood there slack jawed, in amazement."

Stammering to speak at that critical moment, I said, "Boulder, Colorado. Now don't get me wrong. I'm not a womanizer, but my wife would wonder if I didn't look. As she says; 'Look, but don't touch, and if you do, I'll...' Well you get the picture."

"Are you from the university river trip?" I asked her while trying to look as much like a worldly, philosophical sage as possible.

"No," she answered, "I am with a private party." It was small talk. I guess my luck changed when I crossed my arms and leg and leaned against the rock wall. That's when the can of soda in the fanny pack went Phossh! There I was, with foam running down my crotch and pants leg; a great way to impress a girl. "Don't know who laughed the hardest; the young girl, or my wife when I told the story."

The artist fellow who never actually introduced himself, but continued talking anyway finally said, "Most people get into trouble on this river for not taking the simplest of precautions. Last summer a young man in a raft came up to my camp obviously in distress. This fellow's girl friend had passed out; too much sun. Leaving Sand Island they were in great spirits but by the time they had gotten to my camp down around eight foot rapids she had literally cooked. The only clothing she had brought was bikinis."

"I stay completely covered up when I'm on the river. I even take off the river during the hottest part of the day and stay in the shade. Anyway, I carried her over into the shade of the bluff, propped her legs up, and then took a beach towel I usually keep wet over my cooler to save the ice. I soaked it in the river and draped it over her. She immediately came to but then I had to give her my extra change of clothing just to get her down the river. I'll tell you what, I bet that if she ever took another river trip, she brought along a shirt with long sleeves and a pair of long pants."

Kids ran around the campsites until late in the evening. Music was filling the air until after midnight keeping all but the most exhausted awake. Hidalgo, Corey and I decided after that first night that we were glad to be leaving Sand Island.

A Visit from the Bruja

We hung around Sand Island the next morning just long enough to eat breakfast and then submit ourselves to another inspection by a different ranger. This time the ranger was polite, not in such a hurry, and certainly didn't have the arrogance of the previous ranger, in fact he was extremely polite. The discrepancy in the launch date didn't really seem to matter to him.

"How interesting, you say you floated in from Durango?"

"Yes," I answered.

"Hidalgo here," I pointed at Hidalgo, "Is researching a book on petroglyphs."

"Well," replied the ranger while looking at Hidalgo. "As a Native American, he should know more about them than anyone else around here."

There was a pause in the conversation then Hidalgo casually answered, "Well, the people who lived here were as different from my people as your people are from the Greeks. How well do you read Greek?"

"See your point;" said the young Ranger then he abruptly changed the subject, "The purpose of the inspections and permits is designed to make river trips more enjoyable to the public. Too many people on the river at one time cause problems because there are only so many camping spots. Besides, the fee makes it possible to make improvements here. We want you to have a good time"

"What about rock carvings, petroglyphs, asked Hidalgo?

"There are rock carvings, in all the side canyons, all the way down to the Mexican Hat Anticline. I don't know what's below that, but there's probably some at Mexican Hat and of course there are many down in Grand Gulch," answered the Ranger, "You folks enjoy yourselves."

We finally launched, after what was now five weeks on the river, we were finally on a section that was considered beautiful by anyone's standards. The problem was, now we were not alone and we felt like we were experiencing culture shock. For the last five weeks we had usually been completely alone, particularly while floating from Shiprock, now we were tying up on tiny beaches where a huge raft party had already tied off. There was always another party of canoes or rafts coming down the river, again it was a three ring circus.

Stopping at the Kachina panels as well as several other Paleolithic sites, Hidalgo was enjoying himself. The tourists that we ran across were perplexed; they couldn't understand the ambiguity of why an Indian would be interested in Indians.

Hidalgo would try and explain it by asking them, "You spend years in school studying American history, why should this seem so different?" But of course, it was different, but then Hidalgo was different by anyone's standards.

That evening we camped under a large cottonwood at the trail head at the foot of Combs Wash. At one time a thousand years ago, it was the focal point for many families. Hidalgo, Corey and I spent much of the following day climbing up the ridge following an ancient trail that went to other sites such as Butler wash many miles away, until we had a bird's eye view of the magnificent countryside.

We had just started to return to camp when a most peculiar thing happened. I spotted it first. The slight breeze carried a few scattered clouds that day from west to east as it does almost every day, but on the horizon a very dark and angry looking cloud formed in the east and moved across the sky in the opposite direction. Appearing to boil from the inside out, it made no sound but looked ominous with what appeared to be small lightning bolts flying from it. The three of us just stood there and watched it spell bound for several minutes until it disappeared over the Mexican Hat anticline.

"What in the world was that," I asked?

Corey answered, "It sure doesn't look like what Richard described over in Gallina Canyon on that deer hunting trip."

Hidalgo answered the inquiry with, "I have relatives who live south of here that say they have seen such occurrences many times, they would say that we are looking at a witch cross the sky on the way to make trouble somewhere."

I observed, "That didn't look like any witch I have ever seen. Witches are supposed to be old ladies with moles on their noses who ride on brooms."

Hidalgo answered my point with, "Witches are in the eye of the beholder. Native Indians have never encountered the kind of witch you are talking about, but based upon what I have learned about your culture those people are actually Wiccan's, people who use natural herbs and conduct rituals. Those are the same rituals used in early forms of the religion that became Christianity. Anyone who is different such as those who used herbal medicine was considered a heretic to Christians. Your history is full of people who were burned at the stake or persecuted because they looked different, talked differently or even believed differently. Your religion does not allow anyone to be an individual, someone who thinks for himself. You even call our spiritual leaders witchdoctors which does far more to demonstrate your ignorance of our cultures than it does to elevate yours."

Corey looked at Hidalgo and said, "I wonder what science would have to say about that thing that crossed the sky?"

I answered the question with, "Science doesn't say anything about things like that. Science is a tool not a thing or a person; it is a systematic way of discovering the truth about things, the search for facts and information. It is what people do with that information that sometimes has little logic. People do not want to change because it requires the effort to look and learn, and most people are lazy."

Corey added, "That's called politics. Usually if enough people believe something then it is considered truth."

Hidalgo countered this argument with, "Thousands of years ago your people thought the earth was the center of the universe. Then, slowly you began to realize that the sun was the center of this solar system. Now we know that the sun is only one star among billions in this galaxy and there are billions of galaxies out there that make up the universe. Our bubble of galaxies may be just one more bubble in a maze of bubbles, each a universe in itself. In your Christian bible doesn't it say there are many kingdoms in the heavens?"

Not receiving an answer, only curious looks, he continued, "Only a short time ago your culture would see a comet cross the sky and they just knew that God was warning them of certain doom. It would be time to repent your sins or find a scapegoat who had caused the trouble in the first place. Science on the other hand, has increased our understanding of the world but it has done little to cultivate our understanding and interpretation of those facts. Science may be able to describe, even offer an explanation, as to what is was that we saw but that doesn't mean that people actually understand it at all. Who is to say that what we saw wasn't actually the manifestation of a skin walker on its way to do someone harm or even to correct a wrong? Maybe it was like the comet that appears in the sky as a warning, a precursor of things to come. Maybe the ancient people who lived here thousands of years ago were right all along."

Staring into the horizon and hoping something else would happen, I continued my point about science; "Science is not a highly specialized and refined laboratory technique, but rather, general methods which can be used by all people as a tool to cope with problems in an ever-changing world. Living in a democratic society requires that individuals have the ability to make group decisions based upon examining and weighing alternatives and thinking through choices.

"Here we go again. Once you get Penny talking about something like science it is hard to stop her," Corey sighed.

"Therefore, before the civil action and decisions are undertaken, an understanding of the geological processes that determine the physical environment, and therefore the variables for making responsible democratic decisions, is required. Once an understanding of these variables is obtained, the process of scientific problem solving can be used with reflective exploratory thought to resolve issues and make responsible decisions. These decisions must be based upon the scientific method, which is the asking of questions that direct one's observations in such a way as to answer the questions clearly, to test one's beliefs, or assumptions, and to change or revise them accordingly"

I realized that no one was listening to my scientific preaching, in fact they were ignoring me so I reached out and placed my hand on Hidalgo's shoulder and said, "I don't know but I do know one thing for sure; it's getting late and I would like to see what other people down at the river say about what we saw. Let's head back to the camp, besides you promised us catfish for dinner." With that we trudged our way back down the trail stopping every few minutes to look for other aerial occurrences but nothing happened.

The Thief

The next morning we slept in late, eating a late breakfast prepared by Hidalgo that included catfish cleaned and cooked and hush puppies made from corn meal. Then we slowly packed our tents and dry bags after letting everything dry out. We only had a few hundred yards to go as we planned on camping on river left where Chinle Wash emptied hematite red slurries of water into the main channel. We intended to stay there a couple of days while exploring the side canyon which was lined with cavernous sandstone bluffs with ruins in them.

However as the river channel brought them past the camping area on river right they noticed a large crowd of people gathering. People were pushing each other around and screaming at each other. Thinking that they had also seen the apparition in the sky we skimmed along the edge of the river to see what was going on and to talk to them. But evidentially no one had noticed the apparition that we had seen from atop Coombs Ridge. Nobody had time to discuss the issue. This was a mystery in itself as it would have seemed impossible for them not to have seen it. We soon discovered that the crowd was consumed by the tumult of a criminal investigation.

We pulled off the river, secured our canoes, and walked over to the crowd that had grown to about forty people including kids and barking dogs. There, several men stood guard over two young boys who were sitting on the ground. They were both bleeding from numerous scrapes and cuts, as well as one of them had a broken nose. They were accused of stealing things in the camps.

I asked a young lady, who was hanging onto two small children, what the problem was. "Well, you know people come and go here all the time. For a long time nobody noticed what was going on. People would simply discover that their personal things were missing. Wallets with money, possible bags with car keys and guns along with credit cards, personal identifications and cameras are missing from tents all over the area. You can imagine what it is like when we realized that our money is missing. Our only take out is Mexican Hat. If we travel on down to Clay Hills Crossing we are facing a 60 mile walk back to a phone. We can't even use our cars unless we have hidden a key somewhere; and how do we buy gas?"

It was true; the two young boys had been little peeping Toms. They had enjoyed themselves the last week by going from campground to campground and seeing what people were doing. A normal activity of bored young people growing up, but they were caught in the act of doing something at a most inconvenient time. They had caught a young couple doing something that is normally restricted to the privacy of married couples.

There is a world of people out there that demonstrate strange activities when away on a river trip. They are in new situation that allows them to act in ways they normally wouldn't. The boys were caught red handed being peeping Toms but were they guilty of stealing people's personal property?

Hidalgo couldn't stand it. He walked over to where the two boys were being held. Bloodied; one of them was still trying to stop a nosebleed. "Who hit these kids," he said angrily while bolting into the crowd.

"What's it to you?" Demanded one fellow who seemed to be the ringleader and maddest in the crowd, the one who was discovered with the young lady and caught the boys in the first place. He reached up to hit one of the boys again but Hidalgo caught his arm, turning him around. Hidalgo then shoved the man to the ground.

Hidalgo stood over him daring him to get up. "Why did you hit these kids," he asked again?

"Do you have any authority here," the man demanded?

"I am a detective with the La Plata Police, and yes I do have authority here!" He had lied, something that any real Navajo would never do. In Navajo culture there isn't even a word for it, they use the English or the Spanish word, *mentiroso*.

Corey and I said nothing but decided that Hidalgo was usually right in situations like this. The argument continued for a while but with the crowd pushing in they decided to agree to Hidalgo's authority.

"Someone needs to go back to Bluff and call the authorities." said Hidalgo angrily. With that, one young man who was obviously very athletic volunteered to hike out to the main road and hitchhike back to Bluff. It would be a tough ordeal taking many hours to accomplish.

The crowd was getting pushy; Hidalgo demanded that everyone sit down. They did. Hidalgo knew that if he could get them off their feet and sitting down the anger would subside. He needed facts now that he had the crowd under control. He knew the peace wouldn't last unless he could produce answers and he knew he didn't have a clue as to what had really happened.

Jeremy, age sixteen and Thomas, age fourteen were not really bad kids. After searching their tent and finding nothing, Hidalgo talked to them for about forty minutes, one at a time. Their parents, who were headed toward a divorce, had gotten into a heated argument and had made the monumental mistake of taking off down river separately thinking that the children were with the other parent. The mother had left with another party of river runners who were feeling sorry for her. Their father, without even bothering to pack up his tent and gear had taken off with the family raft thinking the boys were with their mother. They were probably just discovering their mistake but it would take a while to correct the problem. The bored and hungry kids had milled around camp several days waiting for their parents to return. They finally had discovered a new game to play which was watching other people. They hadn't stolen anything except some food. Everyone was watching other people. Everyone was guilty.

"I want everyone in this camp sitting right here, and I want to know who has been in this camp the longest."

Everyone just sat there looking at each other. Hidalgo brought their attention back to focus. "If these, pointing to the kids, are not the thieves all of you will be held legally responsible for child abuse." He paused until he was sure of the reaction he would get, and then he said, "Let's get our facts on the table." He now had them a little worried and was working the crowd. Everyone there described what they had lost. "Who has been here more than a week, Hidalgo demanded?"

"I want to see everyone's river permit." The problem was many of them didn't know where their permits were as they kept them with their wallets inside their personal bags that had vanished.

"Well, most of you are civilized people. How long have you been staying here?"

They went through a process of comparing days in camp and checking the river permits, the ones that could be produced. Hidalgo was thinking that maybe the bad guys had been there awhile making a business out of stealing from the local people. The oldest permit was not the boy's but rather Jonathan Jones, an elderly gentleman and his wife who obviously didn't have a need to steal from anyone. The Jones' had been there for two weeks and were in no hurry to get down river as they were actually living there and planned to continue living there until Mr. Jones had written the next chapter of his book, a detective story.

The group was narrowed down to only a few individuals. One, the one who was attempting to strike the young boy, was Jeffery Overholt who was there with his girlfriend from Denver. The one discovered making love while the boys watched and he was also the one that caught them and broke the oldest boy's nose.

John and Susan O'Conner had been there almost a week spending a generous amount of time photographing everything possible. Finally there was Paul Baca who was on a solo canoe trip. He had just gotten out of the military and wanted to relax and explore for a few days. Everyone else was overnighters. The group broke up and everyone returned to their camps as kids were complaining that they were hot and hungry.

A line of cars soon showed up at the Combs Ridge trailhead. After a short hike over to the camping area, the Bluff City Police along with some BLM rangers and a couple of locals from Bluff who were curious and wanted to help arrived at the camps. Everyone again converged upon the camp to see what was going to happen. Everyone had their camp searched. But before everyone had been searched Hidalgo noticed someone missing.

"Where is Overholt's camp?" Everyone started walking over to Overholt's camp but it turned out to be an empty tent with a sleeping bag stuffed with empty wallets and personal bags. He and his girlfriend, along with his raft had vanished.

"There is no way we could catch him now, even if we were prepared to dart down the river," the BLM ranger said matter of fact, "They may be fast but the soonest they can get to Mexican Hat is tomorrow and that would require them to float all night long. Besides, they cannot go faster than the speed of a radio call. The police will be there waiting for them."

"What about those kids?" Hidalgo asked.

The Bluff city policeman said, "We will take them into Bluff for now until we can find their parents. The parents of course, will have to be prosecuted.

Hidalgo said, "You realize that many people will need to make phone calls to be rescued. The policeman answered, "We will set up a shuttle to get people in to a phone but that's about all we can do for them. We have experienced a little thievery on this river, especially in this area, but nothing like this.

The policemen thanked Hidalgo for doing a good job in routing out the suspects and handling the crowd. "It was obvious that they were using the boys as a decoy to cover up for their own actions. We will get them," stated one of the policemen confidently.

I looked at Hidalgo and said, "Do you remember that apparition we saw yesterday?

"Sure," answered Hidalgo.

"I think you were right," I said thoughtfully. "It was a witch looking for trouble, and we found it. Do you realize that not a single person here saw it but us?"

"That's true," agreed Hidalgo, "Maybe we were the only ones who were supposed to see it." With that said we got back into our canoes and made the very short trip across the river to find a campsite under some rock bluffs overlooking the river as it cut through the Mexican Hat Anticline. Hidalgo would now get to explore many miles of Chinle Wash with all the pictographs, petroglyphs and cliff dwellings that he wanted. Corey and I stayed in camp most of the time enjoying the first privacy we had experienced for some time.

Chinle Wash

*H*idalgo came back, late the following day, dog tired and dehydrated. Corey and I went out of our way to make him comfortable. The first thing he did after drinking some water was to go down to the river and lay in the cooling water. Corey and I was both curious as to what he had found hiking up Chinle Wash and even more importantly, had he seen any more apparitions like the one we had all seen while hiking Comb Ridge. While I prepared dinner that evening Hidalgo gave a detailed review of his experiences.

"Actually the country is similar to what we experience around *Serpiente*; granaries, cliff dwellings and classic petroglyphs. The ruins here are not constructed as well as the ones we found at Serpiente and they seem to be isolated and hidden.

One major thing that I discovered was two active pictographs. Someone out there is still applying fresh pigments to at least two pictographs and one of them is not your normal pictograph. The one close to camp here is a normal pictograph like many others that we have seen around here, a classic anthropomorphic with fresh red, white and blue pigment on it. The other one, in a side canyon well up Chinle Wash, depicts some kind of creature that I have never seen before. This pictograph has a creature that truly looks more alien than human. I realize that people are always confused by pictographs." He stopped for a minute to find the words to explain his point. "For example, modern people look at pictographs of humans who have two large structures on the sides of their heads and assume that they must be wearing helmets or antennae or something. Actually all you need to do is look at modern Indians to see that the women often wear their hair in two large balls on the side of their heads. It was a common style in ancient times." He continued making his point. "Artists and of course television shows always show Indians wearing headbands with feathers stuck in the back of them, showing the rank of the warrior. Actually they wore a single feather in the front of the headband to shade their eyes from the suns glare. Only the chiefs wore multiple feathers in bonnets used only in ceremonies and certainly not during a war campaign.

The Apparition

I had prepared a treat that evening; tortellini with the classic cheese sauce. It should have been great. And really it was despite the grit that somehow found its way into the sauce. There was sand in the food, prompting Hidalgo to do something out of his nature, he found himself in the most unlikely of situations; initiating a nervous conversation.

He began by teasing Corey, who had just bitten into something that hurt. Then Hidalgo managed to find another grain of sand that he spit out. Finally I found some grit in a dainty bite that I was working on. I didn't want to break a tooth if there really was sand in the food. For a moment I thought; they were teasing. Sure enough, as I had discovered, there really was sand in the cheese sauce. I had no idea how I had managed the deed. Perhaps I had picked up some sand with the spoon I used to stir the mixture of sauce and tortellini. Sure, I was still learning to cook, and camp cooking was a particular challenge but I actually took pride in my work.

Hidalgo realized the embarrassment that I was suffering though and came to my rescue. "You have to think about it," he replied to me. "It simply isn't that romantic picture that most *bilagannas* have about living out here, especially when it comes to ancient people who lived here. Their clothing was very utilitarian. They used animal skins for breeches and feathers for coats."

"Why would they use feathers for coats?" I asked.

Hidalgo thought about it for a moment and said, "For the same reason that birds fluff up their feathers; feathers make a great insulator. By tying hundreds of feathers together they could make a great coat to keep the chill wind off of them. The people, who lived here in the past, lived on the edge of existence. They had many skills; they could survive here when no one else could. They were all survivalist. Yet they could die from any of a number of things; in fact very few of them lived to what you would call an old age."

"Right now, most people who live around this area depend in one way or another on the petroleum industry continued Hidalgo. "Without petroleum and cheap energy, the only thing that would bring money into this area is a little cattle ranching and tourism. It would be lean pickings for all the natives. In the old days, some natives did make it to old age, but the vast majority of them died young. When their bones are examined by archeologist, most of them suffered from numerous broken bones. Because of extremely limited amounts of sugar their dental work showed no dental decay, but they did show enormous wear from a daily dose of sandy grit that wore their teeth down. They ground their corn between rocks. There simply was no way of getting the grains of sand out of the food as the rock itself wore down. It was impossible to keep all the sand out, just like it is for river runners now. No matter how careful we are, we will find sand in our food, and it will get worse as we go down the river."

Corey broke out laughing. Realizing what Hidalgo was up to. I also saw through his charade but decided to play along; I had other interests in mind. I wanted to learn more and since I was the one who was the most innocent and could get away with it. My question would have to be seriously considered, even if was painful for Hidalgo.

I asked him a theoretical question that I knew the answer to from spending many evenings with Aunt June discussing archeology. "What would it have been like to live here as an Indian a thousand or two thousand years ago?"

Hidalgo had to think about what he was being asked and decided to answer the question a little differently. "Well, obviously there was none of the modern conveniences we enjoy today. Their food consisted mostly of fresh game if they could catch it. They certainly knew how to preserve food but it was without salt and marinades. They did use some spices to flavor up their food but the average Indian person was very thin in those days. My forefathers and elders were all thin people unlike many Navajos today."

"After thousands of years of near starvation we suddenly were living in a world of plenty, that is why most natives are now overweight. Our bodies are not used to the amazing varieties of food available at any supermarket now. Mesquite beans, squash, corn, and meat and here, because of the river, fish were the principle foods they ate. Eating a diet consisting of primarily meat, they suffered from the same problem many modern people suffer from who live in northern climates. A person can starve if all they have is meat protein in their diet. They suffered from a problem that few modern people would consider; constipation."

I reached over and playfully patted Hidalgo on the stomach. "Yes," Hidalgo said with a twinkle in his eyes, "That is why I'm overweight; I truly enjoy good food, especially when you are cooking."

I laughed and said "Please go on."

"Although they suffered through the diseases Europeans brought with them like smallpox, they did have to deal with plague and hanta virus just like we still do. I'm sure they suffered their far share of rattlesnake, spider and scorpion stings. Head lice were always a problem. The only cure was to mix up a batch of thick mud and apply it to your head, let it dry and wear it a few days. The lice would suffocate and you were good till next time. They would occasionally take their cloths and bedding out to ant beds and leave them for several hours. The ants would eat all the lice that were on them."

"Sounds delightful, I laughed; "It must have put a stop to any romantic notions?"

"I wouldn't know" answered Hidalgo with a laugh. He thought for a moment then continued. "When someone takes something that belongs to you, you feel you have been stolen from and the thief did something wrong. Early Indians believed that stealing from others was a trophy, and that is how power was obtained. Of course, they never stole from another member of their own tribe. A skilled warrior who gathered the most things was able to gain the respect of others in his tribe. Actually," replied Hidalgo, "They were the same as all ancient cultures; a successful warrior could afford several wives." Hidalgo looked at me to see if what he had said would get a response.

Corey, who couldn't help himself, teased me by poking me in the ribs and saying, "Most men can't deal with one wife, why in the world would they want more than one wife?"

I quickly countered his point by saying, "I know at least one fellow who may never keep his wife unless he changes his attitude."

Hidalgo was enjoying the playful joust between the two of us but wanted to get the conversation back on task. "To share the work," he explained. "The more wives a warrior had the less work each wife had to do. I'm sure a blushing bride concerned herself little with sharing her husband with other women, as long as the work was also shared. After all, they were all taking care of one person, our noble warrior."

"The Indian world was not a world where you celebrate a holidays such as Christmas or Valentine's Day and then return to your regular work where you forget what you did and look forward to the next vacation." Glancing at both of us he said, "Isn't that what most modern day people do?"

We both nodded, with grins on our faces. Hidalgo frowned, and then continued in a quieter voice. "These people went through every minute of every day doing their daily rituals that were blessed and governed by their ceremonies. Native ceremonies are never scheduled; they are done whenever they are needed. But what separates the ancient cultures that lived here was something to do with their ceremonies. All ancient peoples relied upon shamans, what you call witchdoctors to help them get through life. Certainly in my own culture, we have many ceremonies such as the Blessing Way.

"The Blessing Way," I asked? "All of this was new to me, growing up in Tennessee; I was entertaining a whole new view of the world.

Hidalgo responded, "We have two major rites; the Blessing Way as the name implies, is used to ensure good luck and prosperity and the Enemy Way which is used to exorcise the ghosts of aliens. It came from older ceremonies used to protect warriors from the ghost of those they had killed. Both, of course, are a lot more complicated than the names. In the Indian world, everything has a life force in it. When a person dies, the life force leaves the body and is absorbed by other living organisms. There is power in even the smallest of living things.

Hidalgo took a long sip of coffee, discovering that it was already getting cold; he didn't want to waste the coffee. After several gulps he continued, "I cannot really speak of what happened in the ancient cultures here, however it is obvious that their belief in witchcraft took a dark turn. Sure, they were influenced by other tribes of people all around them, particularly from Central America. We know they traded with those people because of items found in their ruins such as parrot feathers, jade, and shell. Those items come from thousands of miles away. Despite the vast distances, the Chacoan civilization was certainly aware of other peoples. Tribes that lived to the extreme south of them practiced human sacrifice and perfected the power of the dead. There, the dead have more power and are more important than the living. I'm sure they influenced the people here. But," after a long pause, "something bizarre was happening here."

"Almost all ancient peoples did something during the time when the leaves died and fell. Halloween or as in Mexico, celebrating *Dia de Muerto*, they're victorious conquest over fears. Eventually Science won." There was a long pause in the conversation. Hidalgo arose to rinse out his plate and get another cup of coffee then he turned around to face me, and interjected with a quizzical look, "Or did science win? I don't think science won the battle here."

Stirring the powdered milk into his coffee upon his return to the camp chairs, he continued. "Many people who live here believe that the ceremonies didn't just take a turn to the dark side. Long ago, either some shamans acquired real power or we are dealing with something that is not human at all. They could not be humans. There is something out there that is able to do things that no human should or could do. You know, this place is not unique; there are stories of many places all around the world where apparitions or monsters play havoc on humans. This is why witchcraft is so despised and feared by the native people who live here now."

"The pictograph I looked at was well off the beaten path," continued Hidalgo. It depicted a large creature about six feet tall, thin but muscular and almost hairless. It was the head that bothered me, I felt like the eyes were following me. The head looked somewhat like a coyote but with large bulging red eyes, the entire pictograph had a ring of lightning bolts flying from it."

"Like the apparition we saw, I blurted out. "That had lightning bolts coming from it."

"That right," countered Hidalgo, "Many believe that skin walkers are very real, there really is a creature or creatures out here that are skin walkers and shape shifters.

"What exactly is a skin walker," I asked?

Hidalgo looked at me and answered, "Here in the American Southwest, the Navajo, Ute, and other tribes all have skin walker stories. A skin walker is a witch who can alter his shape at will to assume the characteristics of certain animals; usually coyotes, bears or birds. Particularly ravens are often labeled as witches because they are highly intelligent birds."

"Skin walkers are malevolent, transforming themselves into any shape that they want to assume. When the transformation is complete, the human witch inherits the speed, strength or cunning of the animal whose shape it has taken. The Dine people claim the skin walkers use mind control to make their victims do things to hurt themselves or others. Again," says Hidalgo to emphasize the point, "They are purely evil in intent. Maybe all the stories that I heard as a child have a grain of truth to them, not just mythology. Maybe it explains why many of our neighbors, particularly the older ones, have a firm belief in shape shifters or skin walkers. Even the Navajo police take those beliefs very seriously; when bad things happen, the people around here are always blaming the shape shifters rather than other people."

"I don't understand," replied Corey with a hint of doubt in his voice. "Why would the police get involved in the supernatural?"

"Let me give you an example," countered Hidalgo. "When I was a boy growing up just south of here, a relative, Alan Begay had a flock of about sixty sheep that supported his family with their wool and meat. One day just like any other day he walked out to his field where he kept his sheep and discovered they were all dead. They were mutilated, appeared to have been torn apart like chickens after a coyote or dog gets in the pen, yet the police could not find any trace of coyotes or any other animals responsible for the deed. Besides, with that many sheep it would have taken a large pack of coyotes."

"Sure dogs do attack in packs but there had been no traces of any dogs in the area. A pack of dogs would have singled out a sheep or two, but never the entire flock. It simply made no sense. Begay had no enemies and none of the neighboring families even knew where he had pastured his sheep. He blamed shape shifters and the police had no choice but to agree with him."

"I am beginning to understand what a dear friend of mine was talking about several years ago," said Hidalgo with sadness in his voice. "I laughed at him when he told me this story and now we are no longer friends. " Alex Chee was driving a gravel road out in the country on patrol in a Navajo police car when he heard a loud thud against the side of his patrol car. Looking over he saw a creature that looked like a wolf with large glowing red eyes running alongside of the car. The problem was he was going about thirty miles an hour when he first noticed it, and sped up to about sixty. The animal kept pace with him for several miles until he finally pulled over, took out his service revolver and opened his door. The apparition was suddenly gone but the side of his car had scratches and dents all the way down it."

Naturally, when he returned to the station, the sergeant didn't believe a word of his story. Neither did I when he told me, but he would never change his story nor would he admit he had hit something other than the eerie creature who tried to get at him."

Suddenly, despite the parade of tourist that was floating down the river we felt a little intimidated. We were alone with this knowledge and suddenly the canyon that loomed around the sharp bend in the river seemed much darker and spookier. That evening Corey built a small fire in the metal pan. Until that moment it had been a useless item. Why a fire? Maybe to drive away the shape shifters that hid in the encroaching shadows.

The next morning while I cleaned up and guarded the camp, Corey accompanied Hidalgo back up Chinle Wash with camera in hand to document the unusual pictograph. A few people had left sets of tracks while wandering up Chinle Wash but they never went more than a short distance up the wash. In the soft sand it was easy to retrace and track Hidalgo's route, to where the active pictographs were

. To pass the time as they tracked the route Hidalgo had taken the previous day, they talked about all things Anasazi.

"Did you know how an Anasazi knew who they were tracking?" asked Hidalgo?

Not answering, but rather looking curiously up at Hidalgo, Corey waited patiently for the answer.

"Most sandals that they made and wore were of a simple cross hatch design. They were utilitarian and they, like us, needed protection from everything from cactus to ants. But some were different. In Chaco, for example many wore sandals woven with extremely fine weave from a local plant, white dogbane. The thread count so fine a person could hardly detect any weave at all. The soles carry a protruding geometric design. Everywhere the person walked, the identification of the walker was in every track."

"Interesting, replied Corey, like your left boot there; the one that has a notch missing in the heel.

"I guess so," laughed Hidalgo. "We are there." They had arrived at the first of the pictographs. The first one was there as Hidalgo had found it, not far from the San Juan River where undoubtedly many river runners had found it before, but the more bizarre of the two pictographs was not anywhere around the main trails, it was well up Chinle Wash deep in a side canyon which required a several mile hike. Hidalgo's footprints were clearly visible in the soft sand of the canyon, but when they got to the panel wall where the pictograph was, it had vanished.

Hidalgo was awestruck; he couldn't say anything for several minutes. He could follow his own tracks up to the panel where he could clearly see where he had walked around examining it the previous day but it simply wasn't there. He remembered it as a painted surface with no lines cut into the rock but the pigment, he thought, had been made of traditional pigments found around them in nature such as red ochre and yellow cadmium, all readily available colors except for blue. Blue is hard to produce from natural minerals. But the apparition had simply vanished making Hidalgo not only doubt his own sanity but everything he knew about reality. Something was very wrong.

Corey did find one thing that was interesting about the blank rock panel. There, carved into the rock, not just painted on top of the surface, was a small zigzag line with the oval head and two lines representing a snake with its tongue out located along the lowest part of the rock panel. Hidalgo thought it strange that he hadn't noticed this part of the petroglyph the day before. In all, a pictograph had disappeared and a petrograph had appeared. Hidalgo couldn't believe his own eyes.

We settled into camp that evening with far more questions than answers and decided to lay over the following day so I could also make the hike in search of the missing rock art. Both Corey and I were worried. We had never seen Hidalgo in such a state of fear before.

Hidalgo needed time to think, he had never been so perplexed in his life, and now, it was very personal. When Hidalgo refused to take the hike up the wash for a third time we understood and decided it was for the best and we changed the subject.

Sphexishness

Hidalgo could not sleep and was still mystified the next morning. Corey and I found him sitting on the ground next to the edge of the river. He was watching the patterns that the rivulets formed in the fast water. I handed him a cup of coffee, fixed just the way he liked it. He was brooding. On the one hand he felt a little like a fool. He had looked into the eye of a skin walker, and didn't even know it. He should have immediately recognized what he was looking at and avoided its gaze, but he couldn't remember being intimidated by it at all, in fact, he felt like he had been drawn into it. He had been so proud of himself, finding an undocumented glyph. It looked so real, just like what he expected an active glyph to look like. He had even noticed along the edge places that appeared old, as if the artist hadn't repainted that part for a long time. He had stood as close as he could get in order to examine it.

Over a breakfast that only I could eat, I tried to console him. "When I have problems that I cannot answer I always call upon Jesus for answers."

Hidalgo who was obviously not himself simply looked off into the distance and answered, "You are trying to be so kind, I truly appreciate what you are trying to say. Allow me to offer you some thoughts; from the earliest crusades in the middle east to the Spanish Inquisition both in Spain and here again in New Mexico, to modern American politics the name Jesus has been called upon as a rallying call for all kinds of power struggles. From the time Jesus was alive, the ignorant have always screamed the loudest and people have been herded and forced to do the bidding of the elite. Throughout history they have defended everything from worldly desires to wars while citing scriptures they hardly understood. They celebrated their victories with their intolerance of others peoples' beliefs using scriptures as proof of their convictions. Now two-millennium later, mankind has managed to utterly erode everything that had once been so beautiful about Jesus."

"I'm sorry you feel that way," I answered. I was somewhat flummoxed as to what to say, never having seen Hidalgo in such a dark mood.

"I'm sorry," said Hidalgo. "It is a human condition. It doesn't really matter what culture you are talking about, in time all religions, including the beliefs of my own ancestors seem to have eroded. Right now, I don't know who or what to believe, all I know is that what I saw, I saw."

A change of subject appeared as a large raft party floated past, conversation drifted to the tumult that had occurred just a hundred yards up river. There was nothing but questions about what had happened to the two boys, the character who had stolen everyone's personal stuff and even more importantly, how all those people were going to get home after their river trip was over. Then I asked Hidalgo a simple question, "As a detective how do you solve crimes?"

This question brought about a long pause in the conversation, followed by a "Well…" Hidalgo refilled his coffee cup from the coffee pot that was precariously balanced on some burning wood in the fire pan. "Most criminals are creatures of habit and are really dumb."

"I know they are dumb, at least the ones that are caught, but what do you mean by creatures of habit?" I asked.

"Sphixishness," answered Hidalgo.

"What in the world are you talking about," I asked?

"Take for example, that dog that we watched retrieving that stick in the rapid back in Farmington. The owner tossed the stick, probably the same stick over and over, into the rapid. The dog plunged into water, found the stick then returned it to his master to do it all over again. The dog did the exact same motions, flawlessly, over and over. But change the rules such as a different stick thrower or a different rapid and the dog gets stuck. This is because of internal rules that the dog has."

"Internal rules," Penny asked?

"Its' like the female sphinx wasp". Hidalgo was remembering what he had learned while taking a class at Fort Lewis College in Durango. "The wasp will sting and paralyze an insect, stash it in a hole in a tree, and lay her eggs on it. When the eggs hatch, the baby wasps have a fresh meal waiting for them. However, the female sphinx has an internal rule. When she brings the insect to the opening of the hole, she always goes inside for a look around before she drags the meal in. If someone moves the insect a few inches away while the wasp is in the hole, she will leave to get another insect, repeating the process. Like the dog retrieving the stick, the wasp will repeat the process over and over. It's fun to observe this behavior in animals. The trick of course is to be able to recognize it in ourselves, and then apply what you have learned to catching bad guys."

"People have internal rules that they follow, even groups of people like the group called Americans. For example, why is it that Americans, no matter how crazy it should be, are able to purchase a gun to solve problems? Sometimes our internal rules completely overcome common sense. A bank robber will go through the exact same steps in order to rob the next bank despite the fact that an obvious pattern has been established that the police can pick up on. We are creatures of habit."

Hidalgo took off his hat and ran his fingers through his long black hair. "Do you know what locks are for?"

"Sure," answered Penny, "to keep a thief out."

"No", answered Hidalgo, "To keep an honest man honest. A lock never stopped a thief."

Corey entered the conversation with an observation, "You know if a frog is paced in hot water it will immediately jump out. But, if you place him in cool water and slowly heat it up, the frog will stay in it until it dies."

Hidalgo raised his eyebrows and said again, "We are creatures of habit."

I reentered the conversation with, "I remember something that Mr. Dale taught us in science class, He wrote five words on the board and asked us what it meant, 'Then they came for me.' The only answer he got was from a kid in the back of the class who was actually talking about a relative who was on death row at the penitentiary. The kid hypothesized that Mr. Dale might be talking about the feeling that his uncle had each time another prisoner was taken to be executed.

Actually as it turns out Mr. Dale was talking about people who lived in Germany during the rise of the Nazi party. First in Germany, then in Poland, then all over Europe, people refused to believe that anything could happen to them. Usually they were the most professional or wealthy people and certainly not just Jewish people. In time the Nazis brought everyone down including their own people."

Hidalgo continued his point, "Criminals get caught because they do stupid things. That fellow who stole everyone's personal stuff should have known that there was only one way to escape, that being down the river. He is headed toward a bottleneck at Mexican hat. Even if he has a car waiting for him there, there are only three or four places that he can get off the river. The police will be there waiting for him."

Hidalgo said nothing for a few minutes then said, "I remember something a man said to me when I was a small boy."

"What was that" I asked?

He looked straight at me and said, "Indians don't have souls. It bothered me for weeks."

I said, "Obviously this person did not have a soul. The truth of the matter is that you are one special person. Everybody knows it, particularly the members of this family. Somehow, I feel there is a special plan for you. You and I both know that you saw something on that rock. It wanted you to see it. Perhaps you had better think about that. "

Hidalgo smiled and replied, "I have, it's the only logical solution, but for the life of me I can't imagine why it would pick me to reveal itself too."

I looked at him and suggested, "Well, you are a native, you have family roots in this community; you are studying the ancient culture here and deciphering their messages, and again, you are a very special person. Maybe more special than you realize."

Hidalgo paused for a minute then admitted, "This place is making me spooky, let's go down the river."

Eight Foot Rapid

A measure of San Juan River charm requires a psychological test which some pass and there are certainly casualties not up to the task. While floating down river the observant river runner can see signs of lost canoes, kayaks or rafts and occasionally the lost occupants. They can be found puzzling over such trivialities as lost keys, wallets, paddles and bail buckets. After some gentle persuasion they usually consider the situation all with a good nature; an adventure and figure out a way of getting down the river.

They cannot walk out because of the shear canyon walls and unless a raft party comes floating by that agrees to rescue you, the learning of life skills may take on a whole new dimension. After several tumultuous attempts and with great anticipation we historical detectives finally set out down the river entering the Mexican Hat Anticline where the first real whitewater was located.

Our outlook on life improved the further we drifted away from Chinle Wash and like the scenery which was spectacular our mood changed for the better. The San Juan cuts through the Mexican hat anticline which itself looks somewhat like a great Indian blanket with brilliant shades of Permian reds, browns, and white with sheer walls that rise straight up from the edge of a fast river. As we floated into the canyon the first natural formation we encountered was a Perched Meander. In our research of the San Juan, we had found that this is a wonderful but short hike created by the changing course of the river over the centuries. We stopped and while I watched the canoes, Hidalgo and Corey made the hike up a hundred feet to the bed of the ancient river. Water had not flowed down this small meander for millions of years yet it looked just like any riverbed, without the water. A quarter mile circuitous hike and they were back down to the active river bed. This of course was followed by a further walk back up the bank of the river in order to return to me and the canoes.

Four foot rapid was the next challenge. It is not a drop off but rather a short section of river where the water drops four feet in elevation over boulders and gravel. For many novice river runners this is the first rapid they encounter, which is why it is remembered by many despite its tame appearance. As the river flows on toward eight foot rapid the river runner encounters a distinct optical illusion. As the alternating colored rocks rise out of the river at a decidedly steep angle the river drops down through those layers. It appeared incredibly steep and actually it was, but the angle of the rocks made it appear alarmingly so. Then suddenly we were at eight foot rapid.

The river forms a huge round pool, dammed up by the rocks that are washed in from a side canyon that enters there. After entering the pool, the three of us took our canoes across the river to the rocky beach. A paddler was attempting to line up a seventeen foot tandem canoe in order to run the rapid. Naturally we decided to watch from the shore.

The river there loses eight vertical feet in elevation, spilling over a narrow deep chute though boulders. Much of the river then piles against a trailer house size rock, splitting the river in half. It was a perfect rock in the middle of the stream waiting for out of control boaters at the bottom. The paddler had already portaged all the gear stored in the front of his boat. Sometimes this is a great idea, to remove some of the weight but the weight still has to be balanced. Generally a paddler has better control with most of the weight in the front of the canoe but this paddler was in a hurry and decided against unpacking the back of his canoe. As he lined up on the chute, the current pushed the canoe sideways. Panicking, the paddler managed to turn the canoe completely around and he ran the rapid facing upstream. Somehow, the canoe shot off to the left at the bottom of the rapid, which is where he wanted to go anyway. But from where the three of us were, we had no idea whether he made it. After dragging our canoes out of the water and tying them off, we took off down the bank to see what the result to the hapless canoeist was.

Returning to our canoes, we all three ran the rapid with little incidence, however missing the rock at the bottom proved a little more difficult for me. I thought it was like riding a huge roller coaster with the last few feet of the track blocked by a barrier. Then half way down I realized that there were smaller routes to be taken on the left side. My years as a high school athlete helped me as I muscled my way to the left and the safety of the beach. Hidalgo always went first in order to rescue anyone who swamped their boat in the rapid but this time it was unnecessary. This time we easily ran the rapid. We were becoming better river runners.

The Sorceress Raven

A few more miles and rapids later we were searching for a camping spot above Mexican Hat. I flopped down on the sandy ground, river left, and heaved a huge sigh of relief. "We really should have scouted that last rapid. It was deceptive, it didn't look like a rapid at all but I almost lost it when I got too far to the right. If I had known how scary that last rapid was, I would have tried to walk around and made one of you guys hike back up and bring my canoe around. My heart was in my throat the whole time. I don't know that I will be good for anything for the rest of the evening." I of course, was teasing; the rapids on the San Juan are tame by anyone's standards.

The guys laughed and Hidalgo replied, "You never know what you can do until you try; besides I would have caught your canoe at the bottom if you had turned it over."

"What about me?" I asked indignantly.

"You are a good swimmer," replied Corey with a smirk, "We knew you could make it to shore."

"Thanks for the vote of confidence," I said smartly, "But a little less confidence and a little more assistance on the next rapid would be appreciated."

With that response, I stalked off carrying the dry bag with a tent. Corey and Hidalgo agreed with a look, agreeing that it might be better to get busy helping me set up the camp, and let me cool off a little. They enjoyed pampering me and at times I enjoyed being the helpless girl in the group.

We were pleased to find ourselves alone at the campsite, a large sandy area about fifty feet from the river with some small cedars that provided shade until the sun dropped below the canyon rim. The small trees allowed us the option to tie down our belongings. Most of the other river runners that floated past us traveled on down to the town of Mexican Hat in search of cold drinks and warm showers.

After unpacking our canoes we dragged them up to the camp, turned them over and tied them to the trees. We then proceeded to unpack the tents but hesitated when we noticed a fast change in the weather. The sky above us seemed to swirl in a large circular motion, growing darker by the minute. Evidently, we were directly under a huge thunderstorm.

I had set up Corey's and my tent but it was still empty and within the second before I could tie it off, the wind hit and it started to roll across the ground. Tent stakes were never used as they were basically worthless in the soft sandy soil. In the windy southwest, we had discovered long ago that it was better to tie the tent to shrubbery or lacking vegetation to fill it with coolers and heavy objects to keep it from blowing away.

I took a dive toward the tent but missed. Corey, who noticed what was happening, managed to do a fifty yard dash and stopped it from blowing into the river, but just barely. The wind picked up more and he was having trouble just keeping it from blowing out of his grasp. One of the poles snapped as the wind blew it flat to the ground.

Everyone scrambled to keep things from blowing away, but it was almost impossible. The sand that made up the area was all airborne in a maelstrom biting into our skin, stinging our eyes. After securing everything by tying bags, camp chairs and anything that could take flight to the small scrub trees, we took shelter under our canoes, curled up in the bow. Because of the foam seats, the men discovered that this was a very uncomfortable ordeal and the storm only increased in intensity. Lightning bolts hit nearby, causing a rumbling sound as the sound waves echoed off the canyon walls. We three intrepid boaters were pelted by rain and finally hailstones lay about us on the ground. Fortunately we were secure under our canoes out of the stinging sand and hailstones, but as the storm dragged on, I found myself letting out a blood curdling scream. Both Hidalgo and Corey grabbed something to protect their heads from the hail and crawled out from under their canoes and ran over to me. There they found me, a wide eyed and terrified girl.

"There are rattlesnakes in here with me," I screamed. Hidalgo grabbed a paddle and Corey jerked the canoe over. There were no rattlesnakes. They were mystified, was it the wind making sounds like a terrified girl? No, I was terrified. I actually saw, what looked like, a rattlesnake sliding up my leg. I had screamed instinctually. A real rattlesnake would have bitten me.

We spent the next few minutes searching for any trace of a snake but could find nothing. The canoe was an empty shell and there was nothing in any of the bushes around me. Corey dragged his canoe next to mine and within only a few minutes the storm was over. It had disappeared as suddenly as it had appeared.

Hidalgo, attempting to calm me down, asked me a question. "What did you do with the amulet that William Owl gave you?"

"I left it at the ranch so I wouldn't lose it," I answered. My response brought a frown to Hidalgo. He was worried.

We ate sandwiches that night being too unnerved to prepare a real meal. Within a few minutes the wind suddenly subsided, giving us the opportunity to actually set up a camp. It took a lot longer than usual, darkness had already set in and figuring out how to set up our tent, with its broken pole was a challenge. Fortunately we had a roll of duct tape that was used to make emergency repairs. We wanted to be prepared just in case the storm returned.

Unfortunately Corey's and my tent would never be the same, it was looking quite limp. It was obvious that it wouldn't shed water in a hard downpour. We crammed the ice chest against the limp pole and with a little duct tape we taped the chest to the tent pole and were able to erect the tent. That night, we finally went to sleep exhausted both physically and psychologically, the three of us asleep with our camp gear inside our tents. We were not alone. High up on the canyon walls set a lone sorceress raven, looking down, laughing at us.

The Mexican Hat Restaurant

The next day we were exhausted, choosing to sleep in late and getting on the river late in the morning. Traveling only a few miles we camped early that evening across from the Mexican Hat rock formation that looked, indeed like a large Mexican sombrero. Finding campers along the Mexican Hat side of the river we paddled across the river to inquire about the couple who had stolen all the families' personal items and hopefully to get a weather report. No one had heard a real weather report; furthermore they had not heard any reports of bad storms, only scattered afternoon thunderstorms, typical for this time of year. No one was aware of any recent storms like the one we had experienced.

The police had run the plates on all the cars that were parked and had been waiting for Overholt and his girlfriend right where they had left their car. If they had gotten away they would have made considerable use of the credit cards and cash, the car keys were nothing but a delaying action to keep campers from following them too closely.

Hidalgo made the comment, "Most people who run into law problems invariably get caught because they do stupid things." Indeed they were stupid. There is no way to outrun police who are armed with radios and telephones. Many people who get out in the back country think that there is no law out here; actually it just takes a little longer to catch the bad guys."

After floating past a rock formation that at just the right angle looks like Fred Flintstone sitting on a toilet, we floated past the dirt road that most raft parties use to take out and instead followed Dr. Douglas's advice about floating under the Mexican Hat bridge and taking out at the steel ladder that had been constructed years ago against a bluff so that guests at the motel and restaurant could gain access to the river. Tying off our canoes we took care of the responsibilities first; loading fresh water into the water bags. All water on the river had to be taken with us in order to avoid a lengthy process of filtering and boiling the river water. Anyone who fails to follow this simple rule is doomed to spend days in agony due to stomach cramps and dysentery. The other major responsibility was for us to walk across the street to the trading company where everyone rented a shower stall with lots of soap and hot water. I felt like I was in heaven.

Returning to the restaurant that catered to tourist and river runners we discovered it was not very busy in the early afternoon. Navajo tacos were served up to Corey and me while Hidalgo preferred a traditional cheeseburger. Sitting at the table we could count four distinct languages being spoken. English, Spanish from the kitchen, German from the stiff looking couple in the corner and what we guessed was Japanese from several tables away. Corey and I spent some time walking around the place reading and looking at all the western memorabilia on the walls as well as enjoying the panoramic views of the river. Returning to the table where Hidalgo was sitting, Corey said he was feeling intoxicated. The air conditioning was doing wonders for him. I agreed.

As we sat enjoying our food, an ancient Ford Pickup truck drove up into the parking lot. Several Navajos piled out of the back of it and began walking down the road in the direction they had come and an elderly Navajo couple opened the doors to the cab and in slow motion piled out. Nobody paid any attention but Hidalgo chewed his cheeseburger slowly, closely watching. The elderly couple walked into the convenience store. Hidalgo picked up his cheeseburger for another bite. Three minutes later they came out with a loaf of bread and headed back to the pickup. Hidalgo, who could now see the faces of the elderly Navajo couple, bolted out of his chair leaving Corey and I amazed.

Hidalgo returned a few minutes later with the elderly couple, sitting them down at the table with Corey and me. "I would like you to meet my mother and father," said Hidalgo as Corey and I feebly reached out for hands.

Hidalgo's father looked like a typical Navajo with well-worn jeans, a blue velvet looking shirt and a bandana tied around his head knotted on the side, holding back long strands of what had at one time been pure black hair. Now it was long strands of grey hair. A barrel chest and strong arms despite his advanced years, wrinkles on his face told a story of a man who had spent considerable time outside. He could have been a very formidable opponent in another time and place but the expressions his face produced were content and friendly.

His mother was thin and frail yet extremely articulate. She seemed quite different from the typical elderly Navajo lady. Not shy at all. Neither of them had a trace of the customary turquoise jewelry that most Navajos wear. Hidalgo was a little embarrassed and a little angry. "I have sent portions of every paycheck I have ever earned to you so you could live comfortably." He held up the loaf of white bread while looking at Corey and me saying, "This was going to be their dinner."

Hidalgo's mother looked at Hidalgo and said in perfect English, "Yes that is true, however we, she gestured at Hidalgo's father, are very rich by Navajo standards. Others needed the money more than we did. It is not in our nature to see others suffer when we can help."

Hidalgo sat back into his chair perplexed.

His parents were the people that had imbued him with that driving force that made him want to learn and excel. He was a shining star in a sea of despair. His mother and father had worked with him from an early age teaching him not only Navajo culture but all that they knew from all cultures. They had invested vast amounts of their own lives in a process of learning all that they could, not only to help themselves, but to help those around them. They were still doing it. They had planned to settle for a few slices of white bread that evening so that someone else could also afford at least a slice of bread.

Like all of society around them, there were the desperately poor and those who had learned to work the system. To compete, to conquer, getting to the top was not a Navajo trait. In their culture people shared and they were not about to change thousands of years of their culture and nature just because the white culture surrounding them demanded it.

Hidalgo set the loaf of bread on the table and signaled the waiter to come over whereupon he ordered food from the menu for his parents. They ate ravenously. Afterwards, Hidalgo's father reached over and picked up the shreds of lettuce that were left over on Hidalgo's plate. They were starving, not leaving a scrap of food on their plates, prompting Corey and I to clean up the scraps of food left on our own plates.

Between bites, Hidalgo's father says, "I grew up knowing it's wrong to have more than you need. It means you're not taking care of your people. Gathering wealth around you is a *bilagaana* custom, not ours."

Hidalgo answered him, "We have learned to be very careful with our money and as you know I do share most of what I make with others but there is more to life than just living. It is a strange and marvelous world out there. We want to live in it not just exist in it."

At that statement I said, "Jesus said to them, 'Watch out! Be on guard against all kinds of greed. Life does not consist in an abundance of possessions.' Luke 12:19."

Hidalgo's father looked at me and said, "You are a very special person. You do my son honor by being his friend."

Afterwards, while enjoying coffee, Hidalgo got around to explaining what we were doing in Mexican Hat. His parents had learned long ago that Hidalgo could always be found doing something unusual, but floating down the San Juan River was something they had never imagined him to be doing.

"Well, there is really something far more important that we are doing," explained Hidalgo. With that he went into an explanation of what we were doing on this river trip with a brief description of the Gallenas Canyon mystery Richard had encountered and the strange apparition they had seen from atop Comb's Ridge.

Hidalgo's parents just sat there listening quietly with an occasional head bob in recognition of their own ancient memories of such events. Hidalgo finally got around to telling them about the pictograph that appeared to him. At this point Hidalgo's father finally got into the conversation. In broken English, sometimes drifting into his native Navajo, he proceeded to explain that the apparition was meant for Hidalgo. "You are likeminded people, you and the shape shifters, but opposites, perhaps you don't cause trouble in your line of work but trouble will always be around you. Has it occurred to you that the apparition was not an apparition at all? Perhaps it was the real thing; perhaps the shape shifter was as curious about you as you are about it. It wanted to show you something, maybe how strong it is." That was the second time Hidalgo had heard this theory and it didn't set well with him this time either.

Hidalgo's father was special in his own world. He had performed the Blessing Way ceremony many times. Yet many considered what he did a form of witchcraft. In many ways it was similar to witchcraft but produced opposite results. It was obvious that Hidalgo's father had a problem with such discussions of shape shifters or skin walkers. "They appreciate your mind, they both fear you and admire you, but you should beware. They have great powers and have singled you out. You are marked. You can bet they will return."

With that said Hidalgo's parents simply got up and started to walk out of the restaurant. Hidalgo followed them, asking questions. This all seemed a little strange to Corey and I who were used to long goodbyes and hugs, but they had said what they wanted to say and we were dealing with an entirely different situation and culture.

Hidalgo followed his mother and father out to their old pickup. They piled into it but Hidalgo stood there, leaning on the door, having an animated conversation with his father for quite some time. I noticed that he took some money out of his pocket and tried to give it to his father, but his father just waved it off and started up the old Ford truck.

Aztlan

The sun had long ago set on the horizon and we still had to float down the river to find a camp for the evening. Corey and I went down and finished loading the water bottles and food supplies we had purchased into dry bags and patiently waited for Hidalgo who had been sharing a last word with his folks and who would be bringing a bag full of blocks of ice with him.

The three of us finally launched our canoes making one large bend around the river and immediately began to look for a place to camp. We passed an old miners cabin on river right stopping just long enough to make a fast exploration then continued on down the river looking for a campsite. In the next curve of the river, we found shelter in the form of a large cave like structure where the river had carved an undercut providing ample shade from the midday sun. Mendenhall cave isn't really a cave at all, but rather a rock overhang that provides ample shade throughout the day and provides a great camping spot. We decided to camp finding ample room for our camp chairs, bedrolls and cooking materials without bothering to set up tents. The problem was we knew that if the river rose suddenly during the night we could awake with water sweeping all our camp gear and ourselves down the river.

Tired from the day's activities, we all stretched out on sleeping pads under the protection of the megalithic rock and went sound asleep. Corey woke up first as he noticed funny clicking sounds around us. As he sat up he discovered a multitude of ravens had gathered around us. It was a surreal scene. About two dozen of the ravens were walking around our tiny camp with dozens more of them perched on the rocks around us and circling overhead as if waiting for something to happen, but nothing happened. Usually crows avoid people. In fact, on this river one of the things river runners find themselves involved with is tossing rocks at them, purely for entertainment. Crows, being smart birds will usually avoid people, but these birds seemed attracted to our camp.

Without a word, everyone awoke to the scene and watched in amazement at the coven of ravens. Corey tossed some pieces of bread out for them but they ignored the peace offering. As Hidalgo arose from his pad they took flight, circling the camp a couple of times then flying in a large flock back up the canyon toward Mexican Hat.

We, the intrepid river runners, spent the rest of the day in the shade of the canyon walls walking an easy trail up to the miner's cabin and then floating back to our camp. As we floated back down the river to our camp, Hidalgo explained to me that it wasn't a natural thing for crows or ravens, to flock as they did. In the canyons they rarely are seen in groups larger than three. What had happened at the camp was a very unnatural event. Something was surely up. Hidalgo was uneasy.

Despite the fact that there was a brief shower during the following night causing miniature rockslides from the canyon walls above us, we stayed dry under the rock cover and fortunately for us the river actually dropped, leaving us high and dry with a much larger beach to play on. It was the perfect place to stay for a day and explore, watch the natives, and contemplate the ravens that had disappeared along with the scraps of bread. Tiny footprints of mice explained what had happened to the scraps of bread.

We saw a large raft party floating down the river. One raft had large blow up toys, Donald Duck, a pink flamingo, etc. floating alongside of them held to the raft by short tethers. Another raft was loaded with a middle aged couple and a dozen or so dogs, each wearing a lifejacket. One raft floated by with no occupants at all; the raft party was all floating alongside the raft in the river on purpose, a way of staying cool.

Unlike all other desert rivers, this portion of the river did not seem to have a trace of Indian artifacts. Not a pictograph or petroglyph was to be found. Due to the sheer cliff walls around us the remainder of the deep canyon offered only short hikes, but from this site it was possible to hike all the way back to Mexican Hat. Instead the three of us went for short hikes up and down the shelf of rock that formed the roof of the cave we were camped in. The true value of the place was the shade and the comical view of people floating down the river.

I found myself pressing Hidalgo about what his parents had said to him about the apparitions that we and Richard had seen. Hidalgo answered me with, "My father didn't say anything specific about the apparition but he did bring up some interesting points. You see, most Indian stories must be understood from the perspective of the peoples who tell them. For example if you were an Indian living here two thousand years ago in what would become New Mexico and saw a silver disk fly through the sky, you might want to record the event by carving a petroglyph of a bird since birds are the only thing that you know of that flies. But often, those same petroglyphs can be just representations of birds, they are easy to misunderstand.

"Did he make any suggestions," I asked.

"Yes, but you need to understand that Navajos are very secretive about our traditions. They, he stopped himself and added the word 'we' simply don't feel comfortable sharing our cultural traditions and history with outsiders. My father warned me not to get involved with outsiders, particularly concerning skin walkers. However, I will share a few thoughts with you. He made one very specific suggestion."

"Navajo Indians have been in the Southwest, migrating here from Canada, only for the last few centuries, since the 1400s. Our people found mostly a deserted land filled with ruins from a previous people. But the descendants of those people were discovered in many pueblos to the south of what is now the Four Corners Area. Our warriors actually made war on those people, the word Anasazi actually means ancient enemy in Navajo."

Hidalgo continued his explanation, "The earliest people who lived here lived in small mobile settlements as long ago as the last ice age. Finally they acquired skills in agriculture and settled into permanent residences building with the sandstone instead of living in pit houses and skin huts, what you call teepees. By about 1000 A.D. Chaco Canyon became the capital to the world for these people. But let me inform you of a simple fact, it was not a world like many *biligannos* imagine, it was not an equalitarian society. As in all human societies there were the lions and sheep, the rich and the very poor, social stratification. People were coerced into building out of fear. Everyone contributed to the building of Chaco Canyon as well as any ruin found in this area, but much of it was done because they were fearful of punishment from the masses. During the tenth century this area was a beautiful area, growing food was easy and the population grew. Then what geologist call a little ice age occurred and the climate changed. Suddenly this area dried out. The forest disappeared and the streams turned into dry river beds."

"So that is why people left this area," I said.

Hidalgo continued, "The earliest people were Nahuati speaking people who in time would become known as the Aztecs. They began to move south out of what may have been the present southwestern United States in order to settle in Mexico. The pueblos that make up modern New Mexico are the northernmost settlements of those people. There are many theories as to why they left their homes but the most common reason that is given by archeologist is that the area became gripped in persistent drought but there is much more to it than just drought. No one really knows why they left their northern homeland known as Aztlan but by the year 1110 A.D. they had been traveling for almost two hundred years. During this time they roamed throughout what is present day Mexico looking for a place to settle. The empire was controlled primarily by a political body made up of the Acolhua people of Texcoco, the Mexica in Tenochtitlan, and the Tepaneca people of Tiacopan. The Aztec capital was located at Tenochtitlan, which is the site of modern Mexico City. By the year 1500, the Aztecs ruled all of what is now known as Mexico extending down into regions of Central America.

"You do not think it was drought that caused them to move, do you?" I asked.

"No it took a lot more than a severe drought," replied Hidalgo, "They had experienced droughts before. There was a sickness among the people. They had grown proud and self-absorbed; what you would call arrogant. They had also been influenced by Toltec's that came up north from Mexico."

"Toltec's," I asked?"

Corey interjected, "They were the precursors to the Aztecs, a very warlike people who practiced human sacrifice among other things."

Hidalgo continued, "Many archeologists think that all Anasazi people practiced cannibalism, but it isn't so. They feared the retributions of the leaders of Chaco who were under the influence of the Toltec. Some of the shamans in that culture were cannibals, and like any fad, it seemed to spread out among the people. When desperate, people will eat anything. The people here moved into the most inaccessible places that they could. Which is why, we have been looking at houses built into cliffs. The Indian culture that existed here for thousands of years died of fear. Then, slowly the people migrated to the pueblos that dot New Mexico today; Zuni, Hopi, Isleta, Santa Clara and many other places that can be found on any modern road map.

Corey looked up and said, "That's only half of the story, isn't it?"

"Well, yes," answered Hidalgo, looking a little frustrated. "The other half of the story is the part that my father was so sensitive about."

I contributed the words, "Skin walkers."

There was a long pause, Hidalgo thought about changing the subject but then continued with, "The Chacoans themselves became involved in witchcraft and the people moved away. They moved into cliff dwellings to escape the Chaco Canyon witches. It didn't work, they were always found. Something terrible happened here. In the very ruins that we have been exploring, skeletons have been found in which every bone had been broken in a twisting fashion. All the long bones had spiral twist when found. Those people were alive when those bones were broken. A gang of warriors must have attacked people, one at a time, and holding them down, twisted their bones until they eventually died. It must have been agonizing for them. These warriors enjoyed inflicting as much pain as possible."

"Some of the people escaped by moving south, joining up with the Kachina Cults that were developing in the communities that now exist. The people who were here before us became intimately involved in those Kachina Cults, but they had a relationship with our apparitions that extended back thousands of years before. My father recommended that we learn from the elders in Zuni. The Zunis are what archeologist defines as an isolationist culture. Even their language is different than any others around here. They are an ancient culture. They may offer us an insight into the apparitions we are seeing."

Corey who had been relatively quiet up till this moment spoke up, "He is right." We both looked at him with frowns until Corey began to explain. "We need to learn more about the Kachinas." He then began to explain.

Zuni Mud Heads

"The summer before my folks died in an automobile accident I spent an entire summer working for Douglas construction, building houses under a government program in Zuni Pueblo. My first exposure was as a boy of fifteen. It was my first great adventure away from home and completely on my own. This was going to prove to be more than just a grand adventure; it was my first glimpse into cultural differences. From a personal perspective, I learned about something called ethnocentrism. This was the first time I began to wonder about my own orientation to life. My whole outlook on life changed as a result of my visit there."

Hidalgo and I settled down on comfortable sleeping mats, Hidalgo, always sipping his coffee with cream and sugar said, "You must have been a very lucky person to get to live in Zuni for a while. The people there are very particular about who can visit there and that includes my people the Navajos. The Zunis have long memories."

Corey, who had learned to tell a story as well as anyone, took the stage. "The volcanic plains of extreme western, New Mexico are home to the Zuni. Modern Zunis gain their sustenance primarily from agriculture, cattle and sheep herding, and from the production of jewelry featuring inlayed turquoise for which they are famous. They live in one compact village with three outlying hamlets occupied during the crop-growing season. In a singularly inhospitable environment the Zuni Indians have built up an economy with relatively high standards of living."

"The "poor man" at Zuni is one without ceremonial connections. They see life differently than other people and a comparison of views shows the differences in the way we see reality. Modern scientific people regard the notion that reality is to be regarded as a process. The world is in dynamic evolution. Time is in the past, present, and future. Pueblo Culture stresses what appears to be a present time orientation. In Indian time, events do not depend upon a clock so much as they do on weather, unpredictable animal stock and their associated problems, ritual, superstition, marital conditions, and in some cases, hangovers. What is important is what is happening now; tomorrow will take care of itself. Most Zuni Indians can adapt to Anglo time, however most would prefer not to."

Hidalgo entered the story with, "That is true. When I'm on the reservation I don't wear a watch. I don't need one, I don't need one now."

Corey continued, "Clockwork time can be a deadly master, we all bow to it. On a daily basis most people's lives are totally structured around it. Any small infringement into that clockwork world creates a major ripple in what was otherwise a smooth continuum. Linear time isn't so smooth anyway. The typical day I experienced, as a small boy was vastly longer than the days I experience now."

"Educated, scientific individuals tend to be highly competitive. Often this view makes them appear to be aggressive to others, especially to Pueblo people. Pueblo Culture stresses cooperation and anonymity. They want to blend in, to disappear, and to be invisible within a crowd. The effects of this can be seen in reservation schools where non-Indian and Indian students compete for grades. A good teacher uses a different approach when teaching in those schools. Learning that requires cooperation rather than competition usually produces superior results from the students."

Hidalgo, who knew exactly what Corey was talking about, looked up from his view of the river and said, "This is beginning to sound like one of those long winded speeches that Penny would make." I picked up a pebble and threw it at him.

Corey continued anyway, "Scientific living requires a degree in adaptability, a readiness to change as the environment changes. In Pueblo Culture a conservative attitude is retained regardless of changing conditions. Pueblo people tend to follow the ways of the old people. After all, their culture has existed there for thousands of years.

It works for them. Pueblo Culture stresses a call to Pueblo authority. Contemporary pueblos have a tribal council with elected officials to represent them. Often, however, solutions to problems are derived through mythology and witchcraft. Often issues are handled in this manner. Even the concept, or mental map, of the environment for example, has a totally different meaning to Zuni people."

"There is mystery as to where the Zuni people themselves come from. People who study the language of the Zuni say the roots of their language can be traced back to the Jomon of Japan, who had a maritime culture by the last millennia of the Ice Age. Migrating down the coast of the Americas, always seeking resources, they apparently migrated into the present day region long ago. People have lived in this area for more than ten thousand years, shifting from hunting and gathering, to an agricultural life-style and from dispersed villages to big communities. Zuni is one of the most populated areas of the Southwest. Living there, for me, was an education in itself."

"The impressions one gains by actually living with people, not necessarily by studying the relics of their past, produces a far better understanding of the people you are dealing with. As every second year archeology student knows; you can reconstruct a ruin and make some educated guesses as to what a people were like, but you cannot reconstruct a collective consciousness."

"To be honest with you, my first impression, upon arrival at Zuni Pueblo, was that I was going to die. I had a bad case of culture shook. There was only one other Anglo kid, my age, on the entire reservation. I really stood out when doing such mundane things as going to the local Dairy Queen. My fears were dispelled when I realized that the other young people there were as curious about me as I was about them. They weren't afraid of me, but I was of them. Penny's saying; 'Face your fears and they will go away,' comes into my mind when I think back on this now. After a little exploration I discovered that I was far safer there than in most other localities around New Mexico and particularly in the South Valley of Albuquerque."

"I remember that soon after my first paycheck, I began prodding the construction boss to let me work overtime. Sure," he grinned and replied, "But you'll have to get a crew to work with you."

"I went to talk to the local employees. No one would answer my questions or say anything. I spent about a day making a nuisance out of myself in this way. Then after a few days one elderly Zuni gentleman came to me saying that he would happily work overtime with me, if the boss OK'd it."

"The boss assured us it was all right, ignored my question about overtime pay, and then proceeded to ignore us. So away to work we went spending long hours after a full days regular work. We worked on the elderly gentleman's house for about two weeks before I realized that I would never see a dime of the overtime money. The much older, and wiser man, was more than happy to help me construct his future home. He appreciated the gift of my time."

"Zuni Pueblo is unique. Unlike other pueblos in the Southwest, such as the Isleta, Zia, or Santa Clara, Zuni was one of the last holdouts against the Spanish in the Pueblo revolt of 1680. Throughout the 17th century, Spanish authorities destroyed Pueblo Kivas and sacred objects. Religious intolerance, in conjunction with a persistent, although illegal, abuse of Pueblo labor prompted several Pueblos to revolt. The Spanish usually crushed them."

Hidalgo cut him off by finishing the point he was making, "Like I was saying back when we were on our way to Rinconada, in 1675, forty seven Pueblo caciques, or priest were convicted of practicing sorcery and plotting to rebel against the Spanish. Four of these religious leaders were hanged. The others were whipped, had body parts cut off, reprimanded and finally released. Many contemporary Pueblos still harbor strong cultural bias against the race that attempted to enslave them, particularly the Zuni."

After a short stop in the conversation, Corey continued, "One day I was sitting on a trailer doorstep with Raymond Zuni and four or five other young bucks that were off work. We were enjoying a little of the white man's disease: alcohol, in the form of beer. Being illegal on the reservation, beer is still boot legged in and abused. What you can't have is often what you crave the most. Many Native Americans are also extremely overweight due to their adoption of the white man's diet. Diabetes brought on by consuming too much salt, sugar, and fat, kills one in ten of the people."

"Soon, I saw a trio of feather and mud adorned individuals walking up the alley which ran behind the trailer house. They had a purpose to their actions but they seemed hesitant to be seen. I had never seen real witches before and was intrigued. Without really thinking I asked my friend Raymond if he really believed in Indian witchcraft. To me it seemed the correct thing to do since I knew that he had gone to the University of New Mexico, where he had earned his Master's degree in engineering."

"Raymond Zuni, who did not seem at all like the other workers there, simply answered, "Do you see those ruins over there?""

I looked through the screen door across the road to a burned down house, still black from a fire. He continued, "Those people did not believe in the old ways."

"That was all. He refused to explain."

"He probably couldn't," Hidalgo sighed, "trying to explain what Kachinas are to an outsider is a hopeless pursuit. Without the aid of a lifetime of experience in the

Zuni culture there are few reference points in order to aid an explanation."

Corey continued, "Also, my impression was that these people live by following natural laws, the basis by which they make decisions. Natural Laws are very simple. You cannot change them, they prevail over all. There is no court, nor even a nation in this world that can change Natural Laws. You are subject and born to those Natural Laws. The Indians understood the Natural Laws. Their customs coincide with the Natural Laws, and that's how they survived."

Corey finished his story with, "I did learn that they truly believe that many of the Kachinas represent beings that came to earth long ago and were encountered by their ancestors."

I thought about what he had been saying and replied, "I have to admit that I didn't know you had lived in Zuni, nor did I know that you knew so much about the people there. You are full of surprises."

Hidalgo answered, "Like I have said before, we are all geniuses but in different ways."

I continued, "So, I understand that some of the Kachinas represent visitors from other worlds. Do they really believe that space beings came to earth a long time ago?"

"Why does that sound so strange?" asked Hidalgo. "You grew up in a very Christian community in East Tennessee. People who attend church regularly believe in the same sort of things only they call it something else."

"What in the world are you talking about?" I asked.

"Well, think about it," answered Hidalgo, "If an ancient Native Indian saw a UFO he might describe it by drawing a picture of a bird. Your culture shows people who fly and have wings, as if extra appendages would actually sprout out of their backs. Why would they need actual wings? When the Christian bible was being written, it is a given that people could not understand the technology that Elijah attempted to describe. Was he really going up to heaven in a chariot of fire?"

I thought for a minute, then quoted the bible, "And it came to pass, as they still went on, and talked, that, behold, there appeared a chariot of fire, and the horses of fire, and parted them both asunder, and Elijah went up by a whirlwind into heaven."

Corey added, "Like in Ezekiel where he gave a very accurate description which details the movements, the lights, the sound and even how they lifted off in unison. What I don't understand is if they were actual visitors from other planets, why would they need machines that use rocket propulsion which produces fire and flames? If they were supernatural creatures, why would they need vehicles at all?"

Hidalgo continued, "There are many references to unusual or alien things throughout the Bible. While not all of them need to point to aliens or even Skin Walkers, nevertheless, it is enough to allow serious consideration. But as you asked, why would God need a vehicle to ride around in?"

"Yes I see," I said. I paused and then said, "You are a very exceptional person. Why are you so different from most other Navajos?"

Hidalgo lifted his shoulders into a shrug and grinned. "What makes a genius?" I was very lucky as a small child to have a mother and father that valued knowledge and worked with me everyday spending long hours learning languages. I also had to learn from a tiny child how to survive borrowing the best I could from many cultures. I learned to memorize and make games of learning. That was my only real entertainment. As one person said, being a genius is a matter of perspiration coupled with inspiration. Everyone has the ability to become a genius in one way or another. There is really nothing special about me that any child couldn't achieve, as far as I am concerned."

What is Science?

The next two days were uneventful with nothing out of the ordinary occurring. The canyon here was made up of spectacular meanders which meant that the river runners floated down miles of river but actually traveled only a few miles as the raven flies. We found ourselves acting just like all the other river runners who were enjoying their vacations. Finally we camped at Slickrock Canyon, taking a short hike up it until we came to a waterfall that was used as a shower by river runners and would require considerable effort to climb around. Returning to camp we were entertained by small parties of people who were sitting in the shallow pools of crystal clear water. We stopped in our tracks when we realized that a loud roar was overtaking us in the canyon. Three F-18s appeared just above the walls of the canyon. As they flew over the jets flipped over to allow the pilots to get a bird's eye view of the people lounging in the pools. Evidentially they were used to seeing some spectacles in those pools. Then, just as suddenly as they had appeared, the planes were gone and all was silent again.

Back at camp I prompted Hidalgo into a debate; Science versus Native American Witchcraft. Hidalgo didn't want to play but after some prodding and lack of an escape he gave in and let me say my peace. Besides, I didn't want to be left out of the discussions so I blurted out; "I believe in science. What is science and what is it that scientists do? When discussing what science is, there are many meanings to the word science, and what it is to be a scientist. The name "scientist" is usually used to refer to a certain type of person. Often, stereotyped as a slightly balding, squint eyed, middle aged man wearing a white laboratory apron and who is busily mixing chemicals or working away at collecting data in order to complete the requirements of a fat research grant. If this imaginary character spends his time using laboratory apparatus and techniques we naturally conclude that he must be a scientist. Television and other media tend to reinforce this stereotype. Actually, this imaginary person would more accurately be termed a technician. One may be highly skilled as a technician and yet have neither the mental set nor the wit of a scientist."

Hidalgo sat down in a camp chair, wondering what he had done to prompt the discussion but upon reflection, he had to admit that sometimes he learned something.

Thinking back to what my favorite science teacher, Mr. Dale, had taught me, I continued; "Traditionally, science education has tended to be historical compellations of scientific information. This is the same process by which most problems are solved; solutions are based upon experience. Science teachers who teach science as if they are inoculating their students with science are probably doing their students a disfavor. Teachers are usually perceived by their students as experts in the field, yet the net result of this pseudoscientific imitation is to produce more experts in pseudo-science. Ernest E. Bayles may have summed up this process when he said, "We tell 'em what we are going to tell 'em; then we tell it to 'em; then we tell 'em what we have told 'em. Afterwards we give examinations in order to find whether they can tell us what we told them."

"Don't you see what I'm saying? Students are not trained to make decisions based upon examining and weighing alternatives and thinking through choices, there is no test. Besides science doesn't teach anything, experience teaches it. So what is science?"

Hidalgo returned my query with a blank look so I continued. "Modern science contends that all things are in a state of constant change, growth, and decay, energy transformations, and social change, are all manifestations of the process nature of reality. Heraclitus the Greek once postulated that you cannot step in the same river twice. The Greek was asserting that no two things are ever exactly alike, that reality should be regarded as a process. One cannot step into the same river twice, not only because the river flows and changes, but because the one who steps into that river is also changed."

Hidalgo mulled this over for a while then made a simple point, "Throughout all of your history when mysterious or stressful events occurred, humans called upon metaphysical forces such as deities or some form of God to solve the problem. How is that really different from what Native Americans do? Many societies still use this approach. So what is science?"

I thought for a minute then replied, "Science is a tool used to solve problems. It usually involves conducting a test or an experiment whereby measureable, demonstrable, and repeatable results are obtained as an answer to a problem."

Corey looked up and says, "Boy, have I heard that from you before! You made the same speech when you were solving the problem of the rattlesnakes in *Serpientes*. Yes, I believe I understand."

Hidalgo thought for a moment then asked, "So what would a scientific person such as you say skin walkers are?"

I shrugged my shoulders, "I don't have the foggiest idea."

Grand Gulch

At one time in the distant past, a tiny San Juan river emptied it's water onto a vast plain where the river formed huge serpentine meanders as all rivers do when flowing over a very flat plane. Afterwards the land slowly rose and the Rocky Mountains formed, providing a much greater source of water. The land around here slowly rose thousands of feet allowing the river to cut down through the older layers of soft sedimentary rock under it, while keeping its original serpentine route. What is here now is the result of millions of years of erosion.

Along a quiet section of the river, Hidalgo asked Corey and me, "Have you ever considered that maybe we are floating through the insides of a giant serpent? A serpent that came here when the dinosaurs lived, it swallowed us somewhere upriver," he says with conviction.

Corey says, "I only hope it pisses us out downriver."

After a pause without a change in his facial expression Hidalgo says, "Sorry, "I

can't help but see the symbolism in my mind, certainly we are under its influence, we are being influenced by something. We really need to watch out for one another; they both glanced over at me.

"Well, I am having a good time except for one rattlesnake that curled up under a canoe with me. I still remember seeing it. It certainly seemed real to me. Corey is the only other creature that I want curling up with me!"

Floating down the huge meanders of this ancient river, we were all delighted. The long canoe trip now seemed worth all the effort. The scenery was spectacular and constantly changing. The river pours over a bowl shaped valley surrounded with shear canyon walls which tower a thousand feet high. The walls taper over then to a rounded incline all the way to a flat mesa, which is usually out of sight, hundreds of feet higher, it is impossible to find a route out of the canyon. Down the river is always the only way out.

Side canyons constantly appear where after heavy rains, cascading waterfalls empty into the San Juan River. In the alcoves created by those side canyons are many interesting camping sites. Sometimes there is an obvious trail usually ascending the side canyon until at some point or another it reaches sheer cliffs. There an amphitheater is created by the cascading water.

Along this section of the river we noticed many rafting parties and we made many friends along the river and felt that everyone's disposition was improving including our own. We slowly floated around a curve discovering on river right, a huge side canyon, with several rock formations that appeared to look like a giant phallus.

Arriving at Grand Gulch we encountered a problem. The floor of the gulch is about fifteen feet above the water line. The only way to unload the canoes is to unload them while floating in deep, fast water and we couldn't get close to the base of the cliff without walking over several rafts that were tied there. In a moment people started to gather along the rim looking down at us when one of them simply says, "We will be down to help you up."

Clinging to the edges of the raft they climbed down and helped us to tie the canoes to the rafts, then one at a time we unloaded the canoes and people handed our gear up. The dry bags were easy to tie to a rope and pull up to the ledge but iceboxes were another thing altogether. Fortunately, some of the people we had met at Chinle Wash were camped there and they graciously volunteered to help us; prompting others to help. Several of them expressed gratitude for getting their most important things back. We found an ideal camping spot and proceeded to tie the canoes to several small cedar trees just in case the wind got up and we had another weather encounter like the one we had above Mexican Hat.

The side canyon called Grand Gulch is some twenty-seven miles long. With a tiny stream flowing down it much of the year, the entire length of it contains Indian ruins with many petroglyphs, first explored by Richard Wetherill in 1893. It proved to be an archeological bonanza. He took out thousands of relics left by the ancient ones; most of which have now disappeared inside the Smithsonian.

At many sites along the twenty-seven mile stream Wetherill found skeletons far below the surface of the relics he was finding. They belonged to an entirely different people, now known as the Basketmaker people. They were a different race than anything he had seen before and from his point of view, Richard Wetherill had discovered an entirely new culture previously unknown to anyone. The deeper culture had apparently lived in peace but in the upper layers of sand, what he discovered was the evidence of extreme violence; bodies had been massively beaten with bones twisted and broken, the bodies were mutilated and tortured. Examining the more recent cliff dwelling Indians, evidence of extreme violence was everywhere. The upper or surface layers of relics belonging to the cliff dwellers spoke of a strange situation indeed. It was as if the Indians just decided, in mass to leave.

Wetherill documented a people who had lived there thousands of years, then left the area, moving on to Chaco Canyon to do the same thing all over again. In Chaco Canyon, all the personal items of the natives were still there just like at Grand Gulch when Wetherill discovered them. It didn't look to him as if families slowly left the area. Rather it looked as if they suddenly just left one day, perhaps in fear of something, never to return again. In fact, it was his belief, along with many other puzzled archeologists, that the ancient people of the Southwest didn't leave slowly after a long sustained drought but rather they left in a panic. Sure they were suffering from a drought, but they had already survived for thousands of years through worse droughts. Despite their large population, they were surviving. But something incredible had apparently happened here.

Oljeto Wash

*W*e spent several days at Grand Gulch to allow Hidalgo and Corey the opportunity to explore what the canyon offered. I declined the long hikes up the canyon preferring to gossip with the other campers. Usually the ladies hung around their camps rather than making the long and arduous twenty seven mile hike up the canyon, besides now they felt that someone had to watch each camp. We talked of everything but usually every conversation started out with questions about what had happened at Chinle Wash. Questions that arose such as how did Overholt know, in each camp, where all the important bags were? Where was his girlfriend while all the melodrama occurred between Overholt, Hidalgo, and the crowd? Were the boys victims also? Did they ever get back with their parents?

I enjoyed the company of other people. We were all members of an exclusive club consisting of people who had the courage to run rivers for a pastime. We shared stories about other river trips, evaluating the pros and cons of running them in canoes. Soon, my imagination would be on other rivers we could explore. But I envied the iceboxes of cold drinks and food that they carried in their rafts. In our canoes we were limited to one small box per canoe and we certainly didn't have cold drinks. We usually put a few drinks in a net bag and dragged them in the river water as we floated. Lukewarm drinks most of the way down the river but they had soon disappeared anyway and eventually we were left with drinking the melted ice.

When the boys arrived from their hikes they were famished and tired from the walking, which was often in deep sand, to dozens of small ruins. Hidalgo seemed to be intrigued at how artistic the inhabitants had been in constructing their homes. At one time, this must have been a nice place to live.

We had already decided to leave for Clay Hills Crossing the following morning. According to the river runners who walked over to our camp to say hello and bring everyone cold drinks, there were only two reasonable take outs below us and we would arrive at a dirt road on the right which disappears into a forest of Russian olive trees. We were warned that is all there is to it, and if we missed it, we would eventually find ourselves in Lake Powell.

Oljeto Wash was described to us by one fellow as a mysterious canyon. He had hiked up it only a short distance before giving up because of the difficulty. Jim Fulmer explained, "We could have some difficulty just getting into and out of the narrow canyon. On some years the entire landing area is a classic quagmire of deep quicksand

and mud that can be miserable, if not impossible to cross. More than one river runner has had to be rescued out of it. But if you can find a dry trail in and no one has beaten you there is a very nice camping spot some distance up the canyon. The danger of course is flash floods occurring miles away. It is a spooky place!" Downriver from there is a beach on river right with some sheepherder mud structures to explore. Then there is a long stretch of flat water with nothing but Russian Olives to see followed by that single road that comes out to the edge of the river. Don't miss it."

Early the next day, and with a lot of help, we did the reverse of what we did before in order to get down to the river and loaded our canoes. It took a while, even with all the help, but suddenly we were in a fast current careening down the river.

There was a quagmire of mud at Oljeto Wash but there was also a clear trail all the way up to the camp so we decided to take a look. Entry always depended on what's going on throughout the watershed that Oljeto commands.

The well-established camp site was several yards up the wash on a small beach of firm soil. Choosing not to stay there because of the unpredictability of the wash with its uncanny ability to transform into a hundred yard quagmire, we beached our canoes and stashed our paddles. Then we packed our valuables into small backpacks that held everything that we didn't want stolen. Not that we were worried about thievery at this point in the river trip, we were following well established and practiced routines. After tying off the canoes we slipped into our small day packs and began hiking up the narrow slit of rock known as Oljeto Wash. It was to be a short trip, everyone was tired and it was already noon. We just wanted to take just one more walk before the long float to Clay Hills. The first clouds started to gather in the afternoon skies.

The narrow serpentine canyon was a challenging climb. Sometimes there is a way to climb around it but sometimes it is a dead end. Trails like this are always easy at first, and then get harder and harder until it requires technical climbing skills and equipment before reaching the upper mesa. After walking though just a few turns of the very narrow but spectacular canyon, we all sat down on a large rock. We were suddenly struck with a feeling that overwhelmed the three of us. I had felt it before, long ago, while riding a bus in San Jon. An anxiety attack occurred that we have all experienced; that dread one feels when doing something that is utterly wrong and you dread the consequences. The feelings were oppressive, occurring in waves. Perhaps we were just tired from the long ordeal we had been on. Perhaps we just wanted to get off the river for a clean bath and find a cure for a multitude of small pains. Perhaps we were homesick. Perhaps we were ready to return to a comfortable ranch house where there were no demanding responsibilities. We just wanted to turn and leave, to go home.

But just taking that first step turned out to be an ordeal. All three of us could not leave our ledge of rock, breathing hard despite the fact that we had traveled only a few dozen yards. The experience was like diabetics feel when their blood sugar bottoms out. I tried to fight it. In my mind I would will a muscle to move but nothing happened. We were listless with no energy, we were paralyzed. We found ourselves lying back on the ledge and leaning on our small packs. Sitting there had been far too strenuous. It was sudden and drastic, a fear that left us all confused, paralyzed, and defenseless.

The next wave that overwhelmed us was a feeling of extreme panic followed by hallucinations. I could see rattlesnakes everywhere, I was terrified despite the fact that I had long ago gotten over my fear of snakes. Several of the snakes struck me. I could feel deep puncture wounds where the venom was being pumped into my body, in small waves. I was sure that I was bleeding from a multitude of bites. I felt no immediate effect from the rattlesnake bites other than the pain one feels when being bitten. Hidalgo looked over at me and tried to say something but no sound came out. Realizing he wasn't actually saying anything, he jerked his head up and starred at the canyon rims. Corey halfheartedly swung at an invisible opponent that only he could see. We were all experiencing extreme fear and every few minutes our hallucinations changed. We sat there for several minutes experiencing that sensation one has while awaking from a nightmare. Before the conscience brain connects to the body; you gain consciousness yet are unable to move. In your mind during what seems like an eternity, you somehow manage to make your arm drop off your chest or focus all your efforts just to move, to move anything, just enough movement for deliverance from the paralysis. Only that evening, that strategy didn't work. Within a few moments, the only thing we could move was our eyes. Eye contact was suddenly very important. We were paralyzed, each experiencing our own nightmare.

I was the first who could say anything. "Canoes, we need to return to the canoes." It took every morsel of energy I could muster to say each word. Both Corey and Hidalgo were suddenly angry; then I started to cry, loudly like a small child, and then realized what I was doing and immediately stopped.

Corey broke the trance again by uttering, "Do you guys realize this isn't happening? I should be dead by now." I jerked my chin up and looked up at him. Then we both looked at Hidalgo who appeared to be catatonic. Corey and I grabbed Hidalgo by the arms, but we couldn't move him. We did manage to roll him over on his stomach which seemed to slowly revive him. After a period of time had elapsed, just how long, I have no way of knowing, we began crawling, slowly on our knees down the complicated trail we had just casually walked up. After crawling around a meander of the canyon we discovered that we could stand. We wanted to walk down the wash. For the most part, we couldn't. It would take many minutes before we could keep Hidalgo on his feet. Wobbly, he started to drop back down but instead we jerked him into motion. Taking that first step seemed to take a herculean effort.

Only a few precious steps and the trail out seemed to be covered with scorpions. They were waiting there for us, thousands of them covering every possible escape route. Corey says again, "They are not real." They seemed to vanish into every crevasse as we followed Hidalgo, who suddenly took off walking through them. I was thankful that only two more turns and we should be out.

We were still having trouble doing even the simplest of movements; I had to think through every agonizing step. We sat down again, hoping that we could clear our minds. I made the mistake of closing my eyes. Instantly I was in an every changing geometric world that had images of serpents swimming through them. I would see flashes of scenes with Native Americans who were talking to me. I could not understand what they were saying or doing. Then I remember hiking on a long curving trail, I was visiting their homes that all turned into ruins before my eyes. Feeling more confident this time, I may have stayed there with my eyes closed for some time. I was reliving feelings I had felt before. I do not know how long I stayed in those worlds. Evidently, we were all catatonic for a while.

Sometime later, we all seemed to open our eyes at the same time. After asking each other if they were all right, we stood up to continue our exit. Taking only a couple of steps Corey was the first to suddenly stop and turn around to face where we had come. He then dropped his pants and pointed his butt up the canyon. He pulled his pants back up and started laughing while he pointed back up the canyon. Hidalgo started laughing then I started to see the humor in it all. Suddenly we all felt like we were on a sugar high; giggly and humorous. Our chortling and laughter bounced off the walls of the canyon.

Jumping back and retrieving Corey, Hidalgo says to him, "You know that they can control our emotions; we have to get away from here."

It was late evening when we finally got back to within sight of the canoes, but we couldn't account for several hours of missing time. We looked up at the crest of the sheer walls outlined by the darkening clouds and focused upon a single raven. It stared down at us. Then it started making a loud cawing sound, over and over in a humiliating cant. It was taunting us.

Again we had to drop down on our hands and knees, glancing back and watching the raven. It continued to taunt us for some time then flew up the walls of the canyon and over the top and out of sight. Suddenly we were able to walk again, instead we ran. All the previous strange feelings disappeared. We went directly to the canoes, only taking time to tie our small packs into the floor of the canoes, and launched downriver without saying a word.

We floated in the gathering darkness downstream to find a camping spot. Between us we never said a word. Then along river right we spotted the small ruined rock structures. We unloaded our boats and even tied them off but we were all so exhausted all we wanted to do was sleep. Wrapping up in sleeping bags under a tarp, we all feel fast asleep. The three of us didn't want to talk to anyone or eat anything, we needed time to heal. Unfortunately, all three of us had experienced the worst nightmares of our lives leaving us dog tired the following day.

The next day after coffee but no breakfast, we sat off downriver in search of Clay Hills Crossing where after arriving, Hidalgo managed to catch a ride with a fellow Navajo who was working the shuttle services. Four hours later he returned with two different fellows who were dropping off someone's car. The news was that Ken and June would be there sometime late the next day.

The mosquitoes which we hadn't noticed since the early days on the Animas River well above Farmington were terrible and we now found ourselves being eaten alive. Setting up tents well away from the brush that grew along the river and well up the on the take out road helped but we still found ourselves hiding inside our tents in the stifling heat to avoid the pesky little creatures.

Ken and June showed up late in the afternoon the following day. Ken immediately figured out that something was wrong. He found himself making suggestions to us and we would do as he asked. After loading the canoes and equipment, we all settled into the seats of our car, it had been so long that they seemed strange and new to us. As we headed back toward Mexican Hat down the long and monotonous dirt road which intersected the blacktop, we kept nodding off. We were absolutely drained of any energy, physical as well as psychological. Ken and June were worried; they knew when something was terribly wrong. They knew we were hiding a great secret.

After a few miles of road, Ken casually asked us if we would consider camping out one more day. "There is a place down the road called Muley Point. There is a turn off there where this road goes down a thousand feet of rock escarpment, by way of sharp switchbacks. Let's drive out to the point which is on our way home, I think you will find it to be an interesting place, and besides June and I have not been camping out at all, we brought things to cook for dinner and we are tired of driving."

The point was well taken, normally we would have been excited about the prospect of spending the evening at a new place, but all we could do was doze off while they talked to us.

I opened my bloodshot eyes and said to them, "You are rescuing us, we place our lives in your hands," and then I fell fast asleep.

Muley Point is an unregulated camping area that overlooks the San Juan River with panoramic views of Monument Valley. Looking down from the edge of camp, far below, the San Juan River was cutting a deep serpentine course across a vast valley. It truly did look like a huge serpentine creature far below us. It was already very dark down there with nothing but the uppermost edges of the canyon still in sunlight. It was a spooky feeling knowing that just a few days ago we were floating down that river, now enveloped in a shroud of darkness; a surrealistic looking terrain. That evening we enjoyed ice cold drinks and fresh food that Ken and June had brought with them for the occasion. After setting up tents under the local cedar trees we took camp chairs and sleeping pads out to the edge of the rock precipice overlooking monument valley to watch the sunset occur over one of the most spectacular views the southwest has to offer. For hours, we sat and relived the last few weeks to Ken and June, who seemed fascinated, particularly about the apparitions that we had experienced. They wanted to hear every detail. For us, three river runners, this was a very soothing experience. We had not shared our impressions among ourselves and were curious about what Corey was punching at or what had produced a state of catatonic shock to Hidalgo. Was I the only one seeing rattlesnakes all around us? We were feeling stronger and as our minds returned to us we became more talkative. Having an ice cooler full of cold drinks and snacks that only civilization can offer helped to prompt a wealth of conversation as the evening skies were slowly turning dark in a cloudless sky. We were secure, experiencing again, those feelings that can only be shared together in a close family.

The stars came out in the crystal clear evening. By the time we had finished talking about our adventures on the river it was dark, with no moon out. Sitting there in the warm desert air, Ken was the first to notice a light that was moving. Undoubtedly they all thought, just another airplane. But as they watched the plane began a huge sweep across the valley making a crescent toward them. As the first plane came closer another airplane appeared on the distant horizon every few seconds. We were watching the planes making a parabola, flying just a few thousand feet over the valley surface. As our eyes focused it was obvious that there were many tiny dots behind them.

As the jet turned back toward Arizona we could make out that it was a classic

B-52, painted black with only a single light on it. It passed in front of us and in a few moments two more jets passed. Two F-18s, again painted black with one light on them. Then something very different appeared before us, jets crossed the sky in front of us that were shaped like triangles, they looked like diamonds flying, making no noise. We all watched in amazement and became very quiet.

Within a few minutes we noticed points of light that looked like the star that Corey had spotted in White Rock Canyon. They appeared somewhat in pursuit of the other mysterious planes. They zipped along without a sound. The question that everyone was thinking about was; are they ours, or someone else's planes. The dots appeared to dart around, somewhat like butterflies, stopping to hover then darting to another spot in the sky but apparently in pursuit of the stealthy jets just observed. Just as mysteriously as they had arrived they left, heading west to an unknown destination.

"There is one more piece of unfinished business that has to be taken care of that I have not had a chance to take care of," responded Corey," I have gone for a month and a half with Hidalgo watching us, along with tourist, rangers, thieves and skin walkers." At that point he leaned over to me, wrapped his arms around me and asked, "Do you have any idea how much I love you?" He then proceeded to kiss me, a long and impassioned kiss; the kind of kiss of someone who is hopelessly in love gives. I looked over at Ken and June who were grinning from ear to ear.

Hidalgo finally broke the silence with, "A kiss like that means the beginning of something really special, next time a decision is made to run a river, maybe, just you two should go alone, I blush easily.

Ken then pulled out a small box from his jacket pocket. "I realized that you had left this behind and it bothered me for some reason. I thought you might appreciate getting it back."

I placed the owl amulet over my head and that evening both Corey and Hidalgo slept with their heads very close to me.

Evil Intent

The owl offered us protection. We arose early the next morning in great spirits, after the first night of sound sleep without nightmares or even dreams. We hung around the camp about an hour the next day and Ken and June rustled us up a great breakfast. We took turns driving the roads all the way back to the ranch house in *Serpiente*. The road trip was quiet and uneventful. Upon arrival at the ranch everyone was exhausted and there were a lot of chores that needed to be caught up. After cleaning and storing all the gear, including the canoes in a shed, we had nothing but more work to look forward to. We were still exhausted because of all the muscle energy expended while fighting the hallucinations. But we found solace in our ranch work even though we were more tired than usual. It gave us time to process what we had learned. We could not get the apparitions out of our minds; they created too many unanswered questions. In the evenings after the daily ranch chores were done, we sat around trying to come up with a logical answer to those questions, but it would take time.

We had no real answer to the very purpose for our river trip. Why was the apparition that Richard had seen and described at Gallena so different than the apparitions we had seen? The only hypothesis that we could come up with was that the previous culture that existed in Gallena was very different from the Chacoan culture that surrounded them. In fact, according to archeological studies they absolutely avoided each other. Why? There was not a shred of archeological evidence that there was any trade between them yet there are natural trails which connect them. Perhaps the skin walkers that existed in Chaco Canyon found no value in being active with a different culture or maybe, the Gallena culture avoided all contact with the Chacoan culture because of the Skin Walkers and the witchcraft that comes with them. We felt that the apparition that Richard had seen was not a supernatural apparition at all. Perhaps it was a natural physical phenomenon, a plasma ball created by the grinding of subterranean forces that move whole, entire mountains ranges.

What was the apparition that flew across the sky at Combs ridge and did it have anything to do with the tumult at Mexican Hat Anticline or did it have everything to do with the tumultuous things that happened later? Why were we the only people to see it? Skin walkers are rumored to cause humans to act evil; they seemed to enjoy toying with humans. Obviously, things like children being beaten up and personal things being stolen do not happen, normally, anywhere on river trips. Did the skin walkers make Mr. Overholt and his girlfriend, do what they did, or had he planned his actions in advance? The real mystery was how did they manage to steal the most personal possessions from almost every camp in the area? How did they know where all the personal items were hidden in each camp? Did they somehow have help? It all seemed to have happened very quickly. It seemed to be impossible for several thieves to steal as many personal bags as they did in such a short time, but no one was actually ever seen trying to steal anything. It was Overholt who insisted that the boys were responsible for everything. Were the boys working with Overholt and then found themselves victims when Overholt turned on them. Virtually the entire camping area was victimized. If they were smart enough to figure out how to do that, how could they possibly be so stupid as to think they could escape by paddling downriver to Mexican Hat? It is a bottleneck, but then, it can be paddled in several hours if the paddlers are determined and skilled enough.

When the crows visited our camp at Mendenhall Cave, were they all skin walkers or was one animal directing all the other crows to do its bidding. Perhaps they were just crows! They all just seemed to want to look at us, and then they left. The problem was trying to wrap my mind around forty crows all belonging to a single clan that wanted to examine us. Why?

Did any of this have anything to do with the disappearance of previous cultures that occupied the river watershed? Would the violence return in the modern four corners area? Certainly no one can explain the amount of violence that had suddenly appeared after centuries of relative peace. Why did the early Indians turn to cannibalism and head hunting? Were they so desperate that it was the only way they could survive, or were they being directed by evil witches? We all felt like we were seeing something that was invisible to everyone else.

The apparition that Hidalgo saw seemed real enough for him. Why did it then disappear? Was it taunting Hidalgo or had it been examining him? Was it what the Navajos called a trickster? Why did it pick him to appear to? Hidalgo naturally wondered why he had been chosen.

Oljeta Gulch was a profound mystery to us; we wondered how the raven took control of our minds. We kept wondering what could have happened, the raven had complete control of our emotions. Emotions are generated in the oldest and most primitive part of the human brain. What some scientist call the reptilian center. We wondered if there was a connection but were at a loss as to how the raven actually used its power. We found ourselves asking was there a way to combat the powers of the skin walker, or kill them? Certainly if the serpents wanted to kill us they could have easily manipulated our minds into murder. Were we being attacked or being tested? Hidalgo came to the conclusion that the creatures were trying to learn as much about us as possible. They were testing us for something that was to happen. Hidalgo knew deep in his heart that there was going to be another confrontation, sometime, somewhere.

I learned from Hidalgo that all of this witchcraft certainly seemed to have a profound impact on the Navajos who were living there now. They despise witchcraft, yet it has a profound impact on their culture. What do the tribal elders know that they refuse to share with the rest of the world? Or do they? Everyone has different opinions.

The one mystery that didn't seem to bother anyone was the strange dancing lights that appeared in the sky. They didn't seem to do anything but dance in the night sky. For now, they seemed harmless, a preoccupation of modern Americans but they seemed very different from the ancient creatures that were plaguing the people on the San Juan Watershed. One thing we understood was that there was an unnatural, supernatural force in this land, consisting of pure energy with an evil intent.

Researching Zuni

Wanting to find out more about the Zuni culture, Corey and I took a trip to the library at the University of New Mexico. There we read chapters from several books and wrote the most interesting things down to share with Hidalgo, June and Ken.

When the Spanish entered the southwest in the early sixteenth century, two hundred years after Chaco Canyon was deserted, there were over eighty pueblos clustered along the Rio Grande River and its tributaries. In addition, to the far west were the Hopi towns, then to the east of them the seven Zuni villages as well as the sky city of Acoma. Several different languages were spoken in the pueblos, Keresan, Tewa, Tiwa, Towa, Shoshonnean, and the unique Zunian to name a few. The Zuni language is inexplicable. Linguist say that some aspects of it closely resemble dialects found in primitive tribes of people from North Africa in what is now the country of

Libya and other linguist say they can find direct roots in their language to the ancient Japanese.

Due, undoubtedly to the European influence, the eighty pueblos have dwindled to nineteen. Zuni is known to its ancient inhabitants, as Halona I'tiwana, the Middle Ant Hill of the World. Only a single pueblo called Zuni now exist where at one time there was seven. It is located in extreme western New Mexico, some thirty-some miles south of the railroad town of Gallup. The people in Zuni are noted for making inlaid silver jewelry and for their skill at performing at Native American ceremonies such as the Shalako that involves six giant Kachinas called The Couriers of the Gods. There is much more, however, that distinguishes the Zuni Indians.

Zuni first experienced Europeans when Franciscan Father, Fray Marcos de Niza and his Moorish companion Estavan, walked across North America with Cabeza de Vaca searching for the seven cities of gold. Instead they stumbled upon Zuni. Estavan, thinking that he could talk to the Zunis, boldly rode into the Pueblo. He was killed. Hearing of this, Niza fled south to Mexico with the news of Estavan's death, telling tales of a golden city. Hearing those stories, Francisco Vasquez de Coronado set forth to find the Golden Cities of Cibola.

The city he found was gold colored, but only because of the appearance of the natural rocks and adobe mud bricks that were used in its construction. There was no real wealth in the form of gold to be stolen there. He found the villages in 1540, and that is when the trouble began. Afterwards a succession of Spanish explorers stumbled into Zuni, mostly on their way to somewhere else. The natives, who had already fought outsiders such as Apaches and Navajos, now had another invasion to deal with.

Driven by the search for gold and souls to save, Zuni was visited by a succession of explorers. By 1629 Spanish missionaries had settled into Hawikuh and a Catholic mission rose in its midst. By 1680 the Zunis had joined in a pueblo wide revolt from the Spanish. After killing one of the priests, and burning the mission of Halona, they fled to a fortified position. When the Spanish returned to Zuni they settled in a single village, Halona, as a safeguard against the increasing raids.

The first American to have real contact with the Zuni Indians was Frank Hamilton Cushing. Arriving in Zuni in 1889 he spent four years among them becoming a Zuni himself. Cushing was unique not only because he was a brilliant ethnologist associated with the Bureau of American Ethnology under the directorship of Major John Wesley Powell of Grand Canyon fame, but because he became one of the very people he was studying. He became a member of the tribal council and as such a warrior. He learned to take scalps, a curious custom introduced to the tribe by previous Spanish invaders. He took it as a personal responsibility to deal with their real enemies the Navajos and the American politics of the time.

By this time the area was being settled by American pioneers, even the land itself was being stolen. Cushing found himself acting as a court lawyer, fighting the surrounding ranchers who wanted to add pueblo land to their personal empires. They argued that since they would have to pay for any land they acquired, and the Indians had never paid for any of their land, it was an injustice. The Indians had no court documents registered in Santa Fe documenting their land therefore it was up for grabs. Cushing, who had learned the Zuni language and customs, was the only white man who ever got a real insight into what it is to be a Zuni and fought for their rights in the courts.

A Visit to Zuni

*I*n particular, I wanted to return to the San Juan area. My curiosity only peaked once I had the time to think about my experiences. I was amazed, after all, strange things like what had happened to us simply do not happen to the vast majority of people who travel through or live in the Four Corners area or anywhere else. Considering the hundreds of river runners who floated down the river, why did everything happen to us? But I also wanted to go to Zuni. Hidalgo's father had suggested that the only way anyone could find out why the canyons around San Juan were deserted and people left their homes, was by visiting Zuni. When I asked Hidalgo about going to Zuni all he would say is "No!" Hidalgo refused to even discuss going to Zuni. Corey didn't care; he just wanted to be with me wherever I went.

It took almost a month before all the chores were done, particularly medicating the cows for an infestation of deer ticks. We decided to take the arduous trip into the canyon lands behind the ranch house that hid thousands of ruins and of course what was left of the mysterious mountain that at one time was the home of thousands of mysterious serpents. Everything looked rather sad and deserted. Not only had the serpents apparently disappeared but much of the other wildlife from coyotes to rabbits had simply vanished. Walking through the canyons, one would always be entertained by the singing of birds. Now it was a stony silence. The good news was that the entire episode was being forgotten by neighboring ranchers. They were starting to prosper again as their domesticated animals were making a rebound. Everyone seemed happy except for the family at Serpiente Ranch; we knew the hidden, but very real, cost of what was going on.

Hidalgo continued his stubbornness until we seemed to be arguing about Zuni constantly. Finally one evening at dinner, when the subject inevitably came up June stopped the conversation with an announcement that she was going to Zuni alone. June explained that she was the only person among them that had real contacts in the Zuni world. She knew one family at Hopi well and several families at Zuni including clan elders, because of her work there on her anthropology degree. She also had the political contacts in Santa Fe where she had managed to interest certain political parties into the value of assisting in the survival of New Mexico's indigenous populations, if for no other reason, than for tourist trade and of course there were votes in Zuni.

Many Zunis did not take the time to participate in state elections, they have their own problems to take care of and saw little value in the government that represented the outside world. Besides, after hundreds of years of foreign contact not a single foreign entity had offered them anything that would actually help them, only religion; foreign religions that were useless to them as far as most of them were concerned. June had spent many long hours working at the pueblo and even longer hours in Santa Fe where she talked to government officials about the deplorable and ancient houses that the natives lived in. She had missed seeing Corey there years ago by only a few days.

Strangers came and went through the pueblo all the time, mostly tourist who after placating their curiosity drove on. There were no motels in Zuni. Nobody ever stayed, they couldn't. The Zuni tribal council didn't allow anyone but natural born Zuni citizens to live on the reservation. The Zuni people are a very private people. There were a few exceptions to that rule, but newcomers who wanted to stay were really not welcome. One exception to the rule was the trading company that was owned and operated by a white family for the last fifty years or so. It was necessary to the tribe. June knew she would be able to talk to Zuni Indians when nobody else could because her political efforts brought in a construction company that built homes for the people. They used Zunis as the primary source of labor which meant there were jobs, which meant there was money to buy things that were desperately needed by the pueblo people. They might feel compelled to help her.

She knew all about the ancient cultures that lived in the southwest, she knew secrets. She knew that there was far more to their ancient ceremonies and rituals than people realized. After all, at one time the cultures in the Americas were just as interesting if not superior to anything offered in Europe. When the Spanish conquered the civilizations in South America, it was recruited Indians and disease such as smallpox that actually conquered the nations of natives, not Spanish warriors. At about the time Columbus mistakenly wandered into America, the indigenous cultures of the Americans consisted of huge populations of people, who in places like the Amazon, simply vanished along with the traces their cultures which have since been engulfed by the jungle. Only a tiny percentage, usually only one or two percent of any given population survived the introduction of the new diseases. In North America, when Columbus arrived there were some five hundred different indigenous nations, each with traditions and a culture of their own. They raided each other and occasionally intermarried. They were all profoundly affected by the newcomers and their populations plummeted due to diseases.

Apparently gold was never considered a useful metal to the local natives here in the American Southwest. It was too soft. Although there was evidence that they traded gold to natives in the south for ceremonial goods that could only come from present day Mexico and beyond. The cultures the Spanish found were poor in material wealth; the Spanish never found the rich cities of gold that they had hoped for despite their successes in South America, but they were very rich in ceremonial and racial memories. While everyone else measured the cultures using a yardstick that measured the amount of territory they occupied, the megalithic structures they created or the gold they possessed. June was one of the first who realized the vast amounts of energy that was donated to ceremonial activities; material wealth meant nothing to them.

June personally knew several people at Zuni pueblo such as the governor as well as several conspicuous elders. After piling into the most dependable work truck, and making the long journey to the pueblo, she encountered what she expected. They were all polite, she was even invited to share food with them in several of their homes, but they wouldn't answer her questions about Skin Walkers. They either had no memory of the stories from that time or they would simply change the subject, it was a taboo subject, something as one elderly lady says, "a subject the Navajos would have to deal with." Finally one elderly man gently patted June on the knee, leaned over and said into her ear; "We believe that thinking about shape shifters or skin walkers, much less talking about them, might invite them into our community. As far as we are concerned they do not exist." They certainly didn't want to discuss it with a white woman. Despite her political pull within the tribe, she was still an outsider.

The people of Zuni Pueblo had good reason for being so secretive and private about their history. Although Zuni is very old and unique, they, along with Hopi and many other communities are the modern day descendants of the people who left San Juan and Chaco Canyon, the homeland of the ancient Anasazi world. They are the living descendants of those people who left in fear. They may know answers but are unwilling to divulge anything.

After the people left what is now northern New Mexico and Colorado, they took up a whole new religion that was being practiced in Zuni, Hopi and many other southern communities, the religion of the Kachina. For the average person, life had been horrible in the north, a real challenge just to stay alive, while in the southern communities, everyone was prospering. The weather cooperated with the new communities and their gardens produced food to feed a slowly expanding population. The new religion of the Kachina, offered them a whole new way out of the darkness. After only a few generations only a few had memories of what happened.

Finally, just when June realized that she was making a nuisance of herself and started to prepare to leave, her solution appeared to her. She first noticed the small boy in the shadows, watching her. This was not unusual because in the pueblo children learn to avoid outsiders. But curiosity overwhelms a few of them. She caught several glimpses of him watching her, and then she slowly advanced toward him. Finally she positioned herself where he would run into her if he tried to escape and June asked him "What's your name?"

Cornered, he turned to her after looking up and down the street to see who else was there. He then dropped his eyes to the ground and walked over to June and without answering her question said, "You want to ask someone some questions?" June answered, "Yes that's true, but let's answer the first question, first."

"Joaquen Mendoza." said the boy with a smile. "If you really want answers to your questions you should talk to my grandfather. He is a shaman."

June thought she knew everyone in the community who participated in the ceremonial arts. She also knew however, that if she was going to get some real answers she would need to find someone unique, a person who followed their own path instead of following the flock. June knew what would be required, "What would your grandfather want in order to share some information with me?"

Without a moment's pause, the small boy answered, "Food."

With that, June grabbed the boy's hand and headed to her pickup truck. They then drove to Gallup. The local trading company had only a meager amount of groceries, specializing in the tourist trade. Thirty miles away, in Gallup she bought a large bag of oranges, three pounds of coffee, some sugar, twenty five pounds of potatoes, onions, twenty pounds of pinto beans, two loaves of fresh bread and a large precooked ham. With a little coaching from Juaquen she also bought a couple of bags of candy. Loading the groceries into the bed of the truck she then said, "Ok, let's go to your grandfather's house. How do we get there?"

"Back to Zuni," said the small boy. Returning to Zuni, June expected the boy's grandfather to be living in the pueblo but the boy pointed on down the road and so June followed his lead. She kept looking at every house they encountered expecting it to be the house where the boy had come from, but he kept insisting on going further and further out of town on a well rutted gravel road. Finally after they had traveled some ten miles he pointed to a turn off. Two almost invisible ruts circled through a forest of weathered cedar and juniper trees up to the foot of a sandstone bluff where a classic Zuni style rock house appeared. It appeared exactly like so many ruins June had explored but this one was roofed, with a small stream of smoke coming out of a rock chimney. Opening the door made of rough planks, probably from a local saw-mill, she entered a dimly lit room where the boy and his shaman grandfather lived.

Almost being afraid of the answer, she asked the small boy, "How in the world did you get into town?"

"I walk." Walking was the only way they got around, but what was really on her mind was how did the boy and his grandfather know about her?"

Grandfather, the only name he answered to, indeed, looked like an Indian shaman known as a *casique*. Grandfather was not a pueblo elder; he was the town misfit, a hermit. Using any substance he could get his hands on in order to become inebriated, he probably was considered by all, an outlaw, June guessed. He did not follow the Zuni way. June figured that many had already branded him as a witch. They were undoubtedly mean to him, and enjoyed teasing him. Old, and unable to get around and unable to hunt now, he was without family except for his grandson; they were slowly starving to death. The young boy had gotten by, by stealing what he could from his neighbors. He too was not following the Zuni way, and had made enemies in the community, but the boy had no choice.

June had the boy stoke up a fire in the potbellied stove that the family used both as a cooking stove and the only source of warmth on cold winter days. She put on a pot of beans which would take some time to cook and then made some ham sandwiches. Grandfather only ate a slice of ham folded into a single slice of bread; he was afraid to eat more. It had been too long ago since he had eaten, but the boy wolfed down several sandwiches. The shaman then took a long drink from a bottle that was clearly an alcoholic beverage and began a quiet chant.

June said to him, "You know, it is against the law to have any kind of alcoholic beverages on the Zuni reservation."

He looked up at her and said, "That's true, but I know the answer to your puzzle. Besides, holding the bottle up, it was given to me. I have no money to spend on alcohol and no way of going off the reservation to get more."

Since June had not asked any questions she was a little mystified. In her own mind, she felt like she had been taken as a fool, at which point the old man said, "I do not consider your questions foolish!" June was beginning to believe that the old man could read her mind, and sure enough he seemed to have answers for her questions before she asked them. Along with an uncanny ability to know what June was going to say, before she said it, the old man would demonstrate that he had an articulate understanding of the history of his people.

Grandfather apparently had always been a rebel in his own tribe. Every tribe has rebels, but Grandfather was indeed different, he was certainly not afraid to talk to an outsider, if she would provide him with certain things. It wasn't that he wanted to take advantage of an outsider; he appeared to desperately need help, not only for his sake but for the sake of his grandson of whom he had gained custody after his son and his wife had died in an automobile accident two years ago. June could emphasize with him, the same thing had happened to Corey's parents. Ken and she had adopted him.

Grandfather looked at June and said, "We have a bond, you and me, we are both responsible for others. Corey is very much in love with the new girl, uh...Penny, isn't she?

June looked at him in amazement. There was no way he could have known about Corey and me.

"And, what are you doing hanging around a Navajo?" He said it with a big grin on his face, he was toying with her, and she knew it. She was truly mystified. Either Grandfather had incredible connections to town gossip or he had special powers that only a few mortals could claim. She had never talked to anyone about the Navajo, Hidalgo, because she knew how sensitive the Zuni people were about the Navajo. Currently they were at peace under the laws of New Mexico and the United States of America. Before, they had been mortal enemies.

As darkness settled over the ruin early, being in the shade of the bluff behind it, Grandfather began to chant again, he finally stopped and looked at June.

"You have a great mystery that you are trying to solve, something to do with my ancestors."

June gasped, "That's true, but how do you know?"

Grandfather looked at her and solemnly said, "Actually I have heard the town gossip. I do have friends that come and check on me to see if I'm still alive. My friend told me about you. He saw you at one of meetings you had with our elders. He was there, helping serve the food. "He followed up his statement with a grin that showed many missing teeth.

"They didn't tell you what you wanted to know did they?"

"No," June had to admit.

"I will tell you because you have a good heart. My Grandson here thinks my stories are just like all the other stories he hears from people. They are just stories, a way to entertain."

"I am descended from many shamans. My father was a shaman; his father was a shaman and so forth. I am a shaman but what few people seem to understand is that not all shamans are bad people. I am not a witch, or a *bruja*, we simply know things that give us an entirely different view of the world. We understand the futility of doing things that others do. My secrets own me."

June asked him point blank, "What is a skin walker?"

"When we lived in the other world, in Aztlan or in what you call Chaco Canyon, the first people who lived there lived comfortably and in peace. But soon our leaders began to entertain visitors from the south, outsider, warriors, and tricksters from what is now known as Mexico. Outside people came among us, who worshiped evil beings. They were evil creatures themselves, butchering us and even using us for food. We fought back but soon the elders adopted the newcomer's ways. Soon all the elders were living in a dream world brought on by the magic the shamans from the south had brought with them. The youth, within a short time, learned to enjoy hurting others. They roamed in packs, like wolves, preying upon anyone they could find alone. Sometimes, when they found a victim they would simply twist all of their bones until they died. They seemed to have superhuman strength, being able to turn bones into splinters. Children were burned alive while their mothers watched in horror. It was terrible times; people would walk around talking to invisible beings, attacking people, even family members, for no reason. Many people died. My ancestors left in small groups, sneaking away from Chaco Canyon and hiding in cliff houses far away to escape the intruders but after a while they were found by new enemies from the north who preyed upon us. We were trapped between warlike people from the north and the supernatural cruel enemies from our former home, Aztlan. When they found us, terrible deaths occurred."

Finally we heard about peaceful tribes that were visited by star people.

"Star people?" June asked. They came among them and showed then a better way to live. They are what the Kachinas are. They are the creatures in our ceremonies. Star creatures are very sacred and beloved beings just like they are in your culture, only you call them by other names. However, there were rebels even among them. They were not all good people; some of them were evil creatures. These evil ones were despised even among their own people, so they were cast out. Where the Navajo people now live and where our ancestors lived is where they settled. They are the ones who are causing the problems to the people who live there now, the Navajo. They are the ones who were left behind by the star people who returned to the stars. This place, you call earth, is their jail. They left behind because of their evil ways and their evil intent. We discovered that they controlled our minds, our very thoughts. We made war on ourselves for their entertainment. It was the final thing we could deal with, so we journeyed south to this land where the rain was better and there were no Skin Walkers. Here we didn't have to deal with the Ute's and Navajos who were killing us and stealing our land. The Skin Walkers, as you call them, stayed there, I am not sure why, but I don't believe they can't journey far from their source of power, their home.

June asked him, "What is their source of power?"

The shaman thought over the question for a minute then answered, "Your scientist talk about breaking everything down into what is called elements, the tiny things that everything is made of. Each of those elements is further made up of atoms with protons and electrons."

"That is very true," said June. "New Mexico is famous as the birthplace of the atomic age."

"There is a lot more there than protons and electrons," the shaman added.

"There are many things inside the atom that are just now being understood by your scientists."

"That's true," replied June. "They have discovered a whole zoo full of particles inside the atom as well as different kinds of energy."

"When you get to the most elemental levels of matter, there is something there called dark energy by your scientist that they cannot understand; it defies the very laws that your scientist use to describe atoms. Skin walkers somehow use that energy."

"How do you know all this, asked June?

"It is a knowledge we have always known, at least we seem to be safe here. Skin walkers don't bother us here." With that said; the old man turned over on his bed and started to go to sleep.

"Thank you," said June. "Is there any way we can fight them?"

He remained motionless as he answered, "After several hundred years we never found a way to defeat them. They live to commit evil deeds or to have others do their evil deeds for them. They seem to draw energy, dark energy from the fear and sufferings and finally the death of their victims."

June thanked him again and even hugged the small boy. June had her answers but they only created more questions. She thought to herself, by the strangest of circumstances, she had experienced the briefest encounter with a shaman. She wondered how many other elderly Zunis she had spoken to had known the secrets about this land? Based upon what Corey, Hidalgo and I had told June about our encounters, the serpents could control our minds but not our actions.

June thanked the small boy, said her goodbyes and started the short walk to her parked truck. She would have a world of things to talk about when she returned to Serpiente, but the first thing she noticed as she got to her truck was the raven perched on a tree branch directly over the cab. As she opened the door the raven flew away, but as she drove down the ruts out to the main gravel dirt road the raven swooped past her windshield several times, making her wonder.

Part 5

The Fight Game

History is a set of lies, agreed upon.

—Napoleon

There were giants in the earth in those days.

—Genesis 6:4

Clan Protector

*I*t had taken almost a full two hands of the morning sun before Clan Protector began his morning climb up the trail leading to his favorite lookout. From there, he could enjoy a vast panorama and still keep an eye on the cave. He had hoped to get away before it got too hot but before he could leave this morning, he had many things to do. Clan Protector had hoped one of the women would prepare his food. He was accustomed to having this chore being taken care of when he was staying at the cave. None of them seemed interested. They had plenty of food but none of the cave dwellers wanted anything to eat nor did they want to prepare food for others. Some sickness was affecting everyone except Clan Protector. Everyone had diarrhea. They stunk. He did what he could do to help everyone and make the elders comfortable. Then he left to find his own food. More than likely he would go hungry but there was always a chance that a cottontail would make the mistake of showing itself to him.

His stomach was just starting to bother him. He wanted to be alone. Suspecting that the sickness came from something they were eating, he had not eaten anything since he left the lookout yesterday evening. He had not touched anything in the cave having prepared his own food while away at the lookout and he knew how to live very comfortably there, on his own. He felt strong and he was very smart, he had made a conscious decision to vary his routine.

Doing the same thing every day made you vulnerable to an attack. Cats were especially a problem; they sometimes studied you several days just planning how they would get too you. After hiding, when you least expected it, they would attack you. It would be lightning fast and usually fatal.

On his left thigh and ribcage, he had several parallel scars from a not so long ago encounter with a cat. Fortunately, his brother Red Ochre had seen the cat and came running to his older brother with a spear and war cry, the cat ran away. Clan Protector was very lucky. Even the sickness that the wounds caused didn't seem to bother him now. He had healed well but he remembered the sickness that came over him as he healed. Every few hours Elder Women would wash the wounds out with hot water and then pack the cavernous cuts with herbs. It hurt. Now he had full movement and was growing stronger every day. Nevertheless on his journey to the lookout he had to be careful. Every living thing around him could hurt him in an attempt to protect itself. Even the plants yielded spikes and spines that often inflected poisons. But it was all instinct to him, he knew how to survive, but he was in serious competition with many other meat eaters such as bears, cats, and a multitude of teethed and clawed creatures that lived around him.

All his people were in constant danger. Fortunately, most animals avoided places that had been marked by humans, that is, where humans had peed on the ground. Most animals avoid the smell of humans but some cats were attracted to the scent. He had learned as a small child how to keep a spear between himself and a cat. He had been lucky, lucky all his life. He had encountered several cats, and it seemed that usually they would run from him if he could just keep the obsidian tip of the spear between his body and the cat.

Stopping and sitting down at his resting place, a small overhang in the rock where a human could just get in out of the rain and listen, Clan Protector was listening to what was close, hearing nothing unusual he enjoyed the opportunity to feel contemplative. Unfortunately, many ghosts were playing with his mind today. He decided that it would be easier to just continue on, besides he was starting to get hungry.

He rose, stretching all nine foot of his frame. He secured his black hair out of his eyes with a leather head band and continued his casual walk to the lookout. However, from here on up he would be gathering herbs and roots to prepare for his dinner as well as checking his deadfall traps in hope of catching squirrels. He relished his food. He had a large bag of rock salt gathered from the south end of the lake as well as peppers that were hot. He had traded for them long ago from like people from the south. From his lookout, he could comfortably and carefully study his world. Although he couldn't see to the other side of the lake from his viewpoint he could imagine it. He had been there many times. He knew exactly what it looked like because even as a child he had been there.

The first time he tried to follow the hunters there he was caught right away and brought back by his elders, but a year later he had snuck out and followed them on their yearly hunt; alone and invisible, always well hidden in the trees like all great hunters and cats. The elders, of course, knew he was there and that time permitted his rite of passage into manhood.

Before preparing dinner, which would produce a small amount of wood smoke and possibly give his position away to other humans and cats, Clan Protector found himself staring and reminiscing, far below to the waves playing out their cyclic motions on the edge of a vast lake. A thought occurred to him, he was reminiscing about the times he had enjoyed on the other side of the lake. He remembered that on the far side of the lake the waves were much bigger. On windy days he enjoyed watching them crash on the sandy beaches. During the summer hunts he felt safe there. There were such a multitude of game to be killed and eaten; an armed human would be left alone. It would take too much effort for a cat or other carnivore to pester them, the hunting was far too easy. During the winter months it could be a death sentence to be there as the hunger in the wild cats increased when easy prey became scarce.

Clan Protector had been reminiscing that it had been several summers since he had seen other people like himself, across the lake. His daughter was ready to find a mate but there were few clans that he knew of and they required a dangerous journey to visit them. At one time, there were many clans of humans like himself who would make the journey to the southeast part of the lake and hunt each summer, but now except the few members of his own, he never saw anyone. Others that looked like him seemed to be slowly disappearing.

He and his kin had many reasons to journey to the other side of the lake where he knew they would be able to hunt the large animals that grazed there in the deep grass along the edge of the lake. That open area between the water and the forest of trees that circled that lake abounded with lush grass that supported huge herds of bison, mammoths, and even the much larger and prized wooly mammoths would sometimes graze there. Most importantly, there were deposits of salt that all animals including humans relished. They could hide in the trees knowing that their scent would blow away from the prey animals rather than to them. It was impossible to get near them on his side of the lake, the side where the protective cave was, the wind would always blow the humans smells to the animals. Here, on the side where the sun sets, they had to depend upon small animals and an occasional deer. On the side where the sun rises they could easily sneak up on larger animals and deliver a deep lance. They needed the larger animals on the other side of the lake because of the fat content in their meat. The fat could be combined with summer plants making a food that would get them through the long, dark and cold winter months.

Making the journey to the other side was an imperative, the clan depended upon it. He knew the journey there would be a challenge; the swampy lower end of the lake was also the home of saber toothed lions, bears and dire wolves. Sometimes, larger animals became mired in mud, making them easy prey for the carnivores. The trees used for cover was also scarce there; we humans would be exposed at times.

It was the wolves that worried him most. Like the hunters themselves, they hunted in packs, always looking for the solitary beast that would find itself mired in mud, diseased, or simply too old to keep up with the herd. He knew that just like the animals they hunted, in large groups or herds they were safe but once separated from the herd they would enter the food chain of the carnivores. Clan Protector was worried; his herd of humans was becoming smaller every year. There were fewer men who could engage in the hunt and more females, like his daughter, at home to care for.

The mammoth that they hunted would be a welcome relief from the venison, rabbits, and other small game that was easily obtained on the cave side of the mountain where they lived. They knew by instinct that by eating only lean meat they would suffer greatly during the long winter months when no greenery could be found. Despite the huge stores of roots, nuts, wild onion, leaves and fruit they stored inside of their cave, by mid-winter it would all be gone. It would lose its life force, that magic that kept them alive. The food that provided the vitamins and nutrients that would ward off the disease that would become known as scurvy in another day would become useless. They needed stores of mammoth meat that was marbled with fat that would sustain them through the winter. Mammoth meat and pine tree needles, for some reason a hot drink made from these kept the sickness away.

Mixing the fatty meat with berries, vegetable products and nuts and then enclosing it in animal intestines then drying it all produced a food that kept them healthy though the winters. The fat itself provided them with a multitude of necessities that provided them with much more than just food; it powered their lamps that provided them with light that was necessary to live in a cave. It was used as ointment that kept their skin from flaking and itching during the long winter nights and even provided a bit of protection from the wind that always blew from the direction that the sun set. It kept their leather and fur clothing supple and flexible. Without it they would need to move to another cave where game could be found and that would be a very dangerous move.

He knew that there were other men out there, like themselves but much smaller and more numerous. Despite all manner of attempting to make peace with these smaller creatures, they had given up. They were numerous and like themselves, they were all territorial and they had discovered the bounty to be claimed on this part of the lake. Clan Protector knew that they would have to watch for them. Maybe they would have to hide and wait until the other people had killed all they wanted. Most strangers would consider you just another animal, a food source.

After his small hunting party gathered up small leather packs with foodstuffs and cutting implements made from the volcanic glass that was found where there were mountains of black burnt rocks, they gathered up their atlatls and short spears that would be used to wound the beast. No one ever just went up and killed one of the huge beasts; it had to be wounded, then the hunters would follow it until it finally bled to death. Sometimes it took days, even weeks. It would then be cut up into slabs that could easily be transported on travois all the way back to the cave where it would be stored deep within the coolest parts of the cave, away from other prowling animals that surely would attempt to take it away from them. In the deep recesses of the cave it would keep for many moons, until the first green leaves would return in the spring.

It took only two days for the men to arrive at the south eastern edge of the lake, but they immediately spotted a problem where the lake spills over into a shallow winding river. A scout or hunter from one of the clans of small peoples had spotted them. Clan Protector watched him as the warrior ran as fast as he could, fleeing to the eastern shore to where the sun rises and the waves were much larger. Running along the shoreline and then darting into the trees. Clan Protector could see wood smoke from many fires where a large band of people were camped in the small cedar trees that hid them.

The smaller people were superstitious about the much bigger humans that lived around them. They were different. Not human like us. They are animals. Besides they too wanted the rights to hunt game in this ideal place. Although they were much smaller, there were many of them and within a few moments it was obvious they were preparing to give chase. About two double handfuls of them ran out in the open and followed the pointed finger of the scout to where he had spotted Clan Protector and his small band of hunters. In Clan Protectors hunting party there were fewer of them than there were fingers on two hands. There were many-many handfuls of the other smaller but deadly visitors. Clan Protector and his small band of hunters had only one clear choice; to flee back to the safety of the cave. There, they would be relatively safe from even large bands of the new people. Clan Protector had experienced other encounters with the new comers. It had happened before, several winters ago, a band of the smaller humans had followed them to the cave where instead of killing them, the small warriors were killed and eaten by the clan. Unfortunately, this time things could be very different. There were many of them and this time, the newcomers would conceive a diabolical plan.

An Uneasy Feeling

Leaving the Serpiente ranch house that cold December day left everyone in a moody feeling. Suddenly the ranch work was done and a "blue northern" had covered all of northern New Mexico in an icy grip. Here in central New Mexico, where winters were normally mild and wet, it had been spitting snow all day yet the snow never accumulated, only blew across the road drifting in tiny rivulets of crust around brown yucca plants. Driving up the rutted dirt road in the snow was a hypnotic sensation. Only rarely did a glimpse of warming sunlight filter through the dark angry clouds, when it did it left the scene looking like a classic oil painting with the scenery saturated in vivid colors.

With the road almost frozen, the traction was pretty good but there were spots. Wherever a side arroyo crossed the bed of the road, the road dropped down into cold, wet mud. The day before there had been a thin layer of running liquid water. That water was still there but it was in the process of freezing, making traction easier, but now climbing out on the opposite bank would be a challenge.

Everyone was tired, after busting their collective butts rebuilding several structures that desperately needed repairs. Serpiente, the name given to their ranch, had been in desperate need of repairs. The roofs of two buildings were starting to sag badly, looking rather oriental. Constructed years ago, they were built with the easiest to acquire materials, the cheapest that could be found. They had to be torn down and completely rebuilt. Several other small structures required the entire roof structure to be torn off and then new rafters built from re-sawn two by six planks of lumber. Once they were structurally sound they were roofed with long sheets of corrugated metal to make them waterproof.

In New Mexico the question is never whether roofs are waterproof or not, but whether they are wind proof. More than a few corrugated panels had blown off these roofs. Then, of course, there was fencing. On a ranch, fence repair is a never ending job despite using the best barbed wire available. The problem is the post. Much of the ranch was still fenced with cedar post. Cedar posts are slow to rot but eventually all wood rots. Those that did had to be replaced with a steel post.

Cattle needed to be rounded up and taken by a trailer, one load at a time into Belen where they would be shipped to packing houses to feed hungry New Mexicans.

They even had to spend a couple of evenings processing a couple of steers for themselves. The entire family worked to cut, wrap with freezer paper, and store the meat in the twelve foot commercial chest freezer they had recently purchased. They had also purchased a hog from a neighbor that had to be butchered and processed. Then, there were many more jobs that had to be done on a daily basis.

Those weeks leading up to the first major snow had been hectic. Hidalgo was stoic, like the Navajo he was. Whatever was going to happen would happen. Although Hidalgo was completely comfortable, if not downright sociable when around most people, during times like this his Navajo persona came out. As I would say, he seemed to go into a Zen state. Someone who didn't know him might think he was depressed. Instead he was actually in a higher state of consciousness. In his mind he was always several steps ahead, somewhat like a chess player. Often he was in a mental world completely alien to his surroundings.

Corey on the other hand, was impatient, always looking for the next chore. He had long ago lost his childhood notions about work. His work was his life, he enjoyed it, and he had every intention of making the most of it, he always wanted to make a showing.

Sitting there in the truck seat and reflecting upon their situation, Corey and Hidalgo, who had usually worn leather gloves while working with the rough re-sawn wood, had still managed to inflict their arms and hands with a multitude of tiny splinters that required me to use needles in a meticulous effort to extricate them. Blisters had appeared that later had turned into calluses. Calluses are normal for working folks, but with Corey and Hidalgo a whole new set of calluses had formed. Those callused hands were the calling cards of a working rancher.

A working ranch was, and is, a small town. But even in the best of times the ranch was an operating nightmare. Although a good living could be made, it was a tough living, always requiring a multitude of skills. The smart rancher was schooled. He operated as his own accountant, lawyer, farmer, politician, mechanic, carpenter, veterinarian or anything else it took not to have to pay someone else to do it for him.

Operating cash was hard to come by, often coming only during the fall after the stock was sold. On a ranch such as Serpiente nothing was wasted. When an animal was slaughtered for meat, for example, everything was used except the hoofs, hide, and bones. Small bones still flush with fragments of meat on them were used as stock for stews. Ken even enjoyed sucking the marrow out of them like all people before modern humans. Eventually even the waste bone and hoofs were used for fertilizer. The hides were cured and turned into all sorts of leather goods by a tannery in Albuquerque.

Most ranches in New Mexico survived because the owner could earn an outside income; another job, another income. The people who operated the ranch at Serpiente were actually well to do. They were wealthy by nearly all standards. Their adventures as historical detectives had left them with a small treasure consisting of gemstones such as emeralds along with a small amount of gold that they had accidentally accumulated. Most of this had long ago been banked for a time when things might get rough, but it did give them real operating capital and confidence. In the meantime, we lived within our means, off the ranch.

The family was constantly reinventing themselves, adapting to every new situation; typical proud Americans. We wanted to prove to ourselves that we could live within our means on a working ranch. They found they couldn't stick to their vow of frugality, not and attend college as well as do all the things that their detective work required without dipping into the money, but it was their personal goal to try.

The ranch house, called Serpeinte was named after the serpentine canyons that contained a multitude of ancient pictographs or painted rock drawings or petroglyphs, usually of rattlesnakes which is in Spanish; *Serpiente de Casabel*, the serpent with bells on its tail. The ranch was the center of our world. We lived well because of our devotion to each other. We had become a real family. It was a working relationship and working together as a team we had accomplished all that we had set out to do. We were all working on the same game plan, yet as individuals we were all very different both in personality and skill; each of us an expert in our own way. The fact that they were all learned in their individual skills made each of us both interesting and irreplaceable. But there was much more to that relationship than sharing of skills. As historical detectives it was our individual skills that made us effective.

The distant mountains and typical scenery of New Mexico had disappeared in the weather. The only visible scenery which could be used to judge their progress was the small sandstone buttes and volcanic knobs very close to the rutted road. It didn't matter; they had driven the route hundreds of times and knew it by heart. For entertainment they relived old times such as how funny it was when I walked into the kitchen and accidently let it slip that I would like to learn to paint oil paintings. I always thought of myself as somewhat an artist but had never had the money or chance to really learn. June had also expressed an interest in art; she wanted to cover the bare walls of the ranch house in art expressing the families' exploits.

Then a week passed and Hidalgo drove up to the ranch house and came inside as if nothing different was going on. After dinner with coffee he causally asked me if I was really interested in learning to paint.

"Sure," I replied, "I was thinking of taking a class or something."

Hidalgos says, "I got some things for you today while I was in Albuquerque. If you think you can use this stuff, it's yours." We all walked out to the truck Hidalgo had been driving. The entire truck bed was full of artist supplies with dozens of pre-stretched blank canvases.

This all caused quite a stir. Now June and I owed something to Hidalgo and the tease was on. But it wasn't the first gift Hidalgo had given me. That tease would continue until Hidalgo was in debt to me. Like sisters and brothers we couldn't stop a playful tease, we all seemed to be family. Corey and I had developed a real working relationship with Hidalgo and under Ken and June's tutorage the three of us had created a world of adventures in which, we all worked together. The adventures of detective work took the edge off of the drudgery of ranch work.

Within a few days Hidalgo had taught me how to actually paint a landscape painting. I simply did exactly what he said even if it seemed wrong to me at the time. Hidalgo had learned the basis of painting while working in Durango. Before he got his job as a policeman he had lived with a young lady who completely filled the small house they shared with her art work. Hidalgo had watched her paint dozens of paintings and although he had never been offered a canvas to paint himself, which was disappointing to say the least, her point was there wasn't enough room in the small apartment for two practicing artist. After all, she was the professional artist and it was her house she was renting, even though Hidalgo was paying half the rent and stayed in a separate bedroom as for her request. Hidalgo preferred it that way. Hidalgo had taken careful mental notes of how she acquired the effects she got on her canvases, and then found a better place to live.

Following Hidalgo's simple instructions, such as mixing the Cerulean Blue with a little Titanium White to get the best likeness of a western sky, and then adding only the most subtle amount of Payne's Grey to get a sky that is light at the horizon and darker hued as you look up into the sky which is what he taught me to do, all done with a big brush because of all the blending that is done. "Look at the sky," and I would, and then he would say, "Paint it using the techniques I have taught you." I was able to paint a mountain scene; a truly marvelous mountain scene! At this point, I felt like I was ready for the Sistine Chapel.

Hidalgo had also saved my life, several times now. Even historical detective work can sometimes become dangerous work. People want to keep secrets, particularly if they involve great wealth, and particularly if it is purloined wealth, that they wanted for themselves. But now the members of the detective agency had hoped to do something a little less dangerous for awhile. I would normally have gone with Corey and Hidalgo at a moment's notice but this time I was busily immersed in my new hobby and Corey and Hidalgo were relieved to be done with the drudgery of the ranch work.

A jackrabbit darted across the road in front of them and Cory had to jerk the steering wheel to avoid hitting it. All and all, they were pretty proud of their efforts as the ranch houses began to look brand new. At least the animals that lived in those structures would enjoy a relief from the monotonous cold winds that had enveloped the area. Still they had an uneasy feeling. Something else was bothering them, making their moods as cloudy as the weather. They were feeling a foreboding about the trip that couldn't be put into words. They decided to blame it on the weather.

Don and Leslie Nelson

After reaching Los Lunas, Corey and Hidalgo pulled on to the old Isleta highway that splits off just north of Isleta Pueblo. There, between the black volcanic mesas they followed Coors Road until they came out on Central Avenue. They traveled a short distance west on Central where they had decided to find a café to enjoy some New Mexico food to warm them up. Instead of Rio Grande chili they had steak fingers out at Mac's 'Steak in the Rough.' Being used to turning out an amazing amount of physical labor they were famished, both men ordered double helpings of 'Steak in the Rough.'

They were supposed to meet with Don and Leslie Nelson, who were teachers at the University of New Mexico. Don and Leslie were avid outdoor enthusiast, who among other things, were members of the Adobe Canoe club, mountain climbers and avid speleologist. Name an outdoor sport and they were involved in it, which was why they taught recreation and physical education majors at the school, but they were actually much more. To them, recreation and physical conditioning was just a means of preparing them for having real adventures. They had the same mindset as Corey and Hidalgo but worked at it in a more personal if not professional way. I had met Leslie Nelson while taking a workshop at New Mexico State University, immediately developing a friendship. It was only a matter of time until a letter arrived at Serpiente which is why the rendezvous was set up.

After gassing up the Ford Cherokee, Corey and Hidalgo continued northward until they turned East on Eubank Avenue that would take them toward the center of the city. The address was hard to find, and the snow was starting to accumulate which didn't help. They found that trying to find an address, while dodging out of control drivers was a challenge. The streets were snow covered and just slick enough to send an occasional car barreling down the road sideways.

They drove past the entrance several times between two house numbers that left them stymied as to where their meeting house was. Number 208 was easy to find, as well as 216 which was perfectly visible, but where was 209 Eubank? The entrance turned out to be an unmarked and walled in road that curled around to a hidden Hacienda styled adobe house. After driving down the narrow one lane drive for fifty yards or so, the road completely curled around to the right into a very private parking lot. The southwestern adobe walls completely hid the adobe house in the middle of a curve of the wall. After parking, Corey and Hidalgo walked up to a locked gate with a door bell button to push.

Don Nelson, a young man in his thirties appeared clad in only in house shoes, short pants and a tee shirt. After a fast introduction, they followed him though the courtyard to the front door of the house. The courtyard was now covered by several inches of wet snow which gave it an unworldly appearance. As they followed him to the house, Don turned and said to them, "I really didn't expect you to come on a night like tonight."

Ducking under the lentil of the low door, they were instantly warm again. Before anything was said, Leslie offered them cups of hot apple cider with cinnamon sprinkled on top. Hidalgo instantly relaxed but Corey was anxious and still a little curious as to why they had been called out. They were, after all, just hoping for an excuse to travel but they hadn't figured on the snow.

The snow was supposed to go north barely getting into the Rio Grande Valley. Howard Morgan, the weatherman who normally was dead right, had predicted the possibility of one to two inches of snow, there was already four inches of snow on top of everything. Most folks around Albuquerque loved the snow but hated the aftermath, the days filled with accidents both vehicular and pedestrian. The snow storm had stalled over them and it seemed to have no inclination to stop.

Inside the Southwestern styled house, they sat down to a handmade table made of what appeared to be a solid slab of oak wood. Hidalgo started the conversation with, "My name is Hidalgo and this is Corey and speaking for myself, as well as Corey, thank you for the cider. Penny Anderson suggested that we get in touch with you after she received a letter from you. She said that in the letter you didn't explain much about the purpose of a meeting or anything else; just that we had to meet. We are free to answer your questions; you must have some kind of proposal for us, something interesting that requires help."

They all looked at one another for a moment then Leslie blurted out, "We may have something very interesting for you or we may have just wasted your time.

Hidalgo says, "Even if there is nothing we can do for one another, you certainly know how to make a person feel welcome." he held up his empty cup and asked, "May I have some more please?" This seemed to break the ice and Leslie and Don started explaining.

Leslie says, "Like I said, we are not exactly sure if we can afford the work you do...this might be a waste of your time." It was an awkward moment, Leslie seemed afraid to approach the eight hundred pound gorilla in the room; money. Would Corey and Hidalgo charge a large fee for working with them? They were uncomfortable asking this question, but it was important to Don and Leslie. They were university teachers and had a small savings to work with, but they were far from wealthy.

Corey says, "In general, it depends upon the kind of services we get involved with. Generally we charge what it cost us. Penny, for example earns extra money doing genealogical work for people, finding out who their ancestors are. Sometimes they will send her nothing but a letter or picture and ask if she can explain it. Usually, she gets paid and paid well, but if she runs into a dead end, she earns nothing. Hidalgo here is even contacted occasionally to do regular detective work, but ninety-nine percent of what we do have nothing to do with making money and when we do make money it is not from the friends that we work with."

"It really depends upon what you are asking us to do. Think of it as excavating a Sunken Pirate Ship, We share the cost of excavation and we share in the bullion we find."

Hidalgo started to say something else but Leslie broke into the conversation with, "Let's talk about it. We are always looking for new caves to explore." They looked at each other blankly.

Don said, "We found a cave in the Estancia Basin."

Hidalgo asked him, "Well, so why do you need us?"

Leslie explained, "To gain access to the cave. Three years ago a rancher and the local bank agreed that they had picked out a good spot to drill a well. It should have been a wet well but instead they drilled straight down, some thirty five feet and then broke through the ceiling of a natural cave. They pushed the pipe on down another few feet and stopped when they could not find the cave floor. They dropped a weighted plumb bob down the pipe and discovered it was another forty feet to the cave floor. When the plum bob was pulled back out it was bone dry so the drillers lost interest in the site and went to another job."

"Because of the cavity they had drilled into, they left the pipe in the ground. Obviously there is a large cave there or possibly a whole system of caves, dropping off through the bedrock, seemingly dry and completely unexplored," continued Leslie.

"Do you realize what scientific discoveries could be made? There is actually life inside of caves and this is a sealed cave. Just think about it, there are stubborn microorganisms that live deep in the earth and break down rocks into simple chemicals that they live off of. Different caves produce different types of biological materials. The microorganisms there may be used in scientific research in order to develop new products such as medicines." Leslie paused to catch her breath.

Corey asked, "Wouldn't our presence there destroy those isolated strains of biological life?"

"Possibly," she answered, but the value of what we learn is well worth it."

"Really," answered Hidalgo, "speaking as a Navajo, I find that modern scientific cultures are more than ready to go to places that they shouldn't. They tend to destroy everything they touch."

Leslie countered Hidalgos objection with, "You are correct, but cave microbiology has been studied for years without hurting any of the natural microorganisms. I really doubt that anything can hurt them. Even fully desiccated caves have microorganisms that spring back to life as soon as a little moisture is added. They live for years that way, but there is far more that we would like to learn about this cave than about possible microorganisms."

Hidalgo asked, "The likelihood of finding minerals, gold or silver is pretty unlikely I take it."

"Not likely," laughed Don, "But there are true treasures to be found in natural caves."

The Skeletal Hand

*H*idalgo was still playing devil's advocate; he knew the answer to his next simple question. In fact, he had explored many caves during his lifetime. At the Rio Grande Gorge he had been in a natural cave that had an underground river in it. He thought back to the amazing bio luminosity that microorganisms from another world produced in this most unique cave. "Aren't all caves just holes in the ground with a few formations that people like to look at?" he asked with a sly smile on his face.

"Hardly," answered Leslie. In this area of New Mexico several caves have produced fossils of early animals as well as people. Think of Sandia Cave on the back side of Sandia Crest. Dr. Hibbens from the University discovered the remains of an Ice Age culture that lived here in New Mexico way before 'modern Indians' migrated into this area. They may have been here well before the last ice age, certainly well before the Indians that make up the tribes that live here now."

Hidalgo countered her argument with, "My ancestors migrated down into this area only a few hundred years before the Spanish arrived here. What makes you so certain that people were living in the Estancia basin thousands of years ago?"

"Well," answered Leslie, "Would you agree that such animals as mastodon and wooly mammoths are ice age animals? Clovis age arrow heads have actually been found buried inside of mastodon bones. Some very brave and hungry person managed to get close enough to them to stab them with an obsidian tipped spear. Those people wintered over in caves."

Corey says, "Just like our ranch animals, they must have gotten tired of the monotonous and cold New Mexico wind."

"That's true" said Leslie, "But I take it you two are not interested in this, perhaps we have wasted your time."

"Actually," answered Hidalgo attempting to calm the sudden turn of conversation that had just occurred, "We are very interested in your project, but we are still confused as to why you need us."

Don entered the conversation at this point. "The last time we were there Mr. Sanchez who owns the property became belligerent with us and demanded that we leave his property. People who live off of highway 10 are very secretive and private. In the small towns of Torreon and Chilili for example, several people have been attacked by a group of men who claim independence from America. As far as they are concerned, they should be the owners of the entire Estancia basin as laid out in the old

Spanish land grants. They resent the taxes that they must pay just to keep ownership of the tiny plots of land they now own. In many ways I don't blame them. As the population of Albuquerque and other cities around Estancia continue to grow, more and more of the land they once owned is bought up for taxes, subdivided and sold to Anglos."

Leslie added, "They resent the loss of their culture as well as the loss of their land."

Hidalgo, who was smiling the entire time she had spoken, answered her with a bit of sarcasm of his own, "Again, speaking as a Navajo, I think I can relate to that. The Estancia Valley was prime hunting grounds for the indigenous peoples who lived there well before any Spanish king decreed ownership to their conquistadores."

Leslie continued, "We need you to break the impasse we have with Mr. Sanchez. The last time we were there he and another fellow showed up with a trailer behind his truck and released a bull on the property. We gathered up what we could and left as fast as we could."

"Ok," said Corey, "So even if we can get permission to go back to the well site and if Mr. Sanchez agrees to move his bull to another pasture, what do we do then?"

"From a practical point," she continued, "A pipe with a diameter large enough to allow people to drop down it would need to be installed at the site. This of course, would take major equipment as well as time and money. We would need a rescue well drilled, like the ones used by miners in order to get trapped miners out of caved in mines. They drill straight down until they break though then bring the trapped miners out one at a time. A pipe that allows a cylinder to drop down it attached by a steal cable would allow a person to not 'hang up' as they drop down the shaft. Drilling a vertical shaft and installing a pipe would be expensive but it might pay off if the cave is unique enough."

"Just think about it," said Don, "A speleologist would need to dead drop through a pipe, just big enough for a body to fit in. That would be a very scary moment. Just think about it, you would be the first person to descend into an unknown world."

Corey asked, "How old is the rock in the cave?"

Don answered, "If you could get down the pipe, you'd drop into a Pennsylvanian Age seabed, some three hundred and sixty million years old."

"Actually," replied Corey, "You'd find yourself dangling above a pitch black cave and you'd have no idea what is down there."

"Actually we have a very good idea of what is down there," Leslie continued in making her point. Her assurance, coming from a teacher in her prime was showing. She knew her stuff. "In this area, very old Sandia Granite, some 3.6 billion years old, is covered with Pennsylvanian age sea beds. A geological unconformity occurs here because the geological ages of sedimentary rock that should be on top of the bedrock are not there. At one time the area was under a lot of erosion. All of the rock that might have been deposited during the Paleozoic age eroded away until finally oceans and seaways appeared. The sea beds of the Pennsylvanian Age or what is sometimes called the Carboniferous Age have left very interesting fossils there. The earth was several degrees warmer during those times and all manner of life lived in those shallow seas as well as on land. They are, by the way, the same rocks that make up the rind of the watermelon that the Spanish named Sandia Crest that makes up the Eastern Albuquerque skyline."

Hidalgo thought about it, from the west mesa of Albuquerque the observer sees red Sandia granite topped with a grey rind of sedimentary rocks and finally capped by the green of the forest that is on top. It literally looks like a large slice of watermelon. The Spanish were right in naming it watermelon or Sandia.

Don continued, "We think the cave may have formed during a wet period millions of years after the seas withdrew. We think that the cave was shaped by underground streams that were active during the age of dinosaurs. Estancia basin is an old sea bed but geologically new. Sandia Granite is slightly tilted up to the West making up the edge of the Rio Grande Rift Zone. The granite is impermeable to water forming a natural north and south basin with drainage patterns on the side with many tributaries. Actually the slope of the Estancia basin..." he was interrupted by Corey.

"So let me get this straight, which of us is going to put up the thousands of dollars it would cost to drill a hole so humans can get into that cave?"

"Well, actually, Leslie and I have some resources but we are certainly not rich. We live well, but we have to live within our means, and that means the money we make from teaching. But we have connections to some interesting and great friends. They just might be willing to put up the money if we can demonstrate the value of the cave."

Testing them again, Hidalgo said, "We also have some resources but I am not sure that we can afford to put up money for some spelunking club to have its own cave to explore." He strived to make a diplomatic point, he paused then said, "But we will think about it."

This seemed to bring the conversation to an impasse but after a moment, Leslie said, "We are professionals, "What if I told you that we dropped a miniature camera down the pipe last year."

His curiosity peaked Corey asked "What did you see?"

Leslie answered, "Wonderful things, formations, fossils and something really strange, what appears to be the bones of a skeletal human hand, a very large human hand." Leslie brought out the photograph, a black and white photo of a skeletal hand that appeared to have been cut off from the rest of the body at the wrist.

Corey asked, "How would a human hand get into a cave that apparently was formed millions of years ago that does not appear to have a natural entrance, at least not now?"

Leslie answered, "That's one of the mysteries we would like you to help us solve. Obviously at one time or another there was a natural entrance. If it is a human hand down there it must have been deposited sometime since the last Ice Age." Leslie stopped talking for a moment and then added, "We wondered why would there be just a hand there and not a full skeleton."

Corey mumbled, "Another mystery to solve."

They were certainly interested but wanted more information. Because of the snow they were invited to sleepover. Don and Leslie brought out sleeping bags and pads for them to sleep on and they piled out in front of the huge iron, inset stove that because of the thick adobe walls, kept the house toasty even on the coldest of days.

After breakfast with Don and Leslie they agreed to do some preliminary investigations and left to find Corey's relatives who lived on Valley Road off the old Isleta highway in the South Valley of Albuquerque.

The Great Estancia BB Gun Shootout

The next morning the sky had completely cleared off and the temperature rose to thirty eight degrees. The four to five inches of snow that had accumulated overnight was already starting to disappear. They turned south on Isleta Road and drove until they reached Valley Road, a side street. Traveling down the road they turned into Alice and Boone's place. There, they knew they could get a history of the Estancia Valley. Alice had grown up in Estancia and knew the area well.

The Hollidays lived in a small home that had been built by Boone on weekends. For years they had lived in the middle of a construction zone and it was still under construction. Richard; age nineteen was the only one who was at home at the time and after a brief description of their problem over some hot coffee, that Hidalgo relished, Richard began a description of the Estancia Valley from his point of view from a day in the life of a nine year old.

"The small dry pinto bean farming community of Estancia, New Mexico has always been a part of my life. I grew up in Albuquerque, but sometimes my summers were not my own. The summer I turned nine years of age I spent living there. I remember spending other long summers there, while my folks tried to make a living doing construction work in Oregon and California."

"Those were lonesome days. Being the city kid that was dropped off into an entirely different world than the one I enjoyed in the South Valley. I was distinctly the outsider. I found myself at every sunset walking out to the dirt road that separated the house from one hundred and sixty acres of desolate looking countryside. The only time anyone even went over there was when Bo would carry buckets of Grandpa Wilse's spit from his chewing tobacco habit across the road out to the soft sand on the other side and buried it. I spent long days there looking up and down the country road hoping to get a glimpse of Alice and Boone's old Dodge truck coming to rescue me. Rescue me from the boredom that every child feels, especially when feeling deserted, despite the fact that unknowingly they have been lovingly cast into grand adventures."

"At one time Wilse Holliday operated a saw mill on the homestead, and the corrals housed a large string of horses which were used to work all matter of machinery. It was a working ranch but then they had more than the hundred and sixty acres of land to work; they had several thousands of acres to work with and unlimited natural resources. The problem was to utilize those resources such as lumber, meat products and dry land farming on the limited capital available to them. Yet they prospered. During the days of the depression rarely did less than twenty or more people sit around the dinner table."

"During times of hardship it is often the farmers and ranchers who live the best, while the city folks stop by often just to enjoy a home cooked meal. By the time I arrived in Estancia, the old homestead, like most of the other homesteads in the valley was already in decay and like all old and mysterious houses it contained a wealth of mysterious objects and hideaways. My curiosity was piqued by these objects of antiquity. To my delight I discovered that Wilse and Lizzie Holliday, my grandparents, enjoyed explaining the significance and use of those objects."

"Young Sherlock Holmes would have enjoyed the game. Soon, I had several wooden boxes full of small metal objects, which entertained all of us in the discovery of their secret purpose."

Richard put his hand on Hidalgo's shoulders at that moment and said, "Just like you Corey and Penny, I am still playing that childhood game, but on a much grander scale."

Immediately he pulled his hand back. "Again, I am the outsider being not only the 'city' kid but also the youngest. My days were full of simple activities such as carrying water from the windmill to the house, slopping the hogs, and irrigating the fruit trees. However, when the older folks left the homestead things got serious. That was when older boys took great delight in teasing younger boys. I got my fair share and rarely got the opportunity to repay in kind, but finally I got my chance. That summer we all had BB guns and a great BB gun shoot out was arranged. Bo, my older half-brother, who had grown up on the ranch instead of Albuquerque, simply thought that I was defenseless against him. He was wrong."

"The next morning everyone went into town except for me and Bo. Almost immediately the shootout began. Throughout the homestead we went, stealth was my main objective. The longer I stayed unseen the faster rescue would occur. We both traded shots but nothing significant happened until finally Bo made a mistake. Up the windmill tower he went where he figured he had a superior position on me. I nailed him several times as he climbed the ladder then simply secreted myself away into the house where I waited, while eating apple pie, for him to become bored and start back down. Every time he started back down I stepped out and fired a few more shots up at him. Evening and the return of the folks brought Bo down. After this, we had an understanding and at least a minuscule amount of mutual respect."

Hidalgo and Corey both laughed at the story, they had both experienced similar situations growing up. Corey asked him, "What are you majoring in at UNM?"

"Well, actually I'm not sure yet but the classes I'm enjoying the most right now are geology and English. I am miserably behind in my math classes. I only took algebra II and Geometry in high school and frankly, they didn't prepare me well."

Corey who was older said, "I once watched a television show in which a Dr. Kingsfield said to his first year law students that they would need to teach themselves law. All he did was train their minds. Perhaps you shouldn't depend upon anyone but yourself." Corey grinned when he said it. He had been homeschooled for most of his young life.

Richard said, "I'm sure you're right, but calculus, last semester and statistics, this semester is going to be the death of me. I would, however like to relate to you a few details I learned in geology class. Hidalgo settled into another cup of coffee stirring the sugar with the handle end of a fork, and Corey settled into an easy chair with his feet up on a kitchen chair.

Lake Estancia

*H*idalgo and Richard sat at the table with arms crossed as Richard continued his conversation, "The Rio Grande River ran into the Estancia basin for millions of years until the Rio Grande Riff along with volcanism from the Jemez Volcano changed its course to its present position, west of the Sandia Mountains."

Corey looked up and said, "Now you are talking my language, geology."

"Despite its present humble appearance, Lake Estancia has played an impressive role in the history of the earth's weather patterns, today's extreme changes in weather exemplified by hurricanes, tornados, droughts, and flooding is tame compared with normal weather, despite what the media and environmental doomsters say. A short look into the not so recent past has uncovered startling data which indicates that our bad weather is actually tame compared to normal climatic weather patterns. Anyway, sometime near the end of the last Ice Age, Lake Estancia slowly dried out."

"The lake at one time covered several million acres of land and reached a depth of one hundred and fifty feet. Lake Estancia was and is the most complete climate record anywhere in the west for the study of Ice Age changes according to geologist such as Roger Anderson of the University of New Mexico. The lake, in effect, documents seven thousand years of harsh Ice Age weather that swept moisture from the Pacific Ocean over New Mexico. Those storms poured an impressive amount of water into Lake Estancia."

"Indeed, climate history may tell us that relatively stable climate is unusual in the Earth's history. Other climate researchers have found from ice layers in Greenland that the last ten thousand years have been the only stable period out of the last two hundred and fifty thousand years of climate history. In other words, dramatic and even violent changes in weather are the historical norm for the Earth."

"Our experience of relative stability could be short lived, at least on a geological time scale. It is rather a geological mystery as to why our climate has been so stable during the last few thousand years." Corey and Hidalgo listened carefully as Richard continued.

"Paleo-Indians, probably the same Native Americans who left artifacts at Folsom, Clovis, Sandia and probably a thousand other undiscovered sites in the Southwest, undoubtedly hunted mastodons in the Estancia Basin. Since the wind blew from the southwest just as it does now in this area, kill sites were located in the eastern fringes of the lake."

"Later, modern Native American Indians would leave artifacts in the form of obsidian arrowheads and skin scrappers at kill sites on the eastern edges of the playas which formed as Lake Estancia dried up. Much, much later the Salinas Indians of the area got their name from utilizing the salt deposits found there. They used the salt for barter."

"As New Mexico continued to dry out it seems quite mysterious as to how these ancients survived. Even at relatively late settlements such as Gran Quivera, where Spanish churches were built, only small pockets of water can be found some seven miles from the ruins which leaves archeologist pondering how such a large population survived. The water was all deep underground, just as it is today."

Giants

"What about caves under the Estancia basin?" Corey asked.

Richard answered," Well, it doesn't seem too likely. If there are caves there they would all be under water. Ground water is what attracted people there in the first place. The only place there could be real caves is along the edges of the basin. A lot could have happened during the millions of years the ancestral Rio Grande River flowed though there. There is bound to have been caves there on and off over the eons, the entire area is underlain with limestone rock. With a long record of rivers running through the area there is every reason to suppose there are large networks of caves. It is well known that south of there, exist many long north and south running caves."

"Any chance a person could find fossils or bones in those caves?" asked Hidalgo.

"Caves are repositories for all ancient life. Everyone and everything wanted to get out of the wind. Think about it," retorted Richard, "caves are where most fossils and artifacts are found by scientists. Ancient people were attracted to caves for shelter and anthropologists sift through the floor dirt for clues."

For a brief moment everyone was quiet. Corey was proud of the answers he was getting and Richard was proud just to be of help. "Let me tell you another story, said Richard, who was obviously enjoying himself. "Three summers ago, Mom, Dad, and I all took a road trip down to visit Carlsbad Caverns. Naturally Mom," he turned to Hidalgo and said, "Alice likes to talk, and us kids went down there to talk to friends and relatives. You know how Alice is," he said, looking at Corey. "She can nurse a cup of coffee for hours if she has good company." Hidalgo reached over for the coffee pot and poured himself another cup.

"At one of the houses we visited, we mentioned that we were driving down to Carlsbad Caverns, Mrs. Moore reached up on the shelf and grabbed a book about Jim White, the discoverer of Carlsbad Caverns.

He stopped talking then slowly continued, "You remember it was Mrs. Moore that brought Butch with her to deer hunt in Gallinas Canyon. It was with her son, Butch, that we experienced a Gallinas Canyon mystery."

Getting back on subject, Richard said, "Jim White was an itenerate cowboy who found himself on guano patrol at the ranch where he was employed. Every day he and another worker would drive a team of horses and a wagon up to the entrance of the cavern. Then they would scramble down a well-worn trail and haul bat guano out of the bat cave for fertilizer. It was the best fertilizer available, better than manure, valuable stuff to anyone that wanted to grow vegetables. There was real money to be made from the guano but it wouldn't be them, it would be the people who actually sold the fertilizer in stores who made the real money."

"After spending many days there digging the black crud out of the top cave, his curiosity began to wander and he thought about the labyrinth of passages he could see dropping off into the earth. What was down there? As far as he knew, no one had ever actually explored past the bat cave. No one knew what was inside the caverns."

"During the next month each time he made a haul of guano out of the bat cave he would leave things he had assembled to explore down into the cave. Finally after he had gathered enough equipment in the way of ropes, candles and kerosene lamps, he started making short trips into the cave. In time he had explored and memorized all the regular cave passages that millions of tourist, now explore."

"There is some humor in this book too, according to Mrs. Moore, referring to the time old Jim White took off his boots in order to cool off his feet. He stepped into a small pond of water that he thought was only a few inches deep. He stepped right into it only to discover that it was eight feet deep. In caves I guess your eyes play tricks on you."

"What really challenged Jim was keeping a light source; more than once his kerosene lamp went out and he found himself panicking. After he took off a couple of times, managing to smack his head on some of those stalactites he decided to take his time."

"His curiosity brought him to wander about the lower chambers where he was sure no one had ever been before. It required him to drop down a vertical drop that no one knew how deep it was. It would take a rope ladder to get out and it would take Jim White several more weeks before he could manage a homemade rope ladder. When the time came he discovered that the lower caverns were actually deeper and larger than he thought. At least as big as the upper caverns, this was truly a huge cave system."

"While exploring the lower chambers of the caverns, Jim White did make one historical discovery that few are aware of; he discovered a human skeleton."

Hidalgo said, "That is nothing new, Native Indians have always explored caves. In Mammoth Cave in Kentucky they found the mummy of a trapped Indian. They think he was digging crystals out of the cave."

"That's true," answered Richard, "But this wasn't an ordinary Indian. First of all, can you imagine someone exploring that far into a cave without any modern light sources? How did he get down the vertical drop? How did he plan on getting back up? He was found there all alone next to a seep spring. He probably starved to death in that spot."

Hidalgo said, "That must have been one very brave Indian."

Richard then said, "The Indian was an unusual Indian. The skeleton was old with the cranium tumbled down into the body cavity. They estimated the length of the skeleton as best they could and it measured over 11 feet in length. Considering the position of the bones when they found it, he may have stood almost 12 feet tall, and that without cowboy boots," he added for emphasis.

"Is the skeleton still down there," asked Corey?

"According to that book the skull was removed and donated to a doctor in the town that is now called White city, named after Jim White. Since then, the skull has disappeared along with all information about the skeleton."

Corey said, "I don't understand. In the bible there are passages about giants on earth in those days, but now it is understood that they were not real giants but rather unusual peoples among other people. In fact, many people as well as scholars think they were talking about aliens."

"Aliens?" asked Richard.

Hidalgo said, "We spent a lot of time on this subject back on the San Juan River. Then looking at Richard he said, "All Indian's belief systems talk about giants. Not big people but rather star people, beings who came to earth in antiquity for their own reasons. There have been several theories as to why they came, usually something about improving the natural stock of creatures that we refer to as Homo sapiens. Considering how violent humans are, they didn't do a very good job."

Hidalgo continued with a question, "What if there was another cave, say in the Estancia basin, that had human remains in it, possibly like the one found in Carlsbad Caverns?"

Richard answered, "That might become the scientific discovery of the century, at least as far as anthropologist are concerned. It might turn the entire scientific world up-side down."

"Actually," said Hidalgo, "I have seen many reports of giants here in North America. One of the most fascinating cases of giants in recent history was the Smithsonian Giants. During the genocidal conquest of the indigenous peoples of North America, the United States Calvary and many hired mercenaries encountered giants living out among the tribes, and engaged in direct combat with these giants. The mindset used to justify the wholesale slaughter of most, and the forced relocation of the rest of these tribes was that they were sub-human; their living with other darker skinned humans being a key to this gross misconception. The giants they encountered and killed were Caucasian looking with light colored skin. Fearing a backlash from the American people for killing whites, giants or not, the government ordered that all bodies of these giants be retrieved and shipped to the Smithsonian Institute, to hide the damaging evidence."

Corey looks at Richard and says thoughtfully, "Perhaps this is what we are dealing with in Estancia."

"Perhaps," answered Richard.

The Incident at the Mexican Restaurant

After leaving the Holliday house they drove west on Valley road then turned left at Alice's Food Market, a tiny family owned store, then turning right again they drove Blake road out to Coors. From there they headed back to West Central where they hoped they could find a decent restaurant before heading back to Serpiente. Because of the snow many places were closed but they did find one small café. Once there, they slid into one of the tall backed booths that provided some degree of privacy.

Alone, except for three other men who were having an animated discussion several booths down from them. Conversations returned to the mysterious assignment they were engaged in.

In academic circles, stories had gotten around of their exploits as historical detectives, the label that several university professors had given them. The perception of the academics was that they were a trio of detectives who specialized in solving historical mysteries.

We saw ourselves as three friends who were intoxicated by the thrill of adventure. However they had been tremendously lucky in solving several mysteries that few even knew existed. They had concluded that good luck occurs due to hard work.

The plates of food arrived with an extra plate piled high with sopapillas and honey bottles. Two more men walked into the café and joined the other two in that animated conversation. The argument or discussion was in Spanish, a language that Hidalgo knew but Corey had no idea what they were saying. Soon, a small boy about fourteen years old came through the door and walked over to the booth where the men were. He had obviously been beat up, with two black eyes and numerous bandages covering cuts on his face.

Hidalgo looked up from his plate and watched the boy walk across the floor. When he got to the booth the younger of the men defiantly raised his head and shouted at the boy, *"Vamonous tu pollo"* The other men looked at him in disgust then noticed Corey and Hidalgo watching them.

One of them quickly walked over to Hidalgo and said, "You guys are about done here aren't you?"

"No," Hidalgo answered with firmness to his voice.

"You need to mind your own business!" angrily interjected the intruder.

"We are minding our own business," replied Hidalgo without losing eye contact.

The other men motioned him to be quiet, but the young man was disgusted with the boy and willing to take it out on anyone around them.

The boy had lost his fight in a tournament. Much like a cock fight, the boy had been in a fight in which men would bet enormous amounts of money on young boys who would fight bear knuckled in order to win the approval of their masters. Like the gladiators of old, they would fight until one of them couldn't stand up or a white towel was tossed into the ring. Unfortunately, by this time they were usually a bloody mess.

The young Mexican pushed Corey's tea class over making a huge mess. This of course prompted Hidalgo to throw his glass of tea into the Mexican's face and instantly everyone sprang to their feet. The two other Mexican men ran over and grabbed the younger man. The oldest man said a fast "*lo siento*" (I'm sorry) then they forced the young combatant out of the front door of the café and they left.

"What was that all about," asked Corey?

"Well," said Hidalgo, "As best I could tell from the limited Spanish I heard they were relatives of the boy who appeared to have been beaten up. Like cock fighting with roosters, it is illegal to have those kinds of fights. What happens is the boys who fight come out with serious medical problems such as concussions. The winner gets a small prize, usually anywhere from $25 to $100 dollars. The loser gets nothing but distain from everyone who lost money on him. The real money is being passed around in the audience in the form of bets. It is a nasty brutal sport. Something should be done. By the way, it was obvious they were worried that we would find out what they were up to. They wanted to keep it a secret. Otherwise, we really would have had a major brawl on our hands."

Searching for a Sponsor

Back in Serpiente, June and Ken as well as Hidalgo, Corey and of course yours truly sat around the kitchen table while Ken talked on the telephone to mining and drilling experts that they knew. It helped that Ken's brother Tim, who was also my father, was in the oil business.

As it turned out Tim had a vast library of names of small companies who specialized in all forms mining and petroleum work. It appeared that their best bet was to find a company that specialized in rescue work; companies that could sink a large pipe down a hole to allow miners to escape a collapsed mine. If there was someone out there that could put a human size pipe down into the cave Tim would know. As it turned out he did know of one company that specialized in mine rescue work but they were very expensive. In fact, as it turns out putting a pipe large enough for humans to drop down and return would be a major expense, costing many thousands of dollars.

June also was of help. As it turns out the idea of giant Indians is not so far-fetched after all," she told the group. "There actually is Calvary photographs of a tribe of Indians in the Needles, California area who were giants compared to other Indians. Some of the men in the photographs were approaching eleven feet tall."

"Still," said June, "The skeleton that you are talking about in Estancia is probably certainly shorter than those found in Carlsbad Caverns."

I said, "Yes, but the skeleton in Carlsbad Caverns proves that it is a possibility. "What if," I continued, "the California Indians were only a small branch of a much larger group of people who lived in North America thousands of years ago, wouldn't that in itself cause a real stir in the scientific world?"

"Why did they go deep into caves," asked Corey?

Hidalgo answered, "Not for the same reasons people do now days. Mayans actually built huge megalithic pyramids and other structures over natural cave entrances. They thought by going into the underworld they were going to where their Gods were located. Even over in Arizona, the Hopi believe they originated from a cave in the Grand Canyon. They believe they came from a whole different world that existed down there. Many Native Americans believed the earth is hollow."

"Yes", answered Corey, but isn't all of that talk of hollow earth stuff just superstition and mythology. Unlike what some science fiction writers would have us believe, as you drop down into the deepest of mines the temperature becomes unbearable as miners get near to the mantle of the earth."

"That's true," said Ken, "Diamond mines in Africa can only go so deep because the temperatures are so high that far down. Despite pumping tremendous amounts of refrigerated air into them the miners can only work in twenty minute shifts. Obviously what we might, and I do mean might, be dealing with is very different."

I said, "You say Don and Leslie dropped a camera on the end of a cable down into the cave? Exactly how big was that hand? If we could find a way to determine exactly how long the bones are in that hand we can extrapolate how big the entire skeleton is."

June said, "It seems to me that our next step is to find Mr. Sanchez and find out just what it will take to gain access to the property. Then go back there and drop another camera down that pipe and see for ourselves just how big that hand is and if there is anything else down there to look at. In the meantime, Don and Leslie can keep searching for a sponsor who might help us pay to get that rescue pipe down there, if we decide to actually drop into that cave."

The Insidious Fight Game

*H*idalgo had too many things on his mind to enjoy his dinner this evening and for Hidalgo who enjoyed good food better than most this was a remarkable turn of events. I kept pushing him to tell me what was bothering him but he simply shrugged it off. Everyone knew he was having a tumultuous argument in his mind. Finally after spending several hours out on the porch in the bitter cold by himself he came into the living area and made an announcement.

Hidalgo sat down on a kitchen chair which is where most of the family business is taken care of. He brushed the long strands of black hair from his eyes. Usually well groomed, he hadn't been to a barber in several weeks and was appearing more like a wild Indian by the day. I poured him a cup of hot coffee and added sugar and cream to it just like he liked it. Then everyone gathered around him patiently waiting for his thoughts.

Hidalgo spoke very quietly in a determined, slow voice. "All of you remember why I left the La Plata police department and came to work for you."

"Sure," Ken said, "You were disgruntled by the politics of the La Plata judicial system. The police were being used to round up young offenders who were sentenced to spend time in a private jail."

Hidalgo thought to himself about the dozens of young offenders he himself had rounded up; all of them arrogant and mouthy when arrested. They all thought that nothing could hurt them. They believed that they would live forever and eventually get retribution for being inconvenienced by the arresting officer. The act continued during the court proceedings, even as they were delivered to the juvenile facility that they were housed in. Many of them, in fact, were darn right proud of themselves. Deep in their hearts they each knew they could beat the system. But they were wrong. They came out looking like beat dogs.

Ken continued, "Since the jailers were also the owners; they were given the right to decide who had been rehabilitated. All sentences were drawn out for several months, costing the parents one hundred and fifty dollars a day. It cost the jail only ten dollars a day to incarcerate the young prisoners. Needless to say, the jail was a money making operation. The situation came to a head when the local press realized that the judge was selective in who he sent to the jail and even more importantly he was getting a kick back from the jail. He had gotten rich, rich enough to purchase land in the Caribbean where he could hide his wealth and avoid paying taxes on it. The judge left the United States as soon as the problem became public knowledge and is still hiding out, but living like a king. Since then, it has all been hushed up to avoid bad publicity for the tourist oriented County.

Hidalgo answered with a simple, "uh huh."

Again, Ken continued his point, "When Tim, my brother met you there you were already considering quitting and soon you quit your job in disgust and La Plata County lost one of the best policeman they ever had. You were an up and coming star being considered for a lieutenants' position. Tim suggested that if you were looking for work, you could contact me and as far as I am concerned that was the best thing that ever happened to this ranch."

"Thank you," said Hidalgo, "But I have to do what my conscience tells me to do."

"What is your conscience telling you to do?" asked Corey.

Hidalgo took another sip of coffee and looked at Corey saying, "If you search your heart, you know the answer."

Corey shifted his weight in his chair, leaning back while balancing the chair on two legs, smiled and said, "You are still bothered by what happened in that café in Albuquerque."

"Yeah," Hidalgo answered softly.

I was carefully looking in his eyes hoping to find an answer to his mysterious mood and was startled when I saw moisture starting to well up, something that never happens to a Navajo and particularly Hidalgo.

"I have to do something about this insidious fight game that is operating around New Mexico. The real losers are the young boys who are forced to fight for the enjoyment of the spectators. They are breaking dozens of laws but seem to be able to do it without fear of any retribution. Someone is protecting them. I don't know if it is a politician or a corrupt police department but somehow they are able to operate without any real fear. There are too many people involved and I suspect a lot of money changes hands. Someone is making money at the expense of those that are least able to defend themselves and to tell you the truth; I suspect that the fight game is a cover up for something even greater that is going on. Anyway I have to try to get to the bottom of this mystery; I have to do something about it."

I got out of my chair, walked up behind him and draped my arms around Hidalgo in a firm and loving grip and said, "First of all, I don't understand why you feel it is your responsibility to solve this problem. Besides, there is no way you can do it alone."

Hidalgo's voice dropped to a whisper, "That's true, but if I'm going to find out who is promoting the fight game, I will need to do it under cover, silently using stealth. Crimes like these always come with long tendrils connected to many people and places. Somewhere out there is a snake, a serpent making money. Cut off the head of that serpent and the problem is solved."

Several eyebrows went up. June, deciding to play devil's advocate, immediately joined in the conversation by asking, "What I can't figure is how the games produce enough income for a gang or cartel to mess with, in the first place? Sure, the men exchange money while they are betting but the money stays among them. Even a door fee, an admission fee certainly wouldn't cover the cost of a lawyer if the games were busted. There has to be far more going on here than watching boys cock fight. Something else, but I can't imagine what."

"I can." Hidalgo quietly says. Deep in thought, he brought his finger up and pointed it at each of us stopping with me; the gesture for someone making a point, something that was not a gesture I had ever seen him do before.

For your own safety, I need to do this alone.

"What about for your safety?" I implored him. "You are not alone here," I said. "If there is anything we can do, let us."

He was getting a little exasperated as he replied, "I really appreciate what you are trying to say, but trust me; I suspect that this is something that I have to do all on my own. I wouldn't want to have to worry about everyone. It is easier if I am alone."

"Yes," I countered, "But sometimes it is better to have an angel looking over your shoulder." The warm kitchen got quiet for a moment. Then Hidalgo continued, "I can chew gum and walk at the same time, I suspect I can work on this and still help you solve this caving problem."

Corey reached over and put his hand on Hidalgo's shoulder and said, "Well, you know we are pretty good at multitasking ourselves. If this is that important to you, there is no reason we can't help you. Besides, what you are proposing is a dangerous game indeed. You are going to need help, help from all of us, and like Ken said, you are a part of what makes this family. We couldn't operate without you."

June said, "Again, what are you going to do now and how can we help you?"

Hidalgo thought about the question for a minute then answered, "I think I would like to talk to Richard Holliday again. Richard seems to know a lot about what is happening in the South Valley of Albuquerque. I seriously doubt that the South Valley is the center of this problem, but it is a place to start."

Ken asked, "Do you think that this is a problem in other cities here in the southwest?"

"Sure," answered Hidalgo. "If there is real money in this operation then they will be staging fights in many cities across this area, possibly in other regions of America as well."

Ken, who was thinking aloud said, "Well, I knew they did things like that in Mexico but I never dreamed it could be a problem here."

Hidalgo looked up at him and answered with determination in his soft voice, "I think it's time to get our facts together. My bet is Richard or his friends will know something about what is going on and one of them will provide me with a lead. In any case I will need to go under cover. I will have to become one of them to learn anything and in order to do that I will have to work alone. I don't want your help; I don't want to endanger any of you"

Everyone around the table looked at each other, grinned and agreed not to interfere with Hidalgo in anyway whatsoever. We all lied.

Hidalgo's Decision

Hidalgo knew that he needed more information. In doing so he would have to emulate and become the serpent himself. He mentally rehearsed ideas that might give him an introduction. Perhaps, he thought, that by proposing that young Indians also take part in the game? He hated the exercise, always thinking several steps ahead, like a cat stalking its prey.

Early the next morning he set off to Albuquerque with the Jeep Cherokee packed with everything from camping gear to maps and food. He carried anything that he might need in an emergency, including extra cash, cash he had worked hard for on the ranch doing real work for little pay. He knew if he needed it, he had other resources hidden away in the bank of Los Lunas. Money was not the problem; he actually seldom used his own money. He had little use for it, even the gas he burned was purchased out of a common account billed to the Serpiente ranch. The only cash he personally used was for meals on the road and clothes.

Where he really spent his money was in helping his family who lived on the Navajo reservation close to Shiprock and for the Indian Polytechnic Institute, located in Farmington. That money was entered into a blind fund where only a few knew who the philanthropist was.

This time, when he left Serpiente he was alone and the road was bone dry, with the promise, but not the appearance, of those first small bits of greenery that would eventually feed cows and mark the turn of the seasons. When he got to the split in the road above Isleta Pueblo where the flat volcanic hills were, this time he took the right hand turn which was a more direct route through the south valley to Valley Road and the Holliday house.

Shortly he found himself sitting at the kitchen table talking to Alice and her son Richard. They were surprised; Hidalgo had never visited without other members of our family there, something was obviously in motion. They were curious yet polite. They decided they would shortly learn why was Hidalgo visiting them? It didn't matter, the Holliday family had long ago adopted Hidalgo and after coffee along with some chocolate cake with thick icing, Hidalgo offered a short explanation then asked Richard directly, if he knew anything about the fight games being staged in Albuquerque.

Richard blushed and then said, "The last thing in the world I have ever wanted to do was get involved with is fighting. It hurts too much! Trust me; I have gone out of my way to keep a low profile when around fighters. It hurts even if you win the fight, and then it takes time for everything to heal. Then afterwards, there are the years when you hope you do not run into this person again. You do know that I went to Rio Grande High School," Richard sarcastically explained. "Rio Grande is a south valley school in a predominately Hispanic community. My senior year it was eighty two percent Hispanic and ten percent Native American. The Indian kids usually, but not always came from the Isleta Pueblo area. That leaves Ray Maxie who was the only African-American and star of the football team and Lotus Lee who was the only Asian student and who was able to blow the top off of every grading scale in school. She had graduated this last year with a perfect 4.0 average."

"What about you," teased Hidalgo?

"Well," Richard said slowly choosing his words carefully, "Rio Grande is a very multicultural school, if you go to school there, you learn to deal with everyone and everyone learns to deal with you. Don't get me wrong, Rio Grande was for me, a great experience. For the most part, I truly enjoyed going to school there and as far as how well did I do?" Richard blushed again, ever so slightly. "I made A's in most of the classes I liked and C's or D's in the classes that I didn't."

"Then again," there was another redirection in the conversation, "my favorite class was band. Playing the trumpet in the high school band took me far and basically kept me out of trouble. I was lucky, the band needed me. You see, Rio Grande has seldom boasted of winning football teams but everyone there learned to escape to make believe worlds, each created by a good teacher. Our band program was a good example, many people would come to the football games over at Milne Stadium to watch the half time show and then leave as soon as it was over. The only reason to stick around would be to find out how lopsided the score would be. On the other hand, our stage band would actually perform homecoming dances for other schools that were in different districts."

Hidalgo knew he had to approach some family members differently than with others. Everyone is different. Hidalgo had been very polite and patiently waiting for his opportunity then finally blurted it out, "Do you know of anyone who might be able to give me some information about the fight games being staged around here?"

Richard smiled and slowly says, "Finally we get to the point. I'm sure tired of taking a sentimental journey down memory lane, but then, you asked."

Hidalgo frowned and Richard grinned, then enthusiastically says, "Hang around for a few minutes; I want you to meet a friend of mine."

While Richard was gone, Hidalgo asked Alice questions about Estancia. She had grown up there living on the homestead several miles south of town. Hidalgo learned nothing new; he had already seen the family photographs. Stories about the valley were usually colored by the obvious fact that there was a tremendous amount of animosity between the new Anglo culture and the far older Spanish culture and if anyone wanted to construct a pecking order there, Hidalgo would come in last place, somewhere just below the devil himself. Hidalgo completely understood this but considered this notion as absurd because as an Indian, he felt that it was his ancestor's land that everyone was squabbling over. The real war that Alice knew and talked most about was the war her family and the Riley family that lived down the road engaged in. Much like the Hatfield's and the McCoy's, the war had raged despite the fact that they had common ancestors and very little to actually argue over.

After about fifteen minutes, Richard returned with a muscular Hispanic fellow who Richard had known well in high school.

"This is Arturo Jaramillo, he was the one shinning point of light when it comes to athletics my senior year at Rio Grande High School and by the way, a great friend to have. He managed to go to the state wrestling finals four years in a row. He is now on full scholarship and is on the wrestling team for the University of New Mexico." Hidalgo and Arturo shook hands and settled into the seats of the kitchen chairs. Alice offered the young man some coffee but he turned it down, "Don't like that stuff, thank you anyway."

For a while Richard was careful not to tip Hidalgo's hand as to the true nature of what he was trying to learn, talking about many things the two friends had in common. Then Richard casually took the lead in asking the obvious question. "Hidalgo, did you know that last year Arturo was approached by two men who offered him money if he would fight in a tournament?"

"I'm not totally stupid," offered Arturo. "First of all, I would win only a hundred or so dollars if I won. Can you imagine the danger of fighting in a tournament like that?" He didn't wait for an answer, "What if I got really hurt in such a fight? A hundred dollars isn't going to pay the doctor's bill. Furthermore, can you imagine what would happen to my scholarship eligibility at the University if they found out? I would lose everything I have worked for. Besides I'm a wrestler, not a full contact kick boxer. But there is another, even more important reason I have a problem with those people. My cousin Alfredo Sedillo actually fought in one of those tournaments. Not once, but three times in one day! The first two bouts he won easy but on the last bout he was put up against a kid who was older and a much better fighter. The kid he fought had trained as a martial artist, an accomplished karate fighter. He took down Alfredo in only a few seconds, therefore Alfredo was denied the money from the previous fights he had already won. He came out of it with a broken nose and a concussion, and needless to say there is nobody to complain to, after all it is an illegal activity."

"Would your cousin help us," asked Richard?

"I doubt it, answered Arturo, he was beaten too badly and of course they made threats to both him as well as his little brother who happened to be with him, if either of them said anything. They don't really care who they intimidate and threaten. I don't know who is more horrible, the people who promote the events or the vultures who sit and watch them." He paused, thought for a minute and said, "Give me a couple days, I need some time. I'll talk to him. My guess is he can give you some credible leads." With that, there was an exchange of phone numbers and contact information as well as handshakes and Hidalgo loaded himself into the Jeep Cherokee. He was at an impasse. There was nothing he could really do for the next couple of days in order to solve this problem.

The Sanchez House

*H*idalgo's conscience was bothering him. Deep in his gut he knew he was obligated and needed to help the family, to make a showing. On a whim, Hidalgo headed east on central avenue toward Tijeras Canyon to do some preliminary research on the cave. Thinking back to when he made his speech at the kitchen table, he was a little embarrassed and now he wanted to. Besides he thought; if he was too conspicuous he would blow his cover. By driving out to the cave site he could at least get the lay of the land. At worse, if he felt he couldn't accomplish anything, he would have a very scenic and informative drive back to the comforts of Serpiente.

Tijeras canyon is the only practical route through the chain of mountains that make up the Sandias, the higher northern range of mountains and the Manzanos, the longer southern chain of mountains. Both make up the eastern skyline of the Rio Grande Valley for much of the state of New Mexico. After driving though the canyon, he turned south on Route 14 driving down the side canyon past beautiful hacienda homes that lined the road. As he descended the back side of the mountain the trees got smaller until after many miles the terrain became open pastureland and farmland with rolling small hills. Hidalgo drove through the tiny farming communities of Miera, Escabosa and finally Chinle. In each small settlement he would get out and walk around just to see if there were people about. People who would talk, but unfortunately nobody seemed to want to have a conversation with him. People were xenophobic and secretive in those small communities for many reasons. They simply didn't trust anyone they didn't know.

After attempting to strike up a conversation with several people and not getting more than a casual nod, Hidalgo drove on. He was disappointed. He had always learned a lot on forays like this. When he came to the intersection of route 14 and 55, he turned right instead of driving down into the valley where the town of Estancia was located. In only a few short miles he found himself driving into Tajique to find the land owner of the cave site.

Tajique is located in Torrance County, which comprises much of the Estancia basin. It is a very small farming community that also caters to the lumber industry. It was built on the site close to an old Piro pueblo which was one of the more northern of the Salinas pueblos. It was occupied by Salinas (or salt) Indians well before the arrival of the Spanish in the 16th century. As the Apache Indians moved south along the edge of the Rocky Mountains in the mid-17th century these missions came under attacks.

The locals made every attempt to make them defensible but with little luck. Apache raids remained a serious problem until well after the Civil War.

However, as far back as 1677 most of the original settlers to the Tajique and nearby Torreon site had left. There was just not enough surface water there to support a population. Nearby Torreon was named after defensive towers built at Manzano to the south and was resettled in the spring of 1841 by Nino Antonio Montoya and twenty six other farmers under a grant from the Prefect of the Central District of New Mexico. Except for a blacktop highway and power poles, it had not changed much since then.

Dirt and gravel roads were cut from Tajique into the flanks of the Manzano Mountains to such secret places as Fourth of July Springs where citizens from Estancia would go during the hot summer months to enjoy the relief of the cool mountain air. Water from those tiny springs such as Fourth of July and creeks would disappear downstream into the sandy soil of the Estancia basin. Those roads would be impassible now. In the higher elevations there would be deep snow that would allow only the sturdiest of four wheel drive trucks passage. Around Tajique, the roads were still a quagmire winding through rolling hills completely covered with cedar, juniper trees and scrub brush. Hidalgo was glad for his four wheel drive Jeep Cherokee. He also thought to himself, how could anyone make a living there?

The problem was he had no idea where the site was. Leslie and Don had said something about the cave being on the Sanchez farm but they hadn't said exactly where the farm was, much less where a rusting pipe was. He pulled into the mercantile store, the only one in town with a single gas pump and went in to ask for directions.

"*Como estas*, he said to the elderly and balding Hispanic fellow he found behind the counter. The clerk answered in Spanish, *muy bien y tu?* (Very good, and you?) Then turning to see who he was talking to he said in perfect English, what can I get for you?

"Well, I need some directions to the Sanchez farm.

"Which one?" answered the clerk, "There are several Sanchez farms around here."

"The Sanchez farm that has a well on it that broke into a natural cave," answered Hidalgo.

"Oh, yes, I know who you mean, but he will not want to talk to you. He sunk all of his money into that well and got nothing for it. He still owes the bankers in Estancia for it. When the cavers came out to get a look at it, it infuriated him. First of all, he really doesn't like people from the outside, especially white people."

"I'm Navajo, maybe he will speak to me," Hidalgo said.

"I doubt it, not if it is about that infernal hole in his farm. He was friendly at first but when some of those cavers from Albuquerque left a gate open several of his cows got out. It took several days of back breaking work to round them up, and needless to say, this did not help his attitude. He lives alone out there and do you have any idea how hard it is to round up cows in this kind of country?"

"Actually I know all too well what a job that can be. I live on a ranch down in Serpiente. I have spent many a day rounding up lost cows."

"Well," the clerk screwed up his face; "Maybe he will talk to you but don't tell him I sent you out there and don't expect much."

Hidalgo bought some corn chips and a quart of milk that would suffice for his dinner and asked again for directions.

It was getting late in the afternoon before he managed to drive up to the Sanchez house. It was an old structure with a rusting galvanized metal roof and plastered walls that were showing lathing wire where the plaster had fallen off. Across from the yard was a holding corral with a fence built from small cedar limbs all tied together with baling wire. Inside it were a few milk cows. The cows looked like they had seen better days.

Looking down a short trail he could see chicken coups, and finally a pig pin. The stubbles were still visible from a half acre garden plot that appeared to have always been there. He thought to himself; gardening was becoming a lost art in New Mexico. It was always easier just to go to the local store and pay for your food. Those people who couldn't afford food, usually used food stamps. Many families in Albuquerque never even cooked anymore choosing to dine out every meal except for the proverbial bowl of cereal for breakfast.

Walking up to the front door he was met by a large growling dog that was certainly big enough to run any intruder away. He grabbed a walking stick that was leaning against the porch and put it between him and the growling, barking dog. He then pretended to ignore it while keeping careful track of it, a trick he had learned as a boy on the reservation.

The doors, as well as the windows were trimmed in extremely faded turquoise paint, the sign of a superstitious person who wanted to keep the *brujas* or witches away. After some furious knocking on the wooden door, an elderly Spanish man appeared with a rifle in hand. Looking around the yard to make sure Hidalgo was alone he said, "I was hoping the dog would drive you away."

Hidalgo says, "All I want to do is talk to you, then I promise I will leave."

"What are you selling?" asked Sanchez.

"Nothing, Hidalgo answered, "But if you let me in to talk, you might be very glad." They looked at each other for a moment then the elderly fellow opened the door wider to allow Hidalgo in.

Lowering the gun the elderly man said, "I don't have any shells for the gun anyway."

It was a one room house with different areas dedicated to sleeping, eating and just plain loafing. There was trash piled everywhere, even along the edge of the homemade bed that was butted up against a wall. There was no electricity, nor indoor plumbing. Hidalgo set down on a homemade couch that had a Mexican serape blanket over it. "What do you want?" demanded the old man?

Hidalgo answered, "I would like to talk to you about your well."

This brought a look of distain from the old man. In a fiery display of pent up emotion Sanchez talked all about how he had sunk all the money he had into the well for nothing, then to top it off, some gringos from Albuquerque showed up to let all his cows loose.

Hidalgo looked at him, and quietly said, "What if someone was willing to help you, make your troubles go away? What if the people I work with would be willing to pay for that well, and maybe even pay for another well that will produce water a little further down the slope? We might even pay for the cost of your cows, and any other expenses you may have acquired?"

This brought about a long moment of silence from the old man. Finally, with a scrawl on his face he said, "What kind of a lying Indian are you?"

Hidalgo answered his question, "I am a Navajo and I have never told a lie in my life." This produced another long moment of silence.

Finally Sanchez had to admit that, "It's true, everyone I know will lie when it's convenient for them but I have never had an Indian lie to me."

Finally he answered, "I'm just tired of dealing with lying gringos. That banker knew there was no water down there. He stole all my money; and those hombres from Albuquerque let my cows out on purpose, I'm sure of it."

Hidalgo thought about this for a minute then answered him, "Perhaps the banker and the drilling company really didn't know there was no water down there. I understand there is a cave down there that would naturally drain away any ground-water that might be there."

Sanchez pondered this for a moment then said, "Why did those gringos let my cows loose? I'm an old man. I have better things to do than to chase cows on my neighbors' land."

Hidalgo answered, "Maybe they just made a stupid mistake. Everyone makes

362

stupid mistakes, even you did, or you wouldn't be in the situation that you are in."

"Perhaps", answered Sanchez, but I don't want anyone else bothering me or my cows."

Hidalgo thought about this for a minute then said, "What if we built a fence that would keep your cattle in the pasture even if the gate was left down?"

Sanchez pondered this a moment, then ask a simple question. "Why in the world would these gringos be interested in that old well anyway? What is down there? Is there gold or something?"

"No," answered Hidalgo, "But they did drop a cable with a camera down the well and discovered some interesting things down there. They want to cut a shaft down alongside it so they can look around down there. There may be some important scientific discoveries to be made down there."

"I don't give a hoot about scientific discoveries. All I care about is getting out from under the thumb of that infernal banker from Estancia. Mr. McDowell, he doesn't seem to understand that I can't make money unless I can grow grain and hay to raise more cows and that requires water, and lots of it."

Hidalgo was perplexed, "Where are you going to grow that grain and hay, I didn't see anything but scrub trees all the way here."

"Yes," answered Sanchez, "But if I have water, I can then get my good friend Enrique Archeletta who owns a small bull dozer to clear the land for me. He already said he would, all I have to do is pay for the diesel fuel. But right now I can't even afford the fuel."

Hidalgo pondered this for a moment then asked, "Where is your tractor that it will take to till the pastureland in order to plant the grass seeds? Where is your machinery that you use to mow it with? Where is your baler to bale the hay with?"

Sanchez looked a little perplexed at these questions; he hadn't thought that far ahead. Then he answered the question with, "I do have friends around here, we all help each other."

"Here on the foothills of the Manzano Mountains is no place to do that kind of farming," said Hidalgo, you need to do that kind of farming further down in the Estancia basin where everyone else is farming. Maybe there is another way to solve your problem. Besides, this is poor land; you can only put, maybe one cow on an acre of land here. I suspect that the banker knew that your plan was impractical well before he agreed to loan you the money to drill a well. How much money did you put into the well?"

Sanchez answered, "Every cent that I had in my savings." He walked over to a counter where he prepared his meager meals and reached up to a shelf and opened a brown ceramic bowl. Turning it upside down to show that there was nothing in it he said sadly, "The bank is empty, but at one time I had over three hundred dollars in there, the banker got it all."

"Sounds just like them bankers," Hidalgo sympathized.

"Yeah, they wanted me to fail. Many of us can't pay the taxes on this land. I don't understand why I have to pay money just for the right to live on my own land. I don't ask anything from those people." Mr. Sanchez was getting animated if not downright feisty. I don't have electricity, sewage, or any of those things that I'm paying taxes for.

Hidalgo asked him, "Have you requested to have electricity here?"

"Well, you know those poles they use to hang their power lines on?"
"Sure," answered Hidalgo.

"They said they would install the first five power poles for free, after that they would charge me for the poles, do you know how much a single pole cost?

"I can imagine their not cheap." answered Hidalgo.

"I can't afford one of them, much less a dozen of them." Poking his finger at Hidalgo he said "I can't do like those young en's around here that have a bunch of babies just so they can collect checks from the government."

Hidalgo deafly grabbed his finger in mid poke and said, "Aren't you a little old to be jealous of others?" Letting the finger go and reaching out in a handshake, a grinning Hidalgo could empathize with him.

Empathy

New Mexico was changing as a result of money being generated from an ever expanding population. Wages were being generated for many, particularly as a result of the military and scientific communities. Investors and speculators were investing money, particularly in the scenic areas that New Mexico had to offer. This created jobs but at a cost. Bankers who represented investors and speculators come in and assumed properties by paying the taxes, therefore assuming ownership. As the cost of paying for community improvements raise, taxes go up. For people who have lived marginally any increase in the cost of living becomes a significant problem so they sell out. And if nothing else works, they simply buy them out with cold hard cash. Those people are of course, taxed on their monetary gain they made as a result of giving up their land. It is a no win situation for them.

After the new ski area, mountain retreat, or land development is built, taxes are required to pay for the community improvements such as roads, power, sewage, flood control, schools etc. This is all wonderful for the investors, but is of little value to the majority of the local citizens. Jobs are generated by the construction of new developments but as soon as the construction is done, the jobs run out, but of course the taxes never go down. Then a land grab occurs by people who want to make even more money. As long as the population continued to grow money would be generated and the cycle would continue.

Hidalgo thought to himself how this situation was just like what had happened too many of his fellow Native American Indians. After they were conquered by a superior armed foe they developed a dependence upon the goods their conquerors produced. With the government's approval and deliberate manipulation they always found themselves in dept, the American way. The manipulation went all the way to Washington DC where bankers, lawyers and politicians hatched a plan to relieve the natives of their property. When the natives couldn't pay off their debts, they paid with the only thing they owned which was their land. In time, the white race owned nearly everything but the natives peoples never got out of debt.

But even in little backwater places like Torreon or Tajique the process continues to this day. Then there are holdouts, those people who do not want to sell at all. If those people cannot pay the higher taxes levied as a result having to pay for all of those improvements they are forcibly removed from their ancestral homes. Now this process was happening even in the poorest places in New Mexico. If land could be obtained, it would then be subdivided into small residential tracts to be sold to an ever expanding population of newcomers. It was the way the world operated. Unfortunately many of the victims of this insidious growth and expansion never understood what was happening to them.

"May I ask you where you got the money to pay for the water well" asked Hidalgo.

"Well," said Sanchez, "I went into Estancia and talked to a Mr. McDowell. He seemed happy to give me a loan, he took what money I had and made arrangements for a crew to come out and do the drilling."

"Yes, I'll just bet he was," said Hidalgo, "Now you are a slave to the note even though you have no water."

"That's true," says Mr. Sanchez, "I owe him a little over $1400 dollars." He paused a moment then said, "Just look around you Mr. Hidalgo, I am not a rich man."

It was true. Hidalgo had recently torn down better chicken houses than the house he was now in. There was no food in the house other than a few Kerr jars full of stewed vegetables, a sack of corn meal and a smaller sack of flour. "Would you mind if I talked to the banker and see what I can find out?

"Could you do that?" asked Sanchez hopefully.

"Sure," answered Hidalgo, "And if I can prove that he is taking advantage of you perhaps there is some legal things we can do against him."

Sanchez asked, "Are you a lawyer? I never heard of a Navajo lawyer."

Hidalgo answered him, "No, I am not a lawyer, but I have important friends who know people in high places. Anyway, if we can solve your problems and make it possible for you to keep your land would you be happy?"

"Sure," answered Sanchez, "All I really want is to live in peace without constantly worrying about losing my home."

"Can I come back and talk to you some more after I learn some things?" asked Hidalgo. Sanchez answered with a little hope in his voice, "You know I think I am going to like you. I still don't trust you, but I like you. Come back anytime you want." Even the dog was wagging his tail when Hidalgo left. He knew he had a job waiting for him in Estancia but it would have to wait for another day. Outside it was already dark. Hidalgo drove down the road a quarter of a mile, pulled over and, curled up in a sleeping bag in the back of the truck.

The Banker

Walking into the Estancia Valley Bankers Association in Estancia, Hidalgo walked up to the nearest bank teller.

"Mr. McDowell is a very busy man," the perky blond said "But I will see if we can work you in."

He settled into a chair waiting to see the bank representative. After waiting about twenty minutes, John C. McDowell opened the door to his inner sanctum, took a fast look at Hidalgo, and then disappeared again for another forty minutes. Finally the pompous little man reappeared and waved Hidalgo in. "What can I do for you?" He gruffly asked.

Hidalgo had a good idea what he was dealing with and he didn't like it, but he had a game plan. Hidalgo asked the banker point blank without introducing himself, "I understand that you are interested in acquiring land up around Tajique and Torreon?"

"Everyone is interested in acquiring land up there in those little Mexican towns," He answered. "So are you selling or buying land?"

"Neither," answered Hidalgo, "Why are you acquiring land in Tajique?"

Mr. McDowell was flustered, "That is something that I really can't talk to you about."

Hidalgo answered him with one word, "Why?"

The banker was beginning to show even more frustration at Hidalgo's impertinent question. "Everyone knows that people from Albuquerque are buying up small patches of land up there. They all want to raise a horse or two, along with a bunch of kids. They like to pretend that they are operating a real ranch, what's wrong with that?" asked McDowell.

"It depends upon how they are acquiring the land," answered Hidalgo.

"They buy it from us bankers of course," answered Mr. McDowell, "That's our business, now if you don't have any real banking business with me I'm going to ask you to leave."

Hidalgo answered very quietly, "I will leave, politely I assure you, as soon as you tell me how you would feel if a well-documented report was sent to the New Mexico banking commission that over sees your operations here. What if they discovered that you were causing people to lose their property just so you can make money?"

Mr. McDowell was about to go ballistic, "What are you, one of those agitators? You need to leave now, I have work to do. If you want to communicate anymore you will need to do it through my lawyer. Good day sir."

Hidalgo slowly placed his hand on the arms of the easy chair he was sitting in, rose up, and then said, "You will hear from 'us' again sir and I assure you, you will need your lawyer." Mr. McDowell held his hand out in front of him and flipped his fingers back and forth in a dismissal gesture. Hidalgo returned to the perky blond who had avoided him in the first place.

"Can you tell me how much is due on the Sanchez note for the water well that was drilled up in Tajique?" asked Hidalgo.

After looking through several files of papers, she came back with, "He is currently six payments behind. The bank will be placing a lien against the property at the end of this month followed by foreclosure proceedings."

Hidalgo asked, "How much?"

"He is behind some six hundred dollars," she curtly answered him.

Hidalgo pulled out his wallet and took out six one hundred dollar bills and handed them to her. "I'll need a receipt for that," he said. She handed him the receipt and Hidalgo thanked her politely. As Hidalgo was turning to leave, a red faced Mr. McDowell came out of his office and demanded that the teller come immediately into his office. Hidalgo hung around just long enough to hear the perky blond get a royal butt chewing for helping him. Hidalgo left with the receipt carefully tucked away in his wallet.

Mi Casa is Su Casa

Hidalgo drove over to the small mercantile store that provided food for the citizens of the town of Estancia. Walking up and down the aisles he received curious looks from the predominately Anglo shoppers as he filled two shopping carts with all manner of foodstuffs including bacon, coffee, toilet paper and anything else that couldn't be obtained on a small farm. Returning to the Sanchez farm and making friends with the dog again, he unloaded it into the house where a very mystified Mr. Sanchez seemed eternally grateful.

"*Mi casa is su casa,*" said Sanchez. "You can come here anytime you want if you bring groceries like that."

Mr. Sanchez had not seen groceries like that for several years now. Suddenly his life had taken a serious turn for the better and when Hidalgo showed him the receipt for the payments on the well he became ecstatic. Now Hidalgo, as well as his friends could do anything they wanted around the well. "I will have my friend, Enrique Archeletta, come over and get his bull out of the pasture if you promise not to leave the gate open."

"Sounds like a great idea," agreed Hidalgo. That afternoon they drove, in Hidalgos truck, out to the drill site. Just a short drive off the blacktop road, and though the proverbial closed and locked gate, they arrived at the drill site with no trace of a mean bull in sight.

"Actually, he is not a mean bull at all, but those gringos don't know that," Mr. Sanchez grinned as if he had really pulled one off on someone.

The well site actually looked like it could have been a good place to find water. At the bottom of an ancient draw that was bordered by a small limestone bluff that followed the contours of the land, a single four inch capped pipe was sticking up out of the sand.

"Why did they put down this big of a pipe," asked Hidalgo? "It requires either a large diesel powered engine or a good electrical pump to get water out of a well this big."

"I wondered about that myself," answered Sanchez. "The banker was the one that arranged for the drilling company to come out and do the work. I would have been happy with a two inch well. I had hoped that a windmill would work for me."

Hidalgo studied the drill site for clues as to how a shaft could be cut into the ground to reach the caverns underneath. His best bet was to cut a horizontal shaft from considerable distance downhill or to drill a vertical shaft wide enough to allow humans to enter the caverns.

Sanchez continued to press Hidalgo as to what was so important at the bottom of the well. Hidalgo explained that there had been a camera dropped down the pipe.

"What did they see down there," asked Sanchez.

"What appears to be a very large human hand," answered Hidalgo. Mr. Sanchez crossed himself several times with the classic Catholic gesture and murmured something in Spanish that Hidalgo couldn't hear.

Hidalgo walked up and down the ancient wash looking for any sign of an entrance into a natural cave. He found nothing, but in several places he found where the small cliff face had caved off into the floor of the streambed. He wondered if well up stream one of the large piles of rock hid an opening to an underground world.

Criminal Elements

*H*idalgo returned to Serpiente to wait for a message from Richard Holliday. It came sooner than he expected so again he drove the long drive back to the South Valley. When he arrived at the Holliday home, he was surprised to see Arturo Jaramillo as well as his cousin and three other young men, Jessie, Magnelena, and Ricardo. All had their share of experiences to share with Hidalgo but no names and no real leads, only a vague description of two men who confronted them. They had been told that they would be contacted and not to try to contact the men. Arturo did have one clue he could provide, the enforcers were two men from Mexico and both men wore very fancy cowboy boots with silver skulls covering the toes. In Spanish, the boys were told that they shouldn't say anything to anyone because the contacts had connections to a Mexican gang, and not just any gang. This gang was a well-organized Mexican drug cartel.

In Mexico, thousands of poor farmers or *campansanos* who are often Yaquis Indians live in agricultural areas and work for the cartel. Normally the farmers in Mexico live a subsistent existence, eating only what they can grow on small plots of land. The money that could be made from working for the cartels was much more substantial than attempting to live off of the land. By working for the cartel they could do more than just eat, they could put clothes on the backs of their families.

These farmers are slaves to the economics, a way of life. Of course they own no land of their own because it was long ago given to a select and politically active group of pure blooded Spaniards by the territorial government. They were the *patrons*, the *ricos*" Despite the fact that Mexico is a wealthy country if you consider mineral, cultural and scenic beauty, the ordinary citizens there are very poor. In Mexico you are wealthy or desperately poor and the poor often look to the drug cartels for their livelihood. Their allegiance is to them. For anyone who interferes with this system, the cartel could become a brutal pack. The law is afraid of them. Anyone who crossed them would wind up dead.

In Albuquerque and other Southwestern cities, the members of these cartels would propose a fight in which people thought they could win lots of money, but usually it was done strictly by word of mouth with only a few locals who might provide a relative who they thought could fight well. It was obvious that there was money in betting on the cock roosters as the fighters were called. But there were many added incentives for winning. Winners would be rewarded with the pleasure of enjoying young girls brought in from Mexico. Sex slavery was an up and coming business. Winners could become enforcers for the cartel. But there was more to it than meets the eye. Once they were in a community the real reason they were there became apparent as drugs entered the community. The system both promoted and fed upon its self.

Hidalgo had had a dim hope in his own mind that sooner or later word would get out and the fight game would die by its own accord, but now he was realizing that the layers of crime were far deeper than he expected. The Mexican cartels were always using tournaments and events like this as a way of getting into a community. They often invested large sums of money into those communities. The business, whether a restaurant, a car wash, or even a bank, would then seem absolutely legit, but secretly they also acted as fronts where money could be laundered.

Every American community has the opportunity to encounter criminal elements. Once inside the community, marijuana, meth, heroin, and a variety of artificial substances would appear which is of course, how the real money was made. The police and authorities would find themselves overwhelmed while dealing with the problems created by the new criminal element. Addicts would commit all manner of crimes in order to support expensive habits.

The fight game itself was a diversion for the cartel, for them it was more of a hobby, but it served its purposes. For Hidalgo, he had only one clear goal in mind, to have the leaders of the fight game arrested. The police would have to take care of the rest. Hidalgo was no longer a policeman but he still thought like one.

After comparing notes he told the group that he wanted to go back to Lorenzo's, the café where Corey and he had encountered the fight game. The place did have good food, and this time he wanted to enjoy a good meal in peace. They asked Hidalgo about his other pursuits. They seemed interested in his caving adventure and so he told them about his plans to check in with Don and Leslie in hopes of exchanging information. Maybe he could come up with a game plan to get back on the property.

He took the short drive to the same café he had stopped at with Corey. Again, it was almost deserted except for the cook and the waiter. He enjoyed his favorites, cheese and meat enchiladas with real Rio Grande chili, not the cheap sauces that is fed to the crowds of tourist that crowd most commercial restaurants around Albuquerque.

He felt relaxed and ate several extra sapodillas with honey. Totally satisfied and full, he paid his bill leaving a good tip to the friendly waiter then he walked out the door and headed to his parked Jeep Cherokee. His wheels were just four cars down the curb, but just two cars down, three well-dressed young men were just getting out of a car. The first two were carrying on a rather animated discussion and appeared to totally ignore him. They causally passed him, or so he thought.

The third guy acted like he was trying to catch up with the other two when he suddenly lunged at Hidalgo driving his fist directly into Hidalgo's sternum. Another blow immediately came to his stomach. His arms were instantly grabbed and held. He attempted to bend over in an attempt to keep his dinner, but it was not to be. The third man stepped back, took aim and did a front snap kick to Hidalgo's groin. He was held there while the third man beat and kicked at him for several minutes while he vomited, then suddenly and mercifully he lost consciousness from a blow to the back of the head.

Hidalgo woke up in the drunk tank at the Bernalillo County Sheriffs' Department. Laying there, realizing that he was in jail, the first thing that came into focus that he recognized was the square hole in the middle of the floor, a place to vomit. His upper lip was split open. He had no idea what it looked like. He was covered in vomit and he reeked of whisky. The smell of the sweat, whiskey and blood caused him to go into a spasm of dry heaves. It was painful. He vaguely remembered the toe of the boot that kicked him in the face had a silver skull on it and he thought he could remember later being turned over when a pair of handcuffs was put on him. Then he had blacked out again.

It had all happened way too fast; the three of them had done a very professional job on him. With Hidalgo unable to move, the cock rooster had enjoyed himself. The rooster was proud of his ability to inflect pain as he kicked Hidalgo in the chest and face with his boots, the boots with the silver skulls. He was a martial artist, undoubtedly well paid and extremely arrogant.

Hidalgo was mad at himself. He had been entirely too casual, allowing himself to be totally blindsided. As he began to question himself, he concluded he had no one to blame but himself.

Hidalgo knew he was in trouble instantly. As he tried to roll over he discovered that he couldn't breathe; instantly aware that he had a cracked rib. He started to black out again but fought it. He barely remembered one of the men taking out a bottle of whisky and forcing some of it into his mouth, then pouring the rest of the bottle all over him as he slipped in and out of consciousness. Very efficiently they had performed their job, professionally; then they disappeared.

After an hour or so the door of the cell opened and a uniformed jail guard stood over him looking down at him with a disgusted look on his face. "Why can't you Navajos hold your liquor?" He had asked the question not expecting an answer. But Hidalgo had one. "I have not had anything to drink. I never drink alcoholic drinks."

"I can smell you all the way out here in the hall; don't tell me you're not stone drunk."

"I'm hurt," said Hidalgo in a feeble voice.

"You might be, but that is not really my concern right now," said the jail guard. Besides that's not what the folks who called us said. They said you came into their restaurant hog drunk, made a mess and then left without paying for your meal. When you got out into the parking lot you picked a fight with a couple of patrons, wanted money so you could buy more whiskey. They settled it. You lost."

"Who filed the report," ask Hidalgo?

"The owner of the restaurant found you; consider yourself lucky, the owner didn't even press charges when you failed to pay for your meal," explained the policeman with a disgusted look on his face. Hidalgo reached inside his shirt pocket for the receipt he always kept but discovered that he didn't even have a pocket, it had been torn off.

Hidalgo asked, "Who called the police?

"The owner of the café, as well as the other people you attacked. They left.

"You don't know who they are," asked Hidalgo?

"The café owner signed the complaint," answered the guard.

"I want a blood alcohol test," demanded Hidalgo.

"Sure said the guard; in fact; we insisted. The judge would like to know just how much you had to drink. You were immediately shackled and taken to Presbyterian hospital where blood was drawn from your arm. As soon as the test was over, you were brought back here. We'll let you know how the test came out. By the way, you have been charged with public intoxication and disorderly conduct."

"Can I at least get a shower," asked Hidalgo?

"Sure, in two and a half hours. You have to stay in here for at least four hours. Can you make bail?" Hidalgo had no idea where his wallet was, and it contained all those important phone numbers he would need to make bail.

"No," Hidalgo answered.

"I didn't think so, you don't have a job, do you, just came in from the reservation?" The prison guard definitely had some preconceived ideas, probably based upon years of experience, but he was right, like many people a few Navajos subject themselves to this sort of indignation on a regular basis.

Hidalgo had no answers for him; he knew he wouldn't be believed. It would be a waste of time to say anything, much less to argue with the guard, besides it hurt too much. It was a slow night and several hours later Hidalgo was led to a room where he finally got to take off his filthy cloths and take a shower. He was then issued standard prison wear, consisting of striped pajamas with cheap shower slippers, and taken to a community workhouse cell where he spent the next three days sleeping on a cot and doing his best to eat prison food.

Nothing seemed to happen, not even a date with a judge occurred. Then finally early in the morning of his fourth day in jail a policeman came into the community cell and asked Hidalgo to come with him. They went into an office where Hidalgo was directed to take a seat. The policeman's name tag which dangled below his pocket identified him as Sergeant Ron Sedillo. Sergeant Sedillo said, "You used to be a Sergeant with the La Plata police department, didn't you?

Hidalgo looked up, "Yes" he answered, "I worked there for about five years, I now work for Ken Anderson at a ranch down in south central New Mexico known as Serpiente, but the bottom line is I was beaten up by three men whom I have never seen before and I'm not sure why they beat me up."

"What happened," ask Sergeant Sedillo?

"All I know is that I went in for a meal and was beaten up on the way out, and I'm darn sure I hadn't had any alcoholic drinks that day or any other day. I never touch the stuff; I have seen what it does to my people."

The sergeant cut into his explanation. "I know," answered the Sergeant, "Your alcohol blood test came back negative. They found nothing in your blood." After a pause he added, "You realize that we have people come in here every day that look just like you did."

Hidalgo pointed out, "You mean Navajos or some other Indian."

"No, I mean people that look like you when you showed up here. Would you like a lawyer?" Hidalgo was fuming; he knew it would do no good to sue the police department despite the fact that he had obviously been a victim.

"No" answered Hidalgo, "Apparently the people who beat me up knows how the system works. Someone must have set me up pretty well knowing that I would wind up here. My guess is they didn't want me to get too cozy with you fellows; they wanted me to be alone. Well, I just want to get out of here. I have done nothing wrong and resent having to spend my time here."

The sergeant looked down at Hidalgo and said, "Actually you are free to go, however I would appreciate it if you would tell me exactly how you got into this predicament." Hidalgo related to the policeman his previous encounter at Lorenzo's the Mexican Restaurant. The police sergeant continued with his questions, "Do you have any idea why those men jumped you?"

"Maybe," answered Hidalgo, I was trying to track down the men who are promoting the fights that are going on with young people here in Albuquerque.

The sergeant blinked at this statement. "You have made some enemies, but for what it is worth, you have also made some friends here. My son was propositioned to get into the fight game. When he declined he was badly beaten up. Anyway, how can I help you?"

Hidalgo answered, "A snake can only die if the head is cut off."

The sergeant thought about this for a moment then answered, "A snake like that enjoys some protection from arrest. Perhaps we can share some information and if you promise you will work with me, I'm sure I can be of some help to you. We cannot protect you unless you are working with us."

"I have told you all that I know; what else do you want?" asked Hidalgo.

"First of all, there is a lot more to this than a few fight tournaments!" Sergeant Sedillo looked down at Hidalgo and realized that he himself was caught up in the moment, after a pause he continued. "I know that most of the recent activity is located down in the Los Padillas area. Kids are taken to a warehouse and the fights occur in front of a small dedicated crowd of people who must pay a large fee to see the fights. They are sworn to secrecy. We have been trying to bust the whole crowd for several months now but have had little luck. It would appear that they are being told when the police are scheduled to show up. We have a mole among us. As you know from your experiences in Colorado, not all policemen are good policemen, but not all policemen are bad either."

Hidalgo answered, "In Colorado it was not the policemen that were crooked; it was the judicial system. The judge that was involved is still being pursued by the state department. Unfortunately once they are out of the country, it is hard to get an extradition order. Many of the tiny islands out there have no extradition agreement with the United States."

"Yes," answered officer Sedillo, "And they take full advantage of it."

It took Hidalgo all day to get his Jeep Cherokee out of the impound lot. It had been stolen and completely trashed. The rear window was broken out and of course all of his camping gear had disappeared. He had discovered that his wallet was gone as soon as the cuffs were removed from him in jail, which was why posting bail had been out of the question. Now he had his Jeep but no way to move it. Walking around the impound lot he was surprised when Sergeant Sedillo showed up and offered him twenty dollars for gas money.

Hidalgo had to hot wire his Jeep, naturally no one had any idea where his keys had disappeared to. He put twenty dollars' worth of gas in the empty gas tank and made it to within forty miles of the ranch house. He knew he had to walk the rest of the way into Serpiente.

He started walking, but after a couple of miles he discovered a car had pulled up behind him. Stepping aside he discovered that I was driving the car.

"Would you like a ride or do you still insist upon doing everything by yourself?" I asked him. He never said a word, he was too tired. Hidalgo simply slid into the passenger seat and closed his eyes. The walk created a number of new blisters that all had to be taken care of. Hidalgo took the next few days off in order to recover from his beating and the long walk. Needless to say, the whole ordeal had left him in a sour mood. Fortunately for him he was home. June and I nursed him back to health.

Silver Skulls

Somehow the characters who were doing the fight game were on to Hidalgo, his cover had been blown, but how? The only people he had confided in were Richard Holliday and his friends. There of course was Arturo Jaramillo and then there were the three boys who were with him. One of them must have been a mole who informed on Hidalgo.

Someone was working with the fight game promoters, and Hidalgo was mad at himself for his own stupidity. He had always trusted young kids, thinking that they were innocent. But Hidalgo's world was changing. Most of the real crime in the world was currently being promoted by the naiveté or stupidity, and arrogance of young kids. He was becoming cynical beyond his years. He was no longer a kid himself, being almost thirty-two years old.

He confided the situation to Richard and Arturo, and then watched to see what would happen as Richard arranged a meeting with the boys again, but this time Hidalgo carefully choose what he said. He lied, something he normally would never do but this was necessary to set a trap. He told them that the police knew who the perpetrators were and that a major bust was coming down, that evening.

One of the three boys was nervous and sure enough as soon as possible, Magnelena excused himself from the group and Hidalgo followed him. Soon Magnelena found a phone and started a heated conversation with someone. At least now Hidalgo knew who he couldn't trust and why he had received a beating at the Mexican restaurant known as Lorenzo's.

Hidalgo thought to himself, I can use him like a tool to get to the men with the silver skulls on their boots. In his mind, there were several loose ends to tie up, particularly with Lorenzo, the owner of the restaurant. Hidalgo wanted to close him down. He had no use for a restaurant that catered to the Mexican mafia despite the great food that they served. Hidalgo wanted to return for a third time to the café and confront the owner, but he guessed that the owner was being intimidated into cooperating with the enforcers. Instead, Hidalgo contacted Sergeant Sedillo. Sedillo was anxious to help and wanted to find the mole within the Bernalillo Sheriff's Department. Somehow they would need to set a trap for the mole, but this time it would need to be far more complicated than dealing with some young kids.

Sergeant Sedillo did have one morsel of information that would help. Word on the street was that a tournament would occur next Saturday morning at a warehouse in Albuquerque's north valley. The problem was, if they put out word that the tournament would be raided the promoters would just move it to another place in another barrio of Albuquerque.

Hidalgo finally made a suggestion, "What if we put out a false raid. Tell everyone that we are going to raid a warehouse in the South Valley, let's send them on a wild goose chase."

What good would that do?" asked Sedillo.

"Simple, answered Hidalgo, if all the police show up in the South Valley, the fight promoters will think they are safe. What we need is a way of getting our agents into that tournament; some honest agents."

"That's the problem," answered Sergeant Sedillo." We know that at least one officer that works with us is not honest. How will we know which one he is?"

"Maybe we won't need to know," answered Hidalgo.

Planning a Sting

Hidalgo did everything he could do to change his appearance and attended the tournament. Putting grey in his hair and donning a Mexican serape did the job. Laughing at himself in the mirror he liked what he saw. Arriving at the tournament, Hidalgo hid himself in the crowd, wearing clothes that made him a stranger to himself, clothes that he normally would never wear. He also had been to a barber and had his long hair cut in a close cropped style that made him look more Spanish than Indian. He wanted to blend in, to be anonymous. Paying the twenty dollar entrance fee, he passed through the door just as he spotted the two men with the silver skulls on the tips of their boots leaning against a wall. They appeared to be disinterested in the tournament, carrying on an animated conversation among each other.

Hidalgo watched indifferently as several fights occurred usually with one of the contestants being knocked out and bloodied. The winners did not seem to be happy about winning, rather they appeared glad to have survived the ordeal. Then it was all over and people began to empty the small arena. Hidalgo watched the two men carefully then realizing he also had to leave he walked out to his truck and watched the remainder saunter out. After watching the door for about thirty minutes the two men with skulls on their boots finally appeared.

The two enforcers finally went over to a black sedan that was parked at the edge of the parking lot and drove away with Hidalgo keeping a discreet distance behind them. It was a difficult job following them without being spotted but fortunately for him they apparently were still arguing among themselves and never noticed the old farm truck that was several cars behind them.

Hidalgo followed them all the way to the Corrales area of Albuquerque, finally they turned into an upscale hacienda style house that was hidden behind a large adobe wall and locked gate. Driving past the gate he now knew where they were staying and his mind immediately began hatching a plan that would entrap the two enforcers.

It was all too personal to Hidalgo. He knew that he could only put a small dent in the cartel operation but he wanted to do his part. Two items played on his thinking. One, he wanted to put a stop to the insidious fight games that were being conducted against the most vulnerable members of our society; our children. Two, he had a personal grudge against the two enforcers who had given him a beating and sent him to the drunk tank. He admitted to himself that he wouldn't be satisfied with merely having them arrested. He knew they would be out on bail in only a few hours. He wanted vengeance, he wanted to hurt them.

He turned south again traveling to Albuquerque's South Valley to the Holliday home on Valley Road. He shared his new information with Richard after swearing him to secrecy. There he would also make a phone call to Sergeant Sedillo and set up a meeting. He knew that Sergeant Sedillo was the only person he could trust because of the danger of tipping off the moles he had already run into. A lot of time and effort would be wasted and the two enforcers could easily return to Mexico to escape prosecution if he played his cards wrong.

Talking on the phone, Sergeant Sedillo wanted Hidalgo to meet him in person immediately to discuss a sting operation. They met in Old Town at the Placita Restaurant where they could find a discreet corner to disappear into.

When Hidalgo arrived Sedillo was already there along with another policeman who had a personal grudge against the enforcers. Sedillo introduced the stranger as Emilio Blanco whose son had competed in a tournament. Blanco explained that his son had fought in two tournaments until his jaw was broken then he was discarded like so much refuse. It seems that he was goaded into fighting when the two enforcers informed him that they knew who his father was, where he patrolled, and how they could easily kill him if he refused to cooperate or even let his father know what was going on. They spent about an hour discussing a fight game of their own.

The Sting

They all loaded into Sedillo's private car and traveled the route to the hacienda styled house in Corralles. There, they parked a full block away from the house in an obscure place where they would not draw attention to themselves and watched. Returning each day in a different car they kept track of the patterns that the enforcers demonstrated. They realized shortly that the only time the two men left the hacienda house was when they had business to take care of during the day but every night they ventured into the night life of Albuquerque returning to the house by 1:00 AM.

After a couple of days of watching the house, Hidalgo couldn't stand it anymore. He brought Arturo with them and when the right moment occurred he opened the door of the car and Arturo casually walked over to the wall that surrounded the house. Working his way along the wall, he circled the entire structure then returned to the car.

"There is an opening in the back of the wall facing the alley. That is where they keep their trash cans until the sanitation workers pick it up. There is a gate there but the latch is not locked. You can easily get into the compound through that gate. Another thing, while I was there I looked in their trash cans and found this." He pulled a paper bag out of his jacket and poured the contents onto the floor mats. It was full of drug materials, marijuana plant stems, seeds and empty rolling packs. But even more importantly, there was aluminum foil with traces of white powder still attached to it.

Sedillo looked at it and said to Hidalgo, "There is our probable cause, and the police didn't find it. A private citizen found the evidence and reported it. Those hombres are not as smart as they think they are, time for us to get a search warrant."

Hidalgo said back to him, "Even the smartest crooks are creatures of habit they seem to always do dumb things that allow them to get caught."

"That's right," countered Sedillo, "They are caught. They just don't know it yet."

At exactly 4:00 AM the following day several police squad cars along with a police truck that had cages in the back with drug sniffing dogs, slowing crept into the neighborhood from different directions and officers got out with weapons drawn. They were all handpicked by Sergeant Sedillo to avoid problems with the department mole. Every one of the officers present had a personal grudge against the cartel. Sedillo took the lead through the gate followed by Hidalgo and at least a dozen policemen. Coming to the rear door they discovered it was locked, which was what they expected. Two of the policeman then took out a battering ram used to break down doors and with a loud thud the door flew open.

Hidalgo followed the officers in as they cleared the rooms one by one. But as they passed the kitchen which was in a disheveled mess they could hear shuffling sounds coming from the bedrooms. Suddenly the rooster appeared in black pajama-like bottoms. Seeing Hidalgo he immediately assumed a karate position closing the distance on Hidalgo in an instant. When he got within kicking distance he stopped, turned, and went into a spinning rear kick, expecting to connect with Hidalgo's head as he attempted to back away from the kick. But Hidalgo did the unexpected; instead of backing away to avoid the kick, Hidalgo stepped into the kick catching the leg with his forearm, lifting the rooster into the air. Down the rooster came on his back with a thud but Hidalgo was already dropping down on his right knee and with his right fist he hammered the rooster in the groin as hard as he could. Immediately Hidalgo moved up and on to the rooster hitting him as hard and fast as he could in the face.

Sergeant Sedillo ever so slowly walked over to them and caught Hidalgo's arm as he was just about to deliver a death blow. "Let's save a little bit for the judge to have," Sedillo said with a look of satisfaction on his face. Two other men who were wearing nothing but handcuffs were unceremoniously dumped into a pile on top of the rooster who was still unconscious. Emilio Blanco appeared at the hallway door and waved them over. "You fellows need to see this."

Leaving the room with a policeman holding a gun on the three men, they walked into one of the side bedrooms. There, they discovered eleven young girls, all naked except for a locked collar around their necks and a dog chain that chained them to a single large metal framed bed with nothing but a box spring on it. The mattress was on the floor so they could all have a place to lie down. Sharing nothing but a sheet to cover themselves they appeared to be in terror, not knowing what was going to happen to them. Sedillo quickly discovered that the girls, the youngest one a tender age of fourteen, were the prizes that the fight game contestants occasionally won. Several of the older girls had been promised jobs in America in the motel business, cleaning rooms. The remainder of them had simply been kidnapped in Mexico to supply the needs of the enforcers.

The drug dogs soon uncovered several unopened packages of marijuana and what was suspected to be cocaine. The party was over. The young girls would be extradited back to their homes in Mexico and the three cartel men would be spending many years in the New Mexico State Penitentiary where they would be treated to jail hospitality.

Hidalgo felt vindicated. Although he would have enjoyed punching the other two men he felt a personal satisfaction as to what had happened. Two days later they were able to raid a fight that was already scheduled to occur down on Fourth Street. Forty two people were arrested and as word got out the fight games ended, not only in Albuquerque but in many southwestern cities. The cartel would be required to find other ways to get their evil fangs into America.

The Newest Cave Discovered in New Mexico

Don and Leslie's hacienda had become a war room; a place where plans would be generated to get them into the Estancia cave. Unfortunately there was no way that a pipe could be drilled into the overbearing rock large enough to allow a spelunker to slide down it without an extraordinary investment of money, resources and time. Hiring a construction crew and getting the equipment to the site would be cost prohibitive. They debated the size of the pipe. The only way of constructing a pipe would be to enlist the help of a company with the material shipped by trucks all the way from West Virginia where experimental work was being done on a rescue system that could bring people to the surface from deep in the earth. It could be considered as a rescue system for thirty or forty trapped coal miners but never for the rescue of people who had died untold millennia ago. It seemed an impractical move anyway, Ken and June had the money put away but wanted to use it for more practical pursuits. It was the family insurance against all unknown circumstances.

Don and Leslie were devastated. Exploring the cave had been their personal dream for some time years now. "What about a side cut into the caves, from further down," asked Don?

Corey answered the question, "Yes, it is possible, but it would still take a long time and a lot of money. Just talking someone into doing it would be problematic. It would require a lot of blasting to get through the limestone down there. People will not do that much work unless there is a huge payoff at the end. We would have to provide that payoff at the end in the form of cash money. Lots of cash money. In all fairness I just can't see it."

Hidalgo, who had been quiet for some time and who was examining a topographic map of the area said, "There has to be another way into the cave. I cannot believe that people would be in the cave without a practical way out. We have to find it."

Don answered him, "But we have walked up and down that old arroyo for miles and have not seen anything larger than a rabbit hole."

"That's true, I have hiked the arroyo myself," replied Hidalgo, "But we are missing something."

I looked at him and said, "What if we took a front end loader there and dug some of the rock falls away from the cliff faces?"

Don and Leslie, who by this time were grasping at straws, jumped at the idea. "What if there are skeletons down there because someone wanted them to be hid for all times? What if someone killed those people on purpose?"

"That could still be rather expensive," Hidalgo said, "but I may have an idea. Sanchez said something about a friend who had a bull dozer who would clear his fields. Perhaps the cost of a tank or two of diesel fuel will solve our problem. If not, we will have to leave it to someone else to solve."

Three days later, everyone met at the well site with shovels, pry bars and a chain saw as well as camping gear with enough provisions to last them for several days. After setting up tents and building a fire to keep them company, they waited for Enrique and Sanchez to show up with a bulldozer. But they didn't just wait;

they hiked up and down the small canyon looking for likely spots for a cave to be. Unfortunately, it could easily be hidden behind dozens of rock falls.

During the last Ice Age, New Mexico was a colder and much wetter place. The streams that run through this area carried a tremendous amount of water. The only thing they had to go on is that the entrance would have to be above the high water while people lived in it. This was problematic because at one time or another, the stream had to actually flow down into the cave, otherwise there would not be a cave there.

Early the next morning everyone was awakened to the grinding of a large truck carrying a trailer with a small bulldozer on the back of it. While Hidalgo, Corey and Ken helped Enrique Archeletta unload the dozer, June and I cooked a wonderful breakfast of bacon, eggs, and biscuits baked in an iron skillet. We even prepared sausage gravy. After the breakfast it took them over an hour to get the dozer with its dead battery going.

Driving the ancient bulldozer to the first rock slide in a bend in the ancient streambed Enrique began pushing rocks away from the cliff face. Actually it was a harder job than they thought it would be, the highest rocks needed to be pried away from the cliff by hand and then pushed away by the bulldozer. All that they found was an occasional rattlesnake that had made a home between the rocks. Each rock fall would take several hours to clear. One down, they had many more sites to explore. It could take several days of this just to work their way up the streambed. They decided to explore up stream first, since logically the water drained downstream to form the cave.

On the second rock fall, located in a sharp turn of the ancient arroyo, they were luckier, as soon as they began clearing away rocks they discovered a crude rock wall that appeared to have been constructed by human hands. Instantly they knew that they were on to something.

As Hidalgo, Corey and Ken removed one of the large rocks that made up the wall a stream of cold air instantly poured out of the hole. They had found the original cave entrance. Early the next morning they would put on the caving gear that Don and Leslie had brought along and begin exploration of the newest cave to be discovered in New Mexico.

Siege Warfare

Siege warfare was an old art form even thirteen thousand years ago. Clan Protector and his small band of hunters had fled back to the cave where they felt they would be safe. From inside the cave, the elders would be safe from attack no matter how large a force was sent against them. In order to get into the entrance of the cave, an enemy warrior would need to stoop over and walk for several yards that way before he would enter a large room where he could stand erect and throw a spear or weld a club. More importantly, the enemy would have to come in single file, making a mass attack impractical. Several of the enemy warriors would die before they discovered how impregnable the cave was.

The problem for Clan Protector was that despite the fact that the enemy couldn't get in, the Clan members hiding in the cave couldn't get out. This would not be a problem for a couple of weeks. Being early summer, the clan had already begun the labor of stashing the lower chambers of the cave with foodstuffs in order to get them through the long winter ahead. Unfortunately they had just begun collecting food for the upcoming winter and they were still dependent upon stores of mastodon fat in order to preserve the meat they had collected, however a small amount of fresh meat was available. They even dragged the bodies of the enemy warriors that had attempted to get into the cave where they were. These enemy warriors were cut up and eaten. Every morsel of the bodies was consumed. Even the bones were cracked open and the morrow was eaten. It must have been a gruesome enterprise since cooking them would not have been an option. Nothing was wasted.

The clan was trapped and every attempt of escape was met with spears and war clubs and time was on the side of the newcomers. All they had to do was wait the clan out, but this was a time consuming and dangerous job. Besides, they needed to be hunting meat themselves, not getting rid of dangerous competition. But the enemy warriors tried. On one occasion they managed to gain access to all but the lowest levels of the cave cutting off body parts of the clan warriors in the process.

Finally the newcomers decided that the easiest way to destroy the enemy warriors was to seal them in the cave, so they dropped large stones off the bluff that towered above the cave entrance. With those stones they built a wall across the entrance of the cave, they then caved off even more rock from the bluff above the entrance. Once large enough rocks were dropped into place, the newcomers simply left. Clan Protector and his tribe simply starved to death in the depths of the cave.

The Crime Scene

After making sure everyone had three light sources with extra batteries, kneepads, and a clear game plan, the men carefully pried away and removed the last of the blocks of rock that made up the crude rock wall that blocked the entrance of the cave. Immediately they discovered two very large skeletons where bodies had decomposed on the floor of the cave. Only the lower bones around the jaw and the huge teeth remained. The rest of the skeletal remains had turned to a disintegrated powder making up a light grey deposit on the floor. But the outlines of the bones were clearly there. It appeared that the two strongest victims had attempted to remove the fallen rocks. Unfortunately for them there was no way to achieve leverage. They had starved to death in the futile attempt. Now all that was left of them were crumbly traces.

Moving carefully so as not to disturb the traces of skeletal remains, we all crawled into the cave, turned on our headlights and looked around. A narrow corridor was before us that we had to bend over to walk and then suddenly the cave opened up into a room some thirty foot wide and sixty feet long. Everywhere they looked they could see bones. These bones were in a better state of preservation. Hidalgo thought to himself that they were walking into a crime scene. Many of the bones showed the evidence of scratches where obsidian knife blades had removed the flesh. In this one large room eight human like individuals could be accounted for; five small skeletons that had nothing but the lower and upper jaws remaining and three larger skeletons.

Two of the larger skeletons were also cut up and disarticulated as if having been eaten and one eleven foot long skeleton seemed to have simply died in place. They hypothesized that these people had starved to death and the one well preserved skeleton was the last survivor. With nothing else to eat, he simply starved to death, the last member of his clan, probably the strongest and most able to defend himself, perhaps the protector of the clan.

The saddest sight in this large room was the remains of a small child that I discovered under a pile of disintegrated leather robes. It appeared to have hidden under the robes until he too had succumbed to starvation. It would have been a miserable way to die, in the cold darkness with no chance of escape.

After examining the large room for a couple of hours we decided to explore on into the cave. Following a well-worn trail dropping down another long corridor we found ourselves in a very large room. The ceiling was a full forty feet above us and around us we found ourselves looking at curious fifteen foot tube worm fossils that were imbedded in the walls. Ammonite and crinoids were everywhere. Fossil shells of many interesting animals packed so tightly in the rock that the rock seemed to be entirely made of fossils. In one corner of the room a small crack in the wall allowed a trickle of water to pour down into a small rock bowl. From there the water overflowed down a small channel and then disappeared into another opening in the floor. They wondered if this small spring was there, thousands of years ago, providing sustenance for the cave dwellers?

Don and Leslie spent the next three days exploring deep into the cave, photographing everything they could. Their progress was stopped when they reached ground water. Further exploration would now be impossible without using air tanks, something for another time with different explorers. This cave would obviously be a focal point for paleontologist as well as anthropologist for years to come. Pieces of mastodon bones were everywhere. Obviously they had been carried into this part of the cave where they were broken apart for the valuable bone marrow. Only the ends of the bones were still intact. Pieces of human bones were scattered among them. Ken spotted the well pipe sticking out of the ceiling and within moments they spotted the hand on the cave floor under it. Just another hand among many that were found in the cave where a primitive people thought that fellow humans were just another food source, or did they?

The group of explorers was in a quandary as to what they were looking at. Did these people eat each other as a natural way of life or were they reacting to an extreme situation. Even modern humans will commit cannibalism under extreme circumstances. Perhaps they actually hunted the newcomers as a source of food. Perhaps this was the reason the newcomers wanted to exterminate them. Regardless of the circumstances, they were obviously engaged in the ultimate and cruelest fight game.

Part 6

Pride, Deprivation and Providence in New Mexico

Those who don't know history are destined to repeat it.
                                        —Edmund Burke

*History will have to record that the greatest tragedy
of this period of social transition was not the strident
clamor of the bad people, but the appalling silence of
the good people.*
                                  —Martin Luther King

The Black Tie Affair

*M*y life had changed dramatically. Little Penny Anderson was simply not the same little girl as I had been in Tennessee. I was now a professional historian and not someone who just studied history; we as a team were making history. This year the entire crew from the Serpiente ranch attended the affair being held at the University of New Mexico Student Union. Despite the fact that only the elite were attending, it was a relatively large group of people there, more than two hundred, the building was packed with people obsessed with history. During the last meeting less than fifty had attended. It was obviously a growing affair. Being a black tie affair and semi-formal, Hidalgo and Corey were particularly uncomfortable. They were used to wearing working men's clothes, the kind that has many small tears, faded, and usually stained with sweat. Even Ken squirmed uneasily in his seat as the committee from the Southwestern Historical Society made announcements of awards and recognitions of this year's accomplishments.

They finally got around to the announcement that the crew from Serpiente had been waiting for; "We would like to announce this year's winner of the Southwestern Historical Societies award for outstanding achievement in historical detective work. These fine people have managed to write a new chapter in New Mexico history with their work in discovering the Estancia Cave and unearthing what had until now been unknown history of the aboriginal people known as the Estancia Indians who preceded the earliest known American Indians who lived in New Mexico. Not since the discoveries of Frank C. Hibbens has as much been discovered about ancient people who lived in North America before and during the last Ice Age."

The Master of Ceremonies continued, "This work has provided more than just historical documentation about this important and poorly understood era in our history, it has opened up whole new doors for archeologist, anthropologist, biologist and many other fields of academic endeavor. We are grateful for their contributions." June accepted the award for the crew and then with only a few short words she sat down. In her lap she cradled the prestigious Historical Society Award in the form of a plaque suitable for any wall. But also, there was also a check for $10,000 dollars, and she knew that there would be much more money earned after publication of her book on 'Early Estancia Man.'

"This year we would like to propose a new challenge for all our participants." The announcer paused for a moment then added, "We also would like to offer our usual cash award or scholarship that has been put up, compliments of our generous benefactor who will remain anonymous. The first place award this year has grown to twenty five thousand dollars paid to the person or persons who best complete a research project illustrating and enlightening an underappreciated southwestern incident or person." The amount of the award brought forth a round of applause from the group who were all eager to participate in the challenge.

"The rules are; one, it must highlight a person who made an impact on the history and culture of the southwest who has received little or no recognition in the current history books. We would enjoy seeing contributions in the field of biographical history."

"Two, the researchers must document the activities of this person by reenacting or documenting their exploits or experiences and demonstrate why they should receive recognition."

"Three, they must present their research in publishable form that can be used at our discretion." The speaker stopped at this point and looked out in the audience. "You realize," she continued, "The University of New Mexico is begging for new books to publish. There is real money that can be made with publishable research, far more than the formal reward given by the Southwestern Historical Society. Fourth, you should be able to compare and contrast the conditions then and now and lastly, it has to be unique."

Corey and Hidalgo now knew all they needed to know and desperately wanted to escape the formal dinner. As soon as the speaker was through making the announcement for this year's contest, they excused themselves and left. They almost ran to the parking lot, untying the ties that had been so carefully tied around their necks by June and Ken. But they experienced a feeling of satisfaction while waiting for Ken and us women to slowly make our way out. The game was on.

Unfinished Business

We had unfinished business to take care of. I spent several days painting an oil painting of the apparition in the form of a pictograph that Hidalgo had encountered at Chinle Wash on the San Juan River. Hidalgo remembered every detail which I patiently painted onto the canvas fabric under his direction. It had appeared to Hidalgo as a coyote looking animal with thin grey fur. It was almost cartoonish, like the coyote in the roadrunner cartoons, but scary. Standing there on its rear paws, somewhat in a boxing position, the face appeared alien in shape; distinctly canine but with huge oversize eyes that glowed red. Its ears were very long and sharp with black tips. It was the first time in his life that Hidalgo's mind appeared to play a trick on him. On that river trip, the following day when he and Corey had hiked back to reinvestigate it, all traces of the apparition had disappeared.

Hidalgo was still profoundly bothered by it. He had been mulling the apparition over in his mind for months now, but he was at a loss as to what it was but helping recreate the apparition was therapeutic to him, even soothing. He had control over the image, not the other way around.

After the paint was dry, we took several photographs of it followed by day trips journeying to Albuquerque, visiting museums, the university and public libraries in an attempt to discover what the image was of. But to no avail, after looking through hundreds of books and asking as many people as we could, we could not find a single match or anyone who had seen anything like it. They had given up, thinking that the only other option was to go to Shiprock and ask some of Hidalgo's old friends. They dreaded that trip because Navajos don't like to talk about such things as skin walkers. Besides, once they broached the subject, news of it would spread out across the reservation like an epidemic. Gossip traveled like fire on the reservation and the idea of skin walkers could cause more damage than the actual animals. But first, they would have to return to Serpiente for a few days. Stopping at the Blake's on Isleta Boulevard for hamburgers on the way back, Corey got into a conversation with one of the young Hispanic girls who took their order. After a few moments of conversation, while waiting for the food to be cooked, he returned to the Jeep. Pulling the picture of the painting out of the glove compartment and returning to the order counter, he showed it to the young lady. This strange action brought me and Hidalgo out of the car to investigate what Corey was up to. The young lady instantly recognized what it was.

"It is a *chupacabra*, I saw one while growing up in Puerto Rico years ago. Well, I was only eight years old but that is exactly what I saw. It occurred on my family's farm," explained the young Sylvia Vagara. She remembered that something was killing all the chickens and small farm animals, particularly the goats. The goats had been tied on a short leash in order to clear weeds from the land. They were found dead with the blood drained out of them. That is why they call the attacker a *chupacabra* or goat sucker. They seem to relish blood from animals, and of course, what worried many Puerto Ricans was, did they have a taste for human blood?

"When you shine a light on a chupacabra, their eyes reflect back blood red and they flee. They seem to avoid the light and are never seen at all during the day. They are dangerous yet a mystery to modern science. Most people, including scientist, do not believe they exist but I saw one, well, really it was an accident. My grandparents found several dead animals and everyone went looking in the forest for the culprit. My mother sent me out to see if the pigs were still locked in their pen. I then noticed the creature. It had been hiding behind the family house all along. It ran, very quickly but then it managed to trap itself in a corner of an open pen. It stopped, turned around and looked at me then leaped straight up over the pen wire. I watched it clear the wire in a simple bound and it instantly disappeared into the jungle."

I was spellbound by the young lady's forthright story and asked her, "Do they really drink blood?"

"Well yes, they seem to kill the animals, then lap up the blood. We would always find puncture wounds on the animals. The *chupacabra* kills differently than you would expect to find from a dog. Dogs tear up the bodies. The animals killed by the *chupacabra* have not been torn up, but their blood is always drained."

Hidalgo, who was listening to her politely, then said to her, "There is no such thing as a *chupacabra*, they are nothing but dogs, *perros*."

Sylvia answered him, "They may have been dogs at one time, but they are not dogs now. It was no ordinary animal, I recognized that immediately. It was different from any dog I have ever seen."

Their order arrived and the waitress had other customer's to attend to. Hidalgo and I thanked her; Corey thanked her and shook her hand, leaving a twenty dollar tip in it.

They drove down Isleta Boulevard toward the ranch house after wolfing down their hamburgers, discussing what they had learned from the young girl." All I know is that painting of Penny's, shows what I saw." Hidalgo muttered as they drove past the swampland next to the Rio Grande River before getting into Los Lunas. He was having an argument with himself. He had seen what he had seen. He certainly believed the girl had really recognized the creature, but he couldn't understand why his apparition had been a *chupacabra*. Something he had never heard of. He had never seen anything like it, and couldn't understand why a *chupacabra*, considered by most as a folklore item even in Puerto Rico, would be the image he saw on the canyon walls at Chinle Wash. He had guessed that skin walkers couldn't or wouldn't leave the four corners area but what was the connection between *chupacabras* and skin walkers? But then he thought of the other name for them, namely shape shifters. Perhaps they really could change their shape at will. Confusion would be the best description of what was going on inside of Hidalgo's mind. Even if there were such an animal, he didn't understand its significance in his personal apparition. Why him?

A Return to Zuni

After June took a photograph of Penny's painting she announced to everyone at the dinner table that she wanted to return to Zuni and ask the shaman some more questions after showing him the photograph. Over scalloped potatoes and ham the family sat around and discussed the trip. June felt that by confronting the shaman with a photograph he might be willing to share more information but this time she asked Corey if he would like to go with her.

"It is a long drive over there and I get tired of the driving. I could use some help. Besides, the shaman seemed to know Corey. After all, Corey has spent some time at the pueblo, perhaps the shaman remembered him from the time he did construction work there. I suspect that Corey may be helpful."

With that said, early the next morning Corey and June loaded camping supplies into the back of his truck which still had a camper shell on it that June could sleep under. Corey took his standard sleeping gear; a tent, and sleeping bag with pads. He also threw in his river running cooking gear. He and June wanted to be prepared for anything.

After driving most of the day they pulled over to camp thirty miles east of Zuni at El Morro National Monument. The ruins of Atsinna, a thirteenth century Zuni village built like a small fortress, are perched near the rim of El Morro Mesa.

Below, on the sheer bluff, is Inscription Rock, bearing the names and comments of conquistadores, explorers, cowboys and settlers, and many others known only by their signatures. It was an ancient camping spot.

At the base of the bluff is also a large pool that collects runoff water from the mesa. It became traditional, while stopping to take on water at the pool for visitors to inscribe one's name, the date, and sometimes comments on the rock. Covering over two centuries of inscriptions, it reminded them of another place; a secret place, known to only a handful of people, discovered by Corey and me deep in the canyons of Serpiente. The one major difference was at Serpiente there were no Spanish inscriptions, just American Indian pictographs along with one strange inscription that appeared to be early Phoenician. The mystery of that inscription was still to be solved.

The following day they gassed the truck up and had breakfast in Ramah then they traveled on to Zuni. Once there, June wondered around the pueblo rekindling friendships with families she had known for years. Corey did not recognize anyone there but many recognized him. By noon, June had exhausted her supply of friends and they headed the ten miles south to the shaman's home.

With some difficulty they found the traces of the turnoff. It looked like no one had been down it in years yet it obviously was the same tiny road that meandered through the trees that she had been down before. More of a wagon trail than a trail for automobiles, the faint tire grooves were overgrown with weeds, in places hiding them completely, but there was only one way through the small pinions and juniper trees. Their anticipation was growing, but as soon as they came into sight of the house they were taken aback.

The house was not a house but a ruin, not unlike thousands June had seen during her tenure as a working archeologist. With the exception of where a fireplace had once been and where it abutted up against the sandstone bluff, the walls were only two or three feet high. With sheep and mice scat scattered all over the floor it appeared to have not been occupied for several hundred years.

"Are you sure this is the place," asked a totally mystified Corey?

"Sure I am," answered June, "I just can't believe my eyes; I have never..."
Corey finished her sentence with, "Neither could Hidalgo up on Chinle Wash."

They looked at each other feeling the hair on the back of their necks beginning to rise. Finally June slowly said, "But it has the exact same layout. Over there is where the old man laid in his bed, close to the hearth, and over there is where we sat and ate sandwiches."

Corey walked about a mile up one side of the bluff finding nothing and down the other way about a quarter of a mile before he ran out of bluff, looking to find anywhere a house could be hid, but he soon returned without finding a trace of a house. Undoubtedly, the old ruin had to be the correct place.

They returned to the pueblo with the obvious questions but no one there had any idea what she was talking about. They knew there was some old ruins there but had never known of anyone living out there other than an occasional sheep herder. The young boy as well as the shaman was as mysterious to the people of Zuni as to June. They returned to Serpiente with more questions than answers.

Journada de Muerto

After our river trip down the San Juan the credulous might think that we would want to avoid rivers, but just the opposite occurred. Sometimes a myriad of scenarios present themselves in the engineering of an adventure, but adventures have so many prerequisites and realities all requiring hard labor. Hidalgo, Corey and I had all developed a fascination for exploring rivers, and now we had to juggle the responsibilities of working long days at the ranch and helping June with her historical research in the evenings. After much begging and borrowing, June had accumulated many books relating to New Mexico history. We would take turns reading them to educate ourselves and of course, we hoped to accumulate possible ideas and leads for our research. We knew we had to come up with an idea fast.

We each had our own personal interest such as our extended families. Corey had relatives in Albuquerque, I had relatives in Texas and East Tennessee, and Hidalgo's mother and father were living on the Navajo reservation. At times like these my other hobbies such as art and writing have suffered. Not from a lack of interest but rather a lack of time and energy.

We were intrigued by river running and found ourselves talking about a way to sneak away and actually run a new river. During our breaks we found ourselves devising diabolical plots not unlike those all good river runners immerse themselves into as an ever accumulating pile of river guide books piled up in a cardboard box. I guess it is a trait exhibited by all souls who allow themselves to be immersed in the creative art of river running.

After June and Corey returned to the ranch, the next few days we talked constantly about such things as skin walkers and *chupacabras* until the subject finally exhausted itself. Within a few days our lives had moved on. The problem we were dealing with was the historical society's challenge. It was important to June, therefore it was important to all of us. The previous year we had not set out to win the prestigious award, we literally stumbled into it. This year, we wanted to compete for it which meant we had to spend long days running the ranch and evenings doing academic research.

We were being pressured to reinvent ourselves again putting our hard learned skills together and working in a whole new direction. The problem was we were still interested in exploring the southwest by running its rivers. Rather than looking at towns and cities that after a while all begin to look alike, we wanted to explore the southwest the way it was before the floods of people who entered the area. Exploring rivers was the closest to the real west we could get; besides it was truly an adventure, a challenge, and downright fun. We just wanted to deal with challenges we had control over rather than the supernatural, which we had no control over.

June decided it was time to explore a personal mystery. "I don't understand; why do you kids want to explore rivers? What exactly is the allure of running rivers?"

Hidalgo began an answer with, "It is the lazy person's way of exploring the country."

"Lazy?" I countered, "I never worked so hard in my life, but I have to admit, it is a work that I truly love to do. I love an adventure, and with these guys, somehow even a short trip turns out to be an adventure."

Corey says, "Let's face it, we love an adventure and river trips are always an adventure. Besides we are learning new personal habits, we absolutely depend upon each other, yet we learn self-dependency. If you lose something or forget to pack something, you learn to do without."

"That may be true," replied June, "but we need to run this ranch right now, besides we also need to solve the historical society problem right now. We don't have time to play. Besides, you kids always seem to get into trouble when you run rivers. Between the skin walkers and the *chupracabras*, I am worn a little thin."

This time it was Ken who came to our defense, "Rivers are the veins through which the lifeblood of this continent flows. They were the routes that all ancient people traveled, not only for water but for food and shelter."

"Well, that's true, answered June, "however we still have immediate problems to solve, the running of this ranch and the historical society challenge."

For a few days we were worlds apart, thinking of other places, times, and events while all the time spending long hours every day working the ranch. But our thoughts often involved the beauty and complexities of the moving water of rivers. The trial and error method of learning an art like river running could be fatal. You only drown once. All river runners, as a basic requirement of the art, learn that the quickest way to master the art of river running is through the experiences of others.

For many runners, money is often the bottom line, requiring creative thinking and resulting in research hopefully generating and contributing to the general knowledge pool. Fortunately for us river runners, we really didn't care, expenses were irrelevant. We knew we could draw upon the financial resources we had accumulated and banked at Serpiente, but preferred not to. It was great insurance but only if things turned bad. We were by nature, frugal, besides we discovered that the only real expense, after we acquired our basic equipment and food was the cost incurred while traveling to and from the river they were exploring.

Late one day, everyone was relaxing while June and I prepared dinner. I asked everyone what seemed, to me, an innocent question; "Who was the first person who actually used canoes in New Mexico?" No one had the faintest idea except for Aunt June. In her studies as an undergraduate student of archeology she had read just about everything possible regarding New Mexico history. She knew of only one river in New Mexico where canoe use had been documented; the Canadian River located in extreme northeastern New Mexico. In its primal state the Canadian River was actually floated in canoes from parties who were coming and going from what would become Texas and Oklahoma. The river served as a natural route for American Indians who paddled from as far away as Arkansas up to where Conchas Lake is today. From there on up are rapids on the main river which would have been avoided by the Indians. The Indians left their canoes at the confluence of Conchas River and the Canadian River then by following the Conchas River they could find their way into central New Mexico. Given enough water they may have dragged their canoes up the tiny Conchas River. After they did their trading they would float or carry their goods back to the confluence, and ride the Canadian as far to the east as they pleased.

The tiny Conchas River flows through present day Las Vegas, New Mexico from its headwaters high in the Sangre de Cristo Mountains. Suddenly we were intrigued over the idea of running the Canadian River but we still had no idea how to spin it into a historical research project.

Immediately I began to research the practicality of running the Canadian river but quickly discovered that the river of old was simply not the same river as today. Today, only a few sections of the Canadian are run by river runners and then only on high water years. Most of the water that usually runs down the river is now impounded behind dams leaving only certain sections available for the white water enthusiast. Most river runners that we talked to avoided it. Unlike rivers like the Chama, the San Juan, and many other scenic rivers the Canadian is simply too remote and dangerous.

Many of those dangers had nothing to do with the actual river. There were many practical problems that would need to be solved. There are few places where the river and roads cross. Working with a support vehicle would be difficult. They were faced with survival questions, basic questions, such as; 'Is it possible to carry that much food, can we eat the local cacti, fried rattlesnake, rabbit, or perhaps fried grasshoppers served on rice.' If they decided to run that river, deprivation would be the norm. Hidalgo and Corey seriously doubted whether or not I would be up to the job, but I had other ideas. Besides, there were other rivers, particularly in Colorado and Utah which would be more likely great candidates to run but not particularly suited for our historical research involving a New Mexico. Not so secretly, I was investigating the possibility of doing research that involved actually floating down a New Mexico river rather than spending long days searching through dusty history books.

After several days of pondering and research, no one had come up with an idea for historical research, much less one that involved rivers that a person in a canoe could float. So far their best bet was the Rio Grande which flowed alongside the *Journada de Muerto*; the journey of death. Surely they could uncover a story there but unfortunately there were few places to run the river until one gets all the way down to the southern end of the state.

Then after several days June remembered and traced down a footnote she had read years ago in *"A History of Arizona and New Mexico* by Hubert Howe Bancroft,*"* The book was first published in 1889 making it an historical item in itself. In that footnote it was stated that Robert Mc Knight held the honor of being the earliest person documented to use a canoe in New Mexico. His story was dramatic and a likely subject for our research. We could retrace and tell the story of Robert Mc Knight's route up the Canadian River. He was captured by the Spanish and sent in a cart all the way to Chihuahua Mexico where he was dumped into a Mexican jail. After two years he and a friend escaped from the Mexican jail and returned to the Canadian River where he left the state altogether. Everyone would contribute to the writing of the document but Aunt June would be the one who would edit the final manuscript. June had already written several manuscripts and had acquired a world of knowledge about writing for publication. Indeed, as she looked into the oven to see if the rolls were ready, she was already organizing the Robert Mc Knight story in her mind.

Providence

*P*rovidence, that foreseeing care and guardianship of God over His creatures, the same providence which sends snow in the winter and then allows a hot, spring sun to create rivers which cascade down the continental divide carrying life giving fluids to all creatures dependent upon it for survival, including river runners. But earlier river runners have been indulging on the free ride as far as the Mississippi River, for thousands of years. An ancient route, it has only been recently that Europeans from the east have wanted to travel this route, to reverse this travel pattern, venturing up the river and back into the southwest, then returning back to civilization, all for a profit.

For newcomers venturing into the southwest, a long and arduous journey up the river was required. Fortunately, a fast retreat was possible with the river flooding on good snowmelt years providing several weeks where a party could ride the flood of river water in a possible escape route back to civilization.

Because humans, as well as pack animals, require water and food in enormous quantities, which can be found in predictable distances between camps, the ancestral rivers of the desert southwest were the natural routes that all ancient and historical travelers used. We figured that a journey down the river would take us to the same campsites used by travelers from across the centuries. Perhaps traces of earlier travelers could be found. People do have a way of writing their names on surfaces so they can say, I was here.

On the trails between rivers, deprivation was the norm, but there were exceptional locations where there was fresh water, along with raw materials for shelter and easy access that would eventually become centers of trade, perhaps becoming permanent settlements. These communities now provide place names on maps such as Taos, Santa Fe, and Pecos.

Pecos Pueblo was a focal point of trade in the distant past with maps showing easy access to the Rio Grande River system flowing south into Mexico or northwest into the San Juan's. The namesake Pecos River meanders southeast into Texas; and the Canadian River to the Northeast was the natural gateway to the eastern plains. Yet due to many reasons, Pecos Pueblo as well as many other pueblos were becoming ruins even as the first great Spanish *Entradas* were occurring. After smallpox hit the pueblo it was abandoned. Providence may provide the necessities of life, but there are no guaranties in this constantly changing world.

Depravation can provide the keenest and sometimes the cruelest of memories, like inalienable rights and family, belonging exclusively to the psychic of the individual. They are vivid, particularly when experienced by the overindulged, pampered, and civilized. People like us. We have all become accustomed to the material subtleties in life and are hopelessly spoiled. We like it that way but what would our life be like if a dramatic event occurred such as becoming hopelessly separated from our canoe?

What would you miss the most? Perhaps dry clothes and a warming blanket, that morning coffee with a cinnamon roll or bacon and eggs with cereal on the side. With no way to make a fire, even if you found scraps of food say a bag of rice, cooking would be imposable. It would be a bad hair day. Deprivation creates a situation, which challenges the human spirit, and we are forced to become problem solving creatures, driven to return to a civilization and a cup of hot coffee. But for those who came before us, there was no such thing as a return. They themselves were in their own minds the essence of civilization conquering a barbarian land. They carried with them, on horses, mules or in a canoe everything they needed for survival. A fragile environment lay before them and in time their descendants would be amazed at the changes that would occur in this vast land. Those changes would indeed be dramatic.

Spanish Explorations

Pride was the namesake of the Spanish Empire during the days of the conquistadores in New Mexico. They were proud to have conquered a new world which had made the Spanish Empire the envy of all other peoples of the time. They could afford to be arrogant and prideful; they deserved it, conquering a continent of millions with only a handful of very brave men.

It was true that they had better weapons, and of course horses which made them extremely mobile and then there is the matter of all the biological weapons they brought with them knowingly or not. Many modern people tend to stereotype the Ancient Spanish as a cruel people but all one has to do is consider the age in which they came to power. Nations were determined to acquire gold which was the monetary standard of the day. Any nation that could acquire gold also acquired immense military power. Gold paid the soldiers to expand the Kings influence which usually resulted in conquering and occupying new lands occupied by non-believers or just plain heathens who was anyone who was not a Castilian Spaniard.

During the golden age of Spanish exploration, all nations that supported an army were considered cruel. They had to be cruel in order to survive. Slavery was a way of life throughout the world and was considered an institution that would never end. It wasn't so much a consideration of skin color but rather an economic issue, much as it is today. In Africa one tribe raided another tribe for slaves just as in America; one native tribe would enslave members of a conquered tribe as a way of life. Often small children were kidnapped and raised as members of the conquering tribe. All this was considered quite normal so when the Spanish conquered the Southwestern Tribes it was considered quite normal for them to enslave the conquered people. Cruelty, like beauty was in the eye of the beholder. Land acquisition and territory was similarly conducted by the nation with the biggest and fiercest army which was Spain.

Providence has provided scraps of history in the form of documents surviving the centuries to weave a story which eventually ends along the banks of the Canadian River. June's manuscript recounted the story. Because Spain managed to explore and then conquer the New World before other nations such as France or England, they were able to steal the gold and precious gems of the great Indian civilizations, and would become a world power with many of their citizens becoming relatively rich.

As treasure ships crossed the oceans, Mexico City, became capital of the Vice-royalty of New Spain. Prosperity continued, but in time the easy pickings had already occurred and pressure was placed on the Spanish government in New Spain to find more gold in order to finance their constantly ongoing wars. They began to consider persistent rumors of gold and legends of great Indian civilizations. These rumors caused the first Europeans to explore the northern unknown fringes of the New World, into New Mexico and eventually into the Canadian River canyon lands.

In the spring of 1536, four ragged travelers, Alvar Nunez Cabeza de Vaca, Alonzo de Castillo Maldonado, Andres Dorantes and his Moorish slave Estevan, arrived at the city of Calican, Mexico, the sole survivors of the Narvaez expedition. After their shipwreck near present day Galveston, Texas in 1528, they found themselves washed up on the shore of an alien sea, without water, food or weapons. Cold, desperate and starving within days and without the intervention of the native Indians all would have surely perished.

The Indians themselves were desperately poor when viewed through the filter of Spanish ethnocentrism. They had no knowledge of gold, its uses, or why the Spanish had such an interest in such a worthless metal, useful only for ornamentation. The

Indians, however, lived very well, at least through the filter of their own ethnocentrism.

The Indians did attempt to cooperate with the Spanish, orating stories about golden cities a long distance to the north. They kept the Spaniards alive long enough for them to regain their health, then with a probable sigh of relief, allowed them to escape making their way by foot from the Gulf of Mexico though western Texas, to northern Mexico. Along the way, the Spaniards heard tales from other local Indians of great riches to be found in the 'Seven Cities of Cibola,' inhabited by highly civilized tribes to the north. After a long and arduous hike around the Gulf of Mexico they finally discovered a route and made their way to Mexico City, capital of the Viceroyalty of New Spain. There, they were rewarded for telling their stores to Viceroy Antonio de Mendoza who became enthusiastic about the possibility of adding further wealth and fame to his own position.

Mendoza was unwilling to risk a large expedition to the north without further confirmation, and in 1539 the Franciscan friar, Marcos de Niza, led a reconnaissance party from Culiacan, with Estevan as guide, northward through present day Arizona. The advance party of Estevan entered the village of Hawikuh, discovering the agricultural villages of the Zuni Pueblo Indians. Estevan managed to get himself killed, after forcing himself upon as many village girls as he could. Several of his party managed to escape the skirmish and carried a description of the disaster to Marcos de Niza who made a fast retreat back to Mexico City.

Attempting to turn defeat into partial victory, the Franciscan told even more extravagant stories about possible wealth to the north. Along came the aristocratic young Franciso Vasques de Coronado, governor of Neva Galicia, along with 300 soldiers and 800 Indians from Compostela who traveled to Hawikuh in 1540. Again, the agricultural communities of Hawikuh had no intention of submitting to invaders and attacked them, killing several soldiers and wounding Coronado before the superior arms of the Spanish defeated and subdued the natives.

After capturing the Zuni villages, Coronado sent out various expeditions. Garcia Lopez de Cardennas went west to discover the Grand Canyon. Pedro de Tovar found the seven villages of the Hopis who also resisted, and like the Zuni continued to resist throughout the Spanish period as well as into the present. The Spanish made significant discoveries but found only traces of gold.

After visiting other pueblos of the Rio Grande valley as far north as Taos, they wintered at *Tiquex* just north of present day Albuquerque. It was a hard winter. When food and supplies ran short, the Spanish took what they wanted from the thus far friendly Indians who rebelled. After a siege of seven weeks, the natives were defeated and despite their earlier generosity, found their homes and stores looted. Bitterness towards the intruders remained high because all invading armies have a tendency to take advantage of the indigenous peoples, namely lovely young girls.

Castaneda, a scribe of Coronado provided the first documentation of the Canadian River reaching it at high water and calling it Rio Colorado, which it was to be known as for over two hundred years. In doing so, Castaneda made a place for himself in history.

In the spring of 1541 Coronado and his men marched to Pecos, where they enlisted the help of a guide, the Indian El Turco. They spent an exhausting seventy seven days in search of gold marching into what they coined as *Liano Estacando*, or the Staked Plains, in search of a golden place called *Quivira*.

Many rivers in the southwest maintained the name of Rio Colorado. After rain all rivers in the southwest run blood red and many carried the name of Rio Colorado on historic documents. However the use of that name eventually disappeared for this river to another historic river in another state. Since his journeys took him into western Kansas it can be safely assumed that somewhere in the eastern plains of New Mexico, Coronado and his entourage crossed the Canadian river. Exactly where is of debate but the natural place, that first natural crossing where generations of Indians had crossed before, would have been Stony Forde near present day Taylor Springs. From Stony Forde they could have wondered anywhere until they realized the wild goose chase they were on. Some historians insist that Coronado may have turned southeast at Pecos then overland to Gallinas and again overland to the Conchas on the Canadian River, a natural conduit into Texas. No one really knows what route he took. Along the way they became convinced that their guide, El Turco had lured them there to massacre them and the Spaniards killed their guide.

Nature may have provided the explorers' the impetus to return. Somewhere beyond eastern New Mexico, Coronado was set back profoundly, by a baseball size hailstone storm. Inclement weather can cause an extremely dynamic situation in the cap rock country. Tornadoes are common, but evening thunderstorms with lightning storms can make anyone a believer. The winds that accompany them arise suddenly, sometimes with only a moment to recognize the impending wind and tie everything down. It may have been one time the solders, explorers, and priest that accompanied Coronado were glad to have worn the ungainly armor of the time. Lesser hailstorms have left jagged holes in modern trailer houses and automobiles which appear like someone has taken a sledgehammer to them. Many side canyons form a labyrinth of cliffs and badlands that dissect the Cap Rock country. One can only imagine Coronado's march through the tableland country, but it is certain to have been a perplexing experience for him.

The explorers finally returned to *Tiquex*, where the situation deteriorated still further, and Coronado retreated to Mexico in April 1542, leaving behind the Franciscan Juan de Padilla and two lay brothers whom the Indians immediately killed. What happened to the search for *Quivira*? It has yet to be found. Perhaps someday a fragment of history will be discovered lying in the sand along the great riparian waterway of the Canadian or some other southwestern river to tell us more of that early mystery.

What is in a Name?

Current maps of this area bear names that have come down from early settlements and geographic discoveries. But the Canadian River, which is not a Canadian River, is somewhat a nomenclature mystery. Why would a river starting in Southern Colorado and finally combining its waters with the Arkansas River in eastern Oklahoma be called the Canadian? The answer to this question is open to speculation with several theories abounding.

Lieutenant James W. Abert of the Topographical Engineers, US Army, who was commissioned to explore the river in 1845, wrote one of the first documents to have provided a name for this river. The Kiowa's and Comanche's had run off most of the indigenous Apache natives who called the river *Goo All Pah*; the stream that headwaters in the high cliffs of Raton Pass. Abert's perilous journey was part of the Western expansion policy of the U.S. Government. Having been dispatched from Fort Bent to the north on August 9 they traveled south through Raton Pass reaching the Canadian River by September. They were documenting everything they saw, or in other words spying for the Army, in a very hostile country. They made every effort to avoid contact with Indians who had gotten very good at defending themselves from the newcomers. By incorporating the horse into their own culture that the Spanish had brought in, they had become a force into themselves. *Comancheros* as well as the Spaniards all considered the real threat to the territory to be Anglos from Texas who were considered as barbarians by all.

Abert was traveling though country that was claimed by many yet despite his stealthy intentions they managed, while preparing an evening meal at a campsite, to set the local countryside aflame. A huge inferno of a fire, the kind that burns thousands of acres of tumbleweeds and sends up a plume of smoke well into the stratosphere occurred. Everyone would undoubtedly see it but evidently nobody cared, for he and his men survived the ordeal and eventually traveled all the way back into Texas.

To Abert's credit it should be noted that he was a fine artist who meticulously recorded the appearance and activities of the friendly Indian tribes he met as well as detailed topographic maps of the *Goo All Pah* River showing the distances covered and campsites. In 1845, Abert later published his work including trail maps as *"Through the Country of Comanche Indians."* Why he used this name rather than the Spanish Rio Colorado is a little bit of a mystery. This earlier name has since disappeared from all documentation.

Many French explorers came to this area as early as 1719 such as Bernard De La Harpein who was searching for a water route to the Pacific Ocean. They were invariably discovered by the Spanish authorities and ordered out because Spain and France were at war at that time. The name Canadian may be traced back to those French Canadians, the Mallet brothers, who visited Santa Fe in 1739. They later returned east by traveling down the Canadian. Did the circumstances for this visit lead to the name of Canadian?

According to some historians, such as the late T. M. Pearce, an authority on New Mexican place names, thought that 'Canadian' might have resulted from the Anglicizing of Indian words for the river. Many of the Spanish-speaking people of the area refer to the Spanish term *Canada*, alluding to the great canyon that opens below the Stony Ford.

Pike

*I*n the last years of Spanish rule in New Mexico, there was always a governor or acting governor in New Mexico, subordinate to the commandant general of the Provincias. Governor Chacon ruled until the spring of 1805, when he was succeeded by Colonel Josquin del Real Alencaster. Alberto Mainez was named as acting governor in 1807-8, and next on the list is lieutenant-colonel Jose Manrique, whom ruled from 1810-14. Melgares was the last governor under Spain, and was succeeded on July 5,

1822, by Francisco Javier Chavez a politico who ruled New Mexico in 1822 for a year. This constant change of leadership reflected the political situation of the day caused by internal squabbling brought on by petty jealousy between the powers to be. In some instances a promotion to governor of the territory was viewed more as a prison sentence than an honor in a land that was cruel to those who attempted to rule, as well as the people that were ruled. The differences between the Spanish lifestyle and the natives, was enormous. The friendly natives were subjugated as slaves; the more warlike tribes lived relatively well.

Unlike the Spaniards, the Indians never used or took anything from nature that they didn't need. The iron handed governors who ruled New Mexico during these years drew their sustenance from those people, forcing them to live not only as slaves but far below the subsistence level they were accustomed to. They starved, even as the taxes owed the Spanish grew larger and larger. The Spanish however lived fairly well. It was the system of the times. Living well off the sweat and labor of another people who were demonized was a common custom in those times. In fact, it is what all aristocratic young people wanted, their own hacienda, with hundreds of peons to see after your most basic needs.

The ethnocentric Spaniards viewed the native religion, which had been practiced for thousands of years on this continent, as a purely pagan ritual. The native pueblo peoples were often baptized in the name of the holy church not understanding a single word of what was being said, but rather only trying to appease their cruel rulers. After the pueblo revolt of 1680 the Spaniards stamped out literally all religious as well as physical resistance. They tolerated no other point of view and considered themselves more than just conquerors of the land. They considered the native pueblo population as nothing more than property like so many sheep or cattle to be accounted for to the ruling masters.

Paradoxically the Spanish were friendly to the Comanche's at this intersection of history being zealous in bringing information and rumors respecting the movements of Americans, and in particular the barbarian Texans. In time, of course, the Comanche would change their collective opinions as they learned the ways of their Spanish conquerors. Adopting the technology brought to them, many of them became outlaws. Eventually, all the eastern plains Indians of New Mexico would make war upon the Old Spanish lineage causing perpetration's throughout the territory. The Navajos, in particular were hostile to the Spanish rulers, entrenching themselves in the Canon de Chelly, where they deemed their position impregnable. Among all individual tribes there were always those young bucks that could not allow submission by the conquering Spaniards.

Raids became a constant source of friction in the territory with the Canadian Canyon of northeastern New Mexico being one of the better hiding places for the hostile Indians. Between Louisiana and New Mexico there had been no trade or habitual communication before 1800, however from both directions flourishing trade with the friendlier Indians had grown up. All of the old Louisiana territory west of the Mississippi, was ceded by France to Spain in 1762-3 and later returned to France in 1800, and then sold or ceded to the United States in 1803. From this date to 1819 the question of boundary between the United States territory and Spanish possessions was an open one. Rivers that were used as conduits into the unexplored back country became the boundary and front lines between growing powers. The American politicians, without a shred of what would be called right but loaded with lots of bluster, brag and just plain pride, sometimes claimed all the territory to the Rio Grande, and the Spaniards, with but slightly better reasons, all the way to the Missouri. There is a lot of territory to fight over between these two rivers, and as for the upper and lower part of the map; that too was up to men willing to fight for it.

As Lewis and Clark were engaged in their famous exploration of the continent by way of the upper Mississippi, Zebulon Pike, a lieutenant of the sixth United States infantry, was sent by General James Wilkerson with less than two dozen men in 1806 to explore the country of the Red, as the Canadian River was then called. Pike was instructed to explore the upper reaches of the Arkansas and Red Rivers. Like himself, his entire trip was immediately shrouded in mystery and controversy. There apparently was a secret directive to investigate a route to Spanish settlements in Santa Fe. Why Wilkerson wanted Pike to travel into Spanish territory is a bit of a mystery; however there is strong evidence that the general was involved in a conspiracy with former U.S. vice president Aaron Burr to separate the West from the rest of the United States. Whether Pike had a role in this conspiracy is not clear. Even more mysterious, there is belief that Wilkerson betrayed Pike by warning the Spanish authorities that he would be traveling in their territory. If this was true, he had to have planned it months in advance in order to notify the Spanish. All this had to be done well in advance of Pike's actual departure. Perhaps they were all spies.

Pike left St. Louis in July 1806 with 23 men, including Wilkerson's son, who was an Army lieutenant, and one of Wilkerson's agents, Dr. John Robinson. They followed a route up the Missouri and Osage rivers in central Missouri to the Arkansas River. When Pike's party reached the Arkansas River, Lieutenant Wilkerson returned to St. Louis with six of the men to report on the progress of the expedition.

Pike and the remainder of the party crossed to the foothills of the Rocky Mountains in mid-November. A week later they arrived at the site of present-day Pueblo,

Colorado; from there, Pike and three of his companions set out to climb the mountain that was later named Pikes Peak. Although unsuccessful in reaching the top they did climb Cheyenne Peak, a smaller mountain about 15 miles away. After rejoining his men, Pike led the party up the Arkansas River to Royal Gorge, which is known as the 'Grand Canyon' of the Arkansas River.

They then spent several cold months wondering around lost in what is now southern Colorado. By now, several of the men were ill, so Pike built a small fort near the Gorge for those who were too sick to continue on the journey. Pike left the fort in January 1807 with Dr. Robinson and 12 others and, in the middle of the winter, they crossed the Sangre de Cristo Mountains into southern, Colorado. Six men got gangrene from walking through the snow, two so badly that their feet had to be amputated. Pike finally decided to stop after he found the Conejos River. The assumption was; that he was at the headwaters of the Red River near present day Mannasas, Colorado. Now starving, his men constructed a fort and raised the stars and stripes. The fort was a star shaped pole structure with redoubts at the points of the star. Made from the local cottonwoods, any attacker attempting to climb over a wall would need to turn his back on his intended victims, not a good idea.

As soon as the fort was constructed, Dr. Robinson suddenly left alone for Santa Fe, claiming to have business. Perhaps this should have raised some red flags, or who knows, maybe they simply wanted to be rescued, considering their deplorable state. A few days after the fort was completed, a Spanish dragoon arrived to be followed later by a force of 50 dragoons and militia charging Pike and his men for illegal entry into a Spanish territory. Pike resisted, saying that he thought he was on a branch of the Red River that formed a boundary between American and Spanish territories. Pike, upon the realization that indeed, his encampment was deep into Spanish territory where it had been occupied by the Spanish for two centuries, decided to lower the American flag. Historians believe that during this time representatives of different countries were conducting conspiracies unknown to each other or even the country they represented. There is, however, general agreement among scholars that Pike knew exactly where he was and he was simply putting on a show for the Spanish authorities.

Not so curiously, the Spanish were most courteous and kind to Pike's men, supplying the half-starved and half naked explorers with food and blankets. Perhaps the irony of the situation allowed the Spaniards to feel generous and superior or as many believe there was political intrigue on both sides. Pike's party of men was escorted, to Santa Fe where they were indeed treated kindly by the Spaniards. It was never quite clear to any of the Anglo-Saxon blood that a Spanish official might rightfully interfere with his personal freedom to do as he pleased. Yet Pike frankly admits to the kindness with which the Spaniards treated him and his men.

Brimming with confidence, Pike and his men proceeded on March 4th, after a dinner given by the governor in their honor to continue their explorations to Chihuahua, Mexico. The journey turned into a diplomatic venture and the Spanish were astonished at the sight of the barbarian newcomers. A Captain Antonio Almansa commanded the escort and with a short stay over at what was to be Sabinal they continued their journey south. The Spaniards were disappointed, according to their records, that they could not make a Christian of Pike. Pike's party, nevertheless were treated like royalty. In fact, they were welcomed with a dance at Tome, New Mexico where the *Melgares*, the leader of the escort sent out an order for the handsomest girls of the region to be sent in for a fandango. Pike was impressed, if not entertained by the girls, which portrays clearly the degraded state of the Indian people. Many days and pretty Indian girls later, Pike with his men were finally escorted into Chihuahua. Later, upon his return to the American territory, he wrote an account of his explorations, which was published in 1810.

As soon as the newcomers returned to the eastern United States, the Spaniards had a problem on their hands. It was a matter of territorial defense, and national security. Like people anywhere, they worried about their livelihoods. They already were masters of their world but they were afraid of the changes that barbarians might bring.

Robert McKnight

Moved by Pike's account of the New Mexican territory, Robert McKnight with a party of nine men crossed the plains in 1812, crossing the Canadian at Stony Ford and arriving in Santa Fe expecting to be treated as Pike's men had upon their arrival. Feeling boisterous and exuberant as they thought of the profits and good times ahead, they entered Santa Fe where they were immediately arrested, their goods were confiscated, and they were put into chains. A few days later, they were loaded into carts, where they were held like cattle until they reached Chihuahua, Mexico.

After the long cart ride they were held as prisoners in the then as now infamous Chihuahua prison. It took them, on the average, several months until they acquired a command of the Spanish language. Lives in Mexican jails were hell for non- Hispanic inmates then, as it is now, and you are held for as long as possible, until all your resources are used up. The pecking order is clear; all Spanish as descended from the Conquistadores form the top of society, including those in jail. They buy and do anything, and they can arrange anything including your death if they so desire. Mexicans of questionable descent and Indians make up a middle class and lower classes, and a final desperate sub-human group exists; foreigners. Then, as they would smugly say, was the devil himself. Well below that last category are creatures held in utter disrespect, creatures to distain, creatures known as gringos or Americans. And then, there is that last group of individuals in particular, a subgroup of the Americans, the dreaded barbarians named Texans, whom everyone considered to be a rough, ungainly, and uneducable bunch.

Bribery is the system that works in jails now as it did then, and surely it took only a few short days until the McKnight party realized their plight, they had nothing. Two years of constant hunger and beatings passed along with daily heavy labor. Few would escape the work details, but fate provided a unique opportunity for escape.

It must have been providence that allowed the moon and the stars to shine at night when their feeble light could allow a desperate flight to freedom. Certainly it took an extraordinary set of circumstances for the opportunity to escape to occur. McKnight and another of his party escaped captivity by fleeing a work detail by means of hiding under piles of branches then traveling after dark. Always running through the cold night air and holing up and sleeping during the heat of the day, they desperately retraced their path out of Mexico crossing the Rio Grande somewhere near present day El Paso not unlike thousands of later counterparts who go through the same ritual in search of better pay along the United States and Mexico border.

Already emaciated and undoubtedly bruised and battered, it must have been an ordeal, staying just out of sight of other travelers on the already ancient trails of the *Journada del Muerto*. They most likely retraced the route along the east bank of the Rio Grande River, a route they would know. The ancestral Rio Grande was a much wilder and certainly more interesting river than we see now. Allowed to meander across the flood plain of the Rio Grande valley, it provided water for a large cottonwood forest, known as the Bosque. There are lots of cottontails, catfish, grubs, bugs and rattlesnakes there to eat. A basic problem they would have encountered was attempting to cook which would give their position away. Still, living off the land may have been a feast compared to what they were used to in the Mexican jail with every morsel eaten tasting great due to sensory deprivation. Leaving the desert, the pair may have crossed the river south of Socorro and continued north, stealing what they needed as they traveled.

McKnight may not have followed Coronado's footsteps, but they could have crossed trails anywhere. The most logical way of traveling would have been to cut across, as many say Coronado did, turning east at Bernalillo, then to Galisteo, and then to more water at Pecos Pueblo. Due east of Pecos is the Conchas River which eventually drops into the Canadian at present day Conchas Lake. From here down, the Canadian was run in canoes by many of the indigenous natives and is still navigable if they are releasing water from dams.

This is the first recorded incident of the use of canoes in New Mexico, but it is doubtful if that was the way things worked out for McKnight. They most likely were never aware of the lower shorter route. Without maps, and relying on memory, they likely returned to the exact spot they started from, namely Santa Fe. Surely they raided as they traveled, slowly accumulating survival objects and possibly weapons, a blanket, or bags to carry those objects in but it must have been tough to find victims to steal from. Everyone was desperate. It was a desperate land and desperate times. Upon arrival in the outskirts of Santa Fe they may have stolen and accumulated more foodstuffs; jerky, onions, chili, beans, flour and salt. They probably would steal many of the same foods a contemporary river runner would use; dehydrated foods and foods that last. From Santa Fe it would be a short walk to Pecos Pueblo, and on to Las Vegas.

The mystery is where did they return to the Canadian? The natural route, at Stony Forde is the route all had taken, since the time of Coronado. Returning the way they originally came, they could have followed the Santa Fe Trail back to Stony Forde and then overland on what would eventually become a wagon trail, but it is unlikely as they were in flat prairie county and easily spotted. Yet they had many options. There are many tiny streams in the area that become major rivers downstream. They all look alike. Leaving Santa Fe they could have followed a well-worn path to the obvious forks of the Pecos and Gallinas River to the south, which would have taken them back into Texas, or back to a Mexican Jail. They knew that they were being sought by the Spanish authorities, therefore they may have decided on a northerly route that would be less patrolled and would provide more cover.

Upriver and up trail further was another possible route for McKnight. At Las Vegas he could have turned east overland to find Sabinoso, an old Spanish settlement below the whitewater section of the Canadian River. There is also the Mora, Vermejo, and Ocate canyons crossing the Santa Fe Trail to the crossing at Stony Ford but again, unless there was a cache of goods including the canoes at a specific location after nine years, it is doubtful.

Because they were being pursued the most likely route they would have taken would have been to return to Stony Ford, followed by a hike down the Canadian Canyon. Once in the canyon they could easily hide in the same camps thousands of others had hid out in throughout the history of the area. After some 70 or so miles they would reach the confluence of the Conchos River. From there they would have known that eventually it would lead them to Texas and civilization, and provide them with water, shelter, and food all the way down. Canoes could be stolen in the Conchas area, from Indians.

What kind of a trip down the river they then faced, historical records do not record, but a river runner who retraces the route of Robert McKnight down the Canadian, may acquire a glimpse into the past.

The Holliday Home

Knowing that just because a map says that there is something there, at a specific location, doesn't mean that anything is there. Most river runners scout the route that they are going to take before getting on the river. Many state road maps have many historical sites located on them but there is nothing there now. An Indian ruin or a river crossing site does not mean anything if you show up, in your canoe, in dire need of something. The launch sites and take outs have to be planned out, well in advance of an actual attempt down this river or any river.

We needed to scout the Canadian River but June and Ken had no time for suffering through such an ordeal, however they did plan on making good shuttle bunnies when the actual river was run. It would be up to Corey and me to map out all the important meeting places. Hidalgo at the last minute decided he wanted to go along so we packed the Jeep with our usual compliment of camping gear and headed north.

The Canadian can be run in several individual sections, each with individual personalities. In an area of few people, vast distances and little industry with the exception of cattle, the upper Canadian River drains one of the most remote areas of New Mexico. The put in is just north of Raton and the young Canadian river generally follows past what is now interstate I-25 south until the Maxwell bridge where it takes off into the grasslands in an ever meandering and deepening canyon until take out, close to Stony Forde at Taylor Springs on Hwy 56. This section is rated class I – II; upgraded to class II because of the many fences, possible logjams, and the multitude of mandatory portages required. The river is in a shallow canyon, and normally requires two or three days to canoe, depending.

River runners know what happens to a river system that drains a huge region prone to fast snow melt and electrifying summer thunderstorms. Melt water from the nearby snow covered Sangre de Christo mountains trickle down many side canyons but principally the Canadian gains the waters of the Vermejo River, Ocata Creek and the Cimarron Rivers making the river, on a wet year, a force to be dealt with. The most popular section below Taylor Springs is the red wall canyon. Much more than a white water run, this section is remote and undeveloped allowing river runners to enter a world now rarely explored except by diehard river runners. On moderate snowmelt years the river is available for only a few short weeks, usually during the early spring.

The Canadian provides a major challenge to the river runner because of the logistics involved in its running being anybody's providence to get the opportunity to run it at all. Timing is the secret. Arrival on a wet year after heavy rains and the river runner can face a death defying Class V at flood stage. These seventy-five miles of the Canadian is normally rated Class III and IV. Arrive during a dry year, which is most years in New Mexico, and you face a long and frustrating hike, dragging your canoe down the river. Because of the length and remoteness of the trip, as well as rapids one should be prepared for any possibility. The secret is in finding the right water level. As for canoe parties, the Canadian Canyon is one of the toughest challenges in the southwest, but it has been done and under extreme circumstances.

The three of us stopped in Albuquerque at the Holliday home on Valley Road. Planning to make only a quick courtesy visit we thought we would stay there only a short time. But we also knew from long experience, that we could discover real tidbits of information, points of view that we hadn't even thought of. Things that can be learned from a relative are sometimes things that cannot be found in books. Alice was there, so was Richard as well as Helen, a cousin who was Alice's age.

Coffee as usual was served up but Hidalgo was the only one who really drank any. Being his relatives, Corey went through the customary rituals of asking how different people were, with Helen volunteering way too much information. Helen liked to talk, she was country folk, and the Holliday family was a large family to cover. An hour later with Hidalgo and Penny starting to get impatient Corey knew they needed to move on. When he finally got the chance after several attempts, he asked his relatives if they knew anything about the Canadian River. Thankfully, Helen assumed a confused look, slowly moved her head from left to right and then back. Richard grabbed at the chance to enter the conversation.

"We lived in Logan for a while, at Ute Lake on the Canadian River, before dad got sick and we had to move back to Albuquerque in order to be near the veterans' hospital," he said matter of fact. "Besides, when I was a kid in Boy Scouts it was there that, I earned my Fifty Mile patch."

Hidalgo didn't say anything, he simply poured himself another cup of coffee and Corey and I curled up together on the couch. Young lovers, we never missed a chance to be together and we all knew that we were going to be there for a while.

Richard's Exploration of the Canadian

Richard related a story of his first and only experience on the Canadian River. First impressions of rivers can dramatically differ from later impressions. His tender first personal impression of the Canadian River was nurtured while serving in a Scouting program, troop 76, headquartered in Albuquerque, New Mexico. He was the troop bugler, a position that allowed him a little prestige but definitely had its drawbacks. Being available by the clock at 6:00 AM for reveille, dinner calls, as well as assemblies, and taps at 9:00 PM sharp, the thing was he had to be available any time the scoutmaster wanted everyone's attention which was one of the drawbacks.

His job required an intimate knowledge of strange rituals such as learning to sleep with the bugle inside his sleeping bag on winter trips. Very cold mornings are hard on all brass players and then buglers must remember all the different calls, especially for formal ceremonies, when the honor and dignity of the troop is at stake. It was not an ideal position for a lazy kid such as me," said Richard, "In order to remember the bugle calls and therefore win the job of troop bugler, I was taught a fail-safe way to memorize those half dozen or so calls. The bugler simply sings a jingle in the mind, as played. Assembly, for example, could always be remembered by means of this simple song.

"There's a solder in the grass, with a bullet up his ass.

Take it out. Take it out, like a good, Girl Scout."

"Yes, the jingles were all just plain horrible, but they worked. The job also required other responsibilities such as taking the flags down in the evening or before frequent thunderstorms. Once, only seconds after I had taken the flags down, folding them, and taken a few steps toward the ranch house, lightning struck the center flag pole. The three pipe poles were cemented in fifty-five gallon barrels. Afterwards, when I awoke, I found myself among sections of pipe and two 55 gallon barrels full of concrete used to hold the sections of pipe that formed the flag poles. Some of the sections of pipe turned up well down the road and the third concreted barrel was found a hundred yards or so down the road where it finally rolled to a stop."

"We were typical kids, but we didn't think so." Despite the fact that most of the scouts came from lower and middle income families, many of them from the south valley, they felt that it was a distinct privilege to be a member of troop 76. Few of them actually owned scout uniforms. In comparison to other troops, even other scout troops from Albuquerque, their uniforms were always piece meal, made up of what their parents could find at yard sales.

"But we stood out in a crowd. Our bandanas were custom made, a square white cloth with a large red seven, with the tail of the seven curving around to form a six; troop seventy six. All other troops purchased standard scout bandanas that varied only by color to differentiate patrols. Our white bandanas, with the unique seventy six designs, allowed us to stand out with a fashion statement that clearly separated us from other scouts, but also clearly demonstrated that we were a cohesive unit. Perhaps, that is why we competed well against other troops, often winning games such as stealing the flag. There was a pride."

"The dues were ten cents a week, a fee many of the scouts were unable to pay, the rest of us often chipped in to help. Some, including me," continued Richard, "just keep a charge account and perpetually owed dues. By now, and with interest, I probably owe the Boy Scouts of America a small fortune."

"But it was all worth the investment. The troop spent a weekend camping trip out in the wild at least once a month, and the high point of the summer was spending one or two glorious weeks at the Canadian Canyon. Actually it was part of a ranch owned by the Wootens. Tenderfoots and new scouts spent one week but senior scouts could end up spending considerable time with a second week hiking down the Canadian Canyon."

"The Scoutmasters were very creative in creating a camp where we enjoyed some great recreation activities such as horseback riding, twenty-two and shotgun shooting, and dehorning and castrating cattle."

Richard's favorite activity was swimming in the Canadian River but it was an arduous ordeal just to get to the swimming hole. The scouts were transported in the back of pickup trucks singing the monotonous stanzas of 'hundreds of bottles of beer on the wall.' After, what was to them, a long and monotonous drive riding in the bed of a dusty pickup truck down two narrow ruts, and then unloading and hiking over to the edge of the Canadian Canyon they then hiked down a steep trail to the canyon floor where the troop seventy six swimming hole was. The entire canyon floor had been washed clean by floodwaters. The river, tiny at this time of year, had carved a very serpentine path through the solid rock bedrock of the canyon forming a narrow miniature inner canyon. It would be hard to turn a canoe around in it and with the water level just a few feet below the surrounding floor, it would be just low enough to make it hard for an upriver canoe or kayak to see the waterfall ahead, formed where the Canadian plummets over the broken edge of the rock escarpment. At high water you could easily be swept over the blind drop.

"After wading to the far side of the river above the waterfall, the scouts would climb down carved steps in the sheer sandstone, ancient carved steps, to get to the large swimming pool at the bottom. It was there that I had my first experience with crypto zoology. A scaly fin, which looked like an alligator hand, appeared in the water close, to a swimmer. As fast as it appeared, it disappeared, leaving only ripples. I would not swim in the pool the next few days," concluded Richard.

I asked Richard, "What do you mean a green hand came out of the water?"

Richard answered me, "Well, I don't know what it was. There shouldn't be anything like that in the river. Maybe it was just a turtle or something but at the time, it seemed very real to me, too big to be a turtle. You know, Scientists do find new animals in the world all the time."

I asked him, "So this swimming pool has a Loch Ness monster in it?

Richard looked at Hidalgo and said indignantly, "It was like an apparition, it appeared and then immediately disappeared. Hey, believe me I saw something."

Hidalgo smiled and reached over, putting his hand on Richard's shoulder, "If you only knew how much I understand that feeling." While looking at each other, everyone laughed a nervous laugh. Richard continued with one finger pointing at Hidalgo.

"You have to remember that the Canadian flows through the most wild and least populated part of the state. While on my first trip to the ranch as a Second

Class scout I was pretty good at target practice. One stormy evening there was severe weather, and the scoutmaster decided to have the entire troop come up and bunk out on the ranch house floor. Sometime during the early morning, someone managed to step on my glasses. Afterwards, at target practice I just aimed at the center of the blurs, but still managed to do a pretty good job. However, I had a basic problem with skeet shooting, I couldn't find the blur. They didn't let me loose with the shot gun, especially after a couple of really bad shots in which several other scouts complained when pellets landed around them. Instead it became time to spend a little time at kitchen patrol. The rest of my first encounter was spent stumbling around until we finally went home then several weeks later and I got a new pair of Buddy Halley looking glasses, but not by choice, it was an economic consideration."

"Horseback riding was a treat until they had to chase me down due to one of my boots getting caught in the stirrup. Spooky, if you are thrown, you die; no question about it. From memory, to this day I can name most of the parts of a saddle, earning me the Horseback Riding merit badge. But that same day, I learned another important lesson. I learned how not to out run the lead horse, a racehorse owned by one of the ranch hands. The horse was the cowboys pride and joy, his route to economic and marital success. He warned us all not to ever get in front of him. It would not pay to do anything that would have a bad effect upon the horse's success."

"Certainly I shouldn't have traumatized the horse. That was the only cardinal rule on the outing; stay behind the lead horse. Finally, after walking the horses for about an hour, we were going to gallop across a field. Despite my best efforts to slow him, my old plug outran the cowboy's race horse. Soon, as a punishment, I found myself jogging along after the other riders. Leading my horse and doing my best to look where I was stepping, control my breathing, and trying to keep up."

"It was a working ranch. Besides the regular duties of kitchen patrol, latrine, and doing laundry in the shallow seep, of course there was dehorning and castrating the calves. Watching one of those calves come over and eat some throw up left by a not so happy scout was gross. The calf was then dehorned and castrated losing its lunch. But then, there were other calves around."

"It only took a short period of time until the high point of the camp was humiliating each other. Volunteers enjoyed the rocky mountain oysters the cowboy life had to offer. Don't kid yourself, when forty kids are put together in wild country, sadistic tendencies emerge. We pretended to make war on ourselves. Someone eventually took a dump in my hat, I was almost proud to find it before I put the hat back on my head after dumping the contents out. Of course, someday later in life, I will find out who he was and he will fail as an adult, in both business and marriage."

"Okay," says Corey who was starting to get up, but Richard stopped him.

"Hang on, there is more to this story," everyone relaxed.

"There is a special patch that is offered in the scouting program that one can wear on the uniform along with all the other badges of honor that scouts work for. This one is unique and much more difficult than merit badges are to earn. You have to take a fifty-mile hike through the backcountry."

"Our troop that year under the Scoutmaster Smitty, one of the greatest Scout-masters ever, decided to take our troop for a hike down the Canadian River. In places, the Canadian Canyon is in a pristine state. When there is enough water the Canadian is a spectacular canoe or kayak run with continuous rapids through a spectacular wild canyon with tiered sandstone walls reminiscent of the Grand Canyon. In places, it is heavily forested and of course people have been using it as a route to the eastern plains and back for thousands of years. There is evidence of ancient foot trails even in the wildest parts of the canyon."

Hidalgo perked up and exclaimed, "That sounds interesting, tell me more."

"Well for example, the carved foot holes at the swimming hole, they look like Indians made them in order to get down the shear wall." He looked at Hidalgo and seriously said, "Someone took the time to carve them a long time ago and there are other places where an obvious route has been established."

Hidalgo looked at Corey and Penny and said, "You know, that could make an interesting research project; 'Ancient trade routes by Native Americans along the Canadian River'."

Richard picked up the conversation, "So after a week of camp activities and what we thought was training, we were assigned to some pack animals that we dragged down the canyon. Thank heavens they carried most of our food and gear because our hike turned out to be much farther than fifty miles."

"We were each allowed one candy bar per day. One day, another young man and I realized that we were dragging the mule with all the goodies packed on it. My friend wanted to get into the box with the load of candy bars."

"They won't miss just one or two," he kept saying. "Yeah, but I'll have to live with it, I thought to myself. I didn't slip into the candy box. I've been glad for that all my life."

"One of my first experiences with rattlesnakes occurred on that fifty-mile hike. We had been hiking along, leading our pack mules, when in the middle of the afternoon we decided to pull over and rest in a grove of mature cottonwoods grow-ing next to Russian olive, quicksand, and the physical remains of the world's most ennoble creature, the cow. Naturally, we did what all bored young teen-agers do; we got into a fight and not just your normal, everyday fight. The choice of ammunition was obvious: cow plops otherwise known as cow patties or cowslips. Dried plops, wet plops; it didn't really matter since we would all wind up in the river afterwards."

"The fight was on. First, just a couple of dry tosses, then like all wars, escalating into an all our frenzy of aggression until all ammunition was exhausted, a real neat way of rearranging the Bosque, and getting the trail nicely cleaned up. The scuffle lasted maybe ten minutes or so until the bullies had cleaned up on the smaller scouts. By this time I was pretty tired of war games, cow plop style, so I went over to the spreading roots of a cottonwood tree to relax until Smitty would bark for us to go."

"Dodging cow plops is not exactly what every mother wants her child to do when away on an outing. Ka Plop! I always hated the really fresh ones. They stick to you rather than careening off. By this time everyone had noticed that I had given up and had wondered off by myself. They could see that I was in deep thought, wanting to be left alone. So, naturally they came after me, with discus sized projectiles in hand. After all, if it had been someone else, I certainly would have been one of the culprits."

"Spat, got me good all right, time to get even! It's time for the sweet taste of revenge, time to reach for my own anti-ballistic cow plop. I could see the circular shape of the cow plop next to my knee in my peripheral vision; however it was the attackers that I had to watch. Those cow plops can really hurt if you are hit in just the right spot. Especially by those cow plops that are half cured out, soft, wet, and heavy on the inside and hard as a rock on the outside. That's when I finally noticed that the cow plop I was reaching for wasn't a cow plop at all, but rather a tightly coiled, sunning rattlesnake."

"I've always known that most snakes have a built in survival technique. When your see a snake traveling in its classical undulating motion, what you see isn't necessarily what's there. The stripes and markings on your typical snake are there for far more than just decoration. They form an optical illusion. Just try to pick one up while it's trying to crawl away. Reach for the tail, and what you get is dirt. Reach for the head, and you actually grab six inches behind the head, perfect position for the creature to turn around and sink its fangs into your wrist. Trust me; it takes practice to pick up a rattlesnake."

"Just because one is being bombarded by cow plops doesn't mean you want to get in a hurry, particularly when there is an angry rattlesnake just inches from your personal parts. I froze. We just sort of stared at each other. I began thinking to myself all those funny little things that one considers when you are under stress and really don't have time to think about anything but survival. What if the snake is hit by an errant cow plop toss? No time to ask myself dumb questions. I backed my hand away a micrometer at a time. An eternity and several cow plops passed by. Finally the other boys realized that something was wrong. I wasn't fighting back. Even worse, I was ignoring them, which made them focus their efforts on me."

"Determined to get my attention, Taylor, one of my best friends, picked up a huge cow plop and held it up over my head, poised to come crashing down, maggots and all. That's when he noticed the rattlesnake, which hadn't made a sound so far. The snake never struck nor made a sound and could have easily gotten me, yet somehow I think it sensed that I was not actually trying to harm it. The real source of the commotion was the invading Boy Scouts of America and their flying cow plops, why the rattlesnake never struck is still a mystery to me."

"This snake never shook a rattle until after a bullet hole appeared right between his eyes. Snakes can strike completely by instinct for several minutes after they are thought to be dead. Looking up, there was Smitty with a worried look on his face. Then I moved away, at least faster than a dead rattlesnake can strike. It was nice to have the momentary respect of my fellow scouts."

Pecos Pueblo

We finally left the Holliday home that afternoon knowing that we would not get to our destination that evening. We were able to make the drive toward Santa Fe staying on the route that turns east to Las Vegas and on to the Canadian River. Getting late in the afternoon we knew we could travel only a few miles till we could get into some back county and set up an evening camp. We drove out to Pecos Ruins and did a fast tour. Then getting dark, we took a road that ventured up into the mountains in search of a decent camping spot where we could get off the main road and out of sight and sleep.

Pecos pueblo should have been the greatest pueblo in all of New Mexico. It had everything going for it. First of all, its location put it close to several major river systems making it centralized for trade throughout the area. The namesake Pecos River flows out of the lower end of the high Sangre de Cristo Mountains, flowing through the small valley where the pueblo is located. The Pecos then travels for hundreds of miles south until it empties into the Rio Grande far away in Texas. It is close to the Rio Grande River and all the pueblos that had sprung up along it, the original inhabitants having migrated from other areas. Just west of the pueblo is Conchas River which flows east to the Canadian River that flows into the eastern plains. The pueblo, founded around 1300 A.D. is located on a rocky knoll and was built like a fort; defense was obviously a prime concern for the people who lived there. They had access to everything, mountains, rivers and lush green valleys. There was ample food to be found and grown in the surrounding lands and the pueblo grew and prospered for eons.

Pecos was one of the first North American villages to feel the impact of European contact. This was the pueblo's downfall. Less than fifty years after Columbus first set foot in the Americas, this pueblo was visited by Coronado and his followers; He and his exhausted men had endured the hardships of a northern New Mexico winter and inspired hatred because of the deprivations they caused among Indian villages along the entire length of the Rio Grande river system. It had been here, where Coronado enlisted the guide whom the Spaniards referred to as 'the Turk' in their search for the seven cities of gold.

In the following years, the pueblo suffered from constant attacks and deprivations by just about every possible means. In the year 1750 the pueblo's military force was destroyed by the Comanche's; and in 1788 its population was struck by smallpox. Pecos was caught in destructive forces totally beyond its control. Hidalgo thought to himself that, at least, he could understand why this pueblo had died, unlike many others.

When Robert McKnight came through Pecos pueblo on his way to Santa Fe, the pueblo was a ghost of its former self. The community was still there but the deprivations of time had left its mark. Goods and services could still be acquired there even if they had to be stolen; certainly the natives were getting very used to being stolen from. The question that was bothering the history detectives turned river runners was whether or not McKnight had visited the pueblo while making his escape out of New Mexico.

Early the next morning we loaded up our camping gear, stopping only to make coffee, and headed off to find a café for breakfast. Driving into Las Vegas they finally stopped at Ramones, had breakfast and then after two and a half hours of driving we arrived in Raton, Spanish for place of rats. There we grabbed a snack out of a truck stop while we were gassing up, and drove out to the put-in.

We discovered that there was nothing there, just a very small place to turn off the black top road. The young Canadian River meanders across the plains with no trace of a canyon. As the road crosses the river there is a barbed wire fence blocking the river. It would require the canoes and gear to be carried over the fence. Hidalgo wanted to explore taking about an hour to explore down the river, while Corey and I waited in the jeep. Returning, his report was ominous. The river could be run, but there were logjams and fences, requiring portages. They were glad they had come to the most up river section of the river, but after the twenty three portages they had performed on the San Juan trip, they decided to investigate a few miles downriver. Besides, it was highly unlikely that Robert McKnight would have ventured into this part of the Canadian. They knew that the plains could be crossed if they had loaded pack mules and arms for protection, but dangerous afoot. He would have learned from his earlier experiences and from others including the indigenous natives, easier ways to get into Texas.

Driving downriver we stopped at every access to the river. Starting at Springer, New Mexico, we drove out to where state route 56 crosses the river and is a major put in for modern day river runners. The canyon below flows through the Kiowa National Grasslands. The canyon there is wild and spectacular making it the most popular section for modern river runners who have the resources to make such a journey. There are two other access points; one at route 120 where the road crosses from Roy to Wagon Mound and again at route 65, where the road from Las Vegas crosses the river. It remains a grand sandstone canyon all the way to modern day Conchas Reservoir. But first they had to deal with their encounter at the tiny settlement of Sabinoso.

Emilio Romero

The Canadian River is usually run only after infrequent, heavy rains making it a real challenge for the die-hard river runner to find the opportunity to run the canyon. At the time of year that we were scouting the river it was obvious that the canyon is easier hiked through or horseback ridden through. Hidalgo made the point that it could certainly be a great place to find a good hole to put a fishing line in order to catch one of New Mexico's original catfish, the blue cat. There are some huge holes in the river, where with a little work one could pull a large catfish out of the river even in the leanest and driest of years.

The tiny historical village of Sabinosa, Spanish for place of knowing or wisdom, is located just above the normal bridge takeout on Hwy 65 between Las Vegas to the west and Roy to the east. After descending into the shallow canyon there we found ourselves searching for a tiny dirt road that leads to the scattering of adobe houses which make up Sabinoso. The river emerges there from its awesome gorge and empties into a broad valley, measuring 60 to 70 miles in breadth at some points. Below the Canadian continues descending into another deep canyon with almost continuous class IV rapids followed by the extensive mud flats of Conchas Lake. That section of the river is rarely, if ever, run.

The region has always been dangerous, occupied by many warring factions of Indians who succeeded each other conquering and enslaving the former occupants or driving them out. The Spaniards continued this cycle, governing the region for three centuries, and creating large ranches from the land of the native people, who eventually drove many Spanish settlements into extinction. The vast plains are now subdivided into huge ranches, which make up personal kingdoms. Because of geographical isolation, the old timers and cowboys are weary of all outsiders.

Coming to the end of the road we finally met some people with whom we could make inquiry about the area. First there was a young man sitting on top of a horse with a 30-06 in the scabbard, a pistol strapped around his hip and a *cervasa* (beer) in his free hand. Stopping the truck and politely leaning out of the window, Corey attempted to talk to him. The Hispanic cowboy ignored them, turning his horse through a gate decorated with keep out signs. They followed the dirt road past the gate down to the river edge. The river that day was just a rock garden with hardly enough water to float canoes. Moments later, Emilio Romero a local rancher, drove up to their campsite in a vintage pickup truck. He ran some fast razor sharp Spanish past Corey and me. Feebly, Corey answered him with *"Lo seinto, Me Espanol is un poco mal. Habla despacio por favor."*

In perfect English the rancher answered, "What are you doing here, on my ranch? This took Corey back for a second; for he was pretty sure this was a public road that for granted, went to the Romero ranch.

After a short explanation about researching a river trip Romero pointed to the river and said, "The River is just a few rapids like this, pointing to the rock garden we were looking at, then turns to sandy bottom for about twenty miles. After that all hell breaks loose." His Nephew, who was sitting in the pickup truck with several rifles in the window rack, told of some tourist he watched from the ranch house.

After putting on with an aluminum boat with no flotation, collar style life jackets, and a cooler full of *cervasas*; the results were predictable with the wrapped boat, lost equipment, and long cold swim, followed by the horrendous hike out.

Hidalgo who had returned from a short hike then discussed the situation in Spanish which seemed to cure the problem. Romero backed his truck up and then putting it into first gear, drove on down the road without saying another word.

Comencheros

We drove on to Conchas Reservoir stopping at the State Park Office. Again, Hidalgo took the lead by having a long conversation in Spanish which he related to Corey and me. On wet, and dam release years the river overflows the Conchas Dam spillway allowing the river runner to float down this historic section of canyon to Ute Lake, named after its contributory Ute Creek. Ute Creek should probably be called Ute Wash because it really only flows after local rains but it drains a huge area. The danger in running this section is the extreme isolation. If a problem does occur the only recourse a river runner has is self-rescue. Some parties have become marooned when the dam keeper at Conchas unexpectedly closed the release gates. They probably experienced a long walk out, dragging their canoes or rafts assuming they had enough water.

Virtually all-historic buildings along the Canadian River are in ruins; for example the historic Spanish settlements of Conchas are now under Conchas Lake providing a home for catfish. Ranchers in the area tear down all unused buildings to avoid paying taxes on them. Fort Bascom, a historic fort overlooking a bend in the river has now disappeared, literally without a trace. At one time it was a busy place with a large garrison of men stationed there to protect the area from Comencheros. Comencheros and other Indians, staged attacks and were undoubtedly a problem but the Indians, who were victims of ethnic cleansing, were not the real killers of the soldiers at Fort Bascom. As with most forts in the west, the main cause of death was disease, namely syphilis which was treated with mercury.

When water is being released from Conchas there is 50 miles of deep sandstone canyon from Conchas Lake to Ute Lake. Below Ute Lake, New Mexico to Lake

Meredith, Texas it is about 70 to 80 miles flowing through Oldham County, and here the topography changes from a majestic canyon to a gradual slope to a braided riverbed, hundreds of yards across. Through this area, it could be a long and boring walk dragging your canoe behind you.

During high water this entire riverbed would be covered with fast moving water several feet deep. But the river would be overflowing into thousands of acres of scrub forest, each one inviting an entanglement of you and your boat. Below Logan and Ute Lake, the Canadian can theoretically be run on years when there is an overflow. Too much water and it could be a spooky and technical run, in the lower canyons, however there were no contemporary river runners that the Ranger knew about, that had run it. On most years it is too shallow. The entire topography has changed anyway due to human intervention. Historical changes occurred such as the construction of several dams, and the transformation of the surrounding prairie grasslands for a multitude of uses as a direct result of 'mining' the fossil water deposited though the eons in the Ollagawah basin. The ranger also pointed out that we would want to avoid the mud flats in upper Meredith Lake over in Texas.

While Hidalgo talked about what the ranger had said, Corey and I took out road maps that showed that below Meredith Lake, indeed the river showed much braiding of the riverbed until the confluence of the North Canadian south of Oklahoma City. From there, the river is navigable all the way to Lake Eufaula, Oklahoma. After taking out a pencil and doing some addition we figured the river flowed some 655 miles, including the upper canyons or a total of 2000 miles to the Gulf of Mexico.

Logan, New Mexico, 'The Best Little Town by a Dam Site'

A day later, after traveling back to Tucumcari, where I had my first encounter with Hidalgo, we turned north on route 54 and finally arrived in Logan, New Mexico, 'The Best Little Town by a Dam Site,' the sign said. After driving through the tiny town and then out to the lake, we returned into town and stopped at the only place where people where congregating, 'Whiskey the Road to Ruin Bar,' and went in.

It was noisy at first, then suddenly quiet as we walked in. Everybody stopped talking and was looking at us. Then as we walked to an empty table, they turned their gazes away and resumed their conversations. I had felt it before many times, men always looked. Sitting down at the table we quickly realized that, despite the name, the bar was a meeting place for many of the locals who needed a place to hang out. Rowdy was not an appropriate description. Everyone was congenial and friendly and soon we found ourselves talking to a fellow by the name of Freddy Fetzner who took the initiative to introduce himself.

Everyone else, who had been staring at me went back to their conversations about the price of cattle feed, lack of rain and what they would like to do with a group of hippies that were camping down in the park. I seemed to have taken center stage only until the local boys realized I was wearing a wedding band and the two fellows sitting with me looked like people they would not want to deal with. But Fetzner made a point to be friendly anyway. He had grown up in Logan and knew everyone and probably everything about the tiny community.

After I explained what they were doing in Logan, Fetzner's curiosity was piqued.

"Over the years I have learned to listen to other people, it is amazing what people will tell you," said Fetzner with a sly smile.

With time invested in any small community, sooner or later a visitor becomes acquainted with many interesting characters. Often conversations occur with young characters centered around and involving sexual exploits by the men, and the foolishness of those men in conversations with or about women. In many ways Logan is just like all small communities in that everyone knows everyone, but despite that reality there is always something happening there to create an excuse for gossip and entertainment for the bored.

Fetzner directed the conversation to the excitement of stealing. The younger of us want to prove something, usually involving some form of bravado. The competitive male psyche always provides entertaining conversations regarding the assorted mean pranks.

"Take that fellow over there for example." He pointed to a large, Hispanic fellow, who had been looking at Penny, then he would turn to a friend saying something then they would both break up in laughter. "Billy is a friend of mine. One day he just says to me;"

"You know, it is possible to make a sixteen wheeler disappear; it's just a matter of knowing someone with a potato silo."

"A month later two sixteen wheelers actually disappeared and the culprits were never caught. Eventually two different farmers discovered the trucks in their potato silos."

Fetzner says, "The trucks were not stolen so they could be resold. They were stolen because they *could* be stolen and that provided cheap entertainment."

"The most interesting stories around here come from those souls who don't feel the need to brag about their personal exploits. They are the quiet ones, keeping away from people who try to belittle their ambitions. Small people always do that, but wise friends make you feel that you too can become great. They are the ones, those older ladies and gentlemen with leathery faces who know real stories. I have learned to seek out these gentle and wiser folks but sometimes you have to pry the stories from them. The memories of these people are their personal treasures. Each person is a world into oneself and often they jealously guard their memory treasures."

Again, I prompted Fetzner with another beer to get him to talk some more. He obliged us after a gulp. "Take Eloy Casadas over there, he is a good example of someone who is older and has lived a world of experiences all stored between his ears. Eloy is a rancher who lives out on the edge of Tucumcari draw where it dumps its water into the Canadian River. He has spent the last two years raising cattle and selling them to afford a breeding bull. I don't know if you know this, but those bulls are very expensive."

"We live on a ranch," Hidalgo replied.

"Oh," says Fetzner who thought he was telling them something they didn't know, then he continued, "It had taken him two years to save enough money to buy the bull and you can bet your booty he was proud of it. Well to make a long story short, a person has to cross the railroad tracks off of route 54, and you immediately come to a locked gate. Eloy's ranch house is back along the canyon requiring the visitor to go through at least two more gates before they even get to his house. Once there he unloaded his new prize bull out of the cattle trailer and let it wonder into the pasture behind his house. Eloy felt that the bull was absolutely safe there because there was absolutely no access to the pasture without going through several locked gates, one of them actually attached to Eloy's house. The back of the pasture is inaccessible because there are sheer bluffs that drop down into the floor of the canyon. Those cliffs could only be climbed by a mountain goat or someone with climbing gear. Needless to say, the bull should have been safe out in that pasture."

Fetzner stopped long enough to allow Hidalgo to order another beer for him. Then after another big swallow he continued.

"Early the next morning Eloy walked out into the pasture to admire his new bull but was dumbfounded when he discovered the animal was dead. It looked like something had gotten to it but it must have been something very strange indeed. The animal had been drained of every drop of blood in its body; the tongue had been surgically removed along with the rectum which looked like an apple corer had been used to remove it. He could see no tracks or signs of any predator activity around the bull. What he did find was very strange though. In a circle around the animal was traces of a white powder that turned out to be magnesium dioxide, you know, the burned metal they use in flashes for cameras."

"That does sound interesting," says Corey. "What happened then?"

Well, there was a rash of cattle mutilations around the county, then it all stopped. Billy over there was involved in one particular tough incident though."

Everyone turned around and looked at Billy who looked startled when he realized that everyone was looking at him for a change.

"Billy was put on night patrol overlooking a pasture on his family's ranch. He parked his old Buick up on a ridge overlooking a pasture with about three hundred head of cows in it. Being easily bored, naturally he took a cooler of beer with him so he would still be able to enjoy himself while watching the cows."

"All went well until about four in the morning. Slumped down in his seat, he was almost asleep when he noticed the car starting to move. First it was just a little wobble but soon the car was literally bouncing up and down. In a panic and with thoughts of alien abductions going through his mind he grabbed his gun and jumped out of the car."

Fetzner stopped at that point for dramatic effect and to finish off another beer.

"There he stood, face to face with a bull who had been scratching its butt on the fender of the car. The indignant bull blew snot all over Billy and then stomped off.

The story brought a round of laughter from everyone and another beer for Fetzner who continued with his stories.

"Old-timers describe Logan as a completely different world than exists around here now." Fetzner, who has lived in the best little town by a dam site for all of his life, remembered a wild and unpredictable river instead of the one that now lazily seeps through a magnificent sandstone canyon. The character of the Canadian River in New Mexico for at least the next millennium or so was completely changed by the construction of Conchas Reservoir, and later, Ute Lake. Below Ute Lake, the character of this ancient river is now permanently changed. It is now a much more difficult canoe run, due to a multitude of manmade situations and creations such as barbed wire, weirs, dams and artificial lakes."

After redirecting the conversation several times from family genealogies he eventually got back to the town of Logan. "Logan was named after a Texas Ranger but was really founded he alleges, after a train robbery. The story was brief. It was an unsolved train robbery. The thief robbed the train then blended into the Canadian canyons. In a short time he became an influential rancher. Slowly, over the years the money provided the initial economy that built the town. Later, that economy allowed the thief to get involved in politics."

"In those days, there were twenty-two bars in town but only one church. Now there are twenty-two churches in town but only one bar. The town has gone to hell."

Having heard a similar joke before, I took to dragging the conversation back to the river, but he hushed me, explaining that the history of the community and the river are intertwined. He began by asking us to reflect upon the cliffs of the canyon, next to the bridge on route 54. There, much higher than the present bridge, remain cement abutments. The pillars that once served as supports for a railroad bridge vanished years ago.

"Every spring the river becomes a raging flood, with only the old rail road bridge, between here and Tucumcari, being able to withstand the force of the flood. The Mexican's used to gather down at the railroad bridge after the water dropped and haul out great trees that had accumulated there. They cut the trees up for fire-wood and for poles to make pens. Trees, cows, windmills, and everything else would occasionally be swept into the raging and unpredictable current." He then leaned over to me and his voice became less animated and more serious;

"One year a farm house was found down there. No one knew where it came from. There was clothes and stuff still in that house, but no one ever found the people. Afterwards the townspeople searched the canyon for days but never found anyone. Eventually a fisherman discovered a skeleton of a small child way up the canyon but no one could identify who it belonged to."

"Usually, late in the summer the river will drop to a tiny green trickle that won't even cover your ankles. Then after a weather system comes in from the north-west, the river literally explodes into a raging red river, it is dangerous. Now day's the river is pretty tame. But you know, above Conchas Reservoir it can still flood to an amazing degree. On wet years the flood trail from the Canadian, as it dumps into the Reservoir, can be fifteen feet above the level of the rest of the lake."

After the sixth beer, Fetzner's stories began to have more meanders than the river. "Years ago a bunch of Hell's Angels Bikers attacked the town looking for women to have their way with. We had to hang them all because we don't have a jail here in Logan. The worst one was an Indian...." At that Hidalgo stood up and started toward the door followed by Corey and me who could of course see the humor in the situation and were fighting back laughter. We drove back out to the lake, spent the night and after breakfast in town, we began the arduous drive all the way back to Serpiente.

Learning Spanish

By the time we had driven all the way back to Serpiente, we were dog tired and terribly in need of a rest, but to our astonishment we discovered that Aunt June was already making plans to journey into Mexico to both document the McKnight escape and to visit an archeological dig that she was invited to participate in. It all seemed a little much for Hidalgo and Ken who needed to catch up on ranch work and especially Hidalgo was tired of traveling anyway, but the rest of us were game for another trip. We argued for Hidalgo to go because of his command of the Spanish language, but to no avail, he was going through one of his stubborn times. In reality Hidalgo felt uncomfortable going into Mexico. He had already experienced some very negative confrontations with the drug cartels and he didn't want that kind of confrontation. "You will be safer without me."

We took the back roads down to Magdalena then over to Socorro before hitting the interstate that would eventually take us down the *Jornada del Muerto* and into El Paso, the gateway into Ciudad Juarez. Traveling in a car at 65 miles per hour it still took most of the day to get there. It made us wonder what it would have been like for Robert McKnight's crew to have been boxed into crude wagons and slowly driven in the hot sun all the way down to Chihuahua, Mexico. Even more amazing would have been the return trip. They walked the entire route while hiding from the authorities going in the opposite direction all the way back to the Eastern United States and of course it was entirely different back then. There would be no help from anyone.

All the way down we practiced our Spanish with June offering suggestions. The problem was she herself knew only the basics. Corey could recognize more praises than I could but he couldn't really keep up in a conversation. Hundreds of Spanish words were in my vocabulary but I only had the crudest idea how to use them in a coherent sentence. Proper Spanish grammar was beyond my abilities and conjugating verbs was a knotty problem for all of us.

To pass the time we settled on a game where we were figuring out the origin of the words and names that we were sharing.

"Cafeteria," was the first word I tossed out. "Even I know that one. Isn't it the same in Spanish; a place to eat."

"There are many cognates in English which are the same words in Spanish" says June. "The places around here may be one key to learning a few words. Sandia Mountain or watermelon mountain, Manzano Mountain or 'Apple Mountain.' There are names all over New Mexico that have Spanish names that people use. Even surnames are common, Mr. Mantano is mountain, Mr. Luna, or moon, Calderon or caldera or kettle, Mr. Blanco or white, Mr.Cabeza de Baca or head of cow, the examples are endless but a true understanding of Spanish requires an ability to conjugate verbs; I am, you are or *yo soy, tu eres.*"

I mulled all this over for a moment then asked, "How in the world am I going to learn enough Spanish to get around in Mexico?"

"What you are going to learn," answered June, "is that most people that you will need to deal with speak some English. In fact, despite the fact that English is far more difficult to master than Spanish, people in other countries usually speak more than one language.

I frowned then asked, "Shouldn't they all speak English?"

June thought for a moment before answering her. "Yes in America, certainly everyone should speak English but remember you are going to be a guest in another country. We make two basic mistakes here in America. One, we should teach our children foreign languages early in life when they learn like sponges soaking up words effortlessly, and we think everyone should learn English because it is what most people grow up with around here. Actually we limit ourselves in business opportunities around the world because of our ignorance and arrogance."

Hatch, New Mexico

By afternoon we had gotten to Hatch, New Mexico, where growing chili was becoming an up and coming occupation of the community as the value of the chili has been discovered by all of American. In the alluvial volcanic soil the chili grown here developed a sweet taste which is coveted by all those who enjoy Mexican food. Hatch chili has become known as Rio Grande food, a mixture of Indian and Mexican food, with many dishes that are entirely different than those served in Mexico. Every variety of chili is grown there, chili ancho, chile de agua, chili poblano, chili piquin, chili marillo, chili chipole, chili costeno, chili guajillo, and chili morita, but the most common varieties are simply known as New Mexico mild, Big Jim, Sandia, and the hottest chili; Barker.

Over plates of fine Rio Grande enchiladas made from red Big Jim peppers, and while learning the names of the basic implements used in eating such as *cuchara*, *tenedor*, and *cuchillo* or spoon, fork and knife, June changed the conversation and began to educate them on the community that they were traveling into. Paraphrasing her words;

"First of all, archeological work there is considered unimportant by the Mexican government. Since the local ruins at Paquime are relatively new compared to the spectacular pyramids and city complexes found further south there is little to draw the tourist dollars to this site. However, from the point of view of the archeology community, Paquime is a huge archeological site that resembles a maze rather than a Mayan complex and is very important for understanding what happened to the Anasazi who originally left Chaco Canyon.

All archeologists know that the present boundaries that separate the United States and Mexico where nonexistent in the distant past. The early people who lived there were the same people who made up the indigenous peoples who had originated in Chaco Canyon as well as all over the American Southwest. For several thousand years, people who had lived in Chihuahua had trading relations with Native Americans in New Mexico. Yet they were always at war with invading groups of natives such as the Apaches which is why they built their city with many blind alleys and entrances, a maze to confuse and confound invaders.

The Tatahumara Indians were the largest and most defiant group who lived in the area. They were particularly defiant against the invading Spanish, French, and later outside Indian laborers who invaded the area in search of work in the Chihuahua silver mines. As Chihuahua became a center of the silver trade, the tremendous pressures on the indigenous inhabitants inflamed and provoked a flurry of revolts. By the middle 1600s many of the native tribes joined together in an effort to rid themselves of foreign rule but again the indigenous natives were conquered.

When the Great Northern Revolt took place in New Mexico, it did not just affect the Pueblo Indians of New Mexico, as many believe. It spread throughout Chihuahua and Durango. From Casas Grandes to El Paso; Conchos, Sumas, Chinarras, Mansos, Janos, and the Apache Indians all took up arms. The Tarahumaras also revolted once again in 1690 and were not defeated until 1698.

During the Eighteenth Century the Apache Indians became a constant and unrelenting enemy of the Spanish administration as well as to the Indian settlements. The Apaches adapted to a different kind of warfare with the Spanish, being highly skilled horsemen they effectively eluded the Spanish military forces. The Apaches continued to defy both Mexico and the United States for many years until 1886. Then Geronimo, the famous Chiricahua Apache leader was surrounded in the Sierra Madres by American forces that had crossed the border for the purpose of capturing him. He surrendered because he found himself fighting more conscripted Indians than solders. Without the help of native Indians the United States soldiers didn't have a chance of capturing him.

They have always been at war in Chihuahua. When Cortez and the conquistadors came into this area, they brought not only new weapons but new sickness to a people who had never known them. There were some fifteen million Aztec in Mexico before the conquest. They had lived well for the standards of their world, but within fifty years only about three million poor, degraded, and enslaved people were left.

The native religions and cultures were replaced by foreign traditions and the churches of the conquistadors. Now Mexico's political structures and institutions along with its corruption and inefficiency have produced extreme inequity of income. Even now, Mexico has more billionaires than any other country except the United States, but it also has more people living in desperate poverty.

Desperate people do desperate things. Many of the once proud indigenous natives now work for the drug cartels on land their ancestors owned but now they lease it from the cartels. They grow marijuana and other drug producing plants which allow them to live and take care of their children. At least now they can afford clothes for their children. Little has changed since the earliest of days. There is always a fight going on with someone. Now reports of executions, kidnappings, and extortion surface daily. Any archeologist working in Chihuahua takes their life in their hands. The local police are basically ineffective against the drug cartels that actually control just about everything; including the local police and judicial system.

Exploring Chihuahua

*C*rossing the border between El Paso and Juarez, I finally popped the obvious question; "Exactly what are you doing out at those ruins?"

"Well," answered June, "A fellow archeologist has discovered a mystery that she asked me to help solve. As you know, I am pretty good at identifying Indians by the type of pottery they make. Sometimes I can identify the actual individual who makes a ceramic. Understanding pottery is also how we know about their trading patterns. Sometimes when an odd piece of pottery is found at a ruin it is there because of trade with other groups. The polychromatic pottery found here has presented a mystery involving two types of simple everyday use pottery. In the 1200s, a small community of Hohokam, a people who lived primarily in what is now southern Arizona moved into a neighboring valley. The ceramics were made using two distinctive techniques, one from the local culture and the other Hohokam. Interestingly, there is a complete absence of trade between the two groups except for this one site. The theory is that the Hohokam pottery found there was made by female captives. Obviously, if the Hohokam-style ceramics were made with clay composed of local soil, then that tends to support the theory that the Hohokam was prisoners. It will be my job to collect some samples and bring them back to the University where an analysis can be made of the clay they are composed of."

I mulled this over for a while then asked. "What do you want Corey and me to do while you're out at the ruins?"

June produced a big smile and said, "I want you and Corey to explore Chihuahua and enjoy yourselves, I would suggest that you figure out the local bus services and enjoy the sights and sounds of this community. There really are some amazing things to see here and the place we are going to stay at is very nice. Trust me, you will enjoy yourselves, just be careful. Stay where there are lots of people and don't get to far away from the hotel. If you do leave the hotel, leave me a note so I won't worry about you. I'll be in every evening and we can have dinner together."

June smirked at Corey and said to him, "Don't be surprised if some of the local boys come up to Penny and propose marriage to her, promising her a home in million dollar haciendas. Usually they are just kidding around in an attempt to flirt with a good looking girl. Girls that have accepted invitations like that wind up in abject poverty or worse. Those haciendas usually turn out to be adobe houses out in the middle of nowhere. Just laugh it off and avoid them. Seriously, kidnapping is a problem here. Penny is a good looking blond. You don't see too many blondes in Chihuahua, especially when they look as good as Penny. Women have been kidnapped and forced into the sex slavery business. It will only take me a couple of days to solve the pottery problem so again, enjoy yourselves, but be very careful. Go to the tourist places where you will be in crowds, don't leave those crowds if someone wants to show you something or wants to sell you something. We will be out of here in two or at the most three days.

The Drug Bust

I wanted to see everything that involved art, so for the next two days we took bus tours to galleries and museums. Chihuahua certainly had plenty to offer. I was particularly impressed by the Sacred Art Museum where two rooms exhibited beautiful examples of Mexican religious art created in the 18th century. Corey was most fascinated by the Nombre de Dios Caves. The caves feature stalactite and stalagmite formations all made from millions of years of chemical deposits formed from glistening salt but returning to the hotel that evening to meet with June we encountered a problem.

Tony and his girlfriend Valerie were Americans who had been exploring the sights and sounds of Chihuahua just as Corey and I had been doing. Tony was athletic looking despite his long straggly hair. Valerie, with long black hair and matching black fingernails that were too black to match her pan cake skin was quiet, choosing not to participate in the conversation. She acted like she was worried about something, but Tony was very outgoing and jovial and the conversation seemed to be easy for him, particularly since he was talking to a fellow Americans, it was the only English being spoken in the bus. One thing was different about them. Tony had purchased a bag of marijuana and some cocaine from a local dealer and was secretly carrying it with him on the bus. Corey and I, being oblivious to this enjoyed their company on the ride back to the city when the bus pulled over to a stop.

The local police had set up a roadblock to inspect the passengers. It was then that Tony slipped the bag of drugs out of his pocket and into Corey's small backpack without Corey noticing it. The police who had entered the bus directed everyone in Spanish to exit the bus carrying their belongings with them. Once on the side of the road, they basically skipped the natives who were on the bus, ignoring them, but the foreigners had all their personal possessions searched, and of course when it came Corey's turn they found the package of drugs. The search immediately stopped, Corey was handcuffed and put into the back of one of the police cars. Despite what I said and the sheepish looks from Tony and Valerie, I was ignored. The only language that was spoken was Spanish therefore I had no idea what was going to happen.

Tony and Valerie got off the bus at the very next stop and quickly disappeared into the maze of streets that made up this section of town. All I could do was return to the Hotel and wait until June returned. I was perplexed. I really didn't know how serious the situation was nor did I know how to explain the predicament to June. When June did arrive and I explained to her what the situation was, all that I could get out of her for several minutes was, "Oh my."

Officia de Derecho

The following day June and I found ourselves in the *Officia de Derecho*, talking to a lawyer by the name of Alfredo De Vargas. In broken English he explained to June and me that there was little they could do until Corey made his court appearance before the local magistrate. He certainly would need a lawyer, and a translator if he requested one, however it seemed like a sure thing that he would be convicted of drug possession. It was not a problem at all for the natives. In fact, Corey and Penny had smelled and even seen several people smoking marijuana while roaming the city but they were all local. The problem was Corey was an American. Ever since American politicians had begun working with the Mexican federal government to stamp out the drug trade by providing millions of dollars for the war on drugs, the local governments wanted to make the point that the problem was the demand for drugs by the American drug consumers. They wanted to make examples out of as many Americans as they could.

It was useless to try to find Tony and Valerie. They had refused to admit to

anything on the bus. All June and I could do was stay in contact with the lawyer and wait until Corey's court date then we learned that it would be almost a month before that would occur.

Returning to Serpiente, June and I shared the news of Cory's predicament with Hidalgo and Ken; then they all went to the authorities in Albuquerque to seek advice and help. There, they quickly learned that there was little the American government could do to help Corey. For all practical purposes he had been caught red handed and they didn't want to expend time and money on a drug possession charge even though Corey had never even had a traffic ticket on his record. The only advice they really received was to make arrangements with Cory's lawyer to provide him with some money. In Mexican jails, everything such as clothing and food has to be purchased. The jail would not see to his safety or personal needs. Ken and June immediately started wiring small amounts of money, earmarked for Corey's needs and of course the lawyer's fees.

The Jail Sentence

Corey never received any of the money that was sent to him. It didn't matter, as soon as he would have received the money, the thugs in the jail would have beaten him up taking it away from him. In the end it probably saved him several beatings. On the other hand it left Corey in a serious state of deprivation. In only a short time he was reduced to a skeletal figure with nothing but a pair of stained shorts to wear. He learned some of the same tricks everyone there learned. *Mano direcho* (the right hand) was used to eat with and *mano lezuada* (the left hand) was used to clean oneself with. Needless to say, toilet paper was nonexistent along with any other item used for personal hygiene. Breakfast consisted of a bowl of oatmeal served with no sugar or milk. The lumpy grey stuff had to be eaten with your fingers. Lunch was a slice of bread and a single slice of dried out cheese. Dinner was usually a little better with chili and beans served along with occasional canned beets and raw onion. A single tortilla was also served which acted as a bowl to contain the chili and beans. Many of the inmates gave up their dinner to other, more vicious inmates to avoid a beating. Determined to

stay healthy Corey refused to give up his food which cost him an occasional elbow in the rib cage but he did learn to hit back. As soon as the other inmates figured out that he would defend himself they left him alone.

Corey had many enemies in jail but he also had made some friends. Usually they were young Americans who had also been busted for drugs or weapons. Corey learned that only two classes of people in Mexico had access to guns, the authorities such as police and army and the drug cartels. The drug cartels were rapidly gaining on both the army and the police because the poorest of Mexicans were on the side of the drug cartels which were their benefactors. One elderly Mexican man befriended Corey and taught him how to avoid the difficulties of surviving in jail.

Manuel Ortega had been imprisoned two years earlier for holding up a Mercado. It turned out that the food store he had supposedly held up was actually run by a relative of a member of a drug cartel. Manuel Ortega actually was guilty of stealing food to feed his family, but his real crime was not allowing the cartel to use his small farm and family to grow marijuana. Now his farm and family is used to grow the illegal crop anyway. Manuel fought them the only way he could which was by helping other inmates in the jail.

After three months in jail Corey's court date finally came up, delayed because of the overtaxed judicial system. Corey was allowed to take a warm shower, given clean cloths, then handcuffed and driven along with several other inmates, including Manuel to the courthouse to see a judge.

Corey was found guilty of drug possession, intent to distribute drugs, and overstaying his stay in Mexico which seemed a little ridiculous since he really didn't have much choice. His lawyer appeared to be of little help and he was terribly disappointed when none of the family showed up to stand up for him in court. He did not know that they had made other arrangements. The judge ordered a sentence of five years and he was herded back into the prison van to make the twenty minute trip back to the jail.

The Jail Break

The family had been in constant contact with Corey's lawyer, Alfredo De Vargas, but they were given very little hope of getting Corey out. Ken and Hidalgo took matters into their own hands, traveling to Chihuahua and renting a small bungalow where they could work secretly on their own. After a month of quietly making inquiries they made a break though. Vargas suggested that the only way to get Corey out would be to arrange a jail break. But that would require a series of bribes to the guards. The only real chance they had was while the prisoners were being transferred from the prison to the courthouse. Ken and Hidalgo of course was suspicious that they were being set up and changed the plan.

All four inmates including Corey and his new friend Manuel were in a state of desperation and despair as they were shuffled into the waiting van and the journey began. But after only a few blocks a black van suddenly pulled in front of the police van and slammed on its breaks causing the police van to screech to a halt. Out of the van jumped two masked gunmen who held their pistols directly in the faces of the driver and guard who immediately raised their hands over their heads. After removing the keys to the shackles the two prison workers were made to lie down on the asphalt and the inmates were quickly herded into the black car which drove away and disappeared.

After only a short drive of a couple of city blocks the black van drove into a garage, the garage door was pulled down and for all practical purposes they just sat there in complete darkness. Several intense moments passed as police sirens came and then passed the garage. After another twenty or so minutes passed without the police pounding on the garage door a cigarette lighter finally was lit by one of the gunmen who had kidnapped them. As Corey looked up in astonishment the burly fellow slowly turned around exposing his face. There sat Hidalgo with a huge grin on his face.

The Wet Backs

Hidalgo's expression quickly changed to concern. "We need to get out of here fast," explained Hidalgo, "and I don't have the foggiest idea how we are going to get back to Serpiente. It all had happened to fast. We waited and waited for a call from Vargas to let us know when the prison transfer would take place and when it finally did come we found ourselves unprepared."

"Who is that other guy with you," Corey asked. Ken turned around in the seat and another worried grin appeared.

"We are hoping the police assumed that a drug cartel sprung you fellows and decided that pursuing us would only lead to more problems, but I doubt it. It is only a matter of time until Vargas will spill the beans and they will be looking for us. They can't find you with us or we will all wind up in jail with you."

Manuel, who until now had been silent said quietly, "Get me to a phone and I can get us out of here, I have friends who will gladly help us." Moments later all had changed into street clothes. Corey was amazed at the feel of actually wearing real shoes which he had not worn for two months now. After some exchanges in Spanish, Manuel and Hidalgo ventured into the small home that adjoined the garage, then down the street to a pay phone that was in a small store at the end of the block. There, after pushing a peso into the slot, Manuel spoke for several minutes to someone. Two hours later an old farm truck loaded with bales of hay stopped in front of the garage. After quick arrangements it backed up to the back of the black van so the men could scramble under the bales that were held up by a large piece of ply board. As soon as everyone was loaded they travelled to the bungalow Hidalgo and Ken had rented. There the old truck stopped long enough for Hidalgo and Ken to get out and then continued traveling out of the city and into the countryside with the prisoners still inside, including Corey. After what seemed like several hours they arrived at a farm house south of Juarez where the prisoners were unloaded, fed, and told to stay out of sight.

The next day Corey found Manuel despondent. "What's wrong," he asked. "Well," answered Manuel in his broken English, "I have learned that my family has been relocated to southern Mexico. My wife and son have been, as they say around here, disappeared."

"Can you find them," Corey asked.

"There is no way. First of all I cannot show my face around Chihuahua. Not without being arrested by the police. Secondly, if the police don't catch me the cartel men might. I have no money, no idea where to even look for them and no way of getting to them even if I knew where they were. According to my friends who live around my old farm, the cartel now has legal ownership of it. I have nothing."

Why don't you come with me to *Serpiente*," suggested Corey who by this time was beginning to understand the complexities of just trying to live in Mexico.

"What is this snake, Serpiente that you talk about," asked Manuel? Corey described what Serpeinte was and how it might work for him if they could get there. Corey and Manuel immediately began to piece a plan together. He could live in Serpiente for a while until he could accumulate enough money to operate in Mexico. Possibly, with a little luck, he might even be able to locate his wife and son with the resources and connections of friends in Serpiente.

"After all, you saved my butt in Mexico, perhaps we can help you save your family in Mexico," Corey offered.

"This all sounds good to me but first we have to cross the border, do you realize how much more difficult that will be with me along? After all, I will be an illegal coming into your country. When you get there you have your freedom but for me there is only mystery."

"Trust me," Corey replied earnestly, "If we can get you there we will find a way of making you legal, besides my relatives there have political connections. We can and will help you. As you know by now, my relatives have a way of making things happen. They also have a way of making an injustice such as you have experienced become a justice."

"I have to admit they have courage,' says Manuel, "do you really think they can help me?"

With a stern look and firm voice Corey answered him with a single word, "Yes."

The next day Corey and Manuel were each given two gallon jugs of water, a small sack of food and a crude map and in broken Spanish was instructed to begin their journey to America. They were introduced to a coyote, a person who would transport them to the border and show them a likely crossing spot.

Corey thought about the irony of having to sneak into his own country, like thousands of others who yearly make the perilous trip in search of a wage paying job but in Corey's case it was a desperate escape to freedom. He couldn't help but to think about the parallels to Robert McKnight who had escaped from Mexico during a different era.

Two days later Corey and Manuel walked into a service station in a tiny town that served local ranches on the American side, made a phone call, and several hours later were with June and Hidalgo heading north along the *Journada de Muertes*, on their way to Serpiente.

After several weeks of hard work the ranch work was done. Manuel insisted upon doing most of it. Then everyone started to think about the research project that had precipitated their actions during the last few months. They decided to wait on their river trip down the Canadian River. They would need to wait until the following spring anyway so there would be enough water to float the river.

That winter, Hidalgo and June both spent time in Mexico talking to government officials that refused to talk to them regarding Corey's drug case. But pursuing kidnapped indigenous people was a different matter. It seemed an impossible task but the police were actually able to find the young family. A bribe was paid and within only a couple of days, they returned with a young boy and his mother with them. Manuel held them, hugging them over and over well into the night when they were presented to him.

A Return to the Canadian River

Manuel and his family had nothing to return to Mexico for. As soon as he had arrived, he started looking for ways he could be helpful, ways to survive. First after making a thorough survey of the vacant guest rooms then the working areas of the ranch such as the chicken pens and barn, he went to work rebuilding one of the better guest houses. He worked in the hope that someday he would have his family with him and very quickly he did. Manuel and his family were superb at taking care of the ranch at Serpiente, blending into the working fabric of the ranch. Everyone just thought of them as part of the extended family. Besides, it changed our relationship with the ranch. Much of taking care of a ranch is feeding animals and someone has to be there every day. This allowed all of us more time to pursue our professional activities. We suddenly had time to explore our interest whether solving historical mysteries or running rivers.

The adventures in Mexico had become a great diversion for everyone, but now it was time to get back to work. On a warm spring day with June and Ken acting as shuttle bunnies, we loaded our canoes into a trailer and headed to Maxwell Bridge for a launch on the Canadian River. Still mystified by the apparitions that had occurred on the San Juan River; we looked forward to exploring a completely new area and for the opportunity to contribute to creating a comparison of the river then and now which was all part of June's research into New Mexico history.

It was a rugged and arduous river trip, after floating several miles, it was obvious that the further we traveled the bigger the canyon was becoming and so would the innate dangers such as ever increasing difficulty of rapids. We never knew what to expect around the next meander. Often we floated in absolute piece for a mile or two and then there would be a rock garden announcing the next long set of rapids. Then, in the back of everyone's mind was Richard's story of the waterfall to consider. It was on a left meander where the river has cut a path down through the canyon floor rock hiding the drop. Surely we hoped, a waterfall would be obvious. Anywhere there was a line across the water we went through the motions of scouting it out. It is slow moving, exploring a new river and it takes much time and effort.

While floating we would watch for natural sites where it was obvious there had been human habitation. If we came upon a likely place we would either scout it or if a long hike was required, we camped and explored. We were most interested in examining rock overhangs which were the most likely place to find evidence for of early peoples. We found some but little evidence, usually initials scraped into the rock sometimes next to much older petroglyphs. Cliff overhangs do provide shade and shelter even on the hottest or stormiest days along the canyon rims. They made perfect places for people to camp now just like they had though out the history of the canyon. Although they were far from the river and water, they made perfect observation points. A warrior could see you long before you ever saw him and were perfect hide outs or ambush places for the traveler who wandered down the canyon. Names were discovered carved into the rock ledges. However, it would prove impossible to trace the names to the historical characters they were looking for, namely the McKnight party.

There were several near mishaps that occurred on the river. I lost my canoe for a short while after a rock ledge caught me unprepared, however after floating on down the river I found it snagged by the limbs of small pine tree that leaned over into the water. A natural strainer, all the water has to somehow flow through the branches of the tree trapping everything such as my canoe. It would take an extra two hours of hard work before we could get it out.

Hidalgo made a spectacular scene when he pushed ahead of Corey and me in our canoes and managed to spill over a sudden waterfall. It undoubtedly was the same place that Richard had described earlier on his scouting trips, the troop seventy six swimming hole. He had paddled up to the edge paddling backwards furiously. Then he lined himself up and plunged, nose first over the precipice. He separated from the canoe on the way down and they both plunged under the water, canoe and river runner immediately popped back up, winding up on the sandbar formed where the pool overflowed.

Hidalgo was bothered by the incident. In his mind he was sure that this was the place Richard had described, but what if it wasn't? What if that waterfall was still further down the river? After all, Richard only knew about this one tiny slice of the river. There could have been nothing but rocks for him to have landed on. He decided to make a personal commitment to take his time and scout a little better after that.

Once we entered the largest section of the canyon we did experience one incidence that, like the San Juan apparition, would haunt us. We had pulled off the river and made camp in a grove of ponderosa pines where there was plenty of firewood, a perfect campsite. We had learned long ago not to drink the river water without boiling it, an arduous and time consuming process but here, a tiny spring of fresh water trickled over the rocks flowing through the camp making it possible to replenish their depleted water supplies. After dinner that evening we decided to stay the next day and hike up to the canyon rims to see what they could find. As usual we found traces of Native American signs in the form of broken pottery, arrowhead shards and pictographs but no trace of anything they could connect too Robert McKnight nor his party.

The following evening, dead tired from the days hiking we settled down to a camp dinner of cottontails over rice and wild onion. Water cress from the tiny spring provided a much needed salad. While I wrote notes in my daily log and Corey took his turn at the dishes, Hidalgo noticed what appeared to be an old man walking upriver along the rock ledges far above us. He knew that there was a primitive game trail there. They had not seen anyone in the canyon other than an occasional fisherman and that was only at the obvious egress points. Not being in any hurry, Hidalgo studied the man for a while. He was obviously old and stooped over with a walking stick and wearing a large black hat. In fact, he seemed to be entirely dressed in black. Curiosity finally got the best of Hidalgo and he began climbing the trail up through the rock talus piles until he could intercept the old man.

Reaching the trail the old man was walking on Hidalgo waited for a minute until he could catch his breath and waited for the old man to appear, but he didn't. Getting impatient, Hidalgo finally walked around the rock where the man should appear but he wasn't there. Instead Hidalgo watched as a large flock of ravens literally exploded from where the old man had been. Hidalgo was dumbfounded. As the birds flew around him he suddenly felt tired and faint and he decided to step off the path and sit down in the shade of a tree.

Hidalgo curled up and went to sleep waking up on what he thought was only a few minutes later. But when he returned to camp he discovered two extremely worried camp mates. Corey and I had been looking for him since he walked out of camp the night before evidentially walking right past the tree that Hidalgo was asleep under. None of us could explain the time displacement, where Hidalgo had really disappeared to or what had happened to the old man. We were getting a now, all too familiar feeling coming over us. How could they find us here?

An Early Exit

Above Sabinosa the river is gentle, flowing over a sandy streambed through a forest of cottonwoods. We rounded the last major section of the Canadian Canyon carefully picking our way through a rock garden. We tried to imagine what it must have been like for a troop of boy scouts who would find every opportunity to entertain themselves. Just above Sabinosa, we suddenly recognized a familiar truck with the boat trailer on a small beach on the river left. As we paddled up we saw June and Ken were there patiently waiting for them.

Hidalgo, who was always in the lead, yelled "What's up"?

"We have problems, answered Ken who was angling in order to grab the front end of Hidalgos canoe. Let's get everyone off the water and we will try to explain what's going on."

Hidalgo didn't like the sound of the word 'try.' Corey and I finally drifted into view with the same looks of astonishment on our faces.

After beaching our canoes we all gathered around for an explanation. Aunt June took the lead in explaining what the problem was.

"Hidalgo, your parents made a trip all the way down to Serpiente to see you."

Looking like he had bitten into a lemon, Hidalgo asked, "Why didn't they just call the Holliday's in Albuquerque? Richard would have gotten word out to me."

June assumed a worried look on her face. "You see, it is of a personal nature. Do you have a cousin who lives on the reservation, a sheepherder, by the name of Alan Begay who has a son with the same name?"

"Sure," answered Hidalgo.

"He and three other Navajo youths were arrested this week for first degree murder. Your folks are hoping you can help them." With that said, we immediately dropped our goal of floating down the river. We had decided to take out here anyway calling Ken and June to drive us down to Conchas Lake and completing the fifty mile section above Ute Lake but our plans had instantly changed. We unpacked and then repacked the gear into the back of the truck, then loaded our canoes onto a trailer. Then with Corey and me riding in the back of the truck on top of all the gear and under the camper shell, we headed home.

Readers Guide

1. In the preface, what did the author mean when he states, "This is a cautionary tale of evil in serpents and humans, exploring the premise that good and evil are subjective concepts?"

2. In the preface, why did the author include personal experiences while growing up in New Mexico?

3. In the preface, why does the author make the point concerning female attitudes toward science and math education? Why do you think young girls might be socially directed away from science and math?

4. On the greyhound bus, why did the author introduce an elderly lady dressed in funerary attire? Who do you think she was?

5. Why were the main characters revealed in Penny's premonition?

6. Why had Penny done so poorly in school as a small child? If you were Penny's teacher how would you have improved Penny's early education?

7. In many American communities football scores are far more important than academic scores. Is this a true statement? Can you provide examples?

8. Why did the author develop the character of Turner as the antagonist who was the hired farm hand? Where did he acquire the attitude he displayed? Have you experienced young men with the same attitude?

9. Why did Aunt June suggest that Penny return the artifact she found?

10. What was it like to live as an ancient person in Aztlan? Do you think that modern people could exist if placed in the same situation?

11. There have been several theories expressed by archeologists about why the Ancestral Puebloans lived in cliff houses. What is the current, most accepted theory expressed by the author?

12. How did Penny arrive at using the scientific method in solving the problem with the serpents?

13. What is a phantasmagorical experience? Have you heard of others who have experienced such events?

14. Contrary to Penny's earlier attitudes towards boys and marriage, why do you think Penny was so convinced that she must immediately marry Corey while in Tennessee? Why did her mother and Jeb encourage them to wait?

15. Why do you think that the author included Cherokee history in this story? How was Andrew Jackson depicted?

16. It is said that humans always covet what others have. Is this true now in the modern world? Are humans by nature invasive creatures? Are invasions still occurring around the world based upon this premise?

17. Why do you think the author made a point of defining what names of Native American tribes mean as explained in Hidalgo's conversation with Penny's grandmother?

18. Was William Owl an actual person or a shaman? Why do you think so?

19. While driving from Albuquerque to Espanola, why did Dr. Douglas request Hidalgo's point of view in regards to the history of the Pueblo Revolt?

20. It is said that "One cannot judge a book by its cover." Why did the historical detectives and Dr. Douglas think that they were being pursued by three Cholos? What do you think a Cholo is?

21. Why did Penny, Corey and Hidalgo talk about astronomical events so much while they were in White Rock Canyon?

22. Why did Hidalgo tease Penny about his meeting with a bilaganna?

23. What was the main reason the team did not particularly enjoy their trip down the Animas River before its confluence with the San Juan?

24. Why did the author describe the summer time camp site at Sand Island a circus?

25. What is the relationship between the apparition observed in the sky and the resulting tumult that occurred at Chinle Wash?

26. Why did the serpent appear as a chupacabra in a pictograph?

27. What is sphexishness, how is the concept used by detectives?

28. Were the serpents determined to bedevil the team as they floated down the San Juan River or were they just testing them?

29. Why did June decide to visit Zuni?

30. Why did locals not want to help outsiders such as Hidalgo or Don and Leslie Nelson to have access to the cave on the Sanchez farm?

31. Why was the Estancia banker so uncooperative with Hidalgo?

32. Why did Hidalgo become so involved when he realized fighting tournaments were being conducted in Albuquerque?

33. Why did the men hate going to the Black Tie affair at the University of New Mexico ballroom despite the fact that they were honored guest and receiving awards?

34. Upon June's return to Zuni, why did she and Corey discover only ruins when they expected to find a living shaman and a small boy there?

35. Why did they decide to research Robert McKnight's journey into New Mexico?

36. Why did June decide to take Penny and Corey with her on her field work in Chihuahua, Mexico?

37. Why are American drug users pursued and prosecuted so strongly in Mexico?

38. Why did the history detectives decide to run the Canadian River? Did they need to actually run the river in canoes in order to support their research?

39. Why was a correlation drawn between the experiences of Robert McKnight and Corey's experiences in a Mexican jail? How does this story relate to modern problems on the border between Mexico and the United States?

www.ingramcontent.com/pod-product-compliance
Lightning Source LLC
Chambersburg PA
CBHW030850030726
47495CB00005B/1464